BY ANNE FORTIER

Juliet
The Lost Sisterhood

THE LOST SISTERHOOD

THE
LOST
SISTERHOOD

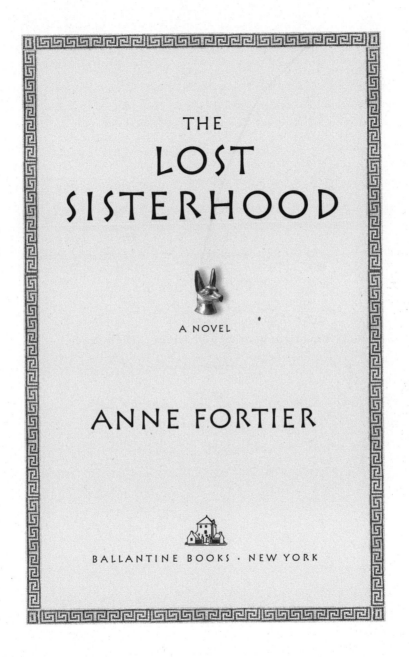

A NOVEL

ANNE FORTIER

BALLANTINE BOOKS · NEW YORK

Copyright © 2014 by Anne Fortier

All rights reserved.

Published in the United States by Ballantine Books, an imprint of Random House, a division of Random House LLC, a Penguin Random House Company, New York.

BALLANTINE and the HOUSE colophon are registered trademarks of Random House LLC.

ISBN 978-0-345-53622-8

eBook ISBN 978-0-345-53623-5

Printed in the United States of America on acid-free paper

www.ballantinebooks.com

246897531

First Edition

Book design by Susan Turner

For my beloved mother-in-law
Shirley Fortier
1945–2013
whose courage under fire
rivaled that of any Amazon

Amazons,

mythical race of female warriors. The name was popularly understood as "breastless" (maza, "breast") and the story told that they "pinched out" or "cauterized" the right breast so as not to impede their javelin-throwing. . . . Amazons have been used as evidence for an actual matriarchy in prehistoric times. This has seemed an attractive counter to modern male prejudices, but mistakes the nature of myth.

—THE OXFORD CLASSICAL DICTIONARY

He who controls the present, controls the past.

—GEORGE ORWELL

THE LOST SISTERHOOD

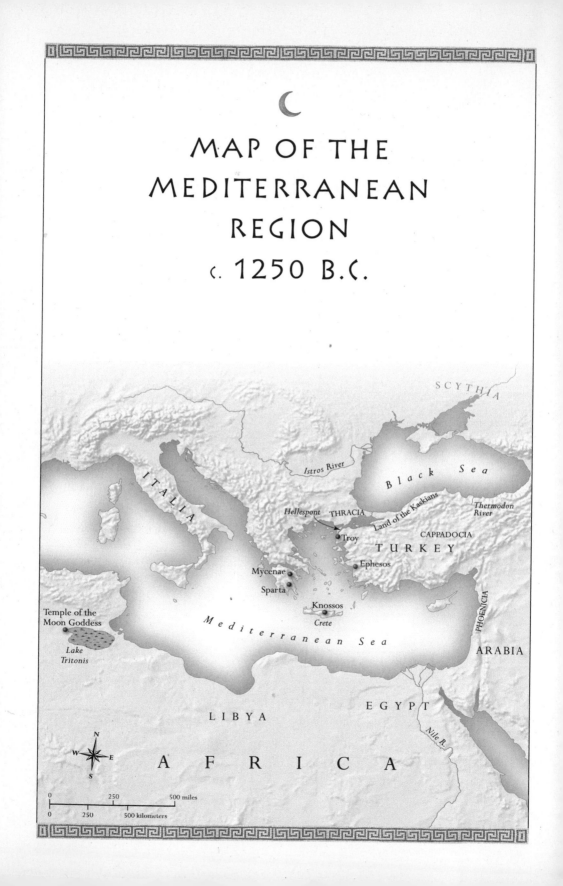

MAP OF THE MEDITERRANEAN REGION
c. 1250 B.C.

SCYTHIA

Black Sea

Istros River

ITALIA

Hellespont THRACIA Land of the Kaskians

Thermodon River

Troy

CAPPADOCIA

TURKEY

Ephesos

Mycenae

Sparta

Knossos

Crete

Mediterranean Sea

PHOENICIA

Temple of the Moon Goddess

Lake Tritonis

ARABIA

EGYPT

LIBYA

Nile R.

N
W   E
S

AFRICA

0   250   500 miles
0   250   500 kilometers

PROLOGUE

THE YOUNG MEN COMPLETED THEIR TRAINING ROW IN RECORD TIME. It was one of those rare bright mornings in Oxford, when the mists lifted off the river right before the bow, as if nature had waited for this moment, this crew, to finally unveil herself.

Haz felt invincible when he and his mates walked back to college together, crossing the Christ Church Meadow in the rising sun. But his elation was cut short by the college porter, who summoned him to the lodge with a brusque wave as soon as the young men entered the quad. "This came for you, sir." The porter pointed an ink-stained thumb at the object sitting on the mail counter. "Not ten minutes ago. I was just about to call the dean——"

"What is it?" asked Haz, stretching to see. "And where——?" But his voice broke off as soon as he discovered the contents of the canvas hamper, for nestled on a cushion and covered with a blanket lay a sleeping baby.

Haz was unable to come up with any appropriate English words to express the sudden chaos in his brain. He had seen infants before, certainly, but had never expected to find one so small in the dank lodge, surrounded by mail bags and forgotten umbrellas.

"Indeed, sir." The porter drew up his woolly eyebrows in awkward sympathy. "But perhaps this letter"—he handed the young man an envelope that was attached to the hamper by a string—"will provide an explanation."

PART I

DUSK

CHAPTER ONE

*Nine days then I was swept along by the force of the hostile
winds on the fishy sea, but on the tenth day we landed
in the country of the Lotus-Eaters . . .*
—HOMER, *The Odyssey*

OXFORD, ENGLAND
PRESENT DAY

IN HER OWN OBSCURE FASHION, MY GRANDMOTHER DID WHAT SHE
could to arm me for the carnage of life. Stamping hooves, rushing
chariots, rapacious males . . . thanks to Granny, I had it more or less
cased by the age of ten.

Alas, the world turned out so very different from the noble battleground she had led me to expect. The stakes were puny, the people
gray and gutless; my Amazon arts were futile here. And certainly nothing Granny taught me during our long afternoons of mint tea and imagined monsters could buoy me for the currents and crosswinds of
academia.

On this particular October afternoon—the day it all started—
I was knocked down by an unexpected gust of wrath halfway through a
conference paper. Prompted by the almighty Professor Vandenbosch in
the front row, the discussion leader sprang to her feet and drew a cowardly finger across her throat to let me know I had precisely zero minutes left to finish my lecture. According to my own wristwatch I was

perfectly on time, but my academic future depended on the favor of these distinguished scholars.

"To conclude"—I stole a glance at Professor Vandenbosch, who sat with his arms and legs crossed, peering at me with belligerent eyes—"it becomes clear that despite all the graphic descriptions of their mating habits, these Greek authors never saw the swashbuckling Amazons as anything more than fictitious, quasi-erotic playmates."

A rustle of enthusiasm went through the auditorium. Everyone had been sodden and rather glum coming in from the rainy quad earlier, but my lecture had clearly done its bit to warm up the room.

"However"—I nodded at the discussion leader to assure her I was almost finished—"the knowledge that these bloodthirsty female warriors were pure fiction did not stop our writers from using them in cautionary tales about the dangers of unbridled female liberty. Why?" I panned the audience, trying to count my allies. "Why were Greek men compelled to keep their wives imprisoned in the home? We don't know. But surely this Amazon scaremongering would have served to justify their misogyny."

As soon as the applause had waned, Professor Vandenbosch short-circuited the discussion leader by standing up and looking around sternly, mowing down the many eagerly raised hands with his gaze alone. Then he turned to me, a little smirk on his venerable face. "Thank you, Dr. Morgan. I am gratified to discover that I am no longer the most antiquated scholar at Oxford. For your sake I hope the academy will one day come to need feminism again; the rest of us, I am relieved to say, have long since moved along and buried the old battle-ax."

Although his charge was disguised as a joke, it was so outrageous that no one laughed. Even I, trapped behind the lectern, was too shocked to attempt a riposte. Most of the audience was on my side, I was sure of it—and yet no one dared to stand up and defend me. The silence in the room was so complete you could hear the faint plunking of raindrops on the copper roof.

Ten mortifying minutes later I was able to flee the lecture hall at last and retreat into the wet October fog. Drawing my shawl more tightly around me, I tried to visualize the teapot awaiting me at home . . . but was still too furious.

Professor Vandenbosch had never liked me. According to a particularly malicious report, he had once entertained his peers with a fantasy in which I was stolen away from Oxford to star in a girl-power TV series. My own theory was that he was using me to ruffle his rival, my mentor Katherine Kent, thinking he could weaken her position by attacking her favorites.

Katherine, of course, had warned me against giving another lecture on the Amazons. "If you continue down this path of inquiry," she had said, blunt as always, "you will become academic roadkill."

I refused to believe her. One day the subject would catch, and Professor Vandenbosch would be helpless to smother the flames. If only I could find time to finish my book, or, best of all, get my hands on the *Historia Amazonum*. One more letter to Istanbul, handwritten this time, and maybe Grigor Reznik's magic cave would finally open. I owed it to Granny to try.

Scuttling down the soppy street, my shirt collar up against the elements, I was too preoccupied to notice someone following until a man caught up with me at the High Street crosswalk and took the liberty of holding his umbrella over me. He looked a sprightly sixty and was certainly no academic; underneath his spotless trench coat I spied an expensive suit, and I suspected his socks matched the tie.

"Dr. Morgan," he began, his accent betraying South African origins. "I enjoyed your talk. Do you have a moment?" He nodded at the Grand Café across the street. "Can I buy you a drink? You look as if you need one."

"Very kind of you"—I checked my wristwatch—"but unfortunately, I am late for another appointment." And I really was. Since it was recruiting week at the university fencing club, I had promised to pop by after hours to help demonstrate the equipment. A convenient arrangement, as it turned out, since I was very much in the mood to lunge at a few imaginary foes.

"Oh—" The man proceeded to follow me down the street, the tips of his umbrella stabbing at my hair. "How about later? Are you free to-night?"

I hesitated. There was something unsettling about the man's eyes; they were uncommonly intense and had a jaundiced tint to them, not unlike those of the owls perched on top of the bookcases in my father's study.

Instead of turning down the dark and mostly deserted Magpie Lane, I stopped at the corner with what I hoped was a friendly smile. "I'm afraid I didn't catch your name?"

"John Ludwig. Here—" The man rummaged around in his pockets for a bit, then grimaced. "No cards. Never mind. I have an invitation for you." He looked at me with a squint of deliberation, as if to reassure himself of my worthiness. "The foundation I work with has made a sensational discovery." He paused and frowned, clearly uncomfortable with the public setting. "Are you sure I can't buy you a drink?"

Despite my erstwhile apprehensions, I couldn't help a twitch of curiosity. "Perhaps we could meet tomorrow?" I offered. "For a quick coffee?"

Mr. Ludwig glanced at a few hunched passersby before leaning closer. "Tomorrow," he said, his voice dropping to an intimate whisper, "you and I will be on our way to Amsterdam." Seeing the shock on my face, he had the nerve to smile. "First class."

"Right!" I ducked away from the umbrella and started down Magpie Lane. "Good day, Mr. Ludwig—"

"Wait!" He trailed me down the alley, easily matching my pace on the uneven pavement. "I am talking about a discovery that is going to rewrite history. It's a brand-new excavation, top secret, and guess what: We'd like you to take a look at it."

My steps slowed. "Why me? I'm not an archaeologist. I'm a philologist. As you are doubtlessly aware, philology is not about digging, but about reading and deciphering—"

"Precisely!" Burrowing into the same pockets that had failed to produce his business card, Mr. Ludwig extracted a bent photograph. "What we need is someone who can make sense of *this*."

Even in the murk of Magpie Lane I was able to see that the photograph showed an inscription on what appeared to be an ancient plaster wall. "Where was this taken?"

"That I can't tell you. Not until you agree to come." Mr. Ludwig stepped closer, his voice low with secrecy. "You see, we've found proof that the Amazons really *did* exist."

I was so surprised I nearly started laughing. "You can't be serious—"

Mr. Ludwig snapped upright. "Excuse me, but I am *very* serious." He opened his arms, umbrella and all, as if to demonstrate the enormity of the matter. "This is your field. Your passion. Is it not?"

"Yes, but—" I glanced at the photograph, not immune to its lure. Every six months or so, I would come across an article about an archaeologist who claimed to have found a genuine Amazon burial, or even the legendary city of women, Themiscyra. The articles were usually headlined NEW FIND PROVES AMAZONS REALLY DID EXIST, and I always read through them eagerly, only to be disappointed. Yes, another weather-beaten diehard with a hooded parka had spent a lifetime combing the Black Sea region for women buried with weapons and horses. And, yes, occasionally he or she would find evidence of a prehistoric tribe that hadn't prevented females from riding and carrying weapons. To claim, however, that those women had lived in a manless Amazon society that occasionally clashed with the ancient Greeks in spectacular battles . . . well, that was a bit like finding a dinosaur skeleton and deducing that fire-breathing fairy-tale dragons had once been reality.

Mr. Ludwig looked at me with his owl eyes. "Do you really want me to believe that after spending, what, nine years researching the Amazons there is not a tiny part of Diana Morgan that wants to prove they really lived?" He nodded at the photograph he had given me. "You're looking at a hitherto undeciphered Amazon alphabet, and get this: We are giving *you* the chance to be the first academic to take a stab at it. Plus, we're going to compensate you handsomely for your time. Five thousand dollars for one week's work—"

"Just a minute," I said, my teeth chattering with cold and the shock of it all. "What makes you so certain this inscription has anything to do with the Amazons?" I waved the photograph in front of him. "You just told me it has not yet been deciphered—"

"Aha!" Mr. Ludwig pointed at my nose, almost touching it. "That's precisely the kind of smart thinking we're looking for. Here—" He reached into an inner pocket and handed me an envelope. "This is your plane ticket. We leave from Gatwick tomorrow afternoon. I'll see you at the gate."

And that was it. Without even waiting for my reaction, Mr. Ludwig simply turned and walked away, disappearing into the flurry of High Street without looking back once.

CHAPTER TWO

Awed by her splendor
Stars near the lovely
moon cover their own
bright faces
when she
is roundest and lights
earth with her silver.
—SAPPHO

MOST OF THE COLLEGE FACULTY WAS ALREADY GATHERED OVER drinks in the Senior Common Room by the time I arrived. Because of my mad dash to the fencing club I had been in too much of a hurry to freshen up, and as I entered the room I could hear a few mumbled comments about Miss America being late for dinner again. But I merely smiled and pretended not to hear them. For all they knew, I could have been at the library, comatose over an ancient manuscript in some dusty corner—a perfectly valid excuse for showing up, as they themselves were wont to do, at the wrong time, in the wrong place, looking as if one had stumbled right out of the Renaissance.

Sadly, I was fairly sure the appellation "Miss America" was not intended as a compliment. While it might be true that I was half a head taller than most people and equipped—as my father pointed out whenever I unleashed my blond curls—with a deceiving angelic exterior, the nickname was almost certainly a comment on my breeding, or perceived lack thereof. It would seem I could never run away from the fact that my mother was American, and that her vocabulary had ruled my childhood home. Even though my father was perfectly British, and I had been surrounded by Brits growing up, there were moments when American expressions came more naturally to me. Evidently, some of the senior faculty members had overheard me turning dustbins into trash cans—or possibly even seen me jogging past college for no other purpose than the rather vulgar desire to stay in shape—and had immediately made up their minds that further investigation into my personality was unnecessary.

"Diana!" My mentor Katherine Kent summoned me to her side with an impatient wave. "How was the conference?"

As always, her machine-gun manner caught me off-guard, and I felt my courage running for cover. "Not bad at all. Quite a good turnout, actually."

"Remind me of your topic?"

"Well . . ." I tried to smile. There was no safe way of phrasing the fact that I had ignored her advice. "I was in a bit of a rush—"

Katherine Kent's eyes became arrow slits. Set in a face marked by mental discipline and framed by hair cropped so short it might have been mistaken for a fashion statement, her eyes were always strikingly vivid, a rare, incandescent turquoise, like crystals set in pewter. More often than not these were sparkling with irritation, but I had come to appreciate this as her natural mode of interaction with people who had, in fact, earned her respect.

Just then, a surge of enthusiasm went through the room. Relieved to find Katherine momentarily distracted, I turned to see who had managed to arrive even later than I and still be the toast of the party.

But of course. James Moselane.

"Over here!" Katherine's arm went up once more, with the impatient flick that never took no for an answer.

"Kate." James greeted the grande dame with the handshake she expected. "Thank you for the review in the *Quarterly*. I am sure I don't deserve it." Only then did he notice me. "Oh, hello, Morg. I didn't see you there."

Which was just fine by me. Because whenever James Moselane entered a room, it always took me a few minutes to rein in my frontal lobes. At a ripe and responsible twenty-eight, it was dreadful to find oneself scrambling to come up with a morsel of sophistication, and—even more distressing—I was fairly sure everyone around me noticed my rosy cheeks and drew exactly the right conclusion.

As academics went, James was an unusually attractive specimen. He had somehow managed to defy the old maxim that being first in line for brains inevitably means ending up last in line for looks. Stuffed with more than your average quota of gray matter, his head was nevertheless crowned with a profusion of chestnut hair, and even at thirty-three his face remained a spotless vessel of boyish charm. As if that were not enough, his father, Lord Moselane, owned one of the finest collections of ancient sculpture in the country. In other words, of all the men I had met, James was the only one who was more prince than frog.

"Diana gave a talk today," Professor Kent informed him. "I am still trying to extract the title from her."

James gave me a knowing sideways glance. "I heard it went well."

Grateful for the rescue, I laughed and wiped a bead of moisture from my temple. It was sweat from the fencing mask, still trapped in my hair, but I hoped James would see it as evidence of a recent shower. "You're too kind. What's new with you? Any more suicidal love letters from your students?"

Just then the dinner bell rang, and everyone started filing out through the common-room door. Conversation was temporarily suspended as our small procession made its way downstairs, crossed the back quad in drizzling rain, and entered the grand college hall in solemn pairs.

The students all rose from their benches while we proceeded up the aisle to the High Table that was perched on a podium at the back of the hall, and as I sat down on my designated chair I was only too aware of all the eyes staring at me. Or, more likely, they were staring at James, who sat down right next to me, looking exceedingly handsome and remarkably at ease in his black gown, not unlike a Tudor prince at court.

"Cheer up, old girl," he said under his breath, while the steward poured wine. "I have it from an excellent source that there was nothing wrong with your talk today."

I looked at him hopefully. By common agreement James was an academic superstar, and his publication list alone made most of his peers look like small moons locked in dying orbits. "Then why didn't anyone *say* anything—?"

"Such as?" James dug into his starter with relish. "You assault them with perspiring warrior women in furry boots and chain-link bikinis. They're academics, for God's sake. Be happy there were no coronaries."

I laughed into my napkin. "I should have made it a slide show. Might have finally gotten rid of Professor Vandenbosch—"

"Morg—" James looked at me with those eyes. The eyes that told me I was seeing only the tip of his thoughts. "You know Professor Vandenbosch is four hundred years old. He was here long before we came, and he will be here long after you and I have gone to the happy punting grounds. Stop pulling his whiskers."

"Oh, come on!"

"I'm serious." Once again, James's hazel gaze cut right through our merry banter. "You're extremely talented, Morg. I mean it. But you need more than talent to succeed around here." He smiled, perhaps to soften his criticism. "Take it from a seasoned chef: You can't boil soup on the old Amazon bones forever." With that, he raised his wineglass in a conspiratorial toast, but he might as well have tossed its contents into my face.

"Right." I looked down to hide my anguish. The words were not new to me, but coming from him they cut straight to my heart. "I understand."

"Good." James swirled the wine a few times before drinking. "Too young," was his final verdict, as he lowered the glass. "Not enough complexity. What a bloody waste."

James and I had been born practically within an apple's throw of each other, but in two completely separate worlds. All we mortals ever saw of the Moselane family were expensive cars with tinted windows going far too fast through our quiet village and pausing for a few seconds while the automated gate to their infinity driveway swung open.

That and, occasionally, through the bramble thicket encircling this private Eden, a glimpse of faraway people playing croquet or lawn tennis in the manor park, their laughter carried by the breeze like empty caramel wrapping.

Although everyone in town knew the names and ages of Lord and Lady Moselane's children, they were as removed from us as characters in a book. Because they were all in boarding school—the best, of course, in the country—young master James and his sisters were never around during the academic year, and almost all their holidays were apparently spent with school friends in remote castles in Scotland.

Little more than an orb of auburn hair in the front pew at the annual Christmas service, Lord Moselane's son and heir had nevertheless lived a perfectly full-fledged life in my daydreams. Whenever I was out for a Sunday walk with my parents—and, for a while, my grandmother, too—I would skip ahead through the forest hoping to encounter him on horseback, his imagined cape fluttering nobly in the breeze . . . even though I knew very well he was away at Eton, and later Oxford, and that there was no one around but me and my frivolous ideas.

But I was not entirely alone in this imaginary world of mine. For as long as I could remember, my mother had been pining to become intimate with the Moselanes, who were, after all, our neighbors. By her calculations, the fact that my father had held the post as headmaster of the local school ought to have placed us in high esteem and thus made us visible even from the manor on the hill. But after spending most of her married life waiting in vain for a dinner invitation with that embossed crest at the top, she was eventually forced to acknowledge that our lord and lady lived by quite a different social abacus than she did.

It was always a mystery to me why my mother—true-blue American that she was—never lost her craving for that sweet manor house, even after all the bitter disappointments. So many years of volunteering for Milady's charities in the hope of recognition; so many years of meticulously pruning some twenty feet of Ligustrum hedge that happened to separate the remotest part of the manor park from our backyard cabbage patch . . . all for nothing.

By the time I moved to Oxford for my doctorate degree, I was so sure she and I had long since been cured of our fruitless nonsense that it took me over a year to grasp her secret agenda in coming up to visit me every three weeks or so and insisting we explore the wonders of Oxford together.

We had started out by seeing every single college in town and had actually had quite the grand old time. My mother could never get enough of those Gothic quads and cloisters, so unlike anything she had known growing up. Whenever she thought I wasn't looking, I could see her bending down to sneak little souvenirs into her handbag—a random pebble, a lead pencil left on a stone step, a twig of thyme from an herb garden—and I was almost embarrassed to realize that, after so many years, I still knew very little of what went on in her inner universe.

After our round of the colleges, we began going to concerts and events, including the odd sports affair. My mother suddenly developed an unnatural interest in cricket, then rugby, then tennis. In retrospect, of course, I should have seen that these seemingly impulsive pursuits were very much part of a campaign that had always had but one single objective.

James.

For some reason, it never occurred to me how perfectly systematical our movements around town had been, and how determined my mother had been to map out our routes beforehand and stick to them regardless of the weather . . . not until the day she finally grabbed me by the elbow and exclaimed, in the voice of a crusader face-to-face with the grail at last, "*There* he is!"

And indeed, there he was, coming out of Blackwell's on Broad Street, balancing a stack of books and a cup of coffee. I would never have recognized him had it not been for my mother, but then, I had not spent the last ten years keeping current with the maturing process of our target through binoculars and gossip magazines. To me, James Moselane was still a pubescent prince in an enchanted forest, while the person emerging from the bookstore was a perfectly proportioned adult—tall and athletic, though completely unprepared for the ambush awaiting him.

"What a coincidence!" My mother strode across Broad Street and cut him off before he saw her coming. "Didn't even know you were at Oxford. You probably don't recognize Diana . . ."

Only then did my mother realize I was not right beside her, and she twisted around to shoot me a grimace that said it all. I had never been the spineless sort, but the horror of suddenly understanding that this, precisely *this,* was what we had been chasing for so long nearly made me turn and run.

Even though James could not see her livid expression, he most certainly noticed her frantic wave and my own crushed demeanor. Only someone uncommonly slow would not have read the situation within the blink of an eye, but to James's credit he greeted us both with perfect cordiality. "And how are you enjoying Oxford?" he asked me, still balancing his coffee on top of the books. "I'm sorry, what was your name again?"

"Diana Morgan," said my mother. "As in Lady Diana. Here, let me write it down." She dug into her handbag and pulled out a scrap of paper, oblivious to my nudges and muttered pleas. "And her college, of course—"

"Mommy!" It took all my willpower to prevent her from jotting down my telephone number as well, and she was extremely cross with me for pulling her away before we had exhausted all her brazen hoopla.

Not surprisingly, we saw neither hide nor hair of James after that. In all likelihood I would never have met him again, had it not been for Katherine Kent. Just before Christmas the following year, she invited me along to a reception at the Ashmolean Museum—a reception, as it turned out, in honor of a recent donation of ancient artifacts from the Moselane Manor Collection.

"Come!" she said, pulling me away from an exquisite statue of the Egyptian goddess Isis and spearheading our path through the exclusive crowd. "I want to introduce you. The Moselanes are very useful." Being a woman of little patience, Katherine had perfected the art of swooping right into a conversation and stealing away her prey of choice. "James! This is Diana. Extremely talented. She wants to know who bleached your Isis."

After nearly choking on his champagne, James turned toward us, looking so tantalizingly handsome in his suit and tie that my fantasies of yore came galloping back in a heartbeat.

"I was merely admiring her," I hastened to say. "Whoever found her and brought her to England must have incurred quite the Pharaonic curse——"

"My ancestor. The first Lord Moselane." Astonishingly enough, James looked as if he had completely forgotten our previous encounter. In fact, his smile suggested I was precisely the sort of woman he had hoped to meet that evening. "Died peacefully in his sleep at ninety-two. At least we like to think so." He shook my hand and was in no hurry to let it go. "Delighted."

"Actually"—I reluctantly withdrew my hand—"we met last year. In front of Blackwell's." Before the words were even out of my mouth, I winced at my own treacherous honesty. It took only a few seconds for the cogwheels to click into place in James's head, and it was not a pretty process to behold.

"Right," he said, slowly. "Right, right, right . . ."

But the word written in his hazel eyes was quite the opposite.

Indeed, in the months to come, whenever we would dutifully meet for coffee—always prompted by Katherine Kent—James's opening question, "How is your mother?" would set the tone for our conversation and remind me why our coffees never turned into lunch. He was attentive, certainly, and would occasionally give me a look that sent hope fluttering through my body. But by and large he kept treating me with unfaltering chivalry, as if I were an untouchable maiden he was sworn to protect.

Perhaps it was all because of my mother. Or perhaps it was partly due to James's being born—as my father had once so very aptly phrased it—with a silver spoon up his arse. Keeping the blue blood pure and all that. In which case I could groom my plume as much as I liked; it would never occur to Lord Moselane's son that we were the same species.

I was stirred from my High Table reverie by a hand taking away the plate with my untouched starter. Next to me, James sat with his head bent as if in prayer, checking his phone underneath the starched dinner napkin. Reaching discreetly into my handbag, I pulled out Mr. Ludwig's photograph and held it toward him. "What do you make of this?"

James leaned over to look. "Approximate dating?"

"I'd say about ten days," I joked, "judging from the bent corner and frayed edges. As for the inscription . . . your guess is as good as mine."

He squinted, clearly intrigued. "Who gave you this?"

"A mysterious man," I said, with deliberate drama, "who told me this picture is proof the Amazons *did* exist—"

"What is that?" Katherine Kent reached over to pluck the photograph from my fingers and study it in the light of a candle. "Where was this taken?"

"No idea." Happily surprised at their interest, I quickly drew up the high points of my bizarre encounter that afternoon. When I circled back to Mr. Ludwig's claim about the undeciphered Amazon alphabet, however, James sat back in his chair and groaned.

"How vexing!" Katherine gave me back the photo with a puzzled frown. "This could be anywhere. If only we knew the name of his foundation . . ."

I shrank under her glare. Clearly, she was blaming me for not extracting more information from Mr. Ludwig, and she had a point. "I think they have an office in Amsterdam," I said. "Because that's where he wanted me to go."

"Does it really matter?" James cut in. "Obviously, you're not going—"

"Actually," I countered, unable to resist the temptation to bait him a bit, "I came rather close to saying yes. It's not every day some stranger in the street offers me five thousand dollars—"

"Precisely." James gave me a look of censure. "Some stranger in the street. And what does that make you?"

I smiled, flattered that he took it all so seriously. "Curious."

James shook his head and would likely have thrown in another derisory comment, had not Katherine—exercising the privilege of genius—held up a hand to silence us both. "And he said he would meet you at the airport?"

Perplexed by her gravity, I cleared my throat. "I believe so."

James could remain silent no longer. "Surely," he intervened, squeezing his napkin into a ball, "you're not encouraging Morg to actually take off with this . . . Mr. Ludwig? God knows what he's up to—"

Katherine sat back with a jerk. "Of course not! Don't be absurd. I'm merely trying to figure out what's afoot . . . who these people are."

Anxious to restore our amicable tone, I laughed and said, "I wouldn't be the least bit surprised if it's one of my lazy students—"

James looked at me sternly. "I don't see the humor in this. You've been targeted, and I don't mean by some sort of student prank. Make sure to lock your door tonight."

CHAPTER THREE

In the face of a true friend a man sees, as it were, a second self.
—CICERO, *De Amicitia*

IT WAS STILL RAINING BY THE TIME JAMES WALKED ME BACK TO MY rooms across the quad, carefully steering us both around the inky puddles on the cobblestone pavement. He had never escorted me home before; if nothing else, at least I could thank Mr. Ludwig for this pleasing development.

"Now, Morg"—James held up an arm to shield me from the rain as I stopped to take out my keys—"I don't think you should leave college for a few days. At least not on your own. You never know—"

I stared at him, hardly able to believe his sincerity. "Don't be ridiculous."

"If you want to go out," he continued, rain dripping from his hair and winding its way down his noble face, "call me and I'll come with you."

Not just the words, but the deep tone of his voice crept right into my ear of ears and reverberated through the caverns of my hibernating hopes. Hungry for more I looked into his eyes . . . but rain and darkness blurred the moment. After an awkward pause I finally managed a stiff "That's very kind of you," to which James merely replied, in a voice as breezy as ever, "Rubbish. We've got to take care of you, don't we?"

And then he walked away, hands in his pockets, whistling a perky tune, while I retreated into my rooms at last. Or rather, the grand, tastefully furnished office apartment was not technically mine; it belonged to the esteemed Professor Larkin, who had conveniently been invited to spend the year at Yale. I had not been the only candidate vying for the one-year lectureship created to replace him, but I was a woman, and the college faculty had long been short on that particular variety of man. At least, that had been Katherine Kent's argument in favor of them hiring me.

I was not paid a full salary, but taking over Professor Larkin's office had afforded me a chance to quit my dank apartment and live in college. The only snag to the lectureship was the workload. My days were so jam-packed with tutorials I had almost no time left over for my own research. And without a selection of fresh, head-turning publications to my name there would most certainly be no college fellowship awaiting me at the end of the year; I would be back in my basement on creepy Cowley Road, writing uninspired job applications and flicking mice off my crumpets.

As I filled up the kettle for a cup of bedtime tea, my mind wandered through the events of the day and ended up—not surprisingly—at Mr. Ludwig. In a matter of minutes this strange man had presented me with a dazzling cornucopia of temptation: academic glory, adventure, and enough money to buy me half a year's freedom, devoted to my own research. Maybe I could even squeeze in a trip to Istanbul, to look up Grigor Reznik in person and talk him into showing me the *Historia Amazonum*—the only original document on the Amazons I hadn't read. My mind bubbled with possibilities.

In return, however, Mr. Ludwig had asked for a week of my precious time, and even if I had been reckless enough to consider his proposition, there was no way I could justify that sort of absence hardly a month into my new lectureship. It would have been one thing if he had shown me some official document, stamped and signed, outlining precisely what his foundation was asking me to do and how marvelous it would look on my curriculum vitae . . . but as it was, the whole thing was just too vague, too risky. Indeed, as both Katherine Kent and James had made amply clear over dinner, one would have to be absolutely insane to fly off like that, into the unknown.

If only Mr. Ludwig had not said the magic word.

Amazons.

He obviously knew of my scholarly obsession with the subject, or he wouldn't have approached me in the first place. But what was I to make of his assumption that I was pining for proof the Amazons had really existed? Surely, there was no way he could know just how right he was.

How could he possibly?

According to most academics, the Amazons had never lived any-where except in Greek mythology, and those who claimed otherwise were, at best, moonstruck romantics. Yes, indeed, it was entirely con-ceivable the prehistoric world had been populated in part by women warriors, but the myths about Amazons laying siege to Athens or tak-ing part in the Trojan War were obviously the product of storytellers looking to mesmerize their listeners with ever more fantastic tales.

The Amazons of classical literature, I would always explain to my students, should be seen as the predecessors of the vampires and zom-bies populating our bookshelves today; they were creatures of the imagination, terrible and unnatural with their habits of training their daughters in the arts of war and mating with random males once a year. Yet at the same time these wild women possessed—at least in the eyes of ancient vase painters and sculptors—enough appealing human char-acteristics to arouse our secret passions.

I was always careful not to disclose my own feelings in the matter; to be interested in Amazon lore was bad enough, to come out of the closet as an "Amazon believer" would be nothing but an act of academic self-annihilation.

As soon as my tea was ready, I sat down to study Mr. Ludwig's photograph with the aid of a magnifying glass. I fully expected to be able to identify the script on the wall right away as one of the more common ancient alphabets; when that did not happen, I allowed myself to feel a tiny tickle of excitement. And after another few minutes of hunched scrutiny and increased confusion, the possibilities began scooting up and down my spine with the urgency of battlefield messen-gers.

What intrigued me the most was the universal quality of the symbols, which made it almost impossible to link them to a particular place or time. They might have been drawn on the cracked plaster wall immediately before the picture was taken, as part of some elaborate swindle, or they might be several thousand years old. And yet . . . the more I looked at them, the more I became aware of an eerie sense of familiarity. It was as if somewhere, in a remote corner of my subconscious, a dormant beast was stirring. Had I encountered these symbols before? If so, frustratingly, the context completely escaped me.

As it happened, my childhood friend Rebecca had been working at an archaeological site in Crete for the past three years, and I was fairly certain she knew precisely which organizations were digging where, and for what. Surely, if someone had come across this kind of inscription anywhere in the Mediterranean region, and had somehow linked it to the Amazons, Dr. Rebecca M. Wharton would have been the first to know.

"Sorry to interrupt your midnight orgy," I said, when she finally answered her cellphone. We had not spoken for over a month, and it occurred to me how much I had missed her when I heard her snorting delightedly at the other end. It was a laugh I would have recognized anywhere; it sounded like a whisky hangover but, in Rebecca's case, was really the rather prosaic consequence of having her inquisitive head buried in a dusty hole all day.

"I was just thinking of you!" she exclaimed. "I have a chorus of gorgeous Greek boys feeding me grapes and rubbing me with olive oil."

I laughed at the image. The odds of lovely Rebecca getting intimate with anything other than ancient pottery shards were, sadly, ten to none. There she was, playing the rebel with her sun cap and cutoff denim shorts, crawling around on her hands and knees in an anthill of fascinating male archaeologists . . . but with eyes for nothing but the past. Although she always talked big, I knew there was still a vicar's daughter right beneath the freckles. "Is that why you haven't had time to call and tell me the big news?"

There was a brief rustle, suggesting Rebecca was trying to hold the phone between her ear and shoulder. "What big news?"

"You tell me. Who's digging up Amazons in your backyard?"

She let out one of her ear-piercing jungle-bird shrieks. *"What?"*

"Take a look." I leaned forward to check the picture on my computer screen. "I just emailed you a photo."

While we waited for Rebecca's laptop to catch up, I gave her a quick overview of the situation, complete with James Moselane's suspicion that I had become the victim of a hoax and might even be in danger. "Obviously, I'm not going," I said, "but I'm dying to know where this picture was taken. As you can see, it looks like the inscription is part of a larger wall, with the text presented in vertical columns. As for the writing itself"—I leaned closer still, trying to position the desk lamp better—"I have this odd feeling . . . but I can't for the life of me—"

A crunching sound suggested Rebecca was chewing on a handful of nuts—a sure sign she was getting intrigued. "What do you want *me* to do?" she asked. "I can guarantee you this photo wasn't taken on my island. If someone had come across a wall like that on Crete, trust me, I'd know about it."

"Here is what I want you to do," I said. "Take a good look at that inscription and tell me where I've seen those symbols before."

I knew it was a long shot, but I had to try. Rebecca had always had a knack for seeing right through the obvious. She was the one who had discovered my father's secret stash of chocolate bars in an old tackle box in the garage when we were children. Even then, despite her sweet tooth, she had not proposed we share one; the mere triumph of the discovery—and of being able to teach me something about my father that I didn't know—was excitement enough.

"I am going to give you another minute—" I said.

"How about," countered Rebecca, "you give me a few days to ask around? I'll forward the photo to Mr. Telemakhos—"

"Wait!" I said. "Don't show this photo to *anyone*."

"Why not?"

I hesitated, aware I was being irrational. "Because there is something about this writing that is deeply familiar to me . . . in an uncanny sort of way. It's as if I can see it in blue writing—"

The truth hit us both at once.

"Your grandmother's notebook!" gasped Rebecca, rustling frantically at the other end. "The one you gave her for Christmas—"

I felt a shudder of alarm. "No, it's impossible. Insane."

"Why?" Rebecca was too agitated to tread gently on what she knew was my emotional Achilles' heel. "She always said she would leave you instructions, right? And that you would get them when you least expected it. Well, maybe this is it. Granny's big summons. Who knows—" Rebecca's voice rose in a defiant pitch as she likely realized the outrageousness of her proposition. "Maybe she is waiting for you in Amsterdam."

CHAPTER FOUR

NORTH AFRICA
LATE BRONZE AGE

TWO FIGURES APPEARED ON THE SHIMMERING HORIZON.
It was the bright, burning time of day, when heaven and earth came together in a silvery haze, and it was impossible to tell one from the other. But slowly, as they made their way across the salt flats, the two quavery forms materialized as women—one fully grown, the other not quite so.

Myrina and Lilli had been away for many days, just the two of them. The purpose of their trip was evident, for all species of prey and weaponry dangled from their shoulders by leather straps, and their steps quickened as they approached the village ahead. "How proud Mama will be!" exclaimed Lilli. "I hope you will tell her how I snared that rabbit."

"I shall leave out no detail," promised Myrina, ruffling her younger sister's matted hair, "except perhaps the part where you nearly broke your neck."

"Yes—" Lilli drew up her shoulders and did the funny turtle walk she always did when she was embarrassed. "Better not mention that, or I shall never be allowed to come out with you again. And that"—she glanced up at Myrina with a hopeful smile—"would be a shame, would it not?"

Myrina nodded firmly. "A great shame. You have the makings of a fine hunter. And besides"—she could not help it, she had to giggle—"you are an inexhaustible well of amusement."

Lilli scowled, but Myrina knew she was secretly pleased. Small for a girl of twelve, her sister had been desperate to prove herself on the trip, and Myrina had been happily surprised at her endurance. Come hunger or fatigue, Lilli never refused a task, never shed a tear. At least not when Myrina was looking.

Being a whole six years older than Lilli, and easily as capable as any man her own age, Myrina had seen it as her duty to teach her sister the art of hunting. The idea, however, had met with visceral resistance from their mother, who had never stopped thinking of Lilli as her baby, and who still sang her to sleep at night.

Walking home with Lilli now, seeing the new pride in her bearing, Myrina could not wait to place it all before their mother's feet: the glorious catch, the many tales, and the youngest daughter returning from the wild safe and smiling, with the bloody mark of the hunter drawn upon her forehead.

"Do you think they will roast it all at once?" asked Lilli, interrupting Myrina's thoughts. "It would be quite the feast. Although"—she looked down at a bundle of tiny fish hanging from her belt by a woolen string—"some things are rather small and perhaps not worth mentioning at all."

"In my experience," said Myrina, "it is the small ones that are most tasty—"

She stopped. They had turned the bend by the pasture, and the Tamash Village lay immediately ahead. This was where the dogs always came to greet her, knowing that her appearance heralded meat scraps and marrow bones.

But today, no dogs came. And when Myrina paused to listen, she heard none of the usual sounds from the village, only the hoarse cries of birds and an odd, persistent buzzing as of thousands of honeybees in a patch of flowers. The only signs of life were a few thick columns of smoke rising from somewhere among the huts and wafting away into the infinite blue.

"What is it?" asked Lilli, her eyes widening. "What do you hear?"

"I am not sure," said Myrina, feeling every little hair on her body rise in apprehension. "Why don't you stay here." She took Lilli by the shoulders and held her still.

"Why? What is wrong?" Lilli's voice was shrill, and when Myrina started walking, the girl followed her. "Please tell me!"

Now at last, Myrina saw one of the dogs. It was the spotted pup that always came and slept at her feet during storms—the pup she had nursed back to life once, and which sometimes stared at her with eyes that were almost human.

One look at this dog—its slinking, obsequious manner, its nervous yawn—told Myrina everything she needed to know. "Don't touch him!" she cried, as Lilli stepped forward, arms outstretched.

But it was too late. Her sister had already taken the pup by the neck and started rubbing it fondly. "Lilli!" Myrina pulled the girl abruptly to her feet. "Did you not hear me? Touch nothing!"

Only then did she see the first tremor of understanding in Lilli's face.

"Please," said Myrina, softening her voice so much it began to quiver, "be good now and stay here, while I"—she cast another uneasy glance toward the silent houses ahead—"make sure everything is well."

Walking into the village, both hands clenched around her spear, Myrina looked everywhere for signs of violence. Certain the place had been attacked by rival tribesmen or wild animals, she was braced for gruesome sights, yet wholly unprepared for what she found.

"You!" A hoarse, hateful voice reached her from inside a hut, and a moment later a hunched woman came out, sweat beading off her body. "It was your mother who did this to us—" The woman spat on the ground, her saliva crimson with blood. "Your witch of a mother!"

"Nena, my friend—" Myrina took a few steps back. "What happened here?"

The woman spat again. "Did you not hear me? Your mother cursed us all. She called down a plague and said she would kill everyone who didn't approve of her whoring ways."

Walking on, Myrina found sickness and grief wherever she looked. Men, women, and children were clustered in the shade, trembling with fear and fever; others were kneeling at smoldering fires, silently rubbing themselves with ashes. And the place where her mother's hut had been was now nothing but a bed of black coals with familiar objects unceremoniously thrown in.

Unable to fully comprehend what she was looking at, Myrina knelt down to pick up a small blackened circle sticking out of the ashes. It was the bronze bracelet her mother had worn on her wrist, and which she had always claimed would remain there until her dying day.

"I am so sorry, my dear," said a faint voice, and Myrina turned to find her mother's old neighbor standing there, leaning on a cane, a ring of open sores around his mouth. "You had better go. They are looking for someone to blame. I have tried to speak reason, but no one wants reason now."

Pressing a hand to her mouth, Myrina began walking away, ignoring the comments following her through the village as she went. "Whore!" yelled the men, not because she had ever lain with them, but because she hadn't. "Witch!" cried the women, forgetting it was Myrina's mother who had come at night to hold their hands and deliver their babies . . . and forgetting it was Myrina who had made playthings for those babies out of animal bones.

When she finally returned to Lilli, the girl was sitting on a rock by the roadside, stiff with fear and anger. "Why couldn't I come with you?" she said, rocking back and forth, her arms crossed. "You were gone a long time."

Myrina stuck the spear into the ground and sat down next to her. "Do you remember what Mother said when we left? That no matter what happens, you must always trust me?"

Lilli looked up, her face contracting with premonition. "They are all dead, aren't they?" she whispered. "Just like the people in my dream." When Myrina did not reply, Lilli started sobbing. "I want to see Mama. Please!"

Myrina drew her sister into a tight embrace. "There is nothing to see."

CHAPTER FIVE

It is a dreadful thing, sir,
To awaken again an old ill that lies quiet.
—Sophocles, *Oedipus at Colonus*

THE COTSWOLDS, ENGLAND

My father picked me up at the train station in Moreton-in-Marsh, looking surprisingly dapper despite the hour. I had expected a bristly grump and was touched to find him dressed in a pair of fairly decent corduroy trousers instead of the pajama bottoms he had started wearing around the house on weekends. It was only a matter of time, I had begun to fear, before those bottoms would venture out in the front yard to get the newspaper, and very possibly even find their way into the car for the odd informal outing.

"One hates to pry. . . ." My father did not find it necessary to complete the sentence. It was his way of saying, "Why on earth did you want to leave Oxford at seven in the morning?"

"Oh—" I looked out the window at nothing in particular, struggling with a childish urge to blurt out the real reason for my visit. "I thought we were overdue for a little inconvenience. Privilege of the only child."

My parents lived in a rambling cottage built with golden stones by some distant ancestor who could not have stood much over five feet tall, judging by the knee-high doorknobs. To him the building must have seemed a lofty mansion; to me—ever tall for my age—it had always felt cramped, and as a child I had often entertained the idea that I was a giantess imprisoned in a small forest mound by two trolls.

After leaving home, of course, even the vexations of childhood had assumed an enchanted glow of their own. For every time I returned to the house now I found that I had grown a little more blind to its shortcomings . . . even to the point of relishing its comforting snugness.

We entered the house through the garage as usual, and paused in the small mudroom to take off our shoes. Spilling over with coats and drying flowers and hundreds of hazelnuts hanging from ceiling hooks in nylon stockings, it was undoubtedly the messiest room in the house. And yet I liked to linger here, for it had such a soothing, familiar smell about it—a smell of waxed jackets and chamomile, and still, years later, of the basket of apples we had once forgotten on top of the furnace.

As soon as he had his slippers on, my father continued into the kitchen and from there into the dining room. A little puzzled by our route, I tagged along and saw him approaching the bay window in a stealthy sort of way.

In the garden outside stood a new birdfeeder, obviously intended for my father's feathered friends. On the feeding platform, however, sat a black squirrel, gorging itself on the seeds laid out for the birds.

"Him again!" My father barely paused to excuse himself before storming out through the garden door, slippers and all, to put a stop to the evil schemes of Nature. Seeing him like this, bustling around in the backyard with his knitted vest on backward, it seemed nearly impossible that this man, Vincent Morgan, had—until recently—been headmaster of the local school where, for many years, he had struck terror into the hearts of little boys and girls. Throughout the region my father had been known as Morgan the Gorgon, and whenever I had left the house alone as a child, I had run the risk of being trailed through town by a pack of boys chanting "Morgan the Mini Gorgon" until the butcher came out in his blood-smeared apron and shooed them away.

It was only after his retirement that my father had turned his cannons on the garden. Never one to embrace change, his persistent narrative about this small, ancestral plot of land was one of lament and nostalgia. The apples were never as tart as he remembered from his youth, nor did the raspberries ever yield quite as much as they had when he was a wee lad, picking basket after basket to bring to Mrs. Winterbottom in the kitchen.

These romantic cameos were always carefully cropped to exclude troublesome details. Gone was the workaholic father and hospitalized mother. Gone was the fact that Mrs. Winterbottom—a housekeeper by profession—was a stern, plastic-gloved presence in whom efficiency and cleanliness left tenderness no quarter. Left was only a little boy and his garden, framed by seasonal foliage and ever so lightly dusted with glitter.

Poking my head into the basement I found, as expected, a handful of women astride stationary bikes that were positioned toward an exercise video. "Hello, Mommy!" I called. "And hello, ladies!"

"Hi, sweetie!" My mother was dressed in the yellow jersey I had given her for Christmas, her silver bob pushed back by a bandanna. She was one of the only women I knew who were not afraid of sweating, and from being a source of tremendous embarrassment this had, over the years, become one of the things I admired most about her. "Ten more minutes!"

As I returned upstairs to find my father still fiddling with the bird-feeder outside, a sudden swarm of nerves hatched in my stomach. Ten minutes. Precisely what I needed.

MY FATHER'S STUDY WAS a dusty cubbyhole with all the trappings of a Victorian gentleman. The walls were completely covered in sagging bookshelves, and here and there among the books sat his special treasures: bugs pinned in wooden cases, worms and snakes preserved in glass canisters, and extinct birds with bright glass eyes watching from the top shelves like predators perched on a crag. For as long as I could remember, I had found the smell in this room dangerously compelling; it was the scent of history, of knowledge, and of childhood trespassing.

Older now but nonetheless nervous, I accidentally knocked over a wobbly mug on the desk, and for a few anxious seconds, pens, rulers, and paper clips skidded in all directions. Jittery with guilt, I fumbled everything back into the mug and placed it on top of the monthly bills, where it belonged.

My father appeared in the door.

"Why, hello there!" he exclaimed, his bushy eyebrows colliding. "Should I be flattered that you find my correspondence so interesting?"

"Terribly sorry," I muttered. "I was looking for my birth certificate."

His brow softened. "Ah. Let me see now——" Sitting down heavily on the office chair he opened and closed a few drawers before finding what he was looking for. "Voilà!" My father took out a fresh new folder with my name written on it. "These are all your papers. I've been cleaning up a bit." He smiled at last. "Thought I would spare you the mess."

I stared at him, trying to see beyond the smile. "You haven't been . . . throwing things out, have you?"

He blinked a few times, baffled by my sudden interest in his projects. "Nothing important, I think. I put most of it in a box. The family papers and all that. You may wish to burn them, but . . . I will leave the decision to you."

THE DOOR TO THE attic was squeaky, and it had always been nearly impossible to keep one's visits to the room a secret.

When we were children, Rebecca and I had kept a small box of keepsakes in a corner of this gloomy room tucked under the roof, and we would sneak up to check on it only as often as we dared. There was a miniature bar of soap from a hotel in Paris, a dried rose from a wedding bouquet, a golf ball from the Moselane Manor Park . . . and a few other treasures that could not fall into the wrong hands.

"What are you two doing in the attic?" my mother had asked one day at lunch, causing Rebecca to spill her lemonade all over the kitchen table.

"Nothing," I had said, with forced innocence.

"Then go play outside." My mother had spent most of a roll of paper towels cleaning up Rebecca's mess, but had not said a word about it.

Rebecca was, after all, the vicar's daughter. "I don't like you being in that dusty room."

And so, just as children learn to please their parents by riding bicycles and falling asleep on Christmas Eve, they furtively work up darker skills, often involving perilously stored cookie tins, and, in my case, the ability to open and close the creaky attic door with no sound at all.

Although I had not needed the trick for many years, I was happy to see I still had it mastered. Pausing on the doorstep, I briefly listened to the sounds from below, but all I heard was the occasional clinking of china. Through the day, my parents really had only one predictable habit, and that was to share the newspaper after lunch. It was no use trying to engage them in a three-way conversation during this time; once the dishes were aside and the coffee poured they were happily lost in a world of cricket and corrupt politicians.

Even so, I was only too aware they were both downstairs as I flicked on the lonely bulb that appeared to be hanging from the attic ceiling by thick strains of spiderweb. As I made my way across the floor I tried to remember which floorboards squeaked and which were safe . . . but soon realized that many years had come between me and the path I had known so well.

Pinched under our steep roofline, the attic was essentially a triangular vault with no source of natural light except a half-moon window in the north-facing gable. Although it was dusty and deserted, the place had always held a strange fascination to me; whenever as a child I peeked into an old leather suitcase or wooden trunk I fully expected to find something magical. Perhaps it would be a forgotten jewelry box, or a ragged pirate's flag, or a bundle of brittle love letters . . . there had always been a promise of family secrets and portals to other worlds in that dusky room and its quaint smell of cedar and mothballs.

And one day, when I was nine years old, the magic door finally opened.

Granny.

I could still see her standing there, back turned, looking out through the half-moon window for hours on end . . . not with the wistful resignation one might expect from someone kept under lock and key, but with active determination, as if she were keeping watch for some inevitable attack.

All I had ever known about my father's mother was that she was ill in a hospital in a country far away. The bit about the country far away had been my own invention, probably to explain why we never visited her, the way we went to see Grandfather during his own long, nameless illness. Without giving it too much thought I imagined her lying just like him, with plastic tubes going in and out of her clothes, but in a foreign setting with whitewashed walls and a crucifix hanging over her bed.

Then one drizzly afternoon, with no forewarning, I came home from school to find a strange, tall woman standing in the middle of our living room, a small suitcase on the floor beside her and a look of uncommon serenity on her face. "Diana!" my mother said, waving at me impatiently. "Come and say hello to Granny."

"Hello," I muttered, although, even then, I felt the greeting to be utterly inadequate. There was something about this long-limbed stranger that was completely out of place, I could see that much, but I remember being unable to determine what it was.

It might have been the fact that she still wore her raincoat, which made her look as if she were merely a random passerby waiting for the bus, and who might be off again any moment. Or perhaps I was confused because, in my experience—obviously rather limited—she did not look like a grandmother at all. Instead of the cauliflower perm favored by the local village ladies, she wore her gray hair in a braid down her back, and her face was almost without lines. In fact, it was almost without expression altogether. My new granny merely looked at me with an open, straightforward stare, and there was no particular curiosity, nor a hint of emotion in her gaze.

I remember feeling disappointed by her impersonal behavior, but I also knew, with the unwavering certainty of a child, that because she was my grandmother, she would inevitably come to love me. So I smiled, knowing we were destined to become friends, and saw a tiny flicker of amazement in her gray-blue eyes. But still no smile.

"Good afternoon," she simply replied, with that curious accent of hers which made it sound as if she had rehearsed the words without fully understanding what they meant.

"Granny has been ill," my mother explained, taking the schoolbag from my back and pushing me closer, "but she is feeling better. And now she is going to live with us. Isn't it wonderful?"

Nothing else was said on that particular occasion; Granny moved into the attic room, which, I now discovered, had been cleaned out and furnished, and although she was unusually tall with—in my nine-year-old estimation—exceptionally large feet, she was so quiet you would never have known she was there, were it not for the attic door's squeal whenever I went to see her.

Years later, I would look back on this period and laugh at myself for having been fooled by that serene air, and for thinking Granny's silence was somehow a consequence of her long, mysterious illness. It used to unnerve me that she could sit on a chair in our parlor for hours doing absolutely nothing while my mother would run to and fro, cleaning and fussing as if her mother-in-law were just another piece of furniture in her way.

"Lift your feet!" she would demand, and Granny obediently moved her feet out of the path of the vacuum cleaner. On a few occasions there was no immediate response, and the vacuum cleaner was unexpectedly brought to a stop, until it eventually occurred to my mother to add "please."

In her better moments, my mother would chastise herself for her own impatience toward Granny, reminding us both that, "It's the medicine. She can't help it," and pausing briefly on her way through the room to pat the sinewy old hand lying on the armrest, even though there was rarely a response.

Several months went by after her arrival before I had an actual conversation with Granny. When it finally happened, we had been sitting in her attic apartment for the better part of a Sunday afternoon, left to each other's less-than-riveting company while my parents were in town for a funeral. I had been laboring over a particularly boring school essay, and for quite a while—somewhat to my growing irritation—I had felt

Granny's eyes on my pen as I wrote. At one point, when I paused for inspiration, she leaned forward eagerly, as if she had been waiting for an opening, and hissed, "Rule number one: Don't underestimate them. Write that down."

Unnerved by her sudden intensity, I obediently wrote down the words in the middle of my essay, and when she saw the result, she nodded her approval. "That is good what you are doing. Writing."

I barely knew what to say. "Do you not . . . write?"

For a moment she looked stricken, and I wondered if I had insulted her. Then she looked down, suddenly fearful. "Yes. I write."

For Christmas that year I gave her a notebook—one of my unused red exercise books from school—plus three blue pens I had bought at the store. She didn't say anything right away, but as soon as my parents were busy with their own stockings, she took my hand and squeezed it so hard it hurt.

I did not see the red notebook again until years later, long after she was gone, when I was eavesdropping on an after-dinner conversation between my parents and my father's old school chum, Dr. Trelawny, who was then a psychiatrist in Edinburgh. Perched on the top step of the staircase I was able to overhear most conversations going on in the living room, and I could also swiftly retreat to my room if need be.

On this particular occasion the subject was Granny, and since all my questions about her were usually met with reproachful silence, I was naturally determined to ignore the biting draft in the stairwell and take in as much information as possible.

My father was evidently showing Dr. Trelawny a collection of medical files, for they were talking about such things as "paranoid schizophrenia," "electroshock treatments," and "lobotomy," most of which was gibberish to me at the time. At one point there was a prolonged shuffling of papers, interspersed with Dr. Trelawny exclaiming, "How extraordinary!" and "This is remarkable!"—all of which made me so agog with curiosity I simply had to descend another few steps and crane my neck to see what was going on.

Through the half-open door I saw my mother sitting on our yellow sofa, nervously twirling the tassels of her shawl, while my father and

Dr. Trelawny stood by the fireplace, their whisky glasses resting on the mantelpiece.

It took me a moment to realize that the object eliciting such excitement from the otherwise exceptionally dull Dr. Trelawny was the red notebook I had given Granny for Christmas six years earlier. Clearly, the three blue pens had been put to good use for, judging by the doctor's fascination with each page, the notebook had been filled from cover to cover.

"What do you think?" my father eventually asked, reaching out for his whisky glass. "I have shown it to a few specialists in London, but they say no such language exists. An imaginary dictionary, they called it."

Dr. Trelawny whistled out loud, oblivious to my mother's warning grimace. "The make-belief language of a delusional mind. I thought I had seen it all, but this is something else altogether."

Unfortunately, the whistle prompted my mother to close the door to the hallway, effectively cutting me off from the rest of the conversation.

Ever since that evening I had been itching to see exactly what Granny had written in the notebook. But whenever I dared approach the subject, my mother would spring up from whatever she was doing and exclaim, "Oh, that reminds me! Diana, I want to show you something—" And off we would go upstairs, to sort through her clothes, or shoes, or handbags in search of something I was old and responsible enough to borrow. It was, I suppose, her way of apologizing for all the unanswered questions.

Once I inadvertently surprised my father as he sat bent over the notebook at his desk, but the clumsy urgency with which he shoved it into a drawer was further evidence that this was by no means an object he cared to discuss. And so I waited and waited, very much aware of the notebook's presence among the family papers, until one day, I could stand it no longer.

Rebecca and I had been alone in the house for an entire day, getting up to all the usual sorts of mischief, when we at last found ourselves on the threshold of my father's study. "You have a right to know the truth,"

Rebecca had insisted, when she saw me hesitating. "They can't keep it from you. It's so wrong. I am sure it's even against the law. You *are* sixteen, you know."

Spurred on by her indignation, I had finally opened the drawer with the family papers, and we had spent the next hour riffling through my father's file folders in search of the red notebook.

During that hour, we found so many shocking papers that our eventual discovery of the notebook dwindled in importance. Yes, indeed, it contained a long list of English words and their apparent translation into a set of bizarre symbols, but Granny's little dictionary, as it turned out, was not nearly as interesting as the letters from doctors outlining ominous-sounding treatments for her, including a stomach-turning description of the surgical procedure involved in a lobotomy.

Somewhat stunned after this unforeseen jackpot of information, Rebecca and I had eventually put everything back in the file folders, including the red notebook, and had walked out of my father's study with a budding appreciation that parents hide things from children for a reason.

I had not laid eyes on Granny's meticulously scribbled dictionary since that day, twelve years ago; in fact, I had barely allowed it to cross my mind. But it had clearly festered there all the same, in some cerebral cranny, and as I stood in the attic on this rainy October afternoon, I knew I couldn't rest until I held it in my hand.

It didn't take me long to find the box with family papers. As expected, my father had done a halfhearted job of hiding it underneath a folded garden parasol, and it was the only box in the room that did not have its contents meticulously scribbled on the side. As I peeled off the adhesive tape one nervous inch at a time, I kept listening for steps on the staircase outside; once I felt confident no one was coming, I knelt down and started going through the file folders.

When I finally spotted the red notebook, I was in such a hurry to test the wild idea that had possessed me since the night before that I nearly missed the two words Granny had written on the jacket: "For Diana."

The discovery that the notebook had always been intended for me filled me with sudden feverous certainty. I opened the cover with trembling fingers and, after a quick glance at the first few pages, could see right away that in her careful blue writing, Granny had left me the key to a language of symbols I would never encounter anywhere else . . . until the day a stranger stopped me in Magpie Lane and gave me a photograph and a ticket to Amsterdam.

CHAPTER SIX

C

W E MADE IT, LILLI!"
Myrina staggered onto the shifting stones of the riverbed.
There was not much of a stream left; what must once have been a roaring waterway was now little more than a long, narrow crack in the
parched landscape. But she was far too exhausted to feel any disappointment, far too exhausted to feel anything other than a faint throbbing as the uneven rocks scraped the last few patches of skin from her
weary feet.

"The river!" Falling to her knees by the water's edge she could finally unfasten Lilli's spindly arms that had been clasped around her
neck since sunrise. "Do you hear me? It's the river!" Myrina eased her
sister's limp body to the ground and began pouring water to the lips
that had been far too silent all day. "Come, drink now."

The desert had been bigger than she thought. Their water-filled
goat bladders had run dry before they were even halfway across it. She
had kept assuring Lilli she saw trees on the horizon, beyond the blazing
plain, hoping her words would come true. Yet as hour after hour went
by without shade or drink, the conversations between the sisters became briefer and briefer, until there had been no words left to speak.

Over the course of their journey those last few days, Myrina con-
tinually heard the patient, steady voice of their mother urging her on,
on, on. "Must reach the river," it said, with hushed intensity. "Cannot

stop. Must keep moving." The words never faltered, never faded; just as her mother had never left her side during all those nights of childhood illnesses and fears, so did she remain faithfully by Myrina's side throughout these last stumbling hours, when there was nothing else to cling to but a few persistent words, throbbing in her head, "Must reach the river. At the end of the river lies the sea. By the sea lies the city. In the city dwells the Moon Goddess. She alone has the power to cure my sister."

When Lilli finally came to, she peered in all directions with her poor, unseeing eyes, then started crying, her narrow shoulders trembling in despair. "This is not the river," she sobbed. "You are just saying that to comfort me."

"But it is! Feel." Myrina guided her sister's hands into the shallow stream. "I swear to you, this is it." She looked around at the dusty rubble. An abundance of trees must have lined this waterway in its prime, but now they were little more than crumbling skeletons toppling this way and that in search of support—the sad remains of a lush world long gone. "It has to be."

"But I cannot hear the water at all," said Lilli, bravely wiping her tears before cocking her head to listen. "It must be a very quiet river."

"It is," admitted Myrina. "An old and tired river. But it is still alive, and it will lead us to the sea. Come, drink now."

For a while they were silent, gorging themselves with water. At first, it was as if Myrina's throat had forgotten how to swallow, but once she had managed to force down the first few mouthfuls, she could feel the cool liquid trickling through her body, restoring life wherever it went.

When her belly was full, Myrina lay back against the rocks and closed her eyes. So many days without rest, and the last, agonizing stretch without water. For how long had she carried Lilli? Two whole days? No, it was not possible.

A startled shriek and a sudden flapping of wings pulled her back upright. Seeing her sister's terror as she kept flinging her arms at some invisible enemy, Myrina immediately drew the knife from her belt.

"It was a bird!" cried Lilli, furiously rubbing her leg. "It bit me! Where did it go? Don't let it bite me again!"

Myrina held up a hand against the sun and eyed the two scrawny vultures circling overhead. "Hateful vermin!" she muttered, putting away the knife and reaching for her bow instead. "Expecting to feast on us today——"

"Why do the gods despise us so?" Lilli rocked back and forth, hugging her knees. "Why do they want us dead?"

"I would not waste my time speculating about the gods." Myrina eased her finest bird arrow out of the quiver. "If they really wanted to kill us, they could have done so forty times." She laid the arrow on the string, rose slowly on her feet, and pulled back the bow. "Clearly, some power wants to keep us alive."

Later, when they were lying by the small driftwood fire under a starlit sky, digesting their unsavory meal, Lilli snuggled up to Myrina and said, "Mama came for me, you know. I saw her so clearly. . . ."

Saying nothing, Myrina merely drew her sister closer.

"She looked happy," Lilli went on. "She wanted to embrace me, but then she saw you, and I think she was afraid you would be upset with her for taking me away . . . so she didn't."

They lay quietly for a while.

It seemed so distant now, their life back home. And yet the memories of their lost friends and loved ones were still strong enough to choke and silence them both, just as Myrina knew that the terrible, evil reek of sickness and death would surely linger in her nose forever.

After leaving the village, they had both been miserably ill with shakes and convulsions. Myrina had been convinced they would die—in fact, she had almost welcomed the thought. But then she slowly began recovering, as did Lilli, although her sister's fever lingered long enough to harm her eyes. For several horrible mornings in a row, the girl had woken up from fitful sleep seeing less and less, until finally she saw nothing at all. "Is it near daybreak?" she had asked on that last day, peering helplessly into the bright sunshine.

"It is not far," Myrina had whispered, drawing Lilli into a sobbing embrace and kissing her again and again, while the awful truth had clawed at her throat from the inside.

But they were still alive. They had survived the pestilence, and now they had survived the desert, too. From here on, things could only get better. Myrina refused to think otherwise.

"Are you sure—" Lilli began, as she did every night. But this time she did not finish the sentence but merely bit her lip and looked away. They both knew there would be no answer to Lilli's big question until they reached their destination. Could the Moon Goddess in the big city undo the damage of the fever and restore her eyesight? No one but the Goddess knew the answer.

"I am sure of one thing," said Myrina, polishing their mother's bracelet with the skirt of her tunic. Underneath the stubborn residue of soot was the jackal-headed serpent she remembered so well, staring at her with blackened eyes. "Mother would be proud if she saw you now."

Lilli looked up quizzically, unable to fix her gaze on Myrina's face. "You don't think she would be angry with me for being useless?"

Myrina drew the girl closer. "Useless is for farmers who don't farm, and herdsmen who don't herd. Remember that you are a sister. A sister does not need eyes to be useful, merely a smile and a brave heart."

Lilli sighed heavily, her shoulders slumping as she leaned on their traveling satchel. "I am only your half sister. Perhaps that is why I do not have your courage; had I had your father, I might have shared your hunter's heart."

"Hush! Fathers come and fathers go, but Earth stays the same. Just as there is no such thing as half a heart, there can be no such thing as half a sister."

"I suppose," muttered Lilli. "But I am still not sure I can ever smile again."

"Well, I am," said Myrina, resting her chin on Lilli's head. "Remember that she who braves the lion becomes the lion. We will brave this lion, and we will smile again."

"But lions don't smile," muttered Lilli, still hugging the satchel.

Myrina made a growl and started biting her sister's neck until they were both giggling. "Then we shall teach them how."

MYRINA AND LILLI FOLLOWED the river for ten days.

They now had plenty of water to drink, but the land surrounding them on all sides was barren. Whenever Myrina came across a living plant that tasted halfway edible, she would munch a few leaves or tubers, then wait a while to observe the effects on her stomach before offering it to Lilli. And whenever the languid stream pooled in a basin of slightly cooler water, Myrina would prowl the perimeter, trying to spear a lonely fish.

On particularly hot days, an animal or two might come down to the river to drink with abandon, and thanks to her bow and a few intact arrows Myrina was usually able to serve up a side of unfamiliar meat for dinner. Those were the good moments. Staying up late, eating as much as they possibly could, the sisters inevitably found themselves circling back to life as it used to be.

How trifling the daily sorrows of their village seemed now. And how much greater all the little pleasures. The comforts of family, the worries and the gossip . . . it all blended together in a bright and happy dream, an impossibly innocent world that survived in words alone.

Since they had both been born in the Tamash Village, Myrina and Lilli had never thought of it as anything other than home. And when the other children occasionally jeered at them for being foreigners with foreign habits, their mother dismissed it as ignorance. "They think it is evil for a woman to have children with different men," she would say, rolling her eyes at the subject. "Little do they know their own father may not be the one they think it is."

In addition to the whoring charge there had been the issue of their mother's mysterious skills with herbs and roots. While the other village women might spend their days gossiping about her sinful ways, as soon as an ailment struck, they would be upon her doorstep, begging for a remedy.

More than once, the village elders had come to the hut with their fine robes and carved staffs, asking that Talla no longer practice her foreign arts. But she had merely shaken her head at them, knowing their wives would never let them drive her out of town. On one particular occasion, Myrina remembered her mother taunting the village chief, saying, "You think I put a curse on your little one-eyed bird, Nholo? Maybe if you didn't sit on it all day long, talking rubbish, it would soar to new heights."

But even those once-unhappy moments were beatified by the golden light of memory. Grudges were forgotten and debts quite forgiven; Myrina was amazed to see how easily death stripped away all the niggling details of life and left an entire village of petty people cleansed and amiable.

As day after day of monotonous travel went by, the sisters would often return to the same few memories over and over, as if the pleasure grew with repetition. "I can still see it," Lilli would say, half-giggling. "Mother trying to catch the old rooster. . . . Oh, she was so mad! And all those young men so desperately in love with you, but too afraid to even smile at you—"

Myrina never corrected Lilli when she spoke like that. She merely laughed along and let her sister roam around in this imaginary past for as long as possible. The present, she knew, would come back soon enough.

ON THE ELEVENTH DAY, the river widened into a delta and now, finally, Myrina began seeing evidence of other human beings. Narrow dug-out canals for irrigation shaped the landscape in spiderweb patterns, and yet not a trickle of water made it into the fields. The soil was as parched here as it had been at home, and there was not a farmer to be seen. "What is it?" Lilli asked at last, unnerved by her sister's long silence.

"Nothing." Myrina tried to sound cheerful, but the truth was, she was sick with worry. Wherever she looked, she saw abandoned farming tools and desolate strips of pastureland. The only animals in evidence were scraggy crows circling the sky. Where were the people?

"Shh!" Lilli stopped abruptly and held up her hand. "Do you hear that?"

"What?" All Myrina heard were the cries of the birds.

"Voices"—Lilli turned her head this way and that—"men's voices."

Infused with hope, Myrina clambered up on a large boulder for a better look around. Before them was a coastline and large body of water—a sight that filled her with relief. "It is the sea!" she exclaimed, pointing without thinking. "It is enormous . . . just as Mother said it would be."

No one back in the village, except their mother, had ever seen the sea. But the elders had often talked of it, all nodding in agreement, sitting in the shade underneath the fig tree. It was big and blue and dangerous, they had said, absentmindedly batting away the flies, and on its distant shores were cities full of danger and suffering, cities full of evil strangers. . . .

Their mother had always laughed at such speech, reminding her daughters that men tend to resent things beyond their understanding. "The city is no more evil than the village," she had once said, brushing it all aside with a hand covered in bread dough. "In fact, people there are a great deal less jealous than they are here."

"Then why did you leave?" Myrina wanted to know, sprinkling more flour on her mother's hands. "And why can we not go back there?"

"Maybe we will. But for now, this is where the Goddess wants us to be."

Myrina had not been fooled. She knew her mother was concealing something to do with the Moon Goddess. But no matter how she phrased her questions, she could not provoke the answers she was hoping for. All her mother ever said was, "We are her faithful servants, Myrina. The Goddess will always be there for us. Never question that."

As THE SISTERS MADE their way through the clingy weeds of the estuary, Myrina found that the sea was surprisingly shallow and marshy. Tall reeds were growing out of the water, and there were no waves to speak of, hardly even ripples. "I don't like this," said Lilli at one point, when they were both knee-deep in mud and slimy sea grass. "What if there are snakes?"

"I doubt there are," said Myrina, lying, as she stabbed the water in front of them with her spear. "Snakes don't like open water."

Just then, a burst of voices made them both stop.

"That is what I heard before!" hissed Lilli, pressing nervously against her sister's back. "Can you see them?"

Myrina pushed aside the reeds with her spear shaft. Through the tangle of green stems she could make out a small boat carrying three fishermen. They were too busy with their nets to notice her and Lilli, and she quickly decided they were hardworking men and thus trustworthy.

"Come!" She pulled Lilli through the water, anxious to reach the boat before it disappeared. The idea of spending another night in the dusty riverbed or in this marsh swarming with bugs was unbearable. Wherever those three fishermen were going, she and Lilli were going, too.

As soon as they were close enough to be seen, Myrina called out to the men, waving her spear in the air. She was in water up to her waist now, with Lilli riding on her back. Not surprisingly, the men stared at her in disbelief.

"They have seen us!" gasped Myrina, wading through the muddy water with unsteady strides. "They are smiling and waving us onboard—" But as she came closer to the boat, she saw that the men were not smiling. They were gesturing frantically, their faces contorted with fear.

Moments later, eager hands pulled first Lilli, then Myrina, onboard the boat, after which the men collapsed in relief and pointed into the water with long strings of explanation in a foreign language. "What is it?" Lilli wanted to know, clinging to her sister's muddy tunic. "What are they saying?"

"I wish I understood," muttered Myrina. Judging by their looks, the fishermen were a father and his two grown sons, and they did not seem like men who were easily shaken. "I think—"

Just then, the riverboat rocked, and the younger men instantly reached to steady their father. Myrina saw them all glancing nervously at the water, and she finally understood the source of their alarm.

A long, speckled form circled the boat, its enormous body sliding through the mire. Was it a large fish? But she saw neither head nor tail, merely a never-ending body as thick around as a human being. A colossal snake.

"What is it?" whimpered Lilli, sensing the sudden tension. "Tell me!"

Myrina could barely speak. She had seen large serpents before, certainly, but never anything like this. "Oh, it is nothing," she finally managed to say. "Just seaweed clinging to the hull."

After a few anxious moments the snake seemed to lose interest in the boat, and the men relaxed and began talking again. They checked a few more traps, but their catch was meager. Only a dozen or so fish and a couple of eels, but even so, the fishermen seemed in good spirits as they picked up their poles and laboriously propelled the boat forward with small, rhythmic jerks.

"Where are we going?" whispered Lilli, shivering with fatigue.

Myrina drew her sister's head to her chest and stroked her grimy cheek. "We are going to the big city, little lion. The Moon Goddess is waiting for us there, remember?"

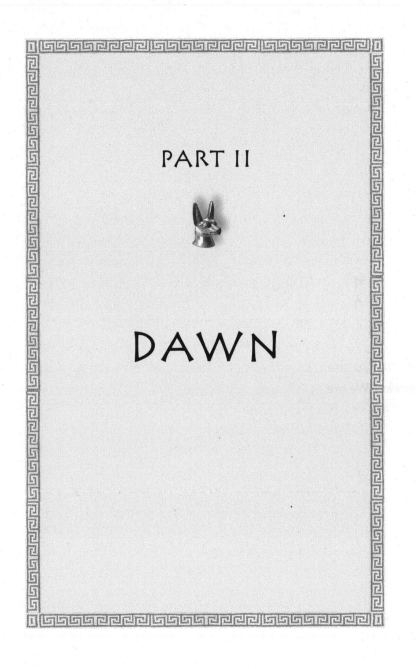

PART II

DAWN

CHAPTER SEVEN

The Amazons will gladly guide you on your way.
—AESCHYLUS, *Prometheus Bound*

GATWICK AIRPORT

IF MR. LUDWIG WAS SURPRISED TO FIND ME SITTING AT THE DEPAR-
ture gate, casually leafing through an abandoned boating magazine,
he didn't show it. He merely nodded, as if my presence was to be expected, and said, "Coffee?"

As soon as he had disappeared, I deflated with relief and exhaustion. For all my assumed calm, the past few hours had undoubtedly
been the most hectic of my life, and I had been at a breathless gallop
ever since finding Granny's notebook in the attic. Fortunately, my father had been perfectly available for a small adventure and had insisted
on driving me all the way to the airport. "Although I do confess to a
slight curiosity," he had said, quite reasonably, while we were parked
briefly in front of my Oxford college and I was struggling to squeeze a
hastily packed suitcase into the backseat of the Mini.

"It's just for a night or two," I replied, sliding into the passenger seat
and tightening my disheveled ponytail. "Maybe three."

The engine was still going, and my father was still holding the
steering wheel, but the car was not moving. "What about your teaching?"

I moved uncomfortably in my seat. "I'll be back before you know it.
It's a research trip. Someone is actually paying me to go to Amsterdam—"

"I take it young Moselane is not your benefactor?" My father was staring into the rearview mirror as he said this, and when I twisted around I saw James emerging from college with a tennis racket over his shoulder.

I suddenly felt hot all over, and it was not a pleasant sensation. There he was, reason incarnate, as gorgeous as ever . . . would it not be wise to inform him that I was leaving, rather than sneaking off like this?

"Oh, bugger," I said, checking my watch. "We really need to go."

My father kept glancing at the rearview mirror as we rolled down Merton Street, probably wondering how to present this inauspicious turn of events to my mother, and I felt the prickly yarn of guilt in my throat grow bigger with every twitch of his eye. But how could I possibly tell him the truth? He had never taken any steps to discuss Granny, had never told me about the notebook she had clearly left for me. To open the subject now on our way to the airport at what was, to him, breakneck speed, could hardly be a good idea. "I'm sorry, Daddy," I muttered, patting his arm. "I'll explain when I return."

We drove in silence for a bit. Out of the corner of my eye I could see his habitual dislike of confrontation wrestling with his growing parental concern, and in the end he took a deep breath and said, "Just promise me this is not some sort of"—he had to do a little run-up to pronounce the word—"elopement? You know we are perfectly capable of paying for a wedding reception—"

I was so shocked I started laughing. "Daddy, honestly!"

"Well, what am I to think?" He looked almost angry as he sat there, hunched over the steering wheel. "You come home for three hours, ask about your birth certificate . . . and now you're off to Amsterdam." He glanced at me, and there was a flicker of genuine fear in his eyes. "Promise me this is not about some . . . man. Your mother would never forgive me."

"Oh, Daddy!" I leaned over to kiss him on the cheek. "You know I would never do that. Don't you?"

He nodded without conviction, and I suppose I couldn't blame him. Although the subject rarely came up, I had no doubt my parents had deduced quite a bit about the motley handful of past boyfriends to whom Rebecca referred jointly as "the Horsemen of the Apocalypse," although none of them deserved so fine a title.

For whatever reason, I had never been good with men. Perhaps the culprit was my own particular preference for solitude, or perhaps—as Rebecca had once proposed, briefly forgetting my childhood crush on James Moselane—I had some genetic incapacity for romance, passed down from Granny. Whenever a relationship ended poorly, with tears and hurtful words, I would even occasionally be left with the suspicion that maybe I simply didn't *like* men, and that maybe this was why I had a growing bundle of farewell letters in my desk drawer accusing me— in more eloquent terms, of course—of being a frigid bitch.

Prompted by Rebecca, long-distance from Crete on occasion of my twenty-seventh birthday, I set out to determine whether my problem might be solved by a simple shift in focus from men to women. But after pondering the question for a week or so I had to conclude that women intrigued me even less than men. The sad conclusion, I decided, must therefore be that Diana Morgan was destined to be a loner . . . one of those ironclad ladies whose legacy did not consist in grandchildren, but in seven-pound monographs dedicated to some dead professor.

Three days later Federico Rivera arrived.

As a longtime regular at the Oxford University Fencing Club I was not easily impressed by posturing males, but I knew right away that the new Spanish master in residence was something else altogether. He was not handsome as such, but he was as tall as I and in excellent shape, and, more important, there was an explosive energy about him that was utterly intoxicating. Federico was a perfectionist, not only in fencing, but in the art of seduction as well, and although I am sure we both knew early on what the inescapable consequence of my private evening lessons with him would be, he spent several months focusing on my lunge and riposte and nothing else . . . before finally following me into the shower and teaching me the *coup d'arrêt* without a word.

Our affair lasted all winter, and despite Federico's insistence that we keep it secret, I fully believed him when he called me the love of his life. One day soon we would make it public . . . get married . . . have children. . . . It was never explicitly said, but always implied. And when he suddenly fled back to Spain from one day to the next, without so much as a goodbye, I was so shocked and heartbroken I thought I would never be happy again.

Then came all the terrible discoveries: Federico's many affairs around Oxford, the furious fiancée in Barcelona, and his ignominious dismissal from the fencing club . . . and yet I wrote him letter after tearful letter, pledging my love and understanding, begging him to respond.

He did. Several months later I received a fat envelope sent from a fencing academy in Madrid; it contained all my letters to him—most of them unopened—plus five hundred euro. Since he didn't owe me any money I was forced to assume it was his way of remunerating me for my services.

I was so furious it took me weeks to decide that Master Federico Rivera, in his libertine wisdom, must have deliberately insulted me in order to cauterize my wound and—perfectionist as he was—complete my fencing lessons with the most honorable move of all: the *coup de grâce*.

Even though I had never told my parents about him, they surely knew I had had my share of secret heartbreak. In fact, there were moments when I suspected that my mother's persistent obsession with James Moselane was simply her own way of consoling us both. And what could be more soothing than the vision of an ideal future in which I lived at the manor just around the corner, happily ever after?

WHEN MR. LUDWIG RETURNED with our coffee, I put away the magazine and moved my jacket so he could sit down next to me. "Thanks," I said, taking one of the cups, relishing its warmth against my nervous hands. "By the way, you never told me the name of the foundation sponsoring our current luxury."

Mr. Ludwig eased the lid off his own coffee. "I'm a careful guy." He took a tentative sip and made a face. "What is it with you Brits and coffee? Anyway, here is a name for you: the Skolsky Foundation. Sugar?"

Moments later, while I was frantically Googling the Skolsky Foundation, I heard Mr. Ludwig chuckle and looked up to find him shamelessly spying on my phone. "You won't find anything online," he informed me. "Mr. Skolsky prefers to fly under the radar. It's a billionaire thing."

Perhaps it was meant humorously, but I was not amused. Around us, the gate was bustling with airline representatives and travelers hoping to preboard the plane, but I was still largely in the dark about our voyage. "I'm embarrassed to say I've never heard of the Skolsky Foundation," I said. "But I am assuming its offices are in Amsterdam?"

Mr. Ludwig bent down to put his cup on the floor. "As I said, Mr. Skolsky is a private man. An industrialist with an interest in archaeology. He sponsors digs all over the world."

I stared at him, waiting for him to elaborate. When he did not, I leaned forward a bit, making it clear I was expecting more. "Such as—?"

Mr. Ludwig smiled, but something in his predatory eyes told me he was getting irritated. "I can't tell you until we get there. Skolsky protocol."

I was so upset by his dismissive attitude that I had a sudden revisitation not only of the vile coffee but also of the well-meant words of warning James had spoken the night before. The supposed Amazon inscription might be a hoax . . . or worse. That was how he had phrased it, and I found myself once again wondering what my own role was going to be. It was becoming painfully clear that Mr. Ludwig no longer felt the need to ingratiate himself with me, and I suspected the rapid decline of his manners foreshadowed the week ahead. Any normal person would heed the flashing signs and walk out while there was still time . . . except I couldn't. Granny's red notebook hidden in my handbag had long since overthrown my common sense.

"Ready?" Mr. Ludwig took out his boarding pass. "Let's go."

Moments later we were walking down the Jetway. I was still not sure why we were flying to Amsterdam, but by this point I knew it would be futile to ask. It did not lessen my confusion when Mr. Ludwig—instead of stepping on board the plane—stopped to exchange a few words with a man wearing a boilersuit and large orange earmuffs.

The man shot me a suspicious look before opening a door in the side of the Jetway and leading us both down a set of rickety metal steps until we were standing on the tarmac, next to the plane. Even outside, the air was dense with noise and exhaust, and when I opened my mouth to ask what was going on, I found myself choking on the jet fumes, unable to make myself heard.

After a short ride in a utility vehicle, weaving between catering vans and fuel trucks, we pulled up next to another plane. Only then, when I saw my suitcase changing hands and disappearing into the baggage compartment, did it dawn on me that our apparent flight to Amsterdam had been nothing but a carefully planned decoy.

There was no time to question Mr. Ludwig about our change of destination, however, for we were hastily ushered up the back stairs to the plane after only the most perfunctory security check.

"Some bangle," said Mr. Ludwig, when the wand beeped next to the bronze bracelet on my arm. "Do you use it as a weapon?"

"Not yet, but I might," I replied, pulling down my sleeve again. He did not need to know that the bracelet had belonged to my grandmother, and that I had excavated it from my underwear drawer only a few hours earlier, as a way of initiating this unexpected adventure. As far as Mr. Ludwig was concerned, I had come along for the money and the possibility of academic glory; I didn't want him to know exactly how personal the trip was to me. If Mr. Skolsky could fly low, so could I.

As the plane taxied to the runway with us both safely strapped into first class, I said to Mr. Ludwig, "Perhaps now would not be an entirely unreasonable moment for you to tell me where we are going?"

Mr. Ludwig touched his champagne flute to mine. "Djerba. Here's to a productive trip. Sorry about the hocus-pocus, but there is too much at stake."

I was itching to take out my phone and look it up, but we were only minutes away from takeoff. As far as I knew, Djerba was a small island in the Mediterranean, off the coast of Tunisia, and known primarily for its resort hotels and pleasant climate. It had never struck me as having much of an archaeological scene, but then, I doubted Djerba was where the actual excavation was. It was most likely in mainland Tunisia.

Which made perfect sense.

Modern-day Tunisia is a relatively small country wedged between Algeria and Libya, but two thousand years ago it was the archrival of the Roman Empire. As a consequence, its ancient capital, Carthage, was eventually destroyed by the Romans, who sold its inhabitants into slavery and annihilated its historical records. Almost no written sources escaped this consummate cultucide; the land of Hannibal might as well have been a myth.

But these were all relatively recent events compared to the time when—according to some—the heroes of Greek mythology walked the earth. Famous figures such as Hercules, Jason, and Theseus belonged to a prehistoric world of monsters and magic . . . and Amazons.

It was true that most ancient writers—regardless of whether they believed in the legends or not—placed the Amazon homeland in the east, most often on the Black Sea coast of northern Turkey, but a few claimed this nation of women warriors originated in North Africa. Part of the problem was that the Amazon tradition fell more or less into three periods, all of which differed enormously, both in time and space.

The last of these three periods had the Amazons entrenched in and around Themiscyra, their legendary capital on the Black Sea, and saw them gradually squeezed from all sides until they either died out or became absorbed by surrounding tribes. One might say this period was a long, slow autumn culminating in one last blossom around the year 330 B.C.E. when an Amazon queen allegedly paid a visit to Alexander the Great, asking that she and her female entourage might spend a fortnight with him in the hopes of conceiving children by this living legend of a man. By the time the Romans showed up—only a century or so later—the Amazon nation was nowhere to be found.

Without a question, their heyday was the middle period, namely the age of the Trojan War, which most scholars would place about three thousand years ago, somewhere between 1300 and 1100 B.C.E. This was the time when the Amazons were skewered by Achilles before the tall walls of Troy, and where Hercules roamed the Trojan hinterland to get his hands on the Amazon queen's girdle as part of his Twelve Labors. It was also the time when the Amazons supposedly raided Athens and finally earned their place on the Parthenon frieze—also known as the Elgin Marbles.

But before that, there was an Amazon springtime of sporadic shoots, the most significant of which grew out of the legendary Lake Tritonis in North Africa. Some claimed this was the homeland of the first Amazons, who were said to have gathered a large army and invaded neighboring countries.

Compared to the later Black Sea Amazons, though, these early shoots came with far less historical framework, and I had often seen Amazon fanatics rolling their eyes at the Lake Tritonis myths, not realizing, perhaps, that to Amazon skeptics it was a little bit like seeing Tooth Fairy believers scoff at the Easter Bunny.

The issue, of course, is complicated by the fact that the climate of North Africa has undergone tremendous changes since the Bronze Age, and that Lake Tritonis—if it ever existed—is long gone. I knew of many archaeologists who were desperate to dig in the area . . . but where to start? The Sahara Desert is an enormous duvet covering all your sweetest dreams of undiscovered civilizations, but your chances of going out there with your shovel and bucket and finding as much as a bedbug are next to nil.

Therefore, the fact that we were presently on our way to Tunisia, which, according to some, was where Lake Tritonis used to be, was exciting indeed. Was it possible the Skolsky Foundation had found evidence of a matriarchal society with women warriors? The potential payoff was staggering.

"Djerba is where Homer's Lotus-Eaters used to live," Mr. Ludwig said, interrupting my thoughts. "Scary zombie types, drugged out on local foliage." He put on his eyeshade, but it only partially covered his smugness. "Sounds to me like the perfect place for an academic."

The observation was so obviously intended to provoke me that I found it quite easy to laugh off. "I have to defer to your expertise on the subject. But you didn't invite me along for the foliage, did you?" I stared at his face, tempted to peek underneath the eyeshade to make sure he was paying attention. "This is about the Amazons, correct?"

Mr. Ludwig adjusted his inflatable headrest and managed to add a few more layers of chin to his ample jowls. "Don't ask me. I never have anything to do with the excavations. Not even sure why I'm in Europe when the Amazon jungle is in South America. But"—he folded his hands over his belly with a shrug—"when Mr. Skolsky tells me to do something, I do it. I don't let my brain get in the way."

It was probably fortunate he dozed off after this little exchange, for we were beginning to get on each other's nerves. Despite his apparent generosity—or at least his readiness to spend Mr. Skolsky's money— there was a self-satisfied pettiness to Mr. Ludwig that was truly offensive.

It did not help that I was aching to take out Granny's notebook. Ever since finding it in the attic a few hours earlier, I had been desperate to test whether any parts of the wall inscription on the photo corresponded with words in the notebook. But between then and now, I had not had a single moment to sit down and break out my magnifying glass.

Perhaps it was silly of me to keep the notebook hidden from Mr. Ludwig, but as I sat there rolling and unrolling the in-flight magazine, listening to all his jerks and snorts as we went through layer after bumpy layer of English weather, I truly felt he was not a man to be trusted. Never mind his worrying flair for secrecy, if not downright dishonesty; was it just my imagination, or had he looked at my bracelet with more than common curiosity?

Shaped like a snake but with a peculiar, doglike head with pointy ears at one end, the bronze band had been forged to coil twice around a woman's wrist, and, to be sure, I couldn't blame my travel companion for being intrigued. But the circumstances of my having inherited this particular piece of jewelry were such as to make me exceedingly uncomfortable with his questioning, however innocent it might have been.

Granny had worn the bracelet as constantly as one would wear a wedding ring, and for all my parents knew she had taken it with her to the grave. I had never dared tell them that one day, about a year into my graduate studies at Oxford, I had found a small padded envelope unceremoniously jammed into my mail slot in the college lodge. The envelope had contained no message, merely this jackal bracelet of hers, which she had once told me "only a true Amazon may wear."

Receiving this special treasure so unexpectedly from an anonymous sender in Berlin had filled me with a noxious blend of fear and bewilderment. Did this mean Granny had died? Or was the bracelet a summons? If so, surely an explanation would follow.

But none came, and I eventually squirreled the envelope away in my underwear drawer without a word to anyone. Once or twice I toyed with the idea of showing it to Rebecca in the hopes she might be able to subject it to some scientific analysis or other . . . but then, that would have meant reopening a troublesome subject. And for all our shared childhood secrets, the truth about Granny's disappearance was something I could never share with anyone, not even her.

It was dark by the time we landed in Djerba. As soon as we emerged from the plane and started down the narrow staircase, we were enfolded in a warm, fragrant breeze that made me almost giddy, despite the hour. It had been many years since I had last felt the thrill of the southern climes, and until this moment it had not even occurred to me how much I missed it.

Rebecca always blamed Oxford for turning me into such a tea-toddling homebody, and I never contradicted her. The truth was, I should have liked nothing better than to jet off regularly like everyone else, to read ancient scrolls in Jordan or scrutinize disputed folios in a grand old library in Rome . . . but I couldn't afford it. Writing convincing applications for funding, apparently, was not my strong suit. And so

I stayed where I was, limiting myself to subjects within bicycle range and living vicariously through the postcards on the shared fridge.

"Hanging in there?" asked Mr. Ludwig, as we walked together through the sleepy airport. "Don't worry, it won't be long before you're rid of me."

A brief taxi ride later, we pulled up in front of a white building that looked rather less majestic than most of the mushrooming resort hotels we had passed along the way. But despite appearances, the modest front door of Hotel Dar el Bhar opened into an alluring realm of elegance and tranquillity, and although its whitewashed walls and porticoes had none of the gargoyle gothic of Oxford, I felt immediately at home.

Beyond the reception area was an inner courtyard with tall trees growing in large flower beds and flickering lanterns sitting directly on the tile floor. Here, more than ever, the air was full of spices, and from somewhere in the darkness of this enchanting garden came the trickling sounds of a fountain.

I am not sure how long I stood there, staring at a potted plant with large yellow fruit and wondering whether I was looking at my first lemon tree, but eventually Mr. Ludwig passed me a room key and said, "You are registered under the name of Dr. Mayo. Just a precaution. If I don't see you tomorrow"—he stuck out his hand—"good luck. My colleague will take over from here."

I looked around, thinking he was going to introduce me, but saw no one.

Mr. Ludwig smiled. "We never connect in person."

"Let me guess: Skolsky protocol?"

His smile turned wry. "More of a scheduling thing. Ahmed lives in his own private time zone."

MY ROOM WAS UPSTAIRS, off the portico that went all around the courtyard and offered a unique treetop view of this private jungle. It was a beautiful junior suite, complete with tasseled red pillows and a welcoming bowl of dates, but at this point I was so tired my eyes were cramping closed. It was only just midnight, but then, excitement had prevented me from sleeping much the night before, and the night prior to that I had been busy into the wee hours finishing my conference paper.

Still, ever since leaving my parents' house that afternoon I had been anticipating the moment when I could turn to Granny's notebook. And so, after a light room service meal of bread and hummus I splashed water on my face and sat down to scrutinize Mr. Ludwig's photo yet again, this time looking for specific sets of symbols that might be individual words, in order to search for them in Granny's dense, handwritten list.

But it was a greater challenge than I had imagined, and my initial excitement at concluding that the two writing systems were, indeed, completely identical was soon squashed by the enormity of the task at hand.

Even with the help of the magnifying glass I was unable to identify any dots or dashes that might have functioned as word dividers. All I had was a long string of letters or syllables in a language I didn't know. Furthermore, Granny's "dictionary" was not alphabetical, neither in English, nor, it seemed, in the other language. The whole thing was, in other words, frustratingly random, and I couldn't ignore a little voice reminding me that I was—perhaps in vain—trying to impose reason on the obsessive scribbles of a lunatic.

After two hours' focused work I was beat. If I were to trust Granny's notebook, the first word of the inscription was either "moon," "water," or "woman." I decided to be content with that and got up to brush my teeth.

Mystery inscription aside, the biggest puzzle of all was how Granny had come to know this ancient language. Perhaps her delusions were simply the unfortunate side effects of once having studied archaeology or even philology like me. It was not unthinkable this writing system had been discovered before, and possibly even deciphered by some obscure university team who never got around to publishing a report. Or maybe they did, and no one ever bothered to read it.

Utterly exhausted but unable to relax, I lay in the darkness, enjoying the soft breeze from the open window. A remarkable variety of insects and birds was already anticipating sunrise with hectic rustling and all manner of shrieks and squawks, and beyond this cacophony of wild-life, from somewhere out there, came the steady, pulsing sound of the sea.

ONE SUMMER AFTERNOON, WHEN I was nine years old, my parents had hosted a garden party for all their neighbors. Several nights before the event, I had sat on the staircase and overheard the discussion about whether Granny should be allowed to attend. "You know it will be a di-saster," my mother kept insisting. "She is bound to insult someone or say something wildly inappropriate. And . . . imagine the looks on people's faces when they realize we have a madwoman living in our attic!"

But for once, my father's stubborn practicality had held sway. "Surely," he said at length, "introducing her to the neighborhood in a civilized manner is the best way of ensuring that she does *not* become some kind of invisible monster living in their own imagination. As soon. as they see her with Diana, our neighbors will realize she is completely harmless."

So it came about that I was tasked with escorting my new grand-mother throughout the party, introducing her to people and helping her at the buffet. By and large, the scheme was a success. Our guests ad-dressed her the way they would a normal person, with polite inanities about the garden, and Granny smiled and nodded, as if she cared.

At one point, however, we found ourselves in a lively group of la-dies who had succeeded in driving the new unmarried churchwarden up against a pear tree. "And you, my dear," the poor man asked Granny, eager to branch out and open up the conversation, "did you also grow up here?"

"No," she replied, calmly taking another sip of the wine I was sup-posed to have exchanged with lemonade. "I come from the Hodna Mountains. My name is Kara. I am the second in command."

The churchwarden stuck a finger into his collar, possibly to let in a little fresh air. "Of what, exactly? If one might be so bold—"

Granny cast him a disgusted frown. "Of the Amazons, of course. Who taught you about the world? You know nothing. Why are you talking to me? Men like you—" She snapped her fingers dismissively and marched away.

Later, safely back in the attic, I asked her if it was really true she had once been an Amazon named Kara. I quite liked the idea of Granny as a young warrior woman, armed and on horseback, chasing churchwardens and gossipy ladies with arrows and war cries.

According to Rebecca's mother, who, being the vicar's wife, considered herself an expert on all things paranormal, the colorful Amazons were nothing but the spawn of pagan ignorance. "The mere notion," she had said, at one particularly memorable Sunday school meeting, "that a group of women should be able to live together without men is both wicked and absurd. I have certainly never heard of such abnormal behavior—"

"What about nuns?" I had countered, sincerely trying to understand, but Mrs. Wharton had pretended not to hear me.

"So is it true?" I asked Granny once more, bouncing up and down on the chair with anticipation. "Were you really an Amazon?"

But now, to my dismay, she brushed it all aside with a groan and started walking about the room, adjusting and readjusting every piece of furniture, every little trinket, with obsessive accuracy. "Don't listen to me. I'm a crazy old woman. I forgot rule number two. Never forget rule number two."

I deflated with disappointment. "What's rule number two?"

Granny stopped, her hands on the back of a chair, and looked straight at me. "Always make sure," she said, slowly, to ensure I paid attention, "that *they* underestimate *you*. That is the key."

"But why?" I insisted. "And who are *they*?"

The question made Granny flinch, and she tiptoed around the chair to kneel down at my feet. "The men in green clothes," she whispered, her eyes suddenly wide with fear. "They look inside your head and cut out the things you're not supposed to think. So you must learn to think nothing. Never let them know who you are. Can you do that?"

I was so frightened by her intensity I nearly started crying. "But I'm not an Amazon——"

"Shush!" Granny squeezed my shoulders so hard it hurt. "Never say that word aloud. You mustn't even think it. Do you understand?" Only then, when she saw that all I could manage was a tearful nod, she cradled my head with her hands and said, more softly, "You are brave. I have high hopes for you. Don't disappoint me."

CHAPTER EIGHT

LAKE TRITONIS

Myrina and Lilli spent all afternoon on the fishing boat, punting along the swampy coastline and checking traps that were mostly empty. But in the hour of evening calm, just as Myrina began to fear they would be spending the night on the water, circled by monstrous serpents, the men finally pulled into a cove rimmed with beach huts.

After their long, solitary wanderings, the sight of busy men and women filled Myrina with joy and apprehension all at once. Their mother had always maintained the people living by the sea were the friendliest of all, but then, she had also spoken of clear blue water and sandy beaches—none of which had turned out to be true. In reality, the hue of the sea was a muddy green, and the water in the cove was a stagnant soup of bird feathers and rotting seaweed.

Once their boat had been pulled ashore and its meager catch handed off to a woman with a large basket, one of the fishermen gestured for Myrina and Lilli to follow him, all the while smiling and nodding, as if to assure them of his good intentions. He took them to see an elderly man in a long red cloak who sat with straight-backed dignity on a straw mat in front of a hut, eating nuts from a glazed bowl. Guessing the man was a village elder, Myrina knelt down with Lilli in the sprinkle of nutshells at his feet.

"Greetings to you," she said, in her own language. When he did not reply, she repeated the greeting in the three other languages she knew—the Old Language, the Language of the Mountain People, and the Nomad Language. None of her earlier attempts had worked with the fishermen on the boat, but when she spoke now in the tongue of the desert nomads, the man brought his weatherworn hands together in excitement.

"You speak the words of the camel people!"

"Only a little," said Myrina. "How do you know the camel people?"

"They came here to trade." The man waved a gaunt arm in the air around him, as if to indicate that things had changed, and not for the better. "There was good trading here when the river ran strong. But no more."

Although Lilli had never learned the Nomad Language, she seemed to instinctively understand what the man was saying, and they sat for a moment in silence, sharing his distress. Then the man offered both girls a drink of water from a calabash and said, in a tone of business, "Now it is your time to talk. How may I help you young women?"

"We are on our way to see the Moon Goddess," began Myrina. "In the big city. My sister was blinded by a fever, but we are hopeful she will be cured."

"I am sorry for your sister." The man shook his head with regret. "Many, many people journey to the Moon Goddess. She is very busy."

"Even so," said Myrina, "we should like to see her."

The man looked a little annoyed, then shrugged and threw up his hands as if to say he had done what he could. "It is not far. I will tell you the way, but first you must eat and sleep."

IN THE HOUR BEFORE sunrise, hovering on the threshold of the waking world, Myrina sensed the sleeping bodies around her, heard the soft whispers of mothers, and for a moment thought she was back home.

Over there in the corner, she imagined, lay her older sister, Lana, with the new baby snuggled tightly under her arm. And here, right here against her chest, lay Lilli, warm and cuddly and sweet. . . .

The stench brought Myrina back to the present. Unwashed for weeks, with cakes of dirt and bloody crusts hopelessly entangled in its curly mesh, Lilli's hair was a cruel reminder of everything they had lost.

Myrina turned her head away and clenched her teeth, forcing it all from her consciousness—the sounds, the smells, and all the dear, familiar forms. "Stop thinking," she commanded herself, over and over, until nothing was left but those two words and their lingering echo.

As THE SUN ROSE and the time for departure came, Myrina took off her necklace and gave it to the fishermen in return for their hospitality. They all shook their heads and refused the gift, but Myrina was determined; although she and Lilli were poor, they still had their dignity.

The necklace was a string of a dozen delicate buds—not from plants, but from the salt plains, which occasionally gave birth to stone flowers of extraordinary beauty. It had been a gift from Myrina's father to her mother on the occasion of Myrina's birth—a small pledge of interest from a nomad who called himself a husband but never visited long enough to be so.

"You might as well take this," Myrina's mother had said one day, when she was going through her finery. "Here." She had closed Myrina's fingers around the necklace with a frown of determination. "Maybe your wearing it will remind him—wherever he is—that he has a daughter."

Since that day, Myrina had not dared take off the necklace for fear its removal would sever her from her father forever. But now, with their home in ashes, she knew he would never be able to find her again, necklace or no.

And so she and Lilli left the fishing village well rested and with full bellies, but poorer than ever. There was not a single good arrow left in Myrina's quiver, and with her necklace gone, too, they were unlikely to procure another meal until they reached their destination. "I suppose we could sell Mother's bracelet," muttered Lilli, as they walked together along the road to town.

"No!" Myrina took the traveling satchel away from her sister. "She wouldn't want us to give it away. And we're so close now—"

But when she saw the city rising before them on the horizon, with its jagged, man-made mountains of building upon building glowing brightly in the morning sun, even Myrina began to wonder whether they were truly that close to their journey's end. To someone who had never seen a town bigger than the village at home, with its three dozen houses and one central common, a settlement as colossal as this defied all natural sense.

Soon, the road became busy, and people and carts pushed past them impatiently, never stopping to greet them or inquire where they were from. Although she did not say it out loud, Myrina found it all deeply discouraging. In such a vast and busy place, where humans seemed no more mindful, no more welcoming, than beetles, she began to fear that she and Lilli—for all their mother's assurances—just might discover that they were of next to no consequence to the Moon Goddess or to anyone else.

"Do tell me what you see!" begged Lilli. "Can you see the temple yet?"

But Myrina saw nothing that looked like the magnificent building their mother had described. The Temple of the Moon Goddess, apparently, was as tall as it was wide, and made of brilliant, otherworldly stone. From the splendor of this lofty dwelling the Goddess controlled the ebb and flood of water, cured the ailments of women, and stood up boldly against the reign of the Sun, defying him by lighting up the night sky behind his back. Throughout their long journey, Myrina had been confident that if she and Lilli ever did reach the city on the sea, the temple of this powerful deity would dwarf any other structure around it. How wrong she had been. Walking through the teeming streets with Lilli in tow, she saw many marvelous buildings, some impossibly tall, but none that looked as if they were made out of anything other than sun-dried mud brick.

The immediate challenge, however, was maneuvering through the unfamiliar and unpredictable movements of other people, which more than once made Myrina reach for the knife in her belt. Fortunately, most of the city dwellers were entirely engaged in their own pursuits; some were carrying tools and ladders around, as if off to build or repair a house, and others were driving mooing, bleating, or clucking livestock through the streets, presumably heading for the marketplace.

A few characters, though, were clearly hovering around with the purpose of striking a bargain with the occasional passerby. Some who had clothing and finery to sell were even bold enough to drape their merchandise around Lilli's neck before Myrina could push them away. Others offered their services in hoarse, hushed voices before retreating into the dark alleys. It did not take long for Myrina's polite newcomer's curiosity to fade into suspicious disdain. She quickly learned to avoid eye contact with anyone seemingly idle, and to duck or sidestep whenever someone approached her with a big smile.

There was no need to explain what she was doing; Lilli instinctively understood. She let Myrina drag her through the tumult, and when the street finally widened, and they could stop and catch their breath, the girl was quivering from top to toe. "Oh, Myrina!" she exclaimed. "To think this place has been here all the time . . . with all these people. It is too wonderful!"

"I don't know what is so very wonderful about it——" Myrina began, but then she regretted her words. She had waited so long for Lilli to regain her usual zest for life; she would not squash it.

"What is that horrible smell?" Lilli held her nose in disgust. "It is foul!"

They stood on the rim of a large, open area crowded with humans and animals. Judging from the presence of old, cracked seashells on the hard-packed sand, this sloping ground had been seashore not too long ago—perhaps even a place where tradesmen pulled up their ships. Everywhere Myrina turned were piles of melons and heaps of colorful spices displayed on mats, and a cacophony of wild shrieks told her butchers were slaughtering animals right there, in the middle of it all. "It is a marketplace," she told Lilli. "Bigger than you can imagine. But there is also"—she stretched to see beyond the commotion—"a house. Enormous. With broad steps in front, and tall, tall columns made of stone."

As they worked their way through the mayhem, heading for the formidable building, Myrina felt a flutter of excitement in her belly. For above the tall columns ran a long, colorful depiction of all the lunar phases, with the full moon in the middle, right above the colossal entrance door. "I am not sure," she said, stopping, "but I think this must be it."

"At last!" Lilli shifted her weight back and forth, anxious to continue. "Why are we standing still?"

"Our task is not an easy one." Myrina looked out over the rolling horde of people gathered in front of the temple, clearly seeking help. She had never before seen so many assembled in one place. "Come." Pulling Lilli along by the hand, she tentatively stepped forward, taking care not to disturb the sick resting on mats or the rawboned mothers trying to console their wailing children. But she did not get far before an old woman rose to block her way, sneering something in a language she did not understand.

"I think we must wait our turn." Myrina looked around at the fetid puddles. The stench was nearly unbearable. "These people have been here for many days, if not weeks. But don't worry." She took Lilli firmly by the shoulders, determined that they would not spend as much as a night in this place, surrounded by shrill lamentations and oozing sores. "We'll find another way."

Pulling her sister along, Myrina walked briskly away from the mob to see what lay on the other side of the temple. She was intrigued to discover that a tall wall extended from the back of the giant stone building to surround what must be a cluster of houses belonging to the holy complex. And even more encouraging: At the rear, ringed by thorny shrubberies, two tall palm trees had been allowed to grow undisturbed, one leaning gently toward the temple wall. An irresistible temptation for anyone with a hunter's heart.

"And you thought the gods were against us." Myrina put her back against the leaning palm tree, testing its strength. "I am telling you, they are on our side. If I am not mistaken, the Moon Goddess has opened her back door to us. Now stay here"—she handed Lilli her spear and bow, slinging their traveling satchel over her shoulder instead—"while I find someone with a friendly ear."

THE MIDDAY SUN WAS pouring gold into the temple courtyard. Its reflection in the artfully tiled water basin set the surrounding walls alight with a myriad of glittering stars, and the few women at leisure in this private haven were mostly asleep on mats in the shade of potted trees, the sleeves of their long, white dresses draped elegantly over their eyes. As a result, it took a while before anyone noticed the figure standing atop the tall garden wall, hands raised in greeting.

"I bring you friendship!" were the words Myrina had chosen for the occasion, and although she did not expect anyone to understand her, she was confident her smile would be enough to convince them of her peaceful intent.

But apparently, the women just saw a filthy, trespassing thief about to jump on them from the garden wall, for within a breath or two the tranquil setting erupted in screaming panic.

"No! Please—" Myrina swerved when one of the women pitched a stone at her. But the dainty arm in the flimsy white sleeve had clearly never practiced, and the rock fell into the water basin with a harmless *plop*.

Nevertheless, Myrina decided to abandon her perilous stand. Running a few feet farther away along the wall, she jumped onto a lower wall and from there onto a heap of straw mats lying on the ground. As soon as she had regained her balance, she put up her hands once more and smiled at the women, saying, "I am here on a peaceful errand. I carry no weapons. This little thing"—she pointed at the knife in her belt—"is just for hunting. Do you understand?"

For some reason, the women started screaming again, and Myrina looked around nervously, wondering where to flee. There were several dark door openings to choose from. . . . But she never got that far.

From somewhere behind her came a gasping shuffle of heavy bodies, and Myrina spun around to see three enormous men approaching her. Unprepared, she tried to duck away, but two of the men had already thrown ropes around her as if she were a wild animal, and while Myrina struggled to free herself, the third forced a sack over her head.

As they carried her off, she tried to protest in every language she knew, explaining she had come on behalf of her sister—her poor little sister, languishing in the heat outside. But the dusty sack filled her throat with grit, and her pleas were soon stopped by violent fits of coughing.

In her desperation, Myrina was at a loss to guess where the men were taking her. Hog-tied and blinded, she could not be sure, but it sounded as if they carried her through long corridors full of mumbling voices, down a set of stairs, and down again . . . before, finally, they dropped her on a hard, cool floor and pulled the sack from her head.

Blinking, Myrina tried to understand the space she was in, but before her eyes had adjusted to the dim, flickering light of a lonely torch, she heard the sound of metal sliding heavily over stone. The men had uncovered a black hole in the floor, immediately at her feet.

Myrina tried to move away, but they would not let her.

Without a word, they shoved her forward over the edge, and she fell with a scream into the darkness.

CHAPTER NINE

That corner of the world smiles in my eye beyond any others.
—HORACE, *The Odes*

DJERBA, TUNISIA

I WAS YANKED OUT OF OBLIVION BY THE PRODIGIOUS RING OF AN OLD-fashioned telephone. It was sitting on the bedside table, within arm's reach, half a world away. "Hello?" I mumbled, still not entirely sure where I was.

"My excuses for ringing so early," said the chipper voice of the hotel concierge, "but Mr. Ahmed is here."

"Who?" Only then did I manage to fully drag myself out of the deep well of slumber. According to my wristwatch I had been out for just over two hours, and the filigree of light on the reddish tile floor confirmed that, outside the shutters, darkness had turned to dawn.

"Mr. Ahmed is waiting," insisted the voice. "He says to come now."

The hotel still appeared to be asleep around me as I emerged on the portico, woozy from having had my much-needed rest cut so short. Despite being commanded to hurry, I paused for a moment to lean on the banister and breathe in the calmness of the courtyard below. A lonely cat was strutting about silently between the potted plants, its tail signaling ownership; the only sound disturbing the morning peace was the faint whisper of a straw broom against a stone floor.

Only then did I notice the figure lurking in the colonnade near the reception area, directly across the courtyard from my room. Clad in a long white garment and a head scarf held in place by a cord, the man looked eminently Arabic, and I felt a dash of trepidation when I realized this must be Ahmed.

As soon as I came downstairs, he walked toward me impatiently, as if I had kept him idling here for hours. I stopped uncertainly in the middle of the floor. If this was indeed Ahmed, I thought, struggling against a surge of nausea, it was hard to reconcile his appearance with his presumed affiliation with the dapper Mr. Ludwig and the evident prosperity of the Skolsky Foundation. Seen up close, the whiteness of Ahmed's robe was compromised by a myriad of stains and rips, and as for the man himself, his murky features were dominated by an unkempt black beard and a pair of cheap plastic sunglasses.

"Dr. Mayo?" He held out a grimy hand.

"Who? Oh—" I was so befuddled, I hesitated longer than I should have. It was only a second or two, I am sure, but long enough for Ahmed to pull back his hand with a grunt of dismay.

"This way," he said, turning to go.

Too shaken to ask a single question, I automatically followed him through the reception area and beyond, blinking against the bright morning sun as we stepped through the front door.

Outside the hotel, right where the taxi had dropped off Mr. Ludwig and me the night before, was now parked a battered monstrosity that could only be Ahmed's jeep—if indeed "jeep" was the right word for the vehicle.

"Please!" He held the passenger door open for me, probably more out of impatience than gallantry. "You travel light. That is good."

I stared at him, blocking the sun with my hand. "Are you saying . . . we're not coming back to the hotel?"

Even though I could not see his eyes through the greasy black plastic, I felt them boring into mine. "Did John not inform you?"

"John?" I zipped up my jumper a little further.

"Yes." Ahmed hesitated, as if he, too, was suddenly questioning our association. "John Ludwig. The man who brought you here?"

"Of course!" I was able to recover a smile. Mr. Ludwig. The man who had promised me academic stardom and five thousand dollars.

"On a good day, it's a twelve-hour drive"—Ahmed brushed off the passenger seat with his sleeve—"and we're already late. So, let's go!"

To HIS CREDIT, MY new escort was considerably more civil by the time I finally emerged from the hotel with my luggage. "I apologize," he said, putting away some species of cellphone in the folds of his ratty skirt, "but they never told me you were coming in so late. Here—" He took my suitcase and flung it into the back of the jeep, over the roll bar, with surprising agility. "Ready to go?"

As we drove away from the hotel, I was struck by the folly of it all. If, at some prior moment in my life, I had been presented with a questionnaire asking how likely I was to get into a car with a strange man of obscure ethnicity, clad in rags, and allow him to take me to an undisclosed location in a foreign country, I would surely have ticked the "very unlikely" box.

Yet here I was.

Even though it was October, the wind blowing against my face and tearing at my hair was warm and dry—so unlike the cool dampness of Oxford that I felt as completely out of place as if I had arrived in Tunisia by time machine. My hastily packed suitcase held primarily clothes intended for Amsterdam, with a few summer items optimistically thrown in. But this morning, in my haste, I had not had the wherewithal to put on anything other than the jeans and jumper I had worn the day before.

"Coffee?" Reaching behind his seat, Ahmed produced two granola bars and a grungy thermos.

"I'm not really much of a coffee drinker," I told him.

"Here." He tossed me a bottle of water instead. "Factory sealed."

While I ate the granola bar, we crossed the bridge that connected the island of Djerba with the mainland of Tunisia. As we drove inland, away from the coast, the landscape changed dramatically. Without the softening effect of the ocean and the valiant efforts of hotel gardeners, the vegetation was slowly drowning in smooth waves of sand rolling in from the south. Fields, groves, orchards . . . although too subtle to be discerned by the eye, the creamy tide of the desert was unstoppable, and the roadside produce stands were dominated by curiously beguiling chunks of sandstone in different shapes and sizes. "Sand roses," explained Ahmed, when he saw me turning in my seat to look. "Minerals. They form naturally here. The tourists buy them."

I sat quietly, taking in the vastness of the desert surrounding us, reminding myself that what I could see was but an infinitesimally small drop in the ocean of sand that was the Sahara. Thousands of years ago, these regions had been fertile, with prosperous urban settlements, but Nature had cast a fairy spell and put them to sleep beneath a blanket of fine-grained oblivion that no amount of scholarship could ever hope to remove.

"Do you mind," I asked at length, "if I make a quick call?"

"As long as you don't tell anyone where you are," replied Ahmed. "And you can't use your own phone. Under any circumstances. Here." He balanced his coffee cup on the dashboard and reached into a pocket. "Use this one instead. It's a satphone, so there'll be some delay."

Despite the coat of sweat and dirt with which it was dressed, Ahmed's phone gave me an excellent line to England and to the one person I knew I had to call: James Moselane. Not only was James unsurpassed when it came to pulling strings around college without alerting the wrong people, but the words he had spoken on my doorstep two nights before dared me to believe he cared more about my safety than I had hitherto assumed.

I was aware, of course, that James would be none too pleased with my absconding, and was frankly relieved when his voice mail came on right away. In the most breezy terms possible, I left a brief message asking him to please, if it wasn't too much trouble, cancel my classes and tutorials for the week. Preferably without Professor Vandenbosch finding out.

When I handed the phone back to Ahmed I spied a smile somewhere within his squirrel's nest of a beard and chose to interpret it as an opening. "So," I said, "what sort of man is Mr. Skolsky?"

"Mr. Skolsky?" Ahmed screwed the cup back on the thermos and pitched it over his shoulder, into the back of the jeep, where it landed with a clang in a heap of propane tanks. "No idea. I've never met him."

I looked out at the desolate landscape and saw a boy driving a flock of goats across a salt plain. "But you work for him?"

"Let's just say they hire me for . . . special jobs."

Despite his dismissive manner, Ahmed intrigued me. He was evidently a paradoxical sort of person with his Bedouin appearance and fairly Western manners. Take away the accent, and his English was suspiciously colloquial. In fact, I was beginning to harbor a suspicion that he was simply some kooky American with a penchant for dressing up when his phone rang and he answered it in rapid-fire Arabic.

"Is something wrong?" I dared to ask, after he hung up.

"When you are dealing with government, how can anything ever be right?" he grumbled, his fingers drumming on the steering wheel. "But no, it's okay. We are just strategizing about where to cross the border."

For no particular reason, my pulse broke into a gallop. "What border?"

Ahmed shook his head. "Dr. Mayo, we are in Tunisia, driving west. Don't they teach geography in that fancy school of yours?"

FOR HER TENTH BIRTHDAY, Rebecca had received a giant jigsaw map of the world from some divorced aunt whose presents were always a bit perverse. She had not been allowed to put it together at home; apparently, the one-thousand-piece folly would have taken up too much space in the humble parsonage.

As we had done with so many other subversive items in months past, we ended up taking the puzzle to Granny's apartment in the attic. We laid it out on the floor beneath the gable window and began by separating the edges from the rest of the pieces. Come dinnertime we had only really managed to put together the four corners and a few bits in between.

When we returned the next day after school, the jigsaw puzzle was lying, fully completed, on the hobby table in the middle of the room.

"Goodness me!" exclaimed Rebecca, clutching her mouth with

graceful affectation and sounding very much like her mother. "Did you do that all by yourself, Mrs. Morgan?"

We both stared at my grandmother, who was sitting in her usual armchair, staring blankly out the window, one of her crossed legs kicking rhythmically at nothing in particular. A little upset with her for taking away Rebecca's pleasure in assembling her own birthday present, I said, "How *could* you?"

Granny shrugged. "It was easy. But the map is wrong—"

"No." Rebecca crawled up on a chair to admire the puzzle from above. "It's perfect. Look, Diana . . . she even did the oceans!"

"It says here"—Granny stood up at last, waving the lid of the box—"that it is a world map. But it isn't." She gestured at the puzzle. "That world is wrong."

"Really?" Rebecca was intrigued. "How so?"

Even before Granny began to articulate her observation, I knew we were in for some convoluted absurdity that would leave me cringing. I did not mind it so much when she and I were alone together, but it pained me whenever I saw that look on Rebecca's face: the look of extreme politeness that comes from finding oneself face-to-face with insanity.

"Firstly," began Granny, leaning over the puzzle with a frown, "what are we to make of this nonsense over here?"

We both followed her finger.

"You mean . . . America?" asked Rebecca, her eyes round with bafflement.

"I mean all of it—" Granny made a sweeping gesture at the New World in general. "And this"—she pointed at the Statue of Liberty—"belongs over here."

Rebecca and I followed the path of her finger once again and saw her placing the famous monument in Algeria.

"I don't think so, Mrs. Morgan," said Rebecca in that confident voice of hers, which I so envied. "You see, this is the Sahara Desert. Nothing much happens there. Unless I am much mistaken—"

"You are!" Granny bent forward abruptly, as if to catch the puzzle in midtransformation. "This is all a cover-up. Three camels and nothing else? Ridiculous! Don't you see?" She tapped a knuckle at the border between Tunisia and Algeria. "We were born here. This is where it all began."

"What did?" asked Rebecca, oblivious to my tugging at her sleeve. "Are you saying you were born in Algeria? You don't *look* Algerian. Not that I have ever *seen* an Algerian——"

A spasm of pain went across Granny's face. Rebecca, of course, did not know that the question of my grandmother's origins was taboo in my family, because my grandfather—bitter old man that he was—had taken it all with him to the grave. As for Granny herself, she was so confused and erratic that no one except me ever bothered to ask her directly about anything. Regardless of the subject, my parents consistently dismissed her utterings as being "merely the medicine speaking" or "what you'd expect from someone who's gone through *that*." They never explicitly referred to the lobotomy when I was present; had I not seen the word in print on the papers in my father's desk that day, years later, snooping with Rebecca, I might never have known.

Sadly, while she was still with us I never fully understood the reason behind Granny's partial amnesia, her sudden fearfulness, and, at times, her mortifying childishness. To me it was primarily a matter of will; if she had really wanted to, *of course* she could remember her childhood. And it frustrated me to tears that there was so much she—in my understanding—refused to share with me.

Where did it all come from, that uncommonly wide mouth and those changeable North Sea eyes I had so obviously inherited from her? I wanted desperately to be able to anchor the narrative of who I was in a nation of people just like us—tall, dreamy, with hair the color of ripe rye—instead of feeling, as I often did, that she and I were a pair of disoriented aliens trying to blend in with narrow-minded earthlings.

"I think," said Granny, poring over Rebecca's jigsaw puzzle once more, "I remember being here." She held a hand over Crete, then mainland Greece, wiggling her fingers as if trying to sense some invisible current. "Or maybe it was over here." Her hand moved to western

Turkey and continued north into Bulgaria and Romania. "I wore fur clothing. Once we were eleven children sharing one egg. I also remember—"

"What kind of egg?" Rebecca had to know.

The question tore Granny out of her trance, and she looked at us both with an expression of disenchantment. "I don't know. A chicken egg, I suppose."

When I circled back to the issue later that night, watching her brush her hair before bed, Granny seemed to have forgotten the conversation entirely. "That is a nice friend you have," was all she said, looking at me in the mirror. "But she talks too much. She is not a hunter."

I never made any further progress in finding Granny's roots. No matter how many different maps and atlases I snuck into the attic under my cardigan, all she and I ever managed to determine was that North Africa was, on the whole, an entirely underrated place.

I WAS PULLED OUT of my snooze by a pat on the arm, and found Ahmed's cellphone hovering in the air before me. "For you. James Moselane."

Tingling with nerves, I pressed the phone to my ear. "I'm so sorry to be a nuisance—"

"Morg!" It sounded as if James was outside, walking through a rainstorm. "Am I to understand you actually went to Amsterdam?"

The direct question made me cringe. I wanted to say "No," but knew it would result in a follow-up question I wasn't allowed to answer. Instead, I said, "Would you mind terribly if I asked you another favor?"

There was a brief shuffle, a metal door slamming, and then the unmistakable swooshing and clanking of exercise machines. "Your wish is my command, madam," said James, in a tone that told me I was overplaying my hand, but that he was being a gentleman about it.

"There is an aquarium in my apartment," I began. "I forgot to mention it in my message. It takes care of itself, more or less—"

"Go on."

I cleared my throat, aware I was pushing it. "There's a thing of fish food in the fridge." I quickly explained my routine of feeding Professor Larkin's guppies, hoping my jolly tone would take the edge off the request.

When James finally spoke, I was relieved to hear a smile in his voice. "I must say, I was hoping for a more Arthurian task. Why not ask your students to take care of the fish? That should keep them busy until you're back."

Our conversation ended on a humorous note, but it left me feeling rotten nonetheless. There was something about James, a sort of old-world integrity that always compelled me to be absolutely honest with him. And yet here I was, lying to him and taking advantage of his kindness.

I had even told him about Granny's illness once, over coffee, although I knew it might make him think—as I occasionally did myself—that my genes were tainted with insanity. With Federico's betrayal still following me around like a distorted shadow, I had taken cover in a state of reckless defiance and didn't much care to keep up appearances, even with James. "On a scale from one to ten," I had said, positioning the cream and sugar at either end of our small café table, "with ten being complete straitjacket ax-murderer insanity and one being you and me, I would say my grandmother was a four." I placed my coffee cup accordingly. "I mean, in the big scheme of things, her only problem was this absurd conviction that she was an Amazon warrior named Kara. It wasn't as if she was plotting to blow up Buckingham Palace—"

"Well, first of all—" James stretched to move away the creamer even further, emanating a very pleasing whiff of sandalwood. "I object to being a one. Do I have your permission to be a zero?"

Our eyes met, and somewhere in his smile, underneath the platonic veneer, I could see that he bloody well knew he was anything but a zero to me. "Secondly," he went on, pushing his own coffee cup forward, "I'm afraid Granny will have to be downgraded to a three, in order to accommodate my uncle Teddy, who was so stark raving bonkers he wanted to marry his horse and penned twenty-nine letters to the bishop arguing for the logic of the union." James's coffee cup snuggled up to mine. "Now *that*, Morg, is a four." He sat back on the chair, legs crossed at the ankle. "Why not a five? Well, you see, Uncle Teddy was originally married to a girl named Charlotte . . ."

By the time James finally stopped talking, the Moselane family had annexed every piece of china available, and Granny had been relegated to the ashtray on the neighboring table.

It was that afternoon, as I bicycled back to college in a rare burst of sunshine, that I first admitted to myself I really *was* hopelessly in love with James, and that there could never be any other man for me, were I to live a hundred years without as much as a good-night kiss from him.

WE REACHED THE ALGERIAN border at noon. Judging by the virgin drifts of sand gracing the road, no one had come this way for hours, if not days, and I began to understand why Ahmed needed more than just four-wheel drive.

As we approached the small border station, I dug into my handbag to find my passport. While I was leaning down over my knees, riffling through my things, the car suddenly swung left, then right, banging my head against the glove compartment. "Ow!" I said, sitting up. "What—?"

The border station was now behind us.

"Are you okay?" asked Ahmed, without sounding too concerned.

"No!" I twisted around in my seat. "You just drove around that toll bar!"

He shrugged. "There is no one there. It's closed."

"But we can't just—" I hardly knew how to express my outrage. Visions of border guards with machine guns flashed through my mind.

"What?" He didn't even look at me. "Do you really want to drive back, find another border post, apply for a visa, wait for two days?" He nodded at my passport. "Trust me, you don't want that kind of stamp in there."

"I also don't want to spend twenty years in an Algerian prison."

Ahmed shot me a broad smile, revealing an impressive set of clickers. "At least we'd be there together."

I had no idea how to reply; the whole situation was absurd, and his sarcasm was perhaps understandable. Behind us was an abandoned building the size of my father's toolshed. The only thing marking the border was a five-foot toll bar that no one cared enough about to be around to operate. There was no wall, no fence, no barbed wire. . . .

Within the blink of an eye I saw myself at seven years old, walking home from school all by myself for the first time. Inevitably, I was cornered by a pair of freckled schoolyard bullies who had recently been chastised by my father. They came right up to me, grinning and pulling at my hair, and one of them used a stick to draw a circle around me in the mud. "Stay here, Gorgon!" he commanded me. "Until we say you can go."

Even after the boys disappeared, laughing and fighting over the stick, I had been afraid to move. After a while it started raining, and the line was washed away, but I had not been sure whether that meant I was free to go.

That was when I had first made friends with Rebecca, who was in the grade above me. She had come skipping down the lane, singing loudly to herself, and nearly bumped right into me as I stood there in the puddle, clutching my schoolbag. "My dear Miss Morgan!" she exclaimed, in the merry, high-pitched voice her mother always used with the vicar's elderly parishioners. "Whatever are you doing out in this dreadful weather? Come." She took me by the hand and pulled me out of the—by now invisible—circle. "Look at you—you're a disaster!"

The memory made me wince. Apparently, even at twenty-eight I still needed others to pull me across lines drawn in the sand by faraway bullies.

Ahmed glanced at me, perhaps wondering whether it was his improper remark that had disgusted me so. "In case you hadn't noticed, we're trying to cover your tracks."

"I have become aware of that," I said, regretting my outburst. "I just don't understand why. Perhaps you would be so kind as to enlighten me? . . . May I call you Ahmed?"

He shifted abruptly in his seat, as if the subject was fraught with discomfort. "Do you have any idea how big the black market in antiques is? Do you know how many people are involved with illegal excavations, tomb raiding, looting?" He pulled out his phone and let it fall into my lap. "Why don't you call your boyfriend back? He can tell you a thing or two about coming to the rescue of other people's history."

I was so baffled I thought I might have misheard him. "You know James?"

"I know the family. Who doesn't? And by the way, my name is not Ahmed. I'm Nick Barrán. You can call me Nick."

I stared at him, still at a loss for words. "As in Nicholas?"

"They didn't make you a doctor for nothing."

This little knee-slapper set the tone for the remainder of our drive. Over the next many hours I sneaked up on the subject of the Skolsky Foundation from every conceivable angle, but to no avail; when it came to evasive tactics and wisecracks, Nick made even Mr. Ludwig look like a dilettante.

In the end I decided it didn't matter. After all, before the day was over, this irritating man's task of transporting me would be complete, and I would finally meet the people who had singled me out and invited me to come.

WE REACHED OUR DESTINATION about an hour past nightfall. I had long since dozed off in the passenger seat, using my handbag as a pillow, and woke to snippets of conversation and the sound of a metal gate opening. The desert night was as black as a broom closet, and it took me a moment to make sense of the gruff voices and sharp white lights flickering across my face.

My first impression was that we had pulled into a shipyard, for we were surrounded by containers and cranes, and men with hard hats and boilersuits were running everywhere, their efforts aided by blinding floodlights on metal poles. But before I could ask Nick where we were, a man with bushy sideburns and a headlamp on his helmet came over to greet us.

"Just in time for dinner!" he barked. "I told Eddie to hold some meatballs." Then he turned to me and went on, more politely, "Dr. Mayo? I'm Craig, the foreman." He shook my hand carefully, as if afraid of crushing it in his massive Scottish fist. "Welcome to the Tritonis drill site."

"Actually," I said, croaky from sleep, "my name is Diana Morgan."

Craig glanced at Nick, a little perplexed.

"Don't worry." I smiled at them both, hugging the handbag that held Granny's notebook. "I *am* the person you need."

CHAPTER TEN

TEMPLE OF THE MOON GODDESS

W HEN MYRINA CAME TO, HER FIRST THOUGHT WAS: *LILLI.*
But Lilli was not there. Instead, in the darkness, there was
something else. She instinctively knew she was in danger. She heard
rustling . . . slithering . . . hissing. Something cold glided over her
ankle. She guessed it was a tiny viper, most likely venomous. And then
came another, not quite so small, and slid right by her ear. Biting down
on her lip, Myrina forced herself not to stir, not to breathe. She was
lying on something mushy. A pile of twigs and rotten leaves? Whatever
it was, the putrid smell of it made her gag. And then the memory finally
struck her; the temple guards had thrown her in a pit.

Ever so slowly, ever so silently, Myrina began liberating her arms
from the ropes. Luckily, the men had been in too much of a hurry to tie
proper knots. They had probably expected her to die in the fall, and she
might well have broken every bone in her body, for judging by the faint
pattern of light coming through the metal grate above, the pit was as
deep as a well—in fact, it probably *was* an old well, now dried up.

Myrina fought back a shiver of fury and pain. Fury at the men who
had treated her like an animal, and pain at the thought of Lilli, waiting
for her, huddled in the scorching sun. Even the throbbing ache in her
back from the brutal fall dwindled by comparison.

Just then, the hissing stopped, and for a few breathless moments all
was silent. The small vipers had fled. Myrina's throat tightened with
dread. Something else was coming.

Listening intently, she finally heard it: a heavy body sliding over stone.

Pulling the knife from her belt, she braced herself. If she guessed correctly, the beast currently circling the outer wall of the pit, looking for a way in, was a large snake of the kind that coiled around its victims, squeezing the life from their bodies before swallowing them whole. Every two years or so, back home, someone had been killed this grisly way. Myrina still remembered the horror of a neighbor's son who went missing—then, days later, seeing a giant serpent cut open to reveal the pallid corpse of the boy.

Mud demons, the villagers called them. Each spring, the elders had walked out to the watering hole in a long procession, with drums and songs and branches from flowering trees, to beg peace from this ancient evil.

From the earliest age, Myrina had suspected the ceremony was in vain. Not because the snakes did not listen, but because it was not in their nature to care. Her father had told her so, the way he had told her many things when they were out in the wilderness together. Snakes did not have the hunter's respect for their prey, he had explained, when Myrina had once cried over a dead fawn; reptiles were not capable of mercy. They felt neither love nor hatred; they were without emotion.

And to fight them, one had to be entirely without emotion, too.

Standing up, Myrina held her arms above her head, waiting for the serpent to find her. Had there been more light in the pit, she might have positioned herself more wisely. As it was, her eyes were useless to her; she had only her ears and the knife in her hand.

But for all her courage, Myrina nearly fainted with terror when the snake finally made its way into the enclosed space. She had braced for the feeling of its cold, smooth scales against her skin, but was unprepared for its formidable size. As the serpent coiled up around her legs and thighs, its sheer weight brought her to her knees with a groan.

Myrina plunged her knife into the rigid body that now wound around her waist. At first, the blade did not even penetrate the tight, scaly skin, but her strength grew with her desperation, and soon she could feel the serpent responding. It paused, as if in confusion, and then, in the faint light from above, Myrina saw a flash of a ghastly, open mouth before it snapped shut around her left arm.

Screaming, she hacked at the snake's head, aiming for its eyes. The pain in her arm was so overwhelming she barely knew whether she was doing the beast any harm at all. In the end, the serpent jerked violently, and Myrina lost her last bit of balance. Toppling over, entwined with the massive body, all air was squeezed from her chest, and she felt the knife slipping from her hand.

She was dying.

And yet, she kept breathing. For all its crushing weight, the giant serpent did not constrict around her any further.

Moving required tremendous effort, but the monster's grisly jaws had become unhinged in death, and she was able to carefully free her arm from its barbed teeth. Then, inch by inch, she wriggled out of its coils, liberating her legs and feet.

She had been lucky, for though her arm was throbbing and slick with blood, there was no massive gushing, and the bone was not broken. . . .

Myrina was too busy inspecting her wounds to notice anything above her, until she suddenly heard the metal grate sliding aside. Looking up, she saw a flickering torch and two faces contorted with disgust. Then came a shower of accusations in a language she did not understand and a glimpse of what looked like her traveling satchel, clenched in a meaty fist and shaken violently in the air. Fighting the urge to scream right back at her guards, Myrina stood up, arm bleeding, to place a foot on top of the mighty body she had just slain and raise her palms in friendship.

"Let me out of here," she said in the Old Language, her voice trembling with the need to make her captors understand, "and I will tell you everything."

For a brief, terrible moment the men disappeared from sight, and Myrina feared they were leaving again. Then something came whipping down from above, its knotted end snapping to a halt right in front of her.

A rope.

WHEN THE MEN PULLED the gritty sack from her head for the second time, Myrina was relieved to find herself in a large temple room under a high ceiling held aloft by massive pillars. There were no windows and no natural light anywhere; the place was lit by countless flickering fires burning atop tall three-legged fire pans, and it took Myrina a while to make sense of the people gathered around, staring at her through the dancing shadows.

Since they were all women and all wore the same white dresses and horrified expression, Myrina assumed they were priestesses serving the Moon Goddess and unaccustomed to the sight of blood and bruises. What confused her were the bows and quivers strapped to their backs, for none of them struck her as having the bearing of archers.

Her rambling thoughts were interrupted by a commanding voice from above, and after a moment's disorientation and several impatient prods from the men standing right behind her, Myrina turned around and saw the fearsome form seated on an elaborate chair on top of a stone podium. Guessing she was looking at the High Priestess, Myrina bent her head in respect. She would have knelt down, too, but the men had bound her too tightly for that.

"You stand accused," began the woman on the podium, perfectly fluent in the Old Language, "of being a trespasser. And possibly a murderer. Do you realize what the punishment is for those crimes?"

Myrina shook her head, too afraid to speak.

"If you do not answer me," the woman went on, "I must assume you are guilty. And I must hand you over to the city officials . . . something I would rather avoid." She held up a small object, and only when it twinkled in the light of the fire pans did Myrina recognize her mother's bracelet. Then suddenly, it all began to make sense—the men furiously waving her traveling satchel above the pit, and then pulling her out for questioning.

Myrina was not the only one who recognized the bracelet; the mere sight of it drew a collective gasp from the priestesses.

"Tell me then," continued the High Priestess, her voice deeper than before, "how did you come to possess this?"

Myrina straightened before the woman's scrutiny. "It belonged to my mother. She wore it on her arm every day of her life."

As soon as the words rang out in the hollow room, they were followed by a burst of mumbling confusion. Only then, when she saw the priestesses turning this way and that in search of an explanation did Myrina notice that they all wore similar bracelets around their wrists.

"Silence!" demanded the High Priestess, looking sternly around the room before turning back to Myrina. "What was your mother's name?"

"Talla."

"Talla?" The High Priestess leaned forward, gripping the armrests of her throne. "Your mother was Talla, and yet you dare come back here?"

When she felt the men stirring behind her—as if preparing to drag her away again—Myrina felt a rush of dread. "Please!" she exclaimed. "I came here because my mother always said we belonged to the Moon Goddess. She served her faithfully all her life—"

The High Priestess stood up abruptly. "Talla broke the rules of this temple. She consorted with a man and was defiled. Had she not run away, she would have been thrown into the pit, just like you."

Myrina was thankful for the ropes that held her so tightly upright. "I understand," she said, forcing out the words. "Throw me back in the pit if you must, but"—she looked up at the High Priestess—"please have mercy on my little sister. She has been waiting outside all this time. She is blind and has no food." Myrina tried once again to bend her knees, but couldn't. "Remove these ropes," she said, "and I will kneel down to implore you."

The High Priestess came down the stone steps with measured dignity. "Tell me," she said, stopping in front of Myrina, "what compels a young woman to become a trespasser?" She reached out to touch the bloody bite pattern on Myrina's arm. "To suffer such agony?"

"I am a sister," said Myrina, biting back a shiver of pain. "That is what compels me. I came here hoping the Goddess would cure Lilli's eyes. . . . Now I see I have been naïve, and that my mistake will damage my sister even further. That is the agony I suffer."

The High Priestess studied her face for a while. "Your courage intrigues me. The eunuchs tell me you have killed a monster?"

"I am a hunter," replied Myrina. "It is what I do."

A faint smile of admiration tugged at the High Priestess's mouth. "Most men would say women cannot be hunters."

"Village men may say so." Myrina stuck out her chin. "But others hold that women are the best hunters. For they are nimble, silent, and patient." She caught herself, then added, more humbly, "My father is a nomad. He taught me how to hunt."

The High Priestess frowned. "Where is your father now?"

Myrina looked away. "He used to come and go, as nomads do. He always said that when I was fully grown, we would travel the world together. But . . . the nomads changed their routes, I suppose, and he stopped coming."

The High Priestess nodded slowly. "How many men have you loved?"

Myrina was so surprised by the question she almost forgot her fear. "None. I have never loved anyone. Except my family."

"That is not what I meant——"

"I know what you meant," said Myrina. "And the answer is none. I do not like men, and they are kind enough to return the favor. No man likes a woman who runs faster or shoots arrows more precisely than he does."

The High Priestess stood quietly for a while. Then she turned around and returned with much grace to her chair on the podium.

The temple room fell completely silent. Everyone was on tiptoes to hear the final sentence; even the three eunuchs stood awkwardly still, their massive arms hanging limply by their sides.

Leaning back on her stone seat, the High Priestess pondered the situation for so long Myrina began to wonder whether she would speak at all. Then at last, the verdict came.

"In all my years," said the High Priestess, "I have never seen so clear a case of divine intervention. By the infinite justice of the Goddess, you have suffered and survived your mother's punishment, thereby clearing you both of guilt. And after hearing you plead your sister's case"—she looked out over the silent priestesses—"I say you have passed every test of worthiness. What say you, daughters of the Goddess? Do you not agree?"

There was a hum of reluctant consent.

Snapping her fingers at the eunuchs, the High Priestess had them remove Myrina's ropes at last. "Your courage has saved you," she said, smiling at her own benevolence. "You *and* your sister. Tonight, when the moon rises, we will welcome you to our sisterhood."

Myrina stumbled forward, out of the ropes. "You mean—?"

The High Priestess nodded. "You will be one of us. Indeed, I believe you already are." Her smile gave way to gravity. "Being a priestess is no easy calling. You saw the unruly mob outside. Their land is drying out and they are starving. Not a month goes by without another report of pirates raiding the coast. These are desperate times"—she made a plaintive gesture at the ring of priestesses—"and we are far too few for the tasks at hand."

"For my sister's sake, I will try," said Myrina. "But I have never delighted anyone with my singing."

The High Priestess shook her head. "You are not here for that. The Goddess has summoned you to her temple in order to shame us. Your strength and courage, your weapon skills—" She made another gesture at the priestesses, this time one of accusation. "Look at us! We are mere waning shadows of the noble figures we once were. We call ourselves generals in the army of the Moon Goddess, but in reality"—the High Priestess fell back on her throne in disgust—"I am surrounded by silly, sweet-toothed slugs, who could not string a bow to save this temple!"

Myrina could feel the resentful glares stinging her from all sides. She wanted desperately to speak up and somehow soften the censure, but she dared not risk it. Lilli was still outside, and the sooner things were brought to a conclusion, the better.

"Now let us all thank the Goddess—" continued the High Priestess, holding out her arms so that the flared sleeves of her garment spread like the wings of a phoenix. "Thank you, kind Mistress, for sending this young woman to train us. Please help her strip away our folly and weakness that we may once again stand guard around your radiant majesty with our bows strung."

CHAPTER ELEVEN

There was once, in the western parts of Libya, on the bounds of
the inhabited world, a race which was ruled by women and followed
a manner of life unlike that which prevails among us.
—DIODORUS SICULUS, *Bibliotheca Historica*

ALGERIA

M Y FIRST NIGHT AT THE TRITONIS DRILL SITE WAS ONE OF DISAP-
pointment. It didn't take me long to realize that no welcome
committee was waiting with bubbly and roses; Nick, it seemed, was the
only Skolsky representative on location.

After a lukewarm meal in the empty cantina Craig the foreman
took me to the tiny trailer compartment that would be my home for the
week. It was a relief to finally be alone, and the door had barely closed
behind him before I broke out Granny's notebook. Despite my exhaustion I was determined to continue my work on it and knew the next
step should be to organize the foreign symbols in some sort of alphabetical order. But the bluish light of the buzzing ceiling lamp did nothing to help my efforts. It was set on a timer that made it necessary to get
up and pull a plastic string of pearls every two minutes or so, and after
having done this at least fifty times without making much progress with
the notebook, I finally gave up and went to bed.

Next morning, right after breakfast, I stepped out of the cantina to
find Craig and Nick waiting for me with three camels. The sky was still
dark, but bursts of purple and orange on the eastern horizon suggested

the sun was on its way. The morning air had a pleasant chill to it; I suspected things would heat up soon enough. "I hope you brought your
riding crop," said Craig, breaking the silence. "We have closed off the
site to motorized vehicles."

I glanced up at the camels, who looked regally bored. "I suspect a
riding crop is not the way to endear oneself to these individuals?"

Craig grinned at Nick. "See? She's not as clueless as you think."

Moments later we were off, and I was happy to discover that the
proud quadrupeds walked at a steady, phlegmatic pace that allowed me
to look up and admire the landscape. Around us, the desert was slowly
changing colors. As the sun rose in the sky, the sand came alive as if it
were a vast tray of embers, flaring up at the first touch of dawn. Sitting
there on the camel, rocking gently back and forth, I felt I had a balcony
seat to a gigantic shadow play in the dunes; for each mountainous sweep
of brightness there was a distorted black reflection on the other side,
but with every passing minute those inky pools shrank into rivers, then
lines, then nothing, as the sun took full possession of the world.

The spectacle of our Sahara sunrise, however, was soon marred by
the debris of human activity. As we crested a dune and looked down
into a deep sand basin, we were met by the unseemly sight of scattered
drilling equipment and a prostrate metal tower. In the middle of it all
sat a brown Bedouin tent with two horses tied outside.

"We discovered the building when we were trying to determine
the best location for the tower," explained Craig as we rode down
toward the lonely tent. "It's right beneath us, just a few meters down,
but for some reason our imaging never picked up on it . . . just took it
for sediment along the old lake."

"There was a lake here?" I looked around, trying to imagine a body
of water in this parched landscape.

"Oh, yes," nodded Craig. "Probably an inland sea that covered parts
of Algeria and Tunisia and was connected to the Mediterranean by
some sort of channel. You can see the shape of it on a paleohydrology
map. But that's thousands of years ago. Over time, the sea became a
lake, the lake became a swamp, and the swamp became desert." He
smiled wryly. "Climates change; that's the way it has always been, and

there's nothing we can do about it. It's the big guy up there"—he pointed a thumb at the sun—"who calls the shots."

As we approached the tent, two men emerged to greet us. They were dressed in paramilitary clothing, and their sizable sidearms did not escape me. Although they both greeted Nick and Craig with smiles and bent their heads politely in my direction, I could not help feeling these were men who, if they thought it necessary, would not think twice about using deadly force—in fact, they might relish the prospect.

The Bedouin tent, it turned out, was not a shelter for the guards as much as a barrier put up to cover our entrance into the underground. At first glance, it looked as if a large steel barrel sat right in the middle of the tent floor; only when I leaned over to look inside did I realize it had no bottom. It was a perfectly circular two-foot-wide hole in the ground, and it took me a moment to grasp that this was where we were going next: down an improvised chute in the middle of an ocean of sand.

I looked up, ready to voice my concern at having been brought this far without being warned about the potential danger of the final stage. But Nick was already handing me a harness and a headlamp, and even Craig looked as if popping in and out of the underworld through a giant straw was a perfectly normal thing to do. "Don't worry," he said to me, fastening my harness with confident fingers. "I'll go first and receive you. Here"—he snapped a rubber band around my head and placed a dust mask over my mouth and nose—"just remember to breathe slowly. You'll adjust in no time."

"Adjust to what?" I wanted to say, but Craig was already astride the rim of the steel pipe, and without another word he whizzed away into the darkness.

Feeling oddly disembodied, as if I were a mere gaping bystander to my own circus act, I let Nick and the guards help me into the tube and plop a safety helmet on my head, as if that would really make a difference. The next thing I knew they lowered me into the hole, and for a few long moments I could hear nothing but the unsettling creaking of the rope attached to my harness and my own panicky breathing amplified by the dust mask and the metal surrounding me.

Then, suddenly, I was through the pipe, and all familiar sounds dissipated into a vast cold void. I dangled, like a grasshopper on a hook, wondering what manner of monsters lurked below in this dark, forgotten world.

ONCE, DURING A SUNDAY dinner, Granny had fallen into a trance over the chicken potpie. Only when my mother had asked her three times to pass the salt did she stir from her reverie and peer at me across the table. "It is all down there," she had said, as if responding to a question of mine, "underneath the surface. You just have to find it."

"There are three pieces of chicken per person," my mother cut in, taking the saltshaker with a huff, "distributed evenly throughout the dish."

"They think it's gone," Granny continued, her gray-blue eyes still locked in mine, "but it is not. They think they can destroy it, and we will forget, but we won't. That is their big mistake."

Only then did it occur to me that she must be referring to the newspaper clippings my father had recently removed from the walls of her attic apartment. To me, child that I was, Granny's growing archive of articles had been too gradual to be truly shocking; every time I brought her one of my parents' discarded newspapers, one or two scraps were added to her collection and ended up hanging from the sloping walls by tiny drops of school glue. "What are they about?" I had asked her once or twice. "All those articles?"

In response, Granny had pointed at a recent clipping that was still lying on the table. The headline read FEMALE WRITER ESCAPES FROM HOUSE ARREST. I read it through twice, carefully, but did not see any connection with my grandmother or anyone else I knew.

Seeing my bewilderment, Granny smiled in that childish way of hers, and whispered, "Amazons!" Whereupon she began walking around the room, pointing up at the clippings dangling from the walls, one after the other. "Amazons," she said, her voice getting more confident. "All Amazons."

I stopped at an article that hung a little lower than the others. The headline read KHANABAD: STONING ENDS IN CHAOS, and there was a black-and-white photo of men and veiled women huddling behind some kind of barricade, clutching their heads. "Those women are Amazons?" I asked, wanting desperately to understand.

Granny came to my side, but only to snort with disgust. "No! Those women are just as bad as those men! But they got what they deserved. Look at them!"

"But—" I barely knew what to think. "What does 'stoning' mean?"

Just then, a sudden draft swept through the room, and the newspaper clippings fluttered like dry leaves.

Spinning around, I saw my mother standing in the door, a hand pressed to her mouth in silent horror. Ten minutes later my father appeared with a bucket and peeled off all the paper scraps without a word, leaving behind nothing but a star map of dried glue spots. As he did so, he didn't look at us once; never before had I seen him so pale, so upset.

Granny merely watched as her carefully assembled archive of imagined Amazon activity was dismantled and taken away, her face hardening a little more for every news story that disappeared.

Although several days had passed since the incident, Granny's eyes were still full of resentment, and she had only grudgingly agreed to come downstairs to join in our Sunday dinner—likely because she knew she wouldn't be fed if she didn't.

"I assume you're enjoying the meal," said my mother at length, never able to pass on an opportunity to point out her mother-in-law's bad manners.

In an unusual fit of present-mindedness, Granny responded right away, in a voice so full of hate it sent a chill through the room, "Rule number three: Never assume."

Understandably, my mother said nothing else on the matter, but the look she sent my father was enough to make the food clog in my throat. Later that night, I sat on the stairs as I always did, listening to my parents arguing in the living room. It was actually not much of an argument—it never was—since my father's contribution came mostly in the form of deep sighs and a restless pacing up and down the floor. "This cannot go on!" my mother kept saying, with growing despair.

"We have to think of Diana. I can't take any more of this obsessive be-havior. God knows what she found in those newspapers. Will you please *say* something, Vincent!"

When they both finally fell silent, I heard the unmistakable creak-ing of the attic door and knew Granny had been listening, too. Cold and miserable, I wanted so much to go up and comfort her, but I was afraid it would only make my mother more upset if she discovered I was not in my bed.

That same night, while I was lying awake in the darkness, my mother came into my room. She probably thought I was asleep, for my eyes were closed, and she bent over to kiss me and whisper against my forehead, "I will never let anything bad happen to you."

From that moment on, I had lived in constant fear of losing Granny. Maybe one day soon, I thought, I would come home from school to find her gone, and my parents would refuse to tell me where she was. They would assume that by removing her from my world, they could extin-guish her influence on me. To them, silence had always been a cure-all, and they applied it generously where needed—usually on me.

That was their big mistake.

As I swung from a rope somewhere beneath the surface of the Al-gerian desert, I was so engrossed in my own primal fears that, when something grabbed hold of my legs, I yelled in surprise.

"It's just me!" boomed Craig as he eased me to the ground and un-hooked my harness. "The bogeyman called in sick this morning."

While I was doing my best to breathe calmly in the cool, stagnant air, Craig lit a lantern and held it up between us, its ghostly light reveal-ing that we were standing in a room so enormous I couldn't see the walls. Here and there lay drifts of sand, which must have come in through cracks in the roof before the entire building, at some point, was swallowed up by the surrounding desert.

"How extraordinary," I said. My voice sounded just as frightened as I felt, and it seemed to travel through the darkness for a long time. "I can't believe the pressure of the sand never made it collapse."

"It's a bit of a wonder," agreed Craig, "but our mineralogist can give you a good explanation. Something to do with the salt concentration in the sand. Depending on the weather conditions it forms a crust and, in this case, apparently, it became its own retaining wall. Careful!"

We both stepped aside as Nick joined us. He monkeyed down the rope as if he had never used a staircase in his life, treating us to a little display of coordination and agility that stood in odd contrast to the bedraggled clothes and scruffy beard. "Still okay?" he asked, blinding me with his headlamp.

When the men started walking, I was too overwhelmed by everything around me to keep up. Judging from the way in which the sound of our footsteps first disappeared, then came back as a faint, distant echo, the building was colossal, its tall ceiling held up by dozens of pillars.

"This is astonishing!" I said to Craig, my voice muffled by the dust mask. "It must have been some sort of royal palace." I walked over to one of the pillars and examined it as best I could in the dim light. "If only I could see better. But I suppose I am too clueless to be entrusted with a headlamp." I took a step back and pointed at the numerous little shelves and hooks fastened to the stone. "Look at that! Maybe it was some sort of covered marketplace."

"We are fairly sure it was a temple," said Craig, holding up his lantern. "And those shelves and hooks were probably for votive offerings. Some of them are still there. Little urns, possibly with human ashes in them. But"—he looked at me with a teasing smile—"that's what we're hoping *you* can tell *us*."

As we continued down the central aisle, trying to catch up with Nick, my initial unease with the place grew into full-blown foreboding. If Craig really wanted to know more about these ancient artifacts, I thought, he would need a whole army of archaeologists, not just a single philologist.

The aisle was flanked by tall metal fire pans, some leaning dangerously, others toppled over completely. And at the end of the nave was a stepped podium with a large stone chair. The presence of this lonely piece of furniture—however stern and impersonal—could not help but make me wonder about the people who had once lived here, and what had happened to them.

Craig sensed my discomfort. "God knows how big this building complex is. We tried to map the basement"—he paused to show me a hole in the floor, with narrow stone steps going down into the underground—"but the boys couldn't do it. There is a whole world of caves down there, and we all got a little freaked out by the . . . animal population."

When we finally caught up with Nick, he was standing in a doorway at the end of the main temple, pointing a flashlight into the dark corners of another, smaller room, checking—I guessed—for unwelcome critters.

"Here we are!" Craig paused on the threshold and held up his lantern. "The inner sanctum. What do you say, Doc, have you ever seen anything like it?"

I had been too preoccupied with Nick's search to look up and realize that I was now, finally, face-to-face with the inscription in Mr. Ludwig's photo—the mysterious symbols that had lured me all the way from Oxford. There they were: three walls covered in writing, occasionally making space for paintings in red, black, and yellow. And in the middle of the floor sat a large, rectangular stone that might have served as an altar.

"It looks as if the paintings were there first," I said, stepping into the room, all thoughts of creeping shadows forgotten. "And the writing came later. See?" I took the lantern from Craig and held it up to demonstrate my point. "Notice how the writing comes right up to the figures?"

Leaving both men gaping at the wall, I took a quick turn about the room with the lantern raised. At this proximity, the inscription loomed over me in an abundance of colors, and I was happy to conclude that Mr. Ludwig's photograph had not done it justice at all. There were interesting variations in the density of the paint and the size of the writing itself, as if the writer had been scribbling the entire thing in great haste, using whatever tints happened to be available and stretching them by adding more and more binder—probably egg or oil—to the point where the symbols became nearly invisible.

Furthermore, my close inspection revealed that there were, indeed, word dividers in the text. The reason why the photograph had not picked them up was that they were very faint in color. They appeared in the form of small yellow asterisks wedged in between individual symbols; most often there was just a single one, and I took that to signal a word break, whereas the presence of two probably meant a sentence break.

I was so excited I couldn't help myself. Reaching out, I touched my hand to the smooth, cold plaster wall and felt a tingle in my fingertips at the prospect of returning with Granny's notebook.

Pulling out my camera I began taking close-ups of the word dividers, but was interrupted by Nick snapping his fingers. "Come on, time to work."

I watched as he and Craig walked up to the stone altar in the middle of the room and started pushing. Only on the third attempt did the top part finally give way, as if it were a giant lid, and together they rotated it ninety degrees, revealing that the large stone block underneath was, in fact, hollow. "Come and say hello," urged Craig, waving me closer.

I stretched to see. "Is that a sarcophagus? I don't usually . . . do sarcophagi."

Nick straightened and brushed off his hands. "I didn't drive you halfway across the Sahara for you to stand there and do nothing. So will you please come over here and tell us what needs to happen next."

I adjusted my dust mask and walked up to the stone coffin, bracing myself for a mummy wrapped in bandages. But there was nothing terribly dramatic inside, merely the outline of a desiccated skeleton at the bottom, resting on a bed of dust. "Oh dear," I said, sorry to be unable to come up with a more respectful remark. "Not much there. No personal treasures, no gifts to the gods of the underworld—"

"Actually—" began Craig, but a look from Nick shut him up.

"Perhaps," I said, "ancient tomb raiders beat us to it?"

"Don't think so." Craig pointed into the sarcophagus. "See the bracelet? They wouldn't have left that behind. But what's more . . . don't you see something unusual about this poor bastard?" When I didn't reply, he pointed again. "Look. No head."

"I don't believe this," I muttered, but my shock had less to do with the missing head than with the bracelet the person had been wearing on his or her right arm, just above the wrist, and which was still there, half covered by dust. The shape was unmistakable, but it almost seemed impossible. . . .

"So," said Nick, taking off his headlamp. "What do you need?"

"Need?" I stood back from the sarcophagus. "Nothing, really. Just time." I nodded at the walls around us. "These things can take a while to decipher."

"Never mind the walls," said Nick. "This coffin was opened last week. We need to preserve the body."

"I'm afraid I can't help you with that," I said, aware that Craig was following our exchange with growing confusion, "I'm not an archaeologist."

"*What?*" Nick glared at me. "I told John to get an archaeologist—"

"Excuse me," I said, determined to maintain my grace, "but Mr. Ludwig *specifically* said you needed a philologist . . . someone who could make sense of this inscription." I made a sweeping gesture at the text crying out at us from every wall. "I don't mean to appear immodest, believe me, but if you want to know what is written here—"

Nick held up a hand, squinting as if I suddenly emanated a bright, piercing light. "All right. You're not an archaeologist. You're here for the inscription. Great. How long will it take to decipher it?"

I shrugged and looked around. "Hard to say. It could take a few days . . . or a few weeks. Or it could take years. It all depends—" I stopped. I couldn't very well tell him it all depended on the accuracy of Granny's notebook.

"Years?" Nick stared at me, the strangest expression in his eyes.

I smiled reassuringly. "Well, in an ideal world—"

"No." He spoke calmly, as if to himself. "This is not going to work. I knew it. Let's get you back to the drill station. Right now."

Realizing with horror I was being expelled from my adventure, I grabbed him by the sleeve. "But you need me! I'm an expert on the Amazons—"

Nick glared at my hand. "The *what*?"

"The Amazons," I stammered. "From Greek mythology. I thought—"

There was a brief but unpleasant silence. Then he simply shook his head, turned, and walked away.

CHAPTER TWELVE

TEMPLE OF THE MOON GODDESS

MYRINA SMILED, BUT NO ONE SMILED BACK.
Already seated at long tables in the dining hall, huddled over their food in intimate clusters, the three dozen white-clad priestesses greeted their two new sisters with silence.

Myrina was not surprised. She saw in their eyes they still thought of her as the violent trespasser who had survived the snake pit just a few hours earlier, and of Lilli as some lesser being whose blindness had made her deaf and dumb as well. It did not help that the High Priestess had shamed them all so thoroughly; had she deliberately sought to stir up resentment against the newcomers, she could have chosen no better way.

Biting back her frustration, Myrina reminded herself that this temple, this sisterhood, was Lilli's best chance of survival in a dying world, and that only the Moon Goddess had the power to restore her eyesight. "This is what Mother would want me to do," she had told herself while the eunuchs put aside her hunting weapons and escorted her and Lilli to a large, subterranean bathhouse. There they were placed in the hands of an unsmiling hag who shaved off their matted hair, threw their clothes on the fire, and scrubbed them both all over with soap and oil until their skin was stinging with cleanliness. To Myrina, the ordeal was particularly painful; the woman had pushed and pulled at her bruised limbs without any sign of compassion. In fact, she almost seemed to enjoy Myrina's wincing and moaning as she cleaned her large bite wound thoroughly with soap and bandaged it as tightly as possible. "Lilli's safety matters more than my freedom," Myrina reminded herself over and over. "For her sake I will endure this, too."

Naked and shivering, Lilli had tried to hide behind Myrina, but there was no escaping the prickly hemp dresses and little pointy caps that marked them as servants of the Goddess. "How fine you look!" Myrina had said, drawing her sister into an embrace. "I am sure I have never seen you so clean before."

"I should much rather be caked with dung," Lilli muttered, rubbing her eyes with angry fists. "And roam about in the wilderness with you."

But they both knew the wilderness was no place for Lilli. Even before the fever, when she still had the use of her eyes, the girl had preferred the comfort of the village to the lonely trail. Myrina had taught her to hunt, yes, but Lilli's joy lay in the tasks of farming, which to Myrina had always seemed tedious: sowing seeds, tending sprouts, and feeding the chickens. Endless routine, requiring precisely the sort of patience Myrina did not possess.

Their mother always used to say her three daughters had inherited the hands of each of their very different fathers. "Those there," she had once observed, nodding at their older sister, Lana, as they all sat around the fire, shelling beans, "are hands that tell big stories. Hands that can make a naïve girl do anything—break any rule." She grimaced at the memory of her first love, whom she had always refused to name, but who had apparently lived in the big city by the sea. "And those there—" She turned to Myrina, next in line. "They take delight in danger, and mark my words, they will follow it to the end of the world."

The girls all sat around, sharing in their mother's wistful silence, until Lilli held out her own hands, smudged with dirt. "What about me, Mother?"

"Your hands," their mother said, kissing the little fingers one by one, "tell wonderful tales of a sweet man." She paused to overcome an onrush of sadness. "They are hands made for nurture and preservation.

But they are no match for the wild animals preying on the herd. So you, my love"—she reached out to draw her youngest daughter closer—"had better stay near the fire, where the lions are afraid to come."

A PATH OF LUMINOUS flower petals had taken Myrina and Lilli directly from the humiliation in the washroom to their initiation in the inner sanctum. The sight of the stone floor specked with merry colors was surely meant to cheer them, but to Myrina it resembled a trail of grains leading into the loop of a snare.

Throughout the ceremony she was in a state of dazed denial; even after their oath, when the High Priestess took the terrible sacrificial knife from the altar and cut a gash across her and Lilli's left breasts, to let out blood for the gilded offering bowl, Myrina barely felt the pain. Or maybe she was too preoccupied with Lilli's reaction to notice her own. The girl was brave, though, and as they stood there together, holding hands, Myrina felt a surge of admiration for her sister.

"Rejoice!" the High Priestess said, as she placed the sacred bracelets of the Moon Goddess on their wrists—bracelets identical to their mother's. "Your blood has joined our blood, and you are now one with us. This armband is a token of our holy sisterhood, and of your promise never to let a man besmirch your purity. Should someone attack you, you will find this sharp bronze an excellent deterrent. But remember: If you betray the Goddess, or your sisters, this golden jackal will become *your* enemy, and *you* will feel its bite. For the hunting hounds of the Goddess are ever faithful; obey her divine commands and they will protect you with their lives; disobey her and they will hunt you down and tear you to bits."

Such had been the speech that welcomed Myrina and Lilli to the temple. Yet as they stood on the threshold of the dining hall, wearing their bracelets for everyone to see, they were met by glares that were anything but sisterly.

At last, Myrina stepped forward. "Can anyone tell me," she said, "who threw that stone at me when I stood on the garden wall?"

Utter silence.

"I am asking," Myrina went on, standing straight before the horde of wary eyes, "because that was a fine throw. My compliments."

A murmur went through the room. Then someone yelled, "Animone threw the stone!" and the murmur broke into full rumpus.

The dining hall would likely have erupted in a bluster of flying food had not Myrina let out a sharp whistle. "Then Animone," she concluded, as soon as she had regained everyone's attention, "is my first friend! And I want her to meet Lilli"—she lifted up the girl for everyone to view—"the sweetest sister you will ever have. There is nothing wrong with her except that she can't see all your sour faces. And that, I think, is a happy loss."

Myrina had the pleasure of seeing shock, even shame, in the eyes of the priestesses as her words traveled around the room in many different languages. A few women remained tight-lipped and hostile, deliberately avoiding her gaze, but they were soon drowned out by general excitement.

Three young priestesses—Animone, Pitana, and Klito—now seemed keen to make friends. "How did you survive the snake pit?" Animone wanted to know, her eyes drawn to the bandage on Myrina's arm. "Tell us how you killed the monster."

"Even better"—Myrina leaned forward conspiratorially—"I will *show* you."

THE STEALTHY MIDNIGHT TRIP by Myrina and her three new friends into the temple basement more than confirmed that the daughters of the Moon Goddess were, indeed, in need of training. Even this trio, who had been willing to come with her, backed away in horror when Myrina threw a rope into the pit and bade them to follow. "But there are snakes down there!" exclaimed the excitable Animone, waving her hands in disgust.

"Why do you think I threw the torches down first?" Myrina nodded into the illuminated grotto where the giant constrictor snake lay coiled in death. "Serpents are afraid of fire. Come—"

"I am not sure I can climb down that rope," said Pitana, a gawkish young woman who was almost as tall as Myrina, but had none of her muscles. "My arms are too long to be strong. I may be able to get down, but I would never have the strength to climb back up."

"Klito?" Myrina turned to the last of the three: a beautiful, wholesome girl with eyes full of adventure.

But even Klito would not go. "I will watch you from up here," she promised, nodding with enthusiasm, "and make encouraging comments."

Myrina shook her head and started down the rope, her newly recovered hunting knife wedged between her teeth. The three women watched with fascination while she skinned the large snake and rolled up the speckled scales in a big bundle.

"That," observed the adventurous Klito from above, "is the most disgusting thing I have ever seen. Please don't bring it upstairs."

"I am going to clean and dry it," said Myrina, "and turn it into clothes. You will see. Now pull it up for me. I promise to give you all a piece to wear."

"You know," said Animone, shaking her head, "I am not even sure I *want* to be your friend."

THAT WAS ONLY THE beginning.

Before a week had gone by, the High Priestess instructed everyone to commence weapon training in the courtyard. "Our exercises will be overseen by Myrina," she told them in the Old Language, in a tone that tolerated no opposition, "and they will take place every day after breakfast. Animone will translate for those who do not understand Myrina. You will be sorted into groups of six, and there will be no exceptions!"

Naturally, the new arrangement was met with fierce resistance as soon as the High Priestess turned her back. Why this sudden nonsense of weapon practice? Why could things not continue the way they were? The older priestesses especially did not understand the reasoning behind the change and soon became masters at making excuses.

But Myrina's greatest challenge turned out to be a handful of younger women accustomed to being in charge. Even though they had no official titles granting them more authority than the rest, these women had somehow managed to assume roles of superiority. For them to submit to the teachings of a newcomer was unthinkable. One of them, a doe-eyed troublemaker named Kara, made a point of missing every single training session—not by staying away from the courtyard, but by pretending to be dozing in a hammock, in plain view of the others.

In spite of these difficulties, Myrina was only too happy to spend her mornings outside, doing what she loved. It had not taken her many days to tire of the ceremony inside the temple building; even the many gold and silver votives on display, glittering so bewitchingly in the light of the fire pans, had soon lost their allure. Furthermore, the High Priestess had ordered Lilli to remain completely silent until the full moon, as a way of endearing herself to the Moon Goddess and earning a cure for her blindness, and Myrina felt she had better stay away, so as not to tempt her sister to talk.

Keeping in mind her father's relentless criticism, which had so often upset her aim, Myrina began the training lessons with encouragement. She complimented her holy sisters on their dancing skills and nimble feet and had them start every day with an acrobatic exercise she knew they would master.

Then, rather than discouraging them with weapons practice right away, she inspected all their bows and shook her head, saying, "How can you be expected to do anything with these? The wood is too old, too dry; we must ask for new ones. Meanwhile"—she had gathered everyone around and lowered her voice—"let us play games and pretend to be training."

And so they had begun by pulling ropes and lifting buckets of water; only when Myrina was confident everyone in the group would be able to pull a bow did she start them on target practice.

But no matter what she did, Kara's little clique remained hostile and did everything they could to obstruct the training. They misplaced their bows and broke their arrows . . . clearly goaded on by Kara herself, who kept rewarding them with snorts of laughter from the hammock.

"Do not concern yourself with her," Animone said one night, when she and Myrina were undressing in the dormitory amid the usual bustle of bedtime intrigue. "Nobody likes her. She always makes much of being the daughter of a chieftain, and I am sure she considered herself quite the mistress of us all until you arrived."

They both sneaked a glance at Kara, who was holding court around the washbasin, handing out sweets to her entourage. "Why should she feel threatened by me?" asked Myrina, struggling to free herself of the still unfamiliar priestess dress. "I have no desire to be anybody's mistress."

"Because you are everything she is not. Look at you!" Animone ran an admiring hand over Myrina's taut skin. "You are truly alive. Almost a man—"

Myrina started laughing, but sobered soon enough. "If I were a man, they would not keep me cooped up like this. In fact, if we were men"—she cast her eyes around the dormitory where the priestesses were still fluttering about, cackling like chickens—"we would not behave like this. Would we?" She searched Animone's eyes for an answer, but saw nothing but admiration.

Had it been the same back home? Myrina was reluctant to think so. While there had often been altercations in the Tamash Village, surely there had never been fisticuffs over a broken hairbrush. A stolen farm tool, yes, or a deceitful lover . . . but such disputes made sense to Myrina, whereas the trivial cares and concerns of her fellow priestesses did not.

I should like to see you all out in the bush with me, she thought to herself as she cast one last, disgusted glance at Kara and her sweets. *You would not last a day. Even if I were to teach you everything I know, it would not be enough. That is what my father would say if he was here now: You can tease its mane all you like, but you can't turn a house cat into a lion.*

IT WAS NOT LONG before Kara's one-sided war with the newcomers culminated in a scene before the High Priestess, whose fatigued expression confirmed to Myrina that temple life in general was rife with such petty quarrels.

"*She* tried to tell those filthy people that their son was assured a seat in the halls of the Goddess!" exclaimed Kara, pointing an accusative finger at Myrina. "Even though *I* kept saying their votive gift was too puny. *I* follow the rules, but *she* just"—Kara shivered at the idea—"says whatever she wants."

"They all became very upset," nodded one of Kara's confidantes, a petite girl by the name of Egee, whose piercing voice more than made up for her small size. "We had to call the eunuchs. It was almost a rebellion."

The High Priestess turned to Myrina, eyebrows raised.

"Frankly," said Myrina, folding her arms, "I do not see why we cannot tell these poor people what they want to hear. How do *we* know who gets eternal life and who doesn't?" She took a step toward the High Priestess, trusting in the kindness of the woman's heart. "They were crying. It was their *child*."

Myrina bit her lip, willing the High Priestess to be more like her mother, to whom the love between parents and children was a sacred thing. She still remembered the day when a group of villagers had gathered secretly behind the dunghill to discuss the fate of a child whose parents were considered deficient. "We think it best," one of them had said, "to take away that boy and bring him up properly, in another home."

Child as she was, Myrina had barely been able to follow the discussion. But she certainly knew her mother was furious when she broke into the discussion, saying, "How can you propose to take a little boy away from the ones he loves most in this world? Whatever else you may think he suffers, it is nothing compared to the agony of tearing asunder the bonds of family. Go home with you, busy neighbors"—she gestured at them as if their very presence was disgusting to her—"and be ashamed of your misguided hearts."

The High Priestess, however, merely drummed her knuckles on the armrests of her throne and said, "We cannot allow ourselves to be moved by pity, Myrina. Imagine if everyone was to live forever in the halls of the Goddess . . . the noise! It would be unbearable."

"But perhaps," ventured Myrina, despite Animone's horrified grimaces telling her to stop, "the Goddess, divine as she is, will ensure that the noisy ones are separated—by a wall, perhaps?—from the quiet ones—"

"That is enough, Myrina!" The High Priestess stood up abruptly. "Go back to your duties and make sure you follow the rules from now on."

What rules? Myrina looked around for the answer, but did not get it. Animone's head was bent in embarrassment, and Kara was smiling— a smug, knowing smile that lasted the entire evening and stung Myrina worse than a whole week's worth of scornful glances.

That same night, over dinner, Animone pointed her spoon at the wall of the dining hall and said, "It's all there. The temple rules. Someone should have told you. I suppose we forgot. We're so used to them."

"Where?" Myrina stared at the wall, but saw nothing except a decorative black pattern on the creamy plaster. Furthermore, her head was still buzzing with the effort of fully grasping what Animone had said; over dinner everyone spoke the official language of the Temple, and although she was a fast learner, Myrina was still struggling to comprehend even the simplest sentences. It didn't help that Lilli was still bound by her vow of silence; even though the girl sat on the bench right next to them, twitching with the effort of remaining quiet, there was no telling how much she understood.

"On the wall!" Animone pointed again. "It is all written there. What we can and cannot do. Do you not see it?"

Another woman leaned in on the conversation. She was older than they, her graying hair tucked neatly into her cap. "It is called *writing*," she explained to Myrina, her eyes full of warm sincerity. "All those little patterns are words." Seeing Myrina's perplexity, the woman took a handful of salt and spread it finely on the table. "When we speak, we use our mouths to make sounds. When we write, we use our hands to make patterns. But it is the same idea. See—" With a finger, she drew two little figures in the salt. "Ky-me. I can say it, but I can also write it. Do you understand?"

"What is a kyme?" asked Myrina.

The woman laughed. "That is me. I am Kyme. My father was a scribe. That is how I learned how to write and read. I wasn't supposed to, of course"—she pointed at herself, smiling—"but I have big ears. Look." Kyme wiped out her own name and drew something else instead, her eyes gleaming with excitement. "My-ri-na."

Myrina gazed at the pattern, fascinated. But just as she reached out to touch it, a gasp went through the room, and Kyme quickly brushed the salt away.

A eunuch stood in the door.

"Eat!" Hunched nervously over her plate, Animone elbowed Myrina. "It is Dais. Don't look at him."

The eunuch made a slow round of the room, pausing briefly at their table, clearly looking for an occasion to pontificate. Finding none, Dais eventually completed his round and left.

"We are not supposed to know the alphabet," Animone now dared to whisper, glaring at Kyme for having brought them so close to trouble. "Or waste salt like that. The rules say so."

Myrina looked from the black writing on the wall to the table where a few grains of salt lingered. "The rules say we are not allowed to read the rules?"

Animone shrugged. "Well, everyone knows what they say anyway."

"Here—" Kyme spread out another handful of salt, ignoring the pleading whispers around her. "This is what *I* think." She drew a new pattern, longer this time, with a firm, defiant finger.

"What does it say?" Myrina wanted to know.

Kyme proudly retraced the words. "Dais—has—breasts."

Soon, the dining room was bubbling away with amusement. The only one who remained stern was Animone. "My grandfather was a sailor," she told Myrina, switching to the Old Language. "He did not waste his time on frivolous games." She cocked her head at the temple rules on the wall. "I know it all by heart, having heard it so often. We all do. What is gained by reading?"

According to the rules, meals were served punctually three times a day, and there were certain chores to be done at certain times. Greet the pilgrims, receive their gifts, hear their prayers . . . and, every day at noon, entertain all the visitors—bumbling foreigners mostly—with a chanting procession to the solemn beat of the ox-hide drum. "What on earth are they *doing*?" Lilli had whispered, forgetting her vow of silence, when she and Myrina had first witnessed the performance.

"A little song and dance," Myrina had whispered back, "in return for all the votive offerings, I suppose."

But not all pilgrims were satisfied with the impersonal spectacle. Some became downright unruly when they discovered there would be no immediate result of their costly gifts to the Moon Goddess. Many had come from far away, carrying the hopes and lives of entire villages upon their shoulders, and they refused to leave the temple until they had seen the Goddess with their own eyes. "Send for the eunuchs!" said Animone, when Myrina asked how one should behave on such occasions. "Whatever you do, never let strangers into the inner sanctum. They would not understand."

Myrina merely nodded as expected. She, too, did not understand. After their initiation on that first day, she had tried to describe the Moon Goddess to Lilli, but had found herself grasping for words. "She looks like a woman, and yet she is not," Myrina had explained. "She is much taller than a real person, and completely black, except for the white in her eyes. You might say she is smiling. A mysterious sort of smile."

Deep in her stomach, however, hidden beneath her hopes for Lilli's eyes, Myrina felt the truth, hard as the pit of a fruit. The Moon Goddess they had come so far to meet was not a living being at all. She was made out of stone.

And unless Myrina was much mistaken, this immovable stone goddess was no more likely to respond to prayers than the holy rock at home, or the snakes in the river. Whatever the sad tales told by the pilgrims, and whatever their offerings, day after day, week after week, the drought did not end, and the rivers did not return. Nor did Lilli, for all her silent pleading, regain the use of her eyes.

But the Moon Goddess, high on her pedestal, kept smiling.

CHAPTER THIRTEEN

Remember: women may not be too weak
To strike a blow.
—SOPHOCLES, *Electra*

ALGERIA

Growing up, Rebecca had a bichon frise named Spencer. To-gether, we took this little dog for hundreds of walks and spent hours pulling burrs from his belly fur. We even brought him to see Granny once, hoping to cheer her with his playfulness. Her response, as always, was impetuous.

"That is not a dog!" she exclaimed, glaring at her four-legged guest. "Look at him! He has forgotten to be a wolf. He thinks the world is fluffy and full of cookies. You must protect him or he will be eaten."

Rebecca's face fell, and I feared she was going to burst into tears—something my grandmother loathed.

"How?" I quickly stepped in between them. "With bows and ar-rows?"

Granny started pacing back and forth, the way she always did when discussing strategy. "Bows," she reminded me, "are long-distance weap-ons. Fine for a skilled archer and an unsuspecting target. But you are not skilled, and your enemy will be fast and unpredictable."

I glanced at Rebecca and was relieved to see her distress turning into round-eyed fascination. "How about knives, then?"

"Knives," Granny went on, her frown suggesting she was ever so slightly upset with me for not remembering what she had told me many times before, "are for close range. And only for someone with a strong arm and a strong heart. My recommendation is that you never walk that"—she glanced at Spencer—"furry thing without a stick in your hand. A good, firm stick, about the length of your leg and pointy at the end." She looked at us both with great seriousness. "Being armed is not a privilege, my little ones. It is a duty."

Rebecca never took Granny's advice seriously. Whenever I joined her for a walk, she would roll her eyes at me for bringing a stick. But one day, while we were poking around in the forest with Spencer, we suddenly heard people yelling nearby. There was an uncanny desperation to the voices that made us stop and look up.

And then we saw it: the small, reddish-brown animal coming at us full speed, flying over rocks and fallen branches, its feet barely touching the ground. Was it a dog? It looked more like a rabid fox.

At first, everything happened too fast. I simply stood by, stunned, while Rebecca instinctively bent down to pick up Spencer and press him to her chest. And because she was in such a hurry, she lost her balance and fell over, just as the attacker launched itself at the white bundle in her arms.

As the beastly, snarling mutt came down on the other side of my friend, flipping around instantly to try again, things finally slowed down in my head. I heard Rebecca screaming, unable to get up because she was clutching Spencer so hard, and I saw the vicious, reddish-brown body once more flying through the air. . . .

I finally remembered the stick in my hand.

Rushing forward, I somehow managed to get it in between them and block the attack, so that Rebecca was merely clawed, but not bitten. And when the furious mutt came bouncing back, this time without a run-up, I had time to swing the stick and deal it a perfect backhand stroke that made it tumble to the ground once more, with a yelp of frustration.

Rebecca later told me I had screamed so many swearwords at the animal that she began to fear I had become possessed by an evil woodland spirit. And when the dog's owners finally appeared, stalking through the dead leaves in their spanking new country apparel—the typical tourist giveaway—they behaved as if *we* were the threat, not their monstrous pet. "Stop it!" the man yelled at me. "Stop it now, or I'll call the police!"

"Yes!" I spat, while the killer dog was swept up and fondled by its doting mother. "Why don't you? I'm sure Constable Murray would *love* to have a word with you."

Not surprisingly, the couple made a hasty retreat and probably spent the rest of the weekend hiding in their rented cottage. At least, I hoped so.

"Oh, Mrs. Morgan! You should have seen Diana," exclaimed Rebecca, when we ran upstairs to tell Granny about the incident later that day. "She was vicious! Almost as vicious as that dog!"

Granny nodded from her armchair, hands folded peacefully in her lap. "That is good." She looked at my muddy pant legs, my ripped zipper and flushed face, and there was a dark satisfaction in her eyes. "I am glad you have it in you."

NICK HAD TOLD ME to pack my suitcase and get ready to leave the drill site after lunch. But I had done no such thing. Instead of dutifully stripping the bed in my small trailer compartment I had sat down on top of the jumbled linen with Granny's notebook, Mr. Ludwig's photo, and my camera, determined to apply my new knowledge of the asterisk word dividers to the inscription.

This time, using the close-ups I had snapped that morning, it did not take me long to solve the riddle of the first sentence. It read: "Moon omen arrive beast men ships," or, if I were to read a little freely: "The Moon foretold that beastly men would arrive by ship."

The double asterisk after "ships" suggested the end of a sentence and the beginning of the next, which simply read: "Priestess pray goddess protect"—a statement that hardly needed interpretation. Clearly, we were dealing with an account of actual events, laboriously traced onto plaster sometime in the prehistoric past. Whatever the narrative unfolding on the wall, the mere fact that I could read it was nothing short of a miracle. Forget Grigor Reznik and his damn *Historia Amazonum.* . . . Granny's notebook dictionary had launched me into a whole new sphere of scholarship.

Armed with my fantastic breakthrough, and a quick dab of lipstick, I wasted no time but scrambled from the trailer and ran off in search of Nick. After our altercation in the temple and throughout the unpleasant ride back to the drill station, he had been completely uninterested in my arguments in favor of staying. For some absurd reason, this man who had driven me hundreds of miles was now determined to be rid of me as soon as possible. Surely, I thought, if I could demonstrate that I was already making headway on the inscription, he would come to his senses.

Craig had pointed out Nick's quarters to me the night before. Apparently, the Skolsky Foundation had found it sufficient to put up their go-to man in the central pavilion in a small village of faded brown Bedouin tents, and the setup brought to mind an image I had come across often enough in ancient literature: the encampment of a barbaric warlord on the fringes of civilization.

A few men wearing head scarves eyed me with apprehensive curiosity as I strode through the dimpled sand. Not entirely sure of the protocol regarding visits to fabric structures, I hesitated underneath the canvas door, which was held open like a canopy by two metal posts. After a few uncertain seconds, I cleared my throat loudly, hoping that would be enough to alert Nick.

When there came no reaction from the tent, I ducked to peek inside, only to recoil at the sudden burst of his voice. By the sound of it, Nick was on the phone; his speech was punctuated by silences, and although I had no idea what was being said, it sounded as if he was being chewed out long-distance.

It was by no means the first time in my life I had regretted not learning Arabic, but I had never felt the need more keenly than now. For, unless I was mistaken, in the stream of Nick's aggressive self-defense the name "Moselane" was repeated at least three times.

Just as I was finally backing away from the tent door, realizing with some delay that I was eavesdropping, Nick came storming out and all but knocked me over. His eyes instantly narrowed.

Sizzling with embarrassment, I held up Mr. Ludwig's photograph and blurted out, "I've done it. The first two sentences. I can do this!"

Without even a glance at the photograph, Nick took me by the elbow and escorted me into his tent. "Take a seat."

I cast my eyes around his lair. Furniture was scarce, and an open laptop sat directly on a Persian rug next to a cantina plate half-filled with scrambled eggs. The only other place to sit down was the rather imposing divan, which, presumably, served as his bed.

"I just came by to tell you the good news," I said, turning toward him. In the dimness of the tent I could see little more than the beard and frown I already knew too well. My sense of smell, however, filled in the blanks. Nick was in need of a shower, and the strong smell of his body made me almost dizzy. "Of course, if you don't care about the inscription, it doesn't matter, but if you *do* care, I suggest we start over." I smiled as charmingly as I could under the circumstances. "What do you say?"

It seemed as if Nick had to summon his thoughts from miles away. "You've cracked the code?" he said at last, his eyes dropping to the photograph in my hand. "That was fast. How were you able to do that?"

I took half a step back. "I'm a philologist, remember? If you were my employer, I could explain my technique." I let the sentence dangle in the air.

"All right," said Nick, crossing his arms. "I apologize."

I looked him over with measured disdain, thrilled to have the upper hand at last. "I'm not interested in apologies. What matters to me is how we proceed from here. Any suggestions?"

In the murky silence following my question, I had a distinct feeling Nick's preferred mode of proceeding would be to break out a riding crop. Without another word, I ducked through the canvas door and started, somewhat flustered, across the sand.

It didn't take him long to catch up and block my way. "How about ten thousand dollars?"

"For what exactly?" I shot back. "To be your punching bag?"

"To stay as planned, until the end of the week?"

Astonished and somewhat suspicious, I held up the photograph against the sun, studying his face to spot the catch. "You are offering to double my pay?"

Even in the blinding brightness, his eyes were dark. "Yes."

"All right, I'll take it. But . . . why?" My relief came with a moment's delay and made me almost giddy. "I would have done it for free."

Nick looked away, his profile inscrutable against the desert sky. "I know."

As soon as I was back in my trailer, I was seized by an irresistible urge to call Rebecca. Of course, during our long drive from Djerba, Nick had made it perfectly clear I mustn't use my own phone, but following his recent boorish behavior I was hardly filled with a warm and fuzzy sense of loyalty.

Seeing that my phone was dead and my plug did not fit the socket in the wall, I walked over to the drill site office to see if Craig could help. "Don't worry," he said, inspecting my clunky three-prong British charger, "we'll get you juiced up." And after a little jury-rigging, my phone sprang back to life.

Three voice mail messages had come in since my departure from Oxford. The first was from my father, encouraging me to savor the joys of Amsterdam. I could hear my mother yelling, "Tell her we love her, no matter what!" in the background, as she programmed the microwave, and that little glimpse of home brought back the only too familiar lump of guilt in my throat.

The second message was from Rebecca, who, in her usual, breathless fashion, informed me she had something totally amazing to tell me but omitted to furnish a single clue as to what it was.

I was thrilled to discover that the third and final message was from James, and that he had left it only a few hours ago. As I listened to it, however, my delight quickly faded. "I don't know where you are," he said, in a voice that sounded uncharacteristically bitter, "but I thought you should know that the phone you used yesterday is registered with the Aqrab Foundation. Do you remember what I told you about the restitution fanatics in Dubai? Well, these are the people." James took a deep breath, as if it was a struggle for him to speak calmly. "I have no idea what they want with you, Morg, but I don't like you being out there with them. Please call me as soon as you can."

When I hung up, my hands were shaking. If James was right—and of course he was—Nick had lied to me. He was not working for the Skolsky Foundation, which, I suspected, didn't even exist, but for the villainous Mr. al-Aqrab—a man whose name alone sent shivers through the British museum world.

A few months earlier, over coffee, James had described in detail the Aqrab Foundation and its ruthless methods. For the past ten years, he told me, al-Aqrab's people had been hounding British museums demanding the return of ancient artifacts to their countries of origin. Threats of violence and terrorism were not beneath Mr. al-Aqrab; apparently this shameless Dubai billionaire absolutely loathed the British—and Oxford academics in particular.

I found myself staring absentmindedly at Craig, trying to make sense of it all. The kind Scotsman had evidently decided to use my presence as an incitement to clean up his desk and was currently inspecting the mold growing in a mug. To what extent was he in on the swindle? I wondered.

But more important: Why was I here? If Mr. al-Aqrab really saw Oxford as his enemy number one, why had he sent Mr. Ludwig all the way up there to hire me? For all my expertise, I was not the only philologist in the world.

Granny's notebook flashed before my eyes. But that was absurd. I was confident her Amazon delusions were a well-kept family secret.

I fully intended to call James back right away, from the privacy of my own room. But I never got that far. As soon as I emerged from Craig's office, I noticed two men snapping to attention across the sandy yard, and moments later Nick intercepted me just as I was climbing the steps of my trailer.

I knew what he wanted as soon as he held out his hand. But I resented the suggestion that ten thousand dollars had bought him the right to bully me—never mind lying to me about his employer—and looked into his sunglasses with feigned bafflement. "Can I help you?"

"Your phone," he said, skipping any pretense of nicety. "I thought I made it absolutely clear—"

"You did," I assured him, taking a bold step up the staircase. "And I heard you. Am I to understand you do not trust me?"

He merely snapped his fingers to let me know he was still waiting. The gesture made my cheeks flood with fury. "What is this? A gulag?"

"With one exception. You are free to leave anytime you want."

There was something about the way he said it that made me realize he secretly wished I would. Despite his halfhearted efforts to make up and move on, it was not Nick who had offered me ten thousand dollars to stay the week. It was someone else. But who? And why?

I placed my phone in the palm of his hand with as much dignity as the situation deserved. "Thank you," he said, slipping it into his pocket. "You know what is down there. You know why I have to do this."

"Quite frankly"—I rolled up the wire from the phone charger with angry fingers and stuffed it into my own pocket—"I'm having some difficulty understanding why your Mr. Skolsky"—I resisted the urge to grimace at the fallacious name—"believes this temple belongs to him personally."

"Is that what you think is going on?"

"What other conclusion can I possibly draw?" I looked at him as earnestly as I could, but the small window of synergy he had just opened was, once again, hermetically sealed.

All he said was, "That is precisely why I have to take your phone."

LATER THAT NIGHT, CRAIG took me out for an evening walk under the stars. Although he did not mention anything about it, I suspected he knew about the phone incident and was trying to cheer me up.

As we walked, I was sorely tempted to confront him with questions about the Aqrab Foundation, but knew it would be a mistake to let on that I had discovered the truth. Even if Craig was not on the Aqrab payroll, he was on their team. Why else had he alerted them—and them alone—when his drilling crew found the temple?

"So, what company do you work for?" I eventually asked, endeavoring to sound as if I were merely making conversation. "And what about Nick? Are you two working for the same people?"

Craig drew on the pipe a few times. "Better ask someone else. I'm just a grease monkey." When he saw my disappointment, his smile turned wry. "Look, I don't know what they've been telling you. I prefer to stay out of it."

"Here's what they've been telling me," I said, a little irked by his cowardice. "They told me this was about the Amazons. That somehow"—I threw a hand in the direction of the buried temple—"this place was proof they really existed. But as you heard this morning, Nick didn't get that memo." I looked at Craig with whatever hope I had left. "What about you? Have you heard any mention of the Amazons? By anyone? At all?"

He shrugged uncomfortably. "Sorry, lass. I'm not the one to ask."

We walked on in silence and ended up by a plain metal gate. Because of the darkness it took me a moment to realize we had arrived at an enclosure, and that there were other people there, too, leaning silently on the fence posts.

Craig nodded without a word, and I looked into the paddock to see two forms moving about slowly—a black horse on a rope and a man dressed in nothing but a pair of white trousers. It took me a moment to recognize the man as Nick, and despite my growing cynicism with regards to his person there was something about this slow, moonlit dance that was utterly mesmerizing. "Look," mouthed Craig, without a sound.

Inside the enclosure, Nick knelt down in the sand. The black horse moved around a bit, then came closer, and eventually stretched its neck to rest its head on his naked shoulder.

A collective hum went through the men gathered at the fence, and Craig beamed at me, the pipe bobbing delightedly at the corner of his mouth. "I put my money on ten days. He did it in five. It's in their bloody genes."

"What is?" I asked, barely able to wrest my eyes from Nick.

Craig gestured with his pipe, a private smile playing in his eyes. "Arabian horses are very clever. They second-guess you. You don't break them; you wait for them to adopt you. Look!"

"Well—" I turned away from the spectacle, the events of the day dragging at my every limb. "I'm afraid I'm more than a five-day job."

Craig's smile disappeared. "If you want my advice—"

"Please!"

"Take the money, do your job, and go. Don't look back. And no matter what happens"—he looked deeply into my eyes, making sure I heard him—"don't mess with these people. They wouldn't be nice about it."

CHAPTER FOURTEEN

TEMPLE OF THE MOON GODDESS

The attack came at night.

Under cover of a cloudy sky, five foreign ships forced their way through the great marsh and drew up on the shore near the Temple of the Moon Goddess. Had they come three months earlier, they would never have made it across the shallow water; they owed their success to a particularly wet rainy season, which had ever so briefly restored the old coastline.

Even as the tarred keels plowed into the sand, no dogs barked, no geese stirred. All sounds were dimmed by the heavy dampness of the air, so characteristic of that time of year, when heaven and earth were at last saturated with moisture. Into this treacherous mist did the five ships disgorge their lethal load: men armed with refined weapons and brute desires, men whose needs had been whetted by long weeks at sea.

So silent was the invasion that Myrina did not apprehend the danger until she was woken up by a small elbow wedged in her ribs. "Did you hear that?" hissed Lilli, sitting up abruptly. "Listen."

Completely against the temple rules—but with the secret blessing of the High Priestess, who appreciated the idea of Myrina keeping watch—the two sisters spent most nights on the roof, preferring the open air to the vaulted safety of the dormitory. Lilli had been hesitant at first, naturally afraid of the perilous climb up the rope ladder. But once she had learned where to put her hands and feet, and with Myrina right behind her, she soon grew to like the nightly escape. For up here, alone on the roof, the sisters could speak privately about the events of the day.

Even during the rainy season they continued to sleep in their high perch, huddled under a small tarp and wrapped in the same blanket. As the much-longed-for water kept rising, the shoreline crept so far inland as to make the vast, green swamp of the ocean visible from the temple roof. Occasionally, in the early morning, Myrina would sit and enjoy the sunrise over the water, trying to describe the changing colors to Lilli, and they would remember their friends the fishermen and speculate about whether their catch had been improved by the weather.

But the rising sea had inspired more than just memories.

As of late, Lilli had been having nightmares about foreign ships, and had woken up crying more than once, convinced the temple was about to be attacked. "It is not a dream!" she kept insisting, whenever Myrina tried to calm her down. "It is a vision. A warning."

The Moon Goddess had given Lilli the gift of prophecy in return for her lost eyesight. At least, that was what the High Priestess had maintained ever since it became apparent that the girl would never see again. Lilli, blind to all things material, could see the future. And in that future she saw blood.

Whenever these nightmares occurred, Myrina simply enfolded her sister in a silent embrace and rocked her back to sleep, just the way their mother used to do. Lilli had always had vivid dreams, and for as long as Myrina could remember the girl had woken up at least every second night, trembling with fear. It was therefore no great surprise to her when Lilli suddenly, on this particular night, sat up on her knees on the temple roof and hissed, "What was that? Do you hear voices?"

Myrina dutifully sat up, too, and looked around. "It is probably—"

She was silenced by a frightened hand on her shoulder. "Men. Weapons." Lilli listened intently. "They are here. The black ships. I have felt it all day."

Still half-asleep, Myrina stood up and squinted into the darkness, trying to make out the coastline. Only when the clouds parted, allowing the moon a brief burst of warning, did Myrina see them—the contours of vessels pulled ashore and the shadows creeping up the bank toward the temple entrance.

"Do you not hear that?" urged Lilli, mistaking Myrina's horrified silence for disbelief. "It is them!"

"Quiet!" Myrina sat her sister down and out of sight. "I must go and warn the others. Stay here and be quiet! Understood?"

As soon as Lilli nodded her frightened assent, Myrina darted off across the roof tiles. There was no time for the rope ladder; instead she jumped down into the courtyard the way she had done on that first day, six months ago.

How sinister the courtyard looked tonight, shrouded in shadows . . . and this time it was she who came for the eunuchs, not the other way around. "Get up!" she cried, banging on their closed shutters as she ran by. "Get up and guard the front door!"

As she passed the tiled basin, Myrina was puzzled to glimpse a series of rhythmic ripples on the water. Stopping to listen, she heard distant thuds of wood against wood, and although she did not know what caused the sound, she understood that its aim was destruction.

When she finally arrived at the dormitory it was completely empty, with sheets and clothes scattered everywhere. Relieved to see that the priestesses had been so swift to perceive the danger and take up their positions, Myrina ran over to check the secret box . . . only to groan with defeat.

There they were, all the weapons, precisely where she had put them after the last training session, four days earlier. Wherever her fellow priestesses had disappeared to, they were as unarmed and defenseless as ever.

Picking up as many spears and bows as she could carry, Myrina continued apace down the corridor to the main temple, pausing now and then to get a better grip. Not until she reached the inner sanctum was she finally met by a squall of shrieks and tearful pleas. Stretching to see, she caught sight of the High Priestess behind the altar, arms crossed in defiance, surrounded by a cluster of wailing women.

"What goes on here?" Myrina dropped the weapons in a pile on the floor. "Make haste and arm yourselves!"

All heads turned at the clatter, but no one motioned to heed her demand.

"She says the Moon Goddess commands her to stay," cried Pitana, towering over the others and waving her long arms fretfully at the High Priestess. "And *they* will not abandon her. Oh, Myrina, do talk to her and change her mind!"

"We have no time for this!" Myrina tore around the altar to seize the High Priestess by the sleeve. "Come! We must position ourselves—"

"Go! Away with you!" The High Priestess brushed off Myrina's hands and reached out for the sacrificial crown sitting on the altar— a massive diadem adorned with a halo of bronze serpents. "I shall stay here. It is my holy duty to protect the Goddess—"

Myrina gritted her teeth. "The Goddess can protect herself. You taught us so, remember?" She took the crown with impatient hands and put it back on the altar. "Now come! You were the one who told me to train everyone and prepare for the worst."

Her bold manner brought nothing but defiance. Without another word, the High Priestess reclaimed the crown and placed it firmly upon her own head, swaying briefly under its weight.

Ducking to avoid the protruding serpents, Myrina seized the High Priestess by the hands. "Why are you so determined to slow us down?" she demanded. "Our hope is dying with every thud on that door. Do you not see that?"

There was a brief silence, in which Myrina could almost convince herself the High Priestess had begun to realize her own tragic mistake, but the sound of splintering wood rendered all such speculation meaningless.

Within the blink of an eye the temple was taken over by hordes of howling demons. Pale, apelike creatures with mangy beards and wild faces hurdled to and fro with their shields and swords, searching for bodies to pierce and treasures to steal. Their presence was so terrifying Myrina made no other attempt at arming her sisters, nor did she even dare to search for her own weapons in the pile on the floor. Trapped as she was in the inner sanctum, faint with fear, there was nothing to do but wait and pray.

For a while the invaders were preoccupied with the riches of the main temple. One by one the votives were pulled from the walls and tossed into a growing pile on the stone floor. Next, the leader turned his eye on the open door to the shrine and the frightened women assembled there. Barking something in a language too guttural to be understood, he made his way through the tumult, kicked aside Myrina's pile of bows and spears, and stepped right over the threshold into the holy room.

And there he stood for a breath or two, staring at them all.

Then his eyes settled on the High Priestess.

"Come, I beg you!" Myrina tried once more to pull the older woman into the anonymity of the crowd, but again she was met with fierce resistance.

"No!" The High Priestess put her hands against Myrina's chest and pushed her away with all her might. "Leave me, Myrina, I command you!"

Held back by Animone and Pitana, Myrina could do nothing but stand by miserably as the man crossed the floor, jumped up onto the altar, and—without the slightest show of respect or regret—swung his blade at the High Priestess.

Impervious to the screaming women, he picked up the terrible, dismembered head and held it high in the air, as if it were a prize and he a deserving victor.

Then came his comrades, pouring into the room like vermin, and before she was able to act, a blow to her head made everything go dark for Myrina.

WHEN SHE CAME TO, she found herself sliding across the floor of the main temple, her body convulsing with shock. Someone was pulling her along by the hair as if she were nothing but dead prey, and she cried out with pain when he continued down the stone steps and right through the dregs of the abandoned pilgrim village.

The man left her in a heap of loot on the beach, and Myrina lay moaning for a while, certain she had broken every bone in her body.

Around her in the gray mist of dawn lay other priestesses, their clothing ripped and smeared with crimson, and whenever any one of them would come to and attempt to sit up, a hairy arm or a leather boot would immediately strike them down. Seeing this, Myrina did not even try to move; she stayed where she was, struggling against the steady trickle of blood and vomit in her throat, listening to the cries from the temple.

Lilli.

She prayed Lilli was still safe on the roof where she had left her. More than ever, Myrina wished she had her weapons. Her hunting knife . . . her bow and quiver . . . but then, what could she possibly have done? What use was a single bow against an army of evil?

As the darkness of a woeful night yielded to the merciless morning sun, the invaders began loading their five ships with the objects they considered most valuable. At one point, an argument broke out between the leader and the rest, clearly to do with the Moon Goddess, whom they had managed to remove from her pedestal in the inner sanctum and lug all the way down to the beach by aid of ropes and lifting poles.

Judging from the men's grunts and gritted teeth, the Goddess was forbiddingly heavy and would undoubtedly compromise the stability of the ship carrying her. But the leader was determined, and on his bidding the unwieldy deity was laboriously hauled onto his personal vessel together with other sacred objects, including, Myrina feared, a bloody sack containing the head of the High Priestess.

Afterward came the division and loading on the ships of other spoils. When all five crews seemed satisfied with their stash, they began filling the remaining space with women. Some priestesses—the beautiful Klito among them—were carried on board immediately; others were stripped naked and inspected, only to be discarded with a sneer.

Myrina was one of the discarded. The sailors took one look at her robust frame and small breasts, and laughed. One of them did seem to make a case for her youthful strength, but he was quickly overruled.

Just as she dared to crawl away, thinking they had finished with her,

Myrina felt a searing pain in her back. Twisting to see what had happened, she caught sight of one of the raiders yanking his spear out of her body. Instead of panic, however, all she felt was a strange sensation of relief as she collapsed in the sand.

THE GODS OF THE underworld received her in their dark halls, cut out her heart, and put it on their scales . . . but found it wanting. Something was missing. Only when they sent her to the chamber of truth, where jackal-headed demons tore at her flesh, did she finally remember.

Lilli.

Clawing her way out of the caverns of death, Myrina returned to the light above and was sprawled once again on the bank of the lake, beneath the ever-hungry sun. When she finally opened her eyes, the world was veiled in a golden mist, and she felt weightless. Standing up, she walked about in wonder, feeling no pain at all. The sky spun around her once or twice, and the beach tried to swallow her as if she were in the sandy funnel of a draining hourglass . . . but she was unafraid.

Seeing that she was completely alone on the bank of the lake, Myrina walked back up the stairs to the temple, wondering if the raid had been nothing but a fantastic dream brought about by sunstroke. But as soon as she entered the building and saw the destruction inside, she understood that it had all been real, and that, for some reason she might never grasp, the gods had held a protective hand over her.

Everywhere around her lay broken pottery and torn garments, and now, at last, Myrina felt the golden mist clearing and her senses returning as she realized that some of those bloody garments were still draped around bodies. Anxious to see who had been so brutally slaughtered, yet fearful of recognizing anyone, she felt a groundswell of despair and kept walking.

The survivors were gathered in the women's dormitory, crouching on the floor in small, cowed clusters. As far as Myrina could see, Lilli was not among them. "Dearest!" Kyme came rushing forward, her graying hair hanging loose and her kind face torn with grief. "We thought you were dead! Oh, what a horrible wound!"

Suddenly, there were hands everywhere, trying to make her lie down, but Myrina pushed them away. "Where is Lilli?" she demanded, feeling the sandy funnel sucking her in deeper and deeper.

"Be calm," urged Kyme, holding an icy hand to her forehead. "Rest."

As she lay down on a cot, Myrina felt herself sliding into darkness, but just as she thought she could hold on no longer, Animone came. Myrina did not recognize her friend right away, for the oval form that appeared in the haze beside her was so broken and discolored it resembled, not a face, but a melon that had fallen off a cart and been left to rot by the roadside. "Look at us," muttered the form, leaning over to press a trembling kiss to Myrina's cheek, "we are the lucky ones."

Myrina tried to speak, but her tongue was too heavy.

"You will die a holy death," Animone went on, "and I"—her voice broke, but she forced herself to continue—"I would rather be raped once by a nameless thug than every day for the rest of my life by someone who calls himself my master. And the Moon Goddess—"

With whatever strength she had left, Myrina grabbed Animone by the arm, just above the jackal bracelet. "Where is she?"

Her friend made a sound of disgust. "The Goddess? Let them have her! What did she do to protect us? We have served her all our lives— been chaste for her. And how did she reward us? By running off with a band of rapists!"

Myrina yanked at Animone's arm and stared at her with feverish impatience. "I speak of Lilli! Where is she? I left her on the roof—"

"Hush now." Pitana appeared, her tall form hunched with anxiety. "You should rest." She stroked Myrina's burning face with trembling fingers. "In truth, you are very ill—"

"Tell me!" Myrina demanded, staring at her two friends. "Where is she?"

Animone closed her eyes and bent her broken head. "She is gone, too. And so is Kara. For all her conniving, I do pity her—"

"They took her?" Myrina tried to sit up, but could not. "Where? Where did they take her? Who were those beasts? Animone, your grandfather was a sailor . . . you must have an idea. Come, help me up. Where is my bow?"

"Bows are for hunters," muttered someone.

"And what are we?" countered Myrina. "Prey?" She managed to sit up at last. "Prey is afraid. Prey squirms. Prey is eaten." She stared at them all in turn, those broken, bewildered faces. "Why such frightened looks? Did not the full moon ever favor the hunter?"

Myrina intended to say more, much more, but her strength had long since burned to the socket. With a groan of exhaustion, she collapsed once more on the cot, and there she lay, still as death, for two days, leaving her sisters wondering what unnatural power kept her alive, and why.

CHAPTER FIFTEEN

I thence arrived to where the Gorgon dwelt. Along the way, in fields and
by the roads, I saw on all sides men and animals—like statues—turned to
flinty stone at sight of dread Medusa's visage.
    —OVID, *Metamorphoses*

ALGERIA

IT TOOK ME FOUR DAYS TO WORK THROUGH THE INSCRIPTION IN THE inner sanctum. Even with my knowledge of the asterisk dividers, and despite spending several yawning hours every night alphabetizing Granny's dictionary, it was still an enormous challenge making sense of the narrative on the wall.

My work was not helped by the fact that the plaster had innumerable cracks and chips, probably brought on by changes in humidity or shifts in the surrounding structure. In some places, large patches had crumbled off the wall entirely, in jagged, irregular patterns, and as a result about a third of the inscription was missing.

What remained was a broken record of apocalyptic events and nauseating violence. Destruction, rape, and murder had marked the end of this ancient, unknown civilization, and even though Granny's list did not contain every single word used by the narrator—far from it— I understood enough to connect the dots.

When I finally reached the bottom of the last wall I lay back on my straw mat for a while, contemplating where this all fit into the ancient world I thought I knew so well. There was no doubt in my mind the temple was at least three thousand years old, and that I was looking at the legacy of a Bronze Age civilization that had left no trace except within the realm of myths. The question was: which myths?

Mr. Ludwig had explicitly told me the Skolsky Foundation had found Amazon remains, and yet the inscription made no mention of female warriors; quite the contrary. Seeing the Skolsky Foundation had turned out to be complete bollocks, should I assume the Amazon connection was, too? Had it all merely been a cunning way of ensnaring me?

If so, why had someone in the higher echelons of the Aqrab Foundation decided to send *me* to Algeria rather than the archaeologist Nick has asked for? Because I didn't have my phone, I hadn't been able to look Mr. al-Aqrab up on the Internet yet. But I remembered James telling me he was one of those typical nouveau riche bastards who had a golf course on the roof and who would happily rent an entire cruise ship for his wife's birthday party. Why would such a man, I had to wonder, give a jot about this patchy wall narrative, let alone undertake such a gargantuan excavation?

And again, my mind returned to Granny. Had she known of this forgotten civilization? It seemed impossible. And yet here I was, holding her notebook in my hand. . . .

My speculations ended when Craig entered the inner sanctum with a smile and a headshake. "I thought I'd find you here. Come on, Doc! It's Friday night and we're killing the fatted calf."

As it turned out, the fatted calf came in the form of yet another mystery stew from the cantina, but it helped that Craig invited me to join him and his mates around a bonfire in the tent village. Above and around us, a myriad of twinkling stars made the infinite blackness of the universe a tad less daunting, and after hours upon hours spent either underground or within the claustrophobic box of my trailer, I was more than ready to savor the desert night, not to mention a bit of human company.

"Now, Doc," said Craig, draping his company fleece around my shoulders, "tell us what you are finding down there. Who's the headless charmer in the coffin?"

Judging by the bemused grunts around me, only a few of the men had known about the skeleton until this moment.

"It's not a man," I told them. "It's a woman. She was beheaded. There was an attack. A small fleet of foreign ships—" Looking around, I saw the men staring back at me with unabashed fascination. "It is always the same, isn't it?" I went on. "Marauding and pillaging. Men bent on destruction, and women—" Even as I spoke, it occurred to me that there I was, a single woman in a camp full of men, unharmed and sharing their dinner. My great-great-grandmothers would have thought it impossible. Truly, in the long history of women stretching between the miserable events described on the wall and the here and now, *I* was the anomaly.

"Most of the priestesses were killed," I continued, drawing the fleece tightly around me. "Some were taken as slaves—the pretty ones, I assume. I'm not entirely sure what happened to the other people living here, but the inscription seems to suggest the raiders set fire to the town before they left." Seeing the expression on the faces around me, I shook my head. "I'm sorry. That was not a very happy tale, was it?"

"And the lass in the coffin?" Craig insisted. "Why was she special?"

"As far as I can tell, she was the High Priestess." I pulled the laptop out of my bag and scrolled through my photos from the inner sanctum. "The earthly representative of the Moon Goddess. Whom they also stole, by the way. The statue, I mean. Apparently, the High Priestess had a headpiece with poisonous snakes." I paused to zoom in on a wall painting depicting an intimidating female figure with coiling serpents sprouting from her hair. "Here." I held up the laptop for everyone to see. "Rather striking, isn't she?"

The men stretched to see the figure on the screen, and I let them pass the laptop around. When it arrived at Craig, he let out a yelp. "She looks like my mother-in-law!"

I waited for the laughter to die down, then said, "In Greek myth, Perseus travels to faraway lands to kill the snaky-haired monster, Medusa. But he doesn't *just* kill her; he cuts off her head and takes it with him, to use as a weapon. Apparently, Medusa was so terrifyingly ugly, the mere sight of her face would turn a man into stone."

"It *is* my mother-in-law!" exclaimed Craig.

Ignoring the ensuing chuckle, I went on, "Medusa was supposed to have lived right here in North Africa. According to Greek literature, these regions were home to many different . . . well, monsters mostly."

"So, where did Perseus take it?" Craig wanted to know. "The head?"

"He carried it around for a bit," I said. "Quite a useful thing, actually. Who wouldn't like to be able to occasionally turn other people into stone? But what is really interesting is that this snaky-haired head ended up as a scary decoration on Athena's shield. You know, the Olympian goddess Athena? She helped Odysseus on his long journey back from Troy."

To this, Craig and a few others nodded in recognition.

"Furthermore," I continued, emboldened by their apparent interest, "the Greek philosopher Plato claimed that the goddess Athena was, in fact, a North African import. Suppose"—I clasped my forehead, trying to hang on to this thread of sudden, euphoric clarity—"this is what happened to the stolen Moon Goddess? What if she was taken to ancient Greece and renamed Athena? That would explain why she carries Medusa's head around on her shield, and why Homer and Hesiod called her 'Tritogeneia.' Don't you see? They arrived in Greece at the same time: the goddess Athena and her secret monster weapon—the only two survivors of a magnificent lost civilization around Lake Tritonis. It makes perfect sense!"

"Were there no other survivors?"

I jolted at the sound of Nick's voice. He hadn't been around for a few days, and I had assumed he was out hunting for an archaeologist to replace me. Yet here he stood, looking at me through the shimmering firelight.

"Well," I said, "those who were taken as slaves were as good as dead. Black women forced into a white world—" I shook my head.

"How do you know they were black?"

I hesitated, taken aback by his combative tone. "As you know, the women depicted on the temple walls are tinted brown, and the inscription refers to the invaders as having pale skin—"

"What about those who were not taken as slaves? There must have been other survivors. Who put the eyewitness account on the wall?"

"Unfortunately," I said, irritated with him for challenging me in front of everyone, "there is a lacuna in the text—"

"What's a lacuna?"

I glared at him. Nick's sniffy manner told me he bloody well knew what a lacuna was. A lacuna was a gap. Something missing. Such as him telling me he was working for the Aqrab Foundation. Or apologizing for his rudeness. Or giving me back my phone.

"It's a hole in the wall"—I flung out my arms—"this big. But yes"—I nodded obligingly—"there were survivors. A handful, no more. And the inscription claims they went in search of their stolen friends."

Nick stepped forward, his eyes reflecting the dance of the flames. "Where did they go?"

I hesitated. I had thought he meant merely to tease me with his persistent questioning; now I understood it had nothing to do with me. "I don't know," I said. "That part is missing."

The disappointment in his face was tangible. Without another word he turned and walked away, and I was left to wonder—once again—about the motivations of the Aqrab Foundation and their objective in hiring me.

When Mr. Ludwig had approached me back in Oxford the week before, he and the foundation had had no way of knowing I would be able to make sense of the inscription. They might have paid me thousands of dollars and transported me through several climate zones for nothing. And on top of that, by choosing me, they had, in theory, alerted the entire Oxford community to the excavation.

My confusion only grew when I returned to my trailer compartment later that night to find my cellphone lying on top of the bed with a note saying, "Call away."

Not surprisingly, my voice mail was jammed with unheard messages. My poor parents were increasingly perplexed at my absence, Rebecca was at a loss to understand why I hadn't called her back, and James was—perhaps not unreasonably—beginning to fear I had been abducted by a desert sheikh, and that he would be dispensing fish-food confetti for the rest of the academic year. "By the way, your students have been talking," he went on, more gravely. "The old hellcat knows you've eloped. You should call her."

The old hellcat was my mentor Katherine Kent, with whom James and I had had dinner the night before my departure. I had hoped to keep my voyage secret from her, since she would most certainly call me a fool for abandoning my Oxford duties in the fray of Michaelmas term, even if it was only for a week.

After a quick glance at the hour, I called her right away. As suspected, she was not in her office, and I left a quick message, saying, "Sorry to dash off like that, but really, I'm onto something spectacular here. Definitely worth it. A whole new writing system—unbelievable stuff. I'm fairly sure I've figured out how to decipher it; can't wait to show you."

That aside, my mind circled back to James's comment about the desert sheikh. Was it possible he knew I was in North Africa? Or was he just playing on the fact that the Aqrab Foundation was headquartered in Dubai? Clearly, to James, historian that he was, the fact that I had been practically abducted by a gang of restitution fanatics made the situation particularly precarious; if indeed the armies of Mr. al-Aqrab were laying siege to British museums, then I had, in a manner of speaking, ended up behind enemy lines.

SATURDAY WAS MY LAST day working in the temple. I had more or less finished with the inscription, and after spending the morning polishing the English transcript, I returned to the inner sanctum in the afternoon to take a few more detailed photos of the walls and, I suppose, say goodbye to the place.

I told neither Craig nor Nick I was going back to the temple after lunch. For all they knew I was hard at work packing my suitcase and, as Craig had put it, braiding my Rapunzel hair before my return to the ivory tower.

After riding back and forth so many times, I knew the temple was not actually that far away from the camp—no more than a brisk half-hour walk across sand dunes. And since we were scheduled to leave for

Djerba in just a few hours, I quite relished the idea of the solitary exercise.

The guards at the tent did seem to find it slightly odd that I returned to the excavation site on foot all by myself. But they were not paid to ask questions, and lowered me readily through the tube.

Soon, the rest of the world became irrelevant. I was back in the temple, far away from the bustle of life and once more alone with my thoughts. Dank, dusty, and dark, it was certainly not the most comfortable of places, physically or mentally, but the wonder of the walls in the inner sanctum soon distracted me from the fact that I was underground, with only a dangling rope connecting me to the world above.

I had come to know the women on these walls, and being down here, breathing the air they had breathed, we could somehow bond outside of time. Whatever the events of the past, whatever had yet to come, this quiet place was our shared refuge, and I could not help but feel a pang of regret that I would have to leave it so soon. Nick had sworn to get me back to Oxford by Monday morning, and considering how keen he was to be rid of me, I knew he'd deliver on his promise.

Soon, I thought to myself, wandering around the inner sanctum in silence, the temple would be bustling with archaeologists, and the media would be clamoring to get access to the sensational discovery. Meanwhile, I would be back at Oxford, doing my damnedest to write a scholarly article about the inscription without giving away the secret of how I had been able to translate these mysterious symbols into English.

Breaking out my camera, I took a few more close-ups of the wall paintings as well as the inscription. In my hurry to decipher the writing, I had spent shamefully little time examining the colorful images, which so clearly predated the text. Most were sacrificial scenes, and one particular tableau seemed to suggest those sacrificed had not always been animals. Here was the picture that had made me think of the Medusa myth: The High Priestess, wearing a headpiece made of writhing snakes, was reaching out for a woman in a white dress, seemingly stabbing her with a large knife. Whatever the ritual going on, and whatever the fate of the victim, I mused, it was perhaps no wonder this snaky-haired lady had gone down in myth as a monster.

Holding up the lantern, I looked more closely at the figure of the High Priestess. The plaster was chipped, but apart from her frightful headpiece I was almost certain she was wearing the same jackal-headed bracelet I had espied on the arm of the skeleton in the sarcophagus . . . not to mention the one I had on my own arm, hidden under my sweater sleeve.

But the skeleton, the priestess, and I were not the only women in the room with a bronze jackal in common. Walking around the entire sanctum with my flashlight trained to the walls, I counted at least eight other figures who wore similar bracelets. They were all robed in white, and although their hair was tucked into small, pointy caps, their bosoms and wide hips suggested they were female.

As I had done so many times before, I found myself wondering to what extent these white-clad women were related to the Amazon legend. Fiery warrior deeds aside, maybe I was looking at a more intimate, perhaps even secret, element of their lives, namely the rituals and beliefs that had bound them together in the first place, as a holy sisterhood. But then, if it was really so, why hadn't they defended themselves against the invaders? Could I possibly be looking at the final hours of a dying Amazon civilization?

Or its beginning?

I still remembered Granny showing me her own bracelet and telling me that the jackal was immortal. Apparently, despite its stillness, the brazen canine was alive and extremely picky about its human hosts. "You can't inherit it," she had explained. "You must earn it. Only then will the jackal choose you."

At the time I had taken it personally, thinking she was referring to me in particular, and had been somewhat miffed at the suggestion that I was not worthy of her jewelry. Well, fine, I had thought to myself, child that I was. Who wants to be chosen by a jackal anyway?

But, in fact, it appeared that this was precisely what had happened: Granny's bracelet had chosen me as its host. Whenever I tried, I was unable to wrest it from my arm; neither soap nor oil would do the trick. Obviously, it had been the first thing on my mind after seeing the skeleton in the coffin; I knew I had to make sure Nick did not spot my bracelet and wonder about the connection. Even in the flurry of everything else that was going on, I kept trying to take it off . . . only, I couldn't.

It seemed to be one of those eerie, irreversible things: Once the bracelet was on, it stayed on. Or perhaps the heat of the desert had made my tissue swell. Then again, down here in the temple I was always cold, but that didn't seem to make the slightest difference. I had put on the bracelet on a whim, and now I was stuck with it.

Had the same thing happened to Granny?

If she had been part of an archaeological team in her forgotten youth, working to decipher this unknown language, it was not unthinkable she had imbibed some of the rituals of the ancient culture she had helped to uncover. Perhaps she had donned a newly excavated bracelet in jest, only to find that she, too, could never take it off again. Or perhaps she had not wanted to.

Walking over to the sarcophagus, I put the lantern on the floor and tried once again to manipulate the stone lid. But, of course, I couldn't. Not even Nick had been able to move it on his own.

All those solitary hours spent in this room over the past few days . . . so close to the skeleton, but physically unable to confirm whether the bracelet on its arm was exactly identical to my own. And now I was going home. . . .

A strange, faint scratching noise interrupted my speculations. Standing still for a moment, I tried to make out the origin of the sound, but couldn't.

One by one, all the little hairs on my arms stood up with dread. Ever since my first visit to the temple six days ago, I had been afraid the whole thing would come crashing down on top of me. But the sound I heard now was not one of mud brick caving in, I decided. It was more of an organic noise, as if someone, somewhere, was dragging a heavy sack across the floor.

As I stood, listening intently, I almost convinced myself I heard voices, too. Not the deep, decisive voices of Craig or Nick, but a faint, ghostly murmur that coiled around me until I could barely breathe.

Too frightened to stay where I was, trapped in the inner sanctum, I crept out into the main temple, just a few tentative steps. I had never been comfortable in that enormous room, with all its umbrage and echoes, and had always kept a wide berth of the square black hole in the floor, which—according to Craig—led down a narrow stone staircase into the unknown.

Pointing my flashlight this way and that, I tried to determine whether I was truly alone. But all I saw were endless rows of columns and shadows, playing hide-and-seek with my beam.

I called out anxiously at the darkness beyond. No response.

From the first time I entered it, the titanic temple building had filled me with dread. And whenever I had returned to work on the inscription, I had always hastened into the relative comfort of the inner sanctum. It was as if the people who had once lived and died here had left contorted, demonic imprints in the air all around—images waiting to spring out at me as soon as I let down my guard. No number of visits had lessened my discomfort with this cold, Cimmerian void that held so many secrets. And now, as I slowly walked through the large gallery with my collar up, chasing elusive sounds, I was so chilled with terror I had to clench my teeth to stop them from chattering.

In my agitation I went farther than I had ever gone before, far beyond the rope exit and down the entire nave of the temple. Craig had told me there was a large double door at the other end, presumably the original main entrance, but I had never actually seen it.

For all his big gestures, Craig had not done the door justice. It was so enormous you could have passed through it riding a camel, and it dwarfed everything around me—not least my presumed knowledge of ages past. What manner of world had once existed outside this door? Had it been inhabited by people like me, or by a stronger, more capable, race? I had no idea.

As I stood there, once again shocked by the engineering capabilities of this lost civilization, it occurred to me there was something odd about the door. It was not the fact that it had so obviously been broken and repaired, but that it was locked in place with an enormous beam.

Barred from the inside.

Whoever had done this, thousands of years ago, had clearly made the choice to remain inside the temple to protect its secrets. Had it been some grand suicidal gesture, I wondered, for the good of the bracelet sisterhood? Or was there another way out of the temple that I didn't know about?

Craig had told me the underground was a labyrinth of caves, and that he had not been able to persuade his men to follow any one of them to its end. Even the drill site roughnecks had been spooked by the place, and I was left to wonder what exactly they had found down there.

Was that where the sounds were coming from? The temple basement?

Once again, I listened intently.

And then I heard footsteps. Right behind me.

Swirling around with a shriek, I raised my flashlight, ready to smash it down on the intruder's head.

"It's me!" barked Nick, his hand clamped around my wrist. "What are you doing here?"

"I heard something—" I began, my voice shaking.

"Come!" He took the flashlight and started toward the rope exit, pulling me along. "Time to go."

My fear morphed into irritation. "I need my jacket."

Running through the darkness, all I had to guide me was the faint shine of the lantern I had left behind in the inner sanctum. Behind me, I could hear Nick yelling at me to stop, his tone increasingly uncivil. But Granny's notebook was in my jacket pocket, and I needed that book more than his good opinion.

When I finally reached the inner sanctum, everything was exactly as I had left it. Except . . .

"Diana!" Nick was right behind me. "We don't have time—"

"It's so strange." I picked up my jacket and made sure the notebook was still there while my eyes scanned the room. "Something happened here—"

"Come on!" Nick tried to take the jacket from me. "Let's go."

"Wait!" I suddenly felt all my nerves snapping to attention. "Look!" I pointed at the sarcophagus. "It's open! Someone opened it!"

Nick didn't even look. He simply took me by the arm and pulled me along, his forehead furrowed with worry.

As we ran from the inner sanctum, I heard a frightful sound that took my brain a few breathless seconds to process. It was of a muted explosion, not far away, and of mud brick collapsing.

CHAPTER SIXTEEN

Women are nothing alone; no Ares is in them.
—AESCHYLUS, *The Suppliant Maidens*

As SOON AS WE REACHED THE BOTTOM OF THE CHUTE, NICK GRABBED the dangling rope and showed me the carabiner attached to it—the carabiner I already knew well from my many previous trips up and down. "In a moment," he said, "you are going to hook this to your harness. I will be up there"—he pointed to illustrate—"and I will pull you up. Do you understand?"

I felt another prickly invasion of panic. "Why can't the guards—?"

"There are no guards." Nick pulled off his baggy shirt and glanced upward with apprehension. "Now give me a minute."

Only when he wiped his palms on his trousers did I realize he was going to crawl up the rope, leaving me behind. "Wait!" I exclaimed, my fear mounting. "What's going on? Why are the guards not there?"

He took me by the shoulders and gave me a little shake. "You'll be fine. I promise. Just keep breathing."

His words were followed by a distant rumble, and I could see in his eyes that he, too, was unnerved by the sound. Without another attempt at calming me, Nick started up the rope. There were no knots to give him purchase; all he had was the strength of his hands and arms and what little foothold he could create by twisting the rope with his feet.

I had never felt as abandoned as I did when he eventually disappeared into the steel tube. Hooking the carabiner onto my harness with trembling fingers, I looked around in the darkness, feeling very keenly that danger was closing in on me from all sides. For every time I took a breath as instructed, it seemed to me there was another sudden rush of rubble falling somewhere beneath me or on the other side of the wall . . . it was impossible to tell which.

Equally unnerving was the faint but growing rumble that made the floor vibrate beneath my feet. In my growing panic, I could almost imagine that a prehistoric monster had been stirred to anger some- where in the caverns beneath this colossal building, and that this fear- some beast was now making its way toward me, one lumbering footstep at a time.

When I finally felt a firm pull on the rope attached to my harness, hoisting me abruptly into the air a foot or so, I cried out with relief. Evidently, Nick had reached the surface and was now doing his utmost to pull me to safety.

Just as I was dangling in midair, there was another explosion, this time closer. Instinctively, I covered my face while my entire body was blasted by pinpricks of flying sand.

When I dared open my eyes again, all I saw was dust and darkness. Breathing through my bundled-up jacket, I tried to make out the faint shine of the lantern we had left behind in the inner sanctum, but it was gone. Nor could I see the assuring dot of daylight at the far end of the tube above me.

Desperate to speed up my escape from the collapsing temple, I grabbed the rope and tried to pull myself up, but of course I couldn't. All I accomplished was to make Nick drop me a whole hard-won foot, and I heard him yelling at me through the pipe.

For what it was worth, the sound of his voice had a calming effect, and I did my best to stop squirming. Moments later I was safely above ground, and Nick was unhooking my harness, his eyes tight with worry.

"Are we——" I began, but whatever I had intended to say was cut short by the sound of yet another underground explosion.

"Hurry!" Nick pulled me from the tent into the blinding sunshine. We ran toward a lonely horse tied to a post. "I'll get up first." He quickly untied the reins and straddled the skittish animal. "Put your foot here." He let me use the stirrup to climb up behind him, and as soon as my arms were clasped around his waist, he spurred on the horse with ferocity.

As we galloped away, a series of explosions ripped through the ground right behind us; it was as if we were being strafed by an invisible airplane. In its panic the horse stopped and reared up, throwing us both heavily into a peaked dune in a jumble of arms and legs.

"Good grief!" I groaned, my head full of sparkles and my mouth full of sand. "Are you all right?"

But Nick was already up, doing his best to calm the horse. And then I saw it, right behind him: the Bedouin tent collapsing and disappearing, sucked into a thundering funnel of sand. "Look!" I cried. "We've got to—"

As soon as Nick saw what I meant, we both scrambled up the dune, not even trying to get back on the horse. Behind us, the roar of destruction rose in a terrible crescendo, and when we finally reached the crest and I dared look back one last time, all I saw was an omnivorous crater of rushing sand. Everything was gone—the tent, the chute, the scattered drilling equipment; the entire valley had become a giant mouth, hungrily sucking in every bit of the here and now, in order to fill the void of lost millennia.

WHEN NICK HAD DONE his rounds and made his phone calls, he found me precisely where he had left me: sitting on a bench in the empty cantina, staring into a cup of tea. "Feeling better?" he asked, sitting down across the table with a mug of coffee. He looked calmer now, almost at peace. Or maybe he was just pretending, to cheer me up.

"I forgot to thank you," I said, straightening, "for saving my life."

Nick nodded. "My pleasure."

"You didn't have to, you know," I went on, turning the teacup around and around. "I haven't exactly been your . . . favorite person. Have I?"

He took a sip of coffee. "I don't want any trouble with the Moselanes."

I was stunned. "Excuse me?" Only then did I realize he was joking.

As always, Nick's beard kept blurring my perception of him, like a ring of thorny bushes around his true self. I shook my head, suddenly exhausted. "Please tell me what's going on."

He shrugged. "Someone decided to blow up the temple—"

"Someone?"

Avoiding my gaze, Nick leaned back and scratched his neck. "Craig got an anonymous call. A bomb threat. That's why I decided to evacuate the guards. And good thing I did, or I wouldn't have known you were down there."

"But that's preposterous!" I exclaimed. "Who would do that? Why? *How,* for heaven's sake?" The possibilities swirled around in my head, and I had to take a few deep breaths to keep down the nausea. "It's madness," I went on, more quietly. "Whoever they were, they must be dead now, mustn't they?"

Nick shrugged. "They probably set it off by remote control."

"But the sounds I heard—"

He shrugged again. "There's no point in speculating. We'll never know."

"Honestly!" I stared at him, desperate for answers. But he merely drank the rest of his coffee in one gulp, pushed aside the mug, and took out a wad of cash. Only when he started counting out bills on the table between us did I realize what he was doing, and I felt an irrational anger at his composure. To Nick, apparently, it was still nothing but business. Bombs, ropes, bruises . . . just another day at the Aqrab Foundation.

"Ten thousand dollars," he said at last, pushing the money toward me. "I believe that is what we owe you."

"Why, thank you," I said, rather fiercely, transfixed by the ridiculous pile of bills. "I suppose that is all I get. No explanations?"

Nick stood up, his eyes completely void of emotion. "We could keep talking. But you would miss your plane."

WE LEFT THE DRILL site in the golden light of late afternoon. Despite everything that had happened, Nick was still determined to get me back to Djerba in time for my flight to Gatwick the next morning—so much so that he was prepared to drive through the night.

As I sat in the car beside him, too exhausted to feel much beyond a welcome numbness, he drummed his fingers on the steering wheel and said, "I thought you might like to know that an environmental group has taken responsibility for the bombing. They sent a fax just before we left—the usual brain-dead anticapitalist bullshit."

I looked at him. The sun was setting behind us, and his face was—as always, it seemed—cast in shadow. "How convenient," I said, surprised by my own sarcasm. "That explains everything."

Nick glanced at me. "You're not buying it?"

"Did you expect me to? You don't believe it, either, do you?"

He shrugged. "I don't know. It doesn't make any sense to me. I was hoping it might make sense to *you*."

"Let's see." I settled back into my seat, appreciating the unexpected invitation to discuss the incident that had nearly killed us both. "You go all the way to Algeria to protest a drill site, but instead of chaining yourself to the drilling rig, or spraying your slogans on the trailers, you crawl through tunnels infested with unmentionable creatures in order to blow up a world heritage site? No, it makes no sense to me. Whoever sent that fax is trying to cover up the truth."

Nick hesitated. "So, what *is* the truth?"

I looked out on a passing oasis, or rather five lonely palm trees huddled against the vast nothingness bearing down on them from all sides. "Good question. I suppose the only thing we can say with any certainty is that whoever did it is a friend of neither of us. After all, friends don't let friends blow up in subterranean temples. Right?"

"I guess," said Nick, without sounding too convinced.

"And while we're at it—" I took off my boots and put my stocking feet up on the dashboard. "I'm still waiting to hear why it wasn't some other philologist who got the privilege of nearly blowing up. Why did Mr. Ludwig come for *me*? God knows *you* never wanted me in the temple. All his talk about the Amazons . . . where did it come from?"

Nick shifted uncomfortably in his seat. "John is a bit of a joker."

"You mean, a jester," I corrected him, determined not to be brushed aside. "A jester has one purpose only: to please the king. So tell me—since you belong to the same court—why did your mighty king tell his jester to goad me on with talk of the Amazons?"

When Nick did not respond right away, I poked him with my left foot. We were, after all, mere hours away from parting forever, and I knew that if I wanted to complete the puzzle of my trip, this was my chance. "Oh, come on," I said, trying to be chummy, "you can't let me dangle like this."

Nick smiled, but rather grimly. "You're assuming the mighty king confides in his lowly knights. Well, he doesn't."

"Then why don't you take that knightly cellphone of yours and call some duke or prince who *does* know?"

"It's Sunday. The office is closed." He gave me a sideways look. "Why are you so interested in the Amazons, anyway? Isn't it enough that you are the only philologist in the world who had a go at an undeciphered alphabet?"

"Which is now lost beneath ten billion tons of sand."

"But still—" Nick took one hand off the steering wheel to count on his fingers. "You have the photos. The text. The narrative. Not to mention ten thousand dollars in your pocket. What more do you want?"

I sighed out loud, frustrated that we were still on square one. "I want an explanation!"

Nick's jaws tightened. "Well, you're barking up the wrong guy. I'm just a gofer. All I can tell you is that the fax from the environmental group was sent from an Internet café in Istanbul." He glanced at me, and I thought I saw suspicion in his eyes. "What do you know about Grigor Reznik?"

I was so surprised by the question, I started laughing. "The collector? Not much." I paused to summon my knowledge, then said, "I've written to him once or twice, asking for access to an ancient manuscript he purchased last year, the *Historia Amazonum*. But he never replied."

Nick frowned. "That's usually what happens when you confront a thief about his loot."

"What do you mean?"

"When Reznik deals in antiques," said Nick, drumming his fingers on the steering wheel again, "it's usually at the point of a gun. Where did the manuscript come from? Who sold it to him?"

Nick's questions made me uncomfortable. My mentor Katherine Kent had said something similar when I made the mistake of mentioning my letters to Reznik, but I had brushed aside her concerns as unfounded hearsay. "All right," I said, yielding to what was apparently majority opinion, "so Reznik is a little unconventional—"

"To say the least!" Nick shot me a look of reproach. "He's a crook! Don't close your eyes to that just because he happens to have something you want."

I was terribly tempted to use this as a segue to confront him about his employment with the Aqrab Foundation, but decided to leave that particular arrow in my quiver for now. "Well, some claim Reznik has had a moral awakening," I said instead. "Apparently, he lost his son in a car crash last year and was absolutely devastated—"

"Let's not put 'Reznik' and 'moral' in the same sentence," said Nick, cutting me off. "And as for his son, Alex, take it from me: The little Satan had it coming. Does 'snuff film' mean anything to you?" Seeing that it did, he nodded grimly. "That vicious punk deserved so much more than a car crash. Makes you want to believe there *is* a hell."

"Sounds as if you knew him?" I said.

"I know *of* him. That's more than enough. In some circles he was known as 'the Bone Saw,' to give you an idea."

"Thanks for that image," I said.

"You're welcome. Now, the more interesting question is why Grigor Reznik bothers with an old manuscript. He is not an intellectual. Explain that to me, please."

"Why? Because you think he was behind the bombing?"

Nick shrugged. "I'm just trying to piece it all together. The fax was sent from Istanbul. Reznik is in Istanbul—"

"But he's not an idiot," I countered, holding up a hand against the dust as we passed a truck on the road. "If he really *did* send that fax, wouldn't he have sent it from somewhere else? *Anywhere* else?"

"Maybe. Or it could be the sender wanted to implicate him. Why?"

"All I can tell you," I said, "is that the *Historia Amazonum* is believed to hold information about the fate of the last Amazons, and the legendary"—I waved my hands in the air to add a little drama—"Amazon Hoard. Not 'hoard' as in a horde of people, but as in a stockpile of valuable objects."

"A treasure?"

"Absolutely. Of course, even Amazon believers think it's a romantic old legend—just like the idea that the Amazons cut off one breast to be better spear throwers." I paused to reassess my own opinion on the matter and decided, as I had so often, that I didn't believe in the Amazon Hoard either. "If this is what Reznik is after, he is not just evil, but crazy. An unfortunate combination. I am not sure where this absurd fantasy came from, that a band of poor, nomadic women warriors would carry around a golden treasure, but I can assure you it is nothing but a fairy tale."

"As are the Amazons themselves," added Nick.

I nodded. "That's what most scholars would say."

"The Amazons whose temple we've both just walked around in."

Stunned, I turned in my seat to stare at him. "Five days ago you couldn't even *spell* 'Amazon.' Maybe now would be a good time for you to tell me what has happened in the meantime?"

"Maybe now would be a good time for you to tell me about your bracelet."

Shocked by the ambush, I put a hand on top of my cuff. "I'm not sure—"

"Did you really think I wouldn't notice?"

I moved uncomfortably, only too aware I was completely trapped in the car with him. "I don't see that it's any of your business—"

"Really?" said Nick, his recent camaraderie falling away as if it had never been anything but a mask. "I see you take after your countrymen. Appropriating ancient artifacts is not even a matter of discussion."

Only then did it dawn on me that he was not, in fact, interrogating me about Granny's jackal bracelet. No, he was accusing me of stealing it from the sarcophagus. However, if I denied the theft, we would still be left with the mystery of how this particular bracelet came to be in my possession. Under the circumstances, that was a subject I would do just about anything to avoid.

And so I made a quick decision and said, as calmly as I could, "If I hadn't taken it, it would have been lost forever. Wouldn't it? But don't worry, I never meant to keep it, just keep it safe for now." I turned my head and looked at Nick's profile again; it was more inscrutable than ever as he listened to my defense. "Anyway, I don't see why it belongs to you any more than it belongs to me. It should be on display for everyone to see——"

"Then take it off. I'll make sure it ends up in a museum. The *right* kind." Nick's scowl told me British museums did not belong in that category.

We sat in silence for a moment. Despite the cool evening breeze I was sweating all over as my brain did breathless laps to save the situation. In the end I decided to stick with the truth. "I can't get it off."

Nick glared at my wrist, clearly not believing me.

I held my hand toward him. "Be my guest." It wasn't a bluff; I knew he wouldn't be able to remove it, either.

He didn't even try.

THAT NIGHT, ASLEEP IN the car, I dreamed about Granny again.

We were standing together on a cliff, looking out over a desert dreamscape. I was in pajamas and Granny was wearing her frayed old dressing gown, her gray hair hanging loose down her back. Behind us, my parents were sitting in the Mini, arguing loudly, thinking we couldn't hear them. "It cannot continue this way," my mother was saying. "This morning I found another one of those drawings in Diana's bed."

She was referring to my sketches of imagined Amazons, most of which were a joint effort between Granny and me, produced in a creative frenzy on those few, precious days when we weren't being watched by the imaginary men in green clothes. Seated at Granny's dining table, she and I would draw Amazon warriors in great detail, using every color of pencil in the jar.

Usually I was careful to stash away all evidence of our cloak-and-dagger activities at the bottom of my wardrobe, but occasionally I would be so enamored with a particular drawing that I slept with it underneath my pillow at night. Undoubtedly, it was one such sketch that had fallen into my mother's hands, and undoubtedly she would have preferred to come upon a note from a lovesick classmate rather than a mounted woman wielding a battle-ax.

"Suppose she were a boy," proposed my father, in a rare moment of objection. "Would you worry about the drawings then?"

My mother groaned with exasperation. She was not accustomed to contradiction, and certainly not from her doting husband. They had met on a sightseeing bus in London some twelve years earlier; she was the American tourist with a checklist, conquering the Old World one snapshot at a time, he the absentminded bachelor who had boarded the vehicle by accident, mistaking it for the N19 to Finsbury Park.

Those roles had never changed.

"It's not easy for me to say these things," my mother went on, in the voice that ended all arguments. "You're her son after all. But she is *ill*, Vincent—"

I pressed my palms against my ears, trying not to hear what came next. But there was no blocking out the inevitable. Granny knew it, too. "Don't cry, my little one," she whispered, touching my cheek. "It was always meant to be this way." She tightened the belt of the dressing gown and squinted against the vastness of the desert. "I must return to my own kind—"

"But I don't want you to leave!" I threw my arms around her. "And they can't make you. If they do, I'll run away from home—"

"No!" She unfastened my arms. "I need you to grow big and strong and wise about the world. Learn everything there is to know about the Amazons, but never reveal that you are one of us." She took me by the shoulders and transfixed me with her blue stare. "Don't forget I have left you instructions."

I mashed away my tears. "What kind of instructions?"

I never got a response. With the surreal panache so characteristic of my dreams of her, Granny stepped right over the edge of the cliff and disappeared. Leaping forward, I caught a glimpse of her dressing gown as it fluttered to the ground far, far below me and eventually came to rest on a pristine wave of sand. Of Granny herself, there was no trace. And within the blink of an eye the dressing gown was gone, too, swallowed up by a sudden whirlpool of sand and disappearing, completely, into the ever-hungry bowels of the desert.

Nick escorted me all the way to the security checkpoint, ensuring everything went smoothly so I wouldn't miss my flight. As I saw him walking away at last, across the barren airport hallway, I felt a brief throb of regret. Despite his demurrals, I was convinced he knew the answers to most of my questions, and now I would never get another chance at extracting them.

Just as I had cleared security, my phone rang. It was Rebecca.

"I've been so worried about you," she said, after listening to my jumbled report. "I couldn't understand why you didn't call."

"Well, here I am," I assured her as I walked to the gate. "Going home."

"Wait! You have *got* to come and see what I've found." Despite everything I had told her, Rebecca sounded jubilant. "And bring Granny's notebook."

I stopped dead in the middle of the concourse. "Why?"

"Because—" As always, Rebecca was torn between her desire to remain mysterious and her compulsion to blurt out everything then and there. "Just come. Change your flight. I really have to show you this."

"Bex!" I was in no mood for additional mysteries. "This past week has been totally mad—"

"It's a clay tablet," Rebecca blurted out, "and on it are the exact same writing symbols as those in the picture you emailed me. It's right here, in our archive. I tried to take a photo, but my phone is hopeless. You need to see it in person, but it has to be *now,* before the team leader comes back—"

Part of me wanted to calm Rebecca down and say that surely, this was no urgent matter, and yet . . . if she had really found an ancient tablet with symbols that matched the writing in the Algerian temple and in Granny's notebook, I could not rest until I held it in my hands. If I flew directly to Crete now, I might still be able to get back to Oxford by Monday. What was another twenty-four hours in the big scheme of things?

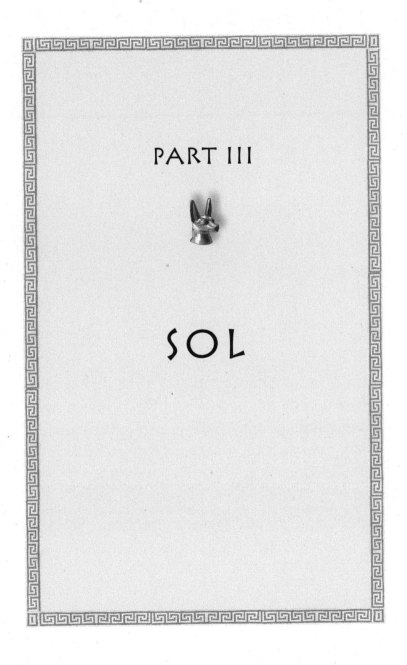

PART III

SOL

CHAPTER SEVENTEEN

ISLAND OF CRETE

T HE SUN WAS IN HER FACE, AND THE WIND BEHIND HER.
Myrina stood in the bow of the boat with her hands on the railing, embracing the rise and fall of each wave and feeling an unexpected trickle of hope. It was her first day without seasickness, her first day of fully appreciating that they were on their way at last.

Aided by Animone, Myrina had worked hard to persuade her surviving sisters to leave their ruined lives and come with her into the unknown. Sweet Lilli, Kara the chieftain's daughter, and the beautiful Klito with the adventurous eyes . . . where were they now? Nine in all had been abducted. Could they be found?

As hopeless as the quest might seem, Myrina was not satisfied until everyone agreed to go. The world the raiders had left behind was a desperate, violent one, with bands of thieves surging through the streets, scavenging anything of potential value, and unburied bodies left as food for rats and dogs. Were not the uncertainties of traveling preferable to the certain misery of passivity?

Crete, claimed Animone, was where they would find sympathetic ears and answers to their questions. Drawing on the tales of her seafaring grandfather, she insisted that this prosperous island in the middle of the great northern sea was favored by sailors as a convenient place to replenish fresh water and food. Surely the evil black-hulled ships were known to the Cretans . . . in fact, it was possible that the raiders, too, would be stopping there on their way home.

Once the decision was made, the twelve priestesses diligently worked together to turn their ravaged temple into a tomb. They removed the sacred objects from the hollow altar stone and placed the dismembered body of the High Priestess inside, cushioned by the ashes of the newly dead and surrounded by their jackal bracelets. After the coffin was carefully closed, Kyme wrote a full account of those last, tearful days upon the walls of the inner sanctum. "In ages to come," she told the others, "people will enter this temple and ask what happened here. I want them to know it all in detail, in order that they may honor our dead sisters who can no longer tell their own story."

Meanwhile, Myrina gathered every weapon she could find, ensuring that each of her sisters had at least a knife, a bow, and a quiver with plenty of arrows. This time, the only one who protested was Egee, the haughty Kara's abiding devotee, who resented Myrina telling her what to do. "What do you keep giving me these terrible things for?" she cried, refusing to take the weapons. "The sight of them makes me ill."

"Ill?" Myrina had to close her eyes to maintain her calm. "And what about the sight of your slain sisters? What does that make you? Or the thought of your abducted friend?" She forced the bow and quiver into Egee's hands. "Do you want to know what makes *me* ill? The sight of a sane, able woman who refuses to defend herself because she believes weapons are evil." Myrina put a hand on Egee's shoulder and gave her a conciliatory squeeze. "Those men who came, *they* were evil. And whoever taught you those false ideas are forever stained with the blood of innocents."

Ready at last, their clothes enforced with snakeskin—once so repulsive even to Myrina's closest companions, but now a welcome armor around their own shaken self-confidence—the women had helped one another place an extra bar across the colossal temple door, bolting it in place as best they could. And after one final prayer to the absent Moon Goddess, Myrina had led the small group away from the temple through the vast system of underground caves—caves she had long since explored on her own while everyone else was enjoying their afternoon rest. "This way!" she beckoned, holding the torch low to keep the snakes at bay. "The flame will soon fade, so make haste!"

With the Moon Goddess gone and the High Priestess dead, it had not taken the women long to fall back upon the skills and passions of earlier lives. Most knowledgeable among the survivors was Animone, who had always claimed to be entirely at home on sailing vessels and the open water, and who now, finally, had an opportunity to demonstrate her skills to the rest. "Why do you not believe me?" she had exclaimed, seeing their hesitation in embracing the abandoned fishing boat she and Myrina had laboriously hauled back along the shore. "I am telling you, I know how to sail this thing. But first, we must repair it. We need ropes"—she had started counting on her fingers, brimming with long-forgotten excitement—"we need poles, we need sturdy string and needles, and we need strong fabric for the sail."

As for Myrina, she stubbornly maintained that she was a hunter. Nothing more, nothing less. Dressed in a snakeskin tunic, with her precious bow and quiver strapped to her shoulders, she made no claims about being in command. But since the others kept looking to her for answers and encouragement, leadership was inevitably thrust upon her. Wherever she went, the others would follow; not even Egee dared to wish it otherwise.

THE LAND OF THE Cretans lay upon the ocean like a giant at rest.

Steep and forbidding, vast parts of the shoreline made landfall impossible; even the most alluring coves were, according to Animone, too treacherous for untrained sailors. Right beneath the sparkling turquoise of those soft waves, she explained, rocks as sharp as teeth and covered in slippery weeds were waiting to toss and lacerate hapless strangers.

Myrina knew better than to argue. Had it not been for Animone, they would have died many times since leaving their homely marsh. Swallowed by giant waves, crushed by cliffs, or shipwrecked on unknown coasts . . . one way or another, they would have perished long before they ever laid eyes on the Cretan coast. It was thanks to this one woman's never-forgotten knowledge of sailing and navigation that they had come this far.

"There it is!" exclaimed Animone, pointing ahead. "This is where the tradesmen land. The king's palace is not far from there. They do not call him 'King,' though. I am sure my grandfather told me he is called the Minos."

Squinting against the sun, Myrina studied the bustling coastline with great interest. All manner of boats were either approaching or leaving the man-made harbor, but none resembled the black ships that had stolen away poor Lilli and so many others. Although a part of her was pining for the sight of them, Myrina also knew she was not yet ready to do battle with those beastly men. As she stood in the bow of their brave little vessel, shielding her eyes with her hands, the wound in her back let her know she had not yet fully healed, and that, for all her grand words of encouragement, and their group archery practice, she and her sisters were still little more than prey.

"You are sure we will be welcomed in peace?" asked Pitana, joining them at the railing, her sinewy arms resting casually on the weathered wood. Despite her gangly limbs, Pitana had turned out to possess a stubborn strength almost equal to Myrina's, and the discovery these past weeks of her own hidden might had all but taken the hunch out of her posture.

"In my grandfather's day," replied Animone, "this was the biggest marketplace in the world. Tradesmen of all colors and tongues would come from every corner of the ocean, to barter their goods in peace and obtain knowledge about routes and wind patterns and"—her voice trembled—"the fate of loved ones."

BUT FIRST THEY HAD to find food. Their meager supplies had long since run out, and for the last three days, they had survived on little more than old water in goat bladders and the occasional fish fastened to a hairpin hook by some merciful ocean spirit.

To make matters worse, a harbor official informed them they had to pay a fee if they wished to stay overnight. He stated his inhospitable message in several different languages before finally striking upon the one used in the Temple of the Moon Goddess—a language Myrina had worked hard to master since becoming a priestess. "I have never heard of such a fee," said Kyme to the man, sounding as if she knew a great deal more about the world than she did. "And who are you?"

The man stuck out his bearded chin. "I am the tax collector. Trading is slowing down, and yet"—he gestured at the havoc all around—"we must ensure the upkeep of this harbor. When your men return, make sure to explain the situation to them."

"Maybe trading would not be slowing down," observed Kyme, "if you hadn't begun charging a fee."

But nothing could be done to change the man's mind. Some manner of payment had to be produced before sunset, preferably in the form of copper tokens, although a delectable food item might also be acceptable.

"If only I could hunt," began Myrina, gazing ahead at the urban sprawl that had left no standing tree in sight.

"Please," said Egee, who still, after so many days of sailing, remained hostile to Myrina, "do not speak the word 'hunt' again. I am sick of it."

"Hunting will do us no good here," agreed Animone. "The same goes for quarreling. Let us think now, and find a solution."

They had left the temple with nothing of value save food and weapons. For all their brutal clumsiness, the raiders had been diligent about removing every gold and silver votive from the shelves and leaving behind no item that would be of value anywhere else. Nor had the priestesses ever been aware of the existence of copper tokens, and had certainly never seen one.

"I do not like the sound of it," said Kyme, turning up her nose and exercising the privilege of being the oldest. "Gold and silver I can understand, but *tokens*? Tokens of what? one wonders. No, let us go into town and barter for food instead. Whatever that odious tax man does not take, we will eat ourselves. For truly, I am so hungry I will eat the barnacles off that pier if we find no other edibles."

"Barter for food," echoed Egee, "with what? We have nothing. Although"—she pulled the knife from her belt—"some may see the value in this."

"We are not giving up our weapons!" Myrina pressed the knife back into Egee's belt. "What a short memory you have. Yes, we have arrived in a city of apparent tranquillity, but we both know how quickly that can change."

And so, with two sisters left behind to keep watch, the women disembarked the boat and made their way across the many interlocking bridges and wharves. When at last upon firm ground, they swayed at the unfamiliar feeling and had to sit a while, waiting for the earth to become steady beneath their feet.

As they sat, a man came over to ask them a question in his own language, his expression so lewd Myrina guessed rather than understood what he wanted. She waved at him to go away, but he merely laughed and stepped closer, as if disgusted refusal was part of the game.

"Come!" Pitana stood up abruptly, pulling her sisters along. "We have rested enough."

As they walked into town, Myrina was reminded of her arrival in the city of the Moon Goddess so many months before, and of Lilli's fascination with it all. Sweet Lilli, who winced at the foul smells but still wanted to continue . . . how Myrina longed to have her that close again, unfailingly cheerful in the face of adversity.

"This is what I propose," said Animone, nodding toward a man with a trained monkey who was entertaining passersby in exchange for food scraps. "Let us sing our sacred songs and delight the Cretans with our harmonious voices." She pointed at an empty space among the teeming market stalls. "Why don't we try here? There is enough room for a small, circular procession, and the noise will surely stop as soon as we begin."

Myrina looked around. The vendors around them sold live chickens and boiled goats' heads, and she saw many goods changing hands in a steady stream of customers. "I wouldn't be surprised if there is yet an-other fee to be paid——" she began.

"So we will pay it!" Animone took off her bow and quiver and checked all her little braids to make sure she looked her best. None of the others had the heart to tell her that even now, three weeks after the temple attack, there was still a mask of multihued bruises on her face. "Just wait and see," she said, with the bravado of someone who has been right about everything else.

But the sacred songs that had drawn such breathless attention from the pilgrims in the temple barely turned a head in the marketplace and certainly did not inspire anyone to lay down gifts of appreciation. Be-fore long, Animone's hopes were crushed by the disinterest of the peo-ple walking by. "What a hateful place!" she hissed, when they had tried every song and every dance step twice over. "These people do not un-derstand our art. What thick skulls they have. They should be forced to pay!"

"Let us return to the boat and try to catch another fish," said Kyme, pale from hunger and fatigue. "Two, I mean. One for us, and one for the man."

"While you do that," said Myrina, adjusting the bow behind her back, "I am going hunting."

BEFORE HEADING FURTHER INTO town, Myrina wound her head with the ragged remains of her priestess dress. With only her eyes visible, she figured, people would naturally take her for a man, for she was taller than most women and her snakeskin tunic was long enough to conceal her thighs. Besides, with the bow and quiver on her back, it would surely occur to very few that there might be a female form underneath it all.

Walking on through the city, she looked for old people sitting in the shade of buildings—talkative codgers who had seen much and were happy to reminisce about it with strangers. Never lingering too long in one place, she asked about ships with black hulls, ships carrying greedy, apelike men to faraway coasts and returning with golden treasures.

But almost no one understood the languages Myrina spoke, and when she was finally introduced to an elderly sailor lying in a hammock, even this speaker of the Old Language had little to tell her. "Many ships have tarred keels," he droned, fanning himself with a fig leaf. "They could be from anywhere. Probably the north, since you say the men had pale skin. My business was mostly in the south, which is why I know your language."

Myrina decided to concentrate on the more pressing matter, namely how to feed her sisters and pay for their night in the harbor. "If I were looking for a free meal," she said before leaving the sailor, "where would I go?"

He replied without hesitation. "The Eastern Harbor. That is where the big ships moor. Try the Trojans; if they are in, you will find them at the far end. I imagine they have something to spare."

And so Myrina made her way there, blushing behind her scarf for behaving like a beggar. But she could see no honorable alternative. Since whoring or stealing were out of the question, and it was unlikely she could make herself or her sisters useful in other ways, Myrina was left with the humble hope of meeting some merciful merchant with goods to spare.

Elbowing her way through strange folk from distant lands—people who had arrived on ships so large she first mistook them for buildings—Myrina eventually arrived at the end of the harbor promenade, where the coast turned to beach again and seagulls circled fishing boats drawn up on the sand. Here, in the slanting orange light of the setting sun, she espied a gathering of men roasting whole chickens and vegetables on sticks over a bonfire, their merriment loud enough to convince her they were friendly. Could they be the Trojans the old sailor had told her about?

Stepping closer, Myrina saw they were engaged in a children's game of throwing rocks into circles—a game she had played with her father when she was still too young to hunt with him, and which she had often played by herself to pass the time and improve her aim.

One of the men—a clean-shaven youth with a strong frame and handsome, embroidered clothing—was particularly good at landing rocks at the center of the circles, and even though Myrina did not understand his language, it was clear to her that he was taunting the others, challenging them to outdo him.

Emboldened by the jovial atmosphere, Myrina picked up a rock of her own and tossed it into the game. It landed with a small thud in the nearest, easiest circle, not precisely at the center, but close enough to make the men turn to see who had thrown it.

When she saw the bafflement in their faces, Myrina pointed at the game, then at the young champion, then at herself to indicate she would like to challenge him. Her gesture set off a rumble of amusement among his mates, and the young man looked at her with eyes full of incredulity, as if he was entirely unused to such bold proposals.

Seeing his hesitation, Myrina pointed once again at the game, then at the chickens roasting over the bonfire, and finally at her own mouth behind the scarf. To which the young man said something she did not understand, his keen amber eyes searching her veiled face for a sign of comprehension. But Myrina merely bent down to pick up six rocks, three of which she held out to him . . . only to have her arms abruptly seized by his companions.

Shocked at the change in humor, Myrina bucked and kicked, anxious to free herself. But a burst of laughter from the young man, followed by a rapid exchange between him and his mates, had them quickly release her again. "Here——" He picked up the three stones she had dropped in the sand. "I will speak to you in the language of the desert nomads, for you look like a nomad to me. Do you understand?"

Myrina nodded. Even though she could have responded to him in words, she was determined to keep her silence lest her voice gave away her secret.

"Good." The man bent his head to look at her sternly, the way bulls look at their adversaries before they charge. "You have challenged me to a duel, and that is no trifling matter." But the sparkle of mischief in his eyes told her his gravity was just for play. "A chicken is at stake. And maybe a carrot. May the hungriest man win." He nodded at the circles drawn in the sand. "After you."

Myrina took aim and threw her first stone, doing her best to ignore the heckling all around. It landed precisely in the center of the nearest of the five circles, putting her initial attempt to shame.

"Well done," said her competitor, making a face of feigned worry. "How am I ever going to match that?" But even as he spoke, his first toss flew through the air and landed right in the center of the second circle. "Ah. I am lucky. Your turn."

Myrina gritted her teeth and threw her next stone, only too aware the man was mocking her. But something in his eyes assured her of an underlying kindness, and even as her second perfect shot was matched by his, filling the third and fourth circle in turn, she remained hopeful she would eventually walk away from this place with something to eat.

No sooner had she landed her last stone in the fifth circle, however, than he pitched the final stone of the game, knocking her right out of the center spot, laughing heartily at her misfortune. "Oh no—" He grimaced in false sympathy. "There goes your chicken, boy. But I will give you a carrot as compensation."

Without a word Myrina bent to pick up another six stones and hand him three . . . but he did not take them. Instead, he said, "I am bored with this game. Shall we try something else?" He looked around for inspiration, egged on by his jeering companions, and his eyes fell on Myrina's bow, sticking up above her shoulder. "Is that just a toy or do you know how to handle it?"

Myrina hesitated. Not only had she been unable to practice properly for months, but the wound in her back was still so excruciatingly painful she had barely shot an arrow since the temple attack, even when she was training with her sisters.

"Let's see how good you are." The man opened a small leather pouch and took out five chunks of bronze. Copper tokens. "They are yours," he went on, "and so is the chicken, if you can hit the seagull sitting on that mast." He pointed at a beached fishing boat lying in the sand some three hundred feet away, its mast at an angle.

Myrina shook her head.

"Why not?" The man looked at her with renewed interest. "I see.

You don't wish to kill a bird for sport." He smiled and made a face at his companions. "What a noble lad! Then how about this: I throw an apple in the air, and you shoot it down?" When Myrina did not protest, he held out a hand and was promptly given an apple by one of the other men. "Ready?"

Before she could even get the bow off her back, the apple sailed out over the water in a long arch . . . and fell into the waves unscathed.

The man shook his head. "You are too slow, boy. But I will give you another chance."

This time, Myrina was ready. Her bow was free before he even had the apple in his hand, and her arrow came out of the quiver just as he withdrew his arm to throw. Had she stopped to think, she would have been too late, or missed. As it was, the arrow flew out with unwavering confidence to split the juicy apple in half before diving, gracefully, into the ocean.

The men were so taken aback by the perfect shot no one noticed Myrina swaying with pain. "What an eye you have!" said her smiling tormentor, slapping her admiringly on the back. "Let us test it further." But when he heard her muffled groan—too unguarded to be anything but the sound of a woman—he pulled back his hand in horror.

Seeing the look of amazement on his face, and fearing the interrogation she knew would follow, Myrina quickly knelt down to gather up the five copper tokens he had let fall into the sand, clutched them to her chest with her bow, and fled. So desperate was she to run away with her prize before he found some new way of detaining her and tricking her out of her winnings that Myrina did not even stop to claim her chicken on the way.

"Wait!" The man came after her, his voice angry enough to make her run faster. Up the stone steps to the harbor she ran, and across the promenade of the Eastern Harbor, jumping this way and that to avoid others along the way. Looking back over her shoulder, she saw him following, his shoulders pulled up in fury, and she made a quick decision to run toward the busy market rather than the Western Harbor, where her sisters awaited her.

She was not sure why the man was tailing her, but suspected it had never been his intention to let her get away with his five copper tokens. Had she stayed, no doubt he would have talked her into some new bet of sorts, and would have made sport of her to amuse his friends.

So busy was she with imaginary events she did not notice the walls of the city closing around her tighter and tighter, until at last she found herself in a dead end piled with oozing garbage. Grimacing at the place, she turned around. . . .

And found him standing right there, blocking her escape. "Trapped," he observed somewhat superfluously, head cocked to one side. "Unless you·are also hiding a pair of wings underneath those scales?"

"Please." Clutching the copper tokens in one hand, Myrina pulled the hunting knife from her belt with the other. "I don't want to hurt you."

The man held up his arms, although his face showed no sincere worry. "I don't want you to hurt me, either. I just want to see your face."

Myrina took a step backward, her heel sinking into something warm and soft. "Why?"

The man laughed. "And why not?"

"These tokens"—Myrina held out her fist—"belong to me. Do they not?"

He looked surprised. "Of course they do."

"Then what is it you want?" Myrina took another step back, but lost her balance briefly in the slippery gore.

"I told you." The man came closer, smiling as if the whole thing was but a game. "I want to see your face. That is all."

Myrina held out her knife to stop his approach. "And then what?"

He shrugged. "Then nothing. You will be free to go."

She hesitated, trying to gauge his sincerity. Then she put the knife back in her belt and quickly unwound the scarf. "There!" She lowered her eyes to avoid—she was sure—his contemptuous stare. "Have you seen enough?"

The man did not reply. And when Myrina finally looked up, she could not guess his thoughts. "May I go now?" she asked, draping the scarf across her face once more. "Please?"

At last, he stepped aside. Without another glance at him, Myrina ran away as fast as she could, the precious copper tokens pressed hard against her chest.

MYRINA RETURNED TO HER sisters just as the sun was setting over the ocean, to find them engaged in yet another argument with the fee collector.

"Wait!" she cried, striding down the gangplank to the outer dock where the boat was moored. "How many copper tokens to stay the night?"

"That depends," said the man. "What do you have?"

Myrina opened her fist and showed him.

"Ah," he said. "Let's say two then. Plus two for tomorrow."

"What?" Kyme stepped forward, her face still flushed from the argument Myrina had missed. "Can we not pay those in the morning?"

The fee collector shook his head. "Then you must leave at sunrise. But you won't be able to. Not the way that north wind is blowing."

Later that evening, after an unfulfilling meal of small crab cakes— one copper token for the dozen—Myrina looked up to find a well-dressed older man standing on the dock next to the boat, staring openly at the women. "Greetings," he said, in the Nomad Language. His accent and bearing reminded Myrina of the game-playing men she had met on the beach earlier.

"Can I help you?" she asked, rising politely in the hopes she was wrong.

"Possibly," said the man, in a tone of dignified patience. "You are the archer who shot down an apple, are you not?"

"What is it?" asked Animone, pulling at Myrina's sleeve. "What is he saying? We have paid the fee for tomorrow; make sure you tell him that."

"Have no fear," said the man to Animone, as fluent in one language as he was in another. "I have come to summon all of you to dinner"— his eyes were drawn to the sorry remains of their meager meal in the bottom of the boat—"or perhaps I should say a banquet, hosted by my generous master, Prince Paris."

When there was no immediate reaction, the man added, with a superior smile, "My master is commonly known as the royal heir of Troy."

CHAPTER EIGHTEEN

When he arrived at Crete . . . having a clue of thread given him by Ariadne,
who had fallen in love with him, and being instructed by her how to use it
so as to conduct him through the windings of the labyrinth, he escaped out
of it and slew the Minotaur.
—PLUTARCH, *Theseus*

DJERBA, TUNISIA

THE PLANE TO HERAKLION WAS PRACTICALLY EMPTY. CLEARLY, Crete was not much of a destination in early November, and the airline representative had only been too happy to change my ticket.

I had already made myself comfortable with my feet up on the empty seat beside me when a man in jeans and a suede jacket stopped in the aisle and began stuffing his duffel bag into the compartment right above my head.

Handsome, I thought to myself as I put my feet back on the floor. Only when he sat down next to me did I realize it was Nick. Without a beard.

"Don't worry," he said, in response to my eye-popping disbelief, "it'll grow back."

I wanted to reply in kind, making light of my amazement with some crisp nugget of British wit, but for some reason the language center in my brain was utterly vacant. The unruly mop on top of his head had been trimmed, too, and what was left was pitch-black. It was the missing beard, however, which held me tongue-tied. There was something absurdly risqué about the unexpected sight of Nick's naked face; I was almost as shocked as if he had stripped down to nothing before my eyes.

"So," he said, beating me to it, "what's in Crete?"

His smugness brought me back to reality. Not only had this man been spying on me after we said good-bye at the airport—how else could he have known about my last-minute change of plans?—but he actually had the nerve to confront me as if *I* were the delinquent one, not he. "How dare you follow me like this?" I said, quickly shoving Granny's notebook into my handbag. "Our business is over."

"Actually—" Nick tapped his passport at my bracelet. "I'm not following *you*. I'm following *him*. For as long as that little doggie is on your arm, you *are* my business."

It was such an outrageous statement, such an absurd situation . . . had we not been on a plane I would have stood up and left.

"Just think of it," he went on, with an irritating smile, "as a little handcuff, linking you to me."

We sat in silence while the plane took off, and I was grateful for the opportunity to rethink my strategy. Nick was here, it seemed, because he thought I had stolen the bracelet on my arm. Suppose I told him the truth? Or at least the bare bones of it, leaving out Granny's notebook?

"Here's the thing," I began, hoping he could sense I was being honest. "I actually did *not* take this bracelet from the sarcophagus. Believe it or not, it belonged to my grandmother—"

Nick shook his head. "The memo I received on you said you have an IQ of 153. Now, either the memo is wrong, or you keep holding back. Why?"

I nearly choked on my own indignation. "Excuse me?"

"And I do. All the time." Nick started leafing through an airline magazine, feigning interest. "What's going on up there? Who's in the prompter's box?"

I sent him a withering stare, but he didn't seem to notice. "Maybe when things stop blowing up around me," I said, "and people stop spying on me . . . maybe then I'll exude more intelligence. I'm not sure you would know how to appreciate it, though. Men of your type rarely do."

Nick batted his eyebrows. "Try me. Say something intelligent."

Piqued, I opened my mouth to do just that, but a small, internal whirlwind of fury tore up every potential retort. Instead, I chose silence.

"After so much thinking," said Nick, "it better be good. I'm still waiting to hear what we're going to be doing in Crete."

"Welcome to the club of unanswered questions," I shot back, somewhat childishly. "What happened to your beard?"

"I don't need it anymore."

"Why not?"

Nick looked surprised. "I thought you'd have understood that by now."

"We've already established I'm not that bright."

"All right." He turned toward me, his braggadocio gone. "Then let me brighten you up. Whenever there is discovery and invention, the parasites are not far behind. Government, of course, is the biggest of them all, but in the world of antiques trading there is a whole separate ecosystem of dealers, smugglers, and tomb raiders. They're all the same; they're all parasites who feed on other people's history and hollow out their cultural heritage." Pausing briefly, Nick found a map in the back of the airline magazine, took a pen out of his jacket pocket, and drew an X on eastern Algeria.

"Now, to the tomb raiders," he continued, handing me the magazine, "I am the X that marks the spot. All they have to do is follow me, and they know I'll take them straight to a new excavation. Even if they can't access the actual site they will start digging nearby in the hopes of finding something we missed. And if they can get away with it, they bribe our diggers to smuggle out artifacts from the official dig before they are cataloged." He rubbed his chin. "I thought a beard and grubby clothes would throw them off. Too bad it didn't work."

I stared at the map, unnerved by the implications of what he had just revealed. When I first met Nick, precisely a week ago, I had taken him for a bumbling caveman to whom the transportation of an Oxford classicist was just another odd job. But as time went on I had begun to realize my mistake, and now I was certain. While Nick might like to appear as if he had crawled right out of the book of Revelation, he was, in fact, a big gun.

"Do you think that is why?" I heard myself asking. "I mean, do you suppose tomb raiders were behind the explosions?"

Nick looked at me, yet I had a feeling it was not really me he was seeing. "Smart parasites generally don't kill the host. The explosions still don't make sense to me. But I have a feeling that's about to change."

I wanted to laugh, but the result was rather sad. "I sincerely hope you're not suggesting I had anything to do with it?"

Nick held my gaze for another few seconds, then shrugged and looked away. "My boss is down hundreds of thousands of dollars in lost efforts. You're up ten K and a bracelet. Not to mention you're the only academic who ever laid eyes on the temple and that you *own* the story now. But no, I'm not suggesting anything, just making sure you get home safely."

REBECCA WAS WAITING AT the rain-battered Heraklion Airport, her red curls splashed against her freckled forehead. As she stood there in her rubber boots and faded flapper dress, waving impatiently from behind the metal barrier, my faithful old friend looked as if she were just about to explode from sensation overload. When she spotted Nick, however, and realized we were together, her agitation quickly turned into speechless bewilderment.

"Bex!" I threw my arms around her. "You're soaking! Thanks for coming out in this ghastly weather. This is Nick Barrán." I moved aside to allow the two to shake hands. "He just won't go away."

"That's what happens," said Nick, "when you start stealing stuff."

For all her signature nonchalance, and despite the blast of rain that hit us as soon as we left the airport building, Rebecca did not recover her cool until we were all crammed into the scratched bench seat of her little van. Nick had offered to sit in the back with our luggage, rocking and rolling in a trail mix of stone fragments, rusty tools, and the odd stick of dynamite. But Rebecca, still at a loss to understand the brassy dynamic between him and me—never mind who Nick was in the first place—had insisted on squeezing him in up front with the both of us. "Apologies for not living up to the tourist brochures," she said, handing out damp squares of paper towel. "I'm afraid you've arrived in the middle of the rainy season."

As the city of Heraklion was presently nothing but a gray blur, we skipped the scenic tour and drove directly out to the archaeological site at Knossos, the squeaky windshield wipers going at maximum speed.

Last time I had been there—a shocking ten years ago, traveling the continent with Rebecca before either of us knew she would end up living in Crete—the weather had been so hot and crispy dry that even the cicadas fell silent. We had walked around in shorts and bikini tops, our burned shoulders a patchwork of pink and peeling brown, until it finally occurred to us that we needed to put a layer of fabric between ourselves and the sun. For lack of better, we had bought a pair of men's shirts and folded them to fit, and in this less-than-fashionable state we walked out to the ancient ruins of Knossos, swaying under our top-heavy backpacks and the pile of library books on ancient Greece I had insisted on bringing along.

Needless to say, I didn't recognize anything in the mint jelly landscape we were currently driving through, least of all my erstwhile thrill in being there.

"Sorry about this," Rebecca kept saying as she leaned forward to frantically rub steam off the window with fistfuls of paper towel. "Normally you can get a good view of the north entrance." Glancing nervously at Nick, she quickly went on to explain that part of the ancient palace had been reconstructed, with striking red columns, and that the dig site was not just the mountain of creamy rubble one might expect. "We even have a monster," she added proudly. "The fearsome Minotaur. But I'm afraid you won't see him tonight; apparently, he doesn't like to get his hair wet."

"The Minotaur?" said Nick. "That sounds familiar."

"Half man, half bull. Used to live here in the olden days." Rebecca shot him another quizzical glance. "Just ask Dee; she's the expert on mythology."

When we eventually pulled into a parking lot, I looked around in vain for the stately villa Rebecca had described to me so often. All I could see was the bleary outline of a whitewashed motel-like complex encircling us in the shape of a horseshoe.

"I know it's not Villa Ariadne," said Rebecca, reading my thoughts. "But I thought it would be better——" She hesitated, probably realizing it was unwise to go into detail in front of Nick, and continued more cheerfully, "The upside is that most of the rooms are empty, plus we're a stone's throw from the actual site. When the fog clears you'll be able to see the palace ruins from here."

DESPITE MY GRIMACES AND whispered hints, Rebecca put Nick in the guest room right next to mine. It was not that she didn't notice my antics; she simply chose to ignore them. "I've just about had it," she hissed, when we were finally alone. "What on earth is going on?"

Only too aware that we were separated from Nick by nothing but a few square feet of plaster wall, I filled her in as best I could, confirming that this was indeed the same Nick I had told her about over the phone—the trickster who had never disclosed that he worked for the Aqrab Foundation. "I still don't know why he is here," I concluded, "but I'm confident the bracelet is just a pretext. He's probably trying to figure out why I changed my flight, and whether it has anything to do with what happened in Algeria."

Rebecca did not look convinced. "I still don't understand. Did you really steal that bracelet?"

"Bex!" I started laughing, but she did not laugh along. In Rebecca's world, archaeologist that she was, keeping excavated artifacts to oneself was in line with murder.

"Well, maybe not murder," she had said once, realizing she had been carried away by a tidbit in a weekly, "but when I read about these things—how some inestimable artifact has been found in the rambling estate of a dead collector—it's like reading about an abducted child who has been kept in someone's garden shed for fifteen years." Naturally, her shock at discovering that her best friend might be one such abductor was considerable.

"Don't be absurd," I said, feeling a twitch of anger that she thought me capable of such a thing. "It was Granny's bracelet; don't you remember?" I held out my arm to show it to her.

"Yes," said Rebecca after a moment. Then she looked up at me, her eyes full of accusation. "I just never knew you had inherited it."

I walked over to the window. Outside, the rain had long since turned the small parking lot into a lake, fed from all sides by rivulets of mud, and a clingy afternoon fog prevented me from seeing more than the silhouette of the units across the yard. Although we were at Knossos, an ancient Minoan palace and the greatest tourist attraction in Crete, the place seemed oddly deserted; notwithstanding the miserable weather this was clearly the time to be here if one wanted to avoid the crowds.

I had walked the site only once, on that glorious day ten years earlier with Rebecca. Interestingly enough, back then it was *I* who had been most passionate about the place; thanks to Granny, I had long since decided on a career in ancient history and already fancied myself a bit of an expert on Bronze Age civilization.

Armed with half a dozen books, plus our shared water bottle, Rebecca and I had spent many hours studying the palace foundation, marveling at the reconstructed royal chambers and the findings from the underground storage rooms. Scoffing at the tourists who hurried to and fro with their guidebook blinkers on, we made our way around the entire perimeter of the site, determined to fully appreciate the enormity of the original building. We had even toyed with the idea of staying behind when the place closed down for the night, in order to get the full moonlit effect of the ruins.

"I swear to God," Rebecca had said, walking wistfully backward as the security guards locked the metal gate behind us, "we will be back, and we will spend a night here, even if it kills us."

As I stood by the guest room window now, peering out into the mist, those merry, sun-kissed days seemed far away indeed. "Well," I said at length, realizing Rebecca was still waiting for an explanation, "it came in the mail one day. I suppose Granny always wanted me to have it."

Rebecca was so shocked, she stood up abruptly. "I can't believe you never told me! Why didn't you . . . how did she——?"

"Bex," I said, suddenly weighed down by fatigue. I had barely slept the night before, and it was all catching up with me—the horror in Algeria, the long drive to Djerba, and the shock of seeing Nick again. "Let's not waste time on this now. Tell me about the clay disk. You took a photo?"

Rebecca clutched her head as if it was physically painful for her to change subjects. Then she walked over to fetch her laptop and show me a few images of a round object. "There. I can't get it any sharper than that."

I studied the screen, but couldn't even verify that the disk was inscribed with Granny's symbols. "You're right. This is useless. Where is the disk?"

Rebecca grimaced. "I'm not sure it's a good idea anymore——"

"Bex! I just flew across the Mediterranean——"

"I know!" She flung out her arms in exasperation. "Okay, so this is what happened: I know you told me not to, but——"

"You showed Mr. Ludwig's photo to Mr. Telemakhos?" It wasn't even a question. For all her professional integrity, Rebecca was incapable of keeping a secret. Even as a child I had been conscious of deliberately keeping her away from my mother when naughtiness was afoot, to prevent her from blurting out our plans at the least convenient moment. And as an adult I sometimes wondered whether perhaps my own slightly worrisome flair for secrecy had evolved as a necessary countermeasure to my friend's clandestine incontinence.

As for Mr. Telemakhos, he was one of those quasi-academic wild cards I did my best to avoid. Rebecca—who had originally fallen under his spell at a graduate symposium in Athens—had repeatedly told me this Greek "oracle," as she called him, was interested in getting to know me and possibly collaborating on a project. But so far I had made no moves to meet this self-taught eccentric, partly because there hadn't been room for a trip to Greece in my budget, and partly because I feared it might taint my scholarly reputation to have my name linked with his. "Do not associate yourself with such a charlatan," Katherine Kent had said when I asked her opinion. "He has no credentials and no publications . . . he's a schoolteacher, for heaven's sake!" For all her obsession with academic purity, Rebecca had no such scruples; Mr. Telemakhos was the convivial uncle she had never had and—I was sure—an enthusiastic recipient of her surplus gossip.

"I emailed it to him." Rebecca did not look the least bit remorseful; in fact, she looked positively triumphant. "And you ought to thank me for it. Had it not been for him, I would never have known the disk was here. I'm telling you, that man remembers *everything*. He recognized right away that the script on your photo is identical to the symbols on a disk in our storage room—a disk he only saw once, twenty years ago. Uncanny. The only problem is"—she looked at her wristwatch and made a face—"the team leader mustn't know about it, and he'll be back early tomorrow morning."

"Why can't he know?"

Rebecca's eyes narrowed. "Because he loathes me. I am positive his entire day is spent concocting reasons to fire me." She turned to look out the window. "You know how I am. When people get their dates wrong, or inflate the importance of a find . . . I just can't keep my mouth shut."

I waited for her to go on, but she merely sighed.

"What a pain," I said eventually, tuning out the voice in my head reminding me I had heard it all before. From the lowliest freshman to the highest professor, no one was safe from Rebecca's passionate love of facts. It was still a mystery to me how Mr. Telemakhos had managed to squeeze underneath her high standards. "But you've been here for three years," I continued. "You practically *own* the place."

She smiled ruefully. "Not anymore." As she stood there in her old dress, her hair still dripping from the rain, Rebecca suddenly looked like the little girl I knew so well but had almost forgotten—the vicar's daughter who desperately wanted to be blasé about the world, but who really, deep down, was rather afraid of it all.

"All right." I stood up. "Then let's look at it right now."

Rebecca shook her head. "It's not that easy. Maybe we should ask Nick—"

"Absolutely not!" I stared at her, wondering how I could have failed to enlist her in my suspicions about the Aqrab Foundation. "Someone in Dubai has a vested interest in Granny's writing system. And until that someone comes to me personally and tells me what the hell is going on, and where the Amazons fit into all this, I am not giving them *anything*. Yes, I deciphered the inscription in the temple, and yes, they paid me for it, but that's it. I will not be bullied into working for them again, and certainly not for free. The disk is none of Nick's business. Understood?"

"If you say so." Rebecca bit her lip in unspoken disagreement. "But we don't have time to see it before dinner."

"Here's what we'll do." I started pacing up and down the floor to clear my head. "You'll keep Nick distracted while I look at it alone. That way I know he's not stalking me. And when your darling team leader flies in tomorrow, I fly out. End of story." I looked at Rebecca enthusiastically, already quite fond of my plan. "Where did you say the disk is kept?"

"Well," Rebecca smiled sheepishly, "that's the pinch."

WE HAD AN EARLY dinner at the Pasiphae Taverna just down the road from the Knossos ruins. The rain had finally stopped, leaving everything damp and rather cool, and as we sat among the dripping olive trees in the patio garden, a tangerine burst of sunset cut through the remaining haze to remind us who was the king of heaven after all.

"So, tell me more about this Minotaur," said Nick at one point, looking expectantly at me. "Half man, half bull. Which half is which? I wonder."

"Oh, never mind." I looked away, still upset by his presence. "It's hardly a dinner topic."

"Why not?" He turned to Rebecca. "I just want to know how you become half bull. It intrigues me."

"All right." She smiled at him, impressing me with her ability to behave as if no secret scheme was brewing. "According to myth, the king here at Knossos had a queen, Pasiphaë, after whom this establishment, somewhat worryingly, is named." Rebecca nodded at the tavern entrance and the sign hanging over the door. "God knows what really happened to this poor woman, but tradition has it she fell in love with a bull, and that the result was a monster with a bull's head and a human body."

"What do you mean, 'result'?"

"Well—" Rebecca actually blushed. "The queen, apparently, commissioned a hollow cow made out of wood and had it placed in the field near the bull. I suppose she figured that would . . . make their courtship easier. Anyway, she eventually gave birth to the gruesome, man-eating Minotaur, who was kept in the dark labyrinth beneath the royal palace. Legend has it the Athenians were committed to sending seven boys and seven girls to Crete every year as food for the monster, and they did so faithfully year after year until the hero Theseus infiltrated the group, killed the Minotaur, and managed to find his way back out of the labyrinth by aid of a ball of yarn."

"How do you explain a myth like that?" Nick wanted to know. "Does it have roots in historical fact?"

Rebecca beamed. This was exactly the kind of question she loved. "Without a doubt," she said, "there used to be a bull cult here on Crete in ancient times, and it is not entirely unthinkable it involved a practice of human sacrifice performed by priests wearing bull masks. Hence, possibly, the frightening figure of the Minotaur."

"And the labyrinth? Is it still there?"

"In a manner of speaking." Rebecca cocked her head in the direction of the palace ruins. "Most archaeologists believe the word 'labyrinth' simply referred to the palace itself. After all, it was an enormous, sprawling building, and must have been extremely intimidating to visitors—even without the added attraction of the Minotaur." She paused to glance at me, and I knew we were thinking the same thing. There was a second labyrinth underneath the ruins, a dark, forbidding place known only to a few insiders.

"It's a hot potato to many archaeologists," I chimed in, afraid Rebecca might be losing her nerve. "How do you explain that this apparently happy, peace-loving Minoan culture had stashes of human bones with knife marks on them, hidden in consecrated caves underground?"

"Those finds could be exceptions," said Nick.

Rebecca nodded. "They could. But as my friend Mr. Telemakhos always says, exceptions are the exceptions, and finds are like ants; whenever you see one, you may be sure there were twenty."

"What about the queen and the bull?" asked Nick, pouring more wine for everyone. "What's the scientific take on that?"

"In all likelihood," I said, hoping to prevent a return to the subject, "it was just another fanciful story vilifying female passion—"

"Or," Rebecca butted in, incapable of putting a lid on her knowledge, particularly on such a juicy subject, "the bull cult also had an element of"—she blushed again—"*hieros gamos,* to use the Greek."

"I don't know Greek," Nick reminded her.

At which Rebecca smiled delightedly, her dimples surfacing for the first time in hours. "I could teach you."

"What?" asked Nick, with half a smile of his own. "*Hieros gamos* or Greek?"

I sat back on my chair, watching in disbelief as the two of them went on to practice a couple of Greek phrases, much to the amusement of both. It was not the first time I had seen my old friend shed a gloomy cocoon after a few glasses of wine, but I was astounded to find Nick playing along so wholeheartedly; had I not known better, I would have said he was truly enjoying himself.

And maybe he was. Maybe Rebecca's clumsy coquettishness had coaxed out some hitherto hidden side of this abstruse man—a side I might never have seen since I did not possess her sweetness. Or was it once again the voice in the sky that had occasioned the change? The

voice who had told Nick to hire me back and double my pay that day in
Algeria . . . and who had, almost certainly, instructed him to clean up
his act and follow me to Crete? Whose was that voice? Mr. al-Aqrab's?
Or was there someone else in the nebulous ether surrounding me who
had instructed Nick to lose the blues?

"What's wrong, Diana?" asked Rebecca suddenly. "Is it the food?"

"I'm so sorry," I said, pushing back my chair, "but I have such a
headache. Please don't let me break up the party—"

"I'll walk you back," said Nick, getting up, too.

"No! No, thanks. Really, I mean it." I motioned for him to sit down
again. "You two . . . stay right here."

RETURNING TO MY ROOM I quickly changed into the old windbreaker
and sneakers Rebecca had lent me for my nightly mission. The clay disk,
as it turned out, was kept in a tablet storage room in that labyrinthine
part of the palace basement we had deliberately not mentioned to Nick.
When describing the scenario to me before dinner, Rebecca had done
everything she could to discourage me from going down there alone,
but pride prevented me from changing the plan I had worked so hard
to sell to her. Furthermore, my curiosity had always had a way of riding
my prudence, and at present it was spurring me on with Amazonian
war cries.

Apparently, the tablet room was considered a bit of a collective
unconscious by the archaeologists working at Knossos. Within its walls
sat hundreds of clay plates, most of them inscribed with Linear B and
found to be old storage lists. The mystery disk with Granny's writing
symbols had been there for years, tucked away in a dark corner; as far
as Rebecca knew, no one had ever made a serious attempt at deciphering the message pressed so carefully into the clay more than three millennia ago.

"I know it's hard to believe," she had said, in response to my skepticism, "but Mr. Telemakhos says there used to be a rumor that this
particular disk was cursed. Some of the people who touched it had ac-

cidents, and . . . well—" Rebecca rolled her eyes dismissively. "You know how these things work. Maybe this is why it's been hidden away for so long."

As I assembled the things I needed for my expedition—my bag, a flashlight, and the ball of yarn Rebecca had insisted I bring along—I heard a little voice saying I should not be sneaking around like this so soon after my fright in Algeria. But I knew it could not be otherwise; I had promised Rebecca I'd be out of the basement well before daybreak, and I was determined to keep the disk from Nick until I knew what was written on it. Not just because of his affiliation with the Aqrab Foundation, but also because Nick—by his own admission—was being followed around by tomb raiders and terrorists, and my chances of solving the mystery of Granny's secret language would be compromised by his involvement.

In fact, after searching in vain for a safe place to hide the ten thousand dollars Nick had given me in Algeria, I decided to zip the money into my bag and bring it with me. I didn't feel comfortable leaving so much cash behind in my room, mere feet from a man who attracted thieves wherever he went.

It was almost dark by the time I headed out. Following Rebecca's instructions, I hurried across the muddy parking lot and stole into the excavation site through a hole in the fence. She had made it sound so easy; as I struggled to squeeze through the tiny opening, the broken metal tore at my hair and clothes, reminding me I was considerably bigger than her.

Making my way across the squishy ground, I tried to use the scattered boulders and protruding rock as stepping-stones whenever I could. But despite my efforts, cool wetness soon began to seep into Rebecca's sneakers, and when I arrived at the shed she had described to me, my feet were soaking.

I fumbled my way along the uneven façade, not yet daring to turn on my flashlight for fear of being seen. When I found the door at last, I slipped inside as quietly as possible, hoping very much no one heard the squeal of the battered old hinges as it closed behind me.

The shed greeted me with that particular, overpowering stench of mildew that usually forebodes spider nests, and I nearly backed right out again. But according to Rebecca, this was the safest access point for descending into the ancient palace basement. There were other entrances, but they were too hazardous; in fact, when I turned on my flashlight and saw the makeshift wooden staircase disappearing into the underground before my feet, I suddenly understood why Rebecca's odious team leader had made it a capital offense to visit the tablet room after hours and without permission.

My heart at a nervous gallop, I took out the map Rebecca had drawn for me and began picking my way down the precarious steps. Vacillating for a while at the bottom of the stairs, I explored the fusty darkness with my flashlight, trying to figure out which way to turn the map.

Stretching into the darkness on either side of me, this ancient hallway—more of a long, jagged cavern than anything built by man—was apparently only a small part of the enormous complex of storage facilities beneath the old palace. Seeing how claustrophobic it was, and how confused it had already made me, I finally understood why Rebecca had given me the ball of yarn.

Taking it out of my bag, I knelt down to tie the end piece to the bottom step of the staircase as instructed. Then I started down the tunnel in what I hoped was the direction of the tablet room, pointing the flashlight ahead of me as best I could, unwinding the yarn as I went. It took all my self-control to stay focused on the map and the few illuminated feet before me; more than once I had to speak my errand out loud to block out the shrill, competing voices of my untamed fears. "Clay disk. Tablet room."

Although I had been brought up to scoff at ghosts and monsters, I couldn't help feeling they were everywhere around, waiting for me to acknowledge them. Every time I turned another black corner or walked past another gaping doorway, picking up a waft of mold or rot, I found myself bracing for a terrible sight. Over dinner, it had been easy enough to dismiss the old legends about a man-eating ogre lurking in the Knossos labyrinth, and to speak in rational terms about masked priests and gruesome rituals. It was quite a different thing to be down here on one's own, tiptoeing through the timeless grottoes that had given birth to such beastly myths.

WHEN I FINALLY ARRIVED at the tablet room there were only a few feet of yarn left in the ball. After unlocking the heavy wooden door with Rebecca's secret key, I tied the end piece of yarn to the door handle and stepped tentatively into the room, pointing my flashlight around.

Following my hunched trek through the dark maze, I was comforted to find myself in a fairly large, angular space with stone shelves covering every wall from floor to ceiling . . . shelves full of clay tablets, hundreds of them, leaning against one another like books in a library.

When I turned on the ceiling lights, I was momentarily blinded by the halogen work lamps hanging from a metal grid by adjustable poles. Most of the lamps were pointing directly down at a table made out of two sawhorses with a large blue door resting on top. This was clearly the rather prosaic workstation for anyone handling the tablets, and yet it was impeccably clean. No papers, no pens, not even an empty water bottle had been left behind, but that was hardly surprising. According to Rebecca, the team leader did an inspection round every morning at sunrise.

After checking the scribbled instructions on my map, I began my search for the clay disk on the shelves in the remotest corner of the room. It sat exactly where Rebecca said it would: comfortably within reach. Wedged between other tablets of a similar size, it was nonetheless quite distinct from them, as it was one of the few round tablets in the entire collection.

Holding it in my hands at last, I took the disk back to the table and put it down on the blue door with extreme care. The reddish clay was chipped around the edges, and a hairline crack halfway down the middle might well turn disastrous if the disk was subjected to vibrations or sudden changes in humidity. As a matter of fact, I thought with a twinge of guilt, I should not be handling it without protective gloves and a portable dehumidifier.

Leaning over the table, I carefully inspected the tiny symbols that had been embossed in the clay in a spiral pattern. Despite the halogen lamps, the writing was hard to make out; it was no mystery why Rebecca's photos hadn't done the job. And yet, it didn't take me long to confirm that she and Mr. Telemakhos had been right; these symbols matched the ones in Algeria and in Granny's notebook.

Unable to resist, I took out the notebook with trembling hands. I had promised Rebecca not to linger in the tablet room longer than absolutely necessary; I would copy the inscription onto a piece of paper, that was all, and not attempt to decipher it until I was safely back above ground. But . . . now that I was finally here, aflutter with excitement, I simply *had* to get a little taste of my catch.

Riffling through the notebook, I scrambled to decipher the first word engraved in the clay. After working with these symbols as intensely as I had, they all felt familiar to me . . . and yet this first word was one I hadn't come across before. "Aha!" I said out loud, when I finally found what I was looking for. "Queen."

The second word, however, was far more elusive. "Queen what?" I mumbled, as I leafed through the notebook once more. "Queen who?"

But the word wasn't there. Disappointed, I turned back to the clay disk, ready to skip to the third word. But there was something about that second word—possibly a three-syllable name—that kept nagging me. . . .

In the end I opened my laptop to check my notes from Algeria. And there it was, among the many unsolved mysteries of the buried temple: the same three-syllable word, appearing near the bottom of the last wall. According to my notes it was almost certainly the name of the priestess who had taken charge after the raid, but whose further actions, unfortunately, had been lost in a lacuna of crumbled plaster.

Yet here she was again at the Knossos palace. Now a queen.

Bubbling over with agitation, I broke out my camera and took several photos of the disk before diligently copying its spiral of symbols onto a sheet of paper. Then, mindful of Rebecca's demand that I hurry back, I put the fragile tablet exactly where I'd found it and packed up my things. My thoughts miles away, or at least back in the guest room, translating the rest of the text before morning, I took out my flashlight and walked over to the door. As soon as I opened it, however, I was pulled rather abruptly back to the present.

For the end of yarn I had so meticulously tied to the door handle was no longer there.

CHAPTER NINETEEN

ISLAND OF CRETE

THE TROJANS WERE MOORED IN THE EASTERN HARBOR, RIGHT BE-
side the beach where Myrina had won her five copper tokens. As
she and her sisters followed the messenger through the evening crowds,
she could not help feeling a growing unease at the prospect of being
once again face-to-face with the young man who had teased her so in
front of his mates. Even worse, she feared his only reason for inviting
her back was to be able to sport with her more.

Be that as it may, she had been helpless to refuse the summons. The
Trojan messenger had painted an alluring picture of food and drink,
and after so many days at sea, and so much disappointment, Myrina
knew her own comfort must give way to that of her sisters.

"Look!" Pitana nodded excitedly at the prodigious ships looming
ahead. "Did you ever see anything so marvelous?"

The three Trojan ships did indeed dwarf most of the other vessels
in the harbor. As tall as they were wide, with curved bows painted in
intricate patterns, they were capable of flying massive sails and each
carried what looked like a house in the stern. "This way, please." The
messenger led them to the middle ship and started up the gangplank
ahead of Myrina. "Fear not; it is quite safe."

He was obviously referring to the long wooden board they were
walking on, which shook a little whenever someone took a step. But
Myrina was less concerned with the gangplank than with the cluster of
stern-looking armed guards awaiting them on deck. "Welcome on

board," said a tall bearded man, whom Myrina recognized from the beach earlier. "Your weapons, please."

It was clear that the guards expected the women to disarm before the promised banquet, and Myrina could feel her sisters staring at her, anxious to know how they should respond. They knew their leader was loath to put down her bow, and certainly her knife, but these were unusual circumstances. "I don't like this," whispered Animone. "Maybe they are slave traders."

"Maybe." Myrina glanced at the bearded man, sensing that behind the armored attitude a kind heart could be found. "But I doubt it." She unfastened her own bow and quiver. "Do as he says."

When they had finished, a pile of weapons lay on the deck, topped by Myrina's imposing hunting knife. "Right," said the messenger, whose eyes had bulged with surprise at every spear and hidden dagger that had been tossed into the pile. "Come with me."

He took them to the house in the stern, which turned out to be a tentlike structure made up with a sturdy fabric attached on either side to the ship's opposing railings and held high in the middle by wooden poles. The result was an open, triangular room lined with low benches and covered in finely woven carpets. Upon those carpets sat dish after dish, overflowing with food, and upon the benches sat a dozen well-dressed men, staring at the women with great curiosity.

At the apex of the room, with his back to the rising bow, a regal form dressed in blue sat comfortably on a chair of his own, golden drinking cup in hand. So it was really him, Myrina thought with a rush of heat as their eyes met across the generous spread of food. The man who had chased her through town for nothing but a glimpse of her grimy face was a highborn prince, and as he sat there nodding his condescending welcome, gesturing at them to sit down, his expression told her he took great pleasure in setting her straight about his status and, more than anything, observing her reaction.

"Go on," hissed Egee, pushing her forward. "I am starving."

Following Myrina's example, the women sat directly on the carpeted floor, nervously squeezing together like hares cornered by foxes.

Although she tried not to look at the men sitting on the benches, Myrina felt their curious, lustful stares, and when she saw Egee reaching out for a proffered basket of bread, she snapped forward to push the girl's hands away. "Do not touch anything," she whispered to her companions, "before we understand our roles here tonight." Then she rose to her knees and bent her head at Prince Paris, saying, "Thank you for inviting us. We do not deserve your kindness, I am sure."

He smiled in response, as if to her alone. "We have a saying in my country: If you must strike, make sure to follow the hurt with a kiss."

The words hung in the air for a while, thrown back and forth between the laughing men. But only Myrina knew Paris's true meaning; the kiss was hers to bestow, since she was the one who had struck at his dignity by running away and pulling a knife on him.

"I understand," she said, sitting once more, warm waves of embarrassment pulsing in her cheeks. "And this is why I must apologize. You see, we are not women with whom any man should expect to exchange kisses. We are holy sisters and as such we have come. Therefore, unless you take pleasure in hearing sacred hymns"—she made a regretful gesture at the food—"we would never be able to properly thank you for this."

Paris's handsome features contracted in irritation. "Once again, your aim is impeccable. Were I a lesser man, I would call myself insulted. But"—he smiled and opened his arms—"I am not. So calm yourselves, ladies, and enjoy our homage to your holiness. Fear not"—he looked directly at Myrina, a teasing challenge in his eyes—"that we seek to fill you with anything other than food."

With that he let them eat in peace, and the chamber filled with the sounds of spoons scraping against clay bowls, and of creaking ropes and sloshing water whenever the surf tugged at the massive ship and tested its mooring lines. Now and then the men exchanged a few mumbled words, but Prince Paris remained silent, his bright eyes fixed on Myrina with the patient vigilance of a resting predator.

Halfway through the meal, two boys came quietly through the room to light a myriad of small clay oil lamps, and the twilight murk was immediately dispelled. The men now reached for the sweetmeats and honey bread, and a brass pitcher with a dark, strange-smelling liquid was passed around.

Although every dish was delicious, Myrina barely paid attention to what she ate. She was too curious about the men not to study them with stolen looks—their language, their appearance, their behavior. Wherever their land of origin, the Trojans were clearly a civilized lot, and their features were as handsome as their manners. Everything about them spoke of wealth and ease—the ships, the furnishings, the food— and the more Myrina listened to the calm tone of their conversation, the more ashamed she was at her initial fears. To think she had sensed lechery and calculation when she entered the room . . . clearly, it had all been in her mind. No matter how long these men had spent crossing the ocean, and how much they longed for a woman's touch, they were not likely to violate the sacred rules of hospitality; nay, *she* was the one who had failed in her duties as a guest by allowing herself such fears.

Toward the end of the meal, Myrina looked up and spoke to Paris in what she hoped was a voice of apology. "You have been more than kind to us," she said, pressing a hand to her chest, "and I cannot bear the thought that we came and went so ungraciously. Will you allow us to sing a hymn of gratitude?"

The prince looked amused at the offer, but managed to turn his smile into a stately frown. "Spare your hymns, dear ladies. You owe us nothing."

Myrina struggled to come up with an alternative. "We must thank you—"

Paris cocked his head. "Will you give me your bow?"

The frank question made Myrina recoil with shock. Politeness demanded that she grant him his wish, but despite her urge to be generous she found herself struggling to speak the word.

Seeing her so flustered, Paris threw back his head and laughed heartily. "Fear not! I should rather tear the heart from your bosom than take your bow, for I believe you would miss it less."

Myrina stared at him, unsure of his meaning.

Still smiling, Paris held out his golden cup to one of the serving boys, who instantly refilled it with wine. "Do not look so mortified. What would I do with another bow . . . or another heart?" He looked around appealingly, and a few of the other men chuckled in accord. "No, holy archer—or should I say archeress? Is it even a word, I wonder?" Paris pursed his lips as if contemplating the issue. "What do *you* think?"

This time, Myrina was not fooled. She understood that Paris was genuinely keen on talking with her . . . yet he could not be perfectly sincere with her in front of his men, lest they think their master a soft and silly man.

The elegant prince struck Myrina as being as different from her as any civilized person could be. Not in terms of strength and ability, for he, too, was tall and able, but rather in terms of spirit and demeanor; where she was dark, he was wonderfully light. His hair and eyes had almost the same coppery brown hue as the wildflower honey her mother had taught her and Lilli to collect, but more significantly, he appeared to be completely unburdened by fate. Even at this hour, with darkness advancing, there was an utterly mesmerizing glow about him. It was as if his body retained the radiance of the sun . . . as if this young man, overflowing with daylight still, was determined to singlehandedly keep the night at bay.

"Surely," she said to him at last, "the word will exist if you allow it to." Seeing she had managed to surprise him, and pleasantly so, Myrina went on more boldly, saying, "Now be kind and disclose what it is you want from us. For you want something, I am sure of it, and yet I cannot guess its nature."

Paris sat back on the chair, impressed by her demand. "Very well," he said with a nod, "I want your story. Where is your home? Are you from a nation of women? Where I come from, the power of the Great Mother has long since waned, and man, proud man, rules heaven and earth." He held out his hands as if to ask her forgiveness. "Can you blame me for being curious?"

"If there exists a land without men," replied Myrina, glancing at her sisters, "we above all should like to know where it is. As you can surely see, we have suffered much, and expect to suffer more, for this world of ships and journeys has not been kind to us." She bent her head as images of the temple raiders passed before her eyes. "Happiness has long since run its course in us. We are now left to choose between danger and regret, neither of which can ever restore the lives we have lost."

When she finally dared to meet Paris's eyes, Myrina was relieved to find that mischief and mirth had given way to an earnest desire to understand the tragedy that had befallen his guests. Leaning forward in his chair, the handsome prince seemed to have temporarily forgotten the men around him; even the wine in his cup was left untouched as he waited for her to continue.

Sensing his sincere interest, Myrina decided to lay out the entire map of their misery before his feet, with all its knowns and unknowns, no grisly detail spared. As she spoke, her sisters came to her aid more than once, reminding her of this and that horrifying moment, or completing a woeful sentence when the dreaded words became trapped in her throat.

"So you see," Myrina concluded at last, wiping a tear from her cheek, "we have no hopes of our own, save to stay alive. Our pulse is beating for those who were stolen, and who are surely suffering far more than we. Where they were taken, we do not know. But we have sworn to find them at any cost."

A deep silence followed her tale. There was not a man in the room who did not look at the women with pity, and Paris now sat hunched, brooding, tapping a pensive knuckle against his chin. "I suspect the raiders were Greek," he said at length. "The tarred ships, the excellent weapons, the language you describe." He looked around at his countrymen and saw nothing but grave agreement. "We share the northern sea with them and know their manners only too well." A murmur throughout the room supported this claim and made it clear Paris had not spoken a compliment.

"The northern sea," said Myrina. "Is it far?"

He gave her a wry look. "It is not the distance. Anyone may sail there when the wind is right. But the Greeks are an ambitious and jealous race. They have founded many cities and guard them fiercely—none more so than Mycenae, home of their great king, Agamemnon.

Perched on a hill well inside a protected bay, it is, I would say, untouchable. Unless, of course, you have a mighty fleet and a land army to spare, which I am guessing you do not."

Myrina's disappointment made a response impossible.

"To the Greeks," Paris went on, "women are little more than livestock, and foreigners are considered more brutish still. This is why Agamemnon's pirates think nothing of attacking a foreign temple and laying hands on a priestess, and why I urge you to forget this quest of yours. If your friends are not already dead, they will be soon. Why add more bodies to the pyre?"

Myrina was so shocked by his words that her growing respect for Prince Paris almost lost its footing. "If I were a man," she said, straightening, "you would not have spoken to me thus. Because I am a woman, you assume my aim in life is comfort, and that my honor lies in my chastity alone. I can't blame you, for you are merely saying what you think I am hoping to hear. But you are wrong. We have higher goals than that—goals that guide us like stars through the darkness, and our endeavor cannot be so easily discouraged."

The words seemed to echo in the air for a while, and Myrina could feel her sisters shifting with discomfort, nervous that she might have dealt the final blow to the goodwill of their host. But in the end, Paris merely sighed and said, "Tomorrow I am meeting the Minos at the Knossos palace. We are to discuss business matters. Perhaps you should accompany me and tell him of your complaints. He is an ally of the Greeks, and they support his rule; if anyone can influence them in this matter, it is him. If your friends are still alive, we may be able to trade for them."

Despite everything, Myrina nearly laughed. "Your generosity has blinded you to my condition. Surely, you do not wish to degrade yourself by escorting a woman in rags—"

Paris held up a hand to silence her. "I see nothing that cannot be overcome by a bar of tallow. Spend the night here, all of you, comfortably asleep in this room, and begin the morrow with breakfast and a sea bath. I wager—for you already know I am a gambler—that after a safe night's sleep and a change of clothes, you just may turn out to be a queen." He smiled, a glint of mischief returning to his eyes. "If not, we shall make you resemble one anyway."

THE KNOSSOS PALACE ROSE effortlessly above the surrounding town with its layer upon layer of brightly colored roofs and colonnades. A harmonious structure, it seemed, without the slightest hint of fortification.

"Is anything the matter?" asked Paris, when he saw Myrina peeking out through the flimsy curtains of the litter. "Do you wish you were riding the formidable creature between my legs?"

The question set off peals of laughter all around. The morning had held no scarcity of amusement for the Trojans, beginning with an improvised satyr play on the beach as they were commissioned to stand guard around the bathing women, and concluding with the comedy of introducing Queen Myrina to her regal means of transportation.

"Goddess!" she had exclaimed, backing up in horror when she saw the animal Paris would have her ride. "Whatever is *that*?"

Taller than cows, but smaller than camels—and considerably more spirited than both—the creatures the Trojans were leading down the gangplank to the pier struck Myrina as being more beautiful, yes, but also more capricious than any other domesticated beast she had ever seen. Clearly skittish after their long sojourn on the ship, they bucked and reared up with the ferocity of wildcats, and when Paris confirmed Myrina's growing suspicion that she was expected to ride one, she backed away, shaking her head.

"Come!" he taunted her, "I have called you fearless. Do not make me a liar. Nothing is simpler than riding a horse. Look." He mounted one with ease, not deterred by its shying and prancing. "All you have to do is hold on."

But no words could persuade Myrina to get up on a horse of her own. Nor could Paris talk her into sharing his. "Please," she said at last, her fingers grappling for the security of her bowstring and quiver strap but finding only the embroidered dress that had been acquired for her—undoubtedly at great expense—in the market that same morning. "Why can I not walk?"

"*Walk?*" Paris nearly fell backward out of the saddle. "Since when did a prince of Troy let a queen *walk* through the streets like a prostitute?"

Looking more than a little irked, he had sent the servant out again, this time to order a sedan. When it finally came, all Myrina could do was climb inside. Her sudden timidity, she decided, was a consequence of being stripped of her weapons and trapped in useless robes . . . and yet, to her secret astonishment she knew it had to do with Paris. The way he had looked at her when he placed the slim gold band around her head and said, "There! I win my bet. You really *are* a queen!" haunted her all the way through town, and no amount of humorous comments could still the foolish flutter in her chest.

THE PALACE GUARDS DID not detain them for long. Without even looking inside the litter, they let the Trojans through the grand gate into the courtyard, and from behind her curtains Myrina heard the horses step from gravel onto tile.

Peeking out once more, she saw the clean angles of the palace buildings against the bright blue sky and the broad stairs teeming with people. It was a magnificent sight, much grander and far more sophisticated than the dwelling of the Moon Goddess at home, and she could not help but marvel at the fact that this sparkling maze of lofty halls and bright red colonnades had been erected for the sake of mortal men—a ruler and his administrators.

Then the curtain was drawn aside, and Paris held out his hand to help her down. "Queen Myrina," he said, with unsmiling cordiality. "Allow me."

As she descended from the litter to find herself surrounded by stony-faced Trojans and self-important palace heralds, Myrina felt peculiarly small. Although the dainty slippers that went with the dress had elevated wooden heels on them, it was as if she had shrunk in stature when she took off her snakeskin tunic and donned the costly guise. Paris was tall, yes, but he had not appeared to tower over her quite like this before. It didn't matter that his golden headband was temporarily on *her* head; the heir of Troy looked every bit the prince as he stood there in his embroidered blue tunic and mantle, while Myrina, for all her borrowed elegance, had never felt so low.

Even if the Trojans had been right in assuring her she had a noble countenance and could easily pass for royalty, Myrina was only too aware of her own graceless gait in the treacherous slippers. And despite her many months at the Temple of the Moon Goddess, where dresses were mandatory, she had never been comfortable fluttering about with the ethereal air of a priestess. "You are not sneaking up on a groundhog, Myrina!" the High Priestess had once scolded her, much to the amusement of Kara and Egee. "You are a celestial body, a star in the sky, a thing without thoughts."

For all her willingness to fit in, Myrina had never quite mastered the art of becoming a thing without thoughts. And as she let go of Paris's hand to clumsily adjust her skirts, she feared the palace guards saw neither queen nor woman, just a foreigner in poor disguise.

If they did, they did not show it. Bowing to Paris and the seven other Trojans with the utmost respect, the heralds proceeded to lead the guests across a mosaic of tiles far more elaborate than any Myrina had seen in the consecrated halls at home. "See the double ax?" whispered Paris, nodding at the pattern. "It is a sacred symbol here."

As they walked up the clean-swept white stairs to the audience hall, Myrina glanced out over the courtyard, wondering why this apparently welcoming open place made her feel so uneasy. At the far end of the tiled square, a red double door stood out against the pale yellow of the surrounding brick, and a golden pattern of bulls' heads and double axes on the lintel suggested the room beyond the door was a holy destination.

"Now, remember," whispered Paris, his hand tight around Myrina's elbow, "when we come into the throne room, we must bow to the Holy Mother first, even if the real power is with the Minos."

Despite its lofty name, the throne room was not big, but it was so full of people Myrina might not have noticed the Holy Mother unless she had specifically looked for her. Seated on a throne against the brightly decorated wall, slumped as if in sleep, the Lady of Knossos gave the impression of a large field mammal dressed up and dragged inside against its nature. Only when Myrina knelt before her did the woman raise her head and fix a weary eye on the golden band crowning the curly hair of her unusual supplicant. Then, with bovine resignation, the Holy Mother raised a bejeweled hand and pointed Myrina in the direction of the true ruler of Crete.

The Minos stood in the far corner, engulfed in a fog of politics. Surrounded by the intense gestures of men with opposing interests, he was clearly a man rarely left in peace. Even from across the busy room there was no mistaking a reptilian cunning in his face; no one could have stood in greater contrast to the Lady of Knossos than this small, fidgety man. As Myrina knelt before him, she found herself wondering about the exact relationship between the two. Were they man and wife? Mother and son? It was hard to determine.

"Today I bring Queen Myrina," said Paris to the Minos in the language spoken in the Temple of the Moon Goddess, his voice and manner completely undaunted by the commotion. "She has traveled far to visit this country and brings a gift of peace." He motioned at his trusted companion, the long-limbed Aeneas, to step forward with the small tablet Kyme and Myrina had composed that same morning.

The change in the Minos was immediate. As soon as he saw the round clay disk with the elegant spiral of text, he opened his arms in a most generous greeting. "Rise, dear queen!" he exclaimed, taking the tablet from Aeneas. "And tell me of your country. From what exotic sphere did you come?"

Myrina did not even attempt to reply. Paris had impressed upon her that, despite all the kind words and gestures, only men were allowed to speak directly to the Minos. "Queen Myrina rules a vast country," he lied on her behalf, "near Lake Tritonis."

"Ah!" said the Minos, his enthusiasm fading briefly, then flaring up again. "I see. You have come for food, I gather. To carry your people through until the good times return." He looked down at the tablet, his brow contracting. "I am not familiar with this language. What manner of pledge is it?"

"Blessings," explained Paris. "And an offer of friendship."

"What? No gift of people? I should think that under the circumstances—" The Minos turned the clay disk over, as if hoping to find the desired pledge on the other side. "These are desperate times for her people!" he pointed out to Paris, ignoring Myrina completely. "Surely she sees that the gods are angry and must be appeased."

Paris nodded, his aspect perfectly calm. "The queen knows that. But she is not here to bargain for food. She is here because she knows Crete is on friendly terms with the Greeks."

The Minos straightened. "Indeed, King Agamemnon's son was just here."

"Is that so?" Paris glanced at Myrina. "Then he must have come directly from Lake Tritonis."

The Minos frowned. "He did mention having to drag his ships through a snake-infested marsh to return to the ocean. And there was some talk of a large, black statue. But may I ask why you are so interested in the movements of the Greeks? I sincerely hope there is not another conflict afoot."

Myrina stepped forward, forgetting in her excitement that she must remain silent. Before she could speak, however, Paris squeezed her arm so hard she cringed. "Three weeks ago," he told the Minos, "Agamemnon's son visited Queen Myrina's palace under a pretext of friendship, but made away with several precious objects, including nine of the queen's maiden cousins."

The Minos took a step back. "I am appalled!"

"Naturally," Paris continued, "the queen is furious. But she would prefer not to launch a campaign."

"But of course." The Minos swallowed hard. His wealth and power, Paris had explained to Myrina, depended entirely on the free movements of ships around his island. A war would stifle such movements and add even more insecurity to the world of trade. For that reason alone the Minos had always been a man of peace.

"It is perhaps not widely known," Paris went on, "but the queen commands an army of thousands, most of which are cavalry." An additional pinch told Myrina that Paris was toying with her, even now. "Surely it is in no one's interest to have such violence unleashed on mankind."

The Minos attempted a smile. "Of course. But why have you come to me? How can I possibly be of help?"

Paris nodded at the clay disk. "The queen is hoping for an agreement, stipulating that you have agreed to an alliance with her. Faced with such an agreement, the Greeks may be prevailed upon to give back what they stole—".

"Oh, dear." The Minos sighed. "That will take a while. The priests are terribly busy, yet they must approve . . . take omens—"

Myrina could bear it no longer. "Please," she exclaimed, before Paris could stop her, "can you not make an exception?"

A gasp of horror all around let her know the severity of her misstep before the Minos was even able to express his dismay. "Perhaps it were better," he hissed, his voice almost failing him, "that the queen made herself comfortable with the other women while the men settle matters here."

It did not take Paris long to finish with the Minos and come looking for Myrina in the other part of the crowded throne room. As he escorted her back out into the blinding daylight, Myrina feared his contemptuous grimace was brought on by her impetuous behavior. "I am so sorry," she began, trying to keep up with his angry steps. "I forgot myself."

Paris paused on the staircase, looking around for the men he had left outside. "If you must apologize, be sorry you did not insult him further. Pinprick of a man. Muzzled by his own priests. Mark my words: This island has seen its heyday."

As Paris and Myrina descended the stairs together, the long-limbed Aeneas came forward to speak quickly and urgently into Paris's ear. Although she could not understand the words, Myrina guessed the narrative was a horrendous one, for Aeneas was pale with agitation, and Paris's contemptuous glower soon gave way to tight-lipped outrage.

"What is it?" she asked him, when Aeneas finally fell silent.

"Nothing," replied Paris, his eyes drawn toward the red double door across the courtyard. "Let us leave this place with no further delay."

"But what is so terrible?" Myrina tried to make out the thoughts that had etched such a dreadful expression across his face. "Is it about the Greeks?"

Paris did not respond until they were reunited with the horses and ready to leave. "It seems we missed them by a hair," he said, with an attempt at levity. "They left six days ago, to return directly to Mycenae."

Myrina stared at him, sensing there was more. "Any word of my sisters?"

"The women never left the ships." Paris took her hand to help her into the litter. "Except one. She was given to the Minos as a present—"

Myrina clasped her mouth. "She is here? At the palace?"

The men exchanged grave glances, and once again, Paris's eyes were drawn to the double door across the courtyard.

Without another word, Myrina let go of his hand and began walking, as fast as she dared, toward the red square crowned with golden symbols.

"Don't go there!" Paris chased after her, but Myrina kicked off her slippers and ducked away from him, breaking into a run. She did not care who might be looking; she could never leave a sister behind.

Finding the door unlocked, Myrina pushed through it without hesitation, entering the holy room with Paris and Aeneas close behind her. And even though the contrast between the sunny courtyard and the windowless cave she had entered was blinding, she stumbled on in the near-darkness, more anxious to escape the Trojans than to prepare herself for what she might find.

The room turned out to be long and narrow, more of a corridor, lined with a few flaming torches stuck in cressets. At the end of the passage, a staircase led down into the unknown.

"Myrina!" Paris finally caught up with her. "We should not be here." But when he saw the determination in her eyes, he said no more, and followed.

They walked down the steps together, with the other Trojans closely behind. At the bottom of the stairs was another, darker corridor, which in turn opened up into a circular room lit by sacrificial fires in brass bowls. It was the inner sanctum of the palace.

Stopping on the threshold, Myrina looked around at the golden bulls' heads mounted on the wall and the altars stacked with meat and bones. She was no stranger to animal sacrifice or, being a hunter, to the sight of entrails and dismembered limbs, but there was something about the unbearably putrid smell of this place that ran counter to all her instincts. . . .

And then she saw the human heads arranged in a small pyramid on the main altar with dismembered arms and legs stacked neatly on either side. Some of the limbs were dark with rot, others were merely gray and bloodless, as if they had been placed there recently. As Myrina stared at them in terror, a shiny object caught the light of the flickering torches. . . . It was a jackal bracelet encircling a narrow wrist.

CHAPTER TWENTY

Now seeing the watchdog deep in sleep, Aeneas
Took the opening: swiftly he turned away
From the river over which no soul returns.
—Virgil, *The Aeneid*

ISLAND OF CRETE
PRESENT DAY

REFUSING TO GIVE IN TO PANIC, I SEARCHED THE ROUGH-HEWN floor of the corridor as thoroughly as I could by the light pouring out of the tablet room. Then, extending my search, I turned on the flashlight and started back the way I had come . . . but it was all in vain. The yarn was gone.

Perhaps, I thought, a sudden updraft had tugged at the flimsy thread and somehow torn my knot from the door handle. Such a draft might have even carried the yarn down the tunnel and out of sight. I worked to persuade myself that this was the explanation. For the only rational alternative—that I was not alone in the labyrinth—was too terrifying to contemplate.

I stood on the edge of the darkness, the beam of my flashlight so feeble I wondered if the batteries were dying. Trembling with nerves, I turned it off and retreated into the tablet room to take stock of the situation. My cellphone was on, but I was not surprised to see I had no reception. There were, after all, thousands of tons of earth and ancient brick between me and the modern world. And what would I have told Rebecca anyway? That I intended to spend the rest of the night in the tablet room—door locked, lights on, barricaded behind the worktable—until the team leader discovered me on his morning round?

No, I decided, I was not that cowardly. I wouldn't risk Rebecca's job. I owed it to her to remove myself from the forbidden basement as discreetly as I had come, without leaving the slightest trace of my intrusion.

Opening the door to the corridor yet again, I stood listening for a while, hearing nothing. There was a faint draft, more of a whisper, but that was all. Taking a deep breath, I unfolded Rebecca's map. Yarn or no yarn, calm logic would lead me back the way I had come, and before long I would be crawling into bed in my guest room, laughing at the whole thing.

But as I started down the tunnel, following the shaky beam of my dying flashlight, calm logic was soon awash in a tide of fear. I couldn't help it; even without the mystery of my yarn disappearing, these stygian caverns made all my instincts run mad. For every step I took, my eyes jumped in panic at some grotesque shadow cast across the jagged wall, and whenever I focused my beam on the map, blackness closed in on me from all sides.

Then, from somewhere deep inside, came a voice that was part mine, part Granny's, reciting the mantra she had taught me so long ago, and which I would always remember. It had been the day after the killer-dog incident, and we had been halfway through our tea when it occurred to me that Granny was treating me differently than before: with less patience but more respect.

"I am an Amazon," she had said, her gray-blue eyes aglow with a feverish, metallic shine, "the killer of beasts and men. Freedom runs through my veins; no rope can hold me. I fear nothing; fear runs from *me*. I always walk forward, for that is the only way. Try to stop me, and you will feel my rage."

She had repeated this high-handed declaration again and again, until I knew it by heart. Then she tested me on it until my voice became firm and confident and I stood before her, as tall as I could, believing every word.

I had occasionally used the mantra before an important exam or a fencing match, but never before had it bolstered me the way it did tonight, walking through the labyrinth. This was what Granny had been preparing me for—not the trifling challenges of modern life, but those rare visceral moments of truth when you are trapped in the web of fate and the real monsters come out.

And so, as I approached the first turn without seeing any trace of the yarn whatsoever, I braced myself for a possible encounter. Someone or something had come through this corridor while I was busy in the tablet room, I was sure of it now. Clutching the bag to my chest, I pulled back the flashlight to be able to strike . . . but when I stretched to look, all I saw was another empty tunnel disappearing into limbo.

Or rather, it was not completely empty, for I spotted something lying on the ground a few steps ahead: the ball of yarn. Neatly rolled up.

I was so flummoxed I didn't hear it coming. In the darkness of the tunnel, I saw nothing other than a sudden, looming shadow, swallowing me from behind. In my terror I ducked instinctively, and I would have started running, had not something grabbed hold of my windbreaker with a bloodcurdling growl of warning.

Desperate to escape, I twisted around and swung my flashlight madly at my attacker. Through a haze of panic I was able to make out a head but no face . . . just a thick brow and two lifeless eyes. Screaming, I struck at the thing as hard as I could again and again until the flashlight was torn from my hands and then came right back with a numbing blow to my temple.

The next thing I felt was the cold, hard floor of the tunnel against my cheek. A second later, something took me fiercely by the arm and flipped me over on my back. Sick with fear and unable to see a thing in the pitch-blackness, I tried to kick at the violent, panting body hovering over me. But my legs were seized and pinned to the cave's floor. Despite my screams and struggles, claws tore furiously at my jacket.

I finally remembered my sharp-eared jackal bracelet and managed a few forceful backhand strokes, one of which made my attacker grunt with pain and let go of me. Fearing the worst, I curled up for protection.

But the strike never came. I heard a rush of feet, felt a trailing draft, and . . .

Silence.

Shaking all over, I stayed crouched on the tunnel floor for the longest time, wondering if it would return, whatever *it* was. The darkness was so complete I wasn't even sure if my eyes were open, and it took all my willpower to get up and start searching for the flashlight.

I couldn't find it. Gasping with panic, I fumbled around blindly on the gritty floor until it eventually occurred to me to take out my phone. Fortunately, it was undamaged and came on right away when I opened it, giving me a few seconds of blue light at a time. Not enough to see far, but enough to read Rebecca's map. Except . . . the precious piece of paper was nowhere to be found. Nor was my bag. My attacker, I realized, had managed to take everything. Even one of my shoes was missing. All I had left were the few items I had slipped into my jacket pockets: my phone, my camera, and Granny's notebook with the clay-disk transcript tucked inside.

On trembling legs I started down the dark tunnel back toward the tablet room. It was only a turn away, I told myself; surely I could fumble my way back there, even without the aid of the map.

I couldn't. Coming into a circular cavity I was sure I hadn't seen before, I knew I had gone too far. Turning, I meant to depart this round chamber the way I came, but absurdly, found myself staring at three identical doorways, unable to identify from which I had emerged.

Nearly in tears from shock and frustration, and too afraid to stand still for more than a few seconds, I finally chose the left one, determined to turn back if it felt wrong. At first, it was impossible to distinguish this tunnel from the one I had been in previously; I kept noticing details that might or might not have been there before, simply because I hadn't looked for them. A pile of rubble, a gaping crack in the wall—

the pressure of finding certainty was so crushing I felt like sitting down right where I was, in the hopes that a search party would find me before the monster came back for more.

No sooner had I overcome this cowardly impulse than the tunnel widened into a proper corridor. Encouraged by the cressets on the wall, I hurried on, holding the phone up before me, eventually ending up in a vaulted grotto. In the feeble light of my cellphone not much could be discerned, but what I did see was promising. I was on the edge of what looked like an underground canal. The ghostly presence of a punting boat and pole suggested the canal had once been passable—it had once led somewhere. Perhaps it had been some ancient form of plumbing; I might be standing on the edge of the old palace sewer. If that were the case, the canal would lead outside. Even the bowels of Hades had to drain somewhere.

Deciding this was my best chance of finding a way out, I picked my way through the rubble, praying I would not end up in a dead end of collapsed stone. I was freezing cold by now, terrified by what had happened and might happen still, and my one stocking foot—throbbing with pain whenever I took a step—was a constant reminder of how vulnerable and human I was.

Stumbling on through the detritus of the palace sewer, I lost my balance again and again and scraped my hands raw by grappling blindly for something to hold on to. Opening my phone with regular intervals, I tried to make out the time, but couldn't. The numbers had lost their meaning. To rally my spirits, I tried to recite Granny's Amazon chant a few times, but my teeth were chattering so badly I had to stop.

At one point, my left hand brushed against a clammy, clingy web of sorts. Flipping open my phone, I saw roots hanging from above. Encouraged by their earthy smell and the evident proximity of the natural world, I strode on and on and on, pushing through rubble and climbing over boulders . . . until the passage became so narrow I had to continue on my hands and knees.

Numb with cold, I wormed my way through that confined space, stubbornly clearing my path by picking up and tossing aside chunks of stone. I was so desperate, so close to losing hope, I barely dared believe my senses when I finally emerged through a chasm overgrown with slippery moss into a different kind of darkness.

Looking up, I cried out with joy at the sight of the crescent moon . . . only to jump aside when a pair of headlights came right toward me before swinging away at the last moment—right into Rebecca's ivory village.

As I LIMPED ACROSS the muddy parking lot and up the stone steps to the shared terrace in front of the guest rooms, I made every effort at stealth. Seeing the lights still on in Nick's room, I tiptoed past his door, trying not to make any noise while searching my pockets for the room key.

It wasn't there. And nor was the key to the tablet room, which Rebecca had put on the same ring, to make things easier. Struck by the stupidity of it all, I leaned my head against the locked door in silent agony.

"Feeling better?"

The shock of hearing a man's voice made me snap upright. Leaning against the wall, not ten steps away, Nick watched me with folded arms. "What happened to your other shoe?"

Although his manner was not exactly friendly, I felt myself softening at the question, and my head drooped with exhaustion. "I'm not exactly sure."

Only then did Nick approach, his bare feet tan against the whitewashed terrace. "What's going on, Diana?"

I glanced up at him reluctantly, in no mood to explain. As soon as he saw my face, his expression changed. Without a word, he took my arm and guided me into his room. "Look down." He inspected my banged temple in the light of the ceiling lamp. "Did you lose consciousness?"

"I don't think so—" I began. Then I caught sight of myself in a mirror on the wall. The bruise looked even worse than it felt; not only was it red and swollen right where the flashlight had struck me, but a dark pattern had spread to my right eye.

"What happened?"

I flinched as he poked the bruise. "A door walked into me."

Nick disappeared into the bathroom. "Do I really have to repeat my question?" he asked when he came back, pressing a damp washcloth firmly against my temple.

His patronizing manner flicked me over the edge. "Repeat whatever you want," I said, pushing away his hand. "I'm under no obligation to tell you *anything*. You have filled me with lies from day one—"

Nick started. "What lies?"

I glared at him, unable to quell the anger that had been festering inside me for so long. "Perhaps you could start by telling me the name of your employer? And please don't say 'Mr. Skolsky.' "

"Why should I waste my time?" Nick was completely unfazed. "You've known it all along."

Momentarily stunned, I sat down on the edge of the bed. I had given him my best shot, but his parry had been effortless. He looked at me with a half-overbearing smile, as if to say, "Is that really all you have?" before shaking his head and handing me the washcloth.

"So," I said, taking it, "you admit to misleading me?"

Nick shrugged. "I'm a liar, you're a thief. Under the circumstances I think we're better off working together." He nodded at my bruise. "Wouldn't your head agree?"

Just then, we both heard a faint knocking sound.

"That would be Bex," I sighed. "We were supposed to meet up—"

Nick walked over to the door. "I'll tell her to get some ice."

"And a gallon of Metaxa," I added, pressing the cloth to my forehead.

Later that night, as I was nested on Nick's bed with a welcome glass of the local painkiller, my lingering shock gradually changed into bitter confusion. Rebecca had been horrified at my account of what had happened, and even though Nick had spoken only a little, I knew he was shocked, too. Sitting in the corner in a tattered gladiolus-blossom armchair, he looked increasingly grim, his fingers drumming loudly on the threadbare armrest.

"Who else knew you were down there?" he asked at length.

I looked at Rebecca who sat on the bedside right next to me, poised to replenish my drink. "Did you tell your darling Mr. Telemakhos I was going down there tonight?" I asked her.

She frowned, looking a little offended. "I don't remember. But surely, you're not suspecting *him*?"

I took another few gulps of Metaxa while Rebecca struggled to explain the phenomenon of Mr. Telemakhos to Nick. This was obviously not the time for an argument, but I highly suspected it was my friend's big mouth that had somehow gotten me into trouble.

"Just to recap." Nick's eyes traveled over my filthy clothes and torn knees before returning to the reddish bump on my temple. "You lost your laptop and a set of keys. What else was in the bag?"

"Oh, not much." I pulled up my sleeve to inspect my throbbing elbow. As I did so, Granny's bracelet appeared in all its timeless grace, reminding us both what a consummate liar I could be. "Just an envelope with ten thousand dollars." I shook my head, ignoring Rebecca's gasp of horror. "Everything else was either in my room or in my pockets."

"Everything else?"

Suddenly chilled, I drew the bedspread more tightly around me. Even though I was telling the truth, my voice sounded false. "Well, I still have my camera with the photos from Algeria." I reached into the black windbreaker, which was lying on the bed next to me. "I hope it still works."

Without hesitation, Nick took the camera from me and popped out the memory card. "With your permission." It was not a question.

Nick's laptop was of the sturdy variety, engineered to withstand grime, desert roads, and minor explosions. An excellent choice considering his employer, I thought as he placed it on the bed in front of me and uploaded my photos directly into his own picture library. The next thing I knew, an entire year of my life played out before us in a cringing slide show of James playing tennis, my father carving the Christmas turkey in his squirrel apron, some early daffodils I had bought at an outdoor market, my mother eating a rare ice cream . . . and finally, all my photos from Algeria followed by the ones I had taken just a few hours earlier in the tablet room.

"It appears," I said, a little irritated at the ease with which Nick had annexed my private life, "I have more or less moved into your computer."

"That's okay." He leaned forward to study the photo on the screen—the last of the batch. "It was getting boring in there. Is that the tablet?" When I nodded, he shook his head. "You risked your life to take a picture of an engraved pancake?"

I decided to let it slide. It was, after all, a relief to see Nick treating the precious clay disk with so little respect; had he seemed truly interested I might once again have wondered about his true motive for coming to Crete.

An odd buzzing sound brought me back to the moment.

"Excuse me." Nick extracted his phone from a trouser pocket and disappeared outside. As soon as the door had closed behind him, Rebecca scooted right up to me, clearly itching to investigate his computer.

"Let's see what he's got on here!" she urged me. "Hurry!"

"Go ahead and hack it. It's all yours." I pushed the laptop toward her. "Be his guest."

Rebecca looked down at the keys, only then realizing they were all in Arabic. "Oh."

"Right." I pulled it back in front of me. "You didn't think he was going to make it that easy, did you?"

"What about his own photos?" Rebecca pecked eagerly at the screen. "Try to open another folder."

I should have said no, but the truth was, I was even more curious than she. After a week of intense coexistence I still knew next to nothing about Nick, except that he was a smooth-talking shape-shifter working for the Aqrab Foundation.

At first glance, his photo library contained nothing outright incriminating. As far as I could see in my guilty hurry, most of the pictures were from archaeological excavations, showing the various stages of digging and cleaning of various finds. Some were burial grounds with skeletons surrounded by clay pots and weapons; others were actual buildings emerging from desert dunes, and the artifacts found here included golden jewelry and drinking vessels.

But in between excavations and artifacts were pictures of armed guards and armored vehicles, stringing the entire photo library together by barbed wire. Even though the guards were often smiling and posing for the shots, a current of latent violence ran through it all, humming right beneath the scientific surface.

Only then did it occur to me to check the most recent folder. As expected, it contained photos from the temple in Algeria, including several close-ups of the sarcophagus in the inner sanctum. Scrolling through the images with trembling fingers, I barely allowed myself to look carefully until I arrived at the very last one.

"Look!" hissed Rebecca. "It's your bracelet!"

I stared in disbelief. The photo did indeed show a coiled jackal lying on a paper napkin, the ancient bronze dimmed by dust. But it certainly wasn't mine. It had to be the one from the sarcophagus. My bruised head throbbing with agitation, I decided there could only be one explanation for its presence here among Nick's photos: *He* was the one who had removed it from the skeleton, and his claim that *I* was the thief had been nothing but a handy excuse for following me to Crete.

Just then, the door opened, and Rebecca—who didn't have my early training in cloak-and-dagger dealings—recoiled with a gasp. Nick took a long look at her, then came over and closed the laptop. "Bedtime."

As I CURLED UP with Rebecca that night, I found myself unable to fall asleep. The events of the evening kept swirling around in my head, and I felt a strange, giddy excitement that didn't make sense at all. I had been through a hellish ordeal, and my forehead throbbed so badly I could hardly lie down. And yet . . . I had survived. I had held my own against my attacker, and had managed to stubbornly claw my way out of the underworld. As delayed reactions went, my perplexing giddiness was tinged with triumph.

Maybe, I thought, I was wired differently than most people. It could be due to Granny's indoctrination, of course, and her obsession with the toughness of the Amazons . . . or it could be that I had inherited some genetic condition of hers; perhaps a whole cluster of nerves was simply missing from my brain. It was not the first time I had nursed this suspicion, but it was the first time I had happily embraced the possibility that I was, in some respects, more like my grandmother and less like everyone else.

WE HAD BRUNCH WITH Nick at the Pasiphae Taverna. After a misty morning, the sun was finally peeking out through the haze, and the brightness did much to dispel the remaining night shadows. Clearly, none of us was in a hurry to reopen the subject of my misadventure in the labyrinth; Nick glanced once or twice at my bruise but didn't actually ask me how I felt.

He was dressed in a loose white outfit consisting of a collarless shirt and drawstring trousers, all of which my mother—in her infinite insensitivity to the customs of others—would have been swift to classify as a nice pair of pajamas. I took this as a sign that he was heading back to Algeria or perhaps Dubai on the next plane and knew I should be relieved to see him go.

"So." He looked at me with a knowing smile. "What does the pancake say? I know you've deciphered it."

I hesitated. Out of the corner of my eye I saw Rebecca tensing, but decided the subject was harmless enough that I didn't have to lie. I had indeed spent the early morning deciphering the tablet by the aid of my paper transcript and Granny's notebook, but had found no mention of golden treasures or anything else that the likes of Mr. al-Aqrab could conceivably be after. "It seems to be a treaty," I replied, truthfully, "or at least a proposed treaty, between a queen and—I am guessing—the ruler here at Knossos."

"Do you see any connection between this tablet and the inscription in Algeria—apart from the language?" asked Nick, his eyes locked on mine.

"Possibly." I was a little unnerved by his intensity. "The name of the queen is identical to the name of a priestess mentioned on the temple wall, and the treaty also explicitly describes the enemy as having 'black ships.' I'm not sure what to make of these similarities, except—"

I broke off, aware that the narrative I had nourished in my own mind—a tale of violated women looking for revenge—was too wild, too embarrassingly fanciful.

"All right." Nick studied me with those dark eyes of his—eyes that kept making me feel *I* was the double-dealer, not he. "How did you do it? You deciphered the text in Algeria in five days. And now this. What's the trick?"

I felt a prickle of anxiety. Although I had not made any great effort to hide Granny's notebook from him, I had not exactly made him aware of its importance either. For all Nick knew, I was simply a gifted code breaker who could find patterns and connections where others drew a blank.

"Don't put perfection on the spot!" exclaimed Rebecca, erupting from her chair to ruffle my hair. "She can't help it. She's a decryptomaniac."

Just then, her cellphone rang, and she excused herself to take the call. While she was gone, the waiter returned with our food and I started eating, only too aware of Nick studying me across the table. "What?" I said at last, unable to stand his scrutiny any longer.

But he merely shook his head and kept looking at me. Although the wooden tavern chairs were rather square and rigid, Nick had managed to make himself comfortable—a specialty of his, it seemed. With one arm draped over the back of his own chair and a beach sandal casually up on Rebecca's, he would have looked like a man completely and utterly at ease, had it not been for the speculative expression on his face.

"I'm terribly sorry," said Rebecca, returning to the table in a flurry of nervous energy, "but I have to go. The team leader has something for me, which apparently"—she grimaced and took a quick sip of coffee—"can't wait."

And then she was off, leaving us with heaps of delicious food—all of which suddenly turned my stomach. For despite my good intentions, this little detour to Crete had been an unmitigated disaster. I had a bump on my forehead the size of Sicily, bitter memories of ten thousand dollars lost, a power cord but no laptop, and, without a doubt, back at Oxford, the Larkin lectureship was imploding in my absence. As if that were not enough, I had managed to get myself tangled up with the wrong kind of people—one of whom was presently looking at me with a suspicious squint, apparently forgetting that *he* was the bad guy, not I.

"Curious to know," I eventually said, poking at my scrambled eggs, "whether you ever managed to find someone back at the office who could explain the Amazon connection?"

Nick shifted abruptly in his chair. He still hadn't touched the food—was merely nursing a glass of orange juice. "Remind me of the connection?"

"Well." I felt a little flare-up of irritation. "Evidently *someone* you work with decided you needed me in Algeria—probably the same *someone* who sent Mr. Ludwig to Oxford to woo me with talk of the Amazons. Now, as it turns out, you *did* need me . . . and yet I am left wondering what is so bloody important about those priestesses in the temple. Were they Amazons? If so, how on earth did that idea get into Mr. Ludwig's head in the first place? And while you're at it"—I pointed at the bruise on my temple—"ask your lovely Mr. al-Aqrab why I keep getting hurt!"

We sat in silence for a while, until Nick finally pushed aside his plate as if our conversation required his undivided attention. "That night at the bonfire," he said at last, leaning on the table, "I heard you talk about a legendary hero who stole Medusa's head. You said it reminded you of the goddess Athena, who could have been a North African import. Any further thoughts on that?"

The question threw me off completely. "No, why?"

Nick shrugged. "I'm just trying to solve the mystery. Who were these women . . . where did they go next . . . how did they end up as Amazons in John Ludwig's head? I think it all hangs together. And here is the fun part"—he picked up his fork at last, stabbed a cherry tomato, and pointed it at me—"I think you already know the answer."

I was so astounded I couldn't even think of a snappy retort.

"Help me out here," Nick went on, eating the tomato. "The priestesses left Algeria and sailed to Crete. Where did they go next?" When he saw my speechless incredulity, he held out his arms appealingly, fork and all. "Come on! Give me something to tell the boss. Anything."

"I have absolutely no idea what it is you want—" I began.

Nick shook his head and leaned back on the chair once more. "You've never worked in a big corporation, have you? Corporations can be like governments: All the little drones have a budget to spend. And because you're just managing other people's money"—he reached out and stabbed another tomato—"deep down you really don't give a shit. It's just a job. And all they want to hear at the big meeting is that you've met your quota."

I was so shocked by his prosaic speech, I wasn't immediately able to determine whether he was lying or at last telling the truth. "So, that's what you are?" I asked. "A drone with a travel budget?"

Nick smiled as if he was quite comfortable with the label. "An overworked drone, in fact. Nice to be on vacation." He looked around at the other tavern guests as if he genuinely enjoyed being there. "I've always liked Crete. People are nicer here."

Nicer than where? I wondered. Was this really the man who had yelled at me because I wouldn't touch his sarcophagus and get things moving? The man who had confiscated my cellphone with the manners of a prison guard? What could possibly have turned such a hell-bent workaholic into a slug ready to bullshit his way to a paid holiday? It simply didn't compute. Yes, Nick could be convincing in his role as al-Aqrab's gofer, making a big show of his slipshod attire and cereal-box wristwatch, but this time I wasn't fooled. I had spent enough time with him to see that it was just another disguise and that, underneath it all, there was a savvy manipulator whose sole responsibility—at least lately—seemed to be to keep an eye on *me*.

"Fair enough." I watched him across the table as he finally embarked upon his toast. "You're on vacation. I suppose it's wonderfully relaxing to see other people getting beaten up."

"Yes," said Nick, frowning, "I'm sorry I forced you to go down into the labyrinth all by yourself. How can I make it up to you?" He pretended to think about it, then said, "Here's an idea: You tell me what to write in my report, and I give you a check to cover your losses. Sound good?"

I was sure I had misheard him. "You're offering to give me another ten thousand dollars?"

He nodded. "*And* pay for a new laptop."

It was all I could do not to laugh out loud. "Right. What's the catch?"

"No catch. Just answer my question. Who were the men on the black ships? Where did the priestesses go next?"

I stared at him, trying—as I had so often—to figure out his game. "All right," I said, ignoring the little voice in my head warning me it was all a trap—that somehow, underneath Nick's playful repartee, a bomb was ticking. "You can write in your report that all the arrows point to Greece. The hero Perseus who stole Medusa's head, the goddess Athena"—I counted on my fingers—"but most importantly: the black ships, which we know from Homer. . . . I'm not saying I'm right, but if I am, and if we allow ourselves to believe that the ancient myths contain a core of truth, then the pirates who raided the Temple of the Moon Goddess were Greeks. In ancient times, the Greeks were a power to be reckoned with—an empire, if you will, consisting of many small states, the strongest of which was called Mycenae. Mycenae, of course, was the home of King Agamemnon who, as you know, launched a fleet of a thousand ships and started the Trojan War. Why? Because the Trojans had—rather stupidly I might add—abducted the beautiful Helen of Sparta . . . and since Helen's husband was great King Agamemnon's brother, let's just say it would have behooved Prince Paris of Troy to be slightly more discriminating in his choice of female abductee. Am I earning my ten thousand dollars?"

Nick nodded, not unimpressed. "Close. Where do the Amazons fit in?"

His sudden interest in a topic that had, until recently, seemed to excite few people but me, was too much of a temptation. "Well, according to myth," I went on, only too aware that my fanciful string of speculation would have made most of my academic colleagues roll over in their leather club chairs, "Medusa's killer, Perseus, was held to be the founder of Mycenae, that is, the capital of the Greek empire in Homeric times. In other words, there just might be a long-forgotten historical link between North Africa and Greece. As for the Amazons, legend tells us they were ardent enemies of the Greeks, to the point of siding with the Trojans in the Trojan War."

"I don't remember seeing them there."

"True. Even Hollywood, for all its female superheroes, has never embraced the Amazons. I've often wondered why. Maybe there is a cartel of modern-day Amazons putting the brakes on all such efforts." I glanced at Nick to see his reaction, but he merely frowned.

"Back to the Greeks. Any other links?"

"Well." I felt my pulse speeding up. Perhaps it was my imagination, but it seemed to me his dismissal of the subject of modern-day Amazons was a little too abrupt. "Interestingly enough, one of the highlights of Amazon lore is their attack on Athens—a sore spot for the Greeks ever after. This was what earned the Amazons their place on the famous Parthenon frieze—"

"I think you mean Room Eighteen at the British Museum."

I barely heard him. "Yes, but the thing is, Athens was no more than a flyspeck in Homeric times; if the Amazons had really wanted to make a statement, it would have been Mycenae they attacked."

"The heart of the Greek empire? Why risk it?"

"Good question." I pondered the issue for a moment. "According to the ancient writer Plutarch, among others, the Greeks had abducted the Amazon queen, and her fellow Amazons were determined to free her."

Nick smiled broadly. "See, I knew you already had the answer. Greek pirates raided an Amazon temple in Algeria, and the Amazons raided them right back in what would have been the Athens of the time, namely Mycenae, to free their kidnapped friends. It makes perfect sense."

I burst out laughing. "You should talk to Rebecca's friend, Mr. Telemakhos. He has a house in Mycenae, and he is *also* insane."

Nick nodded. "I like it. Let's go."

"Where?" I stared at him, thinking he was joking. "To Mycenae?"

"Why not?" He looked at his wristwatch. "We can still have you back in Oxford by tomorrow morning. With your ten thousand dollars. What do you say?"

It didn't take me long to find Rebecca; she was lying across her bed, face buried in a pillow. "Bex!" I exclaimed, rushing to her side, "What's wrong?"

"Everything," she muttered, her voice distorted behind the pillow. "Are you alone?" When I assured her that I was, she lifted her head, and I was shocked to see her expression; never before had I seen such unmasked hatred in her face. "Worthless prick," she sneered, at some specter visible only to her. "I should have told him exactly what I think of him."

The team leader, she went on to explain, had summoned her to his office under the pretext of having something to show her. That something, it turned out, was the shoe I had lost during the attack in the labyrinth. There it was, sitting on his desk, while he himself sat in his swivel chair, beaming with triumph. "And when I said it wasn't mine," Rebecca went on, still hugging the pillow and refusing the glass of water I held out to her, "what do you think he did, the slimer? He took out the keys you forgot in the door lock and dangled them in the air."

"Oh, Bex!" I felt jabs of pain on her behalf, "I'm so sorry—"

"Don't be!" Rebecca's mellifluous voice had temporarily morphed into a crusty growl. "He was just waiting for an excuse to get rid of me. He can't stand the fact that I know more about this place than he does."

"Did he actually . . . fire you?"

She finally boxed away the pillow and took the glass of water. "More or less. He told me to take two weeks off to think things through, or, translated into modern English: Go find myself another job."

"This is awful." I tried to put my arms around her, but she wouldn't let me.

"What happened to you?" she asked instead, her voice understandably terse. "You look positively radiant."

I shook my head. "I think you mean furious. Nick wants to replace the ten thousand dollars I lost—"

"Why, excellent!" Rebecca was too upset to hear me out. "We'll fly to Milan and blow it all on shoes. Okay?" The way she looked at me suggested that, despite her assurance of the opposite, she still largely blamed me for the mess she was in.

"There is a snag," I pointed out. "Nick wants to meet Mr. Telemakhos. He isn't going to pay me unless I take him to Mycenae."

Rebecca's eyes narrowed, and I could almost see the wheels turning in her head. "Interesting."

"Don't even think about it," I said. "I'm not traveling another mile with that man. And I don't give a damn about the money. I'm going home."

In response, Rebecca rose from the bed and walked over to put the kettle on. "I wonder what your grandmother would say to that." She slammed the fridge and pulled the cap off the milk bottle with an angry gesture. "I thought this was about finding *her*. Didn't you say you could feel her pulling at you in a way you couldn't explain?"

"Yes, but—"

"And what about the theory that it was all a summons . . . Mr. Ludwig, the photo, the inscription . . . and that maybe, somewhere out there, she is waiting for you?" Rebecca looked at me as if I had betrayed both her and Granny in one fell swoop.

I stood up at last, my battered knees aching. "What do you want me to do?"

Rebecca came over with the tray and handed it to me. "I want you to be the Amazon I know you are. I didn't lose my job so you could weasel out like this. Sugar Daddy wants to go to Mycenae? Fine, I'll take you there, first-class." She went back to check the kettle, her gestures more gentle now. "And you're finally going to meet Mr. Telemakhos, whether you want to or not."

I put down the tray on a footstool, struggling to come up with an objection that wouldn't upset Rebecca further. "You don't have to do this—"

"I think you're forgetting," she countered, "that the Aqrab Foundation funds digs all over the world." She tried to make a sly face, but came up a little short. "Maybe I can persuade Nick to give me a new job—"

"No!" I shook my head vigorously. "No-no-no—"

"Why not?" She looked me up and down, a spark of resentment returning to her eyes. "Why can *you* work for them, but not me? Where do they dig? How many archaeologists do they employ?"

I sighed. "No idea. I've been meaning to Google them—"

"What?" She glared at me. "You haven't even looked them up? You're traveling around with this man, escaping explosions and getting yourself beaten up . . . without even knowing the *facts*?" She shook her head in dismay, not allowing me to defend myself. "You may rest assured, my dear Miss Morgan, all that is about to change."

IT TOOK ME A while to work up the mettle to call James. Half-expecting him to be at some charity luncheon with his phone turned off and a tiaraed dowager leaning on his arm, I was somewhat startled when he picked up right away. I heard a splash of water, then, "Morg! It's about time." His voice sounded deeper than usual.

"Maybe this is not a good time," I began, losing my nerve.

There was another splashing sound. "Don't hang up! Let me just turn this off." I listened with astonishment as James interrupted what could only be a shower in order to talk with me. "Are you still there?" He sounded genuinely concerned. "What's going on, Morg?"

I quickly drew up the situation, leaving out every detail that might alarm him. The result was a short account, concluding with a promise to return to Oxford in the next day or so. "The thing is," I concluded, finally getting around to the reason for my call, "I have a class tomorrow afternoon—introduction to Sanskrit—and I was wondering if I could persuade you to step in and give your Assyrian Empire lecture instead?"

There was a brief, rather unpleasant silence. Then James cleared his throat and said, "Anything for you. Just promise me one thing. What-ever happens, please don't let these people get into your head."

I was so surprised, I started laughing. "You're worried about my *head*?"

There were no sounds to suggest James shared my amusement. "You're an intelligent girl, Morg. If they can get into your head, they can get in anywhere. Watch out for Kamal . . . he's a bad egg."

"Who?"

"Kamal . . . or Karim, or whatever you said his name was."

"You mean Nick?"

"Yes. The bloke who does al-Aqrab's dirty work. Don't give him an inch."

I was briefly back in the collapsing temple, feeling Nick straining to pull me up into safety. "Don't worry," I said, "I'm practically on my way home."

"That's what you said in Algeria," James pointed out. "You'd better have a bloody good explanation ready for the old hellcat."

My spine froze in place, like an icicle. "I see."

After the call had ended, I remained seated on Rebecca's bed for a while. I simply couldn't move. Something was wrong. Never mind the fact that I was getting increasingly unpopular at home. I was absolutely positive I had never revealed to James—or Katherine Kent, for that matter—that my mystery destination had been Algeria.

CHAPTER TWENTY-ONE

ISLAND OF CRETE

Myrina pulled back in terror at the grisly scene. She knew religion could take many forms, but had never before seen worship in the form of human slaughter. Nor had it even occurred to her that the temple sister she sought had already met such a gruesome end.

"Out," croaked Paris, holding up his arms to prevent the others from proceeding any further. "I never saw such a cursed place on earth."

But their retreat was blocked by the advent of a priestess—at least Myrina guessed she was a priestess from her naked breasts and rich jewelry. Her face contorted with incredulous rage, the woman picked up an ax from one of the slaughter tables and began swinging it at random, narrowly missing Aeneas.

"Filthy, disgusting demon!" sneered Paris, reaching for his dagger. In one smooth, effortless movement the weapon was out of his belt and lodged in the chest of the priestess, who fell against the wall and onto the floor with a piercing wail, her wide-open eyes as ghoulish in death as they had been when she was still alive.

"Quickly!" Paris waved them all toward the stairs. "Others may come."

And they did. Alarmed by the commotion, two other priestesses emerged from a door in the wall—a door Myrina had not even noticed. As soon as they saw the priestess's dead body they fell to the floor, pleading for their lives.

So shrill were their entreaties the Trojans did not even apprehend the bustle behind them. Only Myrina, still immovable with shock, saw the approach of the monster that seemed to have been conjured out of nowhere—from some dark niche behind the main altar. Too tall and wide for normal, human proportions, and made even more beastly by his horned headpiece, this ogre of a man rushed forward with a long spear aimed at Paris's back.

Roused from her petrifaction, Myrina acted instinctively. Deprived of any weapons of her own, she swooped down to claim the double ax that had slipped from the hands of the dead priestess, flinging it with all her strength at the monster.

Thrown with power and precision, the deadly blade lodged itself in his throat, cutting short his round-eyed surprise at having been struck down so easily. Only when his giant corpse dropped to the floor with a heavy thud, throwing up a cloud of dust, did the Trojans spin around to see what had happened behind them.

Myrina was too busy wresting the ax from the neck of her foe to see the expression on Paris's face as he realized she had saved his life. But once she looked up and met his eyes, it occurred to her as well.

"Let's get out of here," said Aeneas, his voice thick with revulsion. "What about those two?" He nodded at the priestesses cowering on the floor, their prayers even more shrill than before.

"Kill them," said Paris, holding out a hand to Myrina and starting toward the stairs. "Kill them as they deserve: like animals."

THE RIDE BACK TO the harbor was a blur to Myrina.

Much to Paris's relief, they returned to the Minos's palace courtyard just as another delegation was arriving, and the royal heralds were too preoccupied to notice the Trojans' emergence from the sanctuary.

Dismissing the litter that had transported her earlier, Paris lifted Myrina up onto his own horse and enfolded her in his cape, even as, all the while, she held firmly to her ax. Moments later, they were safely away from the courtyard and riding apace through the city streets—

downhill this time, toward the sea. It did not even occur to Myrina that this was what she had resisted before: riding on Paris's horse. All she felt was a choking grief at the wickedness of what she had just seen, and a nauseating fury at the Minos, who could receive visitors with the utmost eloquence upstairs while sanctioning heinous acts of cannibalism in the basement.

At the Eastern Harbor, Myrina dismounted the horse with Paris's help and took a few steps toward the gangplank . . . but could not continue. "How can I possibly tell my sisters what I have witnessed?" she whispered, more to herself than to him. "The evil of it all—"

"Come." Paris pried the double ax from her hands and pulled her away from the pier and down to the beach where they had first met. "Let us wash the blood from your face first or you will most certainly make them swoon." Without stopping to disrobe, he pulled her into the surf by the hand, wading out until the skirts rose up around Myrina's waist like petals of a flower. "There," he said, wiping her face with one of them. "It will not do to have a queen carry the bloody mark of a hunter."

Myrina met his eyes. "But that is what I am: a hunter."

Paris took her by the chin and looked her sternly in the eye. "You saved my life. By human calculations, that makes you a noblewoman. And the gods, I am sure, have long ago appointed you a queen." He paused, his eyes dropping briefly to her lips. "As have I."

She pulled away from him. "You would be wise to return me to the gutter where you found me. I may have saved your life, but do not forget that it was also I who put us in peril. And now the Minos will surely be your enemy." She sighed and shook her head. "You are too kind, and I am unused to it. For your own sake, do not stroke my misery. It knows not how to respond, but with a vicious bite."

"Wait." He gripped her wrist. "I have been meaning to ask you." Drawing her closer to him in the water, he spun her around and pulled the dress from her shoulders.

Gasping with indignation, Myrina clutched the garment against her chest. "What are you—" she began, but was silenced by his fingers, touching the old wound on her back.

"This worries me." Paris pressed the skin here and there to assess the damage. "Why did you not tell me?"

Myrina freed herself, pulling awkwardly at the dress to drape it over her shoulders once more. "Because it is nothing. And it is healing—"

"I'm afraid it isn't." Paris began wading ashore. "As soon as we are at sea, I will take a better look."

"At sea?"

He stopped and turned, a crooked smile on his face. "Unless you would prefer to spend the night with the Minos? I expect his invitation shortly."

NONE OF THE WOMEN protested when they saw the Trojans preparing the ships for departure and learned that they had no choice but to stay on board. Even if their futures were still uncertain, Myrina knew her sisters were secretly relieved to leave the hardships of the old fishing boat behind.

Once they were away from land, the large sails filling with a rising wind, she gathered them all around her on deck and explained in greater detail the reason for their hasty departure. As suspected, the account of her terrible discovery at the palace of the Minos put them all in such a state of grief and despair they could barely tolerate hearing the words.

"Could you see . . . who it was?" asked Animone at last, her hands still pressed to her mouth with shock.

"I think it was Neeta," whispered Myrina, her eyes closed against the vision of the numerous severed heads. "But I am not sure."

Neeta had been a quiet girl, had rarely drawn attention; never had her sisters bestowed as much love and attention on her as they did tonight, sitting on the deck underneath an indifferent moon, remembering her sweetness.

"She attended to her duties without complaint," whispered Pitana, staring away into her own memories. "Never broke the rules."

Being as she was the oldest, Kyme tried to remain calm throughout these remembrances. "Above all," she said, shaking her head sadly,

"Neeta showed us there can be as much virtue in the things we do *not* do as in those we do."

The women were silent for a while, wiping away tears that wouldn't stop coming. Then Egee, who unlike Neeta could find a point of contention in any situation, said to Myrina, "I still don't understand why we could not stop to give her a proper funeral. *You* may take delight in breaking the rules, but *I* say there are still rules worth observing. And now we are going to Troy"—her voice turned more bitter still—"that is, I am assuming we are going to Troy?"

"Here is a new rule for you," said Myrina, getting up before she lost her temper. "Assume nothing. As for our destination, I am as ignorant as you and not the conniving tyrant you want me to be. You are here, as are we all, because we have no better place to be."

Later that night, Myrina found Paris alone in the bow of the ship, looking out over the wine-dark sea and the stars above. "Is the map of heaven different where you come from?" he asked.

Myrina looked up at the sky she knew well. "No. I suppose our stars follow us wherever we go."

"That one"—Paris pointed out a constellation—"is named after you. We call it 'the Hunter.'" He looked at her teasingly. "What is your name for it?"

Myrina leaned forward to rest her elbows on the ship's railing. "My mother called it 'the Three Sisters.' She said they were three sisters in love with the same man, and who asked him to judge which one of them was the most beautiful. The result was war and destruction." She glanced at Paris. "My mother was convinced the stars were remnants of a previous world, left in the sky as a warning."

Paris's arm came to rest right next to hers. "A warning against what?"

Myrina straightened, pulling back her shoulders to stop the pain still throbbing in her back. "Stay away from sisters." She gave him a sideways glance. "Especially the holy ones."

Paris turned around, leaning against the railing to see her better. "How holy are you exactly? Clearly not too holy to handle a weapon like a warrior. Tell me, what else do you handle?"

Myrina tried to end the conversation with a glare, but the darkness swallowed her intention.

"Come." Paris took her firmly by the hand. "I want to look at your wound."

"Wait!" Myrina tried to slow her steps, but found herself dragged below deck, through a narrow space filled with men asleep in gently swinging hammocks. Not until they reached a storage space at the stern of the hull did she dare protest in more than a whisper. "Surely," she said, watching him as he lit a lamp, "tending wounds is not the job of a prince."

Paris turned toward her, his face perfectly sincere. "Do you really think I will let anyone else touch my queen? Now, take that off." He motioned at her snakeskin tunic.

When she did not move, he shook his head and came forward. "Must I really do it for you?"

"No!" Myrina backed up, but got no further than to a wall of wooden barrels. "You call me a queen, but treat me like a whore. Is that why you are taking me to Troy? To work your lust on me?"

Even in the poor light, she saw the mortification on Paris's face. "Please," he said, his voice thick with defeat, "rest your ax, woman. I did not mean to insult you. I——" he ran both hands through his hair, as if trying to rouse himself from a hallucination. "I only seek to care for you."

Myrina pressed a hand against her forehead, regretting her outcry. "I beg your forgiveness. You have been noble in every way. Recent events have convinced me that foreign men cause nothing but pain and grief"—she looked his way, grateful for the shadows obscuring his face—"but you are already teaching me otherwise. If all Trojans are as good as you, Troy must be a blessed place for men and women alike. I cannot wait to see it."

Paris smiled at last. "Then it is my unpleasant duty to disappoint you, for we are not going to Troy. How could we? We are going to Mycenae to see if we can rescue your sisters. Now turn and let me see what is to be done with the wound. Fear not that my aim is pleasure; this will sting soon enough."

. . .

SEEN FROM THE SEA, the land of the Greeks was not unlike the island of Crete; alluring to the eye, but deadly to the careless sailor. The knowledge that this coastline—these proud and verdant hills, these soft and happy coves—had borne a race of brutes bent on destruction was enough to make Myrina and her sisters recoil from its beauty, muttering to one another that their green marsh at home, for all its slithering snakes, was superior in every way.

"Behind those hills," said Aeneas, pointing as they sailed by, "lies Sparta, the most ruthless city of them all. The men there are bred for strife and know no greater pleasure than to run their spears into the flesh of living things. Their king is the blood brother of the man we are to visit; they have an unbreakable alliance and are feared throughout these regions and beyond."

Myrina's sisters looked at the coast in silence, imagining what they could not see. Then Animone, who had never ceased to apologize for their presence, or to thank the Trojans for their kindness, said to Aeneas, "Would you even come this way, up this hostile coast, if not for us?"

He shrugged. "The Greeks won't bother us. They cannot afford to make an enemy of our King Priam."

Animone glanced at Myrina but said no more. When it had become clear to the women there was a continuous, pulsing flow of admiration between their leader and Prince Paris, Animone had wasted no opportunity to remind Myrina of her vows and responsibilities. "You may feel kindness toward this man," she said, after seeing a long look exchanged between the two, "and I cannot blame you, for he is as able a fellow as I ever saw. But remember the pact you made with the Moon Goddess. Wherever she is, you may be sure she is still watching you. So, if you truly like Paris, leave him be." Animone touched Myrina's bracelet. "Remember, the jackal is a jealous mistress."

But Animone needn't remind Myrina of the danger; she was all too aware. Due to unfavorable winds, the journey, which should have taken three days, had taken thrice that long. Trapped in this timeless whirl, Myrina found herself sucked into Paris's charms further and further, to a point where she had almost no strength left to kick against the current. Every night, under pretext of tending to her healing wound, his hand would linger on her back a little longer, his breath would come a little closer. . . . Were it not for Animone, thanking him profusely before whisking Myrina away, some touch or sound would surely have passed between them that no words could undo.

As she lay among her sisters on the floor of the dining space at night, rolling and tossing on the waves of her own thoughts, Myrina felt the jackal's jealous fury very keenly. And because she was determined not to pass any of its demonic bile to the man who had been so kind to her, she spent all day avoiding him, bravely suffering on her own.

But Paris, always on deck, always alert, looked as if the poison had found him all the same. His gaze sought Myrina wherever she was, drinking in the sight of her, and his thirst grew worse for every day he kept mistaking the contagion for a cure.

When the three Trojan ships arrived at the Bay of Argos at last, Myrina almost felt there was greater danger lurking on board than could possibly be awaiting them ashore. First to volunteer, she was outraged when Paris would not let her leave the ship, and stood glumly at the railing while he and his most trusted men rowed off to gather information about the harbor.

"But don't you see it would be disastrous if anyone recognized us?" said Animone, standing next to her.

"Maybe." Myrina followed the rowboat with her eyes as far as she could. "Maybe not. I still do not know what Paris's plan is."

As a matter of fact, she was not even sure Paris *had* a plan for their visit to Mycenae. Nor had he made her any promises. "First of all, we must determine if your sisters really are here at the palace," he had said to her before leaving.

But when the men returned from their scouting trip, Myrina saw right away that Paris had news for her. "The Minos did not deceive us," he said, drawing her aside. "King Agamemnon's son has just returned from a journey, and there is much talk of a black goddess to be gifted to a chieftain up the coast. We will move the ships to the harbor, for to-night we dine at court. And yes, you may come"——Paris held up a hand to delay Myrina's raptures——"but this time, you will not be wearing my crown. You will be my slave, and believe me: I shall enjoy ordering you around."

THE ROYAL COURT AT Mycenae was situated inland, some miles from the harbor town of Argos. Between Argos and Mycenae lay a vast and open plain, ringed by protective hills and farmed in long, narrow strips. Now faded and dormant for the winter, the landscape gave every promise of summer ripeness, and Myrina found the contrast between this place and the scorched salt plains of her childhood so staggering she barely knew where to rest her eyes.

"You would like it here," said Paris, looking at her over his shoulder. He sat just in front of her on his giant horse and seemed more preoc-cupied with her reaction to their surroundings than with the road ahead. "It is full of hunters and farmers and boisterous talk. Perhaps not as refined as the world you once knew, but I suspect you would feel right at home."

Myrina merely smiled behind her head scarf, shifting her hands once again to touch him as little as possible as the beast below jostled her. She had resisted the scheme of sitting behind Paris, sharing his saddle, knowing she would enjoy the closeness more than she ought, but had eventually surrendered to common sense.

"To walk will take hours," Paris had told her. "If you want to ac-company me, it will be on my horse's back. And your sisters"——he had nodded at Animone, Egee, and Pitana, who insisted on coming, too——"must suffer a similar indignity." Smiling at her nervousness, he had dared her anyway. "You decide."

Agamemnon's royal residence was perched on a hillside above the Argos Plain, with the small but prosperous town of Mycenae kneeling at its feet. Heavy walls protected town and citadel alike, and in spite of a steady stream of traffic going in and out of the central gate, there was a general atmosphere of fear and suspicion.

As the road grew steeper, Myrina felt her blood rushing ahead with anxious anticipation. Glancing at Animone, sitting behind Aeneas, she suspected her friend was equally filled with fears and misgivings, for she became more and more silent as they approached the gate to the citadel. Although only a sliver of Animone's eyes was visible behind the head scarf, that glimpse was enough to convince Myrina her thoughts were not merely for the women they were hoping to find at King Agamemnon's court. Animone was also thinking about the men they might recognize—the demons who had crushed their idyllic life in the temple, and who had surely never imagined that the evil shadow they had cast abroad would follow them home.

The royal residences at Mycenae were a rambling complex of buildings that had grown over time, not according to a master plan, but heeding the fancies and conveniences of subsequent dwellers. Where the palace of the Minos had been an elegant, angular place, there was something more organic about the court in Mycenae. To a bird flying in the sky, Myrina could not help thinking, it must all resemble a random cluster of white mushrooms sprouting from a putrescent source of nourishment in the ground.

Everywhere she looked she saw yet another set of steps or a covered alley leading away; the place was utterly disorienting. The Trojans, however, did not dally in confusion when they finally arrived at the upper terrace of the citadel. Both Paris and Aeneas knew their way around, for they had visited King Agamemnon several times before, to mend and strengthen the diplomatic ties between Mycenae and Troy. Leaving the horses with Pitana and Egee as agreed, they continued up a wide staircase to the central courtyard with Paris in front and his slaves Myrina and Animone at the rear, necks bent in submission.

Across the courtyard was the entrance to the throne room—a wide door set behind a portico and guarded by four strapping men with spears. Despite her promise to be discreet, Myrina could not help scrutinizing the guards as she walked past them into the building. Although they resembled the temple raiders in stature, nothing about the four struck her as particularly familiar.

"Slave." Paris paused on the threshold to address Myrina under his breath. "Know yourself. And control yourself."

Then a herald came forward to greet them, with ardent bows and hands nervously clasped, and they finally stepped into the room the Trojans had gravely referred to earlier as "the lion's cave." For here sat the bearded king of Mycenae upon his throne, sometimes hungry for blood, sometimes not. He was ever surrounded by men who would do anything—kill anyone—to please their master. To the visitors who came to see him, regardless of their errand, Agamemnon and his cronies truly were like a pride of lions; no one bold or foolhardy enough to enter their cave could be sure to leave alive.

The royal throne was hardly more than a chair among others; the king of Mycenae needed neither pomp nor elevation to be formidable. All the seats in the room, Agamemnon's included, encircled a fire pit large enough to hold an entire ox, and this was precisely what was turning on a spit over the flames—a blackened bull with the horns still attached.

"Paris!" exclaimed Agamemnon, raising his chalice in a friendly greeting. Whatever he said next, however, Myrina did not understand, nor could she follow Paris's elaborate response. It was all in the language she had heard only once before, during a night and morning of unspeakable horror. The cadence of it, to her ears, was the most hideous sound in the world.

Sitting on a bench cushioned with woven wool, Paris motioned for his men to sit beside him—all except Aeneas, who settled down with Myrina and Animone on the stone floor behind the couch, in order to be able to whisper translations whenever he thought the conversation worthwhile.

In the beginning, little more was exchanged than polite remarks and harmless inquiries. Myrina looked discreetly around the room, trying to make out the faces of the men gathered around the king's fire. Many were as old and gray as he, but a few struck her as painfully familiar. More often than not, after nervously following the line of Myrina's stare, Animone would bend her head and nod with heavy certainty.

By the time meat and wine were carried around, Myrina was reasonably sure at least four of the fifteen Greeks in the throne room had been part of the raid on the Temple of the Moon Goddess. She remembered their faces and gestures from the beach, where they had argued about the loot and scuffled over the priestesses. When she saw Animone wincing at the entrance of yet another man, entering the hall from a back room, she instinctively knew her friend remembered more than just his ignoble face.

"Now they speak of your country," whispered Aeneas, leaning toward Myrina. "My master asked the king whether he has seen any evidence of the rumored drought with his own eyes, and the king says his son just returned from Lake Tritonis. He says that because of low water they had to drag the ships overland to return to the sea. He calls it a region of monstrous serpents and ugly witches." Aeneas fell silent for a while, his eyes brimming with embarrassment. And on the couch in front of them, Myrina saw Paris stiffen as he listened to Agamemnon's tale.

"What is he saying?" she urged Aeneas.

The Trojan hesitated. "He says the women of the region are stubborn and haughty. He is shaking his head at his son, the prince, for bringing home so many of them." Aeneas nodded at the fire pit. "The prince sits right over there. Can you see him? Maybe, if you lean over a bit."

When Myrina moved forward to espy Agamemnon's son on the other side of the fire pit, she saw a face she would never forget: that of the man who had butchered the High Priestess and held up her severed head in triumph.

"Now my master says the king's tale has made him curious," Aeneas went on. "He is asking if he may see for himself one of these strange women. And the king—" But Aeneas did not need to interpret further. Agamemnon snapped his fingers, and a hunched servant galloped away only to return almost immediately with a young woman in a white dress.

Myrina recognized her from her gait alone. Fumbling and uncertain, the girl clung to the arm of the servant, depending on him to lead her through the unfamiliar room. The sight made Myrina flinch with pain and relief all at once, for the girl was Lilli.

CHAPTER TWENTY-TWO

O king, my king
how shall I weep for you?
What can I say out of my heart of pity?
Caught in this spider's web you lie,
your life gasped out in indecent death,
struck prone to this shameful bed
by your lady's hand of treachery.
—AESCHYLUS, *Agamemnon*

KNOSSOS, CRETE

POPPING BY MYCENAE TO HAVE A QUICK CHAT WITH MR. TELEMAK-
hos did not turn out to be quite the first-class experience Rebecca
had promised. No sooner had I agreed to go than my friend disappeared
for the better part of an hour; when she came back she was dressed in a
nifty little flight jacket and a tight leather helmet with goggles.

"You didn't think I would do it, did you?" she grinned, referring to
one of our many late-night discussions about the pros and cons of flying
one's own airplane. "Well, I finally got my pilot's license. Or rather, I
am getting one as soon as Stavros gets his printer fixed."

"That's tremendous news, Bex," I said, foreboding gnawing at my
imagination. "I hope you're not planning to actually take off somewhere."

"Absolutely!" She ushered me outside and locked the door behind
us. "It's really the only way to go, in my opinion. You can fly directly
from dig to dig and never have to deal with the modern world at all."

After we had picked up Nick, I saw what she meant. In her van, Rebecca took us on a short, bumpy ride down a gravel road, at the end of which stood a derelict hangar with three propeller planes parked outside. Two looked airworthy; the third struck me as something that belonged in a museum, with a DO NOT TOUCH sign hanging from one wing.

"I rent it through Stavros," explained Rebecca, parking the van next to the hangar. "It needs a little love"—she nodded at the dilapidated plane—"but the price is right."

"Who is this Stavros?" I asked, still too shaken to think straight. "And why is he trying to kill you?"

But Rebecca had already jumped from the van, leaving the door wide open. Nick followed her without a word of protest. So, there I sat, alone with my misgivings, asking myself how an impulsive flight with a doomed airplane could possibly bring me closer to Granny. What spurred me on was the knowledge that I still had unfinished business with Nick. Never mind the money he was going to repay me, which I was determined to split with Rebecca—no, it was my conviction that somewhere in an office in Dubai sat a top-secret folder with the answers to all my Amazon questions.

Rebecca and I had spent a good half hour on her computer earlier that day, looking for information about the Aqrab Foundation. What little we found was enough to fuel my fears and confirm what James had already told me. Violence, shootings, lawsuits . . . the Aqrab approach to archaeology ran counter to everything I had ever held dear in the world of ancient studies. Nowhere did I see a celebration of the beauty and poetry of the past; instead, it was all about money and ownership.

Rebecca and I were so addled by our findings we nearly missed the—for me at least—most relevant news item. Not only had the Aqrab Foundation been suing British museums for years, claiming these had knowingly purchased looted artifacts from the Middle East, but the Moselane Manor Collection had recently joined the list of targets in a veritable blitz of what sounded to me like truly far-fetched accusations.

I now understood why James had warned me, just a few hours earlier, not to let Nick and his ilk "get into my head."

The discovery had added considerably to my already confused state. Had I somehow become an unwitting Ping-Pong ball bouncing back and forth between al-Aqrab and Lord Moselane? Was that why James had taken such an interest in my whereabouts, to the point of tracing Nick's phone and ascertaining that I was in Algeria? I barely knew what to think.

"Hello? Earth to Bronze Age." Rebecca cut short my unhappy reflections by sticking her head into the van. "The Oracle is waiting. And yes, you may die, but at least you will be a martyr for friendship."

FOR ALL ITS VIRTUES—GETTING off the ground and actually flying being the most significant—Stavros's eight-passenger wonder was alarmingly shaky, and the uneven clamor of its engine was absolutely hellish. "It's because he gutted it!" Rebecca yelled when we were aloft at last, her voice nearly drowned out by the roar and rattle of the claptrap plane. "It'll get better when we reach cruising altitude."

"Speaking of cruising altitude," I yelled back, hugging my life vest, "are you not supposed to be in radio contact with some . . . authority?"

"I don't see why we should." Rebecca checked her instruments, seemingly in control. "We're literally flying under the radar. And in the off chance we meet another plane, there are basic rules. It's all wonderfully straightforward."

Nick was understandably laconic during the flight, and yet gave the impression of being at ease. He had taken the seat right behind Rebecca but didn't speak to her at all; he merely observed what she was doing and occasionally glanced out the windows. But then, if I were to believe what I had just read on the Internet, even a rickety plane flown by an amateur would be a safer environment than what Nick was accustomed to as an operative for al-Aqrab. Perhaps, I thought, studying him as I had so often, with reluctant curiosity, he had not even been lying when he said he needed a vacation.

By the time we finally landed on the Argos Plain, only my respect for Rebecca's dignity prevented me from kissing the ground. I was still light-headed when we were picked up by Mr. Telemakhos, and it didn't help that part of me remained hesitant to meet this eccentric man. For the past three years I had dodged Rebecca's attempts to introduce the two of us, hoping the man she had nicknamed "the Oracle" would eventually get the hint. But clearly, despite my best efforts, Fate was determined to have us meet.

"Welcome to Mycenae, barbarians!" boomed Mr. Telemakhos, slamming the door to his rusty convertible. He was a sunbaked, bald-headed hulk of a man, whose natural authority was not the least bit compromised by his open, tie-dyed shirt or the golden necklace meandering through his jungle of white chest hair. "My little Hermes." He waited for Rebecca to come to him before embracing her. "What did you bring me today?" But before she could reply, he cast me a look of triumph and said, "Diana Morgan. Here at last."

I opened my mouth to say something suitably conciliatory, but there was no need. Mr. Telemakhos had already moved on to Nick, a wide smile of recognition spreading across his face. "You're back!"

Both Rebecca and I were stunned; Nick looked positively gob-smacked. "I've never been here before——" he began.

"Yes, you have!" insisted Mr. Telemakhos, frowning now. "You came here to ask me questions, and we talked all night. Don't you remember?"

Obsessed with the memory and determined to be right, Mr. Telemakhos drove us directly back to his home: a fieldstone bungalow on a gravelly hillside, facing the ruins of ancient Mycenae. Muttering to himself in Greek, he went ahead of us into the living room and then returned, almost immediately, carrying with him a large scrapbook. "Aha!" He set down the book on the kitchen counter atop a cutting board with bread crumbs. "Now, let's see."

Beginning at the end, Mr. Telemakhos worked his way backward through the hefty volume, scrutinizing its every photo and caption. The further he got, the more impatient he became. "I know I'm right!" he insisted. "It's right here somewhere."

When he finally found what he was looking for, however, his delight deflated. The photo was thirty years old. Furthermore, despite the washed-out colors, it was evident that the young man pictured in it bore only a vague resemblance to Nick. He was handsome, certainly, but his features were darker, his expression more remote. "Chris Hauser," said Mr. Telemakhos, poring over the handwritten caption. "From Baltimore. Do you know him?"

Nick shook his head but looked uncomfortable. I couldn't blame him. It would seem he had risked his life flying with Rebecca for an appointment with a madman—not to mention the ten grand he owed me. I couldn't help thinking it was all beginning to add up and turn red . . . even to someone working for a billionaire.

Soon thereafter, Nick slipped outside to make his usual dozen phone calls. Half an hour or so later, when his absence was becoming tiresome, I went in search of him and found him behind the garage, striding around through the tall weeds with his shirt open. "Don't even whisper it to the grass," I heard him mutter into the phone. "That's totally off the record."

I backed up a bit, hoping he hadn't seen me. Standing just around the corner, I heard his next words with gut-wrenching clarity: "Well, apparently it's real. People have been looking for it for three thousand years. The experts I'm working with are confident we're on the right track." And then, a moment later, "That I can't tell you. But they say it's bigger than anything we've ever found before. They refer to it as 'the Amazon Hoard.' "

Almost sick to my stomach with shock and confusion, I leaned against the crumbling wall, anxious to hear more. But that was it. After a few added pleasantries, Nick hung up and made another call, this time in Arabic.

I returned to the house in a state of helpless rage. How many times had he lied to me now? When I told him about the ancient *Historia Amazonum* manuscript in the car leaving Algeria, I could have sworn he had never heard about the Amazon Hoard before. He knew about the Istanbul collector, Grigor Reznik, yes, but not about the treasure. That was two days ago. Either he had brilliantly concealed the fact that he already *did* know, or something extraordinary had happened between then and now. But what?

CONVINCED MY SUDDEN MALAISE had been caused by hunger, Mr. Tele-makhos rushed us all to an early dinner at a restaurant down the road, called King Menelaos. It was run by a distant but friendly cousin, and Mr. Telemakhos maintained his own exclusive table on the patio, piled high with newspapers and discarded lottery coupons to discourage tourists or anyone else from sitting down just there.

Hair sprouting as vigorously from his open shirt as it must once have done from his head, Mr. Telemakhos insisted on ordering for us, claiming he knew precisely what we needed. "A young man like you," he said, patting Nick on the shoulder with nostalgic camaraderie, "must eat meat. Remember that. Lots of meat. Otherwise"—he leaned closer to impart his wisdom behind a folded-up newspaper—"you won't have the energy to keep the ladies happy. Eh?" He chuckled at their secret understanding, then added, more gravely, "That's what happened to Menelaos. He didn't eat his meat, and couldn't hold on to his woman." Mr. Telemakhos sighed and shook his head, reaching out for his ouzo glass. "It happens to the best of us."

"His wife was the beautiful Helen," interjected Rebecca, mostly to Nick, "who ran away with the carnivorous Paris and started the Trojan War." She smiled, anxious to maintain the merry tone. Mr. Telemak-hos was recently divorced, she had told us earlier, and desperately needed some cheering up.

"A toast to Menelaos"—our host held out his glass—"who didn't realize what he had until she was gone. Helen, that two-timing bitch."

"To the vegetarian," said Nick, raising his own glass, "who launched a thousand ships."

I glanced at him, amazed at his cool. Here he was, after just jam-ming a knife into my back, looking as if he didn't have a care in the world. If the beautiful Helen had been a two-timing bitch, what was the number on Nick?

"And this," Rebecca went on, passing him a bowl of caper berries, "as you have already guessed, is where Menelaos launched them from. Big brother Agamemnon's pad—the bedrock of Greek power in the Heroic Age."

"Heroic! Pffff." Mr. Telemakhos batted away the word as if it were an annoying fly. "Man will be man; kill first and explain later. That is why we have this big brain, you see." He clutched his head as if he meant to pull it right off. "It is so we can sit around and tell nice stories afterward. Homer was good at that."

"Apparently," interjected Rebecca, who had clearly heard the rant before, "the beautiful Helen never existed. She was a plot device, meant to shine a romantic light on the destruction of Troy."

"Sorry to slow things down," said Nick, leaning back on the chair as far as humanly possible, "but where exactly *was* Troy?"

I groaned inwardly. Was this more of his act? Rebecca, however, was only too happy to plunge into one of the greatest archaeological questions of all times. "Even to this day," she told Nick, "after decades of excavations at Hisarlik, some of my colleagues are still not convinced we have the answer."

"Hisarlik is in Turkey," I added, "on the northwest coast of Anatolia, right where the Aegean Sea meets the Sea of Marmara." I pointed over my shoulder. "Basically over there. Four days by boat in Homer's day."

"And that was precisely the problem." Rebecca leaned forward to reclaim her narrative. "Location, location, location. Troy was prime real estate for anyone who wanted to dominate the Aegean Sea."

"The Trojan War was never personal," Mr. Telemakhos chimed in, looking as concerned as if he were personally to blame for what had happened back then. "We, the Greeks, were building a commercial empire, and Troy was in the way." He stabbed a few slices of sausage and transferred them to his plate. "Call it what you want, but don't call us heroes."

After dinner we took a moonlit stroll through the Mycenaean ruins, marveling at the masonry on this seemingly remote hillside. The contrast between these massive walls and the completely unfortified Knossos palace in Crete was striking. It was hard to believe the two civilizations had been so close both in time and space.

"The Greeks took control of Crete sometime around 1450 B.C.E.," said Rebecca. "Traditionally, the Knossos palace was thought to have been devastated by fire only half a century later, but there has been intense debate over the dating of this fire, and *some* people"—her raised eyebrows suggested she was one of those people—"are ready to swear it actually didn't happen until around 1200 B.C.E. Take for example the Pylos tablets—"

"Where is all this going?" muttered Nick, falling behind the babbling academics on their walk to have a quiet word with me.

"Not entirely sure," I said, although I knew only too well what Rebecca was doing. Despite all my warnings about foul play and ticking bombs, she was trying to impress Nick with her expertise, hoping it would result in a job offer. "Apparently, Mr. Telemakhos has a surprise for us."

And so did you, I thought to myself, watching Nick as he checked a new text message. Even though he was wearing something as normal as jeans and a T-shirt, I knew the normality didn't run deep. He was full of nasty surprises.

"I've been meaning to ask you," said Nick, interrupting my bitter thoughts. "What are you going to do next time someone attacks you? Hope they run away again, like the guy in the labyrinth?"

The question was meant to provoke me, and it did. "I'll be just fine, thank you very much," I said. "I know how to take care of myself."

"Come here." He waved me closer. "I want to show you something."

Thinking he was referring to something on his phone, I did as he told me. But as soon as I approached, he seized my arms in a powerful grip and spun me around so that my back was pressed against his front.

"Got you," he said, right into my ear. "Now what are you going to do?"

I was too shocked to even attempt to free myself. "Count to three—"

"And then what? You can't *talk* your way out of everything."

"One!" I said, with forced patience. It infuriated me that Nick felt at liberty to play games with me like this, and I was determined not to stoop to his level. "Two—"

"You're banking on the fact that I'm a nice guy. What if I wasn't?"

"Three." I waited calmly for him to release me, and just when I started fearing he wouldn't, he did.

"Diana," he said, shaking his head. "You're lucky to be alive. What about next time? How can you not want to learn how to defend yourself or the people you love? I can show you some easy tricks—"

"I bet you can." I glared at him as he stood there framed by moonlit rubble, looking as if he really meant it—as if my safety was his number one priority. "But I don't need your cheap tricks. I happen to be on the college fencing team." Realizing how lame it sounded, I added, with more dignity, "I prefer chivalry and proper etiquette over hooligan methods."

Nick nodded, clearly not unimpressed. "Good. That's great. But where"—he opened his arms and pretended to look around—"is your sword?"

Grinding unspoken retorts between my teeth, I turned away and continued up the path in search of the others. Not once did I stop to check whether Nick was tagging along; I needed to put space between us in so many ways.

Rebecca and Mr. Telemakhos were waiting at the entrance to the ancient citadel. They stood framed by gigantic boulders and a colossal monolith lintel, which I could barely make out in the poor light but recognized from illustrations in books: This was the famous Lion Gate with a relief of two fierce animals sitting face-to-face.

"Built by giants," said Mr. Telemakhos, proudly patting the imposing stone. "The Mycenaeans were mountain bears, you see. Big, hairy men who liked to sit around a roaring fire and talk about war." He scratched his chest and looked around. "They built an empire through force, but were raided by pirates in the end. How is that for poetic justice?"

"Those who live by the sword—" I said.

"Get shot by those who don't," muttered Nick, right behind me.

"Let us not forget their legacy of stories," Rebecca pointed out as we continued up the steep path, "which inspired the Greek tragedies and Western literature ever after. Agamemnon, Cassandra . . . returning from Troy to a dinner with murder. Orestes, who killed his own mother. And Electra——"

Her list continued all the way to the summit. Not until we were finally standing on the foundation of the old royal residence, looking out over the limestone hills toward the distant lights of Argos and the black ocean beyond, did she stop to catch her breath.

"All right, Diana Morgan," said Mr. Telemakhos, who, despite his size, did not seem the least bit fatigued by the steep climb. "Tell us why we are here."

The request would have made me smile, had I not been too preoccupied with conflicting thoughts. I had come to like Nick, I realized, far more than I should, and no matter what I did to change that, it felt as if I were swimming against a massive current that was bound, eventually, to pull me under. Whatever it was he was really after, and whoever was helping him, it was all on a scale that dwarfed my own contribution. I was obviously not one of the experts he had mentioned in his phone conversation, for—as I had told him in the car when we first talked about it—I had never for a minute believed the Amazon Hoard was real, nor did I have a clue as to where such a treasure—if it did, in fact, exist—might be found.

Realizing everyone was waiting for my answer, I said, "Well, there are many unknowns——"

Mr. Telemakhos snorted like a mule. "Suit yourself! Be boring. But if you ask me, there is a playground between known and unknown. And in that playground, everyone has a name. The name of your three-syllable priestess-queen, for example"—he nodded at Rebecca, who had blurted it all out over the phone to him before we left Crete—"is not hard to guess. And you, Diana Morgan"—he shook an accusatory finger in my direction—"should have figured it out long ago. Any old crosswords hound could do it. Amazon queen from North Africa. What's her name?"

I winced before the finger. For all my knowledge of Greek myths and Amazon lore, it had never even occurred to me that the name might be one I already knew. It was such a shock to tumble down this path of inquiry and ram my head against the answer that I almost couldn't get it out. "Myrina."

"Bravo!" Mr. Telemakhos clapped his hands. "See, you *did* know."

"Wait a minute—" I stepped forward, head spinning, to rein in his enthusiasm before it galloped away with us all. "How do *you* know the name? How can you be so sure?"

Mr. Telemakhos leaned back on his heels, trying to look down at me. "I trust the myths. They tell me the Amazons were real; they came from North Africa, and their queen was called Myrina. I believe it all. Don't you?"

THAT NIGHT, AFTER TAKING us back to his house, Mr. Telemakhos launched into the most extraordinary fairy tale about the original North African Amazons. Aided by copious glasses of Retsina, he wove a colorful web of adventure, taking us from Lake Tritonis to Mycenae to the Battle of Troy . . . spun from a bottomless grab bag of obscure, literary snippets and a local oral tradition no one had ever bothered to write down.

We were sitting in his living room, which had no furniture except a dining table made up of a large beat-up blackboard and five mismatched chairs, all of which bore witness to better days. The walls around us were lined with sliding stacks of journals and frayed volumes; it looked as if someone had just moved in . . . or, rather, out.

"She even took the bookcases, can you believe it?" said Mr. Telemakhos when he first showed us around. "Now I can't find anything." He cast Nick a glance of apology. "That is why I get confused about things."

Throughout the rest of the evening, our host kept interrupting himself midthought, to stare at Nick and say, "Egypt?" or "Lebanon?" to which Nick would simply shake his head. Not until Rebecca looked at him pleadingly—to spare us more interruptions—did he finally surrender and say, "Iran."

Mr. Telemakhos slammed both palms into the blackboard table, causing a bowl of olives to tip over. "But I already said that! I said 'Persia'!"

Nick folded his arms. "That is the name *you* gave us. *Our* name is Iran."

"Ha!" said Mr. Telemakhos. "Mystery solved. I knew it. You have a Persian nose, and I said so. But tell me"—he leaned forward to peer at Nick with courtroom intensity—"what is a man from Iran doing with a Christian name and a Brazilian passport?"

I cringed. It had been naïve of me to tell Rebecca about the passport—which I had spied on the plane from Djerba—and not think it would somehow come back and slap me.

"It saves time," said Nick, unfazed by Mr. Telemakhos's knowledge. "Brazilians don't get terrorized by airport security. Iranians do."

"But have you ever actually lived in Brazil?" Rebecca wanted to know.

"Sure, I have. My mother is from Rio. We lived there when I was a boy. My father was a street musician." Nick met my eyes across the table, and for the first time since I had met him I felt he was telling the truth. "The best. Always knew how to read the crowd. And I was the little monkey passing his hat around." He looked at us all in turn, undaunted by our somber silence. "So now you know why I think all talk of borders and colors and nationalities is absurd. People try to pin you down on a map and paint you a certain color to make everything simple. But the world is far from simple, and intelligent human beings don't like to be pinned down and painted by some hand in the sky, whether it belongs to a god, a priest, or a politician."

"So you're not . . . religious?" asked Rebecca, still a little shell-shocked.

Nick thought about it for a moment, then said, "To me, there is only one God. An unnamed presence we'll never understand. Everything else is human politics. It was human beings who wrote the holy books, and human beings who made all the rules and rituals. In other words, it is human beings who turn life into hell. So yes"—he picked up his wineglass—"I try to live by the spirit of God, but not by the rules, because rules are made by man, and man is nothing but a fatally conceited flea on the mammoth of Creation."

Rebecca didn't even try to respond. While she might have been running away from it all her life, she was still, deep down, the vicar's daughter. Well, I thought to myself, at least now she might be a little less eager to ingratiate herself with the Aqrab Foundation and a little more receptive when I told her about Nick's wicked dealings.

By the time Mr. Telemakhos finally put the exhausted butt of chalk back in his shirt pocket and brushed off his fingertips, the blackboard dinner table was populated by a myriad of matchstick women and multilingual scribbles, negotiating their way around bread crumbs and small puddles of olive oil.

"There you have it," he concluded. "Diodorus Siculus was right when he said the Amazons came from North Africa and were led by a queen named Myrina. It was only later they moved to the Black Sea and became the warlike wenches we read about in books."

"Diodorus Siculus was an ancient Greek historian," I explained to Nick, "who worked from many sources that are now lost to us. He probably spent most of his time at the library in Alexandria . . . you know, the famous library that was later destroyed. I've seen grown men cry over the literary and historical treasures that would have been found there."

Nick looked a little amused at my pathos. "Let's hope a lot of Alexandrians were overdue with their library books that week."

"Now you, my half-Persian friend." Mr. Telemakhos leaned toward Nick, staring him in the eye. "Tell us what you are thinking. I can see you are thinking something. Persians always are. Even the half ones. And this Greek would like to know what it is."

Nick smiled, his arms still crossed. "I am thinking you have something up your sleeve. Greeks always do."

"Ha!" Mr. Telemakhos rose from the chair. "Persians are smart. That's the problem." He motioned for us to follow him. "I am going to show you a big secret. You can't tell this to anyone, do you understand?"

Nick was the first to get up and follow our host down a set of stone steps into the moldy darkness beneath the house. Rebecca and I both hesitated before following. "Why does everything have to be underground?" I muttered to her as we picked our way down the treacherous staircase. "I have spent far too much time in the subconscious lately."

Even though I made light of it, the dank stillness of Mr. Telemakhos's secret space was bringing on a visceral déjà vu not only of my recent fright in Crete, but also of the temple in Algeria. Would I ever, I wondered, be able to descend into a basement again without a shiver?

"Many years ago," boomed Mr. Telemakhos from somewhere in the darkness, "when I was a little boy playing in these hills, I found something very special." He turned on a lonely ceiling bulb to reveal that we were in the midst of a small command center with walls and tables completely covered in paper scraps and newspaper clippings. I had never seen anything like it . . . at least not since my father had gone through Granny's attic with a bucket, ripping her archive of imagined Amazon activity from the ceiling.

Walking over to an old safe in the corner, Mr. Telemakhos started dialing a code. "I didn't tell anybody about it at the time because then a greasy little bureaucrat would come out in a van and take it all back to Athens. That is where you have to go to see the artifacts from Mycenae now; they are all in the National Archaeological Museum. Or"—he grimaced with disgust—"at the Louvre in Paris, of course."

Opening the safe, Mr. Telemakhos riffled around for a bit before finally taking out a small transparent plastic bag. "Come and look!" he said, waving us closer. "It doesn't bite."

In the bag lay a jackal bracelet.

"There." He handed me the bag, beaming with the sensation of it all. "I think you will find it matches the one on your arm."

I felt a pinch of surprise at his sudden interest in Granny's bracelet. It had been right in front of him all day, but even as he had regaled us with tales of the Amazons, he had made no mention of it—had barely even appeared to notice it.

"I found this little piece of Amazon jewelry on the hill next to the palace ruins," Mr. Telemakhos went on. "Deep inside a crater that was probably carved out by lightning. I am guessing people went there to make offerings to the gods of the sky."

"I am shocked!" said Rebecca, refusing to touch the bag. "This is a unique find. Should it not be . . . in a museum?"

Mr. Telemakhos's woolly eyebrows shot up in dismay. "When my work is done, I will make it public. But for now, I am saving these irreplaceable treasures from the stupidity and greed of bureaucrats and other thieves."

"Roger that," said Nick.

I put a shaky hand to my forehead, wondering if one could develop a fever from shock alone. "I don't understand," I said. "How can you be so sure these bracelets belonged to Amazons? Couldn't they just be ordinary jewelry, worn by ordinary people? The jackal motif is not that unusual."

Mr. Telemakhos jiggled the bag before my eyes. "This jackal is special and you know it. But let me tell you what happened." He stretched to put the bag back in the safe. "When I found this bracelet, I sent out inquiries. I was careful, but still, a few people found me. Such as"—he nodded at Nick—"your friend Chris Hauser."

"And what did he want?" asked Nick. "My friend Chris Hauser."

Mr. Telemakhos suddenly looked self-conscious. "Well, as a matter of fact, *he* was the one who told me it was an Amazon bracelet. And he wanted to know if I had ever seen others like it. Which, at the time, I hadn't."

"But later," I insisted, "you discovered more of them?"

Mr. Telemakhos gently closed the safe. "Yes."

"Where?"

"That is what I want to show you." He started toward the stairs. "Tomorrow. There is someone you have to meet—"

"Just to be clear," said Nick, casting one last glance at the safe. "Why do you think Chris Hauser was so interested in this bracelet?"

Mr. Telemakhos paused with his hand on the light cord. "What do all men want? To be ravished by an Amazon, of course."

Nick didn't exactly laugh, but it was close. "Speak for yourself."

For once, Mr. Telemakhos was unamused. As he stood there in the basement, surrounded by the evidence of a lifelong devotion to a subject that clearly, by his estimation, ought not be exposed to the light of day, the old Amazon hunter reminded me of the weather-beaten Scots I had seen so often on television, stubbornly maintaining the Loch Ness monster existed, despite all scientific evidence that it couldn't possibly.

"I still don't get it," I said. "How did Chris Hauser know it was an Amazon bracelet?"

The question did nothing to smooth the lines of defiance on Mr. Telemakhos's face. "He wouldn't say."

I looked at Rebecca and saw that she, too, was staring at our host with disbelief. Could it really be that the man she called "the Oracle" had based his life's work on something as insubstantial as this, the flimsy fancy of a young man from Baltimore? Glancing at Nick, I expected to see headshaking skepticism to match my own. But his eyes were fixed on my wrist, and there was not a trace of amusement left on his face. To us all, I suddenly realized, so much more was at stake than the mere unraveling of an old legend.

"You are young," Mr. Telemakhos said at last, squaring his shoulders and looking at us one by one. "You have lots of time to find what you are looking for. But to someone like me, there are more days in the garbage can than on the calendar on the wall. That is why I am impatient"—he nodded at my bracelet—"and why I want more, more, more."

"More what?" asked Nick, leaning over to scrutinize one of the many pieces of paper hanging on the wall.

Mr. Telemakhos made an impatient snort. "I've spent three decades trying to prove not only that the Amazons *did* exist"—he gestured at the mess on the table and on the walls all around—"but that they *still* exist. Every week I find more evidence."

"Of what?" asked Rebecca, her voice uncharacteristically feeble.

Mr. Telemakhos walked over to one of the bulletin boards and took down a scrap of paper. "A girl is molested by a rapist on parole. Two women—strange women, unknown to the girl and her family—find the man, knock on his door, and cut off his testicles." Mr. Telemakhos looked up appealingly. "If that doesn't have 'Amazon' written all over it, lock me away in a padded room."

"Interesting," said Nick, displaying a surprising capacity for forbearance in the face of what must surely, to him, seem like utter folly, if not downright insanity. "I have to say, I like the idea, and I hope you are right. But let me ask you this—" He walked a few steps along the wall, scanning the news clippings. "At what point does it become more than just a feeling? Where is the proof? Where is the UFO in Hangar Eighteen?"

Mr. Telemakhos bristled. "I am not talking about aliens! The Amazons, my friend, walk among us. But they are sly, and they don't want to be found out. Some say they never use telephones or email when they communicate with one another . . . that they use a medium that can't be traced—maybe a printed pamphlet of sorts." He held out his arms as if to say that although he was convinced he was right, sadly, he had no proof. "Think about it. They break the law; they are what we would call vigilantes. Imagine how many people want to find them and stop them. Not just the criminals, but governments, too. Remember, the state has a monopoly on justice. Even when it does a bad job—when the policemen whose salaries are paid by Mr. Telemakhos's taxes do nothing but sit around on their fat asses waiting for Mr. Telemakhos to drive a little too fast on the motorway—even *then* we are not allowed to do what they *should* be doing and chase the *real* criminals. That is why the Amazons don't want to be found out. That is why you will never recognize them in the street. In fact"—he pointed a finger at me—"how do you know Diana is not one of them? She is wearing the bracelet, isn't she?"

Nick turned to look at me with an expression I couldn't quite make out. In the meantime, I saw Rebecca grimacing at Mr. Telemakhos to let him know we were entering treacherous territory, and, thankfully, he got the hint. "But it's getting late!" he went on, clasping his hands abruptly. "And tomorrow morning we want an early start. Adventure awaits!"

For some reason, everyone's eyes turned to me, and I said, with some regret, "Tomorrow is Tuesday. I really must be on my way."

Mr. Telemakhos gave me a long look. "You can't come this far and not see where it all ends. Can you?"

"Where *what* ends?" asked Nick. "The trail of the Amazons?"

Our host looked at us all with a mystical squint. "I will say to you what the scientists say about the small particles in the universe: I can't show you where they are, I can only show you where they *were*. If I have learned one thing these past thirty years, it is that the more you want to find the Amazons, the less they want to be found."

Curiosity and duty were at war in me. I wanted desperately to stay in Mycenae until I had extracted every last snippet of information from Mr. Telemakhos, and I was aching to see where he wanted to take us and why. But I knew I couldn't. It was bad enough that I had abandoned my students for over a week; to postpone my return even further would be unforgivable. "I'm sorry, but I really can't," I said with a sigh. "I *have* to be back in Oxford by tomorrow evening."

Mr. Telemakhos's temporary gloom gave way to a delighted smile. "Tomorrow evening? But that's excellent! We'll have our excursion in the morning, and you can get a flight in the afternoon."

"But I really need——" I began.

"Stamata!" In a rare burst of irritation, Mr. Telemakhos held up a hand to silence me. "I know what you need, Diana Morgan. And you will get it, I promise."

CHAPTER TWENTY-THREE

Myrina's excitement at seeing Lilli alive and seemingly un-scathed was so violent that Aeneas had to put a warning hand on her shoulder. "The king says this girl is the only useful thing his son brought back from his trip," whispered the Trojan, interpreting the royal court's odious dialogue while holding Myrina still as best he could. "She speaks with the voice of a spirit, says the king, and what she says comes true. Apparently, she predicted our visit, saying she foresaw the arrival of friends."

Eager to provide a demonstration, King Agamemnon had the ser-vant take Lilli about the room that she might touch the palms of the dinner guests and read their fortunes. Watching her sister with narrow eyes, Myrina could see the girl was not fully herself; had the servant not been there to steady her, Lilli would have been unable to keep her bal-ance. And yet she was smiling, as if nothing too terrible had befallen her, and the auspices she gave the Greek chieftains sitting around the king's fire were clearly kind, for whenever the servant translated them, the recipients looked suitably pleased.

When she reached the Trojans, Lilli gave Paris's companion to the left—whose name was Dares, and whose frame was so massive he could barely fit on the bench—the same gentle attention she had be-stowed on everyone else. Her expression changed as she felt the lines of his enormous hand, eventually settling in a smile. "You are a man of great courage," said Lilli, and now Myrina could hear that her sister spoke the language they had learned at the Temple of the Moon Goddess. "Your glory will live forever. Thousands of years from now, men will still speak your name with admiration."

Dares chuckled and replied to her directly, before the servant could translate. "I would have settled for a happy life, but thank you all the same."

Lilli looked surprised, then let go of him to turn to Paris. "And you, sir," she said, swaying slightly, "do you care to know your fortune?"

"Is it good for a man to know his destiny?" Paris reluctantly gave her his hand. "I am not sure."

Lilli ran her fingers over his palm as she had done with Dares, her features settling back into feigned amiability. But it was not long before her expression changed, first into a frown of incredulity, then into pure and utter amazement. "Myrina!" she exclaimed, her face erupting in joy. "Myrina?" She reached up for Paris's cheek, feeling her way around his evening stubble with growing horror, as if wondering what deforming malady had befallen her sister. Then, without another word, her unseeing eyes rolled away into oblivion, and she collapsed at Paris's feet, her head in his lap.

The incident occasioned a great burst of laughter from the men around them. "See?" Agamemnon looked mightily pleased as he switched away from the Greek language to tease his guest. "A sweet little oracle, that. Sees right into a man's heart." He raised his chalice at Paris. "And now we know what's in yours."

Paris moved uncomfortably on the couch, not sure how to best accommodate Lilli's limp body. "An intriguing girl," he agreed. "I should like to see her take a turn about my father's court. She might help him read the minds of his wives."

The king laughed and leaned back on his chair. "Not even the gods can do that. But next time your father visits here, I will have her feel his fortune."

"He would appreciate it," said Paris. "He is a man of far-reaching tastes. In fact"—he motioned at Dares to take something out of a leather satchel—"I had to sail to the very edge of the world for this exquisite gift. I am confident it will awe even him. Have you ever seen anything like it?"

The object was passed reverently around the circle of dinner guests to end up in the hands of Agamemnon. It was a golden face mask, embossed with the features of a bearded man and complete with ears and a protruding nose.

"Magnificent, isn't it?" Paris watched closely as the king admired the mask. "Pure Egyptian gold. But in truth, I wonder if my father would not be even more amused by your little soothsayer."

The king raised his bushy eyebrows. "You would trade *this* for that little witch?"

Paris hesitated. "Maybe not. And yet . . . I was commissioned to purchase house slaves, not return home with useless finery." He gestured once again for Dares to take something out of the satchel—this time a pair of golden earrings forged in the shape of dragonflies. "My mother always complains that she has more gold than she can carry . . . but no hands to help her put it on."

"A sad situation," agreed the king, eyeing the earrings across the room. "What manner of house slaves are you looking for?"

Paris leaned back in contemplation, his hand still resting on Lilli's head. "Your account of these women amuses me. I suspect my mother should like to surround herself with such exotic creatures. She was never a friend of the fearful and demure—"

"Say no more!" The king threw up his hands, the golden mask still resting on his knees. "They are yours. All of them. Seven plus the girl. I shall be happy to see the end of their surly presence—" A sudden clamor silenced the king, and Myrina saw the villainous prince step up to his father and speak out indignantly against the bargain.

A brief, but harsh exchange later, Agamemnon turned again to the Trojans, arms out in a casual apology. "Did I say seven? Six is the number. Six plus the girl. As it turns out, my son has taken a liking to one of them, and what father can deny his firstborn a toy?"

As soon as the deal was struck, Paris motioned for Myrina and Animone to remove Lilli from his lap and carry her outside. His expression was one of absolute indifference, as if the whole thing were nothing but a temporary diversion, already half forgotten. And yet the look in his eyes when Myrina knelt down to pick up her sister was so dark, so full of words unspoken, she knew he was just as anxious as she to gather everyone and return to the ships before Agamemnon had a change of heart. But protocol demanded the men remain seated, enjoying honey cake and music, until the king tired of their company and bade them farewell.

Meanwhile, in the courtyard outside, blushing evening turned to murky night. Myrina descended the staircase slowly, insisting on carrying Lilli by herself while Animone led the way. Neither dared open their mouths until they were safely on the lower terrace, where they found Pitana greeting them with a nervous wave. "Egee ran off to scout and has not yet returned," she hissed. Only then did she notice the limp body in Myrina's arms. "Who is that?"

"Lilli." Myrina knelt down to carefully set her sister on the ground. "I think they have drugged her. But she will be herself again soon, I hope."

Seeing Pitana's alarm, Myrina and Animone hastened to lay out the events that had allowed them to carry away Lilli just like that, under the auspices of the gold-grubbing king. And when Egee eventually returned, sweaty from stealth and excitement, she could confirm that news of the negotiation over the enslaved women was already at large throughout the palace. "There is great confusion," she said, undoing the scarf around her head with eager fingers. "As far as I can tell, they have already heard that some of the slaves are to be taken away by new masters, and everyone else is sick with jealousy."

"Did you happen to learn the name of the one who has caught the fancy of the king's son?" asked Myrina. "For she alone must stay behind."

Egee shook her head. "But I saw the room where he keeps her. That is, I saw the door and the guard posted outside. An old woman who knew our language let me understand that the prince comes and goes whenever he pleases, day or night, and that everyone dreads the sounds—" She sat down heavily on a stone step. "I did not realize that behind this door was one of my sisters. What a terrible fate. Apparently, the women he locks in that room never leave it alive."

Their distress was only pushed aside when the Trojans returned. For between them walked six women whose arms were bound, but whose faces were lit, radiant with hope. And when they recognized their four sisters—all with fingers pressed to their lips to prevent an outcry—they ran headlong into a silent embrace, a jumble of interlocking arms that grew denser for every rope severed by the Trojans.

Not until they were well outside the palace gate did the freed women dare speak. Judging from their nervous glances they all fully expected Agamemnon's men to come after them, spears in hand, to cut short their freedom. Down the hill they went, and through the sleepy streets below, their steps so eager they nearly outpaced the horses.

Safely back on the Argos Plain, they were met by the horsemen Paris had posted there in the event they would be needed on the return. Lilli's limp body was carefully handed over to the solid Dares, and the rest of the liberated women were quickly distributed among the other riders. Few words were spoken save the obvious exclamations of gratitude. For what was there to say? They were free, and blissfully so; only one of them had had to stay behind.

Kara.

NONE OF THE PRIESTESSES could sleep that night. After a late meal and much thanksgiving, the Trojans bade the women good night and went below, to rest before their daybreak departure. "Must we leave so soon?" Myrina asked Paris as she followed him out on deck. "Your men are surely tired—"

"My men," he said, holding up his lantern so she could see his face, "are as keen to leave this place as you are. This has all been far too easy. Either the Greeks or their jealous gods will soon regret our luck."

Myrina stepped closer. "How can I ever thank you?"

Paris reached out to touch her cheek. "What you owe me and I you is a subject far too great for one brief good night. Do you not agree?"

She leaned against his hand. "After what you have done for my sisters, I am determined to please you in any way I can."

"That is unwise of you." Paris ran his fingers over her lips. "For I have nearly run out of grace." With that, he turned away, going below deck with brisk strides.

Returning to her sisters, Myrina found them all drawn together, whispering about the fate of poor Neeta, lost to cruelty, and the plight of Kara, still alive. Happy as they were to escape the destiny of slaves, the freed women's relief was tempered by regret at having been unable to save the other two.

"Kara's pride piqued the prince," said the liberated Klito, who had once looked so wholesome, so ready for adventure, but whose beautiful face was now marred by suffering. "The Greeks cannot tolerate women who refuse them. He would surely have thrown her overboard on the first day had not the crew been laughing at him. And so instead, he beat her senseless and—" She shook her head, swallowing the details. "But all of you know Kara. Once she was recovered, she refused him again, even spitting in his face. And since, he has been obsessed with dominating her."

Just then, Lilli stirred on the couch next to Animone before drifting away once more into unconsciousness.

"It has been an evil month," said Myrina, sitting down on the floor by her sister's feet, which were as dirty and worn as they had been that day long ago, when she and Lilli had first arrived at the Temple of the Moon Goddess. "And I doubt the gods have finished with us yet." She looked around at everyone in turn. "Let me ask you this: If we sail away without Kara, will we ever be able to arrive anywhere else?"

The only one who met her gaze was Egee. "What are you proposing?" she asked. When Myrina did not respond, Egee leaned abruptly forward. "Have you lost your wits? You saw that place! I am telling you: Kara would not have gone back for *us*. And especially not for *you*."

Myrina sighed, her head drooping under the burden of all this trouble. Then she straightened and said to Egee, "Had you been trying to convince me to go, you could have made no better case for it. The only thing holding me back is the danger, not to me, or to those brave enough to come with me, but to the men who have saved us all—the men asleep below. If we fail and perish, it was our choice to do so. But they have not been consulted and should not be held hostage by our fortune or lack of it."

"Even now," said a bitter voice, "your thoughts are for *him* and not for us."

Amazed, Myrina turned her head and stared at Animone, who had never before spoken out against her in front of the others. "If my thoughts were not for my sisters," she said, her voice hoarse with disappointment, "I would not be sitting here, proposing an impossible venture—"

"Why not?" Animone stuck out her chin, her eyes red with emotion and fatigue. "What better way to secure *his* admiration than to rush forth on yet another mad hunt?"

"Enough!" Myrina rose on legs weak with exhaustion. "Let us go to sleep, all of us, before we choke on our own poison."

She left the room as quietly as she could, although she felt like yelling out her frustration. Finally outside and away from the staring eyes, she walked over to the railing to fill her lungs with night air. They had come so far, accomplished so much . . . and yet she tasted bitter failure in her mouth. Somewhere in the darkness, beyond the Argos Plain, a woman whose face she knew was being killed, slowly but certainly, by a man who should have been struck dead long ago, had there been any mercy in heaven.

"So what is the plan?" asked Pitana, coming up to lean on the railing next to her. "We still have some hours before sunrise."

"No one would have to know," said another voice behind them. "There is a way of getting past the palace guards."

Myrina turned to see Klito standing there, her hollow cheeks even more pronounced in the darkness. "You would go back?" she asked her. "When you have finally escaped?"

Klito nodded. "If any of the palace slaves are about, the sight of a familiar face will calm them. They all hate their masters."

"It is a long walk."

"Not as long as the rest of my life." Klito tried to smile, but her mouth had forgotten how. "Unless it ends tonight."

Myrina bit her lip. "If anything goes wrong—if someone sees us—we cannot return to this ship. We will be separated from the others, perhaps forever."

"Come now," said Pitana. "Everyone would assume she had run away on her own. No one would accuse the Trojans of such an act of madness."

"Perhaps not." Myrina took a deep breath. "And you are right, it is madness. But sometimes, madness is the only path forward. Let us—" She fell silent as the night guard walked past.

"That was Idaeus," whispered Pitana. "I will ask Brianne to distract him. He has a sweetness for her, poor man."

ONCE THE DECISION WAS made, the three women pushed aside every scruple and fully devoted their thoughts to the venture ahead. They must be armed, of course, yet travel light. After some deliberation, Myrina opted to carry the double-headed ax from Crete instead of her spear. "It is very useful," she explained to Klito, "and gives an advantage to weaker arms." She did not mention where the ax had come from, nor her suspicion that it might have been the very weapon that had killed Neeta.

"But your arms are not weak," countered Pitana, strapping on her quiver. "At sea you arm-wrestled Paris, and I saw the sweat on his brow."

Myrina busied herself with her sandals. Jester that he was, Paris had let her think she was winning over him, allowing her to press down his hand until it hovered an inch over the table . . . only to laugh and force hers over backward, laying it gently down on the wooden boards beneath his own. And until that moment, the only one who had been sweating was Myrina.

"Yes, well." She struggled to purge any thoughts of Paris from her mind. "The palace guards are a different kind of beast. Most men are.

Even the fat, lazy ones have more power in their arms than we. Nature made them that way, I suppose, so that they could more easily overpower us. How else would humankind reproduce? And that is why"—she stuck the ax in her belt, letting it hang from the double head—"you must never put yourself within arm's reach of a man unless you know how to make up for the unfairness of nature."

Klito eyed the ax enviously. "I could have used that many times. To think I used to long for the touch of a man." She grimaced. "As you say, nature taunts us with our weaknesses."

Myrina took Klito by the shoulders. "It is not a taunt, but a challenge."

Once ready, the three women made their way down the gangplank to the deserted pier, glancing back now and then to make sure Idaeus the night guard was still fully preoccupied with Brianne. But just as Myrina thought they were safely away, she heard running feet behind them. Spinning around with a gasp of guilt, she was relieved to see that it was Animone.

"Please!" The woman caught up with them, out of breath, pressing her hands together. "I want to come with you."

Myrina merely nodded and touched a finger to her lips.

As they headed out across the Argos Plain yet again, this time without the advantage of horses, Myrina tried hard to outrun her own doubts. Here they were, discussing how to sneak into the palace and, if need be, kill the guards. Less than a year ago, these very women—Pitana, Klito, and Animone—had been so fainthearted they barely dared follow her into the temple basement to see the dead serpent in the pit. . . .

"Have no worry," said Klito, as if reading Myrina's thoughts as they ran. "Anyone who has seen and felt what I have, believe me, is ready to swing that ax of yours."

Behind them, Animone gasped out her agreement. "All these weeks, I have been imagining what I would do to the boar who—" She broke off with a growl. "For his sake, I hope he does not try to stop us."

Myrina winced at these words, but said nothing to discourage her friends as they egged one another on with visions of revenge. She had not been through what they had, and could only guess the depth of their hatred.

Not until they arrived at Mycenae did Klito and Animone finally fall back into nervous silence. In the pale light of a waning moon, King Agamemnon's abode resembled, more than ever, a ghostly growth of poisonous mushrooms, and Myrina felt her stomach turning at the sight.

Gathering her courage, she headed up the road toward the great stone gate . . . but was stopped when Klito put a hand on her arm and whispered, "This is where we take the other road. The shrine where Lilli laid down her jackal for all of us is up there, near the summit." Klito pointed up the hillside to the left of the palace. "As I said, there is a secret path from this holy place to the palace kitchen, through a hole in the garden wall. The masters don't know of it, but the slave women use it all the time to steal out and lay down gifts to the gods in the hopes of deliverance from this place."

As they followed Klito's lead up the hillside, Myrina heard Pitana whisper in a tone of disbelief, "If you could leave the palace so easily, why did you not run away?"

"And go where?" Klito threw out her arms as if to emphasize the desolate quality of the hills all around. "Live in the wilderness where they would delight in hunting us down?"

"Wicked, wicked, *wicked* people," spat Animone.

Again, Myrina kept her silence, but a long look from Pitana told her she was not the only one struck by the paradox. Their enslaved sisters had been bold enough to sneak out of the palace and pray for salvation, yet were not bold enough to flee. But then, as Myrina knew only too well, it is the loss of hope that kills the prey—the loss of will to keep struggling. Perhaps that, more than anything, was why she would not leave Kara behind; Kara had never stopped believing she should be free.

THE SECRET PASSAGE TO the palace kitchen went through an herb garden with beehives and dormant fruit trees. Even this time of year, far from the hum of summer, the place was so well tended and filled with sweet scents it was difficult to marry its loveliness to the crudeness of the Greeks.

"Through here!" hissed Klito, ducking through a prickly hedge. "Quiet!"

They sat for a while hunched in the shrubbery, listening for any sounds of workers in the servants' quarters. Above, in the darkness, a bird made a warning squawk. Below was a rodent bustle in the dung-hill. Otherwise, all was quiet.

Crawling on all fours, Klito stretched to look around the corner, across the kitchen yard, at the small building where Kara was held captive. Then she fell back, gasping with excitement, and whispered, "The guard is gone. That means the prince is in there with her."

"Oh no!" Animone shifted nervously on the damp ground. "Now what?"

"Wait here." Klito rose to sneak through the shadows along the hedge until she disappeared from sight. When she returned, her eager gestures told the others she had good news. "No sounds," she hissed. "They must be asleep."

"Oh no," said Animone again.

"Oh yes," countered Pitana, pulling the knife from her belt. "The prince may never wake up."

"Wait." Myrina held Pitana back. "We cannot all go in there. Four silent people make a terrible noise. Klito and I will go, while you two stay here."

"But if the door is barred—" protested Pitana.

Klito tightened the scarf around her face. "There is a window. Small, but always open. Since the building is sunk into the ground, a slim person could probably get in from the outside, but no one can get out from the inside: It is set too high above the floor."

After a cautious approach through the shadows, Myrina sidled up to the door and tested it with her hand. To her relief, it yielded readily to her touch. Glancing at Klito, she saw they were thinking the same thing: Would that this small token of carelessness was left by a man far gone in drunken oblivion.

At first, Myrina could see nothing of the room inside, but after a few blinks her eyes adjusted to the narrow beam of moonlight that leaked in through the open window. What she saw confirmed what she had already smelled—the presence of two bedraggled bodies, nesting in their own excretions.

Lying on the same bed, they could have been a pair of lovers . . . except that the prince, fast sleep, was resting comfortably under a sheepskin while Kara—highborn Kara, daughter of a chieftain—lay naked beside him, her arms tied with thick ropes to a bedpost.

Nodding at Klito to guard the door, Myrina undid her scarf and tiptoed ahead to wake their unfortunate sister. To her surprise she found Kara's eyes already open, staring blankly at the ceiling. Feeling a twinge of panic, Myrina reached out to find the pulse on a neck that was cold and sticky to the touch.

She was still alive.

Only then, as Myrina went on to feel her face, did Kara blink and turn her head. But even though she looked straight at Myrina, she showed no sign of recognition. In fact, she showed no sign of thought whatsoever.

Myrina tried to smile. "It is your sister, Myrina. We have come to save you. Come—" But as soon as she took out her knife to cut the ropes, Kara pulled back in fear and started sobbing.

"Shh!" Myrina pressed a hand against her mouth. "Be quiet."

But her plea had the opposite effect; as soon as Kara's hands were free, she used them to push and slap at Myrina as hard as she could. "Go away! I don't want you here! Go!"

"Quiet!" hissed Myrina, pulling at the unwilling arms. "Come! Hurry!"

"No!" Kara screamed the word at the top of her lungs, crouching against the bed that must have been her home for many days. "Leave me!"

At last, the prince stirred.

Sitting up in bed, he peered into the darkness until he caught sight of the three women, now stone still, and noticed the frame of light around the half-open door. Then, with a roar, he reached down to grab his weapon. Myrina, acting by instinct as she would against a charging predator, pulled the ax from her belt and flung it at him with all the force of her fear.

The blow hit the prince right in the chest and threw him off the bed and onto the floor, his deadly cries no more than a beastly final wheeze.

"Disaster!" Myrina was not sure whether she said the word out loud or merely thought it. Their plan to come and go without a trace was thwarted. Had it been any other body they might have tried to hide it, but this was King Agamemnon's son. "Let's go!" she urged the others. "Quickly!"

"Wait." Klito was by her side, spear raised. "We have to make sure he is dead." She bent closer to poke at their victim. "You disgusting plague . . . do you know what the punishment is for defiling a priestess?"

From her state of petrified dumbness, Kara now sprang into being. "Stop!" she cried, trying to wrest the spear from Klito's hands. Then she added, somewhat belatedly, "Please don't hurt him—"

"Enough of this!" Myrina stepped across the man's body to dislodge her ax from his chest. As she did, she saw there was no need for Klito's spear; he was quite dead. "We must be away before he is discovered."

Their retreat, intended to be so silent and full of joy, was the opposite. Wailing over the sudden death of her capturer, at first Kara refused to leave the room, spewing curses at her sisters. Then, when they made moves to depart, she bounded after them with cries of panic.

"Quiet!" Klito clasped Kara's head and mouth between her hands, desperate to silence her. "You will wake everyone—"

But it was too late. Back at the hedge, where Animone and Pitana had been hiding, they were met by an assembly of at least a dozen house slaves—all women—engaged in a furious exchange of whispers and hand gestures.

"I think they want to leave with us," explained Pitana, grimacing.

"Tell them they cannot," said Myrina to Klito, who claimed to have gleaned the rudiments of the Greek language during her brief captivity.

"Just say we will all be hunted down and butchered alive." Without waiting for Klito to impart the message, Myrina continued through the herb garden, dragging along Kara, still sobbing and reluctant.

It was all too confused, too clamorous, and Myrina feared that within moments, there would be men afoot to stop them. "Pull yourself together!" she ordered, tying her head scarf around Kara's shivering nakedness. "We came to save you, and now your hysteria may get us killed."

Expecting they would be intercepted by the palace guards, Myrina hesitated in front of the hole in the garden wall, not understanding why no one was there. Having little choice, she pushed Kara through the hole and proceeded to pull her down the hill as fast as they could both go.

It was not long before she heard voices growing louder behind them. Stopping and turning, she saw that the entire cluster of women was still coming along, despite Klito's ardent attempts at stopping them. Groaning with frustration, Myrina waited for them to catch up, then said as loudly as she dared, "I am sorry. You cannot come with us. Escape if you will, but we have no room for more."

"Please," Klito held out her folded hands to Myrina. "I know these women. They are all good, and are all suffering. Can we not—?"

Myrina clutched her head. "We cannot empty the palace of slaves. Do you wish to start a war?"

Klito turned to the women once more, explaining as best she could, but their appeal was so pitiful even Pitana was swayed. "Must we really leave them here?" she said under her breath. "Their faces will haunt me forever."

Myrina straightened, angry to have her logic besieged by emotion. "Very well. Those who wish may come with us. But tell them they must follow the rules of our sisterhood. They must never again consort with men, must learn to kill rather than love, and"—she paused for inspiration, determined to come up with yet another condition that would surely discourage them all—"they must subject themselves to having one breast seared off, in order to better pull the bow." She nodded firmly at them all. "Such are the conditions for joining us. Now, who wants to come?"

Klito's translation caused a whimper of horror throughout the group, and no one came forward.

"I thought so." Glumly satisfied, Myrina turned to go.

"Wait!" a fawn of a girl, hardly even a woman, stepped toward Myrina, fists clenched with conviction. "I will come."

Myrina glanced at Klito, who stared at the young girl with a puzzled frown, as if trying to recognize her, but failing.

"So be it." Myrina turned to go, making a face at Pitana. "Small as she is, they will never even realize she is missing."

THEY RETURNED TO THE harbor just as the Sun appeared in the eastern sky, driving his golden chariot through the rosy veil of dawn. Even at this early hour the pier was abuzz with activity. The Trojans were hauling on board the last water barrels before departure, and men were running up and down the gangplanks yelling instructions.

At no point had it occurred to Myrina the ships might take off without them; in fact, whenever she had envisioned their return from Mycenae, she had seen a pier just as deserted as it had been when they left, with the ships' crews still fast asleep.

But the Trojan sailors were up and about, too busy to pay attention to the women. The only one of them receiving the odd glance as they boarded was Kara, limping with exhaustion after the journey across the Argos Plain, and whose makeshift dress consisted of nothing but scarves.

As they lugged her up the gangplank—slowly, so as not to lose their balance—Myrina caught sight of Paris on deck, looking their way. Arms crossed, he looked to be struggling to contain his temper, and yet he spoke not a word to his crew or to her. He merely watched the women's approach with eyes that suddenly made Myrina weak with doubt. And then, the moment they were on board at last, he turned away and shouted the order for departure.

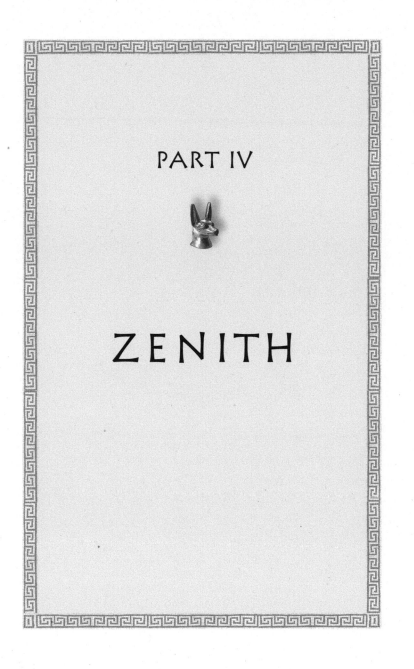

PART IV

ZENITH

CHAPTER TWENTY-FOUR

I was picking fresh flowers
gathering them into my robe, to take
to Athene there in the brazen house
when he caught me away through the bright
air to this unprofitable
country, poor me, made a prize of war
—EURIPIDES, *Helen*

NAFPLIO, GREECE

M R. TELEMAKHOS DROVE US DOWN TO THE HARBOR JUST AFTER sunrise. Before getting into the car I reminded him of his promise to take me to the airport in the afternoon. "Yes-yes-yes," he replied, brusquely opening the back door for me, "I know you have more important things to do." The wounded defiance with which he spoke made me embarrassed to have reopened the issue.

His boat—a two-master named *Penelope*—was moored in Nafplio, a few kilometers south of Mycenae. This ancient town had sprung up around a rocky peninsula that jutted far into the Aegean Sea, and its alluring crescent of vibrant façades made it a favorite stop for yachts and cruise ships. Even at seven in the morning the harbor was bustling with sailors enjoying the sun and looking for breakfast.

The *Penelope* itself was a wooden ketch with cream-colored sails. The boat was clearly a labor of love, every piece of brass fitting polished to a shine, every sail immaculate.

"She saved my life," said Mr. Telemakhos, patting the gleaming golden-brown railing as he climbed on board ahead of us. "Used to be my father's. He practically lived on her for the last ten years of his life. I didn't even know he was still alive, but then, one day, he suddenly walked into my kitchen just as I was opening the letter."

"What letter?" asked Rebecca, helping him carry supplies on board.

Mr. Telemakhos grunted and paused to balance a colossal tin of olive oil on his thigh. "The letter from the oligarchs of school administration, saying they didn't need me anymore. Drink your hemlock, old fossil, they said. Take your scratched-up blackboard and be gone! Young people nowadays want teachers with remote controls."

He disappeared belowdecks with the olive oil, but we could still hear his booming voice as he rummaged around the galley. "So I retired. And the doctor said, hey, now that you're such an old fossil, you can't eat meat anymore. So I stopped eating meat, and that's when everything started going wrong in the engine room. Before I knew it . . . my bookcases were gone."

As we helped him lug this and that on board the boat, I had to bite back my impatience. Why were we stocking supplies for an Atlantic crossing when we were just going to nip up the coast and be back in Nafplio by lunchtime? But when I voiced my annoyance to Rebecca, she rolled her eyes and said, "Will you relax? He has gone out of his way to host us; the least we can do is give him a hand." She shrugged peevishly, still irritated with me for insisting on going home. "The rest of us may go back on the boat once you've left."

While Nick and Mr. Telemakhos juggled freshwater bottles belowdecks, I called the lodge at my Oxford college to assure the porter I would be back in my office, ready to see students, in a few short hours. Just as I hung up, my father called.

"Sorry to put you through the grinder," I said to him. "It's all been a bit hectic, but I'm coming home tonight."

"I'll pick you up at the airport," he replied, in that brusque way of his, dressing his worry in verbal chain mail. "When do you arrive?"

An ear-piercing drilling sound from below forced me off the boat and onto the pier. Rebecca was already there, sitting on a roll of rope, studying a chart of the coastline. "I'm not sure," I confessed, steadying myself against a large anchor. The metal was pleasantly warm from the morning sun, but it would take a lot more than that to thaw out my conscience after leaving my poor parents in the dark for so long. Soon, I knew, I would have to confront them with my discovery that Granny's notebook was not quite the work of madness they had hitherto assumed. Knowing how shocked they would be, it occurred to me that it might be wise to initiate the subject now, long-distance, in order to give them time to recover before we met.

"Here's the thing," I said, pressing a hand against my eyes to block out the distractions. "I know you don't like to talk about it, but a couple of weeks ago, I came across an inscription with an undeciphered alphabet." I could almost hear my father exhaling with relief, thinking it was just about philology after all. "Except it's not actually undeciphered." I cleared my throat, struggling to maintain my nerve. "Because it looks like Granny deciphered it at some point. And wrote it down in . . . that notebook." I gritted my teeth, bracing for his reaction.

But I never got it. All I heard was Rebecca's frightened outcry right behind me. . . . Then the phone was plucked from my fingers by a blond bowstring of a woman who shot right past me on Rollerblades.

It happened so quickly I didn't even fully comprehend I had been robbed until I noticed my empty hand. My body, however, responded instantly.

Without even a look at Rebecca, I took off after the thief, who was making her way down the pier with strides worthy of an Olympian skier. She probably didn't realize I was coming after her; only when she reached the harbor promenade and had to slow down for crossing pedestrians did she glance over her shoulder and spot me right behind.

Because I was running as fast as I could, the woman's face was blurry to me. But even so, it seemed that after that first grimace of surprise, she actually shot me a contemptuous smile that had the benefit of refueling me with indignation, enabling me to run even faster.

"Stop!" I yelled, hoping someone would understand the situation and block the thief's way. But the woman effortlessly slalomed past every obstacle, gathering speed as she went. Eventually, I lost sight of her as she disappeared around a corner, right between two cafés.

By the time I reached the corner, she was long gone. But I was not quite ready to give up. A narrow pedestrian street stretched ahead of me, and I continued at top speed, checking every side alley as I went. Seeing they all ended either blindly or with a steep staircase, I concluded that the woman had shot right through the deserted street to hook up with some main thoroughfare on the other side.

I was right. When I finally emerged into the sunlit exposure of an open square, it didn't take me long to spot a silver Audi idling with its trunk open. Next to it stood the woman I had been following, unlacing her Rollerblades. She was not alone. On the other side of the open trunk stood a woman with a wet suit unzipped to the waist, calmly putting on a T-shirt.

What should I do? Could I take on this pair all by myself? And what about the car's driver, gesturing at them to hurry? Irritated with myself for my indecision, I nonetheless started toward the car. When the two women spotted me, the Rollerblade thief immediately slammed the trunk, and they both jumped into the backseat, half undressed. Less than a second later, the silver Audi sped away with squealing tires, leaving me completely alone in the sleepy square.

Still out of breath, my head throbbing with defeat, I sat down on an overturned trash can to regain composure before eventually making my way back to the boat, my limbs as heavy as if I had run a marathon.

"Hurry up!" exclaimed Rebecca, who was waiting impatiently for me on the pier. "We have to cancel your phone account before she makes all sorts of expensive calls—"

"Bex!" I put a hand on her shoulder, but removed it right away when I realized how sweaty I was. "That was not a random pickpocket. This was planned. By someone far away."

Rebecca's forehead contracted into a rather unbecoming monobrow. "Don't be absurd. Who would—? Why would they—?"

"Two more excellent questions to add to the world's longest list of excellent questions," I said, climbing on board the boat just as Nick emerged from below decks.

"We need to find a police station," insisted Rebecca, staying on the pier.

"And do what? Sit around for five hours while some grumpy clerk misspells my address on a ten-page form that's going right back in the filing cabinet?" I shook my head, aware that Nick was looking at us both, mystified. "Let's just *go,* for God's sake."

Rebecca was clearly not ready to quit the subject, but Nick's presence made her hesitate. I had told her about his clandestine phone call and the Amazon Hoard earlier that morning, and although her first reaction had been to exclaim "How exciting! We're on a treasure hunt. Too bad you're going home," it didn't take her long to agree that something illicit was afoot.

"Pickpocket," I finally said, in response to Nick's raised eyebrows. "On Rollerblades. She took my phone. I almost had her."

"Did you?" His eyes did a tour of my disheveled clothes and red face. "You must be the fastest philologist in the world."

"Not as fast as I would like," I said, more sternly than intended. "Please tell me we are ready to go."

Once we had cleared the harbor traffic, I searched through our pile of luggage for the windbreaker Rebecca had lent me. The sunny lee of Nafplio had been deceiving; as soon as we were away from the protected bay, the briskness of the northerly wind reminded us that it was, after all, early November.

It was then, as I went on to look for my lip balm, that I discovered the full magnitude of the Rollerblade heist. "Bex?" I stood up, tightening my salt-spattered ponytail. "Have you seen my handbag?" It wasn't technically *my* handbag, but a tasseled suede loaner from Rebecca, seeing that my own had disappeared in the Knossos labyrinth. "I was sure I put it right here."

When we boarded the boat, I had made a point of wrapping the bag in Rebecca's flight jacket and tucking it underneath Nick's duffel bag for further concealment. The duffel bag and jacket were still there, but the tasseled wonder was nowhere to be found. Nor could Rebecca remember seeing it since we left port. "Nick," I said, with growing panic, "have you moved things around?"

But Nick had no recollection of touching "the hippie bag," as he called it. While Rebecca and I had been loitering on the pier, he reminded me, he had been hard at work belowdecks.

Maybe it was the choppy sea, or maybe it was the shocking confrontation with my own stupidity . . . but I suddenly felt woozy. Leaning against the boom, I had to fight to keep down the ham-and-sausage omelet Mr. Telemakhos had made us for our predawn breakfast. Granny's notebook had been in that bag. And now it was gone.

"Dee?" Rebecca gave my arm a little shake. "Are you all right?"

"Of course!" I tried to laugh. "Now someone else will have to pay off my credit cards. And my passport was just about to expire anyway."

Despite my efforts at making light of the whole thing, Nick wasn't fooled. He kept glancing at me, as if half-expecting me to blurt out some terrible confession along the lines of having carried around stolen gold coins, sewn into the lining of that unfortunate bag.

Little did he know that, to me, losing Granny's notebook was so much more devastating than any monetary loss could ever be. It was bad enough that I had lost the long list of translated words; I also couldn't shake a feeling that there had been a mystery within the notebook I had yet to grasp . . . a secret message I had yet to find. And now I never would.

ON MY TENTH BIRTHDAY—a sunny Saturday in April—Rebecca had arrived for the party an hour early, her face blotched from crying. "He was hit by a car," she whimpered, as we hurried up the staircase together, away from the inflating balloons and rising birthday buns. "Mr. Perkins said there was nothing he could do. So, my father went out and dug a hole in the garden, behind the strawberry bed."

It took some calm prompting from Granny to make Rebecca sit

down in the armchair and recount the story of Spencer's death in a coherent manner. "Father wouldn't even let me hold him," was the sad conclusion to the dog's hasty burial, "or talk to him. He said I had to pull myself together, because"——she could barely get out the words——"everything happens for a reason."

"That is wrong," agreed Granny, who, to her credit, had either forgotten or suppressed her disdain of Spencer. "Death is a test. This is when we must remember that we are humans, and not animals."

Despite strict instructions to never leave the property without my parents, Granny put on her dressing gown and took us both over to the vicarage. We snuck into the garden via the little wooden bridge connecting it with the churchyard, where Rebecca assured us we were not visible from the house.

"I assume this is the place?" said Granny, stopping at a small circle of freshly turned dirt with two shovels sticking out.

"Yes," nodded Rebecca, still sobbing. "He's down there. All alone."

"Well," said Granny, liberating the shovels. "Let's dig him up."

It did not occur to me to protest. Seeing the determination with which Rebecca embraced the task, I started digging, too, while Granny stood right beside us, overseeing the work. When we finally spotted a tuft of white fur, barely a foot into the ground, Granny pushed us both aside and personally dug out the rest of the dog with her hands. "Here," she said, placing the limp body in Rebecca's arms as gently as if it had been a sleeping baby. "Now you can talk to him." Then she sat down right there, on the little heap of dirt we had just dug up, and waited.

I have no idea how long we stayed there, waiting for Rebecca to stop crying. In the beginning, I had cried, too, over the shock of the whole thing, and later at the sight of the dead dog I had known so well. But after a while all I could think of was Rebecca, and whether she would ever be my happy, funny friend again.

We were all stiff with cold by the time Rebecca finally sighed deeply and said, "I'm so tired." She had been lying on the ground with Spencer in her arms, but now she sat up sluggishly, so pale and worn I was afraid she was going to faint.

"Good," said Granny, looking as if the damp ground did not affect her at all. "Now collect his favorite things. His bed, his best toy, some-thing to eat—"

"His leash?" suggested Rebecca, struggling to focus her swollen eyes on Granny's face.

"Did he like his leash?"

"He always got happy when he saw it," said Rebecca, chin trembling again.

"Off you go, then, both of you," ordered Granny. "Help each other, and come back here as quickly as you can. Hurry-hurry-hurry!"

When Spencer was finally laid to rest on his blue cushion, with his favorite things around him—all snatched from the house while the vicar and his wife were busy with a clogged toilet—Rebecca started crying again, and so did I. But it was a different kind of sadness now.

"Remember," said Granny, "you can always come back and talk to him whenever you like. But now he has to sleep a little. Bow your heads." We dutifully did as she said, while Granny recited a long string of words in a foreign language. We understood none of them, but they had a strangely soothing effect. Then she gave us the shovels and told us to fill up the hole. When we were done, she took a handful of soil and brushed it over our faces with her palm. "You are in grief," she told Rebecca, framing the dirt-smeared face with her hands. "But you have done the right thing."

It was not until we stepped through the front door of my house that I suddenly remembered the birthday party. A few balloons were float-ing about aimlessly, and there was a warm smell of ginger cake, but the whole house was eerily silent. A small collection of gift bags sat on the tile floor beneath the coat rack, but the gift givers were nowhere to be seen. Only then did I hear the clock in the living room strike five. The birthday invitations with the embossed silver horses had said three o'clock.

Just as we were tiptoeing up the staircase, my parents appeared in the kitchen door. They were both grave and pale, but they didn't say anything, merely watched us as we stood there caked with dirt, not knowing whether to go up or down. "I fear this is all my fault," said

Rebecca to them in a feeble, but unfaltering voice. "And I apologize. I know it's all . . . quite unforgivable."

"Well," said my mother, pulling her shawl more tightly around her, "why don't you girls come and have some birthday cake?"

After that day, there were no more nocturnal discussions in the living room, no more appealing glares from my mother to my father . . . merely silence. A pained, exhausted silence, heavy with finality. And within a week, my parents began driving off to meetings in faraway places, only to return with brochures and forms that they were careful to hide from me.

But I knew, with a child's instinctive grasp of adult skullduggery, where all this was going. They were preparing to send Granny away, to some impenetrable building with unsmiling men and large iron keys, and I would never see her again. They would strap her to a bed and put needles in her arm, and it would be my fault—for letting her be my friend.

THE ONLY ONE NOT afflicted by the theft was Mr. Telemakhos, who stubbornly refused to think of my handbag as being stolen. "It will show up!" he kept saying, waving a hairy hand at the wondrous ways of fate. "They always do."

To hide my misery, I threw myself into every available task around the boat and endeavored to ruminate as little as possible. The scheme was so effective it took me over an hour to look up from what I was doing. Only then did I feel a tremor of suspicion. If we were just going up the coast, why was there nothing but bright blue sea in every direction?

I approached Mr. Telemakhos, who was at the helm, laughing it up with Nick and Rebecca. "Excuse me," I said, suddenly feeling like an interloper. "Where exactly are we going? It's already ten o'clock—"

Mr. Telemakhos smirked. "I told you: We're going to the place where it all ends." When I kept peering at him, demanding more, he added more loudly, as if talking to someone with a hearing impairment,

"We are going to Troy. I have abducted you, Diana Morgan. For the next few days the three of you will be the hostage of my obsessive need for intelligent company." Seeing our shock at his boastful confession, Mr. Telemakhos broke into thunderous laughter. "In ten years, ask yourselves: Was he a pirate or an angel?"

"But you promised——" I began, almost choking on my own outrage.

"I promised to get you where you need to go," said Mr. Telemakhos, nodding as if we were in agreement. "And that's what I'm doing. Besides, what's the point of taking you to the airport when you don't have a passport?"

So furious I could have pushed the big man overboard, I turned to Nick. "Will you help me turn the boat around?" I asked him, fully intending Mr. Telemakhos to overhear me.

After a second's hesitation, Nick folded his arms. "I'm not a sailor. Sorry." Something in his eyes—a strange, devilish satisfaction hiding behind the apology—told me he was lying.

I looked at Rebecca, who was strangely silent. "Please explain to your friend"—I nodded at Mr. Telemakhos—"that this is absolutely unacceptable."

Rebecca's dumbstruck expression turned into irritation. "Do you really think he doesn't know that?" She glared at Mr. Telemakhos, who smiled blithely in response, as if our argument was merely birdsong in his ears.

"Bex," I said, struggling to contain my desperation, "for every day I don't keep my commitments around Oxford, a cyclops by the name of Professor Vandenbosch rips another limb off my career."

Rebecca looked away, apparently already resigned to her fate as abductee. "At least you *have* commitments. How wonderful that must be."

Realizing I was completely alone in my ire, and that neither Rebecca nor Nick would help me persuade Mr. Telemakhos to return to Nafplio, I left them and stalked off to the bow of the boat. I had rarely felt this helpless, and I didn't want them to see me like this, almost in tears with frustration.

It was true that I wouldn't be able to board a plane without my passport, but that only made my need to return to shore so much more urgent. I would have to find alternative transportation, and even if everything went smoothly I couldn't possibly hope to arrive in Oxford before the weekend. Truly, my situation was extremely distressing even without the added complication of my being currently trapped on the *Penelope*.

And yet . . . even in my wretchedness, I couldn't help feeling a treacherous tickle of excitement at the prospect of visiting Troy. Was this not, after all, precisely what I secretly wanted? To continue on the Amazon trail? For all my determination to return to Oxford without further delay, I hadn't been able to quell a strong feeling that by doing so I would forfeit my only chance to find the missing link between Granny and the priestesses from Algeria.

Standing in the bow, looking out over the Aegean Sea and the islands materializing in the distance, I decided I might as well come to terms with the situation. We were going to Troy, and there was nothing I could do about it; pouting was a nonstarter. As soon as I returned home, I would make up for all the canceled tutorials and lavish so much attention on my students that they would come to regard my absence as a blessing. With regard to Katherine Kent, I clung to the hope she would forgive me once I explained myself—she always had in the past.

When I finally felt confident of my poise, I returned to the others. By now, Rebecca was steering the ship, giddy with the thrill of it, and Mr. Telemakhos was busy giving her instructions. The only one who paid any attention to me was Nick, who gave me a sideways glance and said, under his breath, "I think you just broke the world record for sulking. Under ten minutes. Very impressive."

Not quite ready to be chummy, I responded with curt detachment, "I don't sulk. I calculate."

Later that night, after putting on a patient face all day, I left Rebecca asleep in our shared cabin and crept up on deck to be alone. Dinner had been jolly—I had even laughed—but I was not yet over my anger. Mr. Telemakhos was so proud of his own power over us, so self-satisfied . . . A childish part of me wanted to teach him a lesson.

We had cast anchor in a quiet bay, and the only sounds I could hear were the waves lapping the hull of the boat and an occasional flapping of wings against water. Earlier, in the golden glow of sunset, the bay had appeared uninhabited, but now, long after nightfall, a few distinct lights shone from windows in the hills. How far away were the houses? I wondered. Were there people on this island who might be able to help me? Or were the specks of light in fact stars, just rising over the forested ridges? Despite the moon, which gave a bit of structure to the darkness around me, I couldn't quite tell where the earth ended and heaven began.

As I sat there on the deck, hugging my knees and meditating on fanciful escape plans, Nick appeared. I hadn't heard his approach, for he was barefoot and, as always, moved completely silently. After a moment's hesitation he sat down next to me and nodded at the gibbous moon. "Almost full."

When I did not reply, he continued, "A wise bosun once told me there is a guardian angel who watches over young men. To me, that angel was always the Moon. She has saved my life many times."

"Really?" I said. Despite the fact that Nick had done nothing whatsoever to help me reason with Mr. Telemakhos earlier, I still preferred his company to my own grumpy solitude. "Did she ever deliver you from boats with mad Greek captains?"

I sensed him smiling in the darkness. "We can try. Maybe she will grant you a wish. What do you want? To be back in Oxford right now?"

For some reason, my affirmative "yes" got stuck in my throat.

"Don't worry." Nick spoke directly into my ear. "I won't tell anyone."

A little annoyed with him for thinking I was won over so easily, I leaned away and said, "I promised everyone I'd be home today."

"Here." Nick handed me his phone. "Call and explain."

"Thanks. Maybe tomorrow. My parents are in bed now."

"What about Boyfriend? Doesn't he pick up after ten?"

Not knowing what to say, I shook my head and gave him back the phone. Nick chuckled. "Relax! They're not going to fire you. They need you. You're smart. In my experience, beautiful women are only attractive until they open their mouths. With you, the more you speak, the more—" He broke off abruptly, then said, more quietly, "I wish I had your ability to focus. To sit in a library for days . . . months . . . and just *read*. But I've never had that kind of patience. And so I've never become really good at anything." Perhaps realizing he was doing himself an injustice, he elbowed me teasingly. "Well, a few things I do well, or so I've been told."

The words, although spoken in jest, crept all the way into my imagination and caused a quiet burst of chaos. "And what else are you good at?" I heard myself saying.

Nick straightened. "Taking risks. I'm a pro at that."

"Give me a for instance."

He pondered it briefly, then said, "How about free-climbing? Or canoeing the Nahanni River in November?"

I frowned. "I don't even know where that *is*. What else?"

"Oh." He slouched a little, as if he wasn't terribly proud of himself after all. "The usual. Trying to push the limits. Impress my friends."

I unfurled my arms, no longer as chilled as I had been before. Part of the warmth, I realized, emanated from Nick's body and lingered in the narrow space between us, luring me closer. "Somehow I imagined you out there in the service of mankind," I joked, grateful for the increasingly humorous trajectory of our chat. "Trucking food aid to starving villagers—"

"I did that, too." He spoke calmly, with a shrug, and didn't even bother to look at me to see whether I believed him. "Until I realized the only people I was helping were the warlords and the pig-headed politicians who had caused the problem in the first place."

"I see." I studied his profile, wondering whether I was finally seeing Nick the way he really was, or whether this, too, was just another role in his seemingly endless cast of characters. "You were demoralized by the malfunctions of civil society and so flung yourself into frivolous pleasure seeking as a result?"

He thought about it for a moment. "More like pain seeking. But yes, that sounds about right. Hey, if you ever get demoralized by the malfunctions of academia, you should go into public relations." He lowered his voice conspiratorially. "I'll hire you as my spokesperson."

"Maybe I'll start by canoeing the Nahanni River," I countered. "In July."

"You'll be eaten alive by blackflies. Or grizzly bears."

I touched a gamesome fist to his thigh. "I'll hire you as my guide."

Nick chuckled. "You may regret that. I wouldn't shave, and we'd be sharing a sleeping bag."

The image went straight to my cheeks, and I was grateful all he could see of me were shades of gray. "Why couldn't we have one each?"

His sweatered shoulder bumped teasingly against mine. "Why do you want to go camping with me in the first place?"

"Oh, I don't know." I cleared my throat, astounded by the flirtatious turn our conversation had taken. "You are quite the amusing conversationalist."

I couldn't help it, there was something about his eyes that made me lean a bit closer, and for a few breathless seconds I was certain he would kiss me. As a matter of fact, at that precise moment—despite how fundamentally at odds we were—I was rather hoping he would.

Instead, he reached for something and handed me a flat, familiar-feeling object. "There. I took the liberty of removing it from your bag this morning, before we left the house."

It was Granny's notebook.

"But——" I was so flummoxed by the reappearance of my most prized possession I burst out laughing. Clutching it to my chest, eventually I worked up the wherewithal to thank him, although a small part of me was dismayed at the fact that he had gone through my bag.

"After the attack in Crete," Nick began, the tone of his voice suggesting he wasn't too proud of himself, "I had a hunch your shadowy thief would try again. I've been meaning to talk to you about it, but we're never alone."

"This is all a bit . . . shocking," I stammered, my perception of Nick doing somersaults in my head. If there had been the tiniest part of me thinking it just *might* have been him, and not the Rollerblade gang, who had made my tasseled bag disappear, then that possibility was now thoroughly buried under a rather clammy avalanche of shame.

"Just be happy," Nick went on, teasing me again, "I haven't paid you yet. I'm not sure I can keep up with the pace of your losses—"

"Ah," I said. "Money again."

"What's wrong with money? Isn't that why you're here . . . with me?"

I shook my head, still too frazzled to play my cards with discretion. "There's nothing wrong with money. In fact, I'm a great fan of it, but it's not why I'm here."

"Then tell me."

I looked at his face, made even graver by the moon shadows. Sitting close to him like this, it did not seem right to have so much deception between us. True, he had his own secret agenda with the Amazons, but then so had I. In fact, I suddenly realized, Nick's perception of me could well be no more flattering than my perception of *him;* perhaps in his eyes, I, too, was nothing but a weasel working for the wrong team.

"In Crete," I said, "you asked me how I did it. The translation. You assumed there was a trick to it. Well——" I rose and walked away from him. "You were right."

Standing by the railing, looking at the moon's reflection in the inky water, I told him of Granny and the notebook and bracelet she had left behind for me. She had likely been an archaeologist, I explained, who had encountered the Amazon writing system in some other dig and been able to translate it into English. "And yet even she," I concluded, "for all her obsession with the Amazons, never tried to teach me this strange language; in fact, she never even mentioned it. She just left me this bloody notebook."

When I finally stopped talking, Nick came over to lean against the railing beside me. I fully expected him to berate me for not telling him the story earlier, but instead, he simply asked, "How did your grandmother die?"

I flinched, frosted by a familiar sense of guilt. "The thing is . . . she disappeared. My parents were about to send her away to an asylum, and she——" I stopped, unable to continue as I meant to. On the rare occasions in the past when I had been forced to tell the story, I had said that Granny ran away, glossing over the locked doors and her being entirely without means. "The truth is," I now heard myself saying, to Nick of all people, "I gave her all the money I had, and walked her to the high road, and helped her on a bus."

"To where?"

I swallowed, ambushed by holed-up emotions. "I don't know. I was ten years old. For the entire rest of my childhood I was tortured by thoughts of the terrible things that might have happened to her. Whenever there was a strange letter in the mail or an unexpected phone call I was afraid it had something to do with Granny. That she had been found dead somewhere." I shuddered at the memory of my old fears. "Only later I discovered that my parents employed a private investigator for two whole years. He came up with absolutely nothing but a horrendous bill."

Nick pulled off his sweater and draped it over my shoulders without a word, folding the sleeves around my neck.

"Sorry about the long epic," I said, staring out over the black water. "I've never actually told anyone about all of this before. Not even Bex."

When Nick finally spoke, his voice was unusually gentle. "Are you sure she was really crazy?"

"I . . . don't know." Once again, the path of his inquiry took me right back to questions I had been wrestling with for years. "The doctors thought so. She was certainly not normal by anyone's standards, whatever that means."

"Do you know if she had any friends? Communicated with anyone?"

I felt a tiny sting of suspicion. "What do you mean? I hope you're not taking Mr. Telemakhos's talk about modern-day Amazons seriously."

"Why not? What do you prefer to believe: that it was all in her head or that there was something to it? You just told me she had an archive, too, with newspaper clippings . . . that she kept seeing evidence of Amazon activity around the world. What makes you so sure she was wrong?" I felt Nick studying my profile in the darkness as he waited in vain for my response. Then he went on, saying, "Apart from all the tough talk, did your grandmother ever actually *behave* like an Amazon? Did she hurt people?"

"Well." I cast my mind back to that stolen day so many years ago, where I had been sitting on the floor with Rebecca, going through the papers in my father's desk. Among them had been a psychological evalu-

ation that recounted the tragic events leading to her initial hospitaliza-
tion. "Only in the beginning, I am sure, before they realized she was
mentally ill. They didn't really have a name for it in those days, but I think
Granny had a postpartum depression that spiraled out of control. In any
case, she was convinced she had given birth to a girl rather than my father
and absolutely refused to hear otherwise. She locked herself in a room
with the baby—my father, that is—and wouldn't come out. In the end,
they had to use force, and she . . . well, she defended herself with a poker
from the fireplace. It was all quite terrible. A police constable ended up
in the hospital." I shuddered, as I had so often, at the thought of Granny
drawing blood from another human being. Then, realizing how shocking
this must all sound to Nick, I hastened to add, "I'm sure she didn't mean
to hurt anyone. Apparently, she had a delusion that it was wrong to have
a boy, and that if *they* found out, they'd take him away."

With his back to the moon, Nick was little more than a dark silhouette, and I felt more than saw the intensity of his stare. "Who was
'they'?"

"Her fellow Amazons, of course. Can't raise a boy, can you now, if
you're a true Amazon. Haven't you read your Strabo?"

Nick didn't answer but merely stuck his hands in his pockets and
did a little tour of the deck, perhaps thinking I needed time to recover.
When he returned, I took off the sweater and gave it back to him.
"Sorry to go on like that. I probably should have told you before, but—"

The sentence hung between us for a while. Then Nick slung the
sweater over his shoulder and said, "You were right not to trust me. I
am not even sure I trust myself anymore." After a pained pause, he
added, "Besides, you *did* try to tell me about the bracelet. But I wouldn't
listen. I thought you had stolen it. I'm sorry."

"Wait a minute." The photos on his laptop did a little bitchy catwalk
in my head. "*You* took it. Didn't you? You even took a picture of it!"

The accusation did not provoke the hoped-for confession. Instead,
Nick said, "When we first opened the sarcophagus, we found fourteen
bracelets."

"*What?*" I stared at his solemn profile, unable to keep track with
him.

"They were just lying there. They were all"—he nodded at my arm—"exactly like yours. And yes, I took photos of them. But I decided to leave the one on the skeleton, because I wanted an archaeologist to do things properly."

I was so baffled by this news I felt an irrational urge to embrace him. "So, if neither you nor I stole that last bracelet . . . who did?"

"How do you know it was stolen?" Nick scrutinized me in the darkness. "Because the sarcophagus was open?"

"Let me rephrase that," I said. "Who opened the sarcophagus and why?"

Nick shrugged. "Don't look at me."

"Why not?" I decided to jump right in. "You're the one who is on a treasure hunt."

I waited for his reaction, but he was completely silent. "Come on," I said eventually, stepping closer. "I heard you on the phone, talking about the Amazon Hoard. What's going on, Nick?"

He finally groaned and rubbed his face. "I wanted to keep you out of it—"

"Well, too damn late!"

With a sigh he sat down, his back against the main mast. "Do you remember what I told you in the car last Sunday? That I am the X that marks the spot? Well, after what happened in Algeria, I'm not exactly the most popular X around the office."

"But that wasn't your fault. How can they—?"

"Oh, it's nothing personal. That's how we operate. I'm a liability now. Lots of crooks on my heels, as we can both testify." Nick opened his arms, just a little. "I apologize. But the Aqrab Foundation has too much going on this month. A new site in Jordan. Some issues in Bulgaria. So, the boss thought it might be an idea to"—he paused to take a deep breath—"send me away for a while. Away from the hot spots."

I felt my chest tighten. "But . . . where are you going?"

Even in the darkness, I could see the embarrassment on his face. "No, you don't understand. They sent me away already. That's why I went to Crete with you. That's why I'm *here*." He paused, clearly waiting for my reaction. When it didn't come, he sighed again. "Diana. You and I both know the Amazon Hoard is bullshit. But *they* don't."

It took a few moments for my fuse to catch. Once it did, the shock threw me backward, into the ropes of the railing. "That's it?" I exclaimed. "Wait, let me get this straight. . . . We're being followed, and basically, you're using me as a decoy . . . to lead the crooks astray? Is that what you're saying?"

Nick stood up. "Look, I'm not proud of it——"

"No!" I held up my hands to prevent him from approaching me. "What a complete and utter ninny I have been! *Of course* you were never interested in the Amazons; you barely knew who they were! But that didn't stop you, did it, from hijacking a penniless philologist and using her as bait!"

"Listen——" Nick took a tentative step toward me, then another. "This was not my idea. And I certainly never wanted you to get hurt. All these accidents——"

"They're not accidents, Nick, they're beautifully planned." I felt an absurd impulse to laugh. "It finally makes sense! Oh man, I thought I was going nuts. . . . I thought I was being chased by Amazons. This is fantastic——" I tried to look him in the eye, but the moon wouldn't let me. "Come on, smile! You should be happy your scheme is working so beautifully. Not only did the bastards take the bait, they took quite a few pieces of *me* along the way. Well done, Nicholas! The X that marks the spot has earned his bonus."

Nick looked stricken. "How can I make it up to you?" But before I could respond, he reached out and touched a finger to my lips. "Not now. Think about it. Go to bed and count to ten."

I pushed away his hand. "How about counting to ten thousand?"

He nodded slowly. "I'll give you a check tomorrow."

"Make it cash," I countered, sidestepping toward the stairs. "And how about adding a handsome tip for putting up with *you* all this time?"

CHAPTER TWENTY-FIVE

Lilli woke up as soon as they were in open waters. Stretching and yawning, she sat up and felt around her with curious fingers. The soft couch with the woven cover . . . the fabric wall bulging inward from the pressure of the sea air: The room in the stern of the Trojan ship was clearly so different from what she had expected that she became quite frightened. "Klito?" she called. "Are you up yet?"

"Indeed I am." Klito kissed the girl on the hair.

"Are we sailing again?" asked Lilli, frowning. "There was a man—a man who smelled like Myrina—"

"I have a surprise for you," said Klito, tears of happiness running down her cheeks. "A surprise that will make you laugh."

Unable to wait any longer, Myrina pushed forward and enfolded Lilli in a firm embrace. The others had insisted on breaking the news gently, so as not to shock the girl, but Myrina understood the extent of her sister's toughness better than anyone and knew this was a shock she would relish.

"Our prayers have been met," said one of the freed priestesses, whose name was Pylla. "Clearly it was Lilli's jackal bracelet that bought our freedom. Let us thank the gods—"

"Maybe you should start by thanking Myrina," said Pitana. "She has not rested, has barely even sat down since you were taken away."

"Might I suggest we are *all* thanked?" interjected Egee. "Let not Myrina carry the burden of your gratitude all by herself—"

No one else cared to argue. After spending the morning hours wrestling with a hysterical Kara—who was now, thankfully, collapsed in sleep—none of the other women had the stomach for more drama. Nor did they attempt to question the new girl they had picked up in Mycenae; she had told them her name was Helena, and for now that was all anyone wanted to know.

After spending the morning in the stern room, unable to take her eyes off Lilli, Myrina eventually went in search of Paris. She found him in the bow of the ship, deep in conversation with Aeneas and Dares.

Not one of the three had a smile for her upon her approach; nodding grimly at Paris, the two other men quickly excused themselves and left. Nor did Paris seem ready to have words with her; turning his back and looking out over the ocean ahead, he gave the impression of being unaware of her presence.

Despite the hostile reception, Myrina stayed where she was and said, "Will you at least allow me to apologize?"

When Paris finally replied, his voice was tense with anger. "What I allow—or do not allow—seems to have little effect on you."

"But still—"

He turned to face her, flushed with exasperation. "Myrina, I am not someone who cares for fine words and intentions—especially not when your actions so blatantly undermine them. If you must apologize, apologize to my countrymen. They will be the victims of my lunatic faith in you. Never again will a Greek trust the word of a Trojan sailor—" Too upset to finish the thought, Paris turned his back to her once more, shaking his head. "I barely have the will to ask you what happened last night. And yet I must know. You managed to free your friend, I see that, but I don't know what price I have yet to pay for her."

"Perhaps they will think she escaped on her own—" began Myrina.

"Are you telling me you were able to enter and leave the palace unseen?"

Myrina hesitated, then threw back her head and met his eyes. "The prince is dead. Dead on the floor of his own prison, steeped in the blood of my sisters. But those who saw us will not squeal. Nothing is as silent as a woman who hates."

Paris closed his eyes. Then he opened them again, ten years older. "Were I a man who lived by the rules—nay, were I a *wise* man—I would turn this ship around and take all of you back there. But I am not. As a god in the sky, believe me, I should pummel evil Mycenae with thunderbolts and pierce it through and through; as a man, it seems I must be content to pummel it with insults and flee as fast as I can."

Seeing that Myrina was ready to weigh in, Paris shook his head. "The kindest thing you can do is to stay far away from me. Go and rejoice with your sisters. Let me not see you in the stern anymore. In two days, if the winds are favorable, we land at Ephesus. I was going to offer you a home at Troy, but under the circumstances I cannot. Where you go next is up to you, but Ephesus is where we say good-bye."

AFTER THREE DAYS OF pained silence and accusatory looks from the crew, Myrina's sisters were naturally relieved when the ships reached the coast across the sea from Mycenae. Thrust forward by a rising storm, the Trojan fleet was blown straight into the harbor of Ephesus, unable to lay anchor. All night the ships rocked and scraped against the docks, and by morning everyone was running around above and below, surveying the damage.

"There is no hurry," said Paris, when Myrina came to bid him farewell. "We will not be leaving until everything is repaired." He glanced at her as he spoke, and she was relieved to see that after two days of stubborn separation, his anger had evaporated at least enough for him to want to look at her again. "But if you and your sisters are ready to go—and I see that you are—let me take you to the Lady of Ephesus and introduce you. As you will soon realize, it is no coincidence I have brought you here."

Leaving the harbor on foot, Paris escorted the women into town. In no particular hurry to complete the task, he gave Lilli his elbow and described everything they passed: the fruit vendors, the clothes dyers, and the old people sitting in the shade, lamenting the way the world was going. More than once, he made the girl laugh out loud with some fresh observation Myrina could barely hear.

Meanwhile, it was all Klito and Egee could do to pull Kara along with the group. Even though she had finally stopped crying over the death of the man who had—she kept insisting—cared for her after all, she still would not speak to Myrina nor acknowledge having been in need of saving. "I loved him!" she exclaimed more than once, to whoever was in earshot. "And he loved me!"

"Is that why he starved you, tied you up, and beat you?" Pitana finally asked. But Kara was deaf to all such voices; she had long since sought refuge in a life that existed only in her own mind.

Set among gentle hills and lush, uninhabited countryside, the town of Ephesus struck Myrina as a sleepy, harmless place. This was where she and her sisters would live until they had gathered the means to leave . . . or until they all grew old together and sat in the shade like these gentle elders, gumming the memories of peaceful lives. It was not a bleak prospect compared to the horror they had left at home, or seen at Mycenae, and yet Myrina found she could take no great pleasure in the vision. For regardless of how she framed it, it was a future without Paris, and although she had known him for only a short time, she felt her being had already attached itself to him. Wherever he went, she yearned to follow. If he disappeared from sight, even for a moment, she felt as unstable as a chair with one leg missing.

It was an odd and worrisome sensation to someone who had long since learned to depend on no one but herself, and yet Myrina had come to cherish it—so much so, that the prospect of parting from Paris filled her with dread. Not the acute, temporary dread that could be conquered by courageous actions, but a dread so profound, so pervasive, it cast a dark shadow over everything she did or said, even over her joyful reunion with Lilli.

What a peculiar thing, thought Myrina as she looked around at the inviting calmness of the quaint town and its dwellers, that she who had seen so much danger, and been within arm's reach of death so often . . .

what a sleight of fate that *she* of all people should arrive in such a blessed place and feel her life was over.

HALF-EXPECTING THE LADY OF Ephesus to live in elegant seclusion on a hill overlooking town, Myrina was surprised when Paris stopped in a seemingly random street to let everyone through an open gate. Entering last, Myrina saw they were in a quiet courtyard framed by buildings and a shady portico, and saw her sisters turning about themselves among the carefully potted exotic plants, eyes wide with curiosity. Clearly, the Lady of Ephesus was someone who prized tranquillity and elegance— two qualities Myrina had yet to master.

Conscious of her own shortcomings—dirty feet being one of them—Myrina withdrew into the shade of the portico . . . and then suddenly all those small concerns were forgotten. For there, among the pillars and coiling vines, stood a figure she knew well:

The Moon Goddess.

Admittedly, she was not smooth and black, but carved of wood, and her body was dressed in a linen tunic that bore a myriad of brown stains—probably drips from the rotting lumps of meat hanging by strings around her neck.

"I see you are already friends." Paris came up to Myrina with Lilli still in tow. "Of all the towns on the Trojan coast, I knew this would appeal to you the most. Here, no man holds sway. The Lady of Ephesus, as you can see, is a protectress of hunters and maidens—a combination I always thought unique for this place"—he shook his head—"until I met you."

"Are those—?" Myrina leaned closer to inspect the lumps of meat hanging around the neck of the goddess. They appeared to be animal testicles—the parts she always cut away and left for the hyenas.

"I'm afraid so." Paris grimaced. "It is a tradition here. Woe to any male who crosses the hunting trail of Otrera's daughters. Stags, bears, men"—he grinned, clearly teasing her—"no one is safe. You will fit right in."

"Who is Otrera?" asked Myrina, but just then, an older woman, stiff-necked with dignity and wearing a long gray dress with flared sleeves, appeared on a balcony overlooking the courtyard, understandably puzzled by the sudden influx of strangers.

"Hippolyta?" she called. "Penthesilea?"

"Lady Otrera," explained Paris to Myrina, while beaming with admiration, "is the High Priestess and my mother's sister. But she detests ceremony, as do all her daughters. They live for the hunt and are masterful riders; in fact, most of them spend their time on a farm just outside town, where they breed and train horses." He looked at Myrina with a bashful smile—a rarity for him. "That is how my father met my mother: He came here to buy horses."

She stared at him. "Your father . . . the king of Troy?"

Paris frowned. "Surely you have realized we take our horses very seriously."

"Yes, but—" Myrina looked up at the woman on the balcony, still not fully understanding. "How many daughters does Lady Otrera have?"

"Probably about thirty," said Paris, "plus the novices." He gave her a sideways look. "Quite impressive for a woman who has never known a man. Come, let me introduce you. I am confident she will recognize the language you speak with your sisters; my aunt is very learned and prides herself on her fluency in most foreign tongues."

It was late afternoon by the time Lady Otrera finally rose from her straw chair on the marble portico. By now the distant mountains were dressed for evening, glowing with tender reds, and a great peace had come over the world as the sun sank into the ocean at last, spent and satisfied.

"It is decided, then," said the noble woman, whose face was still grave with sympathy for Myrina and her sisters after everything she had heard. "You will be our guests for as long as you wish. And should you come to like it here, you may earn your keep and call it home, for there is always work to be done on the farm and in the orchards. As a matter of fact"—she cast a strict glance at Hippolyta and Penthesilea, who had arrived on horseback in the middle of Myrina's tale, sweating and disheveled—"since my daughters are rarely where I think they are, the extra hands will be welcome."

Soon after, Paris took leave of everyone with a vague promise to return, as he phrased it, before the end of the world. Unwilling to commit to a time, he walked off with determination, barely stopping to say good-bye to Myrina.

"Wait—" She followed him through the door and down the street a few uncertain steps. "Will I not see you again?"

He paused and turned, frowning with displeasure. "Otrera has taken you in. You need no longer depend on me. I should think that comes as a relief for us both." As he stood on the sloping street, the setting sun formed a halo around his head; never had he looked more handsome, or more forlorn.

Myrina moved toward him, but something in his eyes made her stop. "I wish it were otherwise," she said.

"What exactly?" Paris cocked his head. "Do you wish we had never met?"

"No! But . . . I know I have caused you much pain—"

Despite his evident decision to be stern, Paris burst into laughter. "True. But that is my own fault." He glanced over his shoulder at the masts in the harbor. "I should have tossed you overboard when I had the chance." Then, seeing Myrina's wounded expression, his own softened considerably. "You want things otherwise, you say." He walked up to her, closer and closer, until they were almost chest to chest. "So tell me, insatiable Myrina, what more do you desire from me?"

She stuck out her chin, bracing against his teasing charms. "You have already spent too much on me. The gold mask in Mycenae—"

"I am not talking about gold."

Myrina hesitated, not sure how to best express herself. "Well," she said at last, seeing he was still waiting, "if you find yourself at ease, with nothing else to do, I should like for you to"—she cast her mind around and reached for the only thing she knew—"teach me how to fight like a man."

Paris's eyes widened with surprise. "Really? I would think you had more than enough practice in that regard. In fact"—he bent his head to speak directly into her ear—"I believe the only lesson you have yet to learn is how to surrender like a woman."

Myrina felt a rush of heat. "Why must a woman always surrender? I am not prey—"

"No, *I* am. Your arrow struck me long ago"—Paris took her hand and placed it on his chest—"right here. And every time I try to pull it out"—he used her hand to demonstrate—"you force it back in."

They stood like that for a moment, her hand pressed so tightly against his chest she could feel the beat of his heart beneath the embroidered fabric. Then Myrina said, "Please don't leave. I cannot bear the thought."

"The thought of what?" Paris looked down at her hand. "Of not having everything and nothing all at once?" He poked at the jackal bracelet with evident loathing. "You make so much of this freedom of yours, yet allow yourself to be enslaved by a piece of metal." Then, letting go of her, he took a few steps back, a challenge in his amber eyes. "If you really wish it were otherwise, make it so. You are the only one with the power to do that."

PARIS DID NOT COME back the next day, nor the day after. And on the third day, when Myrina stole out of the house to look, she could no longer see the Trojan ships in the harbor.

He had gone. Without another word of farewell.

Her disappointment was so great she nearly sat down in the middle of the road and cried. For three days she had dreamed of the moment she would see him again, and had insisted—selfishly and irrationally, scorning the plans of Lady Otrera—that she and her sisters remain in town rather than going out to the farm right away . . . just in case he returned.

Walking back inside now, heavy with defeat, Myrina found everyone occupied much as they had been since their arrival: Some were busy in the kitchen, grinding grains and tending pots, others were crawling around in the inner courtyard, spreading out laundry on the warm tiles. Every single one of them—even Egee—had embraced these simple tasks with grateful relish. After all they had been through, any chore not interrupted by high seas or an abusive master was a happy one.

Even Kara was beginning to show small signs of recovery. She was no longer muttering to herself, and no longer slept through the day, her back turned in hateful protest. But even as she was up and about, taking part in the tasks of the house, she still slipped in and out of awareness. In the middle of sweeping a floor or beating on a rug, she might pause and lean on the broom for the longest time, her thoughts presumably back in Mycenae—not the Mycenae Myrina had seen, but a Mycenae of her own making where she, Kara, was queen.

When consulted on the matter, Lady Otrera had advised Myrina and the others against any manner of confrontation or impatient urging. "Kara will return when she is ready," she said, walking with Myrina in the shade of the portico. "The mind is a changeable thing. It will take on any form it pleases; sometimes it is a lion, sometimes a rat . . . and the more you chase it, the faster it runs, the deeper it burrows."

They stopped in front of the statue of the Lady of Ephesus, and on Otrera's prompting Myrina found herself describing in some detail the rites of the Moon Goddess. To which Lady Otrera—snaking her arm around Myrina's elbow and commencing another turn about the quiet loggia—replied, "Our mistresses are one and the same, I am sure. For we, too, worship the night when men are asleep, and our passions are as pure as the hearts of the does in the woods. Animals are what we love—horses above all—and every one of my daughters knows that man, fascinating as he may be, brings nothing but deceit and destruction. It is man, and man alone, who robs woman of her natural dignity and infects her with despair and death."

"Surely there are *some* good men," began Myrina, thinking not only of Paris and the courteous Trojans, but also of her father, and Lilli's father, too, the latter of whom had rivaled any woman in the village when it came to nurture and patience.

Otrera looked straight into Myrina's eyes, her light-brown gaze as calm as that of a lioness at rest. "I did not say man corrupts woman by

design, merely that it always turns out so. This was once the house"—
she made a loving gesture at the buildings around them—"of a mother
who lost all her daughters to childbirth. Three she had, three darling
girls who grew up, and were wooed and married . . . only to be snatched
away by death at the height of their happiness. This woman—so goes
the story—sat here many a sleepless night at the feet of Lady Artemis,
deep in conversation with the Goddess, until she understood at last that
she had been taught a lesson. And so she decided to open her house to
strangers, inviting orphaned girls from far and near to take refuge here,
as long as they agreed to a pact of purity." Otrera pointed at a fresco of
running horses upon the wall of the loggia. "It was this poor, grieving
mother who discovered the healing powers of the hunt, and I must say,
I have never seen a woman who was not perfectly satisfied with the
exchange of a man for a horse and halter."

As THE WEEKS WENT by, Myrina began to understand what Lady Otrera
meant. Even though it was winter and the farmlands were dormant, the
farm itself—a rambling village at the foot of a hill—was perpetually
crawling with activity.

In the beginning, Otrera's daughters were skeptical of the
newcomers—not because they did not embrace the influx of new blood
and foreign quirks, but because the kind of life Myrina and her holy
sisters had led in the Temple of the Moon Goddess struck them as so
overly regulated, so agonizingly dull, they could scarce accept that any
sane person would willingly lead it.

"And you," said the broad-shouldered Penthesilea to Myrina one
day, while they were feeding the chickens together. "How can you call
yourself a hunter when you do not even know how to ride?"

Myrina had taken the exclamation as a product of language confusion rather than ill will and had smiled at her new friend, saying, "I
depend on my own legs and not those of a fitful animal. Besides, my
weapon is the bow, and I don't see how you can be an archer and a rider
at the same time."

"Then do as we," replied Penthesilea. "Rely on the javelin. Come."

She brushed the last grains of chicken feed from her wiry fingers and started toward the stable. "I will show you!"

Left to her own apprehensions, Myrina without question would have stayed away from the horse enclosures for a good long time, but her pride forbade her from saying so to the dauntless Penthesilea. In fact, it was primarily the realization that these other women—some too waifish to lift a sack of grain—were perfectly comfortable around the temperamental beasts that made Myrina determined to master the art . . . if only to silence their teasing.

No sooner had she commenced her training than her sisters came forward, too, emboldened by her being still alive and—apart from a few bruised ribs—tolerably whole. Aided by Penthesilea and the slightly more sympathetic Hippolyta, they spent the winter months learning how to ride and control the horses, and before the first spring flowers were out of the ground, even Animone was tearing around the pastures with abandon.

Lilli, of course, was clamoring to take part in the games. But Myrina was loath to let her sister ride a horse alone or even be around the animals on the ground, for fear she would be kicked or trod upon. Penthesilea's horse, in particular, was an unpredictable, aggressive beast, and its rider did nothing to curb its temper; quite the contrary. So, instead, Myrina would come to the house on her own horse at least once every day, sidle up to the raised porch, and have Lilli sit either in front or right behind her, holding on tightly. In this fashion they would trot around an uncut hayfield or make their way slowly to the beach for a gallop in the sand. And yet Lilli never stopped talking of the day she would be riding a horse of her own, and Myrina barely knew whether to be happy or worried that her sister—who had never actually *seen* a horse—continued to have such a zest for excitement.

In the beginning, Myrina had tried to encourage a friendship between Lilli and Helena—the girl they had rescued from Mycenae. Close in age, the two could have found solace in each other's company . . . but the girls were so different Myrina might as well have tried to make a cat befriend a dog. For while Lilli was the happy, pleasing girl she had always been, Helena was silent and brooding, her eyes full of spite. And whenever she spoke—which, fortunately, she did rarely—her words were so belligerent Myrina often felt inclined to cover Lilli's ears with her hands.

"I thought you were warriors," Helena had said once, when Myrina asked her rather bluntly to justify her surly manners. "You said big words, and I followed you, because I am a warrior. But you are not. You do not fight."

Even the discovery that she would not, in fact, need to have a breast seared off had only seemed to infuriate the girl. "You lie about everything!" she hissed at Myrina, pointing a hateful finger at her face. "Just like my father."

The exclamation startled Myrina; for some reason she had assumed Helena was an orphan. "Where *is* your father?" she asked, already toying with the idea of sending the unpleasant girl home to her parents, wherever they may be. "Was he, too, taken by the Greeks?"

Helena turned up her nose with disgust. "I am not a slave. And I am not going home. My father will kill me. He *will*. He killed my mother. And my sister. I know he did." Her mouth tightened. "I wish I could kill *him*."

More than once, Myrina caught Helena behind the barn, playing solitary weapon games. Sometimes she would join her, and they would practice together, throwing spears and knives. And yet later, back at the house, Helena would regard Myrina with eyes as cold as ever—as if their sport had done nothing to soften her animosity.

In this flux of new challenges—learning the language of Ephesus being one of them—Myrina hardly had time to spare for daydreaming. And at night, when she lay quietly in the darkness, reaching out for the memory of Paris, she was usually asleep with exhaustion before he could join her. But even so, he was never far away, and the thrill of his imagined presence neither wavered nor waned. Most of the time it made her happy, but occasionally her happiness was trampled by panic at the fear that she would never see him again. For while he had healed her old wound, he had left a mark in its place: a mark of kinship that no number of baths—warm or cold—could erase.

Ironically, these feelings were what eventually enabled Myrina to bond with Kara. One night, when they had cleaned up the kitchen together and sat quietly on the doorstep, stroking the house cats, Kara suddenly said, in a voice thick with defiance, "I am carrying his child. Do you understand?"

And in a strange way, Myrina did. She had heard the others talking about Kara's imaginary pregnancy with headshaking weariness, but had so far not been asked to comment. Klito and Egee, she gathered, had proof it was merely a delusion and had tried to shame Kara into reason, but the result had been a weeklong return to tears and hateful silence.

Sitting there on the doorstep, both of them tired from the day's work, Myrina could almost feel Kara's pain . . . could almost sense the lump of deformed emotions she carried within. And so she put her arm around the woman who—for weeks now—had refused to speak to her directly, and said quietly, "I understand."

EVER SINCE HER FIRST conversation with the haughty Penthesilea, Myrina had harbored a secret ambition. The more Otrera's daughters scoffed at her beloved bow and extolled the advantages of the javelin, the more Myrina became determined to adapt the art of archery to horseback riding. It was no easy task, for regardless of how she held her bow, the horse was always in the way. In the end she decided that since not much could be done to alter the shape of the animal, the solution must be to improve the shape of the weapon.

"What is the matter?" asked Lilli one night, when she heard Myrina grunting with frustration. The sisters were sharing a cot in a corner of the dormitory, and while everyone else was asleep after a long day of chores and training, Myrina worked stubbornly on her new bow in the light of a small clay lamp. "You are in pain. Did you cut yourself?"

"The pain is in my pride," whispered Myrina. "For I cannot contrive of a way—" She interrupted herself, struggling with wood and string. "Go back to sleep. I am sorry I woke you."

"Let me see it." Lilli reached out to feel the instrument in progress. "I thought you said it was a bow. This piece of wood is far too short—"

"It needs to be short," sighed Myrina, brushing thread fibers and wood splinters from her lap. "Or one cannot maneuver it in full gallop. But the shorter I make it, the weaker it becomes. Pull it! It's a child's weapon now. The wood has lost all its power."

Lilli tested the string and ran her hands admiringly over the flawless piece of craftsmanship. "It is beautiful," she said. "Smooth and obedient. But how to make it stronger?" She thought for a moment. "Perhaps, as with humans, strength comes from provocation . . . from being forced and needing to resist. Maybe"—she handed the bow back to Myrina—"you must force the wood in an unexpected way. Try to surprise it and tease out its hidden strength." With that the girl lay back down and fell immediately asleep, while Myrina sat staring at the challenge in her hands, more awake than ever.

SPRING HAD TURNED TO summer by the time she was ready to exhibit her invention. Crafting a bow was no simple task; first, she had to build the tools, then the materials had to be found and cured . . . and above all, it had to be done discreetly, without Penthesilea finding out. For if the product was a failure, Myrina knew ridicule would be her only reward for toiling so hard.

After weeks of clandestine practice, she finally summoned everyone to the horse enclosures. Since only Lilli had been privy to her plans, no one else knew what to expect, not even Myrina's closest friends. All they saw was one of the straw stags set up for javelin practice in front of a vacant paddock. And then, to their bafflement, they saw Myrina mounted on her horse, without a javelin in sight.

"What is that deformed little thing?" asked Penthesilea, nodding at the curiosity Myrina was holding in one hand. It was a bow about half the length of a regular longbow, its tips forced over backward by the aid of horn and sinew; to the eye it did not seem like much, and Myrina could hardly blame the others for laughing and shaking their heads.

"I call it a recurve bow," she told them, with patient defiance, "and

I say it is superior to the javelin as a rider's weapon. Care to put it to the test?"

Scoffing at the challenge, Penthesilea mounted her snorting horse and rode toward the target, javelin pulled back for a mighty throw. With a cry of delight she launched her weapon from a distance, and the spearhead struck the straw stag with such force that it toppled over and fell down with a thud.

"There!" she exclaimed, circling back to Myrina in a triumphant canter. "Now what are *you* going to kill?"

Myrina nodded at the empty horse enclosure. "Those."

Everyone turned to stare, and it took a moment before Hippolyta grasped what she meant and yelled, "Look! On the fence posts!"

Indeed, every third post had a straw ball balancing on top; the paddock was ringed with no fewer than ten targets.

Without another word, Myrina spurred on her horse, gathering as much speed as she could without sacrificing her aim. Then she pulled the first arrow from her quiver and laid it on the bow . . . but her desire to put Penthesilea in her place made her release it too soon, and the arrow flew right by the target without touching it.

Furious with herself for letting petty concerns interfere with her concentration, Myrina rode on and shot the next arrow with great care . . . and the third and fourth one, too. All were perfectly on target, and the straw balls fell into the field one by one, pierced through by her arrows. Encouraged by her success, Myrina rode faster, and her aim remained true despite her speed. By the time she came back around the enclosure on the other side, after shooting down every single target on the way, her speed was so furious the women scattered before her like poultry. Only Lady Otrera did not move; the distinguished woman stood perfectly still while the horse came to a skidding halt before her.

"I missed one," said Myrina, glaring at the straw ball on the first post.

Lady Otrera turned slowly toward the post, then looked at the others, her face inscrutable. "What do you say, Penthesilea? Myrina missed one. Should I pronounce you the victor?"

Penthesilea did not need to reply with words; the red blotches on her cheeks said it all. And although everyone around her was silent, too, Myrina heard their roaring cheers in her heart.

IT FINALLY HAPPENED ON a bright summer morning. Alone in the hay barn, Myrina was chasing a runaway chicken when a long shadow fell across the floor. Looking up, pushing away her tousled hair, she did not recognize him right away, for the sunlight coming through the door behind him was so blinding she had to shield her eyes.

"Still a hunter, I see," said a voice she knew well—a voice she had longed to hear for months and months. "Are you ready for your lesson?"

CHAPTER TWENTY-SIX

There has always been affection in my heart
unfading, for these Phrygians and for their city;
which smolders now, fallen before the Argive spears,
ruined, sacked, gutted.
— EURIPIDES, *The Trojan Women*

THE AEGEAN SEA
PRESENT TIME

WHEN WE REACHED THE ISLAND OF DELOS THE NEXT DAY, MR. Telemakhos took one look at the water thermometer, threw the anchor overboard with a grunt, and announced that it was bath time. "Nineteen degrees!" he assured us, waving the thermometer before tossing it back in the water. "Better than a shower."

In the sunshine of midday the water was a mellow transparent blue, and above were the sandy semicircles of the coastline. I wanted to point out that this was no pleasure cruise as far as I was concerned, but even my fastidiousness had met its match in the allure of this sunny cove. The only thing stopping me from tearing off my clothes and jumping in was pride; I didn't want Mr. Telemakhos to think I had surrendered so wholeheartedly to his abduction scheme.

"Come on, North Sea woman!" he taunted me, clearly interpreting my hesitancy as a form of squeamishness. "Your namesake was born on this island! Not Lady Diana," he went on to clarify to Nick, "but the

Greek goddess of the hunt, Artemis, or, as the Romans knew her, Diana."

"Yes." I gave them both a sideways look. "But as you know, it is not wise for mortal men to behold Diana while she bathes. One tends to end up dead."

I was sure I heard Nick mutter, under his breath, "The name's spot-on, then." We had avoided each other all morning, and whenever our eyes met, he looked at me with a sort of ironic forbearance, which did not exactly encourage conversation. Nor did I particularly look forward to our next exchange; I had spent most of the night cringing at some of the things I had said to him, and yet, upon reflection, would wish none of them unsaid.

Before jumping into the water, Nick handed me his phone and said, "I'm sure you have someone back at Oxford waiting for a report."

As he stood there in front of me in all his tawny glory, it was impossible not to admire his physique, which was as chiseled and polished as a Roman statue and equally inviting to the touch. I told myself that for all his present physicality Nick was so removed from me in everything but time and space that indeed, he might as well have been made of marble. But it was no use; he still made my boreal blood run wild.

"Thank you," I said, looking away. "Should I pass on a message?"

"Tell them you were worth every cent. Here—" He pushed a bank-roll into my hand. "Half and half euro and dollars."

I weighed the roll in my hand. "Is it all here?"

"No tip yet. So better be nice to me."

A splash later, I was left with the money and his phone, and a lingering sense of regret. Earlier in the day, when Rebecca and I had made up the bed in our small cabin, she had demanded to know what was wrong with me. Clearly, my anger with Mr. Telemakhos was only the tip of it. Too tired to fabricate anything more flattering than the truth, I had given her a quick summary of Nick's confession from the night before. "So, obviously," I had concluded, boxing my pillow into shape, "he's a lying, thieving charlatan. Unfortunately, in her fathomless nonsense, your pathetic old friend has managed to become ever so slightly—"

"I knew it!" Rebecca stood up straight, morning hair abristle. "He's the fourth horseman. I knew it the moment I saw him. There he is, I said to myself, there is the man who is going to finally outdo the fencing shyster in the art of breaking Diana's heart."

"Oh, please!" I protested, already regretting having confided in her.

Rebecca nearly jerked the bedspread out of my grip. "Weren't you the one who told me he was disgusting? That he smelled?"

I grimaced at her, fearing Nick might hear us through the wall. "Yes, but the problem is that I *like* the way he smells. Even when he's disgusting, which he isn't." I shook my head, trying to get rid of the blur. "It's as if I'm trapped in some sort of balloon where the laws of physics don't apply—"

"Then allow me to puncture your balloon." Rebecca came around the bed to slap me on the bottom with her hairbrush. "There! Feel better?"

"Ow," I said. "That hurt."

"Good! Now get a grip. This is what happens with people on boats: They forget who they are and what really matters."

AFTER OUR SWIM I called my parents, who, fortunately, were not at home. "Sorry about that," I said to their answering machine, "but my phone just suddenly stopped working." Then I sent a quick text to James, stating simply, "Amazon hunt continues. Next stop Troy. Aiming to be home by Monday."

"So," said Nick, laying out his towel next to mine. "I can't wait to pick up where we left off."

"And where was that exactly?" I glanced at Rebecca and saw her rolling her eyes before disappearing belowdecks to change.

Nick sat back on his elbows, squinting against the afternoon sun. "How about your grandmother's notebook?"

"Oh." Because of the playful overture, I had half-expected him to take me back to the shared sleeping bag by the Nahanni River and was mildly upset to have strayed down that path all by myself.

"Last night," he went on, his frown confirming we were thousands of miles apart, "when you told me about your grandmother, you said that she—most likely—had been trained as an archaeologist, and that the notebook must be the result of her efforts to decipher an ancient unknown language."

"That," I said, berating myself for admiring his recumbent body and, more important, for having told him so much, "seems the only logical—"

"Then how do you explain the modern words?" He turned abruptly toward me. "Tomato. Corn. Cocoa." When I did not immediately react, he smiled. "Come on, Dr. Morgan, don't disappoint me. Those plants all came from the Americas during the sixteenth century. So, explain to me why a Bronze Age civilization in North Africa needed words for them."

I opened my mouth to reply, but the truth was, even if I knew the notebook fairly well by now, I had never paid much attention to these so-called modern words. My starting point had always been the foreign symbols, never the English glossary. In other words, the reason I had never stumbled over the word "tomato" before was that it had never appeared in the text I was actually translating. Nor, I was sure, had "corn" or "cocoa."

"So, you looked through the notebook?" I eventually said.

Nick spun his phone absentmindedly on the varnished wood. "Of course."

"Why? To find traces of present-day Amazons?"

He finally met my eyes, and beneath all the teasing I spied the profound darkness I remembered so well from Algeria. "There are also words for hotel, train, and envelope. I think that's more than a trace, Diana."

Shocked at the fact that he had discovered so much in Granny's notebook, I lay down on my elbow, mirroring his posture. "What are you saying?"

"Do I really have to spell it out?"

I shook my head, refusing to take him seriously. Here I was, a life-long Amazon believer with every reason in the world to embrace the idea of modern-day Amazons . . . yet still frozen with indecision on the edge of that ultimate leap of faith. And here was Nick, coming out of nowhere and jumping right in. "Why do you even care?" I said. "Isn't this all just a big illusion, staged to fool the enemy?"

Nick rolled away from me, an arm over his face. "What matters is that *they* believe. Your laptop, by the way, is in Geneva."

"How on earth do you know that?"

"There's a group in Switzerland that's been on our radar for some time. They're a slick network of smugglers and dealers headquartered in the Geneva Freeport. They have fingers in all the major international markets." He moved his arm to cast me a knowing glance. "I'm pretty sure they're in bed with your friends, the Moselanes."

There was still some warmth in the sunshine, but I suddenly felt chilled. "Honestly, Nick—"

He folded his hands over his chest and continued, "Did you ever ask your boyfriend how his ancestor got the title in the first place? Well, I'll tell you how. It was a reward from the king for bringing back such a huge haul of treasures from the ancient world. Lord Moselane has a proud family history to live up to, and the Geneva network is his faithful supplier. These people are experts at removing dirty fingerprints and creating fake provenances. My favorite one is 'Gift from an anonymous Swiss collector.'"

More than anything, it was Nick's arrogant invective against James that caused a timely flare-up of my anger from the night before. Regardless of whether he was lying—which I highly suspected he was—I knew Nick's jab at the Moselanes had no other purpose than to provoke me.

"How do you know my laptop is in Switzerland?" I asked, studying his face. "And what about my cellphone? Let me guess, you are tracking my personal belongings with some sort of device?" When he didn't contradict me, I shook my head. "And you have the nerve to call other people crooked!"

Nick looked embarrassed, but not for long. "That's the nature of the game," he said, with a grim shrug. "I thought you'd been bought off by Grigor Reznik." Glancing at my gobsmacked expression, he quickly added, "Why else would you pretend to board a plane to the UK but go to Crete instead? I couldn't figure it out. But I know Reznik is obsessed with those jackal bracelets." He nodded at my wrist. "He'd pay good money for that one, trust me. It's not surprising that he wants to see what's on your laptop. Your phone, however"—he shrugged noncommittally—"seems to be on a tour of Spain. Don't ask me why."

I was so disoriented I could barely remember what we had touched on when we discussed the nefarious Istanbul art collector and his deceased son in the car from Algeria. "I never knew the bracelets were part of Reznik's Amazon fixation," I said. "And how do you know that *he* has been after my laptop? I thought we agreed that he was *not* behind the explosions in the temple—that someone else had tried to implicate him—"

Nick looked surprised. "I guess I forgot the most important part: Reznik is the gray eminence behind the Geneva network I just told you about. Whether or not they actually blew up the temple, his people *have* been following us, right from the beginning. I'll bet my life on it."

"But *why*?" I was reluctant to espouse his slapdash theory without a few pros and cons. "Does Reznik really believe in the Amazon Hoard? If that's the case, it would seem his treasure hunt began long before *we* joined in."

"He obviously knows something we don't," agreed Nick. "But what? Maybe the answer is in your *Historia Amazonum* . . . which would explain why he's so interested in you. You wrote to him, didn't you, asking to see it?"

"But he never replied."

"Oh, he did." Nick nodded at my bruised temple. "I bet you've been in his crosshairs ever since. He's probably been tapping your cellphone. That's how he knew you went to Crete."

"But then why would he have his people steal it?" I countered. "It doesn't make sense. Now he can't listen in on my conversations anymore."

Nick was quiet for a while. Then he said, squinting at the hazy horizon, "It seems we have two options. Either we split up, go home, and do everything we can to convince Reznik we've given up. Or"—he shot me a daring smile—"we continue together and find the treasure before *he* does."

WE REACHED THE DARDANELLES on Friday afternoon. The Dardanelles—or the Hellespont, as it was known by the Greeks—is the extremely narrow passage going from the Aegean into the Sea of Marmara. It is rivaled only by the narrowness of the Bosphorus Strait a couple hundred kilometers further east, where the Marmara Sea connects with the Black Sea, and is, naturally, a windy and potentially dangerous place to sail.

After the freedom of the open sea, it was daunting to head into the perilous strait, which soon closed in on us from both sides, until the waterway was hardly wider than a large river. For the last hour or so, Mr. Telemakhos had peppered our progress along the coast with comments such as, "Tenedos! This is where the Greeks supposedly hid the fleet, while they waited for the Trojans to take the bait," and "See the coastline over there? That used to be an open bay, just like Homer described it."

By the time we finally moored in busy Çanakkale—the city closest to the ancient ruins of Troy—Rebecca was fast asleep on a mattress on the deck, oblivious to the portside pandemonium. During our time at sea, she had begun napping at the oddest hours, and I suspected that despite her seemingly high spirits she found the whole situation depressing. Here she was, expelled from her beloved Crete, traveling with a friend whose normally sympathetic ear was clogged with competing concerns; even Mr. Telemakhos was too busy savoring his unexpected windfall of young people to spend much time on Rebecca's predicament.

As for Nick, he had so far been rudely unmoved by her efforts to enlighten our cruise with insightful lectures, and the hoped-for job offer from the Aqrab Foundation remained conspicuously absent. His only proposal had been for me: Treasure or no, Nick was prepared to pay me another ten thousand dollars to continue on the Amazon trail with him.

I had told him I would think about it. It wasn't that I meant to punish him for the uncertainty he had so readily inflicted on me, but rather that I myself was unsure what my next step should be. Despite the frustrations of our detention on the *Penelope,* and despite Nick's deceitful behavior, it was hard to imagine parting from him; he had come to represent everything Granny had divined my life would hold—adventure, danger, and discovery.

In contrast, the reality awaiting me at home had all but lost its luster. After almost two weeks away, I struggled to remember what was so attractive about an Oxford career—why it was so imperative that I hurry back. The more familiar I became with the foreign world around me, the more old Avalon, with its cracked, mossy walls and Gothic rigor, receded into the mists. . . .

"Aha!" Mr. Telemakhos turned his back on the bustling harbor and nodded at the coastline across the strait, less than a mile away. "Where are we now?"

"Turkey?" suggested Nick.

"And over there?"

"Also Turkey."

"Yes-yes-yes." Mr. Telemakhos looked a little irritated. "But in the big, overall scheme of things?"

"This is the famous Hellespont," I explained to Nick, my teeth chattering in the brisk November wind that was funneled down the Sea of Marmara all the way—I imagined—from the Russian steppes. "The juncture of two continents. Here, Europe kisses the Orient."

Nick looked from one coast to the other, hands in his pockets. "More of an air kiss, wouldn't you say?"

"Take a leap of the imagination," I countered. "And sink yourself into the romance. Lord Byron did. Swam across, like so many others."

"Hero and Leander!" exclaimed Mr. Telemakhos, with as much headshaking *tristesse* as had they been his relatives. "She was a priestess of Aphrodite, who lived in a tower over there. Fell in love with Leander, who, unfortunately, lived over here. So, back and forth he swam, until . . . well, he drowned." Mr. Telemakhos shrugged, already thinking of something else. "Who is going to wake her up?"

"Why is it always," muttered Nick, as Mr. Telemakhos began nervously circling Rebecca's curled shape, "the man who must do the swimming?"

"Apparently," I said, inadvertently quoting my mother from one of her many failed attempts at talking my father into a seaside weekend, "it does wonders for the circulation."

"Don't worry, North Sea woman"—Nick took my frigid hands and rubbed them with his own—"there is nothing wrong with my circulation."

I WAS STILL MILDLY flustered by this unexpected intimacy when we were picked up by Dr. Özlem, an old friend of Mr. Telemakhos and curator of a nearby museum. Although they greeted each other with similar joyous abandon, I saw right away that Dr. Özlem brought a soothing touch of yin to the relentless yang of our effusive captain.

Slight of build, and weighed down—I guessed—by a lifelong record of thankless labors, Dr. Özlem welcomed us all with hunched handshakes and wary eyes. We had barely piled into his dusty old Volkswagen minibus before he looked at us in the rearview mirror and sighed with slack-faced despondency. "You want to see the bracelets?" he said, in a tone that suggested we were on our way to a family funeral. "Okay, I will show you."

The Amazon bracelets were on display in a glass case on the main floor of the museum run by Dr. Özlem—a humble set of barracks dedicated to archaeological finds in the Çanakkale region. "There," he said, nodding dismissively at the two coiling bronze jackals, which, at first glance, appeared to be perfectly identical to my own. "Nice work, no?"

Rebecca was the first to break the baffled silence. "Are you saying these are fakes?" she asked. "Reproductions?"

Dr. Özlem stuck out his chin. "I'm afraid so."

"But—" I had a hard time getting my head around the fact that two Amazon bracelet replicas were sitting in a random glass cabinet in Turkey. "How?"

"They were found here at Troy over a hundred years ago," explained

Dr. Özlem, "but in those days, archaeology was primitive, and we don't know what layer they were in. One was found in a tomb near the ancient coastline; the other was buried in the ruins of the royal palace." He looked down at the tile floor, which clearly hadn't been cleaned for weeks. "The past is layered beneath us, as you know, with the most recent times on top and the distant past at the bottom. Now, when our dear Heinrich Schliemann began looking for Homer's Troy in the late nineteenth century, he was sure it must be near the bottom, and he did not care too much about the layers he dug through to get there. So you see"—Dr. Özlem straightened to take a deep, cathartic breath of air, then exhaled very slowly, possibly at the recommendation of his doctor—"things have been a bit of a muddle here ever since."

Looking discreetly around, I saw what he meant. The layout of the room made no sense to me; in one cabinet sat items from several different time periods, and a row of pedestals displayed busts that had almost no features left, and —understandably—did not even have tags of identification.

"I know," sighed Dr. Özlem, following my gaze. "But only a few of our cabinets have locks on them, so we have to put safety above chronology."

"We generally refer to Troy as having nine layers," interjected Rebecca, mostly to Nick. "Schliemann was convinced the Trojan War took place in the very early, deep layer called Troy 2, but nowadays there is a tendency to regard the much later Troy 7a as *the* Troy. Unfortunately, as you can imagine, quite a bit of Troy 7a ended up in Schliemann's junk pile. He did find gold, though"—she made a grimace of reluctant appreciation—"and that did a lot to encourage funding for further excavations."

"So," said Nick, "layer 7a was Homer's Troy?"

Rebecca's eyes lit up. "Don't get me started."

"Yes," I urged. "Get her started. Please."

"The thing is"—Rebecca glanced at Dr. Özlem with timid deference—"we've all gravitated to 7a because it seems to be the least implausible theory. But I promise you, no one would put their head on the block over it. Would they?" Seeing Dr. Özlem's little nod and smile, she went on, with more conviction, "If we are looking for a Troy that was truly spectacular, with tall walls worthy of Homer's descriptions, then Troy 6 absolutely dwarfs the competition. But the problem is that everyone has been looking for a Troy that was destroyed by war . . . *also* in the interest of remaining true to Homer. And that seems to have been the case with layer 7a. However, in my humble opinion, the actual settlement of Troy 7a was only a sad remnant of the spectacular city that once was—hardly worthy of a ten-year siege. Furthermore, Troy 7a was probably destroyed around 1190 B.C.E., which, in many people's opinion, is far too late. How could the Greeks sail off to war with a thousand ships when they themselves were in the process of being eradicated? It doesn't make sense. In fact, the picture that emerges is that those were the final days of civilization as they knew it; illiterate brutes were sweeping across the Mediterranean coasts in waves of destruction, and the whole region was thrown into a dark age that lasted for several hundred years until the Greeks basically reinvented the alphabet around 800 B.C.E."

I clapped my hands. "See? Bex has it all figured out."

"Hardly." Rebecca shrugged a nervous apology at Dr. Özlem. "I am just guessing, like everyone else."

"So," said Nick, "if it wasn't layer 7a, which was it?"

"Aha!" Rebecca held up a finger, eyes gleaming. "Now, as I said, if you look at the actual layout of the city, Troy 6 stands out as the most impressive of them all. This is where the tall walls are, and where the citizens lived in a fair amount of comfort. Furthermore, Troy 6 was destroyed about a hundred years before Troy 7a, namely around 1275 B.C.E., which makes far more sense to me. The *only* problem is that we believe Troy 6 was ruined by an earthquake, not by war. But suppose it was not actually an earthquake—" She flushed charmingly as she neared the climax of her theory. "Suppose it was a battering ram. Or, should I say, battering *horse*?" She pressed a hand to her mouth as if to contain her own exuberance, and looked eagerly around at us all, waiting for someone to get it.

"I see," said Nick, nodding slowly. "You think the famous Trojan Horse was actually a giant battering ram?"

"Think about it!" Rebecca went on, in another rush of enthusiasm. "It *can't* just have been a big, hollow horse made of wood. What Trojan would be so unbelievably daft as to think, 'Aloha! What a nice parting present from those bloody Greeks' and open the city gate to pull it into town? Seriously?"

"I like it," nodded Mr. Telemakhos. "But I always like crazy theories. What do you say, Murat? Could it have been an enormous battering ram rather than an earthquake that brought down Troy 6?"

"I will have to think about it." Dr. Özlem drew up his shoulders a bit. "After more than a century of digging, we have many theories, and I have heard them all." He turned his head to stare out the window, which was grimy with dust and condensation. "Sometimes I wish this was all still just a farmer's field. Why are we so eager to turn a beautiful myth into reality? I don't understand."

Only when he left us to have a word with one of his employees, who had left a glass case unlocked, did Mr. Telemakhos get a chance to explain the circumstances that had so soured his old friend's relationship with archaeology.

"He spent twenty years writing to people all over Europe, trying to have all the Trojan artifacts returned to the area and put into this newly dedicated museum." Mr. Telemakhos gestured at the modest building complex surrounding us. "And he was quite successful. Many things were sent here, among them these two bracelets. But unfortunately, only a few months after the museum opened, it was discovered that some of the most valuable artifacts had been removed and replaced with fakes . . . and suspicion fell on Özlem. For eight years he struggled to clear himself, always in danger of going to jail. Local authorities dropped the case against him only when he became ill, three years ago. Still today, he has enemies who call him a thief, and most of the valuable objects that were left in these buildings have been sent to other museums, where they have better alarm systems." Mr. Telemakhos leaned closer, anxious that his old friend should not overhear him. "I fear they are going to close the museum. That would be his hemlock."

I turned to Nick, who stood right behind me with his arms crossed, looking suitably grave. "Treasures stolen by us evil Westerners," I said to him. "Returned to their homeland, only to be then lost forever. Tell me again, is that really what you want?"

"Oh, they are not lost forever," said Dr. Özlem, rejoining us and carrying a tray of small teacups. "We know where they are. Mint tea, my friends? I'm afraid we have no chairs."

"Have you ever thought of applying to the Aqrab Foundation?" asked Nick, taking a cup.

Dr. Özlem waved the empty tray in the air. "Oh, no. They are bullies. When they give money, they want to throw their weight around, telling you what to do." He shuddered. "I don't like to be told what to do. Not by bullies."

Nick didn't look particularly insulted at the accusation; his wry smile suggested he had heard it before. "Maybe that's what you need," he said, swirling the teacup, which looked absurdly small in his hand. "A few bullies on your team."

More hunched than ever, Dr. Özlem glared at Nick as if he had not really noticed him before and was now wondering whether yet another plague was about to be unleashed on him. "Maybe. But I'm an old man—"

"Excuse me," I said, anxious to save Dr. Özlem and bring us back on topic, "but how do you know these bracelets *are* indeed fakes?"

Dr. Özlem put aside the tray and unlocked the glass cabinet. "There," he said, handing me one of the coiled jackals. "Normally, it takes an expert to tell, but look at the inside, under the head. What do you see?"

I stepped closer to the window and inspected the bronze. "Nothing."

"Precisely." Dr. Özlem held out his hand, waiting for me to give him back the bracelet. "In the originals, there were tiny engravings. Three small symbols in that one, two in the other."

I was so excited, I couldn't let go of the jackal. "What kind of symbols?"

Dr. Özlem looked at Mr. Telemakhos, nodding as if they had planned the moment beforehand. "There you go. Now do your magic trick."

Mr. Telemakhos turned to the cloudy window and drew two symbols in the moisture with his finger. They were both familiar to me—were both from Granny's Amazon alphabet—but the word itself was new. "This was inscribed in the first bracelet," he said.

Flabbergasted, I stared at the two symbols. Here finally, it seemed, was the proof that the bracelets and the symbols were indeed linked. Did all the jackals have these engravings? Did mine? It had never occurred to me to check. "Two syllables," I said, breathless with excitement. "The owner's name? It *must* be."

"It gets better." Mr. Telemakhos drew another three symbols, then turned to me expectantly. "This was the name inscribed in the other bracelet—"

Nick beat us to it. "Our three-syllable priestess queen," he said, sounding strangely disappointed. "Myrina. She really did make it to Troy."

"This is incredible!" I felt like taking Nick by the shoulders and shaking him. "We really *have* been on their trail."

"Yes," he said, with regret. "And this is where it ends. Poor Myrina, who came so far to die."

WE ALL WALKED THE ruins of Troy in the sunset, marveling at the idea that this remote hill surrounded by grain fields, with its confusing rudiments of ancient masonry, had once been a beacon of civilization.

Perhaps in an attempt to spare Dr. Özlem a lecture he had undoubtedly given hundreds of times, Rebecca took it upon herself to walk us through the ruins. "As you can see," she explained, leading the way through a maze of ancient walls and foundations—some still surprisingly tall, "the city expanded over time, and the ramparts spread out accordingly, like rings in the water, to accommodate the growth."

"So, which Troy is this exactly?" asked Nick, looking at the remains of a massive tower.

"Troy 6," said Rebecca, hands on her hips in a posture of ownership. "*The* Troy, in my opinion. That was when this entire outer wall was built, together with several enormous buildings. Don't you agree"—she looked at me for support—"that these are the walls worthy of Homer's Troy?"

"The problem," said Dr. Özlem, "is that nothing significant was found in that layer. At least not to my knowledge."

"Except a gigaton of brick," muttered Nick, mostly to me.

"It is possible," Dr. Özlem went on, ripping a few weeds from one of the walls and absentmindedly stuffing them in his jacket pocket, "the Greeks came many times. And who knows, maybe the earthquake was what helped them take Troy in the end." He looked at Rebecca, slowly but surely cheered by the opportunity to speculate. "Maybe you are right. Maybe it was Troy 6. It was certainly of great importance, strategically."

Mr. Telemakhos nodded. "You saw how narrow the strait is. This is where all the ships would come by on their way to the Black Sea. Sometimes they would be stuck here for weeks, waiting for the north wind to die down. A perfect place to run a business: Your customers can't get away." He picked his way through the weeds and jumped up on a grassy knoll ringed with rubble. "No wonder they were popular, these Trojans. Proud, stallion-breaking Trojans, lords of the eastern sea. Just think of the royal treasury"—he held out his arms at the imagined splendor—"the riches it must have held. No wonder the king of Troy needed his tall walls."

I turned to Nick and caught him staring at my jackal bracelet. On the boat I had felt his eyes on me many times, to the point where the sensation made me as breathless as if he had actually touched me. But now we were once again on solid ground, walking through yet another grass-covered legacy of human endeavor, and his face bore signs of nothing beyond detachment. Did it even occur to him, I wondered, that the shell game he was playing with his enemies might have vast real-life consequences for all of us—not just for Rebecca and me, but potentially also for Mr. Telemakhos and Dr. Özlem, whose sincerity and dedication cast Mr. al-Aqrab's guile into brazen relief?

"You should know," I said to Nick, "that this was the birthplace of the Amazon Hoard. The treasure was believed to consist of gold from the Trojan treasury."

"Not just any old gold," interjected Mr. Telemakhos, who had over-heard my remark, "but the centerpieces of Trojan civilization. Salvaged by the Amazons before the city fell." He smiled whimsically, as if even he, believer that he was, had never fully bought the idea of such a trea-sure.

"But my point," I said, turning once again to Nick and lowering my voice, "is that anyone out there mad enough to think the Amazon Hoard ever existed—and still exists—just may come knocking on Dr. Özlem's door very soon. And they may not be so nice about it. Not if they're the same people who like to mug women in dark labyrinths."

Nick looked at me with raised eyebrows. "Why don't you tell that to the Oxford scholar who started writing letters to Reznik in the first place?"

Still not quite ready to acknowledge my own guilt in the matter, I walked briskly up to the others, saying, "So, do we all agree that the beautiful-Helen story was pure fiction? That to Achilles and all those Greek heroes who gave their lives, the Trojan War was all about gold?"

Dr. Özlem shrugged. "Who knows what their leaders told them. Men always like to blame women for everything that goes wrong. Look at Adam and Eve." He sighed. "If only we had some historical records . . . but we don't. We do have a few ancient treaties made with other countries, but they don't tell us much, and the names are confus-ing. Could the Alaksandu that is mentioned be the historical Paris? Is the 'Great King' of Ahhiyawa possibly Homer's Agamemnon? But where is Hector? Where is Achilles? Were they actually ever here, or were they part of a different story, which later became fused with the legend of Troy?"

"I certainly wouldn't miss Achilles," Rebecca chimed in, as we all continued down a muddy path toward the older ruins. "I mean, what kind of hero rapes the body of a dead opponent in the middle of the battlefield?" Seeing Nick's grimace, she laughed and added, "I am refer-ring to the Amazon queen at the time, Penthesilea. According to tradi-tion, the Amazons sided with the Trojans in the war, to fight against the Greeks. In Homer's *Iliad,* the Amazons are called *antianeirai,* which means 'those who fight like men.' The story goes that Achilles didn't even realize he had been dueling with a woman until she was dead and he peeked underneath her body armor."

Nick turned to me with a frown. "Could Penthesilea be another name for Myrina? Or did the Amazons have two queens at the time?"

It was an excellent question, but his hypocrisy made me cringe. Whatever his reason for being there, and putting us all at risk by his presence, I was convinced he cared little for the actual history of the Amazons. As with the invading Greeks, it was all about the gold. Nick kept joking about the Amazon Hoard as if it was merely a fiction, but I was no longer fooled. He had been after it all along. His recent offer of an additional ten grand to help him beat Reznik to the treasure certainly suggested as much.

"Diana!" boomed Mr. Telemakhos. "Here we are, faced with the question of questions: Did our Algerian Amazons make it all the way to Troy, and was their queen, indeed, called Myrina? To which Homer replies . . ." He gestured for me to complete the thought, but I was too distraught to understand what he wanted from me.

Mr. Telemakhos held up a pedagogical finger. "Never forget your Homer. He is the one who comes to our rescue. He specifically mentions our queen when he describes a small hill on the Scamandrian Plain." Walking up an overgrown staircase ahead of us, arms wide, Mr. Telemakhos recited the passage with panache: "Men call it Batieia, but the gods call it the mound of Myrina, light of step."

I was so taken aback, I felt riveted to the spot. "You believe that verse refers to *our* Myrina?"

Mr. Telemakhos looked out over the old battlefield with a squint, as though he were a surviving officer returning to the scene of a devastating defeat to figure out what he had done wrong. "What do I believe? I believe Homer's *Iliad* is a code, encrypted for the worthy—"

"And the Trojan War?" asked Nick. "Did it really happen?"

"Something certainly happened here." Dr. Özlem zipped up his waxed jacket against the chill of late afternoon. "We're just not sure what it was. But I highly doubt it was caused by a woman." He looked at his wristwatch. "It's getting late. My wife has made dinner. Would you like to join us?"

As we all headed back toward the parking lot and the large wooden horse marking the entrance to the site, the silhouette of a man emerged from the setting sun, walking toward us in a determined manner. Tall and athletic, hands in his pockets, he looked like a reluctant Apollo or some other ill-disguised divinity, dispatched from Mount Olympus to do one last round of duty sorting out yet another errant human.

"Uh-oh," said Rebecca, all her extremities—head included—receding into her flight jacket. "Now we have trouble."

"What?" I began, but then I recognized him, too.

It was James.

CHAPTER TWENTY·SEVEN

Myrina was so shocked at the sight of Paris she forgot to hold on to the chicken she had finally managed to catch, and it fluttered from her grip with a few indignant clucks.

"Here——" He threw her a toy dagger made of wood, but she did not have the wherewithal to catch it before it fell to the floor at her feet, throwing up a little puff of dust. "I am not going to teach you how to fight like a man because you are not a man. You are a woman, whether you like it or not, and as such you have some natural limitations. Never forget that."

Still too stunned to speak, Myrina watched Paris as he held up a wooden toy sword of his own—twice as long as the dagger he had given her—and a long pole with a ball of cloth stuck onto one end. His expression was perfectly serious, perfectly serene; it was as if their long separation had successfully cured every weakness he had once felt for her.

And yet, as soon as Myrina reached up to gather her hair with a string, she saw him struggling to keep his eyes off her body . . . and losing the fight with a grimace. "Never do that," he said, his voice gruff, "in front of a man. One way or another, he will run you through."

Leaving her hair as it was, Myrina picked up the toy dagger and held it in front of her. "And this is how you will have me defend myself? A kitchen knife against *that*"—she nodded at his own two weapons—"and *that?*"

"If this were real," said Paris, showing her the wooden sword, "it would likely be as dangerous for its owner as for the victim. Many a man, in his desire to appear invincible, will carry a sword too long for his strength and meet an untimely death in the backswing. Let not woman, clever woman, repeat his mistake. And this"—he held up the mock spear—"is another weapon your enemy will kindly carry for you. A throwing spear, of course, will fly once and be gone; a thrusting spear, more often than not, will share its fate. For believe me: To withdraw its head from a dead body wearing a leather harness in the middle of a battle, in time to fend off the next assault, is no pleasant exercise."

"And yet," said Myrina, "*you* would go to battle thus."

Paris nodded. "As a man, I must do what is honorable, even if I know it will be my doom. As a woman, you may freely run away, and no one will ever scoff and say you should have done otherwise. But Queen Myrina is not content with that. So come"—he smiled at last, opening his arms—"and strike me dead."

They circled each other a few times, Paris smiling, Myrina still not sure what to make of his presence. Then she stopped, lowering the knife. "You are sporting with me. I know that smile of yours. As soon as I approach with my little wooden claw, you will slap me with those sticks and laugh."

Paris nodded. "Remember what you are doing right now, the way you look. That is how you should always open your fights—by looking as if you have already surrendered. One of the most important rules for a woman is this: Always make sure they underestimate you. They will be naturally inclined to think you a weakling, and that is your greatest advantage."

"A weakling?" Myrina stormed forward, charging at last. But as soon as she did, the wooden sword came between them, right across her throat.

"That was rule number two," said Paris, still smiling. "Here comes rule number one: Never underestimate *them*." With that he pushed her away, and Myrina stumbled backward, nearly tripping over a hayfork.

Just then, as she was contemplating her next move, a third person appeared in the door. It was Lady Otrera, looking far too elegant for the barn and clearly mystified by the sounds of panting and rushing feet. "Nephew?" she called, peering into the dusty shadows. "I heard you had arrived. What a pleasant surprise."

"I was just—" Paris cleared his throat in an uncharacteristic fit of timidity. "I just thought—"

"Yes." Lady Otrera held out a hand to him. "I see that."

For the remainder of the day, Myrina was kept busy with endless tasks, all of which were performed comfortably within hearing range of Lady Otrera. By the time Paris finally left the farm to return to his ship, Myrina was ready to pull out her hair for not having exchanged another word with him.

But as he walked across the dimly lit courtyard of Otrera's private house, heading for the door, Paris made a point of stopping to check his sandal right next to a pillar overgrown with jasmine. Somehow he knew Myrina was right there, hiding from the eyes of everyone, hoping to catch one last glimpse of him before he left.

"Meet me on the beach at sunrise," he said under his breath, not even looking toward her. "And be armed."

MYRINA COULD NOT FIND rest that night. All she accomplished with her writhing and sighing was to have Penthesilea sneer at her to be quiet and Lilli wake up crying, muttering broken phrases to do with ships and fires on the beach.

"It is her!" Lilli hissed, when Myrina tried to soothe her back to sleep. "They are coming for *her*."

"Who, dearest?" whispered Myrina, holding Lilli tightly against her chest, hoping the noise would not wake anyone else.

"*Her!*" replied Lilli, as always upset that Myrina did not understand. "The princess. She is dark now, but she is here."

After a long night of no sleep at all, Myrina finally left the dormitory to creep out behind the barn and saddle her horse. She knew it was still well before daybreak, but she was too anxious to wait any longer. Suppose her scheme was discovered—suppose Lady Otrera tried to stop her? The danger lay not so much in the embarrassment as in the risk of not being able to meet Paris as planned.

The horse, a silver gelding, snorted happily when he saw her, but Myrina hushed him up with anxious entreaties. And instead of riding off with a happy howl as she normally would, she led him past the house by the bridle, hoping to be seen and heard by no one. Not that there was anything sinful about her excursion, but . . . the way Lady Otrera had looked at her the night before suggested that the others might think differently. Paris was, after all, a man.

Riding across the fields toward the ocean, breathing in the soothing coolness of the air, Myrina saw the morning mists lifting off the land with reluctant grace. Although it was already summer, Earth was in no hurry to unveil her splendors before the approach of the Sun; not until he reached out with golden fingers, reminding her of the heat of his touch, did she shed the final layer and welcome him back with a burst of birdsong.

It was the Sun, too, that pushed Myrina forward, urging her on with a warm hand against her back and spreading glorious morning light before her as she rode down from the dunes onto the sand. Within a few loving breaths the bleak expanse of the beach was roused from sleep, changing color from purplish gray to sage honey.

And there, in the middle of it all, she saw Paris riding toward her, holding the mock spear in one hand. But he did not stop when he reached her; he merely grinned and continued down the beach as if he intended to ride all the way to the rocky promontory at its far end.

Riding after him, Myrina did her best to overtake him, and by the time they finally reached a small, protected cove she had never known was there, they both tumbled from the horses, laughing.

"Look at you!" exclaimed Paris, with false disappointment. "I had looked forward to teaching you to ride . . . but I see Otrera's daughters beat me to it."

"Undoubtedly," said Myrina, taking off her sandals, "you see numerous faults with my style. Hippolyta is always after me about my knees—"

Paris smiled. "I would not dare to even notice your knees. All I see is the face of a woman in control and enjoying the ride. That"—he checked himself and turned to unsaddle his horse—"is more than enough."

"Tell me," said Myrina, eager to delay their weapon games until she had received answers to her most pressing question, "have my imprudent actions caused you trouble at home?"

Paris glanced at her over his shoulder. "If they had, I wouldn't be here."

"Then you have . . . forgiven me?"

"I am not sure"—he lifted the saddle from the horse and put it down on a boulder—"what that word means. My feelings in this case are so tangled I have long since given up unraveling them. I tried to cut them off"—he shrugged, taking out his mock sword—"but they grew right back. Are you ready?"

Myrina hesitated, aching to know what he meant, but aware further inquiry would likely yield nothing but more riddles. And so she found her own two wooden knives and crossed her arms before her, in a posture of fear. "There, is that hopeless enough for you?"

Paris nodded. "Not bad. But I know you too well to be fooled. There is something in your eyes—we have to work on your eyes. But first, let us talk about your strengths, because they are your true weapons." He nodded at her legs. "Above all, your litheness. Fast and nimble feet. You could easily outrun a man; in fact"—he smiled—"you have outrun me many times."

Myrina frowned. "I asked you to teach me how to fight. No one needs instruction for how to run away."

Paris held up a warning hand. "You are too impatient. That is a weakness of yours. Strike first . . . and you might as well plunge the blade into your own chest. Wait, wait, wait . . . and then wait again; that is the key."

"Wait"—Myrina grimaced—"while my opponent cuts me into stew meat?"

Paris nodded. "He will try. But you will know how to avoid the blows. And then, just as *he* gets impatient and careless and tired, that is when you strike. But first"——Paris batted the wooden blade against the palm of his hand——"I will teach you how to predict and avoid the sword."

By the time he finally let her rest, Myrina was sore all over with bumps and scrapes. She had become better at blocking and avoiding his lunges, yes, but only after being poked and stabbed again and again, mostly on her arms and legs, but also occasionally in the ribs. Even when she would stumble and fall, he gave her no quarter but slapped her backside with the wooden blade until she was back on her feet.

When at long last he relented, Myrina collapsed in the sand with a groan, not sure she would ever find the strength to get up again.

"Here." Paris offered her water, but she was too exhausted to take it.

"And I thought you were so noble," she mumbled, clutching her elbow. "But you are cruel. When can I have a shield?"

"Did I miss a spot?" He knelt down beside her, taking her arm. "Hmm——" He felt the bruise with his fingers. "How about this?" He leaned forward to press his lips against the spot. "Better?"

She stared at him, words of yes and no at war in her throat.

"Yes? Well, then——" Paris got back on his feet, brushing off his knees. "Up with you, lithe Myrina. We have only just begun."

AND INDEED, FOR SEVERAL weeks Paris met Myrina on the beach to continue her training—sometimes early, sometimes late, in order that no one at the farm saw a pattern in her absence.

True to his word, he taught her how to master the weapons she had—above all her speed, flexibility, and balance—and before long she was able to duck and jump to avoid most of his blows, much to her own amusement and his growing consternation.

"I have taught you too well!" he exclaimed one day, just as the sun was setting on a long, hot afternoon. "Now *you* are the one dealing the blows . . . to my dignity. Wait. What are you doing?" Tossing aside the spear and sword, he lunged at her just as she sat down to rest, mashing her thoroughly into the sand. "What did I tell you? Never think it's over until they are all dead. Even without weapons, even on his knees, your enemy will still try for your throat." He pinned down her arms and legs, putting all his weight upon her. "Now push me off."

Gritting her teeth, Myrina tried to shove him away with all her might, but he was too heavy. "Come on," he urged her. "There is always a weak spot. A careless moment. Find it and use it."

She tried again, and again, but there was no weakness to be found. Groaning with the effort, she looked him in the eye, trying to guess his thoughts. It was not difficult, for they were acutely entwined with her own.

Still breathing hard, she ceased her struggle.

And then he finally kissed her: the kiss they had both craved for so long, a breathless, feverish indulgence that might have gone on forever . . . had not Myrina's heel happened upon a perfect little mound of purchase in the soft sand, enabling her to flip them both over and throw Paris down on his back, one of her mock daggers pressed to his throat.

"And you call *me* cruel?" he croaked, his features torn with humiliation. "You are surely the queen of eternal torment."

Myrina pressed the dagger into his throat a little further. "I haven't killed you yet. Have I?"

Paris frowned. "Why not?"

Instead of answering, she bent down to kiss him again, eager to reclaim the pleasure she had just felt. And when——a few breaths later—— he was once again on top, she did not mind, for it no longer felt like defeat.

Once unleashed, their passion was like two wrestling lion cubs—— at once playful and relentless. Paris did not tire of her lips . . . the lips that had so often teased him and told him no, and Myrina could barely contain her delight in feeling him at last . . . the powerful body she had so often admired, so often longed to feel against her own.

"My beautiful Myrina," he whispered, running a warm hand down her arm to close around the jackal bracelet. "Let us take this off right now——"

"No." She moved her arm away.

"Don't worry." He was still kissing her, and still reaching for the bracelet. "I will do it for you."

"No!" She shrank away from him, twisting her arm behind her back. "We cannot!"

"We cannot what?" He pulled her right back and pinned her, once more, beneath him. "Insult the little doggie? It didn't seem to mind me kissing you, did it? In fact, I have a suspicion it is enjoying itself very much."

But the damage was done.

"Please." Myrina pressed a fist against her face, forcing back the tears. "I do not want to hurt you—"

Paris sat up, flushed and irritated. "Then why is it that everything you do invariably results in the most excruciating pain?" He rose with a groan and paced down the beach, swinging his mock sword at invisible adversaries.

Later, when he was saddling his horse, Myrina walked over to embrace him from behind. "I warned you," she whispered, feeling a sadness so profound she could barely speak. "I have a vicious bite."

Paris let his arms drop. "If only you did. But the gods, in their infinite hilarity, have given you the sweetest taste." Turning, he took her face in his hands and kissed her once more, his face full of distress. "I should go and never come back, but I can't. Meet me here tomorrow?"

For three more days they struggled, until at last, Paris plunged his sword and spear into the sand and fell to his knee with a headshake. "You . . . surrender?" said Myrina, standing awkwardly before him, daggers still raised.

"Myrina." He clutched his face. "My beautiful Myrina. Will you never be mine? Am I destined to be second to a *dog*?"

She knelt down in front of him, desperate to relieve his anguish but afraid of what might happen if she tried.

"I have to return to Troy," Paris said at last. "At first light."

"No!" Myrina threw her arms around him. "Don't leave me again. Please! Promise you will return right away—"

His head dropped. "I cannot."

"But"—she pressed her cheek against his—"are you not . . . fond of me?"

Paris looked up, his eyes full of reproach. "Fond of you? Myrina, you are my *queen*—I want you more than I want life itself." He swallowed, then went on with sudden determination. "Come to me. Come to Troy and be my wife." He touched her chin, his eyes dark with solemnity. "Or stay here forever, enslaved by your imaginary mistress."

Myrina stared at him, pushing back her tousled hair. "You would marry me?"

Paris shook his head. "Do you think I would teach just anyone to fight me to the death? I want you to be my wife. My one and only wife." He took her by the neck and kissed her firmly on the lips. "There is a hill called Batieia just outside of Troy; I will post a man on it day and night, until you come. In fact, I will rename it 'Myrina's Hill' in your honor." Looking straight into her eyes, he took her hand and pressed it against his cheek. "A cold metal dog . . . or a man with a pulse beating in every limb? *You* must make that choice, but I beg you: Do it soon."

MYRINA RETURNED TO THE farm after dark. Never had she felt its appeal more keenly—the wide-open doors and windows, glowing with familiar warmth, and the many voices raised in a chaotic chorus of merriment.

Walking through the garden door, she found everyone busily at work setting the dinner table, laughing at nothing in particular, and absorbed in all things unimportant, and suddenly she felt like a stranger, a trespasser, who had donned a stolen form to be admitted inside.

Not until that moment did it occur to Myrina how masterful she had become at ignoring her own desires—desires that had once been simple, but which had gradually become far less so. A year ago, when she and Lilli had walked through the desert together, she would have liked nothing more than to come upon a dinner table set by friends. And after leaving the Temple of the Moon Goddess in search of her stolen sisters she would surely have fallen to her knees with gratitude had she known that one day soon, they would all—except one—be living in happy seclusion yet again, on a farm near the sea, surrounded by kind people and fertile lands.

But once her task was done and her sisters safe, her own wishes had fallen to the ground limp and obsolete, like the ropes men use to erect mighty walls. And she had fallen prey to the evil that attends every great architect: Once his building is complete, he cannot quietly inhabit it, enjoying the fruits of his labor, but must busy himself with plans for another, and then another . . . until he finally sits down in the shade of the old people's tree, his life having been nothing but a continuous construction, with no time left for moving in.

Or perhaps she was being unfair. There had certainly been times when Myrina sincerely enjoyed the challenges of the farm and the company of new friends equally passionate about hunting. And Lilli, too, seemed happy here. It was true the girl's nights were once again tormented by evil dreams, but her days were merry and full of cats and ducks and joyful tasks. Lady Otrera took special care that those of her daughters who were unable to fully participate in the general mayhem— and there were several such girls, for the locals did not care to raise them—never lacked things to do, never found themselves without responsibilities that were uniquely theirs. So much so that Lilli had developed quite the attitude of being indispensable to the mechanics of the kitchen and guarded her realm with ever-growing ownership.

"I dread to think," she had said to Myrina, only a few weeks earlier, "what they ate before we came. Will you help me clean out the larder? No one seems to care about these things."

Seeing she had little else to do, Myrina had agreed to the project. Together, the two sisters had cleaned out the cellar, finding this and that, tasting and spitting out . . . but most important, they had been able to talk privately about their hopes for the future. By sunset that day, when the larder was finally organized, Myrina had felt confident they were equally fond of their new life and could think of no better place to be.

But then Paris returned. And with him came a swarm of emotions and ambitions that had chased Myrina wherever she went, stinging her continuously, regardless of how many times she plunged into the pond behind the barn, nearly drowning herself to escape them.

Sitting down to dinner that night, after saying good-bye to Paris and seeing him ride off in the twilight, Myrina could almost feel it coming through the open windows: the call of Troy. She had heard it described often enough as a magnificent city with proud walls and towers, but tonight it had assumed a new radiance; it was the home of a man who would deny her nothing, and whose nearness was so captivating, she could think of little else.

Closing her ears to the usual kitchen chatter, Myrina spent the hour after dinner setting mousetraps. It was perhaps not the noblest of pursuits, but she found a strange satisfaction in doing what had to be done with as little suffering to the victims as possible. So intent was she on wiring her cunning contraptions she did not even notice she had an audience until Lady Otrera put a hand on her head and said, "I was wondering why I am no longer disturbed by the screeching of dying mice. All I hear now is a snap, and then silence."

"If only," muttered Myrina, struggling with a knot, "one could wire human hearts as easily."

"Come." Lady Otrera gestured for her to get up. "Let us walk. It is such a calm evening."

Right away Myrina knew what lay behind the invitation. The all-seeing mother of the house had learned of her clandestine trips to the beach, either from an eyewitness or from simple deduction. The Trojan ship had been moored in the harbor for three weeks, yet Paris had only come to dinner once. Why? What did he have to hide?

Bracing herself for the scolding she deserved, Myrina followed Otrera through the vegetable garden to the meadow beyond. Here, bathed in the light of the rising moon and casting a distorted shadow on the wild grains, stood the Tree of Chimes—an old hardwood with wind flutes hanging from its branches. No one had yet explained to Myrina the logic of this tree and its mournful sighs, but she had long since guessed it served as a guardian of the dead, whose ashes—she assumed—were buried in the ground beneath it.

Puzzled by their destination, Myrina stopped beside Otrera, waiting for her to speak. She feared the subject would be sin and punishment, and was already preparing to protest her innocence when Lady Otrera reached out to caress the bark of the tree, saying, "You never met Sisyrbe. She was the finest daughter I ever had. Never broke a rule, never refused a task. A brilliant rider. But she was struck down by a fever before fully grown. And Barkida"—Otrera paused to steady her voice—"fell from a horse and broke her neck. She and so many others died too young. So you see, Fate does not always favor the deserving. All we can do is be honest to ourselves and hope for the best. An unhappy life, cut short by an unfair death . . . surely, that is the greatest tragedy."

They stood quietly for a while, looking up at the silent chimes. Then Myrina, failing to find criticism in what she had just heard, said, "You are telling me to . . . be happy?"

Otrera gathered her skirts and began walking farther into the meadow, following a little path to a stone bench overlooking the sloping expanse of the horse enclosures. "Who am I to divine what Fate has in store for you?" she said at last, sitting down on the bench. "I am merely telling you what is in my heart." She patted the bench to encourage Myrina to sit next to her. "Come, and let me tell you about the man I loved."

Myrina dropped to the seat with a gasp, and her shocked expression made Otrera laugh. "Have no fear. It was a long time ago, and our love never became more than mere admiring looks. For I did nothing to encourage him. I was, after all, devoted to the Goddess." She paused to give Myrina a stern look, then continued, "And so this inconstant man pursued my sister instead, persuading her to cast off her vows and become his wife." Otrera smoothed her skirt with both hands, reliving, perhaps, the sorrow of times past. Then she sighed and said, "Foolishly, they celebrated their wedding here, under the roof of the Goddess, and true to her jealous nature, she gave them a most terrible omen in return. For on their wedding night a fire broke out, and the roof of their building collapsed, nearly killing them both." Otrera shook her head. "You can imagine the seers predicting death and doom everlasting, ad vising them to kill the child that was conceived that night. But, of course, my sister refused to take such a cruel and superstitious measure, and the boy was raised with much love, to become a favorite of his people."

Myrina moved uncomfortably on the bench. She suddenly remembered Paris telling her, upon their arrival in Ephesus, that Lady Otrera was his mother's sister, and that his parents had met right there, on the farm. Was it possible, she wondered, that Paris had been the child conceived in the fire? Could such a capable, smiling boy—now a man—have been born among such evil omens?

"So you see"—Otrera threw up her hands only to let them drop, once more, limply into her lap—"if I had really loved that man, I would be a bitter old woman. I would say the Goddess had punished *me* rather than *her*." She paused, then straightened. "But only the unwise cast premature judgment. Fate is patient. Sooner or later, she will find you."

"The vows I made," began Myrina, "were for the Moon Goddess—"

"And for your sisters."

"True." Myrina leaned forward, resting her elbows on her knees. "But I like to think I have long since paid off my debts to them. As for the Goddess . . . she did nothing to protect us. If anyone has betrayed our holy vows, it is *her*."

"Careful." Otrera held up a hand. "Even the gods must obey Fate. Perhaps there is some grand scheme in heaven . . . perhaps not. But let us not mock powers we don't understand."

"I am sorry," whispered Myrina, bending her head. "I never could hold my tongue in the face of injustice."

Otrera patted her hand. "And for that alone, we shall miss you dearly."

CHAPTER TWENTY-EIGHT

Men whose glory is come by honestly
Have all my admiration. But impostors
Deserve none: luck and humbug's all they are.
—EURIPIDES, *Andromache*

TROY, TURKEY

For as long as she lived with us, Granny had made no bones about loathing men, or, as far as I was concerned, boys. Not because they were necessarily wicked, but because she considered them a waste of our time. "Don't let some fluffy-haired puppy-boy interfere with your training," she kept saying, never tiring of the repetition. "Later, when you are mature and have proven your worth, you may enjoy the company of a healthy male the way you enjoy a good meal. Eat, sleep, and forget."

It might never have occurred to Granny that I needed such explicit advice, however, had not Rebecca—in a typical moment of clandestine overflow—blurted out the story behind the presence of the Manor Park golf ball in our little hidden box of collectibles. "We think it belongs to James Moselane," she whispered, cradling the ball in her hands as if it were a baby bird.

"Huh," said Granny, sniffing the miniature bar of hotel soap with disgust. "Who is James Moselane, and why do his balls deserve to be in this box?"

When Rebecca finally stopped explaining, Granny shook her head and said, "You must rid your mind of these useless thoughts. Both of you. And train harder! Your arms are still too weak." She reached out to test Rebecca's shoulder. "When you are strong enough to pull yourself up, and when you have slain a man in battle, *then* you may play with James Moselane. But not before. And remember to share. Do you understand?"

Now, as we stood together among the Trojan ruins, watching James approaching, Rebecca looked as terrified as she had that day long ago, listening to Granny's instructions. And so, I feared, did I.

"James!" I exclaimed, my heart aflutter as I tried to decide how to greet him. Normally we never touched, except for a brief but possibly accidental caress whenever he helped me with my overclothes. But this time he walked right up to me and kissed me on the cheek.

"Morg," he said, smiling warmly, "I'm sorry it took me so long to catch up." Then he turned to Mr. Telemakhos and Dr. Özlem, greeting them as if they were old friends.

Meanwhile, behind his back, I saw Rebecca glancing nervously at Nick, then at me, as if to ascertain that the feelings I had confessed to her on the boat were in no way so progressed as to leave us in something as sordid as a love triangle. But we had nothing to fear from Nick; he looked at me as if I was not even there, or, perhaps more accurately, as if I were a complete stranger, barely worthy of a change of expression. I could only hope to come across as blasé as he.

In contrast to the rest of us, Nick didn't seem the least bit surprised by James's sudden appearance. "I was wondering when you'd join us," he said, shaking the proffered hand with measured enthusiasm, "ever since your name showed up on my phone."

"Yes, well"—James wrung out a brisk smile—"I meant to come earlier. Oxford likes to keep tabs on its assets. Nick, did you say?"

"You know who I am."

One would have to know James well to see the irritation tugging at his face; it could easily be mistaken for a smile. "I hear our lawyers are getting along famously," he said. "Quite the witty letters going back and forth."

Nick did not return the smile. "I'm afraid I've lost my sense of humor."

There was a brief silence, during which the two men stared at each other as intensely as had they been a pair of duelists waiting for the handkerchief to drop. Then, finally, Nick walked away and James turned to me with a headshake. "Some people," he said, just loudly enough for Nick to hear him, "simply can't be happy with what they have, but *must* try to get their hands on other people's possessions."

I was not sure whether he was referring to me or to the Moselane Manor Collection, but took temporary refuge in the uncertainty. It was clear to me, however, that James had come to Troy to save me from the Aqrab Foundation; my last text to him had been sent from Nick's phone. His presence here certainly seemed to suggest that he wanted to take our friendship a step further. Why else would he go to the trouble of tracking me down in Turkey when he knew I would be back in Oxford within days?

"Do tell me," I said, as everyone started toward the parking lot and we had a chance to fall behind. "How did you know we would be here today?"

James stopped and took my hand. "Morg," he said, looking at me with those hypnotic, bottomless eyes of his, "I have called and called—"

His sincerity made me soften. "My phone was stolen," I told him. "I meant to fly home three days ago, but . . . things got complicated. My students probably hate me by now."

"How did you get this bruise?" James touched his fingers to my temple with uncharacteristic tenderness. I hadn't even realized the bump was still visible. "Don't worry, young Morgan." He put an arm around my shoulders and gave me a little squeeze. "I'm here now, and everything is under control. When I got your text, I thought to myself: You know what, *I* have never actually been to Troy. Maybe now's the time." He glanced at Nick, who was waiting for us next to Dr. Özlem's van, fingers drumming on the faded metal. "Besides, my uncle has a place on the Black Sea. Any excuse to drive his cars"—James nodded at the only other vehicle left in the parking lot: a racing green Aston Martin—"while saving damsels in distress."

The Özlems lived in a tiny farmhouse in the middle of a cow pasture. The more I looked around the humble dwelling, the more convinced I became that it had originally been built to house livestock, not humans.

"I am not going to light the fire," announced Dr. Özlem at one point, kindling my suspicions about the building, "because my wife thinks it smells too much like cows when the walls get warm. As for me"—he gestured sadly at his nose—"I can't smell anything anymore. They say it happens sometimes."

Although she spoke no English, Mrs. Özlem understood the gist of the conversation, and I felt a twinge of pity when I saw the haunted look on her gentle face. Slight of build and dressed in threadbare gray tones, she moved about with the pained grace of an aging ballerina, her every step and gesture devoted to the well-being of her husband. If Mr. Telemakhos had not already more than hinted at Dr. Özlem's illness, the entrenched worry on Mrs. Özlem's face would have told us everything we needed to know about her husband's fragility.

"What a charming cottage," said James, who had readily accepted an extended dinner invitation and was now doing his best to compensate our host with cheery remarks. "I imagine this would be considered traditional Turkish architecture?"

"Yes," said Dr. Özlem, pouring cloudy water for everyone from a three-legged brass pitcher. "Turkish architecture for cows. That was our house, up there." He nodded at a framed photograph on the wall. "We sold it to pay for the lawyers. Our son is studying law, but too late." He began handing out the water glasses, his gestures as dignified as if they had been filled with the finest champagne. "Now I wish he was becoming a doctor. Or a plumber. A plumber would be nice."

Later, over dinner at two small tables put together, James smiled at everyone and said, "So, how is the Amazon hunt going? I'm surprised it has taken you so long to get here. Isn't Turkey supposed to be true Amazon territory? Wasn't the Artemis temple at Ephesus, just south of here, allegedly built by the Amazons? One of the Seven Wonders of the World, if I'm not mistaken?" He glanced at Dr. Özlem for confirmation.

"Some scholars," nodded our host, thankfully oblivious to the teeth-gritting tension around the table, "believe there were quite a few matriarchal societies in the ancient Mediterranean world—for example on the island of Lemnos—but that the spread of the male-dominated Greek culture pushed these societies farther and farther east, until they ended up as colonies on the Black Sea coast. It is possible that Ephesus was a matriarchal society, too, and the many legends and names linking the Amazons to this region suggest there once was a matriarchal tradition here."

"Which is why, I imagine"—James shot me a smile, acknowledging that he was borrowing my turn of phrase on the subject—"heroes such as Hercules considered it their duty to occasionally spearhead a preemptive campaign against them and steal their girdles." Still smiling, James looked at Nick across the table. "Are you familiar with the Twelve Labors of Hercules? It was one of them, you know: stealing the Amazon queen's girdle. Have you had any success with that so far?"

Nick looked at James with the oddest expression, as if his thoughts were far away. Then he suddenly snapped to and said, "I'm not as literate as you when it comes to women's underwear."

A thunderclap of laughter from Mr. Telemakhos finally did away with the doomsday atmosphere. Even Rebecca perked up enough to whisper into my ear, "*Please* let's stick with the myths and not get personal."

Although not in a mood to make merry conversation, I knew she was right. "Allow me to elucidate," I said to Nick and James, "since *I* am the one with a degree in Amazon fashion. A girdle, somewhat disappointingly, is merely a large belt that protects the lower torso. The Bronze Age version of bulletproof granny knickers. A man would use his girdle to carry weapons, such as a sword or dagger, while a woman— at least in literature—wore a girdle as a symbol of protection and virginity. In the case of the Amazon queen, of course, it would mean both. By stealing her girdle, Hercules would in a sense remove both her masculine power and her female dignity. Or, less philosophically, he raped her *and* stole her pepper spray. What a hero."

After the passing around of several bowls and platters, Mr. Telemakhos said to Nick, "If you like, we can continue up the coast and visit the Amazon homeland on the south shore of the Black Sea." He nodded at Dr. Özlem. "Murat knows all the archaeologists digging at Karpu Kale and Ikiztepe—"

At this, finally, Rebecca was able to rally her spirits. "Yes, please!" she exclaimed, looking at the two older men as if they had offered her a seat in a lifeboat. Then something occurred to her, and she glanced nervously at me. "What do you say, Dee? A few more days—?"

Before I could even begin to reiterate all my reasons for *not* continuing another mile on Mr. Telemakhos's floating prison, James leaned into the conversation, saying, "Actually, I'm going to steal Diana away for a party in Istanbul tomorrow night."

I was not the only one staring at him with disbelief. "Thanks for the invitation," I said, "but I'm going to have my own little five-day party hitchhiking back to Britain." Seeing James's confusion, I hastened to add, "I lost my passport."

"Oh, don't be daft!" he exclaimed. "My uncle works at the British Consulate in Istanbul. I can get you a new passport in an hour. It'll be ready after the party."

"*What* party?" asked Rebecca, on behalf of everyone.

James smiled, but mostly to me. "Remember Reznik, the collector you wrote to about the *Historia Amazonum*? He is hosting a bash tomorrow—a sort of masquerade. I took the liberty of annexing a spot on the guest list. Thought it would be a brilliant opportunity for you to meet the man."

I looked at Nick across the table. He had claimed the Moselanes were in bed with Grigor Reznik and his Geneva smugglers. . . . Was it really true? Months ago, when I had first told James about my letters to Reznik, he had not said anything about being personally acquainted with the man.

Meeting my eyes with unusual solemnity, Nick shook his head discreetly, as if to say, "Don't do it."

"Reznik!" blurted Mr. Telemakhos, incapable of restraining his abhorrence for another second. "That son of a donkey has a big house in Istanbul full of stolen antiques. He even brags about it to foreigners and celebrities, to make them think he is somebody. Where do you think Murat's two stolen Amazon bracelets are now? Huh?" He glared at James, evidently holding him responsible by association.

"They say he has a vault in the basement"—Dr. Özlem touched a palm to his chest, as if to calm his heart—"full of gold from Troy that no one ever knew existed. Our boy went to university with Reznik's son, Alex, and says that he bragged freely about his father's crimes. Like father, like son. Poor devil. It all caught up with him in the end."

"Devil, yes," said Nick, his eyes narrow. "Poor, no."

"Well," said James, looking somewhat irritated at my lack of enthusiasm, "*I* am going to the masquerade, and you're welcome to accompany me."

"All of us?" Rebecca straightened with sudden inspiration, then turned to me and exclaimed, "This is fantastic! James and I will distract Reznik while *you* take a look at the *Historia Amazonum*."

"Great idea," I said. "Will you also bail me out of jail later?"

James rolled his eyes. "The manuscript is on display in Reznik's library, for everyone to see. It isn't even wired to an alarm."

"How do you know that?" I asked him, but he didn't seem to hear me.

"Ooooh!" boomed Mr. Telemakhos, shaking his head wistfully. "Would I like to get my hands on that manuscript. They say it holds vital information about the fate of the last Amazons."

"Last?" I looked at him, puzzled. If he sincerely believed Amazons were still around, how could he refer to any of them as the last?

Mr. Telemakhos shrugged, and the whole table wobbled. "I am just repeating what I have heard. That is the thing about the *Historia Amazonum*: We'll never know until it is properly translated and published." He nodded at me across the table. "Eternal fame, my fair-haired philologist, will befall the scholar who accomplishes that task."

"You mean, who steals it from Reznik?"

"Steals . . . borrows . . . sweet-talks." Mr. Telemakhos did not look overly concerned with the legal scope of the act. "When it comes to that man, I would say anything goes."

I could feel Nick's warning glare, but ignored it. "All I want is to have a quick look—"

James nodded to let me know I had made the wise choice. "A quick look and a passport. Consider it done."

WE TOOK OFF FOR Istanbul early the next morning. Despite James's rather toe-cringing attempts at disinviting them, both Rebecca and Nick insisted on coming along.

"Are you out of your mind?" Rebecca had asked, when I urged her to stay on the boat with Mr. Telemakhos and embark upon her Black Sea job hunt right away. "Do you really think I'll let you attend this party alone? No. We'll plunge in and be cut into shark food *together*. You and I can be James's arm candy, and Nick can be his bodyguard—he's so brilliant at being muscled and monosyllabic. Right, Nick?"

On paper it was a seven-hour drive; to Rebecca and me, sardining in the backseat while James and Nick had bigger fish to fry up front, it might as well have been a life sentence. Never mind that we'd volunteered to sit in back; our physical squeeze was nothing next to the rumble of foreboding that rolled through me the moment we left Çanakkale, and which continued to echo through my insides as we drove north along the coast. My impulsive plan to accompany James to Reznik's masquerade had made sense as long as it involved only the two of us. But was it fair of me to keep pulling poor Rebecca along? As for Nick, I was confident he could take care of himself, and yet I worried about him, too. What if Reznik recognized him?

"And what a tragedy," I heard Nick saying to James from the passenger seat, an espadrille up on the wooden dashboard, "if all those little schoolchildren, who so love going to museums, will have to start reading books again, to learn about ancient civilizations. Imagine a world where all the artifacts from ancient Egypt were actually *in* Egypt, and all of ancient Greece was returned to Greece. You mean, we'd actually have to *travel* to see these things? We can't just steal them any-more?"

"But if you go down that road," said James, as he and his family had evidently done many times before, "where do you stop? When the museums are empty? It's a dangerous thing, pulling threads out of the big tapestry of civilization. The whole thing might come apart."

"You know," said Nick, "there are a lot of people who have Monet's water lilies over their couch. But I can safely promise you that not a single one of them is in contortions because he or she does not own the original. Why is that, you may ask? Because—socialists and bank robbers aside—normal, sensible people do not feel entitled to things that aren't theirs." He shifted in his seat, clearly aching to put more space between himself and James. "And by the way, we're not trying to unravel the big tapestry of civilization, just correct the pattern."

James shook his head. "Good luck. If only the world was that manageable. Anyone who attempts to determine which country legally owns which artifact has a lifelong headache ahead of him."

"Tell that to the National Museum of Denmark," said Nick, leaning on the window panel. "They have already repatriated thirty-five thousand Inuit artifacts to Greenland. I think they consider it headache *prevention*."

"The Danes. Always the Danes." James barely looked over his shoulder before pulling out into a busy lane of passing cars. "History doesn't exist anywhere, except in books. Books that *we* write. Think about it. Most artifacts have had many legal owners along the way—to whom should we return them? Should a given statue be returned to Greece, where it was originally made, or to Rome, where it was sold by the artist's agent, or to France, where the Roman buyer went as proconsul, or to Spain, where his heirs moved after his death?" He cast Nick a surprisingly sympathetic glance. "In your rush to justice, you are more likely to open a whole new wormy can of *in*justice."

As I sat there in the backseat next to Rebecca, I wondered yet again why Nick had decided to go to Istanbul with us. While James might be driven by a romantic impulse to be my knight, I doubted Nick's motives were that benign. Something else was at stake—possibly more complex than a treasure.

"I was wondering when you would join us," Nick had said when James met us at Troy. Were those words key to my role in it all? Had my *real* purpose been to draw the Moselanes out of their shady corner and into the limelight? If that were the case, it was no longer strange that Nick had kept referring to James as my boyfriend. Perhaps that was the word used in the Aqrab Foundation memo on Diana Morgan.

And if it was not about the Moselanes after all, then . . . I was right back where I started, struggling to comprehend why Nick was subjecting himself to the torment of spending a whole day in the Aston Martin like this, for no other apparent reason than the dubious opportunity to pose as James's bodyguard at Reznik's party later tonight.

Whenever I closed my eyes, I saw a slide show of contradictions, interspersed with images of Granny, looking at me through a gritty bus window, saying something I couldn't hear before the driver closed the door between our worlds and took her away into the unknown.

JAMES DROVE ALL THE way into Istanbul's historic center and parked right in front of a public bath complex called the Cağaloğlu Hamamı. "I don't know about you," he said, looking at Rebecca and me in the rearview mirror, "but I am ready for a Turkish bath."

As we stood on the pavement, discussing what to wear for Reznik's party and where to buy it, Nick slung his duffel bag over one shoulder and said, "Well, thanks for the ride. Here"—he threw me a small, compact bankroll—"I thought you might like your tip in Turkish lira. Have fun tonight."

"But . . . wait!" I stepped toward him, nearly tripping over the curb. "Are you not coming with us?"

Nick checked his wristwatch. "Not sure I can make it."

Only then did I realize I had spent the last little while in a peculiarly weightless state; suddenly gravity returned with a vengeance. "So, that's it?"

He shot me a completely carefree smile and shook my hand with professional curtness. "Good luck with your future work. And remember." He nodded at my jackal bracelet. "Don't let Reznik see that."

James laughed, clearly relieved at this development. "I thought you were my bodyguard! Does this mean you're not going to take a bullet for me?"

Nick took a step backward, then another. "I already did."

DESPITE ITS DISCREET, IF not downright humble, street entrance, the Turkish bath turned out to be a place of rare magic. Located at the end of a long corridor, deep inside a complex of contemporary buildings, this magnificent old *hamam* was like crystal embedded in rock—a cavern of timeless beauty, perfectly protected from the world outside.

Not until we were sprawled on a marble platform in the otherwise empty women's steam room, dressed in nearly nothing, did Rebecca finally mutter, already sluggish from the heat, "What did he mean by that bullet comment?"

"No idea." I looked at the dome above us, where a pattern of tiny round holes created a mesmerizing starburst of daylight. "Come, thou night in day . . . or is it day in night?"

"That's the spirit," said Rebecca, looking surprisingly comfortable on the wet marble, an arm over her eyes. "I was worried about you, you know. I was sure Nick was going to be the fourth horseman."

"Well, sheathe your worry." I sat up abruptly, in no mood to discuss the subject. "As you saw, he galloped right over me." Before Rebecca could say more, I walked across the floor to one of the marble washbasins on the wall and used the copper ladle to douse myself with cold water.

It was no use. Rather than soothing my throbbing head, the frigid drizzle merely washed away my hastily applied coat of pretense. It was not the water that made me gasp as much as the sharpened image of Nick sauntering away from the Cağaloğlu Hamamı and out of my life.

Had Mr. Telemakhos been there with us—and it was not hard to imagine him at ease on the bath's marble platform, sporting a Homeric loincloth around his ample middle and eating grapes by the cluster—he would undoubtedly have informed me that Nick was bound to show up again sooner or later, in the manner of lost handbags. But so far he had been wrong about my handbag, and I rather feared he would be wrong about Nick, too.

The man who had shaken my hand and walked away from me an hour earlier, casually checking messages on his cellphone, had not struck me as someone likely to show up at Reznik's party or anywhere. After spending the day with three Brits, relentlessly pummeled by James's easy wit, Nick had looked as if he was prepared to swim across the Hellespont to escape us.

Obviously, I would be able to reach him via the Aqrab Foundation; it was not as if he had disappeared without a trace. All it took was a phone call to Dubai. But what would I say? Why was it so terribly important that I got ahold of Nicholas Barrán?

I sighed and filled the ladle once more. As I leaned over, Granny's bracelet scraped against the marble washbasin, and I was overcome by irrational anger toward the coiled bronze for not letting go of me, even here. It was absurd, of course, but I almost felt as if the jackal had played a part in repelling Nick . . . as if it had sensed that, over the past twenty-four hours, he had been steadily outstripping James in a secret race for my heart.

IT TOOK AN ENTERPRISING fashion store owner at the Kanyon shopping mall to finally muzzle the little blighter. In the interest of covering up my bracelet without compromising the necessary look of glamour, the saleslady insisted I wear ruffled satin gloves and a floor-length dress with bare shoulders. And to make absolutely sure no one saw it as more than a fashion statement, Rebecca had to wear the same. With matching shoes, of course.

"Granny wouldn't like it," was the only thing I could think of saying when we stood side by side in front of the gilded store mirror—Rebecca in green to complement her red hair while I wore blue to match my eyes.

"I have to disagree," said Rebecca, whose mood had improved considerably when—during our taxi ride to the mall—I had split my ten thousand dollars plus tip with her. "Your grandmother always said a woman's greatest power lies in her ability to fool the enemy into thinking she is weak and simpleminded, correct?"

A beeping sound interrupted our conversation. It was Rebecca's cellphone, announcing the arrival of a text. "Somehow," she said, frowning at the screen before handing the phone to me, "I suspect this one is for you."

I didn't recognize the number, but knew right away the text was from Nick. "Your laptop is in Istanbul," it said. "Stay away from GR."

"It looks like Reznik *did* steal my computer," I told Rebecca, doing my best to sound amused. "What do you say, should we turn back now?"

"Hell no!" Rebecca glared at our mirror images, arms akimbo. "It's not as if we're planning to steal it back from him. Reznik won't even know it's *you*."

I studied my own reflection in the mirror. Rebecca was probably right; it would never occur to Reznik that I had come to him freely, driven by nothing but a humble hope of seeing the *Historia Amazonum* with my own eyes and maybe, if the party was really hopping, quickly leafing through it. . . .

"Too late," I wrote to Nick in response. "But thanks."

Later, over a stand-up kebab in the food court, I took out the note Mr. Telemakhos had slipped into my hand when we said good-bye. "Here," he had whispered, with uncharacteristic discretion. "There is another jackal bracelet out there. I thought it might interest you."

The note read simply "Museum und Park Kalkriese. Dr. Jäger."

"Germany?" I had said, not quite sure what he wanted me to do.

Mr. Telemakhos nodded. "Near Osnabrück. That woman, Dr. Jäger, knows a lot more than she lets on. She could have the answers you are looking for."

"What is that?" Rebecca pointed her kebab at the note. "A love letter?"

"In a manner of speaking." I showed her the note. "The Oracle wants me to do some legwork for him. Apparently, he's managed to become persona non grata in the German museum world, and if I ever go there I'm not supposed to mention his name."

"Really?" Rebecca looked oddly hurt, and I realized she was bothered by the fact that Mr. Telemakhos had confided in *me* like this, without saying a word to *her*.

"Don't worry." For lack of a handbag, I put the note into my new blue satin evening purse. "I am obviously not going to Germany."

"No." Rebecca busied herself with the dripping kebab. "You're going on a romantic weekend with James. Finally!"

I winced at the image. "Definitely not. As soon as I get that passport, I'm out of here."

Rebecca gave me a long look, but thankfully put no words to her annoyance. For years I had pestered her with my reflections on James; now that he was within reach, I wouldn't touch him.

Although James was still James, he was no longer the man I had known in Oxford. From being the gentlemanly friend he had suddenly catapulted himself into an unspoken engagement with me, completely skipping all the traditional overtures. It was as if, in his mind, there was no need to even inquire about my feelings . . . as if he was so convinced of my devotion that he needn't even bother to attempt earning it anymore. And so he treated me as though it was all a done deal. Every look he gave me, every word he spoke to me, had a tone of ownership. It all felt oddly hollow.

GRIGOR REZNIK LIVED IN a grandiose modern monstrosity in the exclusive Ulus neighborhood. We entered the property on foot, through a tall gate crowded with security guards. As we proceeded toward the house along a garden path lined with torches, we had a sweeping view below of the dark Bosphorus Strait, the illuminated bridges, and the crisscrossing lines of streetlamps on the eastern banks.

"I thought he was supposed to be in love with all things antique," muttered Rebecca, her blue and green peacock face paint contracting at the sight of the angular, completely unadorned house rising ahead. Light poured out at us from three floors of panoramic windows, but it had a cool, fluorescent tint to it—a calculated shine that was more warning than welcome.

"Apparently," said James, brushing peacock glitter from the sleeves of his Aladdin costume, "Reznik believes minimalist architecture provides the optimal framework for art. And torture. Notice the samurai?" He nodded at two austere men in Japanese costumes standing on either side of the door, checking invitations. "Back in the day, Reznik had his own secret police, and these gentlemen—his top officers— followed him into retirement, so to speak."

"Remind me again why we are visiting this creep?" muttered Rebecca, shivering in her satin shawl.

Just then, as James escorted us up the front steps of the house, it finally hit me that he had not come to Turkey to be my knight. He came because of Nick. As with the myth of the beautiful Helen of Troy, the myth of the irresistible Diana Morgan was merely a convenient illusion draped over prosaic facts. The Aqrab Foundation had declared war on the Moselanes by going after their antiques collection, and now, it seemed, they were going after human beings as well. It was all shamefully simple: Whatever his true feelings for me, James was too proud to let Nick carry away as much as a single one of his perceived assets without a fight.

CHAPTER TWENTY-NINE

TROY

THE FARMERS WERE BUSY IN THEIR FIELDS, WEEDING AND WATERING, when Myrina and her little entourage finally emerged from the wilderness. Coming out of the woods rather abruptly, they found themselves on the edge of the Scamandrian Plain southwest of Troy, with a sweeping view across the river valley to the capital they had traveled so far to see.

Glowing in the afternoon sun, the city sat upon the landscape with the grace of a precious crown left in a meadow by a forgetful king. Although fortified with colossal walls and towers—or, perhaps, because of it—there was something bold and unafraid about the place, as if its inhabitants were so confident of their safety they barely even paused to rest their tools and look out over the river delta to the sea beyond.

"Well," said Animone, who was one of the five Myrina had chosen to join her journey, "now let us find the man who isn't here, and turn right around."

It was only that same morning, after a long week of riding north from Ephesus, that Myrina had told her traveling companions about Paris's parting words and the man who would supposedly be posted on the hill called Batieia. "If there is no one there," she had explained, finally putting words to her worst fear, "then it means Paris is no longer waiting for me, in which case we return home. It would not surprise me. It has, after all, been a month."

"What is a month," said Kara who, for reasons of her own, had begged to come along on the trip, "to a couple united by destiny?" She spoke the words with sincerity and yet Myrina could not help wondering—as she often did—whether it could really be true her former rival was now her friend. Still laboring under the delusion of being pregnant, Kara had chosen to remain in her imaginary world a while longer. Perhaps in that world Myrina was the only one who understood her. At least that was what Kara had kept saying when Myrina had tried to dissuade her from joining them.

Besides Animone and Kara, Lilli was there, of course, still grudgingly sharing Myrina's horse. Behind them rode Kyme and Hippolyta, both of whom evidently saw themselves as diplomats of a certain standing—Kyme because of her age and knowledge of writing, and Hippolyta by virtue of being the only one in the group who knew the Trojan language.

"Just leave it to me," she had said when the trip was being planned. "I can speak with the locals, and I know the route . . . all the way into the royal throne room." She had laughed at everyone's gaping awe. "I have accompanied Mother Otrera often enough. The queen is her sister, you know, and used to be one of us. But then she was hit by the poisoned arrow, dipped in honey"—Hippolyta clutched her heart in jest—"and from being a doe flying freely across the fields, she cast off her vows to become a cow tied in a bullpen."

But apart from Hippolyta's teasing, and a few bitter comments from others, the news of Myrina's departure drew far less attention than she had feared it would. Apart from Lady Otrera, the only one who knew what agony and confusion Myrina had suffered before finally deciding to leave was Lilli. No matter how carefully Myrina hid herself from the others in order to think in peace, Lilli always found her. Whether she was in the hayloft, the grain cellar, or the house sanctuary, Myrina could be sure that, sooner or later, she would feel Lilli's soft hands on her arms and be pulled into a welcome embrace.

It was not that they spoke much about Myrina's dilemma; Lilli clearly understood what her sister felt and knew that words would only muddle a situation that, in itself, was relatively simple. Two paths lay before Myrina: one of temporary relief and lifelong regret, and another of temporary pain followed by great happiness. The fact that Lilli was content to merely share her silence told Myrina the girl already knew what the choice must be.

When she eventually announced her decision to leave Ephesus, Myrina found Lady Otrera oddly unmoved by the news. "The less we speak of it on earth, the less will reach the ears of heaven," Otrera said sternly, putting down her basket. "But we *must* remove your bracelet. Let me see now—"

And so it came about that Myrina's jackal bracelet was removed in the vegetable garden without ceremony. "Since we have no moon to-night," continued Otrera, pulling so hard at the metal she nearly broke the wrist it sat on, "the Goddess may not even notice what has happened. There"—she held the bracelet out to Myrina, proud of having bent it to her will—"you are free to dispose of it, as long as you do it discreetly."

But Myrina could not bring herself to throw out this burdensome adornment, nor did she dare keep it, for fear it would strike out at her yet. In the end she gave it to Helena, the Greek girl, to brighten their farewell. "I want you to have this," she said, slipping the jackal around Helena's wrist, "for you are the worthiest warrior the Goddess could ever have. And perhaps, by gaining you, she will think little of losing me."

The girl touched the lustrous bronze with reverent fingers. "How often I hate myself for the things I say," she muttered. "Of everyone here, you are the only one who never turned away from me. Since the night you let me come with you, you have been my steadfast sister. I pray that one day I may return your kindness."

Then at last came the day of departure, with tearful embraces and belated words of gratitude. Myrina made solemn promises to visit often, but nothing changed the fact that she was abandoning the sisterhood. She, who had risked everything to bring them all back together, was going on to new, forbidden adventures, leaving them behind. Despite her sisters' tears and blessings, Myrina saw in their eyes they resented her for it.

THE SMALL HILL CALLED Batieia rose conspicuously from the flatness of the Scamandrian Plain, as if deposited there by a giant mole. Riding toward it ahead of her sisters, across a field of ripening grain, Myrina peered at its contours with narrow eyes, anxious to be the first to pronounce that the man wasn't there.

But he was.

Sitting cross-legged with a spear across his lap, the man first straightened, then stood up expectantly. And when he threw out an arm to wave a greeting, Myrina saw it was the long-limbed Aeneas, Paris's most trusted companion.

Giddy with relief, she jumped from the horse and rushed forward . . . only to stop awkwardly at the foot of the hill. "Does your master still await me?" she asked, squinting against the sun, "or are you here to tell us to go home?"

Aeneas shook his head and bent down to pick up his satchel. "If I told him you had been here but had turned around because of me, this mound would have to be renamed yet again, after my dead bones."

After descending the hill on the other side, Aeneas soon reappeared astride his horse. "Come," he said, starting upriver and away from town, "we will go to my house in the hills. He will meet you there."

The look passing between Kyme and Hippolyta did not escape Myrina. Nor did Animone's scowl of disappointment. They had all, she knew, been hoping for a dignified welcome at the royal court in the manner to which Lady Otrera's daughters were accustomed. To be whisked away instead to a hut in the countryside fell woefully short of their expectations.

The rustic charm of their destination did little to soften the disgrace. Perched on a densely forested slope, Aeneas's home turned out to be little more than a cluster of modest wooden cabins . . . of which the stable was by far the most impressive.

"This is my son," said Aeneas of the boy who came running out to greet them and help with the horses. "And that"—he pointed across the muddy yard at the smallest cabin of them all—"is where my master stays when he is here."

Only then, as he looked around at the women, did Aeneas seem to grasp their apprehension. "I am aware," he went on, a wounded frown passing across his forehead, "we are somewhat removed from town, but this is why he likes to come here. He always says"—Aeneas glanced at Myrina, clearly hoping to win her approval—"this is his true home."

Somewhat softened to the idea of spending the night in the lonely hills, the women followed Aeneas into his own cabin and were rewarded by the delicious aroma of stew. "This is my wife, Creusa." Aeneas smiled at the young woman tending to a copper cauldron by the fireplace. "She doesn't speak your language, but she understands everything and knows what to do. I will leave you with her and return later."

After exchanging a few words and a kiss with his wife, Aeneas left the cabin. Moments later, Myrina heard the sound of a horse galloping off down the forest path and felt a sudden thrill at the thought that Aeneas had left for Troy to let Paris know of her arrival.

Their hostess's immediate concern was the food, but a quick trip by Creusa across the yard—possibly to a storage room—yielded a welcome addition of cheese, bread, and wine. And before long, Aeneas's young wife was ready to sit everyone down at the table with food and drink, while she herself disappeared once more across the yard.

"This stew is not half bad," admitted Animone, as soon as they were alone. "But then, anything would taste good to me tonight."

"Just give me a soft nest," said Kyme, yawning into her wine, "and this old hen shan't utter another cluck of complaint."

They ate a while in silence. Even Lilli was quieter than usual, behaving as if she knew something she dared not put into words.

Creusa later returned, her arms full of woolen blankets. Seeing they had finished eating, she beckoned her guests into another room and pointed at a large bed that could easily hold them all. But when Myrina began undoing her sandals, Creusa tapped her eagerly on the shoulder to make her stop.

"What is it?" asked Lilli, already burrowed into the center of the bed.

"I am not sure," said Myrina. "I think she is asking me to help her."

"Well." Kyme yawned again as she loosened her girdle and let it fall to the floor. "Whatever it is, you are the woman to do it."

Half-expecting Creusa to want help with the big cauldron, Myrina was surprised when the woman went outside yet again, motioning for her to follow. Stepping into the yard, Myrina saw that the summer sun had long since disappeared into the ocean, and yet there was a dewy freshness everywhere that reminded her this night had just begun.

Full of smiling encouragement, Creusa walked Myrina over to the cabin Aeneas had identified as belonging to Paris, and opened the door wide to let her enter. A bit chilled from the unexpected coolness of the mountain air, Myrina stepped into the small kitchen to find a cozy fire burning in the fireplace. The room was by no means luxurious—there was hardly even a mat to sit on—and yet in front of the fireplace stood a large, rather puzzling, water-filled tub made of wood.

Approaching with curiosity, Myrina leaned forward and saw her own shimmering reflection among the flower petals floating around in the water. There did not appear to be anything else submerged in the tub; only when she looked up and saw Creusa's encouraging gestures did Myrina realize that *she* was to get in the water—an undeserved honor for one who was neither a High Priestess nor even a holy woman anymore.

Shaking her head, she backed away . . . but Creusa stopped her. Apparently used to handling reluctant creatures, the woman undressed Myrina with her own hands, nimbly untying this and that until there was nothing left to take off. Only then, urged on by modesty, did Myrina put a foot in the water . . . and found it so pleasantly warm she did not hesitate to step in and sit down.

The water rose around her as she did so, and Myrina was relieved to find herself almost completely covered, with flower petals washing gently upon the shore of her shoulders. Leaning back against the wooden side, however, she could not help wondering about the process of building such a magnificent contraption, and while Creusa was putting her clothes aside—grimacing as she did so—Myrina felt around at the tub, inside and outside, to try to figure out its secrets.

But Creusa took her hands with a smile and put them right back in the water. Then, motioning for Myrina to put her head back, she took a brazen ladle and began running water through her hair until it was completely wet. And after that came the soap—a sticky, sweet-smelling substance that reminded Myrina of nothing she had ever smelled before.

Sitting still, her eyes closed against the suds, Myrina was embarrassed to discover how much she enjoyed the bath: the warm water, the wordless calm of the room, and the gentle fingers slowly working their way around her hair and neck. Perhaps it was because Creusa was a stranger . . . or perhaps it was her, Myrina, whose thoughts and feelings were no longer kept in check by the jackal. If that were the case, she should welcome the change. For had she not left Ephesus and come to Troy precisely for this? Had she not lived this past month in a state of raging impatience, feeling there was so much happiness still to be found in life, so much pleasure?

When the bath was finally over, and Myrina was wrapped in soft blankets, she felt so limp she could barely stand up. Putting a hand behind her back, Creusa walked her through the curtained doorway in the far wall and into the room beyond—a room that was larger than one would expect, but held merely two things: a fireplace stacked full with crackling, burning logs, and a low bed, covered in animal skins.

Pointing at the bed, Creusa let Myrina understand this would be where she slept for the night—away from the others, away from Lilli. And as soon as Myrina stepped into the animal skins, the woman went back into the kitchen to return moments later with a small bowl of hot tea.

After seeing Myrina tasting and nodding with appreciation, Creusa bent forward impulsively to kiss her wet hair, after which she fled the room with downcast eyes.

Shortly thereafter, Myrina heard Creusa leave the cabin, and the door gently closing. Torn between her concerns for the others and her obligation to Creusa, who so obviously wanted her to stay right there, Myrina decided to be patient and drink the rest of her tea before sneaking out to check on Lilli.

But by the time she finished the cup—which contained a curious blend of mint and something else—she was so relaxed that the prospect of getting back into her clothes, bundled somewhere on the kitchen floor, was downright torturous. Sighing deeply, she lay down on the bed to rest for a moment. . . .

And was woken by the sound of water.

Sitting up, Myrina had no idea how long she had been asleep. Her hair was almost dry, and the fire had long since settled into a heap of smoldering coals.

Stepping out on the floor, she tiptoed to the curtain to peek into the kitchen, expecting to see Creusa—indefatigable Creusa—emptying the bathtub. But what she saw made her draw back with a gasp. For it was Paris, completely naked, standing up in the water after a bath of his own, his wet skin reflecting the glow of the embers in the kitchen hearth as he dried his hair.

Unsure what to do, Myrina stayed rooted to the spot, wrapped in her blankets. And when Paris finally pushed aside the curtain and entered the bedroom, barely dressed, she was so struck by bashfulness she turned away. But then . . . her desire to see him was greater than her shyness, and she looked up to meet his eyes.

How long they stood like that, unspoken words passing between them, she was not sure. Then, as though he had been waiting for permission, Paris crossed the floor and took her head between his hands, kissing her with all the pent-up passion she had seen in his eyes—kisses of tender promises and unbending demands that galloped away with her across fields, endless, blooming fields. . . .

But when he tried to pull the blanket from her shoulder, her hand shot out by reflex to close tightly around his wrist. At which Paris smiled and whispered, "Don't fight me. Not tonight."

Myrina slowly released his arm. "It is only what you've taught me so well."

He kissed her neck, right below the ear. "Yes, but there is more."

She closed her eyes, barely able to think. "And what would you have me learn tonight?"

"The most important lesson of all." He drew her tightly against him. "To surrender with grace."

She gasped with surprise. "Once again you are armed and I am not!"

He chuckled but did not let her go. "That is usually why one surrenders."

"If I were a man, you would never tell me to surrender."

"No." He took her by the neck and kissed her again, indulging in her softness. "But you are not a man. You are too lovely, too mysterious—"

Myrina gasped at his skillful touch. "I am not sure I know how to be a woman. I have never tried."

Paris smiled. "If you could see yourself, you would think otherwise."

"Will you help me?"

His eyes darkened. "Does Earth need to ask the Sun to rise?"

Myrina shook her head, willing him to understand. "Earth is new to me. For so long, the Moon has ruled my world."

"I know." Paris took her hand and kissed her wrist—a shade brighter where the jackal bracelet used to be. "The Moon has no power to give life. That is why she is so jealous of our pleasure." He clutched her hand with his, then caught himself and let go. "But first . . ."

Puzzled, Myrina watched him disappear behind the curtain and return a moment later, carrying something wrapped in cloth. After tossing a few fresh logs on the fire he knelt down by the hearthstone to open the cloth and reveal two objects hidden inside. One was a humble clay bottle sealed with wax, the other a golden chalice beset with precious stones. Seeing the hesitant reverence with which he touched the latter, Myrina guessed it was no ordinary royal drinking vessel, but one invested with a certain magic.

"Here." Paris handed her the chalice and peeled the wax seal from the bottle before pouring out the darkest, most viscous liquid Myrina had ever seen. Then he said, with solemnity, "You are the cup, and I am the wine." And when Myrina opened her mouth to ask why it could not be the other way around, he pressed his fingers against her lips with a warning glare. "Drink."

And she did, but just a sip, leaving the rest for Paris, who emptied the chalice with a grimace.

"I am sorry," she said. "I did not realize we were to finish it."

"No." He knelt down to wrap everything back up in the cloth. "Because I did not tell you. The taste of this, I am sure, has haunted many a bride on her wedding night—as if she did not already have her fill of frights."

Myrina started. "Does this mean I am your wife?"

Paris rose slowly, to kiss her with reverence. Then he took the blanket she still had draped around her and very gently removed it. "Almost," he whispered, taking in the sight of her. Picking her up in his arms and stepping directly into the bed, he said, "Before the night is over, you will be."

CHAPTER THIRTY

MYRINA WOKE IN A ROOM BATHED IN SUNSHINE. BLINKING AGAINST the bright light, she looked around to find its source and saw a pair of shutters that had been opened while she slept. Next to her lay Paris, smiling at her confusion. The sight of him sent a bolt of delight through her body, leaving a trail of smoldering embarrassment as all her memories from the night were released at once, flapping away on quivery wings.

Diving back under the bearskin they were sharing, Myrina hid her face against Paris's neck and felt him chuckle. "I thought," he said, kissing her temple, "we did away with this shyness of yours." He ran his hands down her back, drawing her closer. "Perhaps we should try to hunt it down again? Clearly, it is still hiding somewhere."

Myrina giggled when she felt his searching touch. "Unquestionably," she murmured against his ear, "you did away with a lot of things— and thoroughly so—but let me keep my modesty a little longer that I may not be a complete stranger to myself."

"Very well," growled Paris, rolling on top of her. "Keep your shyness if you must, as long as you let this rapacious husband of yours have the rest."

Later, when they were once again calm, Myrina put a hand over his heart and said, "To think I should travel so far away from everything I know . . . and find that my home has been here all along, waiting for me."

Paris turned his head to look into her eyes. "Tell me about the people you used to know. Your parents, your family . . ."

Myrina reached out to cover them both with a blanket. "They are all gone. My sister Lilli"—she paused to stem a sudden sadness—"is the only blood relation I have left."

Paris kissed her on the forehead, then lay back to stare at the ceiling. "You are fortunate," he said, his voice heavy with a burden only he could see. "No one is waiting for you, making demands on you, judging you. You are free."

Anxious to dispel his sudden gloom, Myrina ran a hand underneath the covers. "Not anymore."

"But you are." He checked her hand, not yet ready to play. "This house . . . you and me . . . that is freedom. We have both cast off our bonds to be together, and I wish"—he brought her hand to his lips, kissing it tenderly—"I wish we could lie here, just like this, until the end of time."

THEY STAYED IN THE hillside cabin for three nights. During the daytime, Myrina did what she could to entertain her sisters, but despite their goodwill and humorous comments, it was clear they were all—even Lilli—growing impatient with their mountainous isolation.

When Aeneas returned on the fourth day with orders to bring Prince Paris back to court, even Myrina was secretly relieved to see their rustic sojourn come to an end. She suspected the magnificence of a royal reception would have a soothing effect on her sisters' disgruntlement and free her to once again spend long, delightful hours alone with her husband.

But as they rode back along the Scamander River, with the walls of Troy rising ahead, Paris was so silent she began to wonder whether there was something he had not told her—some terrible reality that would soon undermine her happy expectations. Myrina could not imagine what it might be, other than the obvious risk that the king and queen might be displeased in their son's choice of wife. Whenever she had raised the issue, however, Paris had laughed it away and assured her no one would find fault with *her* . . . implying that, whatever it was, the problem lay with him alone.

In the end, Myrina purged all those futile speculations from her mind and took in the beauty of the landscape around her. The Scamandrian Plain had already struck her as rich and plentiful on the day they first arrived; since then, her appreciation had only grown. For this was her home now; these golden ears of wheat, swaying in the breeze, carried the grains she would eat, and those colossal walls, engineered for eternity, would be the cradle holding her future. And Lilli's future, too, should she decide to stay in Troy.

Riding up to the city gate, Myrina had to put back her head in wonder. Never had she seen walls this tall, or doors made from such giant boards of wood. Nowhere in the city of the Moon Goddess had there been architecture to rival this; even the massive fortifications at Mycenae seemed puny in comparison.

The gate stood wide open, allowing for the constant coming and going of farmers and merchants, the latter of whom were either on their way to the harbor—glittering in the distance—or returning to town with cartloads of foreign goods. There was a great sense of purpose to the place. Myrina could happily have gotten off her horse and sat all day next to the grandfathers on their benches, bobbing in the flow of life.

"When we arrive," said Paris, as he steered them through the mayhem, "there may be some . . . commotion. But please trust me and do not worry." He gave Myrina a reassuring smile. "No one will prevent us from being together, and before you know it"—he leaned toward her and lowered his voice—"I will be chasing you around a bed so big you'll finally have a chance of escaping my satyric lust."

Myrina was not fooled by his levity. Out of the corner of her eye she saw the muscles at war in his jaw and the trenches drawn across his forehead. It pained her to see him suffer, and even more that he did not share his concerns with her, or hint at their nature. But then . . . she also knew him well enough to understand that his silence was, more than anything, an expression of his love for her. Whatever had to be endured, he intended to endure alone. To challenge his decision and argue he was hurting her would be a blow directly to his heart.

UNLIKE THE CITY GATE, the entrance to the Trojan citadel was closed and blocked by armed guards. A steep and narrow ramp led up to it, with tall walls on either side; it reminded Myrina of nothing she had ever seen before.

"We are private people," explained Paris. "So many foreign ships stop here in the summer months—" He broke off to address the guards in the Trojan language, and they immediately snapped to, opening a small window in the door to order the whole thing unlocked from the inside.

As the gate swung out, Myrina saw that the entrance went through a tunnel built with enormous fitted boulders that looked as if they could have been moved by no one but the gods. On the other side of the tunnel, Paris led their party into a vast, sloping yard ringed with magnificent houses. The Trojan citadel, home to King Priam and his court, was a small city unto itself, dominated—at the top—by one particularly large building fronted with a colonnade.

"That is the Temple of the Earth Shaker," explained Paris, following Myrina's eyes. "The all-powerful uncle of the Sun God. This is where he lives"—Paris made a gesture out over the great blue sea visible beyond the walls of the citadel—"when he is not roaming the ocean. But come, I see my father is out. We have a chance of speaking to him without a great echo and a whining choir of doomsday priests—"

Only then did Myrina notice the cluster of men across the courtyard and the handsome red stallion in their midst. As she and Paris rode toward the group with Aeneas and her sisters trailing behind, she saw an old man with a walking stick checking the stallion's teeth and guessed a purchase was afoot.

Dismounting, Paris walked up to another man who stood off to the side and began addressing him with a nod of deference. Because the man was clad in an entirely unremarkable garment, it did not even occur to Myrina that he was the illustrious King Priam until he held out his hand to Paris. After dutifully kissing his father's ring, Paris went on—Myrina guessed—to explain something about the women he had brought to court. He did not get far before the king's serene gaze turned into a squint.

She had done much to prepare herself for this moment, and yet Myrina found herself shrinking under King Priam's scrutiny when he looked at her, then her sisters. Although father and son were alike in stature, and the king's hair had only just started graying, his eyes could have been those of the oldest man in the world.

"Come, my love." Paris helped her from the horse and walked her over to stand before the unsmiling king. Then he took a deep breath and squared his shoulders. "Father, this is my wife. Her name is Myrina."

King Priam's face might as well have been carved in stone, for it was absolutely unmoving, expressing neither anger nor joy. For the briefest of moments, Myrina wondered whether Paris had been wrong in assuming his father would be comfortable switching into the language of Ephesus—perhaps he had not actually understood what his son said to him. But even before she had completed the thought, the king responded in that same language, without even a hint of an accent, "Is it a fact?"

Myrina felt Paris's hand closing firmly around hers. "Yes."

"What say you?" King Priam turned to Myrina. "Are you his wife?"

She nodded, too breathless to respond in words.

"Speak up!" The king was in no mood for meekness. "Are you his wife?"

Myrina swallowed her nerves. "Yes."

Then at last, King Priam nodded at Paris. "So be it. May the Earth Shaker—and your mother!—look kindly upon this union. I will go and forewarn her now." With that the king turned and marched away, leaving not only Myrina, but also her sisters and Aeneas in a state of silent mortification.

"Right," said Paris, addressing all the women at once, his smile defying their shuffling embarrassment. "Welcome to my father's house.

Aeneas will make sure you are comfortably installed, while Myrina and I will do what has to be done—a task you need not envy us."

The queen was not in her courtyard, surrounded by ladies and musicians, nor had she withdrawn to her quarters to bathe and be private. When Myrina and Paris finally found her, she was kneeling in a windowless house shrine in front of a small altar crowded with wax candles and tiny figurines.

After waiting for a moment so as not to interrupt her, Paris leaned down and touched a hand to her covered shoulder. *"Mama—"*

Myrina heard a gasp, then a sob . . . before the queen rose from the small praying stool to throw her arms around her son with a stream of tearful lamentations. Stroking his hair with frantic, trembling hands, she kissed him again and again, unwilling to let him go, and whatever he whispered to her—calm and patient as he was—only seemed to aggravate her more.

Stepping backward, Myrina wanted to run away and hide. She had anticipated fury and accusations, but not tears. It did not seem right that she should witness these intimate emotions; how could she ever look the queen in the eyes after this? She felt anger toward Paris for having involved her in such a critical moment, and yet she could see that he, too, was shocked by the force of his mother's grief.

"Please, Mother," he said, in the language of Ephesus. "When you know Myrina better, you will understand—"

"Myrina? That is how I must address your murderer?" The queen turned reluctantly to face her new daughter-in-law. "Do you know what you have done?" she whispered, as if she were pleading with a merciless hangman. "Do you know what you have done to my son, the only healthy boy that ever lay in my arms?" As she spoke, her voice gathered strength, and when she saw Myrina's terror she fairly slung the last words in her face. "You think you have secured a life in riches, but you have not! Greedy sow! When he dies, I will see to it you burn on the same day, but on quite a different pyre!"

"Mother!" exclaimed Paris, taking her firmly by the shoulders. "Control yourself! Myrina knows nothing of this nonsense." He drew his mother into a tight embrace, trying to still her trembling. "Look at you! What must she think of you? Myrina loves me, I assure you, and would rather die than cause me pain. Just like you."

There was a brief silence. Then the queen mumbled, her voice muffled by his shoulder, "She can never love you the way I do."

"I know, Mother." He kissed her again. "But she is doing her best. She is one of Otrera's daughters and thus your niece. Just like you, she undid her vows to become a wife. Only *you* can know what she has gone through."

This, at last, seemed to have an effect. Wiping her eyes with the corner of her praying shawl, the queen stood back and looked at Myrina once again, her hatred momentarily curbed. "Yet another woman with broken vows under this roof? Then we are doubly damned. But I must take my blame, I see it now. The Goddess has never allowed me to forget . . . and now my judgment is near." She pressed a fist to her chest, fighting back another onslaught of misery. "I should not hate you, child. I was wrong to condemn you. For you are but an instrument of the Goddess. It was not you who killed my son. It was me. In my ignorance and wickedness, I gave him death even before the gods gave him life."

PARIS HAD HIS DOMAIN on the top floor of the royal palace—a vast room with a balcony overlooking the city and harbor. Beyond the harbor, which lay in a protected bay, the sea heaved quietly in the midday heat, specked with the occasional ship coming out of the narrow strait of the Dardanelles to round the Trojan headland.

It was a magnificent, truly luxurious sight, and yet Myrina could not enjoy it. The meeting with the queen had disturbed her greatly, and she was unable to pry her thoughts from the unspoken curse that had cast such a formidable shadow over mother and son.

"This will be your view from now on," said Paris, coming up behind her. "And this will be mine." He kissed her neck, then pushed the dress from her shoulders and ran his hands over her skin. "The finest view in Troy . . . nay, in the world altogether—"

"Please." Myrina held on to her dress as best she could.

"Just as the sun rises on one side of the earth," mumbled Paris, tracing every rise, every valley of her spine, "and spends the entire day traveling to the other . . . so could I spend my days traveling over you, from front to back, from top to toe. And never once"—he pressed against her teasingly from behind—"would you wait in vain for me to rise."

But Myrina could not bring herself to frolic so soon after the drama she had witnessed. "Do tell me," she whispered, looking at him over her shoulder, "what your mother meant by what she said. I cannot forget her sadness."

Paris sighed and released her. "I should have warned you that my mother is superstitious. Do you believe me if I tell you it is nothing to worry about?"

"No."

"Damn it!" Paris walked out onto the balcony. "That is a fine start to our marriage. But then, I suppose I did not marry you because I wanted to be followed around by a cowering slave." He glanced at her to make sure she was listening. "What you must understand is that my mother has carried twelve children, but lost nine of them. Some at birth, others later, due to"—he shrugged—"jealous fortune? I do not pretend to understand these matters."

Myrina shook her head. "Poor woman. To have endured so much grief—"

"Meanwhile"—Paris turned his back on the city, arms crossed—"my wonderful father keeps siring children with his other wives and concubines and is rarely without a babe—or a woman—in his lap." Seeing Myrina's shock, he smiled wryly. "I am sorry. But you were the one who wanted to know."

"And I appreciate your candor." She moved closer to him, not ready to quit the subject. "But why would your mother accuse me of killing you?"

Paris rolled his eyes. "Religious nonsense."

Myrina looked at him intently, willing him to continue. When he did not, she framed his face with her hands and said, "Please let me share more than your bed. Something bears down on you, and it pains me that I cannot help you shoulder the burden. Remember what you taught me . . . and let me fight with you, back to back, until we have driven it safely away—"

Taking her hands, Paris kissed them one by one. "When I was born," he finally said, turning toward the ocean again, "there was no shortage of evil omens. The priests used all their tricks to convince my parents I was an unwanted child—hateful to the gods and therefore a threat to Troy." He threw her a sad smile. "You see, it has always been a fear with us that one day the Earth Shaker will rise and march away from our city in anger, causing destruction as he goes. Occasionally, you will feel him stirring"—Paris ran his hand over a tiny crack in the stone balustrade—"but have no fear, my sweet; he has never been calmer than he is right now."

Myrina studied his profile, anxious to understand. "What could the priests possibly have against a newborn?"

"They never approved of my father's choice of wife. They feared that under a queen raised in Ephesus—a queen used to weapons and independence—the Trojan people might revolt against the new gods and revert to their old ways." Paris hesitated, then continued reluctantly, "I might as well tell you that before my great-grandfather took the throne, Troy was, for many generations, ruled by women. Otrera and my mother are descended from the ancient queens of Troy, and this was why my father chose to ally himself with them through marriage. But the priests have always worried that my mother would challenge my father's authority as king and so, from the moment she set foot in Troy, they began filling her head with superstitious nonsense."

Sensing Paris's pain, Myrina wrapped her arms around him, and they stood like that for a while, looking over the town that seemed joyfully ignorant of its own secret past. "I am sure you can sympathize with my mother," said Paris at length, leaning his head against Myrina's. "Relieved as she was to keep her baby, she was distressed by all the talk of evil omens. And so, as soon as another chorus of scheming priests was installed, riffling through entrails and pronouncing self-serving inanities, she consulted them again, to better understand my destiny."

Paris fell silent once again, his eyes running to and fro across the teeming city, following an oxcart here, a group of roving sailors there. Then he turned and walked back into the room, to pick up his satchel and take out the cloth containing the golden chalice. He did not unwrap it but merely put it gently on a table before walking over to the bed— an enormous divan mounted on a marble podium between four red stone pillars—to throw himself across it, facedown.

When he finally spoke, his voice was stifled by the soft bedding, but Myrina—climbing up beside him—heard every word, although she might have wished she didn't. "Now, to please my parents," Paris began, "the new priests decided my fate was not as evil as formerly thought . . . as long as I never married. My marriage, they claimed, would enrage the Earth Shaker and he would strike me dead. But here I am"—Paris rolled over, throwing out his arms—"married and still alive."

When Myrina did not respond, he sat up on one elbow and tugged teasingly at her hair. "Come now, lovely wife, laugh with me. The ways of the gods may be mysterious but the workings of man are only too obvious."

Myrina, shaken by what she had heard, threw her arms around him. "You didn't have to marry me, you know. I would have happily lived with you—"

"Liar!" Paris rolled over and pinned her to the bed. "From the moment I first called you Queen Myrina and placed a crown upon your head, we both knew there could be no other way. I had to possess you"—he looked down at her body and the dress that was still undone—"fully and completely."

"You speak as if you own me," protested Myrina, partly relieved to quit the sinister topic, yet also piqued by the patronizing tone in which Paris had addressed her ever since their arrival at the palace.

"Do I not?" He smiled at her frown, then began caressing her as if to demonstrate his ownership. "I think I do."

"Allow me to disagree." Myrina sneaked a hand underneath his tunic and soon found what she was looking for. "For all your cocky posturing, it is man's lot to be possessed by woman, not the other way around." Her touch made Paris lie back on the bed with a gasp of pleasant expectation, and she straddled him triumphantly. "Now that I understand the mechanics of things," she said, hovering over him, "I wager that for every rapacious bandit who takes his pleasure at the point of a dagger you will find a hundred husbands bound by the whims of their wives." Myrina moved teasingly against him, enjoying Paris's groans of impatience. "No, my love. Yes, my love. Not now, my love." She leaned forward to catch his eyes, making sure he acknowledged her power over him. "We possess *you,* my prince. Nature wanted it that way. Never forget it."

MYRINA'S FIRST WEEK AT the palace was a confusing web of intense, almost euphoric, happiness intertwined with embarrassments and frustrations that left her—the killer of lake monsters, the savior of enslaved sisters—secretly in tears at the end of every day.

Her primary concern was Lilli. Sadly, Myrina's ideas of how to ensure her sister's comfort went far beyond what Paris was prepared to do. *"What?"* he exclaimed, when she first set a tender foot on the subject. "You would have your innocent sister sleep in our room, where she will hear everything we say and do?" He shook his head with disbelief. "Why do you want to strangle our pleasure like this? You know we would never be at ease with her so near."

Myrina saw his point, of course, and did not repeat her request. But she could not ignore the heartbreak looming ahead. Soon, Hippolyta would want to return to Ephesus, and Kara, Animone, and Kyme would undoubtedly go with her. When they left, Lilli would be sleeping all by herself among strangers in a dormitory in this foreign land. As much as Myrina loved her sister and hated to imagine life without her, there were moments when she felt Lilli might be happier in Ephesus, surrounded by friends.

It did not help that Paris, eager to demonstrate his brotherly love in a more agreeable way, offered to teach Lilli how to ride her own horse. Seeing the excitement spreading like rings around his proposal—involving not only Lilli but everyone who cared for the girl—Myrina could not bring herself to naysay the plan. And so, every evening, after completing his affairs for the day, Paris would come looking for them in the queen's courtyard, to give Myrina a quick kiss on the cheek and steal away Lilli for an hour of raucous fun behind the horse stables.

Another blow to Myrina's contentment was the rampant expectation that she would act the princess in all things and be a hunter no more. Before they had arrived in Troy, it had not even occurred to her Paris might want her to change her ways, but no sooner had they settled into his room before he implored her—in between adoring kisses—to let him put away her weapons for the time being and wear only the clothes he gave her.

"Please understand," he had said, after teaching her how to use the golden brooches that held her new, flimsy garments together, "I love your hunter's heart and would never want you otherwise. But people here are old-fashioned and I don't want them to laugh at me—"

"You mean, they are *new*-fashioned," Myrina corrected him. "Did you not tell me that in the olden days, before the Earth Shaker came—"

"Shh!" Paris looked around nervously, although they were completely alone. "We just need to give them time to adjust to the change—"

"What change?" Myrina held out the frilly dress with dismay. "Look at this useless fabric; it is already torn! I might as well walk around naked."

Their discussion had, perhaps predictably, ended right there, but it was by no means over, at least not for Myrina. She had not exaggerated when she told Paris on their wedding night that she did not know how to be a woman. And although he had been exceedingly accomplished at introducing her to certain aspects of womanhood, he had not prepared her for those many hours of the day where she would have to walk and sit and talk like one, enduring the relentless boredom of female propriety.

While Paris spent his days with the king, either in the throne room or out and about, Myrina had no choice but to remain with her sisters in the queen's courtyard. In the beginning, she thought the place beautiful; a wide portico went all around a small rectangular garden with a sparkling water basin in the middle—a basin thrice as large as the one she had known in the Temple of the Moon Goddess. But after walking the labyrinthine seashell garden paths a few times and realizing they all ended up exactly where they started, she began to suspect the heavily guarded seclusion was intended as much to keep the women in as to keep strangers out.

Reclining comfortably in the shade of the portico, the queen spent most of the day with her eyes closed, nodding along to gentle music played by elderly courtiers and sipping tea handed to her by silent servant girls. She rarely engaged anyone in conversation, yet expected all her ladies-in-waiting to sit faithfully by, sharing in her graceful indolence.

Myrina could scarcely believe it was the same woman she had met on that first day, spewing bile in front of the house altar. Not once had the queen mentioned the episode; in fact, when Myrina and her sisters were first brought into the courtyard and officially introduced, it was as though the woman had completely forgotten that initial exchange—as if she had imbibed some elixir that dulled her memory and made her world more agreeable.

"Ah, yes," she said, when Hippolyta had recited the elaborate greetings sent by Lady Otrera. "My dear sister. How kind. Do thank her and make up something lovely to tell her in return."

And that was it. Hippolyta was waved aside to make space for a tray with fruit, and no one said another word of welcome. Understandably disappointed, Myrina's companions soon began to talk longingly of the chores awaiting them at home, and it took all her eloquence to talk them into a full week of such pompous boredom.

"I cannot believe you have chosen this life," whispered Animone one day, glancing across the courtyard at the king's concubines and their children, roaming rather noisily under the opposing portico. It had not escaped Myrina's notice that several of the women were pregnant; what truly bothered her was the look of pity in Animone's eyes suggesting that one day, she, Myrina, would be the old queen dozing off in the chair, exhausted by nights and nights of sleepless solitude.

That evening, she returned to her quarter with a stash of toy weapons and waited for Paris with new excitement, ready to pounce on him the way she had done so often on the beach in Ephesus. But when he entered the room and looked down at the wooden sword sliding to a halt at his feet, Paris merely laughed and shook his head. "Where did you get these?" he asked, oblivious to Myrina's dueling stance.

"I stole them from the boys," she replied, deflating with disappointment.

"My half brothers?" Paris frowned. "Poor lads. I had better go explain—"

When he finally returned, Myrina was lying on the bed, staring at the painted patterns on the ceiling. Vines, eggs, and fruits . . . all symbols of fertility. "We are nothing but mares, are we?" she said. "Walking around daintily in our little enclosure, waiting to be bred."

Paris was too astounded to reply right away, and before he could even bend down to kiss her, Myrina rose from the bed. "Hippolyta may have her weapons," she continued, "but Myrina may not. And Lilli may ride, but Myrina may not—"

"Of course she may!" Paris came around the bed with a smile, but she turned her back to him.

"A horse!" she said, arms crossed. "I want to ride my *horse*."

He laughed and seized her by the waist. "My little hunter princess. Weary of luxury already. Wishing she was back in Crete, begging for food scraps."

Myrina fairly erupted from his embrace.

"Wait." Paris tried to rein her back in. "I meant it kindly."

"I know." She turned to face him, struggling to swallow her distress. "And you have been nothing but kind to me. I am an ungrateful rat—"

Paris smiled and took her by the chin. "Such a lovely one."

Myrina swallowed again. "Please let us go back to your cabin in the hills? Just for a few days?"

He nodded. "As soon as your sisters have left, we will go. You will hunt for food, and I"—he pulled her back into his arms—"will hunt for *you*."

Just then, as they sealed the plan with a kiss, there was a knock on the door.

"The king requests your presence in the temple," said a voice.

When he saw Myrina's disappointment, Paris said, "Why don't you come with me? They might as well get used to you being there. Where is the crown I gave you? Better put it on. The temple is where we receive our enemies."

THE TEMPLE OF THE Earth Shaker was a stern and forbidding place. Built with the same giant boulders Myrina had noticed at the entrance to the citadel, it did indeed give the impression of being the home of an immortal being who took no pleasure in human comforts. There were no furnishings, no finery of any kind; even the pillars holding up the tall ceiling were plain and unadorned, impressive merely by their vast girth.

The only one seemingly at ease in this stony vault was the deity himself: a gilded colossus reclining—as if asleep—on an elevated stone shelf that ran along the entire back wall of the temple. There was no food put out for him, no leafy wreaths or votive presents laid out beneath his couch; his only entertainment were four flawless yearlings walking freely around the temple, eating hay off the floor.

Entering the building by Paris's side, Myrina found King Priam poised on an elevated platform in the middle of the temple room, surrounded by an assembly of armed guards and somber noblemen.

When she had first met the king, he had struck her as being just another man; today, however, he wore a horned crown and a fur-lined robe and looked majestic indeed. "Father," said Paris, joining him on the podium with Myrina in tow, "what is the occasion?"

"It is good that you have both come," said King Priam, gesturing at a herald, "for your first well-wishers are waiting at the gate: the ever-prowling lions of Mycenae."

Myrina felt Paris stiffen, and she sensed the thunderous surf of the ocean beyond the city walls. She had worked hard to forget the grisly events in Mycenae, but now it all returned to her in an attack of breathless panic: the dead prince on the floor, the stench of blood, the wailing slaves left behind. . . .

There was nothing she could do to slow the steps of Fate. A tumult at the temple entrance prompted Myrina to turn to see a group of men struggling to restrain a white horse. When they finally had the animal under control, two men—one old, one young—came forward to address King Priam, the elder leaning heavily on the younger.

Only then did Myrina recognize the old man as Agamemnon, Lord of Mycenae. It was less than a year since she had seen him enthroned before the great fire pit in his reception hall, but those few months had gnawed at him with the hunger of decades.

"My friend," said King Priam, stepping forward with open arms. "You have blessed my country with your presence."

To which Agamemnon, stooped with age, looked up and said, "Would that someone bestowed a blessing on *me*. For your son's last visit marked the beginning of an evil time."

"I am grieved to hear it." King Priam donned a frown of concern. "Grieved and surprised. My son"—he held out a hand to make Agamemnon aware of Paris's presence—"told me he found Mycenae thriving."

"Yes, well"—Agamemnon paused to cough, and the sound reverberated throughout the temple—"your son left my country before the tragedy became apparent. He must therefore be ignorant of my woes."

"Indeed I am," said Paris, stepping partly in front of Myrina, perhaps to obscure the men's view of her.

"That mask you gave me—" Agamemnon fought back another cough. "It has marked me for the grave. But I do not blame you. Nay, I have come to ask for help." Gesturing at the men behind him, Agamemnon had them bring the white horse forward. "And to pay tribute to the Earth Shaker. For months we have had unfavorable winds and high seas, or we should have come earlier."

"A handsome present," said King Priam. "Now, tell me who you have with you. I see it is not your son."

Agamemnon grimaced and patted his young companion on the arm. "This is my nephew, the heir of Sparta. Menelaos is his name, and he was betrothed to my daughter. But"—the old king paused for air—"my daughter has been abducted from my house; no one knows where she is. And my son—" Unable to go on, the Lord of Mycenae gestured for his nephew to speak on his behalf.

Young Menelaos of Sparta was not an unattractive man, but as soon as he began talking, Myrina sensed that here was someone who had been brought up to kill without reserve and to whom authority was synonymous with truth. "A foul attack," he began, with staccato obedience, "was launched against peaceful Mycenae. The enemy was a tribe of women who fight like men and cut off one breast to better throw the javelin. We call them *Amazones*—women without breasts. Some say they have found shelter here at Troy."

"That is outlandish!" exclaimed King Priam. "I have never heard of such women. Have you?" He stared at Paris, who shook his head, equally shocked. Fortunately for Myrina, no one bothered to question her on the matter; she would almost certainly have been unable to feign ignorance.

"Do you give me your word?" asked Agamemnon, straightening. "For I have sworn to come after them with sword and fire."

King Priam spoke without hesitation. "My word is yours. If I ever see such unnatural creatures—why, I will likely kill them myself."

"They murdered my son," Agamemnon went on, his anger giving him renewed strength, "and stole away my daughter Helena, the only child born of my loins who may survive me. I do not have much life left in me, but what breath I have I will use to get her back. Will you join hands with me?"

Myrina looked on in horror as the two kings shook hands. Could it really be true that the surly Helena—presently in Ephesus, wearing Myrina's jackal bracelet—was King Agamemnon's daughter? "I am not going home," she remembered the girl saying, her face white with agitation. "My father will kill me. He *will*. He killed my mother. And my sister. I know he did." If that father was indeed Agamemnon, Myrina could well believe it. She could even forgive the girl for running away— had it not been for her spiteful subterfuge.

What was to be done? Myrina scarcely knew. Glancing at Paris, she wondered if he knew that the abducted princess had left Mycenae on board *his* ship. But Paris was no longer following the exchange between his father and Agamemnon; he was staring at a slender silhouette standing in the temple door, hair in disarray. Kara.

Lashed by premonition, Myrina seized Paris by the arm, willing him to rouse the guards. But it was too late; Kara could not be stopped.

Running up the aisle to Agamemnon, she threw herself at his feet, hugging his knees so violently he had to put a hand on his nephew's shoulder to steady himself. "Kind Father!" she cried, even as the guards dragged her away. "I am here!"

"Wait!" Agamemnon waved at the guards to leave her. "I am not a man who kicks away a woman in supplication. Speak up!"

"They took me away against my will." Kara looked up at Agamemnon through tears of fear and relief. "I never meant to go."

The Lord of Mycenae looked down at her, speechless. Then his eyes narrowed. "I have seen this madwoman before—"

"Enough!" exclaimed Paris, stepping forward. But it was too late; Kara had been recognized.

"How did this moonstruck creature end up here?" Agamemnon asked, his voice rising in fury. "She was the one who—" He buried a hand in Kara's hair and pulled her up with all his might, drawing a panicked scream from her. "Who killed my son, you miserable whore? Did you?"

"No!" cried Kara, trying to free herself. "No! I told them not to—"

"Where are they?" Agamemnon pulled her by the hair again, flinging her across the floor. "Tell me! Where are they?"

"Stop! Please stop!" Kara held a protective hand over her belly. "I am carrying your grandchild—"

Agamemnon stalked forward to slap her across the face. "Then I will kill two with one blow. Speak up, madwoman! Where is my son's murderer?"

Sobbing beyond control, her face smeared with tears, Kara at last raised her hand and pointed a trembling finger at Myrina.

CHAPTER THIRTY-ONE

Wonders are many, yet of all
Things is Man the most wonderful. . . .
He can entrap the cheerful birds,
Setting a snare, and all the wild
Beasts of the earth he has learned to catch
—Sophocles, *Antigone*

ISTANBUL, TURKEY

AT LEAST THREE HUNDRED GLITTERATI HAD ACCEPTED THE INVITA-tion to Reznik's masquerade, and the whole house reverberated with migrating crowds and echoed laughter. There was no furniture or décor to soften the noise—no sofas, no rugs, no curtains; it was all concrete, steel, and glass, with marble sculptures self-consciously poised in every corner, artfully illuminated by spots. Had someone told me the building was still under construction I could well have believed it; it took a certain kind of person to feel at home in an étagère of naked concrete, even if the view spanned two continents.

The guests, by contrast, were everything but monochrome. Not just the women, but also several of Reznik's male guests were attired in grotesque, theatrical dress that made James look reassuringly handsome and normal, even in his Aladdin costume. There were half-naked supermodels wearing scant costumes glued directly onto the skin and designer werewolves with diamond-studded collars; as it turned out, the shimmering, swirly peacock face paint Rebecca and I had commissioned at the Kanyon shopping mall was ridiculously understated.

"There he is," said James, pointing out a man dressed as a Spanish bullfighter in the flamboyant crowd.

Tall and rigid, his white hair tamed by a brush cut, Grigor Reznik stood out among his dazzling entourage as a man of impeccable fashion and military discipline, whose smile never extended beyond his lips.

Suddenly chilled by foreboding, I said, "Perhaps we should forget about that manuscript—"

"Don't be such a stink, Morg!" James deftly snatched three champagne flutes from a passing tray. "Here, drink this and loosen up. Both of you. We do *not* want him getting suspicious."

Between sips of champagne I wondered how many of Reznik's guests knew who he really was and what he had done before moving to Turkey. Did they know about his secret police and the rat-infested asylums where, as a Communist Party boss, he sent political prisoners? Did they know that even now, in his so-called retirement, Reznik left broken men like Dr. Özlem in his wake, and that he had ignored warning after warning from the Turkish authorities regarding his criminal involvement with the antiques trade? Any moment now, I couldn't help thinking, an Interpol SWAT team might kick down the designer door and haul everyone away to jail in a haze of tear gas. And yet here we were, Reznik's supposed friends—all three hundred of us—drinking his champagne and validating him with our presence.

As we made our way through the crowd, I saw a vaguely familiar figure weaving in and out of sight before disappearing through a doorway. "Did you see that tall blonde in the silver mouse suit?" I whispered, pulling at Rebecca's arm.

"Who?" She stretched left, then right, but couldn't spot the woman.

"She's gone now," I said. "But I'm positive it was the one who stole my phone in Nafplio. She obviously works for Reznik."

Rebecca's eyes widened, but I couldn't tell whether it was because she actually believed me or because she questioned my sanity.

James turned to look at us both with raised eyebrows. "What's wrong?"

"Oh, nothing," I muttered, making sure my evening bag was still securely closed—the satin purse with Granny's notebook, which I now kept close to me always. "Excuse me."

Retreating into a strobe-lit powder room, I leaned against the marble counter and tried to calm my nerves. The feeling I had had when we first arrived—of impending disaster—was back in full force. In an optimistic cranny of my heart, I had nurtured the faint hope that Nick would attend the party after all and had primped accordingly. But . . . if he was really there, how would I even recognize him among so many masked people?

As I stood there in front of the mirror, a beautiful Latin woman in a tight-fitting cat suit emerged from the toilet stall. A silver pixie crop made her look old and young all at once, and I was momentarily mesmerized by the almost palpable power emanating from her body. When our eyes met in the mirror, however, the woman shot me a glare that was nothing short of venomous. Only after the door had closed behind her did it occur to me that I might have seen her before, somewhere else. There was something oddly familiar about her eyes. . . .

When I emerged from the bathroom, Reznik was addressing his guests in fluent French. I caught only the tail end of his speech, but it concluded with a somber toast. "To Alex," said Reznik, holding up his champagne flute, "who died a year ago today. And to justice."

"What's wrong?" whispered Rebecca, as music and conversation resumed. "You look as if—"

"Enough dawdling!" said James. "This is our chance."

It required some determined elbowing to get access to our host, but once we succeeded, James was rewarded with a firm embrace. "Moselane!" exclaimed Reznik, in a clipped Slavic accent. "I am glad you are here. I want to talk with you." He gave James a meaningful look and would likely have said more, had he not been distracted by my proximity. Glancing at me, he looked irritated at first, but then his eyes widened in appreciation. For a few breathless seconds I thought he had somehow recognized me, but his next words suggested otherwise. "Very nice," he said, looking from me to Rebecca. "I see you share my appreciation for rare and beautiful things."

"I do indeed," replied James, with admirable calm. Then, after introducing us to Reznik with false names, he went on to say, "I have told these lovely ladies that you have quite a few . . . unusual artifacts. They are both *very* excited at the prospect of seeing your library." The way James said "library" suggested he meant bedroom. "I hope you won't disappoint them."

I could see Reznik's fingers tightening, ever so briefly, around the stem of his glass. Then he chuckled and said, looking first at Rebecca, then at me, "I can't refuse the interest of one beautiful woman, much less two. If you like, I will show you my little . . . museum." He cast a casual glance around the room. "But let us wait until the ambassador leaves. I will find you."

WE PASSED THE NEXT hour in mindless conversation, pretending to enjoy ourselves. James was a natural; he had something to say about every sculpture and every other guest, and made sure we were never without champagne. "That is Reznik's son, Alex," he said at one point, nodding at a large marble sculpture of a young man modeled after Michelangelo's *David*.

"Beautiful," said Rebecca. "He must have been young. How did he die?"

James glanced around to make sure we were not overheard. "The police said it was a car accident, but Reznik didn't believe them. He's convinced Alex was murdered, and that the crash was a cover-up. Who knows? At some point Reznik has to stop chasing ghosts. This party is a good sign. At least he has taken the gun out of his mouth for a night."

We looked at a few more sculptures before Rebecca excused herself to go to the bathroom. No sooner had she disappeared than James leaned toward me and said, with cheerful detachment, "I fear Bex is lamenting the absence of our bodyguard."

I stooped down to study three small busts that turned out to—yet again—be of Alex Reznik, aged five, ten, and fifteen respectively. "I can assure you she was as relieved to see Nick go as you were."

"Really?" James tried to catch my eyes. "She seems a little . . . pensive."

I suspected he was fishing for my own feelings on the subject, but I was in no mood to indulge him. After two days with full exposure to James's sparkling egotism, my patience had long since ebbed. "Bex has been under a lot of stress lately, and it's entirely my fault."

"Don't be absurd." He put a hand on my naked shoulder. "No one could have a better friend." When I didn't react, James stepped in front of me, blocking my view of the busts. "I mean it, Morg. You're very special to me."

As he stood there in his sagging Aladdin turban, for a moment James actually looked as if he meant it—as if he truly wanted to be in love with me. When I didn't respond, he smiled uncertainly and said, "We've both been playing the long game, haven't we?"

His expression was so hopeful I couldn't help feeling sorry for him, not just because I didn't love him anymore, but because he seemed completely unaware of the fact that he didn't love me, either. In his rush to defeat Nick he had assumed a role of protector, and now— rule jockey that he was—James felt obliged to speak the lines that came with the part, forgetting to ask himself whether he really meant them.

"I always knew you were a keeper," he went on, taking my hand. "Queen material. I just didn't want to start something and then . . . mess it up." When I still didn't respond, he continued, almost angrily, "I love you, Morg. You know I do. Why else would I come to rescue you?"

"*Rescue* me?" I pulled back my hand. "Who told you I needed rescuing?"

James flinched, perhaps just then realizing how upset I was. "Katherine Kent. Why would she say that if it wasn't true? What have you told her?"

I was so baffled it took me a moment to produce a reply. "Nothing,"

I said at last. "I left her a message in Algeria, but I haven't spoken to her at all since I left Oxford. Not a word."

James frowned, clearly irritated that our conversation had been sidetracked by such a minor concern. "You must have told her *something*. How else could she know you'd be arriving in Troy on Friday or Saturday?"

Just then I saw Rebecca making her way back toward us, looking more than a little frazzled. But I was so preoccupied with James's revelation of Katherine's knowledge and interference that it took me a moment to regain my senses and pay attention to my friend's dramatic account of a pickpocket apparently working the crowd and a woman being carted away by ambulance after an allergic reaction.

Half-listening, half-not, I became aware of someone staring at me across the room. Looking up, I saw a man in a dark suit, no tie, standing by himself against the far wall. When our eyes met, a current of warm excitement ran straight through me, from head to toe.

It was Nick.

But instead of greeting me or coming toward us, he turned around and walked up the stairs to the second floor.

"Excuse me." I handed my glass to Rebecca. "I'll be right back."

Gathering my skirts around me, I hastened across the room to follow Nick upstairs, only to see him disappearing, yet again, up glass steps to the next level. Slightly out of breath, I, too, continued to the top floor of the house, half of which had been laid out as a rooftop garden. Seeing Nick nowhere inside, I stepped tentatively through the open panoramic door, trying to spot him among the potted plants and trees.

Only a few other guests had found their way to the dark terrace— men mostly—and they were all silently smoking, taking in the dazzling nightscape of the only city in the world with one foot in the West and another in the Orient. It didn't take me long to determine that Nick was not there, and I felt myself drooping with disappointment. He had *seen* me all right, but for some reason he didn't want to talk with me.

I turned to go back inside . . . and there he was, standing right behind me.

"You!" I exclaimed, shocked and relieved at the same time. "Why did you walk away like that?"

Instead of replying, Nick pulled me into the shadows. A firm hand behind my neck, another around my waist . . . and then his lips fell on mine with unstoppable voracity. Long gone was all his levelheaded languor, or any pretense; what he wanted was perfectly apparent. And I wanted it, too. The moment he let go of me, I took him by the lapels and drew him right back in.

We had been too close for too long, and something had to give, starting with the chastity belt that had girded my passions ever since a certain fencing master had cut me to the quick and cantered back to Barcelona. If Nick was indeed, as Rebecca had predicted, horseman number four, then—I decided then and there, with a scorching gush of exaltation—I was more than ready to straddle the apocalypse.

"I like your costume," I whispered after a while, realigning his lapels.

To which Nick replied, his voice ragged, "I'm not dressed up."

"You are *always* dressed up." I looked him in the eye, trying to guess his game. "What's going on?"

He pushed a renegade wisp of hair behind my ear. "You didn't really think I would leave you just like that?"

"I wasn't sure—"

"Brave, beautiful Diana." Nick leaned his forehead against mine. "Goddess of the hunt. Will you tear me to shreds now? Isn't that what happens to mortal men who get too close?"

The question made me laugh despite myself. "Only when they see the Goddess naked. Which you haven't. Yet." That little extra word jumped out, all by itself, before I could stop it, and it made Nick pull me right back against his chest and bury his face at the crook of my neck, as if he was going to take a bite of me.

"I think I just did."

We would undoubtedly have stayed on the rooftop terrace for a small eternity, unable to call any one kiss the last, had not James and Rebecca eventually come looking for me.

Nick saw them stepping through the glass door before I did, and managed to pull me further into the shadows before James called out, "Morg? Are you here?" Seeing there was no answer, they soon gave up and left, their voices babbling with confusion as they headed back downstairs.

"Oh dear," I whispered, my gloved fingers pressed against my mouth. "This is all so terrible."

"Why?" Nick let go of me. "You don't love James. Isn't it time to put him out of your misery?" When I didn't reply, he reached into his inner pocket and took out a checkbook. "When you make up your mind," he said, scribbling an address on the back of a blank check, "you can find me here." He tore the check in half and handed it to me.

"For how long?"

"Until tomorrow morning." He put the pen and checkbook back in his pocket. "That's when I get new orders." He smiled wistfully. "The boss thinks I've been enjoying myself too much lately. Time to pull for the team again."

I stared at the handwritten address, not really seeing it. "Could I reach you through the Aqrab Foundation? . . . If I don't catch you before you leave?"

Nick's smile disappeared. "This is it, Diana." He put an arm around me and pointed toward one of the illuminated bridges over the Bosphorus Strait. "The narrowest point between our worlds."

"I appreciate it," I said. "But——"

He kissed my temple softly, right where the old bruise was hiding beneath the serpentine glitter paint. "Go back inside, find your friends, and get them out of here."

"Wait!" I tried to hold on to him, but he backed out of my embrace.

"I mean it," he said. "Leave now. There *will* be trouble."

I found James and Rebecca on the second floor, waiting outside one of the guest bathrooms. "There she is!" exclaimed James, taking a step back at the sight of me. "We were worried about you."

"This house is very confusing," I replied, hoping my face was not as flushed as it felt. "I've been looking for you two everywhere."

"Well, here we are," said Rebecca, not meeting my eyes. There was something about her tight lips and one raised eyebrow that told me she suspected exactly what I had been doing and with whom. From where she stood, I realized, she would have had a perfectly unhindered view of Nick returning downstairs . . . preceding me by no more than half a minute.

"Wonderful," I said, taking them both by the elbow. "Come, let's get out of here. We're obviously wasting our——"

I was silenced by a hand on my bare shoulder. "James. Ladies." Reznik looked at us all with the gamesome gravity of a haunted house usher. "The ambassador has left. Are you ready?"

Reznik's little museum, as it turned out, was right on the other side of the concrete wall. A humble and utterly ignorable metal door served as gateway between the two worlds—one public, one private. Through the evening, I realized, I had walked right past the door several times thinking it was just an emergency exit.

"Normally, this entrance is electrified," explained Reznik, reaching into his trouser pocket. "But, of course"—he produced a small bundle of keys, held together by a golden chain—"I don't want to electrocute my guests." He tested the door with a fingernail before unlocking it. "Excuse me for going first."

We followed him into the darkness and heard the door drop shut behind us with an inauspicious clunk. Then a small green light came on as our host stopped to punch in a code on a wall panel. With increasing impatience, he did it three times before exclaiming, "Chyort voz'mi! I just upgraded the alarm system. Idiots!" Reaching out abruptly, he flicked on the ceiling lights in what turned out to be a narrow room— apparently a sort of air lock chamber between the two sides of the house. "Strange," he went on, waving his hand before a wall-mounted sensor. "It says it's on but it isn't. Oh, well." Perhaps reminded he had an audience, Reznik turned toward us with a forced smile. "In the old days, things worked. You know what I mean?"

We all nodded. I guessed from Rebecca's pallor that she, too, was reminded that to this hardened Marxist, culture and the arts went hand in hand with theft and coercion.

Frowning with apprehension, Reznik opened another door and walked ahead of us into a perfect replica of an old-world London townhouse, complete with brass chandeliers and a carpeted staircase going up all the way, I assumed, to the top floor.

Every piece of décor suggested that, by walking through the two fortified doors, we had stepped back in time one hundred years. Paneled with dark wood and lined with glass cabinets full of antiques, the room where we stood had the air of a gentlemen's club; the only feature missing was a stony-faced butler in white tie and tails, asking whether we should like to take our tea in the library as usual.

Alarmed by the dysfunctional security system, Reznik trotted ahead, giving us a quick tour of all the artifacts on display on the first floor. One cabinet held a gilded samurai costume surrounded by four swords, and on his way past, Reznik stopped to take out one of them. "Just to be safe," he said to us, giving the impression that he was only too accustomed to walking around like this, armed against potential foes. "So far nothing is missing. I think we are okay. Come with me."

We followed him up the first flight of stairs, and as we walked, Reznik said to James, "While I remember, I want to talk with you about a friend of yours, Diana Morgan."

I was not the only one who jolted at the sound of my name; Rebecca shot me a grimace of pure panic and nearly tripped in her long skirt. Fortunately, Reznik was walking ahead and didn't notice. The first to recover, James said, "What about her? I haven't heard from her for a while."

"Huh," said Reznik, as if he sensed James was lying. "Do you know where she is?"

Coming up the stairs we found ourselves in a library that took up the entire second floor and framed the grand stairwell with a gallery of built-in bookcases. "What a magnificent room!" exclaimed James, doing his best to change the subject. "How many volumes do you have here?"

But Reznik did not even register the question. Rushing across a large Persian rug, he lunged himself at a bookstand with a yelp of outrage. "No! The bitches!"

Beneath a green velvet cushion, illuminated by miniature spot-lights, was a brass sign that read P. EXULATUS: *HISTORIA AMAZONUM*. The cushion itself, however, was empty.

EVEN THOUGH THE ALARM system was down, a dozen strategically posi-tioned surveillance cameras were apparently still operative. They were all controlled from a computer on the windowless top floor, which turned out to be a Louis Seize bedroom, complete with a colossal paint-ing of Marie Antoinette as well as a miniature guillotine for cutting cigars.

Judging by the stale, rather sour smell of the place, this dark cave was where Reznik slept, and I couldn't help feeling we shouldn't be there—that we were quickly becoming too intimate with a capricious tyrant.

"I've got you," muttered our host, excavating the mouse from a pile of paper. "I've finally got you. Satan's bitches. Very clever—distracting my boys with the pickpocket and the ambulance. But ha! I have you on tape!"

While we stood behind Reznik, not sure what to do, Rebecca nudged me and nodded agitatedly at two mannequins in the corner. One was dressed in a chain mail bikini, the other in a short snakeskin tunic; judging from their weapons and furry boots, this was how Reznik imagined Amazons.

Except . . . both had lost their right hands. And it must have hap-pened recently, for the two eerily realistic pieces of plastic lay discarded on the floor. Looking at Rebecca, I realized we were both thinking the same thing. Those mannequins had lost their jackal bracelets.

Just then, Reznik made a sound of great consternation, and we were all drawn to the computer screen. "Who the hell is that?" he ex-claimed. Freezing the image, he zoomed in on the person caught on camera, then said, even louder, "Can someone *please* tell me who that is?"

We leaned forward to study the blurry black-and-white image of a man standing in front of the bookstand with what could only be the

Historia Amazonum in his hands. Despite the poor resolution and the fact that the thief wore a mask over his eyes, I recognized him immediately. I had, after all, been in his arms just fifteen minutes earlier.

"What do you think?" James looked at me with a highly unattractive blend of anger and triumph. "Do we know this worthless piece of shit?"

I was so shocked I couldn't conceal it. Without a doubt, I was the blindest, most gullible victim into whom the Aqrab Foundation had ever sunk its perfidious teeth.

"Not worthless!" Reznik glared at the screen as if he wanted to beat it to smithereens. "That manuscript cost me a fortune. And now it's gone."

I felt James's eyes on me as he cleared his throat and said, "Not necessarily. Maybe a phone call to Dubai would clear things up?"

Even though I heard him speak the words, I was still so paralyzed by the sight of Nick on the screen that I didn't fully realize what James was doing until Reznik grunted with surprise. "You think al-Aqrab is behind this?"

James shrugged, ignoring my horrified grimacing. "We both know his people never play by the rules. Who else would dare do this to you?"

As NEWS OF THE break-in spread to the other half of the house, the fashionable gathering devolved into chaos. Security guards ran to and fro, barking belated orders, but the confusion was nothing compared to the mayhem in my head as I elbowed my way through the guests, desperate to get out and away.

"Morg!" said James behind me, as he had done several times already. "Don't be such a bore. Where's your sense of humor?"

I didn't bother replying. No matter what I said to him, and no matter what he made up in answer, the mere fact that James could serve Nick up to a notorious sadist like this had made me so incredibly furious I felt like picking up one of the creepy busts of Alex Reznik and hurling it at him.

"Fine!" said James, fed up with me at last. "I'll get our things in the wardrobe. We'll meet back at the car in five. Those who aren't there can find their own way home." With that he walked off.

"I have to pee," said Rebecca. "Give me *one* minute——"

As I waited for Rebecca to return, I again became aware of someone staring at me, this time from the open terrace door. It was the young woman in the silver mouse suit—my Rollerblade nemesis.

Through the pandemonium, our eyes met. Then, with an impudent half smile, she produced a bag and casually slung it over her shoulder, making it impossible for me to miss the obvious.

It was my handbag, the one lost in the Knossos labyrinth.

"Hey!" I exclaimed, instinctively stepping toward her. But as soon as I did, she turned and fled into the garden.

I followed. The silver suit was eminently visible against the greenery, and although the woman looked supremely fit, I was able to stick with her all the way to the property line despite my shoes and the dew that made the grass treacherously slippery. Once there, she squeezed through a tear in the tall wire fence, paused to see if I was still at her heels, and scampered down the road, bag swinging.

The odds were not good, but I wasn't about to let this woman get away again—not without a fight. Muttering curses I had never known existed, I squeezed through the fence, sacrificing my hairdo, shoes, and common sense in one fell swoop, to follow the long-legged heister down the steep road in the direction of the water.

It was strangely liberating running barefoot on the rough concrete pavement, my long skirt clutched in a bundle around my hips, and I was amazed at my speed. Even as lamppost after lamppost flipped by, the gap between me and my quarry never grew, and the woman kept looking over her shoulder until, at one point, she turned a corner and disappeared.

It didn't take me long to reach the corner, but when I did, she was nowhere to be seen. I was standing in a quiet residential neighborhood with parked cars everywhere. The possibilities for hiding were plenty. Stopping, I listened for footsteps or any other sounds suggesting she was still close by . . . and that was when I saw it:

A British passport. Lying on the pavement, at my feet.

Puzzled, I stooped to pick it up. It was my own.

Walking down the silent street with an absurd sense of accomplishment, I espied another object lying on the sidewalk ahead, directly under a streetlamp.

My wallet.

Perhaps it should have occurred to me then, but it wasn't until I also found my diary—lying conspicuously under yet another lamppost, just around the corner of yet another side street—that I realized what was happening.

She was baiting me. First the bag, then the passport, then the wallet . . . and I, like a ninny, was playing along, flattering myself that *I* was the hunter.

Looking ahead, I saw on the pavement what looked very much like the key chain with all my precious Oxford keys. But this time, I did not run toward it. Instead, I very carefully backed up, half-expecting to see a band of strongmen pour out of a van to gag and bind me.

I backed up all the way to the corner before daring to turn around. My head spinning with jumbled questions and nonsensical answers, I ran as fast as I could up the street, back as I had come, until finally reaching the Reznik property. Relieved to recognize the chicken-wire fence I had squeezed through earlier, I walked along it until I came up to the tall entrance gate where guests in costumes were still milling around, sparring over taxis.

Weaving through the crowd on throbbing bare feet, I continued down the road on the other side, still so busy making sense of what had happened that I walked right past the empty parking spot twice before the truth hit me. . . .

James's Aston Martin was no longer there.

Unwilling to believe it, I looked up and down the road several times, my pulse at a frantic gallop, but it changed nothing. The magic carpet had left without me.

CHAPTER THIRTY-TWO

THE NORTHERLY BLEW WITHOUT RESPITE FOR THREE LONG WEEKS. To Myrina, they were three weeks of hateful room arrest, and of watching from her balcony the distant Aegean shore fill up with ships unable to round the headland until the wind changed. Paris assured her they were all merchant ships commanded by peaceful sea captains, and yet their growing presence was threatening all the same. Were not all sailors in constant need of food and entertainment? And had she not seen with her own eyes how readily such men would steal their pleasure at the point of a sword?

"I never thought there were so many ships in the world," she said to Paris one day, when they were standing on the balcony together.

"When the wind turns," he assured her, his hands on her shoulders, "they will all be on their way."

Myrina leaned against him. "Except for the Greek ships."

"I wager," said Paris, kissing her neck, "even *they* will have had enough."

Agamemnon, Lord of Mycenae, had given King Priam one month to punish the Amazons allegedly hidden behind his tall walls, and to hand over the innocent Helena, who had been so cruelly abducted from his house. As for the fate of the man-killing Myrina, it would obviously not do to demand the punishment of a princess of Troy, at least not while she was still young enough to be of interest to her husband. But perhaps atonement for her sins could come in the form of a reaffirmation of the good relations between Mycenae and Troy—relations that ensured the free passage of ships and goods through the Hellespont.

Myrina had never fully grasped the origins of the enmity between Agamemnon and King Priam, but she knew that for ten years a Greek pirate named Achilles had been raiding the Trojan coast. "His men carry away our crops like an army of ants," Paris had told her, "and, most grievously, they steal freeborn citizens and sell them into slavery. Agamemnon, of course, claims these raids are outside his control, but it is common knowledge he benefits greatly from them." Paris had shaken his head with disgust. "My father eventually decided to put pressure on Agamemnon to leash Achilles, by levying a tax on all Greek ships going in and out of the Hellespont. These sailing restrictions have understandably infuriated all the Greek sea captains who make a living in these waters. Believe me, I have had many discussions with my father about the wisdom of his policies, for I fear they will lead to nothing but further enmity."

Considering this history of reciprocal grievances, it should perhaps surprise no one that Agamemnon had decided to use the issue of his abducted daughter to pressure King Priam to abolish the Hellespont tax. But the request had a cauterizing effect on Priam's sympathetic ears; repelled by the grieving father and scheming administrator rolled into one, the king of Troy sent Agamemnon and his delegation away with no promises whatsoever. Yet in the same breath he turned to Myrina and demanded she produce both Helena and the Amazons immediately, to ensure the Greeks had no excuse to start a feud.

And so it came about that Hippolyta and Animone were sent to Ephesus to explain the situation to Lady Otrera and prevail upon Helena to come to Troy and face her father. Once the two had left, there was nothing Myrina could do but wait. Locked in her room by decree of King Priam, she received all her news through Paris. Poor Kara's attempted suicide, Lilli's gentle intervention . . . it all came to her secondhand, and although she could understand why the king felt an urge to punish her for the trouble she had carried into his house, Myrina hated her own helpless confinement.

"Be patient," Paris had begged her many times. "The more noise you make, the longer his anger will last. My father is a man who must have his way; the only effective response is silent submission."

As for the queen, she had come to see Myrina only once, to stroke her cheek with cold, bloodless fingers. "My poor child," she had whispered, her eyes brimming with sadness. "I knew it would be thus. I knew it from the day you came. My poor girl. My poor boy."

All Myrina could do was cling to the hope that her sisters in Ephesus would know how to act and rush to her rescue. Surely the arrival in Troy of Helena—appearing after so many months as wholesome and virginal as ever—would calm Agamemnon and win his forgiveness on behalf of them all.

When a group finally returned from Ephesus, Myrina watched eagerly from her balcony, trying to make out the faces of her sisters. She counted twelve women altogether, but was at a loss to recognize anyone before they disappeared into the stable to attend to their horses.

Unable to contain her excitement, she ran to the door and banged on the wooden boards. But there was no response until Paris finally came to fetch her and take her to the throne room. "Do you realize," he said, his face set in a frown, "your clatter can be heard in the entire building?"

"Then why does no one answer?" Myrina rushed ahead of him down the corridor. "What must my sisters think? That I am a slave?"

Paris caught her by the elbow and stopped her abruptly. "There may come a day when you will remember this time of enslavement and wish it back."

Myrina stared at him, suddenly chilled. "Do not speak like that—"

"Then let us both be silent," said Paris, putting his arms around her, "and not pollute these hours with jaundiced words."

WHILE THE TEMPLE OF the Earth Shaker was where King Priam received his enemies, the throne room was where he welcomed his friends. Seated on an elevated marble chair against the far wall—a chair with armrests carved as talons and a back fanning out like the wings of a bird—he was already absorbed in the news from Ephesus when Myrina and Paris arrived.

If Myrina had anticipated a sisterly greeting by the group she was sorely disappointed. Standing in the middle of the floor, speaking to the king with bold gestures, the broad-shouldered Penthesilea barely acknowledged her presence, except for a stern nod that said, plainly, "This is your fault." And around Penthesilea stood mostly women Myrina had spoken to only rarely at Lady Otrera's farm: hardened riders and hunters who had considered themselves vastly superior to the newcomers and spent no time trying to make their acquaintance. The only truly familiar faces were those of Pitana and Helena, the latter of whom looked just as resentful as Myrina remembered her. But at least she had come.

"I am not surprised," said King Priam, shifting in his marble seat, "to hear of these new raids along the coast; the Greeks grow bolder every day. If Agamemnon ever did attempt to leash that pirate, Achilles, he has most certainly unleashed him again now. It is wise of your Lady Otrera to give up the farm before it is overrun. Where does she plan to go?"

Penthesilea straightened. "We will travel east, to settle among the horse-breeding Kaskians on the rocky shores of the Black Sea. It is a region that lends itself to independence; as you probably know, the Greeks call it the Inhospitable Sea, and it has never been conquered by anyone. Even you" —she looked boldly at King Priam, as always incapable of humility—"would not dare send an army through those narrow valleys."

"Why does Lady Otrera not consider settling here in Troy?" countered the king, whose even tone suggested he was intrigued rather than annoyed by the provocation. "It is much closer, and our walls are unbreachable."

Myrina knew Penthesilea well enough to spy something as rare as embarrassment in her eyes. Embarrassment, she guessed, on behalf of the king whose city was not good enough for Lady Otrera. "That is very generous of the Trojan people," said Penthesilea, looking down.

"But . . . Lady Otrera is determined to remove us from this coastline altogether."

"I see." King Priam drummed his fingers on the marble armrest. "I see."

There was a nervous silence, full of stolen glances, then Myrina stepped forward, unable to keep her peace. "What news of my sisters?" she asked. "Where are they now?"

Penthesilea turned to her reluctantly. "We are camped up the Simoeis River, northeast of here. Those who preferred to stay behind in Ephesus were free to do so. No one did. It has become too dangerous. And those who wanted to stop at Troy, to deliver the little firebrand to her loving father"—Penthesilea shot a glare of disgust at Helena, then made a dignified gesture at the group—"are those you see. No one else felt they had business here."

Myrina winced at the unforgiving look in Penthesilea's eyes. Naturally, she could not blame Otrera's daughters for resenting the situation that had forced them to abandon their home, but she had hoped they would at least still look upon her as a friend, even if she was no longer their sister.

"Now," Penthesilea went on, "with your permission, King, we will ride out to the beach and return this girl to Agamemnon that we may rejoin Lady Otrera as soon as possible—"

"Wait!" said Myrina, angered by Penthesilea's imperious manner. "Should we not confer with Helena about the wisest conduct in this matter? She knows her father better than anyone."

Penthesilea snorted. "Do not speak to me of wisdom! You were the one who stole her away, and you will be the one to formally give her back."

"I certainly intend to," said Myrina, "but—"

"Absolutely not!" exclaimed Paris. "I forbid it."

No sooner had King Priam approved Penthesilea's plan to let the women deliver Helena to the Greeks than he ordered the palace guards to seize Paris and lock him in his room. Too shocked to even try to intervene, Myrina followed the men down the corridor and overheard the furious exchange between father and son as Paris was dragged away.

"I am doing what must be done," said King Priam, gesturing at the guards to be firm. "You will thank me when you regain your senses."

"You are a murderer!" yelled Paris, struggling so hard it took four strong men to restrain him. "You are sacrificing these women—and my wife! At least provide them with a detachment of guards—"

"And make it look as though we intend further aggression?" King Priam shook his head grimly. "Have not these women angered the Greeks enough? As a king, I must wash my hands of them. As a father—"

"Do not speak the word!" cried Paris, as the guards closed the door in his face. "I swear to heaven, I shall never share a meal with you again!"

The terrible exchange still ringing in her ears, Myrina returned to the throne room where Penthesilea and her companions were waiting, impatient to depart. Upon their backs sat recurve bows modeled after her own and quivers with arrows she had designed . . . and yet they looked upon her as a traitor not worthy of a single conciliatory word. Even the fact that she was coming with them despite Paris's wishes did not earn her as much as a nod of approval.

Once mounted on their horses, grudgingly equipped with the crested helmets and half-moon shields King Priam had forced upon them at the last moment, the women left the citadel in a gallop. Towns-people and poultry dispersing before them, they sped through the streets of Troy with eyes for nothing but a swift conclusion to their loathsome mission.

THE FOUR SHIPS THAT had brought Agamemnon and Menelaos to Troy were drawn ashore among hundreds of other foreign vessels in the protected west-facing bay opposite the island of Tenedos. To get there, the women had to cross the Scamandrian Plain with the setting sun in their eyes, and Myrina was not the only one to ride with her shield up against the blinding light.

Approaching the coast, she was amazed to see the sprawling city of tents that had grown up around the beached ships. Had she not known better, she would have guessed the many thousand sailors had come together on this vast shore primarily to celebrate, for over every bon-fire hung a side of meat on a spit, and there was not an unhappy face to be seen.

When they reached the Greek camp, however, a few guards came forward, spears in hand, to hear their errand and ascertain that they were not carrying other weapons than the negligible bows on their backs. But as soon as the men realized they were dealing with women, their amazement grew into a tempest of hooting ridicule and bawdy invitations.

"Take off your helmet," said Penthesilea to Helena, "that they may recognize you and cease this intolerable jeering."

But Helena did not remove her helmet. She had remained silent since arriving in Troy and was clearly insulted to be cast from the sis-terhood with so little ceremony. Despite her determination not to be swayed by sympathy, Myrina felt a throb of pity for the girl now that the handover was imminent.

As they approached Agamemnon's tent, the handsome Menelaos emerged first, carrying a spear. After him came the Lord of Mycenae, leaning on a silver staff. "There he is!" exclaimed Penthesilea, drawing her horse to a halt. "Now take off your damn helmet——"

Riding slowly ahead, Helena reached up . . . to toss aside the shield and free her bow. Before anyone could intervene, she had an arrow on the string, pointing straight at Agamemnon. "Father!" she yelled, in a voice too feeble to carry far. "I will come with you on one condition——"

But what she had meant to say was cut off abruptly by the unfeeling blade of Fate. For a spear, hurled by Menelaos to protect the king, struck Helena right in the chest and threw her off the horse with a sound too terrible to be called a scream. Landing on her back in the sand, the girl kicked once, then went limp, her head falling to the side without another word.

Too horrified to be prudent, Myrina jumped from her horse and threw herself at Helena, desperate for any sign of life. But the spear sticking out of that slender chest was an unforgiving sign that death had arrived before she.

With a violent outburst of regret, Myrina embraced the limp shoulders she had patted so often during their weapon training and began raining kisses on Helena's unresponsive face, barely conscious of what she was doing. Only when she finally sat up and closed the girl's unseeing eyes did Myrina hear Penthesilea's furious command, "Get back on your horse, you imbecile! Do you want us all speared like fish?"

No sooner had the women pulled away from Helena's body before the Greeks clustered around it, curious to see who had dared aim an arrow at their king. Even Agamemnon himself came forward, leaning on Menelaos's arm.

"Back!" yelled Penthesilea, motioning for the women to retreat at once. "It will not be long before she is recognized."

But even Agamemnon did not know his daughter until the men had kicked her around a bit. Then suddenly, there was a shrill outcry, and the Greek camp erupted in horror and fury. Horses were called, weapons were found. . . . Within moments, the women were riding for their lives, galloping back across the Scamandrian Plain to escape a shower of spears and roaring curses.

When they reached the river, Myrina and Penthesilea fell naturally behind to ensure that all their companions got over the bridge safely. As they did so, a spear flew right by Myrina's ear so close she felt its hissing draft. Instinctively turning in the saddle and holding up her shield, she felt the thunderous impact of two more missiles—spears flung with such force they nearly knocked her from her mount. Seeing the spearheads had lodged themselves firmly in the ox hide, making the shield too unwieldy to be of further use, she tossed it aside and reached for the bow on her back.

One . . . two . . . three men did not have the wherewithal to avoid her arrows; a fourth managed to duck and ride next to Penthesilea, his bronze sword catching the last few rays of the setting sun as he forced aside her shield with his free hand.

Too busy trying to calm her panicking horse, Myrina did not witness the strike; all she saw was Penthesilea's body falling into the Scamander River in a gush of blood and being taken, limply, by the current.

And then Myrina was cut off. Two men blocked the bridge, and others were coming, closing in on her from behind. Pulling the Minoan ax from her belt—a weapon that Paris had confiscated early on, but which Lilli had managed to track down with innocuous inquiries—Myrina looked around to see who would come at her first . . . and narrowly missed a sweeping blow from the man who had killed Penthesilea. It was mere instinct that had her lean aside at the exact moment he struck, and the shock of it upset her balance so much that she slid right off the horse and fell headfirst down the riverbank.

Laughing at her accident, the man followed her on foot down to the water's edge, clearly expecting to send her right after Penthesilea with a single slash of his sword. But just as he thought he had her, cowering as she was in the mud before his feet, Myrina got him in the backswing, ramming her ax directly into the midsection he had carelessly exposed.

Perhaps because of the angle, the ax did not actually cut into the man's flesh, but the impact alone was enough to make him double over with a grunt and lose his balance. Without even thinking, Myrina grabbed him by the shoulder strap, pulling with all her might . . . and then he was gone, too, just like the woman he had killed, tumbling headlong into the rushing river.

Gasping from the exertion and lightheaded with panic, Myrina barely knew whether she should stay where she was, dangerously near the water, or try to make it back up the muddy slope. Either way, she would have to face a dozen men . . . not a promising situation. She was tempted to simply jump into the river, feetfirst, and let destiny take over. . . .

But then she heard them: the shrill, ululant hunting cries of Otrera's daughters. And the men heard them, too. Faces raised in disbelief, they started backing away from the slope, looking around for their horses . . . but it was too late. Twisting around, Myrina saw Penthesilea's band of sisters returning toward the bridge in full gallop, their bows up. Within a single breath, their arrows had pierced every man through.

But more Greeks were coming—some on horseback, others on foot—every one of them bent on revenge. And among them was Menelaos, armed with several spears and, surely, after discovering his terrible mistake, enough hatred to raze a city.

Gathering the reins of her horse, Myrina made for the bridge while she could, dreading the missiles she knew would soon follow. Over the bridge she went, howling her appreciation at Otrera's daughters while wondering how far they would get before they were stopped again.

But the men, armed as they were with spears and swords, sat so heavily in their saddles that the women were able to remain out of reach and even increase their lead as they spurred on their horses and raced across the Scamandrian Plain heading for the safety of Troy. "Close the gate!" cried Myrina, when they were all finally inside. "Immediately!"

As the enormous wooden doors fell shut, locked by a colossal, fortified crossbar, she heard the fury of the Greeks locked out on the other side. "Open the gate, you slinking cowards!" bellowed someone, banging on the boards. "Is this the famous Trojan courage? That you let women do your fighting?"

Later that night, when Myrina returned to the palace with her mournful companions, she found Paris waiting by the stable. He did not speak: merely looked at her with an expression she had seen traces of before but never fully understood until that moment. It was more apology than accusation—a dark stare of acknowledgment that told her he had long since seen his own fate in her actions, and had long since ceased to hold her responsible.

MYRINA WOKE FROM TERRIBLE dreams before dawn, to feel around frantically in the dark until she found him. He was still there, asleep right next to her.

They had been in the hillside cabin for three days. Three days to mourn a Greek princess, three days to prepare for the noble trial that would determine who was to blame for her death. Menelaos had been the one to suggest a duel between himself and Paris. Agamemnon, he had explained to King Priam, was too distraught to return to Mycenae without justice, and he was the one who had requested the young men settle the matter in the traditional way.

Before his father could even react, Paris accepted the challenge. And Menelaos went away as quietly as he had come, head bent in mourning for a bride-to-be whose face he had never seen until she lay before him, transfixed by his spear.

That night, Paris took Myrina back to the cabin in the woods, to give them three nights together before the dreaded day. But neither of them could fully embrace the rustic escape they had craved for so long. For although Paris behaved as if nothing was the matter, Myrina was so sick with worry she could not enjoy his caresses without tears.

On that last morning, waking before sunrise, she truly wished she had never met him—that his life had never been infected by her misfortune. If it meant he would grow old in peace, she would have happily seen him married to someone else, some sweet, obedient girl.

"What is it?" he whispered, sensing her sadness and pulling her into his arms. "Bad dreams again?"

Myrina tried to swallow her tears, but there were too many. "Why must it be this way?" She pressed her face against his chest. "Why can we not stay here, in the forest?"

Paris sighed. "It is the way of the world, my love. Men fight, and women cry. Some things never change."

"I would happily fight in your place," muttered Myrina. "He would kill me, but at least you would live—"

"Shh—" Paris ran his fingers through her hair. "You speak as if I am dead already. Have you no confidence in my fighting skills?"

Myrina sat up abruptly. "You know I have nothing but the highest regard for you. No one could be more perfect in any way. But the Greeks are fickle and wily, you have said so yourself. And this Menelaos—" She shuddered. "In his eyes is a coldness, as if life and death are all the same to him."

"Come here"—Paris drew her back into his arms—"and tell me more about my perfections."

"Oh please," whispered Myrina, kissing his bristly cheek and breathing in his scent—the smell that was uniquely his, and which no bath had ever taken away—"cannot we, too, go off and live among the Kaskians? We have our horses and weapons. We can hunt—"

"We could do that," said Paris, running his hand over her skin. "We could live in a hut in the wilderness, where no one speaks of honor and disgrace. And when we have our first child, I will have to hunt alone, leaving you behind with an infant in your arms." He sighed. "Do you not see, my love, such a life is no life at all? The city has its laws and traditions because they are necessary for humans to thrive."

"But——"

"Myrina." Paris took her by the chin. "I have chosen this. No one is forcing me. I am free to walk away, but cannot. You may think this is proof I love Troy over you, but the truth is the opposite. The man you married is a man of honor. And for your sake, he intends to remain so until the end, whenever it may come. I would rather have you pitied for losing a brave husband than have you ridiculed for living with a coward."

"They will not pity me," whispered Myrina, leaning against his hand, "for there will be no one left to pity. Without you, I would not want to live."

Paris growled. "Is that what marriage has done to you? Proud Myrina . . . where did she go?" He patted her cheek, as if to wake her from sleep. "How can I be brave if you have already buried us both? What will happen to Paris if there is no one left to remember his perfections? Who will set the paid singers straight when they spew all their rhyming falsehoods?" He smiled and touched his nose to hers. "You, my queen, must live and remember. That is my blessing, and your curse."

THE DUEL BETWEEN THE prince of Troy and the prince of Sparta was to be fought at noon, when the blinding sun was at its zenith. It was to take place, furthermore, outside the Scaean Gate to the north of the city, in order that the Trojan nobles could watch from their great tower on the citadel.

Perhaps not surprisingly, Paris's mother had been unable to find the strength to rise from her chair in the inner courtyard and walk up the steps to join her husband that morning. Not just one, but three servants had been on tiptoes to fan their mistress with palm leaves since the day the duel was agreed upon, and it was commonly known that the queen of Troy had already lit candles to the gods of the underworld, to ensure a hearty welcome for her son.

As for Myrina, it did not matter how fiercely she implored Paris to let her remain close to him throughout the ordeal. She had proposed hiding herself among the guards chosen for his escort—an idea he immediately dismissed. The top of the tower was where she must be, squinting to see her husband fighting in the road dust, on behalf of the people cheering from the wall.

None of her sisters had been allowed to come aloft and support her. Ever since Helena's death and the fighting at the Scamander River, King Priam had been keen to keep his troublemaking Amazons out of sight of the Greeks.

Lady Otrera's daughters—still mourning the loss of Penthesilea—would have left earlier, had not King Priam pointed out that it might be prudent for them to stay in Troy until the outcome of the duel was known. Menelaos had sworn that if he were to lose, Agamemnon would see the defeat as an act of divine justice and return home without further complaints. In which case Lady Otrera might wish to reconsider her decision to flee like a rabbit, running from foxes to settle among wolves.

But even if they were not with her in the tower, Myrina knew that Lilli, Kyme, and Pitana were praying for Paris in the palace below. Kara, too, had been in tears when Myrina left them all sitting so miserably by the kitchen hearth, and had apologized again and again for the grief she had caused.

Myrina, however, had yet to believe Kara was truly sorry. "Why did you bother to save her and bind her wrists?" she had asked Lilli, after Kara's attempted suicide. "You have done her no service. She wanted to die."

Lilli shook her head. "She never wanted to die. She merely wanted a new life. And that is what I am trying to give her." When Myrina opened her mouth to protest, Lilli put a hand against her lips. "You were not with us on the ship to Mycenae. There is something you don't know. When the men discovered I was blind, they wanted to throw me overboard. But Kara wouldn't let them. She managed to convince the prince I had sacred powers. That was how she caught his eye. From that moment on, she became the sole object of his perversity." Lilli's face contracted with anguish. "Saving me became her doom."

THE TWO COMBATANTS ARRIVED at noon as agreed.

Menelaos came roaring up the beach in his horse-drawn chariot, cheered on by a running mob of yelling supporters. Paris, emerging from the Scaean Gate, stepped off his own chariot almost immediately to allow his opponent the satisfaction of having made the most spectacular entrance.

But the heir of Sparta was not so easily spoiled. Walking into the large circle drawn in the gravel, he hardly seemed to notice the cheers from all the foreign sailors who had gathered around to watch the entertainment. Nor did he flinch at the insults that were slung like missiles from the city wall. Had Myrina been able to make out his face, she knew she would have found no emotion in it whatsoever, and that he was regarding his opponent with the eyes of a butcher carving up a carcass.

Both men carried a sword and thrusting spear; neither had bothered to bring a throwing spear, since the circle they would be fighting in was hardly even wide enough for a run-up. Of the two, it seemed Menelaos was by far the better protected, for although he carried no shield, he wore a suit of armor that not only covered his torso, but went up around the neck as well, and hung well below his loins. In addition, he had on a peaked silver helmet with a red plume and guards on his legs and arms; apart from the face, elbows, and knees, almost no body parts were left exposed.

By comparison, Paris wore only light plates of armor, choosing to protect himself by holding a shield rather than wearing one. This left him more vulnerable, but, presumably, also more limber. On his head sat a solid bronze helmet with a half-moon crest of horsehair, but his movements were so free and untroubled it looked as if he barely knew he was wearing it.

Only when the two men planted their spears in the ground to show they were ready did it occur to Myrina she had never before seen Paris use real weapons against anyone. She knew he trained every morning with several different men, and had often seen him sparring with Aeneas and Dares on the ship, but it had never been more than a game. . . .

Myrina's musings were interrupted by agitated voices.

Agamemnon had arrived.

In a gesture of friendship, King Priam had offered the Lord of Mycenae a comfortable seat on the Scaean Tower, but Agamemnon had politely declined, citing the plight of a grieving father. The man who had just arrived at the battleground in his two-horse chariot, however, looked more the warlord than the father, for he was dressed in a radiant bronze panoply, as if he himself was entering the duel alongside Menelaos.

With Agamemnon present at last, the fight could begin.

Someone pitched a stone into the middle of the circle, and as soon as it had landed—throwing up a small cloud of dust as it did—the two fighters began circling each other, their spears poised to strike. As if to demonstrate the advantage of carrying no shield, Menelaos tossed his spear from one hand to the other a few times, apparently equally capable with them both.

Watching from the tower, Myrina remembered one of the rules Paris had taught her: Always make sure they underestimate you. Judging from Menelaos's posturing, the Spartan was already making his first mistake, thinking himself untouchable in his armored suit. But as soon as he charged, she realized Menelaos had good reason to think himself the champion, for he moved with such swiftness and power his initial thrusts had Paris stumbling backward, barely able to block them with his shield.

Strangling a cry with her hands, Myrina watched with growing panic as the Spartan kept coming at Paris, over and over, thrusting from every possible angle. Yet Paris kept moving, as adroitly as ever, ducking and jumping to avoid the stabbing spearhead.

A heavy hand on the shoulder reminded Myrina she was not alone in her woe. "Have faith, woman," said King Priam, a strange smile around his unsmiling lips. "That is my son. The finest warrior Troy ever saw."

For all his power and determination, Menelaos was unable to finish the duel as quickly as he had undoubtedly anticipated. It was not long before he had to pause and wipe sweat from his eyes, and there was a collective cheer from the Trojans on the wall when Paris used the opening to turn the fight around. As Menelaos stumbled backward across the sand, Paris dealt him blow after blow with the spear . . . but the armored suit withstood them all.

Next to her, Myrina could feel King Priam anticipating every move Paris made. And for every time his spearhead was foiled by the flawless plates of Menelaos's panoply, the king made another grunt of frustration.

After these initial offensives, both men stepped back to catch their breath. They now knew there would be no swift end to their fight, and when they began circling each other once more, dealing a blow here, then there, it was clear they were mapping each other's strengths and weaknesses.

Occasionally a charge would be followed by a brilliant, rapid exchange, but more often than not, Menelaos would duck and try his luck at Paris's legs—earning for himself nothing but howls of displeasure from the crowd. "Foul, foul," muttered King Priam, his hands pressed white against the parapet. "Get rid of that spear."

It was as if the son heard his father's order. For when Menelaos's spearhead became briefly lodged in the leather edge of Paris' shield, the latter did not hesitate, but swiveled the shield so fast and so forcefully Menelaos lost his grip on the wooden pole.

Without even pausing to disentangle the two, Paris tossed both shield and spear outside the circle and immediately went for Menelaos with his own spear. Aiming high, he was clearly looking to strike in between the armored neck and the helmet, but the need for precision compromised his momentum, and when he finally thrust the spear forward, Menelaos was able to bring it down over his armored thigh and break the pole in half.

"Oh no!" whimpered Myrina, covering her eyes.

At which King Priam turned to her and said, "Look up, woman, and be with your husband in spirit. It is far from over."

Indeed, after a brief retreat, both men drew their swords and began their slow dance once more, this time a little closer. Myrina knew Paris's sword well and had always thought it forbiddingly long and heavy; Menelaos's blade, however, was even longer, and although he once again—clearly to provoke—shifted it back and forth a few times, it was evident he needed both hands to wield it.

Had Paris followed the instructions he had given her on the beach in Ephesus, he would have let Menelaos charge and charge again, waiting for the right moment to catch him off-balance. But it soon became clear to Myrina that Paris had drawn up quite a different code for himself—a code that placed honor over safety.

Lunging at Menelaos over and over, Paris gave him no chance to make use of his giant blade. Soon, the crowd began to jeer at the Spartan for being too slow, and—perhaps in desperation—Menelaos began doing what he had done before: lunging at Paris's thighs, which were the least protected part of him.

"Enough!" sneered King Priam, shaking his head. "Finish him."

And Paris did.

Pausing, as if to catch his breath, he let Menelaos pull back his sword to prepare a mighty strike . . . so far back it took no more than a foot against his armored midsection to make the man topple over backward and fall down with a thud that could be heard even at the top of the tower.

Suddenly, it was over. Menelaos's colossal sword came skidding through the gravel, and Paris stood over him, holding the point of his blade against the Spartan's neck. But he did not kill him. Despite the frantic cries all around, Paris merely kicked sand in Menelaos's face, sheathed his sword, and walked over to pick up the rock that had been tossed into the circle to start the duel. Kissing the rock, he held it up in triumph, his helmet flashing in the sun, and looked straight at the top of the Scaean Tower as if he wanted Myrina to be the first to know.

Tumbling down the stairs, breathless with jubilance, she found him in the palace courtyard, surrounded by cheering supporters who had pulled off his helmet and were splashing him with wine, while teasing him for not killing Menelaos. "Marriage has made you soft!" yelled the mighty Dares, punching Paris on the shoulder. "He would not have spared *you*—"

Paris laughed, pulling Myrina into his arms as freely as if they had been alone. "You are wrong!" he yelled back, sweat and wine dripping from his hair. "Marriage has made me hard." And then he kissed her, much to the delight of his mates, and picked her up in his arms the way he did when they were alone. "Fear not," he said with a grin to Dares. "We will have our feast. Go ahead, I will join you soon."

But when he started toward the palace, Paris suddenly stumbled and fell to his knees, nearly dropping Myrina on the ground.

"What is it?" she exclaimed, grasping his face, which had all at once become deadly pale. "Are you hurt?"

"No." Paris struggled to get back on his feet. "He barely touched me. Come"—he took her arm—"give an old man a hand." But again, his legs refused to carry him, and he fell back down with a groan of frustration.

It did not take long for the others to realize something was wrong.

"Shade!" cried someone. "He needs shade. And water."

By joint effort, the men half-dragged, half-carried Paris into the Temple of the Earth Shaker, which was the nearest building to where they stood. Here, they put him down directly on the stone floor and fanned him as best they could. "Water is coming," said Aeneas. "Just lie still."

"Enough of this nonsense," growled Paris, trying to sit up. "What are you? A bunch of old nurses? Don't let my wife see me like this—"

"Oh please," cried Myrina, weighing in with the others. "Lie down and be calm. Tell me where it hurts."

Paris grimaced. "It doesn't hurt. But . . . I can't feel my legs."

Within moments, they had stripped the armor from his shins and pulled off his sandals, hoping to restore his strength. Then suddenly, Aeneas picked up something from the floor and said, "What is this?"

It was a small, polished bone fragment that looked like the tip of a broken arrowhead, except that it was curiously hollow, with a tiny opening at the end.

"Damnation!" exclaimed Dares. "It is a poisoned dart."

After a quick search, they discovered an oozing puncture on the back of Paris's heel, and Myrina was shocked to see the gravity in everyone's faces—it told her they had seen men hit by poisoned darts before and had learned to fear the worst.

"You stay here," said Dares, patting Paris on the shoulder, "and don't move. It's just the heel; I think you'll be fine. And don't worry." He got up, gesturing for the others to follow. "You will get your vengeance. We are going to ride ahead and give those bastards their poison right back. Damn Greeks and their tricks. No doubt Agamemnon ordered this." He paused, his face drawn tight with emotion. "Join us when you can."

The men disappeared in a rustle of angry energy, and Myrina and Paris were left alone. "Lie down, my love," she begged him, stuffing her shawl underneath his head. "Do you feel any better?"

Paris lay back obediently. Then he took a deep breath, forcing the air in and out. "A little."

"Would you like me to fetch the servants?" she asked, stroking his pale cheeks. "Your father?"

"No." He tried to touch her face, but could barely control his hand. "They will come soon enough."

"Please tell me you will be well," begged Myrina, kissing his hand.

"Come lie with me." Paris was able to open his arm so she could rest her head on his shoulder. Then he tried to take another deep breath, but his chest was too heavy. "Will you stay with me," he whispered, touching his lips to her forehead, "just like this, until the end of time?"

Only when she nodded did he close his eyes.

CHAPTER THIRTY-THREE

To me it is clear that you are very rich, and clear that
you are the king of many men; but the thing that you asked
me I cannot say of you yet.
—HERODOTUS, *Histories*

ISTANBUL, TURKEY

I AM NOT SURE HOW LONG I STOOD THERE ON THE PAVEMENT IN MY bare feet, staring at the empty space where James had parked the car. Had they really left without me? I couldn't believe it. Yes, James had been furious with me, and had likely grasped that his vindictive strike against Nick had forever smothered my regard for him . . . but how could he bring himself to leave me behind? Or rather, how could Rebecca have let him do it?

Partly in denial, I walked back to Reznik's house to check whether maybe Rebecca was still there, waiting for me. But the tall gate was now closed, and apart from a few security guards stalking around with walkie-talkies, all was quiet. As I stood there, swaying with indecision, I heard one of the guards say, in French, into his radio, "No, there's no one here. They've left." And then, clearly in response to a question, "Yes, sir. The blue *and* the green woman."

Breathless with fear, I withdrew into the shadow of a dense vine spilling over the fence . . . then, as soon as the guards were facing the other way, I ran down the street as fast as I could, my bare feet thankfully soundless against the concrete slabs of the sidewalk.

If Rebecca was no longer at the house, she *must* have gone with James. In fact, it was beginning to make sense. The guards had started asking inconvenient questions about the theft of the *Historia Amazonum,* and James and Bex had understandably fled. It was even possible they were circling the neighborhood in the Aston Martin, trying to find me.

And so I kept walking, clutching my precious evening bag to my chest. The chase and all the anxiety had made me hot and sweaty for a while; now the cool November evening struck my naked shoulders in full force, making my teeth chatter. By the time a taxi finally pulled up next to me, I knew I had to get in. "Thanks for saving me," I said to the taxi driver, as we sped down the street, hot air blasting from every vent. "I didn't realize Istanbul gets this cold in the winter."

The man sighed and shook his head. "After Reznik's parties, there is always a woman crying outside. Where do you want to go?"

I peeled off the satin gloves and wiggled my numb fingers. As soon as I found a pay phone, I would have to call James and Rebecca and clear things up. "The airport, please," I said to the driver, well knowing there might not be any flights to England before the morning. But at least, I figured, if I spent the night at the airport, I would be first in line.

If Reznik was really as connected as Nick had led me to believe, it wouldn't take him long to piece things together and start suspecting Diana Morgan of having played a part in the theft of the *Historia Amazonum.* When that happened, I had better be thousands of miles away from Istanbul.

Taking out my passport with trembling fingers, I checked yet again that it was really mine. With this crucial document in hand, I would have no problem buying a plane ticket; the only challenge was to stay clear of Reznik's goons until the plane took off.

As I flicked absentmindedly through the passport, I became aware of a yellow Post-it sticker hidden among the pages. Two words were scribbled on it in capital letters: "GO HOME." No exclamation point, just those two words, written with a black ballpoint pen.

I stared at the sticker for a while, trying to see beyond the rather obvious message. Then it occurred to me to check my wallet. Opening it, I braced myself for the sight of empty card slots, but to my amazement everything was still there. In fact, the pouch that had held but a few creased pound notes when I left England two weeks before was now bursting from the addition of two thousand euro in crisp new bills.

Dumbfounded, I took out my diary to see if it held any other clues to the objectives of the people who had held my things hostage all this time. And there it was again, the same unmistakable message, scribbled across the empty space of the week ahead: "GO HOME."

I felt myself bristling at these people's arrogance. So, they wanted me to return to England and were even prepared to facilitate my departure with money and the return of stolen objects . . . but had they given me a single reason to trust them, whoever they were? They still had my laptop and my phone, were still responsible for the bump on my forehead, and their agenda was still obscure to me. Unless . . .

Sitting back in the cold leather seat, I summed up what I knew.

There was a treasure at stake, and I was already acquainted with two of the hunters. Reznik was after the Amazon Hoard, and so was Nick. The fact that my beguiling would-be lover had stolen the *Historia Amazonum* from Reznik amply cemented his guilt. But who were the women in the silver Audi who'd robbed me in Nafplio? Did they actually, as Nick had suggested, work for Reznik? Or could they possibly be . . . Amazons? I felt a prickle of excitement at the thought, as crazy as it was. *If* they were Amazons, was it possible that their objective had always been the same: to prevent Reznik and Nick—among others—from finding their treasure? Was this why they had kept bullying me? To stop me from helping Nick?

I sat quietly for a while, staring into the oncoming headlights of inevitability. It was a bizarre, infuriating sensation—the notion that I had been moved around on a titanic chessboard without knowing whether I was black or white—and as I sat there in the taxi, shivering again, I felt an irresistible urge to rebel against the game.

The jackal had tried to warn me many times, hadn't it? But in my hurry to placate everyone around me I'd ignored its silent vibes. Now it was stirring again, having recalculated our position, and whispered in my ear that I could not go home yet—not until I had the *Historia Amazonum* in my hands. So, the Amazons didn't want me on their side.

Go home, they said. Well, too bad. In my agitated state I could almost convince myself that this one manuscript would redeem all my tribulations . . . that it would lead me to Granny at last . . . but I also had to admit that part of the attraction was its current owner, whose coordinates were scrawled on a folded-up check in my purse. Even if Nick had not stolen the *Historia,* he still had something I wanted badly, namely my heart back in one piece. How exactly I was going to wrest the two from him I wasn't yet sure, but I had to try.

THE AQRAB FOUNDATION SAFE house was not, as I had imagined, located in the heart of a medieval maze near the Grand Bazaar. It was, it turned out, a suite at the Çirağan Palace Hotel—a building which, according to my rerouted taxi driver, had formerly been the summer residence for Turkish sultans.

Notwithstanding my missing shoes, capsized hair, and peacock face paint, it was probably fortunate I was wearing my party dress as I was escorted through the hotel vestibule and into the separate palace reception area by a liveried footman. With ceilings easily as tall as those of the Sheldonian Theatre—scene of my doctoral graduation in May—the vestibule was clad in white marble with accents of dark wood hemming the upstairs galleries. Above, an enormous chandelier hung—it seemed—from heaven itself.

Just then, as I approached the reception desk, I saw a familiar figure emerging from an elevator. He had grown a mustache since I last saw him, and acquired a pair of tinted glasses, but I had spent enough time with Mr. Ludwig to recognize him anywhere.

He was not alone. Next to him walked an athletic man wearing a red baseball cap and a fleece vest, whose face was strangely familiar to me.

No sooner had I crept behind a flower arrangement before it hit me: The eyes underneath the baseball cap had stared out at me from a photo in a scrapbook only the week before. Obviously, the face had aged a few decades, but there was no mistaking the tense jaw and piercing gaze of

Chris Hauser from Baltimore—the man who had long ago convinced Mr. Telemakhos that the jackal bracelet was of Amazon origin.

It took me a while to calm my heart. Coming here tonight, it seemed, had enabled me to spot one of the hidden players behind Nick, and although I was still too frazzled to draw any useful conclusions from Chris Hauser's presence, I knew there was no turning back now.

I deliberately waited a while before approaching the reception desk to call Nick and let him know I was there; it would not do to make him suspect my arrival had overlapped with the departure of his two cronies. And yet, when he finally came down the grand staircase to greet me, I saw in his expression he was wondering exactly how much I knew. It was certainly not the face of someone anticipating a night of carefree carnality; rather, Nick looked like a man who had had one too many surprise visitors already. I knew him well enough to see that he was frustrated, and the fact that he was still wearing the dark suit more than suggested he had not had a moment to himself since returning to the hotel.

"Hello, Goddess." He kissed both of my cheeks while his eyes scanned the room. Then he put a hand behind my back and escorted me toward the elevators, nodding at the receptionist on the way. "*Sağolun, Gökhan.*"

That was all it took, Nick's nearness and the gentle pressure of his palm, and I nearly forgot that I was not there to surrender to him; quite the contrary.

"Rough evening?" he asked, as the elevator doors closed.

"Reznik certainly knows how to party," I said, trying to conceal a rusty tear in one of my gloves. "You shouldn't have left so early."

Nick looked down. "You lost your shoes again."

"Did I?" Trying to make light of it, I lifted up my skirt as if to see for myself. "I hadn't even noticed."

The elevator doors opened again.

"After you," said Nick, holding out an arm.

We walked down the gallery together. Even though we had gone up only one floor, the enormous chandelier that had seemed so distant from the lobby now gave the impression of being within reach, and I felt an onrush of vertigo. Forcing my eyes from the blinding splendor, I chastised myself for being so easily overawed. Here I was, being seduced yet again; it was time to buck up and rally my Amazonian self.

Coming around to the far side of the gallery we arrived at a fortified double door, which Nick had not bothered to lock. "I haven't promised to stay," I said, before stepping inside. "I just wanted to say a proper good-bye."

As soon as the door had closed behind us, Nick took my hand, pulled down the glove, and pressed his lips to my naked wrist right beneath the jackal bracelet. "Good-byes are unpredictable. They can take all night." Then he turned up the lights to reveal a sumptuous parlor with three tall windows framing the night sky over the Bosphorus. "You must be hungry."

I saw him glancing at a half-open door, through which a dinner table with used china and crumpled napkins was just visible. "Not really," I said, pretending I hadn't noticed the debris of his previous visitors. "But I'd love to get rid of this face paint."

Nick nodded, seemingly relieved, and took me into a plush Ottoman-style bedroom with an en suite bathroom. "This is all yours," he said. "If you need anything"—he pointed at a gilded rotary telephone on the bedside table—"just call housekeeping and tell them what you want."

I smiled in response, thinking: If only it was that easy . . . but he had already left, closing the guest room door firmly behind him.

AFTER A QUICK FACE wash I sat on my bed for a bit, pondering the situation.

It was clear to me Nick was besieged by a whole host of problems this evening, and I was bursting with curiosity to know what had transpired before my arrival. Had Mr. Ludwig and Chris Hauser been dispatched by the Dubai office in order to pick up the *Historia Amazonum* and bring it back to Mr. al-Aqrab before Nick—accustomed as he was to racing down harm's way—risked losing it again? If that were the case, I thought with a twinge of worry, I had already failed in my recovery mission.

Turning the door handle as quietly as I could, I peeked out discreetly only to discover that Nick was nowhere in sight. But a majestic door on the other side of the vast parlor was ajar, and I had a feeling that was where I would find him. Tiptoeing across the plush carpet, I listened for familiar sounds and was rewarded with a rustling of paper. After that . . . silence.

Despite everything, I was stupefied. Was this the man who, only two hours earlier, had ravished me on a rooftop and invited me to stop by his hotel for more? Even if Ludwig and Hauser had been the bearers of bad news, I couldn't help feeling Nick was displaying a most unexpected lack of interest in my presence.

I tapped on the door.

A few moments went by before Nick finally appeared with a slightly haunted look, his shirt buttons all undone.

"Hello again," I said, striking a seductive pose. "Aren't you supposed to give me a tour?"

He looked bemused. "What would you like to see?"

"How about *this* room?" I pushed past him through the door, my eyes already on the prowl. It was, as I had assumed, the master bedroom—a fantastic space, definitely worthy of a Dubai foundation with a golf course on the roof. But even more important: On top of the sultan-size bed lay a big envelope with sheets of paper spilling out.

Seeing he had already caught me staring at it, I said casually, "You got your marching orders already. I thought you said you weren't expecting them until morning."

"I wasn't," volunteered Nick, walking over to remove the large envelope from the bed, either to prevent me from taking a closer look or to make space for something other than business. "But things don't always go according to plan, do they?" He put the papers away in a drawer, then turned toward me with an attempt at a smile. "'It's all a chequer-board of nights and days . . . where Destiny with men for pieces plays. Hither and thither moves, and mates, and slays. And one by one back in the closet lays.' Omar Khayyám."

We stood like that for the longest time, each, I was sure, trying to figure out what the other one was thinking. Finally, I leaned against one of the bedposts and said, "Maybe we should just quit. Imagine the freedom—"

Nick's eyes darkened. "Some things you can't quit."

I waited for him to elaborate but he didn't. The way he looked at me suggested he was referring not just to himself but to us both; it was as if, between the Reznik party and now, something immovable had come between us . . . as if he suspected I bloody well knew about his thieving shadow side and was wondering why I had accepted his invitation anyway.

"Quite the proportions," I said, turning to the room to admire the antique furnishings. "I wonder how many harem ladies one can fit into this bed." Glancing at Nick over my shoulder I caught him staring at my derriere.

"What happened to your dress?" he asked. "And your shoes?"

"Good question." I casually peeked into his wardrobe. "Ah, lots of space."

But no *Historia Amazonum.* At least not in plain view.

"Diana." Nick walked up to me. "What's going on? Talk to me. We've been through too much—"

"I know." I turned around reluctantly. "And this is the closest point between our worlds, isn't it?" I looked him straight in the eye. "How come you're still so far away?"

I saw surprise in his face, followed by regret. Whereupon he framed my face with gentle hands, his expression softening. "I'm right here. I've been here all the time." And then he kissed me . . . a slow, heart-rending kiss that drew a moan of longing right out of my soul.

"Divine Diana." He released me with a grimace of pain. "If you knew how you torture me—"

I took him by the open shirt. "Show me."

Nick looked at me with exasperation. "I'm trying to be a gentle-man."

"Why start now?" I ran my hands over his naked chest, indulging in his warm solidity. "I didn't come here to have a polite conversation, did I?"

The words made him stiffen. Or maybe something in my eyes gave him pause. Frowning slightly, Nick looked down at my hands, or rather, my jackal bracelet, as if he was worried it might bite him. "No," he said at last. "I guess you didn't."

Afraid he was going to start questioning me, I leaned in and kissed him again—a kiss I hoped would silence any more inquiries. "Do you know what your problem is?" I murmured. "You *think* too much."

His eyes made one more foray into mine. "Do I?"

"Oh, yes." I ran a hand down his abdomen and beyond. "Far, *far* too much."

Only when I heard his sharp intake of air did it occur to me to slow down a bit. There it was at my fingertips, Nick's imposing pièce de ré-sistance, and when I looked up and saw the somber, uncompromising desire in his face, I lost my mettle momentarily. "Excuse me," I said, with what I hoped was a smile of enticing reassurance, "I just need a minute."

Retreating into his bathroom, I locked the door and leaned against it, trembling all over. The role of seductress was so completely new to me I couldn't even disentangle it from my own feelings. Yes, I wanted to steal the *Historia Amazonum* from Nick, but I also wanted very badly to make love with him; were the two mutually exclusive?

I stepped over to the sink to wash my hands and face with cold water in the hopes of clearing my head. But the woman looking back at me from the large mirror did not want to hear reason now. It's true, she seemed to be saying, you might never see Nick again after daybreak, and you may cry all the way home to Oxford. After all, he's not exactly a man with whom one can expect to have a normal relationship. But come on, whether or not you get more than a single night with him, and whether or not the *Historia Amazonum* changes hands along the way, you've got to go out there and grab him, girl!

Looking around for a toothbrush, I saw a razor resting on a bowl of shaving soap and a zipped bath kit sitting on top of Nick's duffel bag on the floor. Unzipping the bath kit I found a toothbrush and a tube of toothpaste . . . and four passports, held together by a rubber band.

Puzzled, I pulled off the rubber band and opened the passports one by one. The nationalities and dates were all different, and so were the photos, but there was no mistaking Nick's face in each and every one of them.

"Frank Danconia from Canada," I muttered, leafing through them. "Nicholas Barrán from Brazil—I know *you*. Gabriel Richardson from New Zealand. Fabio Azzurro from Italy—"

I sat down on the toilet, struck by surprise and sadness all at once. Which one was his legit passport? I wondered. Judging by the stamps, he used them all regularly. And what about his name? I had always felt "Nick" didn't fully capture who he was—that there was something amiss in the way he introduced himself to people. Perhaps it was because I sensed he was lying.

And so what? whispered the woman in the mirror. What difference did it make that Nick had false identities? In all likelihood it was a requisite for working with the Aqrab Foundation. Had I not just convinced myself we had no future together anyway?

When I finally emerged from the bathroom, the lights had been dimmed and music was playing softly in the background, but Nick wasn't there. I stood for a moment, waiting for him to appear; when he didn't, I walked over to peek out into the parlor. And sure enough: There he was on his cellphone, pacing back and forth in front of the windows.

This was my chance. When I had left the bathroom I still wasn't completely sure what my next step should be, but now, finding myself alone, I knew precisely what to do. Wasting no time, I ran over to the chest of drawers to investigate the big envelope Nick had been so intent on keeping away from me. Only . . . it wasn't there anymore.

Where could he have put it? I commenced a hasty search, but found all the drawers empty. Aware I didn't have much time, I knelt down and checked underneath the bed. Bingo. A metal briefcase.

Pulling it out with trembling urgency, I was encouraged to find it unlocked and flipped it open in the hopes of seeing a stash of secret documents . . . only to recoil with shock. Nested in black foam sat three handguns with extra clips and ammunition.

My head spinning, I quickly closed the case and shoved it back underneath the bed. What did it all mean . . . the passports, the guns? Getting up without a sound, I tiptoed across the floor to check on Nick, but stopped short when he came through the door.

"Where do you think *you*'re going?" he asked, blocking my exit. The question was teasingly meant, but it unnerved me all the same.

"It's been a long day," I began, hoping he didn't guess the reason for my sudden change of heart.

"And it's just about to get longer." Nick drew me into his arms with a suggestive smile. "I'm glad we've done away with the gentleman; now let's see if we can top off the Amazon." He started kissing me again, but my mood was so completely altered I couldn't play along.

"I'm sorry," I muttered, leaning away. "I really *am* exhausted."

Nick's recovery was swift enough to suggest he had expected me to bow out all along. "If you're really so tired," he said, letting go of me, "you'd better go to your room. Because if you don't—" His eyes completed the sentence.

I DIDN'T SLEEP A wink that night. Nor, I am sure, did Nick. Just as the sun began to rise, I heard a door closing and suspected he had given up trying and decided to go out instead.

It was an odd feeling, lying in my grand bed, not at all sure how the new day would unfold. After my initial panic at finding the handguns, I had slowly managed to lull myself into a warm and fuzzy fantasy in which Nick would come to my room before daybreak, unable to stay away, to tell me that he was crazy about me and promise to let me in on everything.

We would spend the day on a romantic Bosphorus cruise, I imagined, during which Nick would apologize for all the secrecy and confess his numerous sins. He would be reluctant to describe the Reznik heist in much detail, of course, but I would be understanding, and it would all end with kisses and a candlelit dinner at some dark intimate restaurant downtown, where we could hold hands across the table while he told me his real name.

But the sun rose, and he didn't come.

There was just that little *click* of the door . . . and then nothing.

Padding out in the parlor in my monogrammed hotel pajamas, I found a small scrap of paper lying on the sofa table. "Back soon. NB."

"NB?" I said out loud, feeling a spark of irritation. "Not just N, but *NB?*"

Poking my head through the open door to the master bedroom, I saw that Nick was indeed gone. After only the briefest struggle with my conscience—more of a jousting match, really, in which my scruples were soon unhorsed—I crossed the floor and knelt down next to the bed.

The metal briefcase was still there, but now it was locked. It hardly mattered, though; I knew what was in it.

All the while listening for any sounds suggesting Nick's return, I commenced a hasty search for the big envelope and quickly exhausted all natural hiding places—atop the wardrobe, inside it, under the bed pillows—before my eyes finally fell on an enormous red Ottoman vase with a bright white floral pattern. Nick was just the sort of man to hide something priceless in plain view.

And there it was, all of it, wedged unceremoniously just inside, at the top of the vase: the fat envelope, the wad of passports, and the *Historia Amazonum*. Bound in a soft leather cover so worn it was held together by only a few threads, the pages were covered in handwritten Latin that had, over time, faded to resemble watercolor. Despite the precarious circumstances, I was filled with giddy relief to discover that Nick had not yet surrendered this precious manuscript to Mr. Ludwig and Chris Hauser. Here it was, at long last, safely in my hands.

As for the envelope, I had not actually intended to take it with me, merely sneak a peek at its contents. However, as soon as I pulled out the documents Nick had been reading the night before, I knew I couldn't leave them behind. For right there, black on white, was the answer to my greatest question: What was Mr. al-Aqrab really after? The bright morning light made it all frighteningly evident, and I knew with nauseating certainty that I had to get out of there before Nick came back. Not just out of his room, or out of the suite, but out of his life entirely.

THE ISTANBUL ATATÜRK AIRPORT was in the throes of the morning rush when I arrived. Men in business suits crowded every counter and self-serve machine, and I waited in line for half an hour only to be told that the first available seat to London was on a plane leaving at three that afternoon.

"But are you sure there is absolutely no faster way of getting me to England?" I asked the attendant. "I don't mind the stops."

"I'm sorry," she said, checking the screen one more time. "All I have is Amsterdam at eleven thirty."

Now, wouldn't that be the supreme irony? I thought to myself as I wound my way through suitcases and cellphone zombies, looking for a café where I could pass the hours until my flight. Ending up in Amsterdam after all. Especially now that I was dressed for the fashion show circuit, complete with a wide-brimmed hat and sunglasses the size of Milan . . . all thanks to the exclusive clothes boutique around the corner from the Çirağan Palace Hotel that had gobbled up half my fortune in less than five minutes.

Sitting down in a secluded booth with my guilty stash of papers and a breakfast tray, I took out the document that had shocked me so when I first laid eyes on it in Nick's room two hours ago. It was a short typed cover letter that bore neither letterhead nor signature and which read as follows:

Attention Jumbo,

We are putting jackals on the menu. A rock per head. Fresh meat only. Take a look at our selection. If supplies run low, we are open for alternatives. Half a rock per bracelet, a quarter per tattoo. Delivery through Pavel.

Stapled to this brief peculiar letter were three sheets of paper, all of which were cluttered with blurred black-and-white photos and lopsided text. The images showed three women caught—I guessed—on surveillance cameras, and there were grainy close-ups of one jackal bracelet and two barely perceptible jackal tattoos. The text identified the women as "Amazon 1," "Amazon 2," and "Amazon 3," and guesstimates were given for their heights, weights, and ages.

My first thought had been that the letter was a coded message from Mr. al-Aqrab to a hit man—possibly Nick—ordering the killing of three women presumed to be Amazons. However, after reading through it several dozen times, I was no longer so sure. As ready as I was to vilify Mr. al-Aqrab, I had a hard time seeing Nick as a willing executioner.

Putting aside the letter at last, I began flipping through the rest of the documents in the envelope, hoping to find something more straightforward.

I didn't have to search for long. There they were, washed out yet unmistakable: dozens of gray-toned photos of my father, my mother, and me. . . . The discovery chilled me even more than the letter to the hit man.

What I had found was a stapled detective report of the kind my parents had commissioned after Granny's disappearance, but whereas theirs had contained nothing but useless fluff, this one seemed loaded with information. Although the text was in Arabic, the illustrations spoke for themselves, and I peered once more at the grainy photos of my father quietly fiddling with his bird feeder . . . my mother stretching after a jog . . . blissfully unaware they were in the crosshairs of a telescopic lens.

Almost all the images were sniper shots, and most of them had been taken through windows or shrubberies. It was downright sickening to realize that my parents and I had been under surveillance by a pair of invisible eyes, even in our most private moments. Yes, there were photos of me lecturing to students and filling the blackboard with Egyptian hieroglyphs, but there was also one of me singing to Professor Larkin's guppies after a few too many solitary glasses of wine.

Even though my mother was in it, too, the report was clearly focused on my father and me, and it was not difficult to guess why. Obviously, the Amazon question lay at the core of it all. For on one of the pages was a familiar old wedding photo I had scrutinized many times growing up: the only existing picture of Granny and Grandfather, both of them looking strangely unhappy, as if they already knew their marriage was doomed.

What exactly had this nosy detective managed to dig up about them? I wondered. My own knowledge about their courtship was limited to the extremely terse account Granny had once given me after persistent needling—an account I was convinced she had never shared with anyone else.

If I were to actually believe Granny, she and another Amazon had—in their rebellious youth—attended a scientific conference in Copenhagen with the sole purpose of singling out the most intelligent male participants. "You can't have everything," she had explained to me as I sat wide-eyed at her feet, "so I chose to find a *smart* man. And I did. It was your grandfather. But I made a mistake. I fell in love with him." Granny gave me the cautionary eye, as if to warn me never to do the same. "Instead of being Kara, I became his wife. I should have known better, but . . . I left the sisterhood."

"Why was that so terrible?" I asked, brimming with the child's need for happy endings. "If you really loved him."

"You must understand." Granny rose and walked over to the small gable window where she stood so often, gazing—I imagined—into her own broken memories. "I grew up as an Amazon. It was the only life I knew."

Because she so rarely spoke coherently about her Amazon self, I jumped to my feet with nervous excitement, desperate to extract as much information as I could before the door between her childhood and mine slammed shut again, perhaps forever. "Where was that, Granny? Do you remember?"

She hesitated. "It is not safe for you to know. Not yet."

"But when? When will it be safe for me?"

She looked down at me at last, love and admonishment doing battle in her eyes. "When you have proven yourself. When I can trust you."

That was it. She never told me any more than that.

Pushing the detective report aside at last, I dug into Nick's envelope once more. Slipped into a plastic sleeve was an article that had appeared in a medical journal some ten years earlier, and it took me a few seconds to realize the author was my father's old chum Dr. Trelawny. Comparing five different cases of schizophrenic paranoia, his point seemed to be that they all shared the same core elements: parallel personalities and an imagined language.

Even though the perfidious Dr. Trelawny had changed the names of the patients mentioned, it was obvious that one of the cases cited was that of my grandmother. Not only did the article describe her Amazon personality in great detail, it also mentioned her jackal bracelet—which Dr. Trelawny referred to as a "worthless trinket invested with emotional value"—and spoke, I was sorry to see, at length about the handwritten "Amazon dictionary" she had left for her granddaughter.

Here it was at last, the link I had been missing since Mr. Ludwig first approached me in Oxford and baited me with an undeciphered Amazon alphabet. Clearly, someone at the Aqrab Foundation had known of this article all along and had specifically set out to get me on board, guessing—correctly—that I would bring Granny's notebook along to the party.

I was so upset I had to get a second cup of coffee simply to warm my hands and stop shivering. How devilish of Mr. al-Aqrab to use me like this—to set me upon my own kind and turn me into an unwitting Amazon hunter.

There were other documents in the envelope, but I had seen enough to know I had done the right thing in getting the *Historia Amazonum*—and myself—out of Nick's clutches. At this point, my most pressing question was what I should do next. Was it not naïve of me to think I could return to Oxford and never hear from Mr. al-Aqrab again?

Slipping the envelope back in my new, ridiculously expensive handbag, I walked over to the nearest pay phone kiosk and called Rebecca. I had been meaning to contact her for the past twelve hours, and had almost dialed her from my guest room at the Çirağan Palace Hotel . . . but something had held me back. Wasn't it enough that everyone had been tracking *me* through my phone? I didn't need them to start teaching Rebecca, too.

"Hello?" muttered a timid voice that didn't sound familiar at all.

"Bex?" I said, half-thinking I had punched in the wrong number.

An explosion of relief at the other end set me straight. "Dee? Where are you? What happened?"

I was so happy to hear her voice my knees nearly gave in. "I'm fine. Actually, I'm not. But never mind. Where are *you*? Are you with James?"

Rebecca whimpered. "It's so terrible——"

I felt all the little hairs on my neck rise with foreboding. "What is?"

"James." She could hardly speak for agitation. "He's with Reznik."

It took me a while to sort out what had actually happened to Rebecca. To my tremendous relief she had managed to take an overnight bus back to Çanakkale and had spent the morning on the boat with Mr. Telemakhos, staring at her cellphone, desperate to hear from me.

The hour preceding her flight to the bus station, however, had been nothing short of horrendous. She and James had waited for me in front of Reznik's bathroom for a good ten minutes before realizing I wasn't coming. Eventually, James had concluded I must have eloped with Nick, and it had turned into quite an argument.

Seeing they were the last guests left in the house, they had decided to walk out to the car to see if perhaps I had been waiting there all along. Rebecca had walked ahead, still too irritated with James to say a single word to him—so she told me between sobs of guilt and regret—and just as she walked through the gate, someone started yelling behind her. Turning around, she saw Reznik's guards walking up to James, preventing him from leaving. Having no idea what it was all about, Rebecca had instinctively felt they were in trouble and had started running . . . leaving James to fend for himself.

"I feel so terrible," she muttered, reliving the moment. "I should have stayed with him, but . . . I just freaked out. I ran to the car to see if you were waiting for us, but the police were there with a tow truck. They said something I didn't understand—something about needing a resident sticker to park there, I think. But I feel so bad about James."

"I'm sure he'll be fine," I said. "It's understandable that Reznik wanted to talk with him. You saw them—they're old friends. And James is Lord Moselane's son. Reznik would never dare——"

"I've been calling and calling, but his phone is off——"

"Well, stop calling!" I said, getting a little impatient. "That's how Reznik tracks people. There's no question he'll come looking for the *Historia Amazonum* soon, so you and I should lie low for a while and not communicate with each other. The best thing you can do is to sail away with Mr. Telemakhos."

"What about you?" Rebecca wanted to know. "Where *are* you?"

I looked around at the busy airport, wondering how much to tell her. It was only a matter of time before someone would be hot on my heels . . . the only question was, who would get to me first? Nick had my scent; Reznik had James. I could make a point of returning the *Historia Amazonum,* of course, but to whom? And how? No, it was too late for grand gestures, I decided; all I would accomplish was to draw more attention to myself.

It was a strange feeling, to stand there at the pay phone kiosk, surrounded by confident travelers who knew precisely where they were going . . . and realize I was on the run.

"I can't tell you," I said at length. "But I'll find a way of ending this, I promise."

After hanging up with Rebecca, I deliberated for a moment, then called Katherine Kent. We had not spoken since the night before my departure; I had left her a message from Algeria; that was all. And yet this all-seeing mentor of mine had known enough about my movements to send James to Troy precisely the day I arrived. How was that possible? I had a feeling the answer to this question might help guide my further movements.

I called her number thrice with the same result: a shrill signal telling me the line had been disconnected. This, more than anything, made my growing fear ripen into panic. Since the invention of the telephone no Oxford numbers had ever changed; the fact that Katherine Kent had been rendered unreachable was a sure sign my world was coming apart.

Retreating into a bathroom stall, I sat down to clear my head. Trouble was coming my way, no doubt about it. Where could I possibly hide until things calmed down a bit? So exasperated I felt like banging my forehead against the door, I started riffling through my satin evening bag to see how much money I had left. As I did so, I came across the note from Mr. Telemakhos with the name of the German museum where—according to him—the last remaining jackal bracelet was kept.

Staring at the unfamiliar name now, overwrought as I was, I almost felt my own jackal responding to its distant call. And within a few short breaths—the sort of breaths one takes before plunging into a cold lake—I decided the answer to my present squeeze was right there in front of me.

CHAPTER THIRTY-FOUR

TROY

EARTH WAS IN MOURNING.

The sun had set forever, and the moon reigned supreme. Nothing would ever sprout, grow, or bloom. There were only the tides of the ocean, coming in, going out, pounding, never-ending. Earth no longer cared.

Curled up on the temple floor, Myrina felt the tremor but assumed it was her own. A deep rumble in the core of her being, a silent, splintering scream of sorrow—it seemed only natural her grief should reverberate through the cavernous structure around her.

Lying with her head on Paris's unstirring chest, she had long since decided never to rise again. She wished someone would light a pyre right there, that it might consume them both at once and free her from the burden of ever having to open her eyes.

A hand on her shoulder demanded otherwise.

"Myrina," said a voice. King Priam. "We must be strong now.".

She pretended not to hear him.

"Myrina. I cannot delay any longer. His mother must be told."

"Please." She could barely speak the words. "Let me go with him."

There was another tremor, this time followed by distant screaming.

"My dear," said King Priam, his voice wavering, "I need you to be strong for my son. Do you hear me?"

Myrina opened her eyes and nodded.

"Good." King Priam clasped his head as if bracing against unspeakable pain. "The time has come. Troy must die with Paris—it was always so. Our walls will crumble. There will be chaos."

"Why am I still alive?" whispered Myrina. "I who caused all this—"

King Priam shook his head in pity. "You think you are stronger than Fate? We are all cups, and our destiny is poured according to measures we cannot understand, cannot influence. Even the Earth Shaker must rise against his will and destroy his home." Priam sighed deeply. "This I must believe. How else can a father look upon his dead child and have the will to breathe?"

The king fell silent, battling tears of his own. Then he said with brusque efficiency, "Come with me, daughter. The Earth Shaker has granted us precious time. We must use it. You and your sisters will leave Troy before the final hour. And you must take with you something precious."

"Why me?"

King Priam knelt down by her side. Only then did she see his eyes, swollen with grief. "Because he chose you. He chose you to carry the future of Troy. And I know you will guard it better than anyone."

KING PRIAM TOOK MYRINA deep into the rocky caverns beneath the citadel, to show her the treasure chamber, gleaming and sparkling in the light of his torch. Never had Myrina seen such splendor, such golden magnificence, and she looked around with reverence while Priam unlocked the door to the innermost vault.

"This is what I want you to take away," he said stepping into the darkness ahead of her. "The soul of Troy. It must not fall into the hands of the Greeks."

After only the slightest hesitation, Myrina followed him into the vault.

And then she understood.

EMERGING FROM UNDERGROUND, MYRINA saw that the chaos had already begun. Wailing women had descended on the Temple of the Earth Shaker, to mourn the dead prince and beseech the deity to spare his city.

Hurrying into the palace, she found Pitana and Kara in the kitchen, tending to poor Kyme, who had suffered a blow to the head and who now lay pale and moaning in front of the fireplace, her gray hair smudged with blood.

"It was a large pot," explained Kara, as soon as she saw Myrina. "It fell from a shelf when the earth shook, and struck her as you see—"

"I am so sorry to be trouble," gasped Kyme. "Please do not worry about me. I will be up and about in a moment."

"Where are the others?" asked Myrina. "We must leave."

"We know," said Pitana, nodding firmly. "We are ready."

"Please," whispered Kyme to Myrina, "this time, I would like to stay."

"No." Myrina took her hand. "You are coming with us."

Kyme smiled. "I am asking to be excused. Just this once. I am weary of traveling. I like it here."

Myrina shook her head. "Come morning, Troy may no longer exist."

"Nonsense!" Kyme tried to laugh. "The earthquake is over, the Greeks are leaving. . . . By sunrise, all will be well."

Myrina bent her head, unable to hold back her tears any longer. "All will not be well. We must be away now, while there is still time. Please come with us. Without you . . . we might lose the art of writing."

Kyme sighed. "Only kings are put in writing, you know. Kings and heroes. The rest of us are but fading echoes in the valley of eternity." She closed her eyes as if drifting off to sleep. "Now leave me, children. All I ask is that you remember my name and speak of me fondly from time to time. Will you do that?"

As soon as Aeneas arrived at the citadel, King Priam walked up to seize his foaming horse by the bridle, saying, "Dismount. I have a task for you."

"I beg to be excused, Master," gasped Aeneas, dripping with sweat from his ride through town, his arms crisscrossed by bloody scrapes. "I must bring reinforcements to our men. There is much violence on the Scamandrian Plain. We rode out, as perhaps you know, to take our vengeance on the bastards, but all of a sudden, at the height of the battle, the horses panicked." He reached down to accept a drink of water. "The Greeks tried to launch their ships to return home, but they are all trapped in the violent surf. They, too, have felt the tremors and fear it is the Earth Shaker coming to punish them." Aeneas grimaced and spat on the ground. "They've slit the throat of every horse they could get their hands on—hundreds of them—and have left the sorry beasts to bleed to death, presumably as a gift to the Earth Shaker."

"The Greeks and their gifts!" growled King Priam. "Hateful race. All they know is blood and burning. But come"—he patted Aeneas on the thigh—"you need a fresh steed. I have a special task for you."

"Where is Paris?" asked Aeneas, looking around. Only then did he notice Myrina. One glance at her face told him what had happened, and he brought both hands to his eyes in wordless anguish.

ON THE KING'S ORDERS, Aeneas was to guide Myrina and her sisters out of town. They left just before midnight, in a tempest of activity. Priam had given them extra packhorses to carry the treasure he wanted the women to safeguard, and by the time of their departure, the group was composed of fourteen women and twenty horses. In one last tribute to Paris, Myrina let Lilli ride the mare he had given her, and which he had so diligently trained her to master.

Leading them through the Scaean Gate to avoid the fighting on the Scamandrian Plain, Aeneas rode with the women all the way to the Simoeis River. Here, he took leave of them, and said to Myrina, "A dark day this has been for both of us. You have lost your husband, and I my friend. Your consolation must be that his funerary pyre will be lit by heaven itself, and that he will have ample company on his last journey. My consolation"—he reached out and placed a hand on her shoulder—"is that, in one short month, you gave Paris more love than most people find in a lifetime. He was as happy as a man could be, he told me so himself. No grumpy old age for him, wondering why the pleasures of the world had passed him by. Although young, he had his fill, and he knew it."

Unable to say more, Aeneas turned his horse around and started back toward Troy. And the women, no longer sure who should be the leader after Penthesilea's death, continued up the river in silence, respecting Myrina's grief by leaving her alone.

They reached Lady Otrera's camp at daybreak, to find everyone already up, trying in vain to calm the horses.

It came just as they ran forward to embrace their sisters: the wrath of the gods of heaven, clashing with Earth. It felt as if a giant hand pulled the very ground from beneath their feet and shook them all— women as well as horses—into the air like grains on a threshing mat. There was a demonic roar as the trees of the old forest pitched and yawed . . . and then the terrible thudding of massive trunks and dismembered branches falling everywhere.

Screaming with fear, the women huddled together, waiting for the sky to collapse and fall. For surely, this was the end of everything—the moment much-enduring Earth finally shook off the wickedness of mankind.

MYRINA WOKE WITH A gasp of hope . . . only to fall back down with a sob of disappointment. For she was in the forest, surrounded by damp darkness and sleeping women, and the person whose nearness she had sensed was Lilli, snuggled up beside her as close as she could get.

"Here." Animone put an arm behind Myrina and held a cup of water to her lips. "You have been senseless all day. Are you in pain?"

"Paris," muttered Myrina. "Is he still—?"

Animone stroked her cheek. "There was another earthquake. A terrible one. Pitana and Hippolyta rode back to—" She hesitated. "Troy is no more. There is not a house still standing. And the raiders are everywhere."

Myrina lay back down. "I am so tired. Forgive me."

She slept again until morning, when Lady Otrera came to wake her in person, saying, "We must break camp, Myrina. We have been here for too many days and the horses are restless. Come." Otrera took her by the hand and walked her down to the river. "Wash your eyes and clear your head. Remember that you are Myrina. Your sisters depend on you to be brave."

Myrina fell to her knees at the water's edge, burying her face in her hands. "How can I be brave when my courage leads to nothing but destruction?"

Lady Otrera knelt down beside her. "Without your courage, your sisters would still be enslaved in Mycenae."

"Without my damned courage"—Myrina doubled over, sick with sorrow—"Paris would be alive."

"It was not your courage that made King Priam tax the Greek ships," Lady Otrera pointed out, "or that made those ships raid our coasts. Nor did your courage make the north wind blow or cause the earthquake. Do not flatter yourself you have such power over life and death. Without you . . . who is to say Paris would not have died in his bed under a collapsing roof?" She leaned closer, a conspiratorial look in her eyes. "Do you not think your husband will look more dashing in the halls of Eternity, coming straight from the battleground, drenched with victory?"

Myrina closed her eyes, relishing the sweet image before it was swallowed once again by the all-consuming memory of Paris dead in her arms, his body still warm against the cold temple floor. "Perhaps."

"Good." Lady Otrera began scooping up water, splashing it against Myrina's face. "Now come, and let us continue on our way. We will not be safe from the Greeks until we are in the land of the Kaskians."

As THEY CONTINUED EAST along the coast, it occurred to Myrina that Lilli had fallen unusually silent. Even after many tearful days of shared grief and tender words the girl continued uneasy, and when Myrina eventually questioned her about her concerns, it took much urging to make Lilli express them.

"We have seen so much sorrow and destruction," she said reluctantly, as they lay awake one night, holding hands. "I am loath to predict more."

"But you must!" Myrina put an arm around her sister. "I have long since learned to trust your misgivings. What do you see?"

"Darkness," muttered Lilli. "The land of the Kaskians holds nothing but agony. We will prevail for a while, but after then . . . oblivion. The only light I see comes from the north. We must cross the waterway; I know we must."

Myrina could not conceal her dismay. "You would have us fend our way through the wilderness of the northern lands? Go where no civilized person has ever set foot?"

Lilli nodded. "I see rivers and mountains and endless forests. And"—her voice quavered—"I see you smiling again, urging us on."

When Myrina shared Lilli's visions with Lady Otrera, however, the older woman would not even consider a change of plans. And when Myrina kept insisting on going north, Otrera finally looked at her with eyes full of bitterness and said, "Do you realize what this means?"

Myrina nodded heavily. "It seems Fate is determined to part our ways."

THEY REACHED THE CROSSING after another three days of travel. It was a bustling place, full of sailors and fast-talking vendors, but the women rode their horses through the crowd in silence, glumly ignoring the raucous comments that followed them wherever they went. For this was where the group would have to separate; some to follow Lady Otrera and sail east into the Inhospitable Sea, the rest to cross with Myrina here, where the strait was narrow.

To most, the choice was simple. None of Lady Otrera's daughters had any desire to extract themselves from the web of people they had known all their lives, and certainly not to venture into lands inhabited—

as Otrera had phrased it when she presented the choice to them—by "blood-sucking witches and howling wolf men."

But to the women who had come all the way from the Temple of the Moon Goddess on the banks of Lake Tritonis—and in particular those who had been rescued from Mycenae—it was an excruciating choice between comfort and loyalty. "How can you ask this of us now?" complained Klito, after Lady Otrera and Myrina had explained the situation to everyone the day before. "We have been delivered from the greatest calamity the world has ever seen, I am sure, and now"—Klito threw out her arms, one toward her holy sister, the other toward the woman she had come to think of as a mother—"you want to force us apart, just when salvation seems within reach."

There was a mumble of agreement in the group. Breaking from their journey to water the horses and rest awhile, they had gathered on the banks of a large river, and Myrina and Lady Otrera had taken turns stepping up onto a large boulder to address the women seated on rocks around them.

"Let us not be fooled into thinking there *is* such a thing as salvation," said Myrina, forcing herself to speak loudly although grief lay like a noose around her neck. "I am making no claims about the safety of the northern lands, but I would not have you run for the Kaskians only to be slaughtered like beasts. Even if you have no faith in my sister's visions, at least consider the warnings of King Priam—"

"Listen to her!" exclaimed Egee, jumping to her feet in anger. "First she abandons us for a man . . . now she pretends to care for our safety. And look at her." Egee pointed her hunting knife directly at Myrina—the hunting knife she had once sworn never to carry but which was now her dearest possession. "Does she inspire confidence? She is sick and beside herself; she hardly knows what she says or does. Clearly, the Goddess is taking her vengeance now. Suppose she dies? What would we do then? No." Egee folded her arms, knife and all. "I say, she may go her own unlucky way, and we shall go ours."

A loud discussion followed Egee's unforgiving speech, but everyone—even the dissenters—fell silent when Kara stood up. Showing them all the scars on her wrists, as if they were an argument in themselves, she looked to Egee and said, "You speak of luck and vengeance as if you know what you are talking about. But you have no idea. You were never violated or taken away on the black ships. You never endured the slime of Mycenae." Her face torn with fury, Kara pointed at Myrina. "*She* was the one who came for us. *She* put our happiness before her own. You think the Goddess hates her? Wrong! The Goddess loves her. Admires her. That is why she has made her an example to us all. That is why she has given her back to us. You think she walks an unlucky path? Perhaps. But I saw a princess of Troy with a crown on her head, and *I* was the one who—in my madness—threw her to the lions." Kara clasped her own face, struggling once more against the demons within. "And therefore I must walk that unlucky path with her, wherever it leads. We may meet flying witches and half humans, but it cannot be worse than what we have already seen. And we are survivors, are we not?" She looked around at them all, hands raised in appeal. "Myrina could have died many times, and so could I, and so could you. But we didn't. We are still alive because we have each other, and we have an obligation to fulfill." She pointed at the packhorses King Priam had given them. "A man who ruled over one of the greatest cities on earth has asked us, with his last breath, to be the guardians of a treasure. I would choose that challenge over any comfort the world could offer. I, for one, have a great deal of shame to wash away, and can think of no better place to do so than in the wild rivers of the north, where I will never again hear Greek spoken."

After Kara, no one else had dared to stand up, and the group had continued toward the coast in a hum of anger and indecision. Even as they approached the harbor, studying all the ships pulling up, Myrina still did not know if she would be crossing the strait with three or thirty.

King Priam's treasure, however, would remain under her control. There had been some murmuring about the unjustness of her keeping it all to herself, but the jealousy had ceased as soon as Myrina disclosed the nature of the treasure and let women see for themselves.

"In truth we do not envy you this burden," Lady Otrera had said, speaking on behalf of everyone. "We only pray that your labors will be rewarded."

THEY STOPPED AT A beached ship that looked promisingly empty. A bulky bear of a man lay in the shade of the hull, chewing on a root. His only weapon appeared to be a wooden club, but Myrina did not doubt he could wield it to great effect. When he noticed the women, the man sat up with a wary nod.

"How much can your ship carry?" Lady Otrera asked him, using the language of Ephesus. "I assume you are for hire?"

The big man grinned, the root bobbing at the corner of his mouth. "All yours, luv, if the price is right. Where are you going?"

Lady Otrera frowned. The man was obviously a brute, dressed in a mangy lion skin and not much else, and yet he looked robust and willing, spoke their language, and his ship was clearly available. "Some of us are merely looking to cross to the other side," she said, "while the rest will want to sail east until we reach the mouth of the Thermodon River. It is my understanding that there are few passable roads between here and there, and that sea passage is infinitely faster and more secure than land travel. Is that correct?"

"You've got it, luv." Standing up at last, the man took a good look at the group. "That's a lot of horses. I'm not a great horse lover. Produce a lot of dung. I've shoveled a lot of dung in my time." He spat out the root and brushed off his hands. "But I have a couple buddies, and I've got Theseus and his rowers working for me now, so that makes four ships in total." He smiled again, baring his teeth in an accommodating smile. "Let's start with the easy trip. How many, altogether, are going across?"

It was the moment they had all dreaded—the moment they had postponed until it could be pushed out no further. "Well." Lady Otrera turned to the group. "Speak up, girls. How many will go north with Myrina?"

Lilli and Kara put up their hands right away. Then came Klito, and Pitana, and half a dozen more. But that was it. Animone was not among them. Sitting on her horse with her head bent, she could not look at Myrina; had she been brave enough to do so, she would have seen forgiveness in her friend's eyes.

"Right." The man picked his nose, inspected his findings, and wiped the finger on his lion-skin tunic. "If that's all, I can take the first group across right now, and then we'll figure out the rest when my buddies come back."

"How about payment?" said Lady Otrera.

"Well." The man scratched his burly neck. "Why don't we see what kind of rowers I can get and how long it takes us to get you ladies where you want to go?" He ran his eyes over Hippolyta, taking in her embroidered girdle and shapely thighs. "I'm sure you'll turn out to have something I like."

And then came the time for parting. Embracing everyone in turn, Myrina ended up in Lady Otrera's arms, unable to put words on her emotions.

"There is no need to cry," said Lady Otrera, half-laughing. "For I am sure we will see each other again soon. You will realize the northern lands are no place to be, and you will rejoin us well before the baby comes."

Myrina stiffened, taken aback. "I do not understand—"

Lady Otrera smiled and kissed her on the forehead. "I may not know men, but I know women. You are carrying something far more precious than King Priam's treasure. You are carrying his grandchild."

STANDING IN THE STERN, Myrina saw her world, and most of the people she knew, shrink with every oar stroke until there was nothing left but the knowledge that her sisters were still there, waiting for the ships to return.

And yet her sadness was dulled by confusion after Lady Otrera's parting words. Could it really be? Had a small, immortal part of Paris survived inside her? She barely dared hope it was so, lest she should discover it was not true and lose him once again.

Pushing aside the thought, Myrina looked at her wrist where the jackal used to be. When she gave it to Helena—poor, star-crossed Helena—she had never imagined wanting it back, but now she missed its reassuring presence. After everything that had happened, she craved forgiveness—forgiveness for loving Paris, for leaving the sisterhood, for bringing grief wherever she went. She just wasn't sure whom to turn to. The Moon Goddess? Hardly. Even the jackals, surely, had long since lost all loyalty for their former mistress.

No, thought Myrina, she would have to find forgiveness in herself and in her ten faithful companions. They would have to reconfirm their sisterhood under new terms. Once they were safely settled somewhere, they would sit down and talk it all through, and maybe, if she was lucky, they would come across a coppersmith who would be able to fashion a new bracelet.

A gruff command interrupted her speculations. The man whose ship they were on—the brute who had been so jovial when they spoke with him on the shore—was walking up and down the deck with his giant club, urging on his rowers and looking as if he would have no qualms about crushing the skull of a slouch. "I don't trust him," muttered Pitana, coming up beside Myrina. "There is a cruel and calculating look in his eyes just now. I wonder if we should ask him to turn around."

Myrina thought for a moment. "Lady Otrera is not naïve. And I am confident her daughters can hold their own. If you had seen what I saw at the Scamander River that day, you would agree with me they have as much will to kill as men do."

And yet, when they had safely crossed the strait and landed on the northern shore, Myrina found herself lingering on the beach, looking to exchange a final word with their club-wielding captain. Feigning admiration, she asked him, "How did a man such as yourself end up in this desolate region?"

He shrugged, no longer too concerned about stoking her regard for him. "I killed someone. Figured I'd better leave town before his friends found out."

Myrina smiled, carefully concealing her alarm. "Who was it?"

The man looked out over the water with narrow eyes. "A man I worked for. Cleaned his stables. Lots of dung. He wouldn't pay me. So, I knocked his teeth out. Unfortunately, they were attached to his brain. Or . . . they were when I was done with him." The man snorted with laughter, looking around to make sure the rowers were laughing right along.

"That's good," said Myrina, adjusting the ax in her belt. "Make sure you tell that story to my friends on the other side. They'll like it. Now, before we part"—she held out her hand—"tell me your name, and I'll tell you mine."

The man threw her a sarcastic look, as if he suspected her of making fun of him. "You want my name? Why? Are you going to squeal on me? Me and the others"—he made a general gesture toward shore— "we're not looking for any trouble. We're just . . . staying away for a while." He finally took her hand. "Nothing wrong with that. Name's Hercules."

Myrina nodded. "You and I have a lot in common, Hercules. We are both killers, and yet we both want peace. Here is some advice for you: Don't touch my sisters. We are the Amazons, killers of men. Only the feeble-headed try their luck with us."

"Killers of men?" Hercules looked at her with a capsized smile. "Say it again, and we may put you to the test."

Myrina was only too aware of the sudden burst of energy among the rowers. She saw them eyeing her with apparent greed and elbowing one another with nods of agreement. "You want to test me?" she asked them, raising her voice. "Do you see that bird?" She pointed at a seagull perched atop a ship's mast a bit farther down the beach. Then, without another word, she liberated her bow and sent off an arrow with such speed and precision the bird didn't even squawk as it fell from the mast and dropped to the sand, pierced right through.

"We are the Amazons," said Myrina again, more firmly, while the men gaped incredulously at the dead bird. "We are the killers of beasts and men. Wild ourselves, we inhabit the wild places. Freedom courses in our blood, and death whispers at the tip of our arrows. We fear nothing; fear runs from *us*. Try to stop us, and you will feel our rage." With that she turned and walked away from the men, through the tall grasses, until all they could see was the tip of her bow.

And then, just as they remembered to breathe again, she was gone.

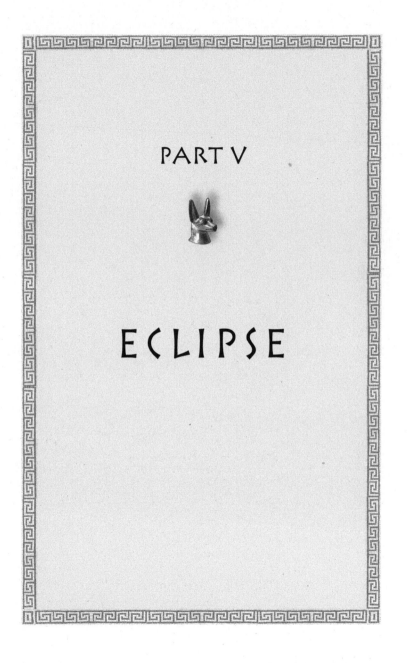

PART V

ECLIPSE

CHAPTER THIRTY-FIVE

It is well known that none of the German tribes live in cities, that even individually they do not permit houses to touch each other: they live separated and scattered, according as spring-water, meadow, or grove appeals to each man.
—TACITUS, *Germania*

OSNABRÜCK, GERMANY

THE DRIVE FROM THE MÜNSTER AIRPORT WAS BARELY THIRTY minutes—just long enough for me to come down with a case of second thoughts. "I blame you," I told the jackal as we went through a flat dark-green landscape saturated with moisture. "You were the one who wanted to hide up here. Now what?"

It was a drab, rainy afternoon of the sort northern Europe does so well in November. Even though I had never been to this part of Germany before I felt instinctively at home in the chilly misery of it all, and it fit my current mood perfectly. With my panic behind me, I was left with a nagging feeling it might have been wiser of me to fly back to Oxford and simply go to the police. And yet . . . what would be gained by that? A temporary sense of security? Although I still felt doubt clawing at my resolve, I told myself I was doing the right thing in following Mr. Telemakhos's lead on the bracelet in Kalkriese. Both Reznik and al-Aqrab were hell-bent on finding the Amazons, and the only way I could escape them, it seemed, was to beat them to it.

I had spent the flight from Istanbul going through the rest of Nick's top-secret documents. What I found had done quite a bit to clear up my confusion, but absolutely nothing to still my worry. Digging into the envelope with some apprehension, I had discovered yet another Arabic detective report, even thicker than the first. But this time it was not about me and my family; it was about me and Katherine Kent.

There were several grainy photos showing the two of us in her Oxford office, looking incredibly suspicious although the subject of our conversation was almost certainly some Greek historian who had been dead for two thousand years. But there were other photos of Katherine, far less innocuous. One had her in front of a punching bag, sweating and grimacing, boxing gloves on, and another was of her in a taxi, wearing a hat and a pair of large sunglasses that had "covert operation" written all over them. But the series of photos that nearly knocked the in-flight pretzels out of me showed her and someone else exchanging a small package at a crowded train station.

That someone was, without a doubt, my blond nemesis.

I am not sure how long I sat there, leafing back and forth through the photos, trying to come to terms with the truth. Here, surely, was the explanation for Katherine's interest in my movements: She was connected to the people responsible for the attack in the labyrinth and the heist on the harbor in Nafplio. Did this mean she was an Amazon? I had never noticed a jackal bracelet on her wrist, and none showed in the photos.

In a hideous flash of clarity, I saw our entire relationship unraveling before me, all the way to our first meeting five years earlier. Much to my flattered amazement, this celebrated Oxford professor had approached me at a student symposium in London and expressed interest in my future plans. "If you decide to pursue an academic career," she had said, with the bluntness so characteristic to her, "I would be happy to be your thesis adviser. Here." She had graciously scribbled a telephone number at the top of my lecture notes, and I had called her within a week.

It had been such a magical opening, such a welcome gift. . . . Even if Katherine's gesture had been dictated by outside forces, I refused to think of it in a purely negative light. She had helped me, and we had enjoyed some fine times together; I flattered myself that our relationship had been gratifying for her, too. But then something had happened. I flew away with Mr. Ludwig against Katherine's will, left her a message from Algeria, and now her number—the very number she had given me that day in London—was disconnected.

Not until I embarked upon the final document in Nick's envelope did I begin to grasp the complex wickedness of what was going on. The stapled papers were a compilation of newspaper articles, typewritten text, and grisly police photos showing molested corpses, confiscated weapons, and video equipment, as well as a smashed-up car at the bottom of a ravine. Only well into the first article did I come across a name I recognized: Alexander Reznik, known in snuff-film circles as "the Bone Saw." Evidently, I was looking at the depraved death trail of Reznik's beloved son, who had managed to squirm out of several murder trials thanks to his father's political connections.

I scrutinized the pages for a while, nauseated by Alex Reznik's suspected crimes, some of which involved mind-bogglingly bestial acts of cannibalism. In one memorable passage he was quoted as saying, "It's not a crime when *they* come to *you* and agree to be eaten."

Surfacing from the bottomless pit of real-life monsters at last, my eyes settled on a newspaper tidbit announcing that Grigor Reznik had put a million-dollar bounty on the "Amazon bitches" who had killed his son. He was quoted as saying, "I have it on tape, God help me. They should know I won't rest until I have them impaled."

The gruesome report—combined with the discovery that Reznik, too, was hunting Amazons with murder in mind—had made me so shivery with dread I had asked the flight attendant for a blanket. Neither Reznik nor al-Aqrab, it seemed, was looking for the Amazon gold after all; the pursuit in which I and the *Historia Amazonum* had become embroiled was much deadlier than a treasure hunt.

I WAS STILL FREEZING by the time I checked in to my modern but soothingly comfortable room at the Idingshof Hotel in Bramsche—the town closest to the Kalkriese Museum. Peeking through the drawn curtains,

I counted eleven cars in the parking lot below my window, and while I stood there, another pulled in. It didn't park—just stopped and idled for a while before slowly backing out again. In the twilight I could vaguely make out a man behind the steering wheel, and the way he kept looking up and holding a hand to his ear suggested he was on the phone.

Pulling back, I felt my pulse quicken. Could it be one of al-Aqrab's detectives? Or one of Reznik's security guards? Surely, even those kinds of people could not have found me so quickly. Furthermore, as far as Reznik was concerned, could I not be fairly certain that James had worked hard to smooth out everything before returning to Oxford? Even if he was still upset with me, surely he would not allow Reznik to believe I was in cahoots with Nick. Or would he? I was still not sure.

Once the car drove away, I paced the hotel room back and forth a few times, trying to calm myself. Of course the car's driver had not been looking for me. It was just my imagination turning every shadow into a fiend. In fact this, I thought with another shiver, must be what it was like having paranoia. All I needed now was to let the jackal convince me I was actually an Amazon in disguise, and I would truly have found Granny . . . by becoming her.

I looked at the time. My original plan had been to go to the Kalkriese Museum right away, but it was already five o'clock. Tomorrow, I decided, I would drive over there first thing and have the whole day to find and interrogate the woman Mr. Telemakhos wanted me to meet.

After making sure my door was securely locked, I ordered an early room service dinner and sat down, at last, with the *Historia Amazonum*. I told myself it was a big moment; three weeks ago I could have imagined no greater triumph than to hold this ancient manuscript in my hands. Under the circumstances, however, I just might have been tempted to exchange it for one of Nick's handguns.

The washed-out writing on the brittle title page announced that the *Historia* was dedicated to a friend and fellow exile, the Roman poet Ovid, which suggested it had been written in or near Tomi on the Romanian Black Sea coast. The remoteness of its place of origin might well explain why the text had never entered the official corpus of Latin literature, but had been passed down privately until it was transcribed into its present form sometime—I guessed—in the early eighteenth century.

The narrative—a festive cocktail of hearsay and pseudoscientific speculation—set out by relating an array of theories about the rise and fall of the Amazon nation. Most were familiar to me, but a few were not, and I was grateful to escape my anxiety-ridden present, if only for a time, on the southeastern shores of the Black Sea.

"The people of this region relate the following story," I muttered to myself, translating a particularly interesting passage out loud, "which they all hold to be true. They claim that after the Amazons had suffered their devastating defeat at the hands of mighty Hercules, the band of humiliated women fell into a terrible disagreement, as women are wont to do." I rolled my eyes and took another bite of my room service Wiener schnitzel before returning to the text. "Anyway . . . in my stuffy old Roman understanding, this was the time when the young Amazon nation first split apart. The most violent half, they say, fled into the Black Sea and founded the illustrious city of Themiscyra, while the rest, weary of destruction after their tragic losses in the Trojan War, ventured into the great woods of the north and fell into utter obscurity."

I sat back in the armchair to digest this unexpected twist to the familiar legend. The part about the Amazons splitting into two groups was completely new to me, and I wondered why no other author had ever mentioned it before. It must, I concluded, be either because it was bollocks, or because no ancient writer but P. Exulatus had cared to record the oral tradition of the region.

Only later that night, after I had brushed my teeth and crawled into bed, did the *Historia* finally get around to the subject I had been keeping an eye out for from page one: the Amazon Hoard.

"As for the famous Amazon treasure," I read, by now accustomed to the pompous rhetorical style of the text, "a few well-informed men hold the opinion that it was never taken to Themiscyra, and that only fools continue to look for it in this violent region. They claim the Amazon queen with whom King Priam entrusted Troy's most precious objects was among those who fled into the black woods of the north. For this reason it is generally believed the treasure was long since lost, because these Amazons, by removing themselves from the map of the world, removed themselves from existence altogether. Nor have any of our brave Roman legions garrisoned in Sarmatia or Germania Magna ever reported seeing treasures there other than those primitive"—I paused to ponder the appropriate translation—"*knickknacks* the barbarians hold so dear, and which no army commander with a sense of shame would ever carry back to Rome in triumph."

The text continued with more sassy observations about the barbarians of the north, but the writing was so hard to make out in the light of my bedside lamp that I decided to put it aside for tomorrow.

As I lay down, my thoughts wandered off in search of Nick. I tried to imagine his fury upon discovering that I had run away with the *Historia* and his secret envelope . . . but couldn't. Too agitated to sleep, I reached into the bedside drawer and took out the document that had shocked me so in his room that morning and scrutinized—yet again—the cover letter ordering the killing of Amazons. Was it possible I had been too rash in assuming it was a message from al-Aqrab to Nick? Now that I knew of Reznik's million-dollar bounty it made more sense if *he,* and not al-Aqrab, was the author.

Reluctant to draw any conclusions I put away the letter and lay down once more. It was time, I decided, to question everything I thought I knew. P. Exulatus spoke of Amazons moving north . . . and why not? Was it not true that European folktales occasionally spoke of maidens devoted to the art of war? Hitherto I had scoffed at figures such as the medieval Amazons living along the Danube River and their female general, Sharka, who allegedly beheaded hundreds of men in a single battle and raped several dozen male prisoners after hours . . . before killing them, too.

Perhaps the Amazons really *had* lived on, in the wild woods of central and northern Europe, but with new appellations. Might the Valkyries and shield-maidens of Norse mythology be the proud descendants of ancient Amazons? This enticing idea kept me awake for a while, and at least it got my mind off Nick.

THE KALKRIESE MUSEUM WAS set in the middle of farmland and forest, with tall fir trees bearing down on it from all sides. As I pulled into the deserted gravel parking lot I had an uncanny feeling the trees were watching me, wondering who I was and why I had come so far to disturb their peace.

It had been raining all night, and although the sun was doing its best to find a crack in the clouds, the morning mists were still lying heavily over the landscape, filling up every dip in the dormant fields and clinging to every cluster of coniferous trees.

Half-fearing the museum and its historic park had closed down for the winter, I left the car in the parking lot and continued on foot up a slippery, muddy path to the welcome center. Only then, as I approached the building, did I see the bicycle leaning against the wall and notice there were lights on inside. Encouraged by this humble evidence of human life I opened the door and was rewarded with a warm waft of coffee.

Seeing I was the first visitor of the day—and possibly the only one—a young archaeologist by the name of Felix was kind enough to pour me a cup and tell me this and that about the place. I was tempted to ask him about Dr. Jäger right away, but felt it would be unwise to disclose the reason for my visit before I had gathered a little more information.

As I strolled outside through the soggy archaeological site, I was once again aware of the fir trees creaking overhead and whispering behind my back. Obviously, the terrain had changed considerably over the past two thousand years, but it was hard to shake a feeling that I was walking—as the Roman Army had done before me—on treacherous ground.

I had often come across the Battle of Teutoburger Wald in Roman history books, but had never thought I would visit the site in person, nor that the trail of Granny's jackal would lead me to such haunted hinterland.

According to history, in the year A.D. 9 three Roman legions plus auxiliary forces—altogether as many as twenty thousand soldiers—had perished in the woods of northern Germania, and the Roman Empire had never successfully expanded beyond this point. Latin historians referred to the event as "the Varus disaster," implicitly blaming the Roman commander Varus for the shocking annihilation of his entire army.

What I had never fully appreciated was that the battle had been a brilliantly executed ambush by local tribesmen, in which the Roman legions had been tricked into terrain that rendered their superior weapons useless and made battle formations impossible. Marching along a narrow forest path, the army had been stretched to a point where there was no strength in numbers, and the soldiers—no doubt unnerved by the immensity of the German wilderness—must have felt unusually small and exposed even before the attack began.

Not only had the Roman legionnaires found themselves wedged between a treacherous swamp and a densely forested ridge, they were also pummeled by a rainstorm and blinded by fog. Waterlogged and disoriented, they became easy targets for the tribesmen, who attacked them from the woods above in order to drive them into the great bog below.

After touring the park, I finally entered the museum—an oblong rust-colored building with a tall tower at one end. I could have spent all day there, but was so anxious to find the Amazon bracelet and see what the local archaeologists had to say about it that I hurried through the exhibition in twenty minutes. After that, I spent another twenty minutes going through it again the other way, only to confirm my depressing conclusion.

The bracelet wasn't there.

Walking back through the archaeological site, I noticed the weather had taken a sinister turn. The sky was dark as lead, and the trees were swaying violently in the rising wind. In my agitated state, I almost got the impression they had sensed the presence of someone more threatening than me, and that they were now—in their ghostly, wordless way—trying to warn me.

Racing the first raindrops through the door of the welcome center, I was happy to see that Felix was still on duty, and still not too busy to chat. "This may sound a little strange," I said, pulling up my sleeve discreetly, "but someone told me you had a bracelet just like this on display in the museum."

"Really?" Felix studied my jackal without recognition. "I'm sure I have never seen anything like that before. Interesting."

"I understand there is a woman here"—I looked at him hopefully—"by the name of Dr. Jäger."

Felix brightened. "Kyme? She used to work here. She still comes in sometimes." Mumbling to himself, he checked a laminated list of telephone numbers lying by the cash register. "Jäger . . . Jäger."

A quick phone call later, all in German, Felix put down the receiver and beamed at me. "She has invited you for coffee this afternoon at three o'clock, and she looks forward to telling you all about the bracelet."

AFTER LEAVING THE MUSEUM I passed a few rainy hours in downtown Bramsche, shopping for clothes and other essentials. When I eventually returned to the hotel I made a point of entering through a side door, just in case someone was keeping an eye on the comings and goings of guests.

My room had been cleaned in my absence, and I quickly checked that my little all was where I had left it. Granny's notebook and the *Historia Amazonum* I now carried around everywhere I went, of course, but the envelope I had stolen from Nick I had left in a bedside drawer, and yes, it was still there. Only . . . I was sure I had put a tourist brochure on top of it, in order to conceal it a bit. The brochure was still there, but now it was lying underneath the envelope.

Jittery with nerves, I quickly went through the documents but found nothing missing. Was it possible, I thought, that the maid had moved things around? Or did I misremember how I had left the envelope?

Walking into the bathroom, I made sure everything was still there, and apart from the fact that the maid had turned my toothpaste upside down in the glass, I saw nothing to suggest a break-in.

Angry with myself for being so fanciful, I decided not to do anything too hasty. My appointment with Dr. Jäger was only an hour away; if I still felt uncertain about the room when I came back, I could always move out then.

As I drove my rental car away from the hotel, I kept checking the rearview mirror to see if anyone was following. But in the grime and gloom of this rainy November afternoon, all the vehicles seemed to blend together, and the Mercedes that worried me one moment was gone the next.

Dr. Jäger lived more or less across the road from the archaeological site I had visited that morning. Apparently, she had spent her entire life in the same small house in the woods, and it was a great and unusual honor to be invited inside. "Look out for a long driveway belonging to an abandoned farm," Felix had explained. "Continue all the way to the end and park there. That is where the path begins. I've never seen it, but that's what she told me."

I parked my car as instructed and continued on foot into the forest beyond. As I walked up the steep dirt path, squinting against the spitting rain and striding over the little rivulets of water winding down through the uneven gravel, it occurred to me that this forested ridge must have been a key part of the woodlands from where the German tribesmen had launched their attack on the Roman legionnaires trapped on the edge of the great bog below.

Some historical sources held that a few years after their disastrous defeat the Romans had sent yet another army to the area to recover the sacred eagle standards of the lost legions and, if possible, patch together a realistic account of what had actually happened. According to the Roman historian Tacitus, even the hardened soldiers of the recovery party were horrified by what they found, for the forest surrounding the old battlefield had been turned into a gruesome monument for death and destruction. Heaps of human bones lay unburied, and severed skulls had been nailed to trees, perhaps as part of religious rituals, or perhaps as a warning to future invaders.

Walking through the forest now, still unable to shake a feeling of being watched, I could easily sympathize with the apprehension the Roman soldiers must have felt so long ago. Down by the museum the fir trees had seemed dense and looming, but up here the woods were mature and majestic—intimidating in quite a different way. Colossal centuries-old pines stood just meters apart, shrouded in fog; despite the vicious weather there was a silent solemnity about them that made me feel they had witnessed much violence in their time and had long since learned to keep their silence. Even at three in the afternoon the place had an otherworldly feel to it that was even more chilling than the rain.

When I finally found Dr. Jäger's house—a modest fieldstone cottage set in a small clearing and surrounded by a thicket of tall weeds—it was a quarter past three. What was supposed to have been a five-minute walk through the forest had taken me more than twenty minutes, and before knocking on the rough-hewn wooden door, I resolved to leave well before sunset, to avoid having to make my way back to the car in complete darkness.

"Welcome, welcome!" A petite elderly woman greeted me with smiling enthusiasm before the door was even fully open. "Come in! I am making pfefferkuchen!" Wiping her hands on her brown corduroy trousers, she closed the door behind me and ran back to the kitchen as if something was on fire. "Keep your shoes on. The floor is cold."

Until that moment I had been mindful of Mr. Telemakhos's assertion that the woman I was about to meet "knew more than she let on." As a consequence, I had half-imagined Dr. Jäger to be a closet Amazon and had even managed to worry myself with visions of a six-foot battle-ax determined to stop me at last. Now I felt like laughing at my own fears. Although trim and seemingly energetic, Dr. Jäger did not strike me as someone who would round up the likes of Alex Reznik in her spare time.

After hanging my soaking jacket on a coatrack made out of deer antlers, I stepped into the living room and looked around. It really was a very old house, with uneven stone walls and a sagging whitewashed ceiling held up by wooden beams. Every available surface was dominated by some part of an animal; the walls were covered in hunting trophies—heads of stags, wild boars, and even bears were staring at me with alert glass eyes—and every chair was lined with skins and pelts. One of the armchairs facing the open fireplace had a deep-brown bearskin draped over it, with the paws and claws still attached.

"Who's the hunter?" I asked, when Dr. Jäger returned with a coffee tray.

She laughed delightedly and put down the tray on the stone edge of the fireplace. "Hunting runs in the family. At least, it used to. There aren't bears here anymore." She straightened and looked up at the wall. "Some of those are ancient. I should probably throw them out. But"—she shrugged and poured the coffee—"they keep me company."

Grateful for the open fire, I followed her example and sat down in one of the armchairs facing the burning logs, my feet up on the brick.

"Try one of my pfefferkuchen," insisted Dr. Jäger, offering me a bowl with cookies. "They are a traditional Christmas treat, and I am baking them now so they can ripen to perfection before the holidays." She smiled conspiratorially, a pair of girlish dimples emerging. "To tell you the truth, I bake them all year round. But don't say that to anyone."

We talked a bit more about the pepper cookies before my hostess finally clasped her hands and said, "So, you have come to Kalkriese because of the bracelet. Tell me, where did you hear about it?"

I wrestled briefly with the truth, which would have involved mentioning Mr. Telemakhos, who—by his own admission—was persona non grata in the German museum world . . . and ended up merely saying, "I can't remember. Apparently, two similar bracelets were found in Turkey. And as it happens, I have one, too." I showed her the jackal on my wrist.

Dr. Jäger leaned closer, clearly intrigued. "That looks like bronze. How interesting. The bracelet we had here was made of iron." Seeing my surprise, she nodded cryptically and sat back in the chair, draping a shawl over her legs. "It was worn by a woman who fell into the great bog two thousand years ago. When we found her at the site, we suspected she had fought in the Battle of Teutoburger Wald, but no one believed us. Women didn't take part in the war, my fellow scholars said. Women are victims, not warriors. But it was clear to me her skull had been broken by a sharp blade. Also, her compressed spine and bent tailbone showed signs of a life on horseback, and seven arrowheads were clustered beneath her lower back"—Dr. Jäger demonstrated with her hands—"which to me suggested she had been carrying a quiver with arrows. Furthermore, she had stress fractures on her bones, which had healed up while she was still alive—fractures from fighting and strenuous physical training. Of course, everyone agreed with us about everything right until the moment we told them it was not a man, but a woman. Archaeologists always assume—or at least, they used to assume—that skeletons found with weapons were male. It would never even occur to them to ask the question, and admittedly, sometimes it can be hard to tell the difference."

"Well, how do you know it *was* a woman?" I asked.

Dr. Jäger leaned forward to stir the fire with a long poker. "Her pelvis. She had clear signs of what we call 'diastasis symphysis pubis.' She must have been in a lot of pain. It was a unique find. The only problem was, she disappeared. We sent her off to a forensic lab for further analysis, but she never arrived. It was quite a scandal at the time. All we had left was the bracelet. And two weeks after we put it on display at the museum, that disappeared, too."

Getting up, Dr. Jäger went over to a brass cauldron in the corner to fetch more wood for the fire. "So, you see," she continued, stretching to place the logs where she wanted them, "I know almost as little about it as you do. That is why"—she smiled an apology at me—"I was hoping you could tell me more."

We sat for a while in silence, listening to the sap popping in the fresh logs. Then I said, "All I know is that some people claim to have seen quite a few of these bracelets—the bronze variety—scattered all over the ancient world. In fact, I have even heard a theory that they were worn by"—I cleared my throat and tried to sound casual—"the ancient Amazons."

I suppose I could not blame Dr. Jäger for laughing out loud. "I am sorry," she said, "but that is too wonderful! Now I understand. You have been talking to that old *spinner* in Greece, Yanni Telemakhos."

A little embarrassed by her ability to see right through me, I scrambled to come up with an explanation, only to have it waved aside. "Don't worry," she said, still chuckling. "I know it is not only crazy people who dream about the Amazons, but also people who love mystery and adventure." She studied my face with a knowing smile. "Are you one of those people, Diana?"

Perhaps it was the cozy fire, or perhaps it was her kindness . . . whatever the reason, I suddenly felt an overwhelming urge to tell Dr. Jäger everything. Right from the disappearance of my grandmother eighteen years earlier to my arrival in Germany the day before. Even if she was not an Amazon, and even if she did not know more than she let on, I still had a feeling it would be worthwhile to tell her about my tribulations and discoveries.

After talking nonstop for at least an hour, I finally sat back and shook my head. "Sorry to go on like this——"

"No, no, no," said my hostess, her face full of sympathy. "You have been through a lot. Made important discoveries. And now you are wondering whether your grandmother was right after all. Whether she really was an Amazon." Ignoring my halfhearted protests, Dr. Jäger went on, staring off into the fire, "You are thinking to yourself, 'If I follow the Amazon trail to the end, will I find her again?' It is only natural that you are thinking like that, Diana, because you loved her very much. But you know, it can be dangerous to live your life waiting for a summons from another world. You begin to see things, hear things . . . make something out of nothing." She reached out absentmindedly to take another pepper cookie, only to find the bowl empty. "Tell me, this notebook of hers . . . does it mention any names? Places? Anything that could explain why all these different people seem to be so interested in it?"

"That's the thing," I said. "I'm not even sure they *are* interested in it, or why they would be. There's no message in it—no treasure map, if you will. It's clear that Reznik is looking for revenge. What al-Aqrab wants with the Amazons I honestly don't know, but I am quite sure he

has been using me to try and find them. As for the Amazons"—
I glanced at my hostess, suspecting she still didn't believe these mythical women were walking among us—"they are doing everything they
can to stop me."

Dr. Jäger broke into a smile. "But here you are."

All around me, the animals were watching intently from their
perch on the walls, as if wondering what I would do next. "Yes," I said,
as much to them as to my hostess. "But this is the end of the trail; it
runs right into that bog. The *Historia Amazonum* says a small group of
Amazons went north, and maybe it's true. Maybe they lived on here in
Germany for another thousand years, forged new bracelets out of iron,
and fought against the Romans the way they had fought against the
Greeks. But how will we ever know?"

Dr. Jäger reached over and gave my hand a squeeze. "Return to
Oxford and try to forget all these terrible things. I am glad you came
today. You have done more than any grandmother could hope for. With
this journey, I am confident you have finally given her peace, just as
you, yourself, will now be at peace. Go home, my dear, go home."

The absurdity of her advice left me speechless. It was as if she hadn't
understood what I had told her . . . as if she thought my fear of being
hunted down was completely unfounded. However, it was getting late,
and I didn't feel like reiterating my worries about Reznik and al-Aqrab
to someone who clearly didn't care after all.

Before leaving, I asked Dr. Jäger if I could use her bathroom, and as
I washed my hands I couldn't help peeking into the medicine cabinet.
On the shelves I spied all the usual creams and pills . . . and then a
lineup of phenol, diethyl ether, and morphine . . . plus two mugs full of
surgical instruments.

It was so surreal, I almost started laughing. What on earth did a
sweet, elderly woman need all this doctor's equipment for? Wounded
pets? Hunting accidents? Illegitimate medical procedures? My laughing
impulse quickly turned to unease. Diethyl ether was an old-fashioned
anesthetic, used to induce unconsciousness. But on whom? Nosy guests?
I left the bathroom with my pulse pounding in my ears.

In my hurry to return to the living room I mistook the doors in the tiny corridor and accidentally entered a crepuscular cubbyhole of an office. A single lamp stood precariously on the edge of a small desk covered in sliding stacks of paper, its green glass shade casting an eerie, supernatural shimmer upon the jam-packed bookcases lining the walls.

But the most unsettling thing about the room was not the ghostly light, or the fact that there were no windows—no, it was the look of the bookshelves. For there were no books on them, just brochures. Completely identical white brochures piled on top of one another as densely as possible . . . some even spilling out of open cardboard boxes on the floor.

I couldn't help it. I had to take a closer look.

Stepping over to an open box, I bent down to examine the front cover of the brochure lying on top. It was an auction catalog with a Greek vase on the cover, fresh from the printer. The layout was beyond boring, and yet it stirred a memory. Had I not, quite recently, spotted precisely the same sort of catalog on Katherine Kent's desk? The only reason why I remembered it so well was that she had whisked it into a drawer with inexplicable urgency.

In a flash I was back in Mr. Telemakhos's basement, hearing him saying, with spirited defiance, "Some say they never use telephones or email when they communicate with one another . . . that they use a medium that can't be traced—maybe a printed pamphlet of sorts."

Unable to resist, I picked up the catalog and started leafing through it, hurriedly scanning the pages for Amazon writing. But all I found were narrow columns with numbered entries and the occasional black-and-white photographs of antique vases, paintings, and other objects for sale. Except . . .

Stepping closer to the desk lamp, I scrutinized the picture of an Oriental rug, looking for any sign of writing or code. Was it my imagination, or had an almost microscopic paragraph written in Granny's Amazon alphabet been transposed onto the photograph, to blend in perfectly with the pattern of the rug? A paragraph so itsy-bitsy you would need a magnifying glass to read it?

In my excitement, I nearly forgot that I was trespassing. Not until I heard a floorboard creaking did I quickly put down the catalog and spin around to leave the room.

And found Dr. Jäger standing right behind me, her kind face distorted with fury and suspicion.

"I'm so sorry!" I exclaimed. "I have a dreadful sense of direction. But what a marvelous collection of journals." I forced out what I hoped was a disarming smile. "German archaeology, I presume. Are you an editor?"

"Yes," she said eventually, her features softening a bit. "I am the editor in chief. A thankless job. But someone has to do it." Putting a gentle hand on my elbow, she escorted me back into the living room. "Would you like another cup of coffee? Or tea perhaps?"

"It's getting late. I really ought to——"

"I insist!" She practically pushed me back into the chair I had sat in before. "It is a cold evening out; you need something warm." With a smile that was almost as friendly as before, Dr. Jäger disappeared into the kitchen, and I heard her putting on a kettle.

Looking down, I saw my ritzy new handbag sitting on the floor right beside the chair. It was precisely where I had left it, but in my heightened state of anxiety it now struck me as being suspiciously erect. Had my hostess done a quick search through its contents, I wondered, and made sure to puff it up again afterward?

Checking the bag with trembling fingers I confirmed that everything was still there: Granny's notebook, the *Historia Amazonum,* and all my remaining money, wound with a tight rubber band.

I barely knew what to do. Part of me wanted desperately to get up and leave, but as always, my curiosity was so great it temporarily drowned out my better sense. Had I accidentally laid eyes on one of the secret Amazon pamphlets Mr. Telemakhos had talked about?

A sound from the kitchen pulled me back to the moment. Or perhaps I should say it was the sudden absence of noise that alerted me to a furtive broken mumble betraying a secret phone conversation.

This time I didn't even think about it; my body rose from the chair all by itself. Swarmed by worrisome images—Dr. Jäger's incensed expression, the surgical equipment, the hundreds if not thousands of auction catalogs—I fled across the floor as silently as I could, my panic increasing with every step. My hostess was clearly determined to keep me in her house for a while longer . . . but why? And why the secret phone call? Whatever lay behind her odd behavior, it boded no good for me, I was sure of it.

Grabbing my wet jacket on the way, I burst outside without even pausing to close the door behind me. And then I ran, as fast as I could, back down the path toward my car.

By now the forest was almost completely dark and even foggier than it had been at the time of my arrival, and when I finally heard Dr. Jäger yelling after me from the house, I knew she could not possibly see me anymore. "Diana!" she cried, her voice shrill with anger. "Come back here! I command you!"

But of course I kept running. Even though I could barely see five feet ahead, I knew all I had to do was follow the path and keep going downhill. And so I continued down, down, down through the misty darkness, splashing right through mud and freezing puddles while trying to steer clear of low-hanging branches.

I was so sure I remembered the way that it came as a shock to me when the path suddenly split into two. Stumped, I ran back and forth a few times, trying to determine which of the two new paths was the least wrong one. They both appeared to be going upward, back into the forest, albeit in two completely different directions. All I could see of their further course was a gauzy gray film covering pitch-black nothing, and neither felt right to me.

It was then, as I stood there uncertainly, I heard a sound that sent a gust of dread through my entire body. It was a long howl followed by barking—perhaps not quite the sound a wolf would make, but close enough. And in the silence following the last bark I heard something else—a familiar sound that, under the circumstances, was extremely unsettling.

It was the heavy, rhythmical thudding of galloping horses.

CHAPTER THIRTY-SIX

While the Romans were struggling against the elements, the barbarians suddenly surrounded them on all sides at once, stealing through the densest thickets, as they were familiar with the paths.
—CASSIUS DIO, *Roman History*

THE FOREST WAS FULL OF DEMONS: HOWLING, HISSING, INVISIBLE DE-mons with the legs of horses and a frightening ability to weave in and out of the fabric of reality. It sounded as if now they were here, then over there . . . and for a few utterly confusing minutes, nowhere at all.

But in that brief quiet, I picked up deep human voices tangled with confusion, bouncing back and forth between the trees in a language I could not just then make out—a language that seemed to dissolve in the fog and reach me only in fragments. Then came gunshots, ten at least, in rapid succession . . . followed by the most harrowing scream I had ever heard.

Perhaps because I was so terrified, it took a while for the sounds to make sense. If I were to trust my ears, there were men, dogs, horses, and the chilling death cries of a wild beast I could not name. The only logical explanation, I decided, as I stood there hiding behind a massive tree trunk just off the path, was that it was hunting season, and that all the demonic screeching and hissing were the natural sounds of fleeing prey.

Desperate to get out of the forest before I was overrun by fright-ened animals, or even worse, by their pursuers, I dived into the nearest thicket and began clawing my way downward through the under-growth, in what I hoped was the direction of my car. Perhaps it would have been more logical to head the other way, in order to make myself known to the hunters and maybe even ask for directions, but something about these men's ferocity—their growling voices and violent manner of riding—told me I was better off if they didn't realize I was there.

Crawling through the brambles, I was soon drenched by the rain-soaked foliage. My teeth chattering with cold, I found myself pleading with the forest to forgive my intrusion and let me go . . . but it kept gripping me with clingy grasses and vicious thorns, doing its best to prevent my escape.

Because the thicket was so dense and I was preoccupied with avoiding the vengeful brambles, I did not even register the approaching horses until I heard a loud snort right behind me.

The sound so unnerved me I instinctively dropped to the ground, forcing myself not to move. And then came the voices, not the deep male voices I had heard before, but rather a crisp exchange in German between two women.

"Where is she?" said one.

"I thought I saw her," replied the other, "but now I'm not sure."

There was another snort, a sneered sentence I didn't understand . . . and the women were off again, galloping back into the forest, urging on their horses with guttural commands.

So shaken I could barely coordinate my limbs, I scrambled on all fours as quickly as I could, then got to my feet briefly, in order to get away faster . . . only to step right into nothing and tumble down a slope several meters before sliding headlong into shrubbery sprouting from a mud puddle.

Gasping with shock, I extracted myself from the slimy bush and wiped the mud from my face. Amazingly, my new handbag still hung across my shoulders, and although it was as soaked as I, at least it was there.

Huddled on my knees, I tried to make out my surroundings. Once my eyes became sufficiently accustomed to the dark I saw a faint light ahead. It turned out to be the illuminated sign marking the entrance to the museum parking lot across the highway. I had quite literally fallen out of the woods and into a fallow field, no more than a few hundred meters from the driveway of the abandoned farm.

By the time I finally got my rental car started, heater going full blast, I was so weak from cold and exhaustion I could barely sit up straight. Backing out the gravel driveway, it took all my focus to steer the vehicle around another car that had been parked there sometime since my arrival.

A dark blue Mercedes. The same Mercedes I had noticed before in downtown Bramsche, when I had left the hotel earlier that afternoon. Now I saw that it had Geneva plates.

Within a few heartbeats my fury had outrun my fear. Whoever these people were, they would follow me no more. Almost intoxicated with anger, I pulled over and attacked the first-aid kit in the backseat, looking for something useful. There were no knives, of course, and nothing else that might help me slash the tires. But there were bandages and adhesive Band-Aids . . . enough to make two tight balls that fitted perfectly in the Mercedes's tailpipes.

"If it's an old car, don't waste your time," had been Granny's advice when she told me how to do it. "It only works if there's no leak in the system."

When I drove away at last, it was all I could do to bend my cold fingers around the gearshift and press my numb toes against the gas pedal. But a sense of defiant accomplishment soon began to warm me from the inside out. Something evil had happened in that forest, but *I* had survived. There had been men and women with horses and guns, but none of them had been able to catch me. And now I had won myself a little extra time—at least I hoped so.

BACK AT THE HOTEL, I stepped right into a hot shower with all my clothes on. Peeling off the muddy layers one by one, I thought through my options. It didn't take long, since there was only one thing to do: leave immediately.

If there had been a small part of me dreaming of a joyful reunion

with Granny at the end of all my tribulations, or at least a friendly encounter with people who had known her, the events of this afternoon
had thoroughly cured me. Assuming Dr. Jäger had mobilized the
women hunting me in the forest, then I had to conclude these present-
day Amazons—for it was hard to call them anything else—were as
threatening to me as Reznik.

Wrapped in a towel, I tore around the room for a few minutes,
gathering up my things. There was no time to check whether Granny's
notebook or the *Historia Amazonum* had survived the mudslide
unscathed—what I needed was to find my map of Germany. Where the
hell was it?

Three quick knocks interrupted my frantic search.

Petrified, I stared at the door, half-expecting it to burst open. But
instead, I saw something sliding in underneath and realized it was a
piece of paper.

Inching closer, I stretched to read the message scribbled on it:
"You're in danger. I can help. Nick."

A quick glance through the peephole confirmed that it really was
him outside my door, unshaven and frowning with impatience.

For a few breathless seconds, my mind was awash with indecision.
I had stolen a top-secret envelope from this man, together with a priceless manuscript, and I knew I should be afraid of him—knew he must
be livid. And yet the sight of him set off a completely unexpected sense
of relief and, dastardly hiding behind the relief, an overwhelming, incandescent joy that made it impossible for me to dismiss him.

My heart beating wildly from the suddenness of it all, I reached out
and opened the door. Only then, as he entered my room, did it occur
to me I was wearing nothing but a towel and that it might be wise of me
to find some means of self-defense, just in case.

Nick scanned the room suspiciously before turning to me. His
eyes darkened as he took in my sparsely wrapped form and, I am
sure, the emotions still at odds in my face. Then, as if realizing I was
waiting for him to speak, he said, somewhat stupidly, "I am here to save
you."

"Actually——" I closed the door behind him. "You're slowing me down."

I am not sure who started it. Nick certainly didn't mean to, nor did I . . . but suddenly we were in each other's arms, closing the torturous, soul-destroying gap between Istanbul and Bramsche.

It was frightening how quickly everything else—even all my doubts and deceptions—faded away to nothing as soon as his mouth was against mine. Groaning, it seemed, at his own weakness, Nick kissed me with frenetic abandon, as if I were the only other human being in a world of brutes and he had spent his whole life searching for me.

"Welcome to Germany," I whispered after a while, in a vain attempt at catching my breath. Even through his sweater, I could feel the warmth and energy radiating from his body, and the thought of letting go was extremely unappealing. "Feel free to stay, but I'm afraid I have to leave."

"Not so fast, Goddess," muttered Nick against my ear. "This time we leave together." But the way he held me trapped between himself and the wall suggested he was in no hurry to make tracks.

"You're a bad man." I ran my hands through his hair, still unable to fathom it was truly him—that he had come this far to get me back. "I should have left hours ago . . . and never let you find me."

"Oh, I would have found you anywhere."

I tried to look him in the eye. "What does al-Aqrab want from me?"

Nick leaned in to kiss me again. "He doesn't know I'm here."

I gasped when I felt his hand underneath the towel, indulging in my nakedness. It was shocking to discover that while there was still a distinct jackal's voice in my head warning me to stay in control and demand an explanation, there was also a rogue, fatalistic part of me that wanted nothing more than to let Nick right in, all seventeen versions of him. "Aren't you afraid," I whispered, "of being skewered by my Amazon sisters?"

"Yes." He began kissing my naked shoulder, all the way to the angle of my neck, drawing from me an involuntary accompaniment of treacherous little sighs. "But you're worth it."

Just then, the room phone rang.

"Damn!" I pushed him away. "See who's outside."

While Nick looked out through the closed curtains, I picked up the receiver with a brisk "Hello?"

There was no response, and the line went dead.

"What do you see?" I asked Nick. "A blue Mercedes?"

"Not sure," he replied, peeking out still. "A dark Audi just pulled in."

"How about this," I said, as I raced around the room, throwing on random pieces of clothing. Much as it pained me to even contemplate, I thought of one possible strategy of retreat. "What about we leave the *Historia Amazonum* right here, on the bed?"

Nick shook his head and came over to help me gather up my things. "Reznik doesn't give a shit about the manuscript. That was just bait to catch the Amazons who killed his son. Now he thinks you're one of them."

"How on earth," I yelled from the bathroom, quickly scraping together my newly purchased—and rather pricey—toiletries, "can he think I'm an Amazon?"

"Because Reznik is a paranoid son of a bitch," Nick yelled back, "who takes X-rays of his guests without their knowledge. He is looking for hidden weapons, of course, but jackal bracelets happen to show up, too."

Moments later we were rushing down the quiet hallway, headed for the emergency exit. But just as Nick reached out for the white metal door, it was torn open from the other side, and two women emerged.

Since they were dressed in jogging suits and had towels over their shoulders, my first thought was that they were simply hotel guests returning from the exercise room. But no sooner had I nodded a friendly greeting than one of them punched Nick right in the stomach and brought his face down hard on her knee.

I was so shocked at this explosion of brutality, it took me a moment to comprehend what was happening. Despite a bleeding nose, Nick fought back admirably, dealing his attackers a few solid blows they were clearly not expecting . . . but then a third woman appeared.

I had just managed to lift a heavy painting from the wall with the intent of using it as a weapon, when I caught sight of other people approaching from the far end of the corridor.

Only then did it occur to me to yell for help, but it was already too late. The two men coming toward us were reaching into their jackets, and I could see in their faces we were precisely what they were after.

Crying out in fear, I managed to alert the three women to the danger, and they immediately dropped Nick and darted down the hallway to intercept the men before bullets started flying.

"Come on!" I urged Nick, pulling at his arm. "This is our chance."

Picking up whatever bags were within reach I scrambled down the emergency staircase ahead of him. Seconds later we erupted through the back door to find ourselves in the hotel garden.

"This way," said Nick, and in the darkness all I could see was his silhouette as he ran in front of me through the dewy grass. Ducking under an electric fence, we continued across a bumpy, sodden field full of silent sheep until reaching a small gravel road and a car parked in the lee of a toolshed.

"No!" I said, when he opened the passenger door for me. "*I* drive. You just focus on your nose."

We didn't exchange another word until we were on the autobahn. I was too busy making sure no one was following, and Nick had put back the seat as far as it would go in an attempt at stopping his nosebleed.

"Is it broken?" I asked eventually.

Nick groaned. "It takes a lot more to break this schnozzle. What the hell happened back there?"

"I've asked myself the same question twice today," I said. "I think we've gotten trapped in crossfire. Some of Reznik's goons from Geneva have been trailing me in a Mercedes, and I'm quite sure those three lovely ladies were Amazons. What do you think?"

Nick made a pained sound that might have been intended as a chuckle. "Well, you did warn me not to piss off your Amazon sisters. Here." Opening the middle console, he took something out and handed it to me. "This is your new passport. We'll have to play dead for a while. Your name is Artemis Panagopoulos. I thought we should be Greek. You can do the talking. I'll just be your doting husband. How about a beach hut on a nice little faraway island, compliments of the boss?"

It was all I could do to focus on the road when really, I wanted to take Nick by the collar and shake him. "I thought you had quit your job! You said al-Aqrab doesn't know where you are—"

"He doesn't. But I'm still working for him." Nick looked at me uncertainly. "If it's any consolation, I almost got fired for stealing the *Historia Amazonum*."

"Really?" I felt my mood improving at this little curveball. "But if al-Aqrab didn't order you to take it . . . then why did you?"

Nick sighed. "Apparently, Reznik had that manuscript stolen from a small archive in Romania. A janitor was framed for the theft."

"But that's not why you took it."

"All right." He put his seat up a bit. "This is what happened: I had strict orders *not* to attend Reznik's party, but I couldn't resist the temptation to see you again. However, before I could make contact with you, I was sidetracked by a woman in a cat suit who stared at me as if she knew me before running off with a friend in a mouse suit—"

"Wait a minute." I tried to recall the hostile cat woman I had encountered in Reznik's bathroom. "I saw them, too. The mouse woman stole my phone in Nafplio. And I bet she was the one who mugged me in the labyrinth."

"I don't think so." Nick moved in his seat and winced with pain. "The person who attacked you in the labyrinth stole your laptop, and your laptop was in Reznik's house well before the party started. I'm pretty sure those two women broke in to steal it *from* him. Now it's on the bottom of the Black Sea, sleeping with the fishes *and* your cellphone. But anyway—and I'm sorry if this bursts your image of me as a hardened criminal—I saw these lovely chicks sneaking into Reznik's little antiques collection during the party. I decided to follow and could hear them going all the way to the top floor. This gave me a chance to check out the library. And there it was, ready for the taking: Diana

Morgan's academic future. I wanted to give it to you that night, as a present, but then things got a little . . . strange."

I glanced at him, softened by his frank confession. "I appreciate the gesture, except now we have a bunch of Reznik's thugs plus some hard-hitting Amazons riding our wake."

Nick made an unhappy grunt. "Okay, I made a mistake. I was sure they had disabled the security cameras together with the alarm system. However, if I hadn't pinched the *Historia,* then your noble boyfriend would never have ratted on me, and Reznik would never have con-tacted my people in Dubai about the theft, *and* I would never have learned about the X-ray that turned you into an Amazon. Show me the Greek tragedy that can rival that one."

We drove for a while in silence. Here, away from the Teutoburger Wald, the night was calm and clear, with stars twinkling around us and a shimmering scythe of moon hovering on the horizon. But the clarity outside did not penetrate to my interior. Layer after layer of confusion continued deep into my consciousness, and it frustrated me that even now, sitting right here next to Nick, I still didn't know what lay behind the Aqrab Foundation's interest in the Amazons. But I knew enough to not ask him while we were going 130. Instead, I said, "How did you find me?"

"Let's see." Nick sounded amused. "You traveled under your own name, rented a car in your own name, and registered at the Idingshof Hotel under your own name." I sensed he was smiling at me. "I'm sorry, Dr. Livingstone, but if you really didn't want me to come, you shouldn't have left a trail as wide as the Nile . . . or should I say the Amazon?" When I didn't respond, he sighed and added, "I called Rebecca. She was more than happy to help. Said Mr. Telemakhos had told you to go to Kalkriese. After that, all I had to do was call around to hotels nearby——"

I felt a twinge of outrage. "Bex trusted you?"

"Why shouldn't she?"

A thousand reasons sprang to mind, but they all looked rather pathetic next to the fact that Nick had defied the mighty al-Aqrab and come all the way to Germany to save my life and have his nose squashed.

It took me the rest of our drive to relate my misadventures in Kalkriese, including my suspicions about the auction catalogs and Dr. Jäger being an Amazon newsletter distributor. "It would make perfect sense, wouldn't it?" I said, as we exited the autobahn at last. "*Of course* the Amazons can't risk someone discovering their secret means of communication—especially not with Reznik's million-dollar bounty on their heads."

I was so absorbed in our conversation I barely noticed the blackness around us until I heard the unmistakable crunching of a dirt road. Nick had given me directions, and I had done as he told me, but . . .

"This is not the Frankfurt Airport," was all I could think of saying as we pulled up in front of a dark cottage.

"No fooling a philologist," said Nick, getting out of the car. "I thought we needed a little peace and quiet."

I heard him unlocking the cottage door with an old-fashioned key.

"Where exactly are we?" I asked, getting out of the driver's seat and trying in vain to make out the landscape around us. It smelled like forest, and the only sounds were the hoots of a distant owl, but I couldn't remember seeing many trees along the dirt road. "The Aqrab safe house in Frankfurt?"

"Anything but," replied Nick, turning on a few lamps inside. "Welcome to *my* Germany. This is the Taunus, not too far from the airport. You can't see it now, but there's a great view of the Main valley from up here." He smiled at me over his shoulder. "I've slept off a lot of jet lag in this house. It's actually the only piece of real estate I own."

I entered the small cottage after him. Besides a large bed there wasn't much furniture. One small desk and a rickety chair stood facing a window, and the only other place to sit was on a large cushion in front of the fireplace.

"What is it?" asked Nick, kneeling down to crumble up an old newspaper. "Not posh enough for Dr. Livingstone?"

I looked around at the rough stone walls and wooden ceiling. There was something utterly seductive about the helpless rusticity and faint smell of charred wood hanging in the air. It was not the Çiragan Palace Hotel, but given the choice I would still rather be here.

When I returned from the tiny bathroom, Nick was leaning on the mantelpiece, waiting for the fire to catch.

"Here." I handed him a wet washcloth. "Your turn."

He shot me a wry smile. "I know I'm a mess—"

"No more than usual." I helped him pull off the blood-spattered sweater and saw him cringing at the motion, favoring his shoulder. "Are you in a lot of pain?"

"I've been in a lot of pain since the day I met you." The way Nick looked at me made it abundantly clear what he meant.

"You should have fired me when you had the chance," I whispered, running my hands underneath his T-shirt. "Or left me to die in the temple."

He silenced me with a kiss. And another. Then he said, with an exasperated headshake, "I did everything I could to *not* fall in love with you."

His words made me ridiculously happy. "And the result?"

Nick took my hand, palm to palm, and after a few seconds I could no longer tell whose pulse it was I felt. "What do you say, Goddess?" He looked me in the eye. "Will you allow this mortal to love you?"

I leaned closer. "It's dangerous. But you like danger, don't you?"

Without hesitation, Nick drew me into his arms, and we fell on each other ravenously. I still had questions, but could no longer remember them. All I wanted to know was *him* . . . how his skin felt against mine, whether he was as frantically impatient as I. Clothes were yanked off, hands found their way at last. . . . Our urgency to be together was so great we both forgot to be gentle. I heard Nick groaning when I clung to his shoulders, but wasn't sure if it was a sign of pain or pleasure. It didn't stop me. I craved him more than I had ever craved anything and claimed his body with rapacious greed. Not even fully undressed, I was up against the wall with a significant part of him inside me, so ecstatic I nearly passed out.

"Oh my God," he groaned, when we finally collapsed together on the big cushion on the floor, his nose bleeding again. "What have you done to me?"

"I think you mean 'Goddess,'" I muttered, gently wiping the blood from his lip, still awash in awestruck fulfillment. "Since when did you become so religious?"

Nick ran his fingers over my sweaty skin, his eyes full of reverence. "Only the immortals can pull at a man the way you pull at me."

"You weren't so keen on me in the beginning."

He smiled, aware I was angling for a compliment. "I'm not sure dragging you into my tent and unzipping my pants would have been the best way of welcoming you to Algeria. Do you?"

"Maybe if you had shaved off that mangy beard first."

Nick laughed. "Careful. If you don't behave, it may grow back."

LATER, WHEN WE HAD made ourselves comfortable in bed, I finally asked the question that had been at large in my mind for days. "What did you mean that day in Istanbul," I said, running my fingers over Nick's chest, "when you said you had already taken a bullet for James?"

Nick smiled and kissed me. "You know what I meant. If it hadn't been for him, I'd have treed you long ago."

I burst out laughing. "Didn't your boss tell you not to harass your employees?"

Nick made a grunt. "Harassment is part of the package."

"Tell me . . . do you like working for Mr. al-Aqrab?"

He thought about it briefly. "No."

"Then why don't you quit?"

"It's not that easy." Nick looked uncomfortable, if not downright sheepish. "I guess now's the time to tell you. Mr. al-Aqrab is my father."

"What?" I would have erupted from the bed if he hadn't held me back.

"Come on." He kissed me in the neck. "It's not as if you're in bed with the devil."

"I don't know." I wasn't sure whether to laugh or cry. It was hard to be upset with Nick for telling me the truth at last, and yet the idea of him surrounded by the inevitable playboy retinue of fast cars and bikini models made me sad. "Define 'devil.'"

"I do have some redeeming qualities, don't I?" Nick took my hand and guided it underneath the duvet. "Such as a very big . . . heart."

"How about a very big explanation?" I countered, reminding myself of all the excellent reasons why I had run away from him in Istanbul. "Your people were spying on my family! You actually had some . . . sleazy detective crawling through hedges and shrubberies to take photos of my parents in their home. And what about those guns under your bed? I'm assuming you use them to shoot people." I stared at him to see if my words had any effect and was somewhat gratified to see his smile disappearing. "So, excuse me if I'm a little disgruntled to say the least. From day one, you have been lying to me, bullying me, manipulating me—I don't even know your first name!"

Nick sat back and folded his arms across his chest, the firelight casting ominous shadows over his face. "My name is Nick. I told you so. My dad named me Kamal, but my mother called me Niccolò."

"Your Brazilian mother?" I proposed, eager to help him along. I remembered well our conversation in Mycenae, over Mr. Telemakhos's blackboard dinner table, when Nick had regaled us all with vignettes— all fake, I now realized—from his destitute childhood.

"No." Nick sighed and closed his eyes. "My biological mother."

As he sank into silence, my lingering confusion grew into complete bewilderment. I had been so sure we would be talking about the contents of the envelope I took from him, starting with the detective report on me and my family. The realization that I might, in fact, merely be a secondary character in Nick's big explanation was strangely sobering.

"My dad was born in Iran, in an old and wealthy family," he began at last, his eyes still closed.

"The al-Aqrab family, I assume?"

"No, no, no." He brushed the suggestion aside with a tired gesture.

"Al-Aqrab is an Arab name. It means 'scorpion.' My dad changed his name when he was cast out of the family at twenty-two."

Perhaps sensing my surprise, Nick opened his eyes. He looked so miserable I felt a throb of pity. Only then did it occur to me that maybe the underlying reason for his protracted secrecy with regards to his real identity was not so much a desire to fool *me* as it was a need to maintain a mental buffer between himself and his father. All the different disguises and moods, all the different passports—could it be that he was hiding not just from looters and smugglers, but from himself as well? Leaning closer, I kissed him on the cheek, and he smiled in response.

"Thirty-four years ago my dad made the Oxford rowing team," Nick continued. "He and his mates went into London to celebrate. There, he met a woman, and they ended up spending the night together. But she was gone before sunrise, and he never saw her again." With that, Nick got out of bed and disappeared into the small pantry, completely naked, leaving me to wonder how I could possibly have kept my hands off this gorgeous man for so long and, slightly more relevantly, whether that was the end of his story.

Minutes later, he returned with a bottle of red wine, two glasses, and a box of crackers. Only when we were both equipped with a full glass did he touch his to mine and say, "One year later my father received a baby in the mail. That was me. With a note attached. The note said, 'Dear Hassan, this is your son. His name is Niccolò. Please forgive him. He can't help what his mother is.' There was more, but nothing that matters now. The note was signed 'Myrina.'"

I stared at him, speechless.

"As you can imagine"—Nick took a swig of wine—"my dad has spent thirty-three years trying to find this Myrina again. He is convinced she was an Amazon. She was so beautiful and strong, and the circumstances of their meeting was bizarre. My dad was walking back from a nightclub with his friends when a beautiful Latin woman joined them and took him by the elbow. It wasn't until later, when he was thinking the whole thing through, that it occurred to him there had been several police cars in the street just then, sirens going. Anyway, the woman walked into the hotel with them and followed my dad all the way up to his room. He was so mesmerized by her he didn't object. As soon as they were alone, she excused herself and went to the bathroom. When she had been there for a while, my dad knocked on the door and asked if she was okay. No response. When he tested the door and found it locked he kicked it in, thinking maybe she was doing drugs or committing suicide. . . . All kinds of things went through his mind. He found her sitting in the shower, crying hysterically. At first, he thought she was hurt, because there was blood on the hand towel and in the sink, but he couldn't see any wounds. Then he noticed the hunting knife in her pile of clothes." Nick grimaced at me. "My dad, of course, was intrigued. Who is this woman? What has she done? He tries to talk to her, but she pushes him away and sneers, 'Do you know the punishment for defiling an Amazon?' In the end, she gets up and dries off, and my dad persuades her to spend the night in his room. I don't know the details, but seeing that I was conceived that night, I am deducing my dad did not sleep in the armchair. And yes"—Nick nodded at my arm—"she wore a bracelet just like yours. That's why my dad went to Mycenae thirty years ago, to talk to Mr. Telemakhos."

At that, the long row of dominoes finally began falling in my head. "Of course!" I exclaimed. "That was your father! Mr. al-Aqrab! *He* was Chris Hauser from Baltimore, wasn't he? That's why you were so strange that day."

"I was?" Nick looked a little bemused. "Well, can you blame me? I had no idea my dad had been there before, under a false name. Even now, I still don't understand how Mr. Telemakhos made the connection. I don't look like my dad at all. Do I?"

"He is the Oracle after all," I said, diplomatically dodging the issue. "He said my handbag would turn up again, and it did."

Nick glanced at me as if he wasn't entirely sure to what extent I had forgiven him yet. Then, touching a hopeful hand to my cheek, he whispered, "He told me you were my soul mate. But I already knew that."

I kissed the palm of his hand. "I wish we had had this conversation before we went to Istanbul. Or at least before we *left* Istanbul."

Nick shook his head. "Diana. I didn't *know* all this until last night. After you disappeared, I flew to Dubai to have a word with my dad in private, which is always a challenge—"

"You flew to Dubai? But I just saw your father at the Çirağan Palace Hotel with Mr. Ludwig—"

"He's a slippery one," said Nick, pouring us more wine. "I had asked him to explain everything to me—what the hell we were doing, what role you were playing, why Reznik was after your grandmother's notebook—and that's why he gave me that envelope, which *you* then appropriately stole from me." Nick gave me a sideways glance. "He also, by the way, gave me the guns in case Reznik came knocking. It's his way of showing his love."

Struck by sympathy, I leaned my head on his shoulder. "I'm so sorry—"

"Don't be. If you hadn't run away like that, I'd never have gotten the truth out of him. I always knew my mother wasn't the woman who gave birth to me, but as you said yourself, before I met you I could barely spell 'Amazon.' It wasn't really until that night on the boat, when you told me about your grandmother and said something about Amazons giving up their baby boys that I began to suspect our trip had something to do with *me*. My dad had sent me on this strange mission—basically to stick close to you and see who came out of the woodwork—but hadn't explained what it was he wanted."

"Why not?" I asked. "Why all the hugger-mugger?"

Nick sighed deeply. "My dad is like that. He always says that those who control the present can rewrite the past. I just never realized he was talking about himself. I suppose once you start lying to people, and constructing an alternative reality, you can't just suddenly pull it all apart." He shook his head again, looking just about as glum as I remembered him from Algeria. "I know it looks like I've been lying to you from the start, but the fact is I was just passing on the lies my dad told *me*. I had no idea he had been looking for the Amazons for thirty-three years, and that his foray into archaeology was just an excuse to dig up every anthill in the Mediterranean—"

"Maybe he thought he was protecting you?" I suggested, thinking of my own parents. "But then . . . why did he want *you* to track down the Amazons? I'm assuming that's what he was hoping I would help you do."

"He claims he wanted to give my biological mother a chance to meet me." Nick frowned. "Personally, I think it's a power game. He wants to prove he was right after all, and that the Amazons *do* exist. He told me to keep an eye on you . . . follow you around . . . see where you wanted to go."

I felt a stab of suspicion. "But you fired me. On day one. Why would you fire me if you were supposed to—as you say—follow me around?"

Nick nodded, acknowledging my point. "When you and I first met, my priority was the temple. I thought you were a liability because of your connection with Oxford and the Moselanes." He smiled, perhaps in recognition of how dramatically things had changed since then. "I'll admit it: I couldn't wait to get rid of you. But when I talked to my dad, he made it clear that you were more important than the temple." Nick put an arm around me and pressed a kiss to my forehead. "He had no idea how right he was."

"Even though I'm a liability?"

"A liability with an Amazon bracelet." Nick flicked a finger at the jackal. "That really heated things up. My dad was convinced that, sooner or later, you would lead me to the big Amazon mother ship. And when that was slow in coming, he figured we could somehow provoke the Amazons into action. That's why he wanted me to give you back your phone that night in Algeria; he wanted to see who you would call, and what would happen. He already suspected that your connection at Oxford, Katherine Kent, was involved with the Amazons; he just didn't know what role she plays."

"Lovely," I said. "Running scientific experiments with his own son. Boom! He certainly got some bang for his buck with that one. I gather this is also why he wanted you to spread the word about the Amazon Hoard? To make the Amazons feel some pressure?"

Nick hung his head, looking just about as penitent as he ought to, on behalf of his father. "To think I kept playing his hand, getting you into trouble. I simply didn't realize what we were up against. And nor did he. Apparently, he was convinced that, at some point, my mother would realize who I was and make herself known to me. And if she didn't . . . no harm done, since I knew nothing about her anyway. He certainly never imagined we would get caught up in the war between the Amazons and Reznik."

We were silent for a while. It was odd to sit and watch the flames dancing in the fireplace knowing that while those logs had been burning, my entire universe had tilted on its axis. In the end I snuggled up to Nick and said, "You told me your father was a street musician. I liked it that way."

Nick sighed. "Well, he was. And I really *was* the little monkey passing his hat around. When his family back in Iran heard about the baby—that is, *me*—they were furious. They wanted him to give me away and continue his studies at Oxford as if nothing had happened; when he refused to do that, they cut him off completely. And when he talked to his college, offering to work for his board and tuition, they told him no, he couldn't stay there with a baby—it wasn't 'the Oxford way.' He had no money, couldn't go back home . . . and so he put me in a backpack and joined a group of traveling musicians. That's how he ended up in Rio, where he started his first business and met the woman who became my adoptive mother. He's a self-made man through and through. Very exhausting to be around. Needs to control everything."

"Even you?"

"Especially me."

I tried to smile. "He's not exactly a favorite among people in Oxford. I get the impression he is quite . . . ruthless?"

Nick squeezed my thigh. "He's not as bad as people like to think, just goal oriented. Have you ever heard of a successful capitalist who was *not* considered ruthless? It's the unthinking herd's favorite prejudice."

"Even so, I'm guessing he won't be too pleased if he discovers you're dallying with an Oxford academic."

Nick turned to look at me with a crooked smile. "He would understand my need to conquer the ice princess who wouldn't even shake my hand." His smile fading, he ran his fingers down the length of my body as if to demonstrate the liberty with which that once-scorned hand could now travel.

"Is that what you've done?" I asked, when he leaned in for a kiss. "Conquered my glacial sovereignty?"

"Haven't I?" Nick rolled on top of me. "Do I sense a rebellion?" He smiled when I softened beneath him. "It doesn't feel like it."

"Careful," I warned him. "It could be an ambush. Any moment now, my Amazon sisters may kick down the door—"

"You're right." He pinned my arms to the bed. "I'd better hurry."

CHAPTER THIRTY-SEVEN

So far (and here rumor speaks the truth), and so far only, does the world reach.
—TACITUS, *Germania*

I WOKE UP SUDDENLY, MY HEART RACING, FEARING IT HAD ALL BEEN A dream. But when I saw Nick right next to me, sound asleep, I felt a relief as great as had I woken from a nightmare. Snuggling up to his savory warmth, I looked at him as he lay there bathed in the soft light of a dawning day. How was it possible that this glorious man who hadn't even known me for a month had nonetheless discovered sides of me—if not an entire continent—I never knew existed? "Just give me a moment, Goddess," he muttered. "I'm a mortal, remember?"

Despite his bruised nose, Nick looked statuesque even in his sleep, and it occurred to me that, for all his secrets, his body bore no marks of its unusual history. No scars, no jewelry, no tattoos gave any clues to his origins or the hands he had passed through before he fell into mine. Kamal al-Aqrab lived with a forged provenance and had by his own admission spent his adult life running away from preying sycophants who couldn't see beyond the ritzy label to the man underneath.

In this, we were more alike than I had first acknowledged. Yes, we had grown up around very different campfires—if not in different sets of caves altogether—but we also had so much in common, most of all the running and the searching. While Nick had trekked across the farthest edges of the earth looking for an exit from his father's imperial ambitions, I had galloped into the past to do battle with those who claimed the Amazons were nothing but fading names on brittle parchment. How odd—how wonderful—that our paths had come together like this.

Too agitated to go back to sleep, I crawled out of bed and went over to the fireplace to see if I could coax the embers back to life. Then I turned to my grubby handbag at last, bracing myself for the devastation I might find inside. It was the third bag I had been using within the space of two weeks; would that the evil handbag fairy tire of me soon.

Fortunately, the *Historia Amazonum* had sustained only minimal damage; the object that had borne the brunt of my mudslide was Granny's notebook. Limp and soggy, it had all but assumed the texture of a wet dishrag, and I felt like crying when I peeled away the front page and saw that the blue writing had been washed out so completely it was no longer legible.

Sitting down at the desk by the window, I carefully separated the middle pages in the hopes that the moisture had not penetrated to the core of the book . . . but it had. Of all the hundreds of words Granny had meticulously translated for me, not a single one was left.

Heavy with regret, I leafed around at random to see whether some trace of the words still lingered, and whether I could somehow reconstruct them. And then I saw it . . .

The invisible writing.

Just a single word drawn across every third page or so, but that was enough to make me jump up and bounce around with silent exhilaration.

What had Granny used? White crayon? Whatever it was, it had been imperceptible while there was blue writing covering every page. But now, with nothing but smudges remaining, the white crayon— greasy as it was—stood out by repelling the watery blue. So simple.

All this time, I thought with a cringe, I had been carrying around Granny's secret message, and had it not been for my ordeal in the wet Teutoburger forest the day before I might never have discovered the truth.

Sitting down again, I began working my way through the sodden notebook from the beginning, holding up each individual page against the sun rising over the meadow outside in order to make out the hidden scribbles.

But it was not as easy as it seemed; at first glance, none of the words made sense. Intrigued, I searched the desk drawer, found a notepad and pen, and started transcribing the words in the exact order I found them:

PHIN XPO LEMS AHI PP LA PAD OB REMS
APA NTA RIT ETH ERMO DO AMR PE SI AACI
BI EINY THYI AMO LP AD AV AB URUS I

After my initial confusion, I started attacking the list with all the textbook code-breaking approaches I knew: shuffling the letters around, moving syllables around, taking every first letter, or second letter . . . but none of my attempts resulted in anything remotely intelligible.

Particularly frustrating was that the words were vaguely familiar to me just as they were, even if they didn't make any sense; I had a feeling that with some minuscule tweak or change of perspective everything would become beautifully clear. And yet, at the same time, the list had both a Greek and a Latin feel to it, and I doubted Granny had mastered those languages. Even if she had been trained as an archaeologist, would she really, after so many years, have been sufficiently fluent to compose a message? Furthermore, if it was indeed written in a mix of ancient languages, how could she be sure I would ever be able to read it?

Whatever the case, clearly she had wanted to make sure the message did not fall into the wrong hands. The question was, what did it take to qualify as the *right* hands? What knowledge had Granny wanted me to acquire before I was deemed worthy of her trust?

But of course.

There they were, as clear as the constellations on a cloudless night.

I was so absorbed in my discovery I jumped with surprise when Nick put his arms around me from behind. "If you don't come back to bed right now," he mumbled into my hair, "I'm going to report you to Amnesty International."

"But I'm just on the edge of an enormous breakthrough," I protested. "Give me one second—"

"Sorry." He lifted me from the chair and carried me off, notes, pen, and all. "*I* am the god of enormous breakthroughs, and this is where they happen."

Only later, after excavating my papers from the jumbled sheets, was I able to engage Nick in an actual conversation about Granny's secret message.

"I figured it out!" I told him, waving my notes in the air. "It's basically a list of Amazon names broken into pieces, with one letter missing in each."

Scratching his unshaven cheek, Nick took the list, which read as follows:

PHINX POLEMSA HIPP LAPADO BREMSA
PANTARITE THERMODOA MRPESIA ACIBIE
INYTHYIA MOLPADA VABURUSI?

After reading through the names, Nick handed the notepad back to me. "That explains everything."

"Only someone familiar with the Amazon legends would be able to figure this out," I explained. "The names are not obvious. See." I handed him the last piece of paper, which looked like this:

SPHINX POLEMUSA HIPPO LAMPADO BREMUSA
PANTARISTE THERMODOSA MARPESIA ALCIBIE
MINYTHYIA MOLPADIA VABURUSI?

"Sphinx?" said Nick. "Isn't that an animal?"

"Yes." I took the list from him again. "I'm guessing it's a warning: 'Beware of riddle.' After that, it's simply a list of Amazon names. If I remember correctly, Polemusa and Bremusa fought with Penthesilea, Molpadia took part in the raid on Athens and so on and so forth. The only name I don't recognize is the last one: Vaburusi. But never mind. Look at the missing letters. They spell out 'Suomussalmi.'"

"Which still needs unscrambling," said Nick, getting wise on the game.

"No!" I poked him with the pen. "Where did you go to school? It's a town in Finland, just south of the Arctic Circle."

Nick's eyes narrowed. "Please don't tell me you want to go there."

I sat up straight, still giddy with excitement. "Why not? Isn't this amazing? Granny is telling us to go to Suomussalmi. I can hear it."

"That's strange." Nick cocked his head as if listening to a distant call. "To me it sounds like she's telling us to stay right here . . . in this bed. In fact—" He reached out for me, taking me by the arms.

Although I was mildly upset that he seemed so uninterested in my discovery, I couldn't help laughing when he pulled me on top of him. "What happened to the faraway island?"

"Why don't you start with *this* island?"

Just then his cellphone rang. He ignored it.

One minute later, the phone started ringing again. When Nick eventually checked the display, he grimaced and handed the phone directly to me. It was my parents.

"Oh, thank goodness you're safe!" said my father, sounding unusually shaken. "We weren't sure we could call you back on this number. Where are you? Whose phone is this?"

I hesitated, equally loath to answer either question.

"Never mind!" interjected my mother. "Sweetie, we got a call at four o'clock this morning, and we don't know what to make of it."

"It was a very unpleasant person," said my father, "who instructed us to inform you that"—he paused to recall the exact wording—"you have three days to hand over the notebook. There was mention of a specific park bench in Paris. If you do not comply"—my father cleared his throat, trying to sound businesslike—"harm will come to people you love."

I was so shocked, I didn't even try to pretend the situation wasn't serious. "I know it sounds frightening," I admitted, "but we're working on a solution."

"Who's 'we'?" my father wanted to know. "Is this all about Bex?"

"No," I said. "It's all about Granny." I suppressed a childish impulse to add, "And we wouldn't be in this pinch if we had just *talked* about some of these things." For really, that was unfair. Instead, I said, "But don't worry, it's not as bad as it sounds. I'll explain when I see you. Meanwhile, isn't it time you finally had that seaside weekend? I know it's November, but why don't you drive out to some cozy little B&B in Cornwall and stay there for a while? Under a different name. Please."

"Reznik," said Nick, as soon as I had hung up. "Always a bench. Always a crowd. And classic Moselane to tell him where your parents live."

I felt an absurd sting of irritation. "Why not the Amazons?"

Nick got out of bed and started hunting around for our clothes. "The Amazons are not at war with us; they're at war with *him*. If they had really wanted that notebook, you can bet they would have stolen it a long time ago."

"Perhaps they didn't know it existed."

Nick pulled the T-shirt over his head, grimacing in pain. "Good point. How does *Reznik* know about it? Through James?"

"James knows nothing about the notebook," I said. Then something occurred to me, and I groaned. "The envelope! The one I took from you. The thugs from Geneva must have checked it out in my hotel room in Bramsche. If you recall, there was a medical article written by a Dr. Trelawny—"

"I never got that far," said Nick with a scowl. "All I saw was the detective report on you and the letter from Reznik to his informant network—"

"You mean the letter to Jumbo? I thought it was a message to a hit man. Actually, I thought it was for *you*."

"Jumbo. Big ears." Nick demonstrated with his hands. "Reznik was trying to gather information. The million-dollar bounty came later. Because he's paranoid, he has cameras everywhere, and the poor bastard caught his own son's murder on tape. I'll spare you the details. Let's just say Alex Reznik knew who was killing him, and why. That was what triggered Reznik's Amazon fixation. I don't know how close he is to tracking them down, but his interest in your grandmother's notebook tells me he is hot on their trail."

"Not as hot as we are," I said.

Nick looked at me with narrow eyes. "Meaning?"

"Think about it." I sat up on my knees, urging him to understand. "If we give Reznik the notebook, he'll see the secret writing right away. And considering his Amazon obsession he just might be able to unscramble Granny's riddle, too. God knows, maybe 'Suomussalmi Vaburusi' is all he needs in order to find the big Amazon mother ship, as you call it, and"—the thought made me shiver—"blow it up."

Nick walked over to me, graver than ever. Lowering his hand to touch my cheek, he said, "And are you sure that would be such a bad thing?"

WE BROKE THROUGH THE clouds to find Finland covered in snow. Even as we walked to our rental car, large, fluffy flakes kept falling from the sky like a welcoming puff of confetti. "Not exactly the sandy beach you were hoping for," I said to Nick.

As we rolled out of the parking lot, the snow fell so heavily against the windshield I had to put the wipers on top speed. "Isn't it wonderful, though?" I said, doing my best to be jolly. "I can almost hear the cheers of Finnish children."

"You hear a lot today." Nick turned on the cabin lights to better see our map. "Are any of the voices telling you whether to go left or right when we hit the Oulun Lääni—whatever that is?"

I touched the brake a few times to determine exactly how slippery the road was. "I told you we should have taken the GPS."

"Real men don't use GPS," he reminded me.

"And that," I pointed out, "is why we have so few real men left. They keep crawling out of the gene pool and can't find their way back."

We were silent for a while. I knew Nick was still irked by my decision to go to Suomussalmi, but then, he hadn't been able to propose any viable alternatives. The one positive thing was that he hadn't deserted me, and for that I was immensely grateful.

Before leaving his cottage that morning, I had called the Kalkriese Museum to ask for Dr. Jäger's phone number. She was, after all, the closest I had been to a humane Amazon so far. But Felix told me she had left unexpectedly, to stay with a sister no one knew she had. Not surprisingly, she had given him no contact information.

Considering the way they had treated us both, neither Nick nor I were particularly fond of the Amazons anymore. But unlike Nick, I felt an obligation to side with them, if only out of love for Granny. I simply couldn't give Reznik—or anyone else—the notebook. And yet if I didn't, I would forever worry about my parents' safety.

In the end, even Nick grudgingly agreed we had to go to Finland. If only from the morbid principle that the enemy of your enemy is your friend, it seemed our best chance was to find the Amazons before Reznik did. Maybe they were in Suomussalmi, maybe they weren't . . . but it was the only lead we had. Also, as I kept telling Nick, convincing myself in the process, I was confident my grandmother would not send me there for naught. Admittedly, her white-crayon summons was almost twenty years old, but surely she had not written it on a whim. In fact, the more I thought about it, the more certain I became that Granny had entrusted me with the magic key to an impregnable Amazon fortress, and that once we got there, our troubles would be over.

"Chin up!" I said to Nick as we sped through the slush. "Soon you'll be having vodka martinis in a hot tub, surrounded by busty superwomen in ridiculously small bikinis."

As we drove inland from Oulu Airport, however, I could feel the grimness of our situation bearing down on us from all sides. In the silent snowy murk of Finnish winter it was impossible to tell whether we were driving through farmland or tundra, for everything was frozen in place—every post, every shrub, every weed. Above this hibernating landscape hung an old sun, too fatigued to dispel the twilight although it was still only midafternoon.

"I have an idea," I said at last, pulling over in the middle of the dense Kainuu forest. "You drive and I'll read us a story."

I didn't propose it merely to cheer us up. The truth was, I was itching to return to the *Historia Amazonum* and see how it ended. Even though P. Exulatus had written it two thousand years ago I couldn't help thinking that perhaps, in some roundabout way, his knowledge might help us when or if we actually managed to find the Amazons. And so, translating from the original Latin as I went, I read the rest of the ancient manuscript aloud to us both. It went something like this:

"Of the barbarians in Sarmatia and Germania Magna much remains to be said, but I will restrict myself to those accounts that concern the Amazons. Many claim to have seen women fighting on horseback in those regions, but whether they can rightfully be called Amazons is a different matter. Women who consort with men on a daily basis I do not consider Amazons, nor would these barbarian wives, who carry weapons to protect their families and the fruits of their labor, refer to themselves as Amazons. They are simply acting according to"— I paused to ponder the appropriate translation—"*common sense, and in these wholesome people it is still possible to find virtue in men and women alike. They do not pretend to hide behind written treaties backed by distant armies, but wake up every day prepared to defend their own rights.*"

"I like this guy," said Nick, when I stopped briefly to make sense of a blurry part. "Too bad nobody reads him anymore."

"Well," I said, "let's hope we can change that." Then, after skimming the next few pages, which gave examples of famous Sarmatian and Scythian warrior women, I jumped forward to where the action picked up again. "Okay, here we go: So much for the exemplary tales from those horse-riding peoples. We are now nearing the end of our history, for of all the legends of Germania Magna only one concerns the Amazons. It was told to me by a soldier stationed there during the Varian disaster, who only narrowly escaped the slaughter."

I gasped and quickly went over the last sentence again. "The Varian disaster! That was the Roman name for the Battle of Teutoburger Wald—the big ambush I told you about, where Dr. Jäger's bog woman died. Now we're getting somewhere! Listen to this: The soldier swore that he had been an orderly for the commander of the Nineteenth Legion." I was so excited, I grabbed Nick by the arm. "A survivor! Those three legions were thought to have been annihilated to a man. But here is an eyewitness!" I returned to the text, barely able to contain myself. "On the eve of the disastrous battle, a woman disguised in men's clothing came late at night to request a favor of the commander. She demanded to speak to him privately and alone. Intrigued, he sent away everyone except his orderly."

"I smell trouble," said Nick.

"When requested to name her errand," I went on eagerly, "the woman asked the commander whether he was familiar with the legend of Alexander the Great and Thalestris, the Amazon queen. When he acknowledged having heard the story, she told him hers was a similar errand. It was her desire, she explained, to spend a night with him; by dawn she would be gone forever."

Nick whistled. "I didn't even know you could *say* that in Latin."

"The commander was naturally astounded by the request," I continued, poking Nick in the ribs. "As a Roman he was not used to such forthright womenfolk. But at length he decided she must have been sent to him as a humorous present from his officers, and, being a proud man, he resolved to make the most of it. To his surprise, when dawn came, the woman rose from his bed and prepared to leave as promised. And when the commander, who had enjoyed her . . . um . . . company, invited her to stay, she responded as follows: 'Roman, our paths have briefly crossed, as do sometimes those of the Sun and the Moon, but now we must once again part. Such are the rules we both live by. But today, when the darkness comes, you may comfort yourself with the knowledge that your strength will live on.'

"Not content with her obscure response, the commander urged the woman to stay, making the sorts of promises that usually work with women. But now she showed him the bracelet upon her arm and said, 'You are a man of many virtues, a strong and unblemished man, which is why I chose you. But this sacred jackal dictates my fate and reminds me the Moon is my mistress. I cannot close my ears to her demands. She forbids me from sharing the daylight with you.'

"To which the commander said, 'You speak with such confidence that I am compelled to challenge you. Are you a German noblewoman? Perhaps, during peace negotiations, I will see you again.'

" 'You may see me again,' she replied. 'But it will be no happy reunion. We both know there can be no peace without blood.' Standing on the threshold, she looked back one last time and said, 'Because the sight of you is still sweet to me, I would tell you to save your own life. But I know that is contrary to your nature. Your bravery is why I chose you from amongst thousands to be the father of my child. And so I will leave you with this: Roman, you live to kill, and your honor feeds on the flesh of others. For as long as this golden band is upon my arm, and upon the arms of my sisters, we will steal your strength but despise your power, and the power of others like you. For there will be others; every century breeds another hungry master, but they will all be turned to dust while we, the Amazons, will live forever.' "

I lowered the manuscript, almost breathless with agitation. "It actually mentions a jackal bracelet. There has *got* to be some truth to this story. What do you think?"

Nick's brow was plowed by deep thoughts, and for a moment I thought he had not actually been listening to the last part of the translation. Then he said, "Would you mind reading that passage again? The one where she tells him why she can't stay?"

And so I did, whereupon he fell silent once more, fingers drumming on the steering wheel.

"What is it?" I asked. "You're making me terribly curious."

"I am almost certain," he said eventually, "my Amazon mother told my dad something along the same lines. Some poetic hogwash about the jackal and the moon and not being allowed to share his daylight."

I put a hand on his thigh and gave it a squeeze. The forest surrounding us was dense and all consuming, covered in frosty silence, its manner everything but welcoming. And yet the wry Moon that had accompanied us on our drive to Frankfurt the night before was now directly ahead. The undisputed monarch of Arctic winter, it seemed, was beckoning us.

"Well," I said, leafing through the last few pages of the *Historia Amazonum,* "the rest is just obsequious drivel meant to persuade some emperor—probably Tiberius—to let the author return to Rome. But poor P. Exulatus very likely died in exile, like so many others, and no one back home ever knew of this manuscript."

"Too bad," said Nick. "I like that last story."

"Even if it doesn't explain anything?"

"But it does." He looked at me. "'Only we, the Amazons, will live forever.' What more do you need to know?"

THE TOWN OF SUOMUSSALMI was little more than a small contingency of shops and buildings huddled against the unfathomable wilderness bearing down on it from all sides.

When we stopped at a gas station to ask for directions to the nearest hotel, it struck me that the locals seemed rooted in the same mystical element as the silent Kainuu forest. They looked at us as if they knew precisely who we were and had only been wondering when we would finally arrive . . . but even so, their eyes betrayed no emotions. We might be friends, or we might be foes. It would take more than the halting exchange of a few stock pleasantries over a cash register to find out.

Nor did the hotel room greet us with any particular enthusiasm, although one could choose to see its vacant college dorm aesthetic as an example of modern Nordic elegance.

"Just for the record," said Nick, putting down our bags on the birchwood floor, "in case this comes up in the future . . . and I know it will"—he swept me off my feet and growled right in my ear— "it was *you* who ran away from my decadent suite at the Çirağan Palace." Walking over to the bed, he set me down on top of the spartan comforter and hovered above me. "What is it with you Brits? Why are you so afraid of comfort?"

"Comfortable people lose their edge."

"You know—" Nick started kissing my neck. "It's lucky I never taught you any self-defense techniques. And I still don't see your dueling sword anywhere. Now I can do whatever I want with you."

"You seem to forget I just dragged you all the way to the Arctic Circle."

"Oh, I'm aware of that." Nick lay down on his back, arms behind his head, smiling a challenge at me. "And now I get my reward. Don't I?"

I laughed. "You're such a caveman."

"And you should be thankful for that," he pointed out. "It wasn't cavemen who invented misogynist metaphysics. It takes a little bit of civilization to come up with that kind of evil."

Later that night, after some wonderfully uncivilized hours in bed and a long, sensuous shower, I was once again reminded of the fragility of our present happiness.

"What's that?" asked Nick, when I began brushing my teeth, his smile fading. "Where did you get that toothpaste?"

I stared at the innocuous tube lying by the sink and felt a creeping panic. Before we boarded the plane that morning, he had instructed me to get rid of everything that had been lying around in my hotel room in Kalkriese while I was out. But somehow the toothpaste had escaped my attention.

"What are you doing?" I asked when he began squeezing out the white paste in the sink.

"There . . . feel that?" He let me touch the bottom part of the tube, where a small, hard nodule appeared to have lodged itself.

Our eyes met. Was this a tracking device?

"Do they know where we are?" I asked, chilled by the thought that we might have to flee yet again from Reznik's goons, so late at night.

"Not necessarily," said Nick, getting dressed. "But I don't want to take any chances. Keep the bed warm. I'm taking our fluoride friend for a little drive."

CHAPTER THIRTY-EIGHT

Let us make a firm agreement
That we will not hurt each other,
Never in all eternity
While the golden moon still glimmers.
—*The Kalevala*

SUOMUSSALMI, FINLAND

THE WINTER WAR MONUMENT IN SUOMUSSALMI WAS SO UNUSUAL
that we drove right by it several times before realizing what it was.
Making the most of the noon sun, we had been on the lookout for an
army of identical tombstones lined up in marching order, but what we
found was stunningly different.

It was the grocer across the street from the hotel who had suggested we visit the Raatteen Portti, as the war memorial and museum
were called, since that was apparently the gateway to Suomussalmi history. Earlier that morning we had chatted with the hotel receptionist,
who had informed us that "Vaburusi" was, in fact, not one but two
names. "Vabu" was a Finnish girl's name, and "Rusi" was a surname.
Unfortunately, there was not a single Rusi in the regional phone book.
That was how we had ended up at the grocer, who claimed he didn't
know of anyone with that name, either.

"But try at Raatteen Portti," he had suggested, drawing a quick map
of the route. "Marko, who works there, remembers everything about

everyone. Even the things"—the man had looked away, hardened lines of strain around his eyes—"we don't want to remember."

And so we drove out to the Winter War Monument around lunchtime, when the sun was at its strongest, quickly realizing that nothing about this place was predictable. Despite its modest surface—or perhaps precisely because of it—I sensed that Suomussalmi had a deep, dark soul full of well-kept secrets.

Entering the memorial park, we were met by a teeth-chattering east wind that had us both pulling up our hoods and putting on the thermal gloves we had bought that morning before heading out on our excursion. The coats we had purchased at the Frankfurt Airport simply weren't enough in a country where the November sun barely made it into the sky before plunging headlong into polar night at three in the afternoon.

"Let's go inside," said Nick, his voice muffled by the hood.

"Not until we've seen the park. I'll warm you up later."

Around us, thousands of rough boulders, each with its own individual shape, sat in a large clearing in the forest, reminding us that every fallen soldier commemorated here had been an independent human being—someone whose last thoughts were likely not of international politics but of his loved ones and the buddies around him. At least that was my interpretation, offered from behind my scarf as we picked our way across the icy gravel.

Walking toward the small bell tower at the center of the monument, we saw a man approaching from the nearby museum building, carrying a ladder. When he realized we were headed the same direction, he put down the ladder, adjusted his glasses, and came forward to greet us. Even though he wore only a leather jacket and nothing woolly whatsoever, his handshake was as warm as his smile.

"I am Marko," he said, flipping up the collar of his jacket. "I was just going to clean the bells. There are one hundred and five, all different sizes." He pointed at the top of the bell tower, which was not really a tower, but rather four curved beams of wood leaning together to form a gigantic Y-shaped chime. "One bell for each day of the Winter War.

You can hear them when the wind blows. But come inside and have a coffee. We have *karjalanpiirakat* this week." Seeing we did not understand him, Marko smiled and held out his arms. "Don't worry. It is a Karelian specialty."

There were few people at the Raatteen Portti museum that day. A couple of talkative women were working in the café, and an elderly man in a wheelchair sat at a table by the window, quietly sorting through photos.

Although Marko was clearly curious, he didn't ask where we were from but merely walked us quickly through the exhibition, assuming—as he likely did with everyone, and for good reason—that we didn't have the faintest clue about the dates or circumstances of the Winter War that was his passion.

"It was Stalin's attempt at invading Finland in the winter of 1939–40," he explained, pointing at old laminated photos of the Red Army hanging on the wall. "We were outnumbered ten to one, and Stalin thought that with all his modern machinery he could take little defenseless Finland in two weeks. He didn't even bother to give his soldiers winter uniforms."

We walked through the exhibition in silence, looking at mannequin tableaux with Finnish ski patrols wearing snow camouflage and bone-chilling photos of dead Russian soldiers frozen in place, their bloodless hands forever raised in surprise and self-defense.

Seeing our horror, Marko stopped to explain. "It was a very cold winter that year. In minus forty, you must not sweat, even with fear, because the moisture will turn to ice and freeze you. But at the same time, you must keep your pulse up. The moment your blood slows down"—he nodded at the grim photos around us—"for example, when you are hit by a bullet, or someone slits your throat with a knife strapped to a ski pole, your body simply freezes the way it is . . . sitting, standing, it doesn't matter. If you read our national epic, *The Kalevala,* you will see that we Finns have learned to respect the frost, and that we have made a pact to live with it. Stalin did not respect the Finnish winter. He sent his soldiers here for murder, and they found it."

We stopped to look more closely at some of the personal objects that had been carried by the dead Russians, and I understood that Marko pitied them just as much as he pitied the Finns. Just like the Romans at Teutoburger Wald, they had been sent into hostile, unfamiliar territory by arrogant leaders only to be torn to pieces by underdogs refusing the leash of empire.

"What exactly happened here at Suomussalmi?" asked Nick. "You would think Stalin would go for Helsinki first."

"He did," said Marko. "He went for everything. He bombed Helsinki without even declaring war, and after that he attacked the border with airplanes and tanks, causing terrible carnage. And what did *we* have? Brave men who ran right up to the tanks and threw Molotov cocktails at their air intake." He straightened with pride. "We invented them, you know. In the Winter War. That was why we named them after the Russian foreign minister." Perhaps feeling he had been carried away, Marko squeezed both hands into the pockets of his leather jacket, elbows sticking out dismissively, before continuing, "Here at Suomussalmi it was mostly guerrilla fighting. Many of the old veterans still refuse to talk about it, even now. They just say they did terrible things." Marko ground his shoe into an imaginary cigarette butt. "Two Russian divisions came across the border right here, east of Suomussalmi, along the Raate Road. They had many armored vehicles, so they had to stay on the road through the forest, in one long line, in frigid weather. The Finns were on skis, wearing snow camouflage. The Russians were sitting ducks. Twenty-three thousand bodies, frozen like statues, kilometer after kilometer along the Raate Road."

Arriving at the cozy cafeteria at last, sitting us down with coffee and cake, Marko went on to say that even today few people wanted to live near the Raate Road. There were wolves and bears in the forest, but even more disturbingly, thousands of Russian soldiers were buried in mass graves along this route of slaughter. In his usual fashion, Stalin had wholly denied the defeat; by refusing to take the bodies of his soldiers back, he had left it to the Finns to bury the men sent to destroy them. Some graves were marked; most were not. According to Marko, any cluster of healthy birch trees among the scruffy firs was a sure sign of a mass grave beneath; Nature had erected her own memorial to the lives cut short in this haunted forest.

"I don't suppose," I said after a silence, "you have ever heard of a woman named Vabu Rusi?"

Marko thought for a moment. "No. But Aarne might know." He got up and walked over to talk with the man in the wheelchair.

I didn't realize quite how on edge I had been until I saw the old man perking up and responding animatedly to the query. And then Marko waved us along, taking us into a room with metal archive cabinets and a slide projector trained at a white pull-down screen.

Talking quietly in Finnish, the men started riffling through drawers full of slides, until, eventually, Aarne held up a narrow box, checked the handwritten notes on the sides, and nodded an unsmiling confirmation.

While the projector warmed up, Marko explained that Vabu Rusi had been a wartime Lotta—one of the many female volunteers helping the Finnish soldiers behind the lines. "Aarne says Vabu was an excellent nurse, and that she always helped with the amputations. The young men liked to"—Marko frowned—"look at her pretty face instead of the doctor . . . you know." He shook his head sadly. "But her story was a tragic one. Vabu's husband fell in the Winter War, and she and her little daughter were taken hostage by Russian partisans—at least Aarne thinks so. As with so many other Finnish mothers and children, no one ever saw them again. But take a look." Marko shoved the first slide in the projector, and we saw an old black-and-white group photo of women standing in front of a building, wearing nurses' uniforms.

Aarne leaned forward to study each individual face, then shook his head. Only when Marko put the fourth slide in the machine—yet another group photo of smiling nurses—did Aarne finally nod and point excitedly at a young woman sitting on a long bench in the front row.

"There!" said Marko. "That is Vabu Rusi. She was an only child, says Aarne. A shame, for all the young men would have liked to marry her sisters."

I walked as close as I could to the grainy projection, studying the sweet, smiling face. It was impossible not to feel a connection with Vabu Rusi after hearing about her sad life, but I wasn't sure if the knot of tears in my throat bespoke more than just sympathy. Did this woman bear any resemblance to my grandmother? It was hard to say. I could not remember ever seeing Granny smiling.

"And the daughter?" I asked the men, holding up my hand against the beam of the projector. "I don't suppose you have a photo of her?"

Marko shook his head with regret. "She was so young when they were taken. Aarne doesn't even remember her name." I could see he was itching to know why it mattered so much, but politeness prevented him from voicing his curiosity. Perhaps living his life surrounded by Winter War veterans, I thought, had long since taught Marko when to stop asking questions.

WHEN WE LEFT THE museum, the sun had long since disappeared below the horizon, and the air had a touch of night to it that chilled me to the core. Walking to the car with Nick, I couldn't help wondering if I would ever be completely warm again. It was not merely the disappointment of discovering that poor Vabu Rusi was in no position to help us unravel the mystery of my grandmother; the truth was that the whole place made me profoundly sad. I could not wait to leave this frozen wasteland and its thousands of homeless ghosts. "So much for talking to Vabu," I said, burrowing my hands into my pockets to find the car keys. "Where to next? The city archive?"

But Nick was oddly unresponsive, glancing now and then across the road at a motorcycle and rider, idling in the shadow between two street lamps. "That," he said eventually, "is a KTM motorcycle. Just won the Dakar Rally. Again." Perhaps realizing I was waiting for the punch line, he added, "I saw one this morning, when we were at the clothes store. I bet it's the same one. There are only so many people who would ride a bike in weather like this."

No sooner had he said that than the motorcycle sped off into the darkness, in the direction of the Russian border.

"Reznik?" I said, feeling another shiver, this time of fear.

"I don't think so." Nick was still staring into the black void of the Raate Road, a small quartet of muscles playing in his jaw. "But I do think we're being watched."

Back at the hotel, I pulled Nick into another shower, desperate to have him to myself one more time. Although we had made no plans to either stay or leave, I knew the sirens would be calling out for Kamal al-Aqrab soon—not to mention the unforgiving paternal Cyclops that ruled his life.

"Exquisite, rare Goddess," he said, stepping into the tub. "We both know what happens to mortal men who see Diana bathing."

"Yes." I drew him into the hissing stream of warm water, longing to indulge in his perfections and forget the imperfect world around us. "But I promise to make it worth your while."

"I would never have imagined," he mumbled, pulling me tightly against him, "I would be engaging in *hieros gamos* in Finland in November—"

I laughed with surprise, only too well remembering our naughty dinner conversation with Rebecca in Crete. "I thought you didn't know Greek."

"I had to look it up, didn't I? Although your red face that night said it all." Nick stroked my cheek, his eyes full of sincerity. "I have never looked up so many words in my life. . . . You're good for my vocabulary."

I frowned, feigning dismay. "That's all?"

He ran his hands down my slippery body. "Let me think. What else are you good for?"

"I could whip you with a birch branch?" I proposed, slapping him teasingly on the gluteus maximus. "That's what the Finns do when they go to the sauna. It's very refreshing, apparently. And then they dash out and roll in the snow afterward. Sound good?"

Nick gave me a wicked smile. "We'd melt all the snow in Finland." Then, turning me around, he drew me against him with mischievous, indulgent hands and murmured over my shoulder, "I have a much better idea. And we won't even need a birch branch."

It wasn't until we were ready to go out for dinner that I noticed the envelope that had been slipped underneath our door. It was addressed to Mr. and Mrs. Panagopoulos and contained a folded piece of heavy bond paper with a hand-drawn map and a brief message at the top:

Please come and see me right away.
Yabu Rusi

Nick was the first to recover from this little game changer. "Congratulations," he said, kissing me in the neck. "You found the Amazons."

I examined the directions with apprehension. "Would they really make it that easy? Suppose it's Reznik? His men did find me in Kalkriese. . . . At least I assume they were sent by him. The Geneva plates."

We talked about it for a while and decided that what had made it possible for Reznik to track me down in Germany was precisely what had enabled Nick to do the same, namely Rebecca's blurting out my interest in the Kalkriese Museum over the phone. Undoubtedly, Reznik had been screening her calls ever since the night of the party. The fact that he had now resorted to threatening my parents—if indeed that was him and not the Amazons—was a good indication that presently he had no idea where we were.

Assuming the letter really was from the Amazons, the big question was whether they truly wanted a friendly meeting, or whether they were leading us into a trap. Their directions had us driving out the Raate Road, past the Winter War Memorial, heading for the same black void in which the motorcycle had disappeared. I knew I had to go.

"You don't have to do this, though," I said to Nick when we walked to the car together. "It's *my* grandmother, *my* problem."

He opened the trunk and dumped in our luggage. We had decided to pack up everything, just in case things went awry and we had to get out of Suomussalmi fast. "You're not really getting it, are you?" he said, slamming the trunk. "I've already found what I was looking for. This is my happy ending, and I'm going to enjoy it even if it kills me."

I leaned over to kiss him. "Don't say that."

As we drove off through the sleepy town and continued out toward the desolate Russian border, the forest closed in around us with sinister resolution. Gone was the backdrop of beaten paths we knew so well; before us lay the Cimmerian no-man's-land at the end of the world. We were entering true Amazon territory at last.

"You didn't happen to bring any of those guns from Istanbul, did you?" I asked Nick, mostly to break the silence.

But he was preoccupied with something in the rearview mirror, and when I turned in my seat I saw two faint sets of headlights on the otherwise empty road behind us. "Are they following us?"

"I think so," he said, grimacing. "Let's see if we can't get rid of them."

We drove another kilometer or so, until we came to an intersection. Vabu Rusi's directions said to continue straight, but as soon as we had done so, Nick suddenly turned off the headlights and pulled into a narrow, rutted trail going straight into the forest. As soon as we were hidden by the trees, he pulled the handbrake and turned off the engine.

We halted so suddenly I didn't have time to brace myself before flying forward and being caught with a jerk by the seat belt. "Are you okay?" he asked, touching me in the darkness. "Sorry about the bumpy ride."

Moments later, two cars went by on the road behind us. "Now let's see." Nick twisted around in his seat. "We'll give them three minutes."

But less than a minute later the cars came back the other way, going considerably slower this time. "Stay here!" said Nick, opening the door.

Getting out of the car, too, I followed him back along the rutted trail until we were within eyesight of the two cars. They were idling in the middle of the intersection, their drivers evidently discussing where to go next.

When they finally sped off, choosing the road going west, Nick put his arms around me, and we stood like that for a while, just breathing. Without a word we returned to our vehicle and drove on, chastened by the close call. There was no need to discuss who had sent the two cars; we both knew it must be Reznik. The night before, Nick had persuaded a northbound trucker to take the tube of toothpaste all the way to Lapland . . . but too late, it seemed.

Turning my focus to Vabu Rusi's instructions, I had Nick go down one side road, then another, all the while marveling at the fact that anyone had bothered to put up legible street signs in this forsaken place. It wasn't until we pulled over to check a capsized sign that I realized they were merely temporary ones made out of wood.

I am not sure how long we had been driving when we finally rolled down a long snow-swept driveway. Something about the moonlight shadows and the deserted forest roads made me lose all sense of time. And the gnarled branches clawing at the car as we wound our way through a ghoulish honor guard of trees did nothing to dispel the sensation that we were entering a place hovering on the very edge of the physical world.

The two-story mansion at the end of the winding trail looked just as abandoned as the unkempt driveway would have us expect. In the bouncing beam of our headlights I saw a grand but peeling clapboard façade with boarded-up windows; only when we got a little closer did I notice the half dozen pairs of skis leaning against the wall. While clearly not completely deserted, the building certainly did not strike me as the unassailable fortress we had both been expecting.

"That's it?" Nick leaned forward in his seat with a grimace of wary incredulity. "Where's the raptor fence and the piranha moat? Can I see the directions?"

But there was no mistaking Vabu Rusi's map; this was indeed where we were supposed to go.

"It's obviously just some random meetinghouse," I said, hoping my disappointment didn't show. "They'd never give away the location of their actual headquarters."

Getting out of the car, I walked ahead up to the house. The front steps were cracked from decades of unrelenting winter, and the brass horseshoe knocker had long since surrendered to green old age. What exactly went on in this dilapidated building? I wondered. Was its purpose to greet people . . . or to say good-bye to them? As soon as Nick joined me on the front steps, I shook off my doubts and knocked firmly on the door, making it clear that, no matter what happened, I was responsible.

We waited for a while. When the door finally opened, my worries dissipated as if they had never been, for the light that emanated from the house was warm and abundant, and the woman who greeted us exuded nothing but the friendliest of intentions. Tall and trim, she wore jeans and a chunky sweater with a pattern of white reindeer, her gray hair gathered in a tight ponytail. At first glance her open, lively face suggested a woman in her sixties, but the gaunt, sinewy feel of her handshake made me suspect she was older than she looked. "At last!" she said, in what I now knew was a Finnish accent. "Come inside. And do excuse the look of the place. Winter here is a crushing thing."

She let us into a grand hallway with a curved staircase going up to the second floor. A few pieces of antique furniture and a large painting of grazing cows suggested we had entered the home of a cultivated family. And yet, something told me it was all for show.

"Are you Vabu Rusi?" asked Nick, unzipping his ski parka.

The woman smiled. "My name is Otrera." She took our coats and hung them from brass hooks on the wall, right next to a gun rack with six standing rifles. "Bears, wolves, wolverines," she said, in response to our silent observation. "I bring a shotgun when I take out the garbage. Or this." Our hostess pulled a rusty rapier out of the umbrella stand. "The wolverines know that this one doesn't feel so good up their nose. But come." She put the rapier back where it belonged and walked ahead of us into a high-ceilinged parlor with an antique three-tier woodstove at one end. "Let's warm up."

As we entered the large room, a handful of teenage girls immediately got up to slip soundlessly out another door. Dressed as they were in sweatpants and long-sleeved T-shirts, and with worn textbooks and pencil cases tucked under their arms, they gave the impression of being a study group meeting casually in someone's home. Moments later we could hear them talking loudly among themselves as they bounded through the house. A book left behind on a chair gave away the subject of their meeting: advanced Russian.

Despite the stately dimensions, the parlor had a utilitarian feel to it;

all the windows were covered by shutters, and the only furniture was a collection of mismatched chairs. Some were plush, some were straight-backed, others were mere stools; all, however, were oriented toward a large map of the world hanging on one wall with a whiteboard right next to it.

"Sit down!" urged Otrera, swiftly erasing the multicolored scribbles on the whiteboard. Then she grabbed a side chair and straddled it, casually resting her arms on the back. I couldn't help marveling at her physical confidence and felt a little flutter of hope. Had Granny aged as well as Otrera? I wondered. And if she was indeed still alive, could she possibly be here, in this house, waiting for the right moment to come and greet me?

Just then, I heard something approaching the house with a long-winded growl before coming to a roaring halt right outside. Glancing at Nick, I saw he had heard it, too. The motorcycle.

Eyeing the door to the hallway, I waited nervously to see what manner of person would enter. But no one came. All we heard were heavy steps going upstairs, a burst of agitated voices, and a door slamming.

How many people were in the house? I wondered. And who exactly were they? So far I had seen no one who fitted my image of an Amazon, nor did the house give the impression of being a meeting place—never mind command center—worthy of a powerful, international organization. Glancing at Otrera, I saw her staring at Nick with a speculative frown before finally saying, "You have a question for me."

"I have many questions." Nick leaned forward to rest his elbows on his knees. "I'm assuming it was you who summoned us here."

Fine strings of amusement—or maybe nerves—pulled at Otrera's lips. "Let me start by telling you about the woman in whose name you were invited tonight," she said. "As you learned at Raatteen Portti, Vabu Rusi and her little daughter, Enki, were among the civilians taken hostage by Russian partisans in retribution for Stalin's defeat here in Suomussalmi in the Winter War. Most of the time, the partisans simply killed the civilians—women, children, babies—but Vabu and Enki were taken by truck into Russia and put into a prisoner camp called

Kintismäki. I was there, too, with my sister, Tyyne. Our father had died in the war, and our mother was killed when they took us." Otrera plucked a piece of fluff from her sweater sleeve and let it fall to the floor before continuing more softly, saying, "Vabu's little Enki died in the camp. She had not eaten a full meal for many weeks—none of us had—and her mother could no longer keep her warm. When two guards came to take away the body, Vabu stabbed them both to death with a kitchen knife."

I was so shocked by Otrera's curt, matter-of-fact narrative that I could scarcely believe she had really been there. Once again, something in her manner reminded me of Granny, who had also been able to speak of gruesome things with uncanny detachment, as if the words were merely utensils in a drawer.

"This caused a great uprising in the camp," Otrera continued. "During the fighting, Vabu gathered some of us girls who had no parents, and in the confusion she was able to get us out through a hole in the fence. We walked all day and all night, and by morning we had no strength left. We just wanted to sleep, and Vabu could not make us go on. But we were lucky. A Russian lumberjack saw us lying in a snowdrift by the roadside, and he picked us up and brought us home. He and his family gave us warm clothes and food, and when we were strong enough, they smuggled us back across the border."

At this point Otrera took a deep breath, and now at last, in that forced, trembling inhalation, did I begin to grasp the extent of her self-control. "I was only eight years old," she explained, with renewed calm, "but I remember it so well. I remember that Vabu did not want to go back to her old house, because she knew the partisans had burned it down. In fact, there was so much fear here in Suomussalmi that many people had moved away. Whenever we went to a house, we found either a ruin or strangers living there. It felt like the end of the world. My sister Tyyne took it very hard. 'Why can't we go home?' she kept saying. 'What did those men do to Mommy?'"

Otrera sat for a while with her eyes closed, as if the narrative fatigued her. But just as I felt compelled to suggest we save the rest of the story for later, she looked up again, a spark of fresh energy in her eyes. "What I didn't realize," she went on, "was that, all this time, Vabu was searching for someone: a woman she had met at the hospital during the Winter War, just after her husband died. This woman—a violinist by profession—had told Vabu that if she wanted a new beginning, she and little Enki could come and join her traveling circus, which was wintered that year just outside Ämmänsaari." As if sensing our skepticism, Otrera hastened to add, "I know it sounds unusual, but Vabu had nowhere else to turn. After losing all the people she loved, she was now responsible for seven orphaned girls—me and Tyyne, and five others. And this violinist had told her the circus took in young women who had no other place to go and taught them more than just acrobatics—taught them how to get by in the world without having to depend on anyone. Oh, indeed, when we found it, it was heaven!" Otrera finally smiled, relishing this tiny palatable part of the past. "The horses, the music, the costumes . . . It was such a different way of life, so exotic for a young girl like me. The contortionists and trapeze artists could do incredible things; I remember watching them and thinking, how is it possible to make your body do that? And of course"—she gave us the conspiratorial eye—"they were all women."

Clearly enjoying our engrossment in her story, Otrera dismounted her chair and walked over to the three-tier woodstove to add more logs. There was a new spring to her step now; seen from behind, in her jeans and high-heeled boots, she certainly did not strike me as a woman in her eighties.

Behind her back, I glanced at Nick but found him preoccupied with the sounds of the house. There were distant voices . . . the clanging of pots and pans . . . even piano playing . . . and yet he was staring at the door to the hallway as though he fully expected an ambush.

When she returned to us, Otrera flipped the chair around and sat normally. She was more stern now, her emotions once again exiled to the distant past. "You, of course, know where I am going with this," she said. "The traveling circus was the Baltic chapter of the Amazons."

I was so agitated, I couldn't help exclaiming, "So, you *are* the Amazons?"

Otrera smiled cryptically. "We are some of them, yes. For generations, the Baltic chapter had been living like Gypsies, never committing to one place and rarely connecting with their Amazon sisters elsewhere in the world. The war, of course, made life so much more uncertain for them——"

We were briefly interrupted when a young woman wearing a sports bra stuck her head through the door to make an announcement in Finnish. "Ah, yes," said Otrera, waving at the girl to leave again. "There is someone who wants to speak with you before dinner. But let me finish my story first. You see, it was Vabu Rusi who convinced the Baltic Amazons—our chapter—that it was time to settle down and think strategically about our potential contribution to the modern world. We, the new generation, didn't just want to perform for money and get into a random fistfight here and there. Instead, we wanted to join forces with the other Amazon chapters to fight for the liberty and safety of women worldwide. So, after World War Two we started organizing ourselves and strengthening the contact with our sisters in other countries. We've been so successful in streamlining the mission of our organization and facilitating communication between the different divisions that the international Amazon headquarters were eventually moved here twenty-five years ago."

"How many chapters do you have all in all?" asked Nick.

Otrera shook her head lightly. "I obviously can't divulge any details, but rest assured we have people on the ground from Alaska to Fiji. Each of our chapters has its own organizational chart and its own queen. We don't believe in centralization, but we do need to work together; it's a difficult balance. Human trafficking, rape, and other atrocities do not abide by borders and jurisdictions, and neither do we. It is our hope, however, that young women living in open, tolerant societies, such as yourself, Diana, will need us less in the future—that you will become your own Amazons. You have the freedom to learn, the freedom to train." She smiled wryly. "You just need to wean yourselves off the State and its false pledge to protect you. Stop taking the bait; the hook will rip out your guts. But come." She rose and walked over to the door ahead of us.

Nick and I exchanged puzzled glances as we followed our hostess across the hallway and into a spacious library with a grand piano in the center. There were several sofas in the room, surrounded by jam-packed bookcases, but the only person present was a brush-cut woman sitting at the piano, playing a melancholy sonata with her eyes closed.

It was Katherine Kent.

CHAPTER THIRTY-NINE

We cannot live with your women. For we and they have not
the same customs. We shoot the bow and the javelin and ride
horses, but, for "women's tasks," we know them not.
—HERODOTUS, *Histories*

A S SURPRISED AS I WAS TO ENCOUNTER MY OXFORD MENTOR IN THIS
remote and unusual place, I waited silently for her to finish the
piece. What shocked me the most, I realized, was not so much Katherine's presence here among the Amazons as it was her intimate manner
of playing the piano. She touched the keys as if they were the sensitive
parts of a living being; I had never thought her capable of such emotional subtlety.

When she finally rested her hands, she sat for a few seconds with
her head bent, then looked up at me with a wistful smile. "I did my best
to avoid this moment. But I underestimated you."

From somewhere deep inside, I felt a rumble of advancing anger.
"For someone who is rarely wrong about anyone or anything, you certainly choose your moments."

Katherine stood up slowly. "I thought it would be better for you not
to know. Knowledge can be a dangerous thing—"

"Not as dangerous as ignorance."

Otrera stepped between us. "Diana, you must understand that this
has been a difficult situation for us. We have strict rules that forbid us
from speaking openly about who we are, *especially* over the telephone.
Under the circumstances, Katherine did what she felt was right: She

kept a close eye on the developments without revealing anything. Keep in mind we didn't know about your grandmother's notebook until you met with Dr. Jäger in Kalkriese. You never told Katherine how you were able to decipher the temple inscription in Algeria in only five days. She was horrified that our secret language could be translated into English so easily."

Nick put his hand on my other shoulder, as if to assert his right to weigh in. "And so you decided to blow up the temple," he said, his tone bitter, "and get rid of us both in the process."

"No!" boomed Otrera, looking at him with reproach. "The mission was carried out by our North African chapter. They obviously didn't know you were down there. They specifically issued the bomb threat to make sure the site was evacuated first."

Katherine came around the piano. She looked smaller than I remembered her—less formidable, more human. "We've always known the temple was there," she said, "and we've been on high alert since al-Aqrab discovered it. But it wasn't until you left me the message about deciphering the inscription that we fully realized what a liability the building was to us." She searched my face for understanding, maybe even forgiveness. "If it's any consolation, the temple is still there. It's just full of sand." She walked up to me, and I almost thought she would reach out and touch me. "We never intended to hurt you, but you had to be stopped. You were unwittingly helping Reznik. Later, after his people stole your laptop in Crete, we had to get it back, in case it held the key to deciphering our language . . . just as we had to prevent you from using your phone, since that was how he was tracking you. I was convinced you would give up and go home after Nafplio. But as I said"—she smiled, and I saw a rare glimpse of admiration in her eyes—"I underestimated you."

"Excuse me for stating the obvious," said Nick, "but why don't you change your way of communicating with one another? Ancient symbols, paper pamphlets, no cellphones . . . it all seems so amateurish. Isn't it time to go digital?"

Otrera straightened with irritation. In her high heels she was as tall as me, and age had clearly done nothing to shrink her authority. "We have corresponded in this manner since the days of Gutenberg. You yourselves have seen the dangers of using telephones. If you want to survive—especially in this day and age of cradle-to-grave surveillance—you have to be analogue. Don't tell me you're unaware of the fact that your own government is tracking digital communication with impunity?" Otrera flared her nostrils, then held out her arms as if to make us aware of the room with its antique lamps and well-worn volumes. "It's the printed book," she went on, "not to mention the pre-computer car or the old antique pocket watch, which will live forever. Time and again, a mindless rush to modernize has displaced better methods. Never mind the possibility of an electromagnetic pulse that will fry all electronic circuits and leave anyone under twenty-five raving and drooling in a padded room, completely disconnected from the world as they know it." Otrera looked Nick up and down with disgust, as if she was referring to him personally. "No, never mind the approaching apocalypse of which most people never give a second thought, but ask yourself this: Who is more amateurish, more vulnerable—those who rely on machines that need to be plugged in, or logged on, or in some other way connected in order to be more than a useless slab of plastic . . . or those who have learned to master life without?"

Otrera paused to give us both a meaningful look. Despite all, she was evidently delighted at the opportunity to share her view of the world and went on in an almost gleeful crescendo, "You came here looking for a modern fortress with blinking machines and retina scanners at every door, didn't you? Some pentagonal lair with people in orange uniforms driving around in little golf carts?" Her lips curled upward in a devilish smile. "Well, I'm sorry, but we're not running an off-the-rack secret society the way men like to imagine them. Here, we chop wood to keep warm. If you think that's amateurish, all I can say to you is this: You are more vulnerable than you think."

At this point Katherine stirred with impatience and said, to me and Nick, "Obviously, we're always striving to improve our system, and very soon the catalogs will be obsolete. Our communications team has been developing a new system for some time now—"

"Carrier pigeons?" proposed Nick.

Otrera's eyes narrowed. "The laughter of the ignoramus. We do use messenger pigeons to communicate, but only internally within the region."

"But the point is," Katherine went on, her lips tight with annoyance, "that these past few weeks have been catastrophic for us. If the likes of Reznik get their hands on our classified memos *and* the means to decipher them, they will be able to document our activity in the past and possibly predict our future movements. When our elite team broke into Reznik's house to steal back your laptop, Diana, we found a collection of our internal publications on his desk. This confirmed to us that he had indeed managed to tap into our private lines of communication." Katherine gave me a grim look. "All he needs is your notebook and he'll have exactly what he needs to decrypt our conversations."

"That night after Reznik's party," I said, "when your blond wunderkind was baiting me with my wallet and passport, what would have happened if I had kept going? Was it a trap?"

Otrera and Katherine exchanged glances. Then Otrera said, evasively, "Our objective was to get you safely back to Oxford as soon as possible."

"What about Dr. Jäger in Kalkriese?" I went on. "Why didn't she level with me and explain all these things? Or was she actually hoping to get me killed?"

I knew Katherine well enough to see her cringing. "Kyme has lived in that house all her life. She will do anything not to compromise it. She was hoping you would simply go home to Oxford, leaving the explanations to *me*—"

"And maybe I would have," I pointed out, "if I'd been able to get in touch with you. But your phone—"

"Is disconnected. Yes." Katherine rolled her eyes with impatience. "I obviously couldn't risk you calling me, asking questions. It would compromise my cover."

I shook my head. "Kyme could at least have hinted she was on my side."

"Believe me," said Katherine, "she was extremely unhappy when we called to let her know you were being followed by Reznik's hit men, and to instruct her not to let you go until they had been neutralized. If you hadn't run away like that, everything would have been sorted out, and our German chapter wouldn't have——" Her eyes strayed to Nick's face.

"Broken my nose?" he suggested.

"Yes, well." Katherine took a step back. "Our German chapter hadn't been briefed about *you*. They were there to rescue Diana, and they didn't realize——" She glanced at Otrera, suddenly flustered.

The sound of an old-fashioned bell cut short the awkward moment.

"Dinner!" said Otrera, visibly relieved.

Nick didn't move. "Why did you invite us here tonight?" he asked them both. "I'm not really hearing an apology."

Otrera gave him a look that would have made lesser men wince. "You are the first male to *ever* have been invited into this house. Please bear that in mind, Niccolò."

Nick flinched at the sound of his real name, but Otrera merely turned to me and said, with the superior benevolence of an all-powerful despot, "Your grandmother's notebook. I'm sure you can appreciate that we would like you to leave it here with us."

I felt a stab of disappointment. Ever since arriving, I had waited for the subject of Granny to come up. Not wanting to force the issue, I had let Otrera move through the past at her own pace. Now, sadly, it looked as if her only remaining concern was the notebook. It was time to acknowledge that my childish hope of being reunited with Granny tonight was just that: childish.

"I understand," I said. "However, Reznik has given me an ultimatum. If I don't give the notebook to *him,* he will go after the people I love. Now, as it happens"——I took the water-damaged volume out of my bag and handed it to Otrera——"this notebook is no longer a dictionary of your language. The only message left in it is 'Suomussalmi Vabu Rusi,' and since Reznik already knows we're here there's really no point in concealing it from him. However, seeing that it's now totally useless, he will be angry with me regardless of whether I give it to him or not."

Otrera leafed through the book, frowning. "This is disturbing news. I did not know he had given you an ultimatum, nor that he knows where you are." She looked up at us. "How can you be sure?"

"Because two cars followed us tonight," said Nick. "We were able to shake them, but they're still out there, looking for us."

"I see." Otrera handed the notebook to Katherine. "This changes things. I'm sorry. We no longer have time for dinner."

THE DINING ROOM WAS at the back of the house, and in contrast to the meeting room and deserted library it was warm and abustle with activity. Its main feature was a table as long as those in Oxford dining halls, with space for at least fifty people seated on wooden benches on either side. At the far end of the table stood a throne-like chair with an ornately carved wooden back.

"Normally the house is full of people," explained Otrera, closing the door behind us, "but because of two separate emergencies on the Russian side and delays at Arlanda Airport, there's only a handful of us here tonight. These are our trainees." Walking ahead of us down the length of the room, Otrera gestured at a steady traffic of young women carrying steaming dishes and armloads of firewood from a nearby kitchen. "We rescue thousands of girls every year, and some of them choose to stay with us. Currently we have four hundred trainees worldwide, divided between our individual chapters."

She singled out a lanky young woman dressed in a pair of denim overalls, and nodded with pride. "That is Lilli. At seven years old she was stolen from an orphanage in Estonia and sold into prostitution. But we saved her, just as we have saved many others. I hope you will forgive her." Otrera gave both Nick and me a meaningful look over her shoulder. "Lilli is forceful, but she means well. She is in training to become our next queen, which is why we occasionally send her on missions outside the region." Perhaps realizing she had disclosed more than she should, Otrera frowned and added, "The queen is our most exposed operative—the one who takes the greatest risks. First into the field, last to retreat. If all nations held their elected authorities to this basic principle of leadership, I guarantee you we would have significantly fewer wars in this world. Look at Lilli." Otrera nodded once more at the young woman. "We are not training her to hide in an air-conditioned bunker and lead her troops by pushing buttons. She will never declare war to distract us from her own cock-ups. Nor will she send her sisters into battle with insufficient equipment, for if things go wrong, she will be the first to die."

Puzzled by the long, ardent introduction, I took a closer look at Lilli. She wore a red bandanna around her head with two blond braids hanging out. It wasn't until she cast a stolen glance at me across the room I felt a spark of recognition. "It's *her*!" I whispered to Nick. "The mouse who baited me in Istanbul! The Rollerblade thief from Nafplio!"

"Pitana! Penthesilea!" Marching impatiently ahead, Otrera approached four women standing at the head of the table, talking over a bowl of nuts. "We need to act. Reznik is closing in."

The women turned toward us with squints of suspicion. They were no taller than me, but there was something about their build and posture that gave away their unusual inner strength. One wore knee-high boots with a matching suede jacket. A pale scar through her left eyebrow stood out against her tan face. Another was dressed entirely in black, her trim body poured into shapely leather trousers and a tight turtleneck. The contrast between her dark, youthful body and the proud lines of gray at her temples was striking; she could easily have dyed her hair and passed for a woman my own age, but the artificial way was clearly not the Amazon way.

All four carried themselves with the confidence of women in excellent physical shape, and the sight of them filled me with emotions I had not felt since Granny and I had traveled the Amazon world in fanciful drawings and thrilling tales. Those emotions were now so fused with real-life childhood memories that I could almost recall the actual smells and sounds of that golden realm of stamping hooves and rushing chariots.

Skipping introductions, Otrera quickly drew up the situation and concluded, saying, "We assume it's Reznik, but we have no proof."

The women exchanged glances. They were clearly upset by the news, but there was more to their silence than that. I could see in their eyes they were angry, not only at us, but at Otrera as well. They had never wanted us there, I realized; in all likelihood, they had advised against the invitation, and now reality had proved them right.

"I'm surprised you didn't know Reznik was here," said Nick, undaunted by the cool reception. "You've been watching us all day." He looked at them one by one. "Who's driving the KTM? Doesn't it attract a little too much attention here in the winter?"

His brazen manner accomplished nothing but to agitate the Amazons further. At length, the woman in the black turtleneck said, with heavy Slavic deliberation, "Finnish men are not afraid of strong women. Only weak men want women to be weak. What about you?" She ran her dark eyes over Nick's body, pausing at all the major muscle groups. "Are you afraid of women who can kick your ass?"

"I'd prefer that you kick someone else's," he replied. "Aren't there people out there who deserve it more?" He cast me a poignant glance, as if to say, "Better not provoke these ladies any further."

"You may think of us as outlaws," said the woman with the scar through her eyebrow. She spoke with defiance, in a canorous Swedish accent. "The truth is, we *are* the law. Not the whiny, counteractive, impotent law sitting around in big volumes on fake mahogany shelves, but the law that lives in the human heart. The law that says bad people will be punished. The law that says might is not right, and that murderers and molesters will not walk free."

"There are police officers out there," interjected the woman in black, "who pray that *we* will find the creep before *they* do." Her eyes narrowed in a menacing smile. "We don't grant parole. And we're not slowed down by a titanic, gluttonous bureaucracy."

"I'm all for limiting the power of the state," said Nick, "but aren't you worried that your vigilante justice is going to take down a few innocents?"

At this, Otrera finally weighed in, speaking with unbending resolution. "We may make mistakes, but not in that. Those who rape the rights of others forfeit their own. But now is not the time for political philosophy. Pitana——" She looked keenly at the woman with the scar. "We need a plan."

"It's too bad," said Nick, ignoring Otrera's impatience, "that you're missing so many people tonight." He nodded at the throne-like chair at the head of the long dinner table. "Who sits there? Your queen? What's her name, I wonder?" He looked intently at the Amazons. "Myrina?"

His words were met by a silence so profound you could hear a drawer closing upstairs.

"Come!" Otrera took both Nick and me firmly by the arms. "I have something to show you. Katherine, stay here."

As we walked away from the others, Otrera shook her head and said, "It is not easy for us to open our house to strangers."

I saw Nick frowning. "Is that what we are? Strangers?"

Otrera gave him a long look. "Your father changed his name when he left Oxford. We had no idea who you were." She broke off to let us through a back door with an old-fashioned bolt. "It wasn't until Reznik's masquerade that we began to suspect the truth. Someone noticed you in the crowd and thought you looked——"

In the brief quiet of Otrera's unfinished sentence, I was reminded of the cat woman who had glared at me with inexplicable hatred in Reznik's powder room and who had later—according to Nick—been part of the break-in. Even then, in the flux of everything happening around me, I had found her dark, penetrating eyes eerily familiar. Now it finally dawned on me where I had seen them before. They were the eyes of the man walking right behind me.

"But that didn't stop your people from beating me up at the Iding-shof Hotel," Nick pointed out as we followed Otrera into a dark, musty-smelling corridor lined with overclothes and footwear.

Otrera turned on the lights. "Our German chapter is very efficient. They did what they felt was necessary. At least, after that, we knew who you were."

"How? Because I fight like my dad?"

Starting down a narrow basement staircase, Otrera said over her shoulder, "How do you think? We have a lab. All they need is a drop of blood—"

"They certainly got *that*." Nick pressed past me and followed her closely down the staircase, apparently not sharing my apprehensions about our underground destination. "And then what? You have my DNA, you know who my parents are. What comes next? Are you going to show me a box with my old teddy bears? Is that what we're doing down here?"

Instead of replying, Otrera continued ahead of us through a narrow basement storage space with spears, bows, axes, and snowshoes either hanging on or leaning against the walls. As we walked past a door slightly ajar, both Nick and I paused to peek into a room that had an entire wall covered with television screens set on different news channels. Oddly, the only sound coming from the room and its maelstrom of flashing images was the rhythmic trot of a strapping woman running on a treadmill with a headset on, intently observing the changing screens.

Realizing she had lost her retinue, Otrera came back toward us with a strained smile. "Obviously, we have to know what's going on," she snapped, mostly to Nick. "But we have no computers online in this house. Our research team is one hundred percent mobile and operates exclusively out of random Internet cafés. But please come with me. We don't have much time."

Walking ahead once more, Otrera took a large key out of her trouser pocket and stopped at the end of the armory to unlock a massive door. "There," she said, pushing open the door with her shoulder and flicking on a light switch inside. "This is our sanctuary."

We followed her into a vast dimly lit room, which had the temperature and feel of a crypt. The only light came from illuminated shelves on the walls, and the darkness in the rest of the sanctuary was so pervasive it took me a moment to make out the presence of an enormous ironclad coffer in the center of the stone floor. At least five feet wide and three feet deep, the coffer was sealed with a medieval-looking padlock, and despite Otrera's impatient waving, both Nick and I had a hard time wresting our eyes from it.

"What's in there?" asked Nick. "The Amazon Hoard?"

Seeing she could not coax us away from the enigmatic receptacle, Otrera came back toward us again, folding her arms against the cold. "It's not what you think." She looked at us intently, almost nervously. "It is not gold."

My pulse quickened. "But it *is* King Priam's treasure?"

Otrera hesitated. "We believe so." She put a hand on the coffer's lid, as if to ensure it remained closed. "Only the queen has the key."

As much as I knew she was uncomfortable with the subject, I could not walk away. Here I was, a faithful Amazon believer, within arm's length of a treasure even *I* had dismissed as a legend. . . . It was too wonderful. And so I nodded and said to Otrera, "I understand. But at the same time, I must take issue with the idea of safeguarding history in this manner. Assuming King Priam really did entrust the Amazons with the most valuable artifacts of Trojan civilization . . . well, why did he do that? Presumably he wanted to ensure they weren't destroyed. And he was wise. The Greeks annihilated the Trojans so completely we're not even sure what language they spoke. To this day, the nature of Trojan civilization is one of the greatest mysteries of the ancient world. In fact, for hundreds of years, scholars believed Troy and the Trojan War were nothing but a grand fantastic myth. Was that what King Priam had in mind when he asked the Amazons to safeguard his treasure? That his realm should be erased from human history for three thousand years? No!" I slammed a palm against the lid of the coffer and saw Otrera jump at the sound. "It would be his greatest wish, I am sure, that these things be known to the world. For if they are merely festering in a frozen basement on the fringes of nowhere, they might as well have been destroyed by the bloody Greeks."

Otrera recoiled at my exclamation, then said, stiffly, "I did not invite you down here to discuss mythology. As you can see, this is a place for memories and meditation." She gestured at the illuminated shelves all around us, and only then did I notice that the objects on display were bronze urns in different sizes and shapes. "Vabu Rusi and all her girls are at rest here. I am the last one. Come." She took me by the elbow and walked me over to one of the shelves, which held seven urns. On the wall behind them hung a framed black-and-white photo of a somber lady seated in an armchair with seven young women clustered around her. "There!" Otrera pointed at a girl in the picture. "Do you recognize that little angel?"

I leaned closer, expecting the girl to be Otrera herself. But instead, I saw a face with two serene eyes that I instinctively knew.

"My sister, Tyyne," said Otrera. "She was your grandmother."

The revelation came as such a shock to me that I could not hold back my tears. It was not just the photo and the sudden realization that *this* was why Otrera had invited us. . . . Most of all it was the unexpected weight of finality. Granny was dead. I had suspected it ever since I received her bracelet in the mail, but now I knew it for certain. Here was the urn with her ashes. I touched it with a profound sense of loss.

Overcome, I wanted to embrace Otrera and thank her for making this moment possible. Beating me to it, she slipped a hand into her trouser pocket, took out a small, sealed envelope, and held it out to me, as if to prevent me from coming any closer. "Take it!" she said, clearly in a hurry to quicken the transaction. "Writing to outsiders is strictly against our rules. But Tyyne—or Kara, as she was called here—was a rule breaker. She made me swear that if you ever came to Suomussalmi in search of her, I would greet you as family and give you this letter."

Nick put a comforting arm around me, perhaps sensing how overwhelmed I was. "You call us outsiders," he said, "but we are your relations, even if you don't think of us that way. There must be others like us—especially male children like me—who have tried to find you."

Otrera shook her head. "It is extremely rare that we consort with men. No one wants to risk conceiving a boy and having to make a terrible choice between the child and the sisterhood. But sometimes Nature takes over." She smiled at us both, as if to say she understood the power of romantic love even if she had lived her life in defiance of it. Then her expression changed. "Oh, that reminds me." She held out a hand toward me. "The jackal bracelet. Tyyne gave it to you, and therefore it is yours. But she did not intend you to wear it like a piece of jewelry. It represents a pact, Diana, and it comes with rules and responsibilities. Yours is one of the original bronze jackals; we only have a few of those left. Some of us wear an iron or silver jackal, and some wear bronze replicas, but more and more, we are moving away from metal. It is too detectable. Most of our younger operatives choose a brand or tattoo these days. The queen still wears a bronze jackal, but she takes it off on missions." Otrera gave Nick a knowing look. "At least she does *now*. When your father met her, she was still in training and wore her bracelet wherever she went. I'm guessing that was what gave her away."

Nick's arm tensed around me. "Correction: She gave *me* away. Is that part of the queenship test, choosing the sisterhood over motherhood? Myrina clearly passed with distinction."

Her patience running out, Otrera turned to me with a frown. "Here." Taking my arm, she pulled up my sleeve and removed the bronze jackal from my wrist in one expert movement. Then she handed it to me with a grave nod. "Should you ever choose to wear it again, Katherine Kent will be your contact."

I barely knew what to do with the bracelet. "Do you think that was what my grandmother wanted?" I asked. "That I become one of you?"

Otrera gave me an obscure, sideways glance, before starting back toward the door. "I don't know. As I said, Tyyne was a rule breaker. And when she returned to us after all those years, she was scarred. But she was still the best mentor our girls ever had. Unpredictable, yes." Otrera smiled at me over her shoulder. "I'm sure I don't have to tell *you* this, Diana. She was a brilliant teacher, and I want you to know that her last years here with us were very busy, and very rewarding."

"How did she die?" I asked.

Otrera paused to look at me with a tender smile. "The way she always wanted: She died riding."

"Did she ever talk about me?"

Otrera began walking again. "All the time. But read the letter. And when you have read it, please destroy it."

"Wait!" said Nick. "What about me? Don't I get a letter?"

Otrera stopped to pull open the heavy door. "Human hearts are complex, unpredictable mechanisms."

"She's here, isn't she?" He glanced up at the house above us. "Why doesn't she want to meet me? Is the noble Queen Myrina embarrassed about her past?"

Leaning against the open door, Otrera turned to look at him, sympathy and austerity at war in her face. "What she did to your father was no worse than what men have done to women since the beginning of time. Just be happy she let you live." With that she turned off the lights and waited for us to follow her upstairs. "Clear your minds. We need to prepare for battle."

The others were still assembled in the dining room. As soon as we entered, Pitana came toward us, giving the impression of a pirate captain with her tall boots and the scar running through her eyebrow.

"Any news?" asked Otrera.

Pitana replied with a curt nod. "Breakdowns and delays. None of the teams can be here before morning. If Reznik comes tonight, we can't attack him head-on until we know what he's got."

"Of all the nights." Otrera took a deep breath. "So, what's the plan?"

Pitana turned to the Slavic woman in black who had taunted Nick earlier. "Pen?"

Penthesilea stepped forward, a challenge in her eyes. "That depends on you two," she said, looking from me to Nick with cautious expectancy, "and how willing you are to fight with us."

CHAPTER FORTY

And there's no heaven above to punish you?
—Euripides, *Andromache*

WE DROVE AWAY FROM THE HOUSE IN STUNNED SILENCE. IT WAS all so new, so confusing; only two things were certain: Granny had hoped I would find her in the end, and I did. I could not wait to open the letter she had left for me, and yet part of me dreaded the emotions it might unleash.

"Don't be sad," said Nick, putting an arm around me as he drove. "Be happy for her. She made it back home, thanks to your piggy bank savings."

I wiped my eyes. "I just wish I had known . . . instead of being so upset with her all the time. When she talked about the men in green clothes, she was not thinking about doctors, but about murderous Russian partisans. What horrible memories she must have had—"

"But how fortunate she also had *you*," said Nick. "You gave her a happy space where she could hide from it all for a while."

Outside the car, new snow was falling on the silent forest, tumbling toward us in the pale glare of the headlights. It all felt ominous and unreal. We had found the Amazons, and I had finally learned the truth about Granny, but at what price?

"How about you?" I glanced at Nick's profile in the blue glow from the dashboard. "Are you okay?"

"I will be," he replied, without conviction, "once all this is over."

Just then we both noticed an unmoving dark form blocking the road ahead. A delivery van. Slowing down, Nick changed the lights to see better, but the snow was falling so heavily they just reflected back at us. "Here we go," he said grimly, bringing us to a skidding halt on the icy road. "Are you ready?"

From one second to the next I was filled with violent, stomach-turning fear. And then we were suddenly bathed in light—the blindingly bright beams from two other cars pulling up right behind ours, preventing us from turning around.

"Now please—" Nick turned to look at me, his features distorted by the ruthless light. "Don't provoke them. Just play the game."

As soon as we got out of the car, at least a dozen men in black combat gear spilled out of the other vehicles, quickly surrounding us. Half of them had guns pointed at us. The others might as well have, for their expressions were as cold and hard as any weapon.

"How cute," said Reznik, stepping leisurely out of the shadows.

Dressed in combat gear just like his men, the retired Communist boss looked quite at home in the frosty wilderness, with snowflakes falling on his gray crew cut. "You're a lovely couple. I have some nice footage of you." Stopping right in front of us, he smiled that measured, forced smile of his that had unnerved me when I first met him in Istanbul—the grin of a calculating killer. "The Aqrab prince and his Amazon princess. *Complimenti*. You had me fooled, both of you. I didn't realize Amazons could be so"—he looked me up and down with amused disdain—"meatless. Oh, well." Reznik looked over his shoulder. "See? I told you we would find them together."

Only then did I notice who was standing behind him.

James Moselane.

Hunched with cold and squinting against the flying snow, my old friend looked so reluctant and miserable that I first assumed he was Reznik's prisoner. But then I noticed that James, too, had a gun.

"What on earth?" I exclaimed, so appalled I almost forgot to be afraid. "This is absurd! You know I'm not an Amazon."

James made a weary grimace and said, mostly to Nick, "Come on, hand it over. Let's be grown-ups."

I glanced at Nick, sensing he was struggling not to punch James in the face. "Here." I eased the *Historia Amazonum* out of my handbag. "We did mean to return it—"

Reznik grabbed the volume only to toss it aside with a sneer. "Not that useless piece of shit. The notebook!"

"I don't have it," I stammered. "We left it with Professor Seppänen—"

"Who the fuck is Professor Seppänen?"

I glanced at Nick. We had rehearsed the story with Pitana, and she had insisted it sounded more authentic coming from me. "He's an expert on ancient languages," I explained, my teeth chattering from fear and cold and the need to be convincing. "We just had dinner with him—"

"Where?"

I waved an arm at the blackness behind us. "Just down the road."

Reznik looked at me with narrow eyes. Then he turned to James. "What do you think?"

I didn't dare take my eyes off Reznik. Did James know me well enough to see that I was lying? If so, he didn't let on.

"All right!" Reznik waved at his men. "Let's go—"

"Wait!" James walked up to him, and the two men had a brief, avid exchange. I was sure I heard James saying, "We had an agreement!" to which Reznik responded with muttered reluctance until, in the end, he growled with annoyance and turned around to issue an order to four of his goons.

Without hesitation, the men came forward to seize Nick by the shoulders and drag him away from me. I tore at their arms and yelled at them to release him, but Reznik restrained me with a crushing grip. When I kept writhing and pulling, he slapped me across the face with the back of his hand.

It was a numbing blow, and for a few seconds my world went black. I faintly registered Nick calling my name, but didn't have the air to respond.

"I lost two of my best officers in Kalkriese," sneered Reznik, right into my face. "It has not been a good week. You Amazon bitches are all the same—"

"Please!" I croaked, trying to regain my balance. "Don't hurt him!"

Reznik snorted with mirth. "Isn't that touching? The Amazon is in love. That makes it all so much more fun." Snapping his fingers, he had the men yank off Nick's ski jacket, then his sweater as well, leaving him in nothing but trousers and a T-shirt. "How do you like that?" he asked me, his eyes bulging with the need to dominate. "Your hot date is getting very cold very fast. Now, let's see . . . ninety kilos, six feet one inch, thirty-five years, minus ten degrees." He wagged his head in mock calculation, then snapped his fingers once more.

"Stop!" I cried, when the men started tearing at Nick's T-shirt. "You're going to kill him!"

"Wrong." Reznik took me by the jaw, a sardonic smile on his face. "*You* are going to kill him if you don't—"

Nick threw himself at one of his guardians—the one holding a submachine gun to his ribs. The man fell down with a hiss of pain, clutching his throat, while the gun changed hands. It happened so rapidly I could barely follow the movements. Within a heartbeat, the three other guards were backing away, fumbling for their weapons.

"Don't!" yelled Nick, aiming at each of them in turn. "No blood. Okay? No blood. Let's keep this clean. You don't want to piss off my dad, do you?"

For a few tense moments, the forest was so silent you could hear the howl of a distant wolf. Then Reznik let go of me and waved at everyone to calm down. "We're just having fun. Back to business. No need to fuck with al-Aqrab." He gestured impatiently at the man holding Nick's clothes. "Give the man back his jacket."

Reznik was too busy issuing orders to notice that James, pale with fury, raised his own gun and aimed it at Nick.

I burst forward and pulled down James's arm, but the gun went off with a hellish, ear-rending blast that had Reznik leaping forward and tearing the smoking weapon from James's hand with a barrage of swearwords.

Horrified, I ran toward Nick, who had fallen to his knees with a groan of agony, clutching his hip where a red stain was spreading. Sick to the stomach at the sight of his blood, I threw myself down next to him, tore off my coat, and draped it over his shoulders to shield him from the cold. "He needs to get to a hospital!" I yelled. "Please!"

I heard Reznik grunt. "You want to go to the hospital? Sure! I'm an old romantic. You can spend the night together in the morgue. Maybe they will even zip you into the same bag."

"Don't be a moron," said Nick through gritted teeth, still clutching his hip. "It's the notebook you want, right? Diana already told you: It's just down the road. But you need her to guide you."

"No!" I threw my arms around him. "I won't leave you here like this!"

Nick looked at me pleadingly. "You *have* to. I'm counting on you."

"Enough!" Reznik tore my coat from Nick's shoulders and sent a shock wave of pain through my scalp as he yanked me away by the hair. Then he yelled an order to one of his men, who went to our rental car, got in the driver's seat, and drove the vehicle off the road into the ditch.

Reznik turned to James. "You're a fucking idiot. Now we have a hell of a mess to clean up. Just pray al-Aqrab doesn't find out who did this. Better buy yourself a one-way ticket to Mars, little Lord Mose-lane."

I glared at James, disgusted with this slithering snake of a man. Although Reznik had long since taken his gun away, James still stood with his arm half-raised, apparently frozen in place. "I didn't mean to shoot him," he whispered, the words barely audible. "I just—"

"Too late!" Reznik gave James another whack on the back of the head as he walked by. "Let's go find that notebook. We'll deal with the body later."

That was how we left Nick: crouching in the bloodstained snow. The next thing I saw was the dirty backseat of a car as the men shoved me inside, headfirst.

"All of this is your fault," said Reznik, getting in after me. "If you had given me the notebook in the first place"—he grasped my face with one hand, looking into my eyes with a mocking smile—"we would all still be friends."

I said nothing. It was all I could do not to throw up when we sped down the road, leaving Nick behind in the freezing darkness.

The drive was a blur to me. I told the driver exactly where to go with unthinking certainty, while the only thing racing through my mind was Nick's blood, draining from his body as fast as his warmth, leaving him helpless against the arctic night. He had been shivering when we left him, and he would shiver for a while longer as he fought off hypothermia. Then the shivering would stop. And that's when I had to be back there to save him. If I wasn't, his body would shut down, organ by organ, until there was no life left.

When we finally drove down the bumpy path to the Amazon hideaway, I was so frantic with impatience I leaned forward to push at the driver. "Keep going! Faster!" As I spoke, the peeling house façade and boarded-up windows became visible in brief flashes, and the ghostly effect of the place was enhanced by the erratic flicks of our headlights and those of the two vehicles behind us.

"That's it?" Reznik leaned forward, peering at the run-down building. "It's an empty house." He stared at me, twitches of anger pulling at his eyes. "You little whore—"

I was too distressed to hold back my fury. "Nick is freezing to death back there!" I exclaimed. "Why would I lie to you?"

Getting out of the car, Reznik took stock of his men and instructed the three drivers to stay behind and keep the engines running. Then he jammed the muzzle of his gun into my back and made me walk ahead up the stone steps to the front door.

I had no idea what awaited us inside. Pitana had not divulged this part of the plan to Nick and me. How would a mere handful of Amazons—most of whom were barely of age, not to mention Otrera at eighty-plus—fare against a gang of heavily armed brutes?

When I had knocked several times without result, Reznik shoved me aside and banged on the door with his fist. Then, when there was still no answer, he tried the door handle . . . and found the door unlocked. As James came to join us, Reznik grabbed my shoulder. "Go, go!" he hissed, pushing at me to enter the house first.

With a tentative "Hello? Professor Seppänen—?" I stepped across the threshold and entered the dark house. Because the cars outside were idling with their headlights on, greeting me as the door swung open was only my own shadow, stretched out across the wooden floor-boards. The hallway was all but empty. Every piece of furniture had disappeared, including the rifle rack. The only object left was the um-brella stand.

Frazzled as I was, I nearly cried out with frustration. The Amazons were gone. Their headquarters had been compromised, and the planned ambush had been nothing but a way of getting rid of us. I felt my chest tightening; never had I felt so forsaken. Even James's betrayal dwindled by comparison.

Reznik poked me again hard with the muzzle of his gun. "So, where is it?"

"I don't know." I looked around, trying to figure out what to do. "It's so late. I'm sure Professor Seppänen has gone to bed."

Turning to his men, Reznik gave instructions to search the house. Two were sent into the congregation room, two into the library, and the rest upstairs. Then he nodded at the door to the dining room, which was straight ahead and slightly ajar. "What's in there?"

"I don't know," I said. It was just the three of us now—me, Reznik, and James. My head was racing with possible ways of escaping the two of them and leaving the house.

"Ladies first." Reznik took me firmly by the arm, his gun digging into my ribs as we walked across the floor together.

The dining room was almost dark. The headlights outside that had made the entryway so bright were helpless to illuminate more than just a few feet of the long dining table, which, in the murk of night, ap-peared to continue indefinitely in either direction.

Just then, we heard a noise from upstairs, right above our heads. It was the sound of a rushing scuffle . . . then a muffled shriek . . . then silence.

Stiffening, Reznik pulled out a walkie-talkie and barked a question. There was no reply.

"Turn on the lights!" he said, prodding me with the gun. I heard in his voice he was beginning to have misgivings about the place, and it didn't help that no lights came on when I flicked the switch. "Try again!" he sneered.

"Shh!" said a heavyset thug of a man wearing a ski cap and pointing a gun—he was one of the four men who had searched the rooms downstairs and who had now rejoined us.

Everyone listened intently.

The house was perfectly still. The only noise to pierce the impression of utter abandonment was a faint neigh from outside. The sound drew a grim curse from Reznik. "Out!" he barked, pushing at everyone. "Out, out, *out!*"

Just as the men began to back up, however, the front door slammed shut behind us, and we found ourselves in total darkness. Too shocked to act on anything other than instinct, I ducked out of Reznik's grip and moved away from the men. Pressing myself against the wall, barely registering the pain when I hit my head on one of the coat hooks, I could hear the cursing and trampling of heavy combat boots as Reznik's goons tried to locate the door, and then suddenly . . .

A blinding burst of light from above and a horrible, frenzied whipping sound engulfed us for several seconds, reminding me of nothing I had ever heard before.

Shielding my eyes from the violent rays of light, it took a moment to make out the bodies lying sprawled on the floor by the door, pinned in place by dozens of arrows. It was a grotesque, sickening sight. Most of the arrows had been aimed at their heads and faces above the armored vests. Already pooling on the floor was the blood streaming from the gruesome wounds.

The only two men who had not been hurt were Reznik and James, who both stood pressed against the wall to the dining room, hidden, as was I, from the eyes of the archers on the gallery right above us.

It took Reznik a moment to fathom that all his men were dead, upstairs as well as downstairs, and that we were the only three left alive. When his eyes met mine, his face became so contorted with fury he no longer resembled a human being. "You tricked me!" he growled, charging toward me along the wall, staying clear of the archers' target zone.

I didn't even have time to wonder about his intentions. The gun in his hand and the livid expression on his face were all I needed to reach out for the umbrella stand. Fortunately, the rusty old rapier was still there.

Unprepared for the sight of me holding a weapon, Reznik kept coming forward without seeming to register the danger. "Come on!" he barked at James, who was still petrified with shock. "We'll use her as a hostage!" Still pointing the gun at me, Reznik reached out for my arm with his free hand, but I managed to get the rapier between us.

"Don't you dare!" I said, my voice so calm it surprised even me. Somehow, holding a weapon I knew so well made me able to think straight again. "I'm going back to Nick—"

"The fuck you are!" Reznik forced the blade aside with his arm and aimed the gun at my face. "You're coming with *me*."

At that moment, a woman armed with a machete emerged from the door to the dining hall right behind him. Pitana. She did not charge Reznik, but pulled back silently, realizing the danger I was in.

That was all it took. Reznik glanced over his shoulder to see what had caught my eye, and I lunged forward, disarming him with a thrust to the wrist. Crying out with surprise and pain, he clutched the wound with his other hand. The gun fell to the floor with a clatter, right between us.

Roaring with fury, Reznik bent to retrieve it, but I kicked it aside. I was so focused on keeping Reznik away from me that I didn't grasp what James was up to until he darted forward and picked up the gun.

"What the hell are you doing?" I cried, when he pointed the gun at me and began backing toward the door, striding over the dead bodies.

"Come on!" James motioned frantically for Reznik to follow. "Let's get out—"

The sentence ended in a cry of pain. For the second time, the gun fell to the floor with a clatter. An arrow from above had struck James right in the hand, penetrating his palm, and he doubled over with groaning agony.

"Gentlemen!" roared a voice of great authority.

Looking up, I saw Otrera—my terrible, beautiful great-aunt Otrera—standing on the gallery with her bow raised, the string still vibrating from the perfect shot. Around her stood a group of young Amazons, among them Lilli.

Opening her arms, bow and all, Otrera said to Reznik, "You wanted to find us. Here we are."

I did not wait to see Reznik's reaction. Without another second's hesitation, I bolted across the floor past James, picking up the handgun on the way. Barely stopping, I tore open the front door, so eager to get out I stumbled over the threshold and fell down on my hands and knees on the gritty stone steps.

I got up, still clutching the gun, but felt a hand grasping at my ponytail and realized that Reznik was right behind me. Twisting around, I hit him in the face with the gun and managed to pull my hair out of his grip. His eyebrow was spurting blood as I turned and started to run.

Despite his wounds Reznik followed me down the steps and staggered after me through the snow. "The gun!" he growled, his voice as forceful as ever. "Give it to me!"

Two furious snorts and the rapid thudding of hooves made us both jump with fear. A horse and rider, blending into a single black magnificent form, came galloping out of the woods and pounding right between us—so close the rider's long leather coat whipped me across the cheek. I saw her face for only a split second as she rode by, but that was enough to recognize Penthesilea, the Slavic woman who had masterminded the ambush.

Squealing with triumph, Reznik bent down to pick up something she had tossed into the snow right beside him when she rode by. A revolver.

His fingers closed greedily around the weapon, and yet I was not afraid. You moron, I thought as I backed away from him. Don't you know Amazon rule number four? Never kill an unarmed man unless you have to.

Before Reznik could fire a single shot, Penthesilea turned in the saddle, raised a long gun that had been concealed by her coat . . . and a deafening blast threw Reznik and the revolver backward, into a snowbank. All I could see of him were his hands and feet, but I knew that neither they, nor the man himself, would ever stir again.

"Morg!" A frenzied call stirred me from shock. James stood on the threshold of the house, waving wildly. "Come back! Please!"

I turned and ran.

Clutching my own pistol with both hands, I raced down the driveway. Expecting Reznik's brutish drivers to be barricaded in their vehicles, armed and desperate, I was relieved to find that they weren't. Both the cars and the van were empty, with the front doors left open, and the only signs of Reznik's three remaining men were the bloody furrows in the snow where they had been dragged away.

Getting into the last car—a brand-new SUV with leather seats—I fumbled around for the key and finally found it on the floor, smeared with blood and melting snow. I was so agitated I could barely control my hands and feet, but managed to get the car started and in reverse before backing up as fast as I could out the winding driveway.

Once back on the main road, I began retracing my route with breathless urgency. The only thing on my mind was Nick, waiting for me minute after agonizing minute.

The image of him crouched in the snow in silent agony was so powerful it had stayed before my eyes all this time. And when I finally approached the spot where we had left him, I fully expected to see him kneeling by the roadside still, huddled against the cold.

But he wasn't there.

Getting out of the car I turned about myself several times, yelling his name at the top of my lungs while the frosty ball of panic rolling around in my stomach grew bigger and bigger. The snow was no longer falling, and the forest was absolutely quiet—certainly quiet enough to convince me no one was responding to my calls.

Running over to our rental car in the ditch, I pulled open the door to see if Nick had crawled inside for shelter. He wasn't there, either.

Only then did it occur to me to look for tracks in the fresh snow . . . tracks of someone walking, or crawling . . . but the headlights that were my only source of light made everything so bright it took me a while to discern that there was, indeed, a fresh pattern—a single tread mark—going down the road toward Suomussalmi.

I felt a rush of hope. Had a motorcycle picked up Nick?

Getting back in the car, I drove on as fast as I could, following the tread mark. Only when I reached the city limits did other patterns begin to weave in and out of the one I was following, and yet, thanks to the late hour and the scarcity of traffic, I was able to follow it all the way through town to its only logical destination.

CHAPTER FORTY-ONE

And a man may say, who sees you streaming tears,
"There is the wife of Hector, the bravest fighter
They could field, those stallion-breaking Trojans,
long ago when the men fought for Troy."
—HOMER, *The Iliad*

THE HOSPITAL WAS A SLEEPY PLACE, WITH JUST A HANDFUL OF PEO-ple on the night shift. When I stepped through the emergency room door everyone on staff looked up. I guessed from their wide eyes I was no pretty sight.

As soon as I had confirmed that Nick was really there, a sympathetic nurse walked me to a small waiting area with a dozen empty chairs. "There is warm water for tea in the thermos," she said. "I will tell Dr. Huusko you are here."

"How is he?" I asked, studying her face to glean whatever knowledge she had. "Is he okay?"

She looked away. "Dr. Huusko will speak to you."

I have no idea how long I sat there, anxiously waiting for news. There was a radiator right behind me, hot to the touch, but I still couldn't stop shaking. The night's events had chilled me to the marrow, leaving me almost catatonic with shock and exhaustion. I didn't even have the wherewithal to get up and wash my hands, even though they were still sticky with Nick's blood.

When Dr. Huusko appeared at last, he didn't walk up to me right away but first stopped and peered at me across the waiting area. And when he spoke, it was in a voice so deep it sounded like a rumble from earth itself. "You better have a good story for me."

I rose on stiff legs, looking in vain for a soft spot in the doctor's face. He was the sort of looming, oaklike man who gave the impression of having withstood several ice storms and lightning strikes, and to whom human beings such as I were little more than a passing annoyance. "Please tell me he will be all right," I said, the words nearly clogging in my throat.

Dr. Huusko pointed at his stethoscope. "This is not a crystal ball. This is science. But science is on our side." He finally walked up to me. "If I was not a rational man I would say your boyfriend has a guardian angel." He showed me what he was holding in his hand.

It was Granny's bracelet. Or rather, I assumed it was, for the head of the jackal was so distorted it didn't look like an animal anymore.

"This was in his trouser pocket," Dr. Huusko explained. "It stopped the bullet. I've never seen anything like it. It probably saved his life."

"But he was bleeding," I whispered, fighting back tears of confusion and relief.

Dr. Huusko looked at me with dismay. "Of course he was bleeding! How do you think it feels to have this punched into your tissue with the power of several hundred pounds?"

I looked into Dr. Huusko's eyes, anxious for him to confirm that Nick was out of danger. "So, will he be all right?"

But now the doctor's face hardened again. "He's in a coma. We shall see. He had severe hypothermia. His heart stopped; I don't know for how long. There could be cell damage." Dr. Huusko's furry eyebrows contracted even further. "With no oxygen flowing to the brain—"

I didn't faint, but everything went dim for a few seconds. "Can I see him?"

"When he is stable." Dr. Huusko fished something else out of his lab coat: Nick's cellphone. "This was in his other pocket. Maybe you would like to call someone. The woman who brought him here said she was his mother, but she didn't tell us anything else. We tried to detain her but"—Dr. Huusko grimaced—"she didn't want to stay."

I PACED THE HALLWAYS, almost too sad and shocked to cry. In the end I sat in the empty cafeteria with Nick's cellphone and the mangled jackal bracelet on the table in front of me. A lonely neon tube was buzzing over the empty food counter nearby, occasionally blinking as if it was just about to burn out. For some reason it brought me back to my trailer compartment in Algeria, and I was briefly assaulted by pointless thoughts of turning back time to a point when Nick and I were still at odds, and where I never in my wildest dreams would have imagined sitting in a hospital like this, crying over him.

Taking a few sharp breaths of air I eventually managed to push those useless thoughts aside and focus on the phone. Although the last thing I felt like doing was talking to strangers, the situation was serious enough to warrant a phone call.

After scrolling through Nick's endless contact list without recognizing anyone, it finally occurred to me to check the speed dials and see whom he considered his closest and dearest. Surprisingly, a number he called "Office for an Argument" was at the top of the list. Next came "Boy Wonder" and "Goldfinger." In the end I gave up speculating and dialed the first number.

The phone rang for a while before someone picked up, and I had already braced myself for a Dubai answering service when a sleepy male voice said, "It's about time."

"This is Diana Morgan," I quickly countered. "Calling on behalf of Kamal al-Aqrab. I assume you know him."

There was a violent rustle at the other end. Then the man said, in a voice somewhere between worry and anger, "What's wrong? Where are you calling from?"

I looked around at the abandoned cafeteria. "Finland. The Suomussalmi Hospital." I paused to steady my voice. "I'm afraid there's been—"

"Is my son alive?"

The question hit me right in the heart. "Oh! You're—"

"Answer my question."

Mr. al-Aqrab's hostile tone jolted some of the courage out of me. "Yes, but we don't know—" Again, my voice faltered. "He had severe hypothermia—"

"Stay where you are. I'll be right up." Mr. al-Aqrab ended the call.

And that was where Dr. Huusko eventually found me—lying over Nick's phone in the empty cafeteria, too heavyhearted to move. "Here." He held a gray photo printout in front of me. It showed a woman in full stride, pulling off a motorcycle helmet as she came through the glass doors of the hospital. "This is the person who brought your boyfriend here. Do you know her?"

I leaned forward to scrutinize the photo. It was taken from above, but I recognized the silver pixie crop right away. Nick's guardian angel was the angry cat woman from Istanbul. She had tried to avoid us by staying upstairs all evening, but Fate had found her nonetheless, to put her to the test. Had she passed with distinction this time? It was a matter of perspective. Breaking the rule of being first in battle, the queen of the Baltic Amazons had left her sisters alone with Reznik's goons in order to save her son.

"Well?" said Dr. Huusko.

I shook my head, avoiding his eyes. "No, I'm sorry."

"Come." The doctor motioned for me to get up. "I'm going to let you be with him. He's still in a coma, but the brain is a strange thing."

Lying in a hospital bed in a room by himself, Nick appeared to be connected to every piece of medical equipment in the building. And he was so deathly pale I should never have recognized him if I hadn't known it was him.

Walking to his bedside, I placed my hand gently upon his, carefully avoiding the intravenous line. There was no reaction. Nor did he make any discernible movement when I bent over and kissed him on the cheek.

Dr. Huusko took Nick's pulse the old-fashioned way, ignoring all the expensive machines. "He's a strong man with a strong heart," he said, making a note on a chart. Then he turned to face me, the look in his eyes a little less severe. "I don't know what happened to you two. I'm not sure I want to know. But the police will have questions. You better start thinking of answers."

Alone with Nick at last, I lay down next to him on the narrow bed, inching as close as I could. Despite everything, he still smelled like him. I tried to cast my mind back to that morning, when I had woken up next to him in our warm cocoon of hotel comforters. I'd had a strong feeling then that nothing outside our little nest really mattered too much anymore; I had finally found the center of my universe.

"I love you so much," I whispered into his ear, hoping the words would reach him, wherever he was. "Please come back. I'm so sorry."

It was I who had wanted to go to Finland, who had been hell-bent on following Granny's trail to the end. And when things went wrong, I had hesitated and fumbled while Nick took on Reznik's men.

"How can you not want to learn how to defend the people you love?" He had asked me in the ruins of Mycenae. "I can show you some easy tricks."

I had been too angry to listen. And now the grand machinery of heaven had taken my arrogance and slammed it right back in my face with blinding accuracy.

MR. AL-AQRAB ARRIVED AT daybreak. When I heard the gruff demands and indignant outcries in the hallway outside, I assumed it was the police coming to interrogate me. But then the door to the room was pushed open and four men came in, with Dr. Huusko and two agitated nurses trailing closely behind.

With his stern, all-business manner Mr. al-Aqrab looked so unlike the man I had seen the week before, walking through the Çirağan Palace reception in a baseball cap, I had to reach all the way back to the intense face in Mr. Telemakhos's scrapbook to be convinced it was really him. Dressed in a suit and tie almost identical to those worn by his three associates, he paused in the middle of the floor without even acknowledging my presence, then walked up to Nick's bed with a grimace of helpless fury.

"Who did this?" was his first question, addressed to no one in particular.

"Reznik and James Moselane," I replied, glancing at Dr. Huusko. "They followed us here."

Mr. al-Aqrab muttered a curse.

I waited for a moment, expecting him to try to talk to Nick, or at least touch him. When he didn't, I said, "It shouldn't really surprise us, though, should it? Wasn't that the plan all along—to use us as bait?"

Mr. al-Aqrab turned toward me slowly, as if he could barely believe my nerve. "And you are?"

"Diana Morgan." I held out my hand. When he did not take it, a bubble of helpless fury burst in my head. "Surely, you remember me from the detective report. I imagine you and your"—I nodded at the other men, who all stood around with frowns of latent aggression—"intelligence department know more about me than my own parents do."

"Right." Mr. al-Aqrab reached into his jacket. "How much do I owe you?"

I stepped away from him. "For what exactly?"

He pulled out his checkbook. "For walking out that door right now"—he pointed over his shoulder with a gold fountain pen—"and erasing it all from your mind."

Although the tone of our exchange had hardly been civil, I was so baffled by his rudeness the room became a blur around me. "I wouldn't take a penny from you," I said, forcing out the words, "if I were a beggar in the street. You were the one who did this to Nick. And had it not been for his mother, pulling him out of a snowbank and bringing him here, he would be dead now."

I spoke with furious passion, and Mr. al-Aqrab swayed briefly before squaring his shoulders and tightening his tie. "This is neither the time nor the place—" He gestured at someone else, and only then did I see the medical team coming into the room behind Dr. Huusko.

"What are you doing?" I asked, stepping a little closer to Nick.

But it was only too clear what they were doing.

I tried to block their access. "Don't take him away! Please! Dr. Huusko has everything—" Seeing that no one was taking any notice of me, I turned to Mr. al-Aqrab and exclaimed, "Haven't you done enough to him? It's freezing cold out there." When he continued to ignore me, I blocked his way, forcing him to pay attention. "All right. You're taking him back to Dubai." I was so upset I couldn't even soften my voice. "I'm coming, too."

Mr. al-Aqrab could not have looked more appalled. "You? Why?"

I glanced at Nick, struggling to hold back my tears. "Because he'll ask for me when he wakes up."

Another contemptuous once-over put me in my place. "I doubt it. Now, excuse us—"

Working without hesitation, the medical team unhooked Nick from all of the equipment in the room and efficiently rehooked every line to their own portable devices. When they wheeled the bed out of the room, I ran after them down the corridor. "I'm serious," I said to Mr. al-Aqrab. "Don't you dare—" I reached out and tried to grab the bed rail. "Stop! You don't understand!"

In a smooth, effortless maneuver, Mr. al-Aqrab managed to cut me off right there, while the medical team continued down the corridor and disappeared around a corner. "Oh, but I understand completely," he said, putting a patronizing hand on my shoulder. "Nick is my son. He has that effect on women. Here." Reaching into his jacket, he took out a wad of money and pressed it into my hand. "Buy yourself a little something from him. He would like that."

I DROVE REZNIK's SUV back out the Raate Road in the morning sunshine, only to find that the rental car was no longer stuck in the ditch and that all traces of violence had been erased by new snow. Gone was our luggage, my coat, the *Historia Amazonum,* Granny's letter . . . not even a footprint was left.

Driving on, I managed to doggedly retrace my steps to the Amazon safe house despite the fact that everything looked different in the daylight and the makeshift street signs had disappeared.

As I rolled down the winding driveway I saw right away my trip had been in vain. Not only were there no vehicles left in the driveway, just a jumble of half-erased tread marks, but the house itself was gone. Where the sad old mansion had stood there was now a pile of charred rubble.

Getting out of the car, I walked around a bit in the knee-deep snow, looking for signs of life. There were still thin columns of smoke coming from the burned remains of the building, but no identifiable objects stood out among the slag.

Standing there, staring at the ruin, I felt oddly numb. What had I expected? That the Amazons would still be here, busily scrubbing bloodstains off the floor?

Making my way around the foundation of the house I noticed an old gray barn tucked away in the woods. It was a long, tall building—perhaps even bigger than the house itself had been. Approaching through the snow, I opened the barn doors with cautious curiosity.

Inside the building were dozens of empty horse stalls and heaps of soiled straw on the floor. More than anything, an overturned wheelbarrow and a broken sack of fodder suggested a hasty evacuation.

At the back of the stable, another door stood open. On the other side of it was an enormous empty room with a concrete floor. My first impression was that something crucial had been kept in this grand space with cathedral ceilings—something that was now gone. But then I noticed the three ropes hanging from roof rafters and . . . the trapezes.

I suddenly heard Otrera describing the traveling circus that had once been the Baltic chapter of the Amazons, and I understood that this lofty room had indeed held something special: women training. Not a single mirror or floor mat softened its severity; this had not been a showroom, but a place for focus, exertion, and pain.

The graffiti covering the walls supported my suspicion. Most were in languages I didn't understand, but two were in English. One read,

"They that can give up essential liberty to obtain a little temporary safety deserve neither liberty nor safety." The other read simply, "A nation of sheep will beget a government of wolves."

Walking over to a chin-up bar on the wall, I grabbed hold of the cold metal and tried to pull myself up. I couldn't. I had done it as a child, playing Amazons with Rebecca in the garden, but then . . . as an adult I had happily listened to those who said women weren't expected to do that kind of thing.

Walking back through the stable, I looked everywhere for forgotten items—any small souvenir to give me strength to go on. But everything had vanished. In the end I picked up a handful of grain from the leaking fodder bag and put it in my pocket.

Where was the Baltic chapter of the sisterhood now? I wondered. And what had happened to James? Did he go up in smoke like the other Amazon secrets in the house?

Chilled at the memory of the bloody conclusion to Reznik's war with the Amazons, I turned to walk back outside. As I did so, I caught sight of something hanging from a nail next to the door. My coat. Baffled, I took it down and inspected it. And sure enough, there they were in my pockets, all the things I thought I had lost: my money, my passport yet again . . . and Granny's letter.

Sitting on the overturned wheelbarrow, I opened the envelope then and there. The letter was not long, and the shaky handwriting suggested Granny had been weak when she wrote it.

Diana—

How old are you now? I am trying to see you before me, but I cannot guess how long it has taken you to find me. I wanted to talk with you again, and explain everything, and hear how you are doing, but it is too late now. Katherine Kent says you are happy. This gives me peace.

I am going to give you my jackal bracelet, but don't assume I want you to become an Amazon. I just want you to have the choice. Too many women grow up without choices. My greatest wish for you is a life in liberty. Remember to keep your choices alive; don't let them get weak. And don't let others convince you that you have none. Remember: Courage has no age.

I don't know where I will be when you read this, but if I can, I will find you and whisper in your ear. The first thing I will whisper is this: Never give up. Goodness will always outrun evil in the end.

With all my love, Kara

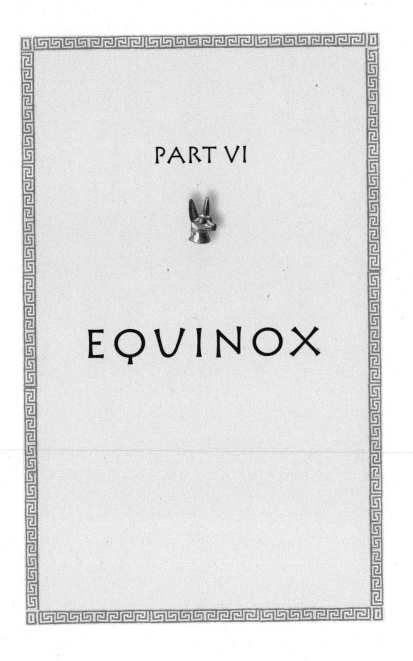

PART VI

EQUINOX

CHAPTER FORTY-TWO

Then much-enduring Odysseus, in his hand accepting it,
easily strung the bow, and sent a shaft through the iron.
He stood on the threshold, and scattered out the swift shafts before him,
glaring terribly, and struck down the king Antinoös.
Then he shot his baneful arrows into the others,
aiming straight at them, and they dropped one after another.
—HOMER, *The Odyssey*

OXFORD, ENGLAND

WITH RAIN-STREAKED INDIFFERENCE, THE DREAMING SPIRES greeted me as if I had never been away. The November air was a bit cooler than it had been when I left three weeks ago, and everyone looked a tad more miserable as they scuttled from building to building, hugging their books. Apart from that, everything appeared much the same. The porter barely looked up from his sports section when I stopped at the lodge to get my mail.

"Hello, Frank," I said as I excavated my pigeonhole, amazed at the scarcity of letters after what felt like a long absence. "Any news to report?"

He shook his jowls with feigned commiseration. "Can't think of any. We're supposed to have sun today. But we'll see. Oh—I almost forgot." Frank stretched to pluck a note from a bulletin board. "James Mosclane called last night. Said it was urgent. He left a number."

We both looked at the digits scribbled in lead pencil. "Switzerland?" I asked, staring at the country code in surprise.

Frank shrugged. "Just said it was urgent. Here." He handed me the scrap of paper with a grimace, eager to rid himself of the responsibility. "Better call him right away."

Professor Larkin's office was no more welcoming than the lodge. A haze of dusty abandonment hung in the air, and the poor guppies were belly up in the fish tank. Dropping my mail on the desk, the first thing I did was march out into the bathroom and flush James's number in the toilet along with the guppies. Coming back a little calmer, I turned on every working lamp and filled up the teakettle in preparation for a long afternoon of beating down my misery and getting my life back in order.

I had spent the weekend looking for my parents in every B&B in Cornwall and had finally found them in a tearoom in Falmouth. We had driven back to the Cotswolds together last night, talking about Granny all the way. After eighteen years of damming it all up behind a wall of nervous silence, my parents' world was now so flooded with memories they barely knew which to cling to. Together we established what we already knew and patched it together with what I had learned in Finland. The picture of Granny that emerged was of a woman marred by loss and hardship, who was a lot stronger, and a good deal saner, than they had hitherto believed.

As heartsick and exhausted as I was, I should have liked to stay at home with my parents for a while, hiding in this refurbished world of memories. But I couldn't stay away forever. I had students to face, colleagues to appease: It was a battle I could postpone no longer.

And so I had taken the Monday morning train to Oxford I knew so well, hoping to fall right back into my old routine. But as I sat there in my usual window seat, it felt as if everything had somehow changed around me—the colors were darker, the air strangely dead. Even the sounds of other people had changed from major to minor.

Before leaving Finland, I had tried to call Nick's second speed dial . . . only to discover that his account had been canceled. No matter what I did, all I got was the same brief automated message in Arabic. I

THE LOST SISTERHOOD · 563

didn't understand the words, but the meaning was clear: I had been cut off.

While crisscrossing Cornwall in search of my parents I had hogged every Internet connection I could find, searching for a direct number for the Aqrab Foundation office in Dubai. When I finally found it, I had jotted it down on a piece of paper in preparation for calling as soon as I returned to Oxford.

Staring at the number now, poised to make my big call on Professor Larkin's antiquated telephone, I felt a familiar twinge of revulsion at the memory of my clash with Mr. al-Aqrab. But I couldn't allow it to delay me any longer; my concern for Nick was so great I couldn't eat, couldn't sleep—I felt as if my soul was at war with my body, calling it a traitor for defaulting to Oxford rather than scouring the streets of Dubai.

The telephone rang only once before a receptionist picked up and transferred me to a Frenchman who—probably from his corner office, looking out over the Persian Gulf—made it abundantly clear the Aqrab Foundation and the Aqrab family were two separate entities. "I have no information to give you," he said repeatedly, clearly following office protocol, "but I can connect you with our press office if you are interested in learning more about the foundation."

The moment I hung up, the phone rang again. "Hello?" I said hopefully, my mind still in Dubai.

"Morg!" James's joy in catching me was explosive. "Look, I'm *so* sorry! I really am! You hate me, don't you? I can't blame you. But listen—for old times' sake." He managed to lower his voice. "I'm in trouble. Your lesbo friends set me up big-time. Can we talk? Are you listening to me?"

When I didn't respond, James laughed nervously. "Fair enough. How about this: Money. I know things are tight for you. Name your price. All you have to do is come to Geneva"—he lowered his voice even further—"and tell these wankers that I didn't kill Reznik. Okay? I'm at the central police station—I'm in fucking handcuffs, Morg!"

I hung up.

When the phone rang again, I unplugged it.

Evidently, the Amazons had known precisely how to deal with James and with Reznik's dead body, and frankly, I didn't feel the slightest need to interfere with their justice.

MY TEACHING OBLIGATIONS, AS it turned out, had been taken over by some overachieving grad student, and everyone I spoke to seemed extremely reluctant to go through the trouble of changing things back to the way they were. Apparently Professor Vandenbosch—the department chair who had long ago made it his mission to squash me—had personally signed the papers. There was even a suggestion that this industrious replacement of mine was now the rightful tenant of Professor Larkin's quarters, and that I had better start looking for lodging elsewhere. I could see the point, of course, having neglected my duties for three weeks, but I was not in a frame of mind to give up my hard-won perch without a fight.

It did not help that Katherine Kent had not yet returned from Finland. I had stopped by her office first thing, but there was no answer to my repeated knocking, and the porter had no idea when she might be back. "You never know with Professor Kent," he said to me with a conspiratorial smile. "I think she works for MI5. But no one believes me."

On Tuesday afternoon I returned to college from a cathartic training session at the fencing club to find my apartment door ajar. My first thought was that the cleaning lady must have come, but when I heard no vacuum cleaner or clanging of trash cans, only silence, I felt a familiar frost on my spine.

Opening my gym bag as silently as I could, I took out my foil. It was designed for sport only, with a flexible blade and a blunt tip, but it was better than nothing. In the right hands, even a sporting foil could be lethal.

Taking a deep breath, I pushed through the door at last . . . and found myself face-to-face with Rebecca.

"God!" she shrieked, clutching her heart at the sight of me. "Are you trying to kill me?"

I lowered the foil, and we fell into each other's arms. "What are you doing here?" I said after a moment. "Didn't I tell you to sail away with Mr. Telemakhos?"

Rebecca stood back and mashed away her tears. "If that's the kind of friend you want, put an ad in the paper. You need help, and here I am. I received a courier envelope with your keys in it, and I thought I'd make use of them."

We compared notes over single malt at the Grand Café. Neither Rebecca nor I were whisky drinkers, but I am sure we both felt a change was necessary. Seated on tall stools at the bar, we worked together to unravel the tangle of people and events that had forced us apart . . . and now back together. Naturally, James Moselane loomed large in this motley mix of friends and foes.

"I still can't believe it," said Rebecca at length. "To think we used to worship the louse. What do you think they're going to do with him? Let him rot in jail? Chop off his head with a sword? Isn't that what they used to do in Switzerland?"

I shrugged and swirled my drink. "I have no idea how they managed to pin Reznik's death on him, but you know what? He deserves it. If I ever see him again, he can have his golf ball back."

When we finally walked home together, arm in arm, Rebecca knew everything there was to know about my ordeals in Germany and Finland. And although she had peppered my regretful narrative with encouraging remarks such as "I'm sure he'll be fine" and "Of course he loves you!" I knew her well enough to sense that she shared my fear I'd never see Nick again.

"Why don't you come to Ikiztepe with me?" she said, matching her pace to mine on the uneven cobblestones. "It's a wonderfully exciting place, and Dr. Özlem says they're desperate to hire people." Rebecca glanced at me to see whether I was in a receptive mood. "I'm telling you, getting fired from Knossos was the best thing that ever happened to me. What about you? Isn't it time to wean yourself off Oxford?"

I shook my head. "Not until I've taken a course on self-defense."

Then I saw it. A delivery truck was idling in front of the college entrance, and beside it stood a figure I recognized only too well. In her long boots and tight clothing my Amazon friend Lilli stood out against the medieval street like a defiant perennial growing on a rock face.

When she caught sight of us, she nodded to me as if we had a secret understanding and walked around the truck to get in on the passenger side.

"Wait!" I cried, bounding forward, but it was too late. The truck rolled down the street and disappeared around the corner into Oriel Square. Standing there at the college entrance, Rebecca and I were left bewildered.

"Honestly!" I stepped through the gate and hurried past the lodge, images of Professor Larkin's Roman coin collection and ancient pottery shards flashing before my eyes. "What can they possibly have taken this time?"

In my hurry to get back to my apartment I didn't notice Frank the porter calling me until he came out into the quad in his shirtsleeves and suspenders. "There's a delivery for you!" he yelled, clearly disgruntled at being pulled out of his man cave. "You'd better take it right away. I can't even move in there."

He was not exaggerating. On the floor of the lodge sat three wooden crates the size of washing machines, and they were so heavy it would take several people to move them. "Came just now," Frank told me. "For you personally. They wouldn't leave until you were here."

"They who?" I asked, curious to know what exactly Lilli had told him. But Frank was already on the phone, trying to find some strong arms to help us.

Half an hour later, the three crates were sitting on the floor of Professor Larkin's office. "I'm not sure I would open them," said Rebecca, chewing her lip. "Remember Pandora's box? Unleashing sorrow on mankind and all that?"

I riffled through the drawers in the desk to find something that could serve as a crowbar. "Call me an optimist, but I can't imagine there being much sorrow left to unleash."

It wasn't until I had borrowed a hammer and chisel from a head-shaking Frank that we were at long last able to pry the lid off the crate marked "1." A few creaking nails later, Rebecca and I peered into the sawdust, transfixed by the leather binder nested on top. "Let's see." I took the binder, which turned out to contain a longish, typewritten text, conveniently in English.

"This is the story of Myrina"—read Rebecca, over my shoulder—"the first of the Amazons, founder of our sisterhood. Oh! Mr. Telemakhos will love that!"

I sifted through the pages to see if an explanatory note was hiding somewhere. But of course not. The Amazon way was the silent way.

Putting aside the leather binder, I stuck my hands into the sawdust and rummaged around for a bit, while Rebecca looked on with wide eyes. Whatever else was in the crate, it was cushioned extremely well, and I had to dig in deep before my fingertips brushed against something hard.

"Hold on!" Rebecca pushed me aside as soon as she saw me straining to pull out the object. "Let's proceed carefully."

Soon, the floor of Professor Larkin's office was covered in heaps of sawdust as Rebecca embarked upon her excavation. And when the object was finally uncovered, she didn't take it out, merely leaned over the edge of the crate to study it. "That," she observed, "is ancient. It must be."

We stood in silence for a moment, staring at the clay tablet. Then I went over to fetch a lamp and hold it over the crate so we could see better.

"It's not the Amazon alphabet, is it?" asked Rebecca after a while.

"No, it isn't." I held the lamp as close as I could for the straining power cord. "I think it's Luwian." No sooner had I said it than the plug snapped out of the outlet, leaving us in sudden obscurity. But the vision left in my head was bright as day. "Oh, Bex!" I whispered, feeling the long-forgotten prickle of scholarly excitement. "Can this really be it?"

Just then, the phone rang.

"I have a journalist on the line," said Frank, sounding appropriately suspicious, "who wants to talk to the person responsible for finding the Trojan tablets. Is that you?"

CHAPTER FORTY-THREE

T ALLA WAS BORN UNDER THE FULL MOON.

She was healthy and hungry, and had her father's eyes. For days and days, Myrina did nothing but lie with her in her arms, looking into those little eyes whenever they were open. "Have you seen him?" she would whisper, letting Talla hold the tip of her finger. "Is your father looking at us? I think so."

They had spent autumn traveling up the Istros River. These northern lands were a world without grandeur, without sophistication of any kind. The people they met were simple and easy to understand. Sometimes they were friendly, sometimes not; there was nothing puzzling about their ways.

So far, Myrina and her sisters had come upon neither witches nor wolf men; in fact, whenever they arrived at a new village, it was evident that *they* were the unnatural ones: women with different faces, different hair, different clothes, but most important, women with different customs. . . .

Women without men.

They decided to spend winter in a valley, a place where there were not too many other hunters to contend with. Here, they built huts for themselves and for the horses, and buried King Priam's precious tablets in nests of straw underneath the floors.

Not a day went by where they did not speak of the future. They had one dream in common, namely that of a fertile and welcoming land where they might farm and hunt in peace without the constant fear that what they had would once again be taken away. "When we get there—" they would say, to themselves and to one another, and none doubted that one day, they would.

"It is out there, waiting for us," Lilli always maintained, smiling at the horizon she couldn't see. "We shall have our village, nay, our city. A city of women."

Through the long winter, they spent evenings around the fire, huddled under pelts and skins, laying out that city in words. The question of men arose occasionally, but since no one could imagine ever desiring any intimacy with the inarticulate males that roamed these northern lands, the response was usually laughter.

"I will never ask you," Myrina said once to her sisters, stoking the fire with a stick, "to live without such pleasures. But I do believe men and women are so different we should not try to live in each other's worlds. If you must, go and frolic with a herdsman under a starry sky, but do not attempt to share his daylight. For the sun works on men as an elixir—it blears their eyes to the worth of women and makes them dare to think they should rule over us. Even the kindest of men"—she bent her head as the memories stirred—"will think they are doing us a favor by locking us away."

"Surely not all men are tyrannical masters," objected Pitana, busily carving a wooden toy for Talla. "I for one remember how you used to smile." She looked up at Myrina, gauging her mood. "I should like to know how it feels to smile that way. It seems to me men bring out sides of us that would wither away if we lived our lives without them."

"Had it not been for the Trojans," agreed Klito, "Kara and I would still be enslaved in Mycenae. Surely *some* men deserve to be praised as liberators."

"I do not deny it," said Myrina. "Many good men, I am sure, have lost their lives—or at least their happiness—because of a woman. This is why I say that the kindest thing we can do for them is to leave them be. We, too, will benefit from such precautions. For man's primitive response to our complex power is to yoke us and make us believe we should be yoked. He calls it an act of love and protection—so speaks the cunning tyrant. And when we believe him and willingly leash our-selves and our sisters"—she sighed deeply and shook her head—"then our tragedy becomes *his* ultimate triumph."

"Indeed," agreed Kara, who had embraced their new life more heartily than anyone. "Love is a treacherous thing. We give men strength, but they do not return the favor. Even those of us who con-sider ourselves superior in spirit lose our bearings when a male spreads his plumes. It is a noxious spell they cast on us, is it not?" She looked around at the others for confirmation.

"Once again I am the lucky one," said Lilli, smiling as she rocked baby Talla in her arms. "I cannot see those noxious plumes that lead you astray. Count yourselves fortunate, sisters, that you have at least one person in your midst who can maintain a steady course."

"I propose, then," said Myrina, when at last the discussion waned and she was nursing Talla, "that our city shall admit no men, lest some plumed cock tries to lord it over us. We will all be free to come and go, of course, and spend our nights howsoever we choose; no jealous Moon Goddess shall rob us of that choice." She pointed at the raised scar on her breast—the permanent reminder of her initiation at the Temple of the Moon Goddess. "From now on, these scars shall mean freedom, not enslavement. Our days shall be ours alone, devoted to industry and improvement; while the sun is up, no male and no stone deity shall be allowed to confine us."

As TIME WENT ON, their numbers increased. Even the world of forests and mountains had no shortage of women ready to exchange a husband for a horse and halter. Always on the move, Myrina and her growing band of sisters refused to settle down until they found the perfect place for their city.

It eventually fell to Talla to challenge her mother's nomadic nature. "We cannot be hunters forever," she said one day, when they were all gathered around a stag roasting on a spit. "Aunt Lilli is right, some hands have a need to plant and harvest. I know we are reluctant to found our city only to have it move again, but is that not the way of the world? The tide will come in, and go out, and we will be in another place." She looked at each of them in turn. "Let us not be enslaved to an inflexible idea—"

Myrina silenced her daughter with a tired gesture. "The ages to come hold no shortage of enemies, I am sure of it. To survive we must be ever ready, ever lithe of foot—"

"And we will be!" exclaimed Talla, throwing up her arms. "But even the strongest runner needs to rest. Let us not imitate those animals who expire from exertion. We may be the Amazons, but we cannot be at a gallop from here to eternity."

And so they settled for a while, and moved, and settled again, never fully rooting in one place, always merely passing through. And wherever they went, the clay tablets from Troy—which none among them could read—served as a symbol of their promise to King Priam and to themselves: Never forget.

Through the years they worked hard to remember the writing Kyme had taught them, but more than anything, they never stopped telling their stories. Even as time went on and their group split into many, each chapter stubbornly clung to the history that was their common root. For in that history, they knew, lay the wisdom that would protect the seed from the hungry beetle—the promise of a new and better world.

CHAPTER FORTY-FOUR

There still may be another Troy.
—EURIPIDES, *The Trojan Women*

OXFORD, ENGLAND

THE SHELDONIAN THEATRE WAS ABUZZ WITH GUESSWORK. IT WAS
rare the humble field of classical philology attracted worldwide
media attention, but the press conference had turned out to be one
such occasion. Less than a month earlier, Mr. Ludwig had promised me
I was about to write history. In his lie, he had been absolutely right after
all, I thought to myself as I walked to the podium.

"Thank you, Professor Vandenbosch." I smiled at the poor old back-
biter, who had been given less than twenty-four hours to compose a
eulogistic introduction listing my credentials, personal virtues, and inestimable value to the scholarly community at Oxford . . . in fact, from
this day on, to scholarship everywhere. Despite a little muscle spasm at
the corner of his eye as he spoke to the ladies and gentlemen of the
press, the venerable department chair was pleasingly convincing in the
role of my committed friend and colleague.

Over the previous three days, since the crates had arrived, Professor Vandenbosch and everyone else with a stake in the ancient world
had run me through an understandable gauntlet of questions, accusations, and insults, and he in particular had been terribly disappointed
when I emerged alive on the other side. From being the self-anointed

anchorman of the whole affair, he had soon been sidelined by journalists and authorities who had no patience for his patronizing mediation. In the end, the vice chancellor had stepped in, and a press conference had been arranged overnight.

"As you already know," I continued, looking out over the swaying field of faces, "an anonymous Swiss collector has entrusted me with twelve clay tablets inscribed in Luwian—a language spoken throughout the Hittite world in the second and first millennium B.C.E. My working theory is that these tablets contain historical records from ancient Troy—records that were removed from the city before it was destroyed more than three thousand years ago. The significance of such records is enormous. As you all know, the legendary Troy continues to intrigue not just scholars but everyone with an interest in ancient civilizations. I hope these tablets will lay a foundation for rewriting what we know about King Priam's city."

I had intended to say more, but as soon as I paused, a wilderness of arms shot up, vying for my attention. Focusing on the core group of media heavyweights in the audience—carefully pointed out to me by the vice chancellor—I took a few questions in rapid succession, without leaving room for follow-ups.

"You say the donor is an anonymous Swiss collector," asked a gravel-voiced London reporter with slicked-back gray hair. "Can you give us any more detail than that?"

"I'm afraid not. I have agreed to maintain the donor's anonymity."

"Dr. Morgan." A female journalist whose face I recognized from television was next. "When I look at your articles and research, I see a lot of"—she grimaced—"Amazons, and not a lot about Troy. Has there been any discussion about whether you are qualified for this new challenge?"

I forced out a smile. "Since you've taken a look at my work, you already know I am not unfamiliar with the Luwian language."

"What exactly do the tablets say?" asked an American in a frumpled brown suit—the only one of the lot who seemed remotely friendly.

"I received them only three days ago," I replied. "But as far as I can see, we are dealing with historical records listing specific events and names."

I meant to go on, but was stopped by a wild-eyed pit bull of a Frenchman who just couldn't wait his turn. "This past week," he barked, not just at me, but at everyone, "there have been other so-called incidents in artifact trading circles. A well-known collector by the name of Grigor Reznik was killed in a warehouse in the Geneva Freeport. Apparently, he was shot by the son of a rival collector during an illicit artifact exchange. Some speculate that Reznik was the previous owner of the Trojan tablets. Also, three days ago, an ancient manuscript called the *Historia Amazonum* was returned anonymously to the Romanian archive from where it had been stolen—allegedly also by Reznik." The Frenchman fixed his accusative stare on me. "What has been your role in these events?"

The question nearly made me choke. "This is all news to me," I said, as calmly as I could. "But I highly doubt the Trojan tablets have been sitting in a Geneva warehouse all these years. Next question, please!"

By the time the most aggressive journalists had had their fill of me, my hands were shaking so badly I had to cross my arms. Until the last minute I had hoped to see Katherine Kent appear out of nowhere for the press conference. But apparently, this was a battle I had to fight on my own.

I suspected my little speech to Otrera in Suomussalmi had been instrumental in convincing the Amazons it was time they did their treasure justice. And yet, their faith in me was so deeply moving I hardly knew how to respond except to make sure the tablets were safe and their texts translated and publicized. That the anonymous press release had been issued on the same day the crates were delivered to me confirmed my belief that I was not merely to be another tablet guardian; I was to bring King Priam's lost city back to life.

"Last question?" I looked out over the crowd again, trying to choose between dozens of eager arms. Among the people lining the walls was a contingency of men in gray suits—so discreet in appearance I had not even noticed them until that moment.

Secret Service? The thought made me stiffen with fear. Had they come to question me about Reznik? Or James?

Glancing at the men again, I wondered if they were planning to arrest me right after the press conference and whether I should try to escape. . . . But then I finally noticed *him,* standing right in the middle of them, looking just as unforgiving as he had done the week before, when he came barging into his son's hospital room and kicked me aside like a dog toy. He, too, wanted to ask me a question.

"Mr. al-Aqrab?" I heard myself saying, into the microphone.

The name set off an earthquake in the audience, with everyone stretching to see the fiend from Babylon, so unexpectedly present in their midst.

"Dr. Morgan," said Mr. al-Aqrab, not unaware of the flashes going off around him. "I would like to congratulate you on rescuing and reviving this forgotten body of history. No doubt it will mark a turning point in the relationship between your university and my foundation, which have regrettably been at odds in the past." He paused to allow the significance of his words to sink in, then continued, "I know you have already been in touch with the Turkish authorities, and I commend you for taking the initiative. With that in mind, who do you consider to be the legal owner of these tablets? Will they now, like so many ancient treasures, become the property"—he held out his arms in a gesture of prosecution—"of the United Kingdom?"

The question caused a series of afterquakes, with photographers vying to capture the image of the day. I barely registered the commotion; all I could think of was Nick. Surely Mr. al-Aqrab would not be here if his son was still in critical condition.

"The tablets were entrusted to me personally," I replied at last, belatedly realizing that everyone was awaiting my response, "and I consider it my duty to ensure their safety. But no one can own other people's history, even if those other people are long dead. To keep Trojan artifacts of any kind here in Britain, so far from their place of origin, would be to fall back on an outdated praxis." I straightened, doing my best to rise above the crescendo of scholarly discontent threatening to drown me out. "The donor has tasked me with choosing the future home of the tablets, and it is my intention to return them to their place of origin as soon as possible."

In the groundswell of anger following my statement I was sure I heard Professor Vandenbosch yelling, "Absurd!"

Mr. al-Aqrab looked around, evidently enjoying the uproar. "Suppose I offered to build a museum for them?"

The room fell immediately silent, and all heads once again turned to me, as if the Sheldonian Theatre was full of sheep watching the unloading of a fodder truck, which might, or might not, be heading for the slaughterhouse next.

"There are museums at Troy already——" I began.

"A *safe* museum, Dr. Morgan. Overseen by a man I think you know: Dr. Murat Özlem. What do you say?" Mr. al-Aqrab smiled, and it changed his face completely. "Isn't it time for a joint venture?"

"Obviously we'll have to clear it with the Turkish authorities," I said. "But . . . that is generous of you. Perhaps we should plan a meeting."

An entire jungle of arms shot up among the debris of our exchange. Professor Vandenbosch was halfway out of his chair, poised to step in and seize control of the podium and microphone.

Uncertain as to whether I should take another question, I looked up and saw Mr. al-Aqrab and his cohort making for the door, their business done.

In a sudden attack of tunnel vision, everything else faded to gray around me. I didn't care what would happen; I was not going to let that man walk away from me again.

"Thank you," I said into the microphone. "Professor Vandenbosch will be happy to answer the rest of your questions." With that I stepped down from the podium and hastened down the central aisle without taking my eyes off the door. I didn't run, but it was close.

As I burst outside, an unexpected downpour of freezing rain confused me just long enough for Mr. al-Aqrab to nod a devilish farewell, get into a black limousine, and drive away, leaving me soaked, inside and out.

I stood paralyzed, staring into the blur of Broad Street. My feet simply wouldn't move.

"You'll have to forgive my dad," said a voice behind me. "He was never good at making apologies."

I spun around to find Nick, standing there, as soaked as I, but smiling nonetheless. His smile faded, however, when he saw my expression. "Hello, Goddess," he said, reaching out to touch my cheek. "Are you not happy to see me?"

And then I was in his arms at last, clinging to his warmth with every shivering ounce of my being, so desperate to assure myself of his wholeness it did not even occur to me to kiss him until his mouth found mine and routed all my fears.

"Don't worry," he whispered after a while. "I'm fine. And I won't disappear again, I promise. Not unless you want me to."

I was not yet ready to laugh. "I've been miserable," I muttered, pressing my face into the crook of his neck. "Why didn't you call me?"

Nick took my head between his hands. "Because I had to see your eyes——"

Just then, the door to the Sheldonian Theatre burst open, unleashing a multitude of follow-up questions.

"Oh no," I said. "I don't want to go back there."

Nick laughed. "Oh why not? Of course you do." He spun me around to face the crowd. "String your bow, Diana. I'm right behind you."

NICK HAD RESERVED a room at Claridge's in London, but we never got that far. Escaping the post-press-conference crowd on foot, we fled down New College Lane underneath the Bridge of Sighs and ducked into the nearest alley. Pulling Nick along by the hand, I led us through a shady labyrinth of timeworn walls until we reached the sneakiest hideout in Oxford: the Bath Place Hotel. A polite inquiry and a key later, we tumbled into our room, ripping off each other's wet clothes with corybantic furor. Only when I saw the stitches on his thigh was I reminded of Nick's recent brush with mortality.

"Wait!" I gasped. "Are you all right? Maybe we should——"

"What?" He drew me tightly against him, his eyes locked in mine. "Wait until the sun sets? I'm ready to break the rules if you are."

I pushed him down on top of the bed and straddled him with a kiss. "The only rule around here," I whispered, indulging in the feel of him, "is that you stay alive from now on."

Later, when we were lying together in a state of sweaty felicity, Nick looked at me with a puzzled frown and said, "Wait a minute. Don't you have an apartment here in Oxford?"

"Yes," I sighed, "but Bex is there. And my parents are stopping by. In fact"—I checked his wristwatch and groaned—"we're all supposed to meet up for tea in an hour."

"Am I invited?"

I laughed and snuggled up to him. "At your own peril. Remember, my father used to be a headmaster. He knows how to ask questions."

Nick kissed me on the forehead. "I'm prepared to stand at attention. I know I'm the embodiment of your parents' worst fears. With a bull-headed Dubai businessman and an Amazonian biker chick thrown into the gene pool, God knows what their grandchildren will be like."

Not sure how much to read into his words, I put my hand gently on top of his wound and said, "My jackal took a bullet for you. My parents will, too."

Nick was silent for a moment. Then he said, with unusual solemnity, "Maybe now would be a good time for you to ask me to marry you."

I was so amazed, so thrilled, I started laughing. When he didn't join in, I sat up and looked at him. "You're so wonderful. But you know, academics don't propose to billionaires."

"No worries." Nick sat up, too, and gave me half a smile. "My dad believes—and I agree—that the surest way of destroying a man is to pay him to do nothing. I have to work and pay my bills like everyone else." His smile broadened. "But I'm not too concerned. I'm planning to team up with a world-famous philologist. And if she won't ask me to marry her, I'll just be her trophy boyfriend." When I didn't say anything, he pulled me into his lap and said, more earnestly, "Come on, help me out here. How do I ask you to share my days and nights for as long as we both shall live . . . without upsetting Granny? I know she is sitting up there, in Amazon heaven, shaking her fist at me." He reached for his jacket lying across the bedside table and produced a smallish, square jewelry case. "But I'm hoping maybe I can appease her with *this.*"

"Oh, Nick," I said, feeling a pinch of discomfort, "you mustn't give me anything. Please."

"I know, I know." He held up his hands in self-defense. "No rings, no diamonds, no patriarchal down payments. I get it. But"—he pushed the box into my hand—"you could at least take a look."

"All right, then, but you really shouldn't—" I opened the box.

It was empty.

Puzzled, I lifted the blue satin lining to see if anything was hiding underneath. But nothing was there.

Looking up, I saw that Nick was enjoying my perplexity. "It's for the jackal," he said at last. "A little doghouse for our best friend."

Too happy to speak, I leaned over and kissed him. "Easy!" he said, laughing. "This daylight lovemaking is new to Granny. I don't want my nose punched again."

I slipped out of bed to locate my latest handbag and the mangled jackal I was still carrying around. Nick watched me as I came back and placed the bracelet on its new blue satin bed. As soon as I had closed the lid, he pulled me into bed with a demonic laugh. "Now you're *mine!*"

"Careful." I held up the jewelry case in mock warning. "This is no retirement home. My jackal may have been blinded by the bullet, but she can still bite."

"I certainly hope so." Nick drew me into his lap once more. "How do you want to spend the next half hour? I still haven't told you about my death ride to the Suomussalmi hospital with my arms frozen into place around my mother's Kevlar waist . . . but that's more of a dinner conversation."

"And I haven't told you about your mother's namesake, the original Myrina." I glanced at my handbag, wondering if this was the time to show Nick the leather binder with the meticulously recorded memoirs of the small band of sisters who had—three thousand years ago— traveled before us from Algeria through Troy to the freedom of the northern wilderness. "Maybe if you're lucky, I'll read it to you *after* dinner."

"I have an idea," said Nick. "Why don't you lure me into another shower?"

I gave him a long look. "Remember what happened last time."

"Yeees." He pulled me in for a kiss. "But it was still worth it."

WE DIDN'T GET AROUND to actually reading the story in the leather binder until two weeks later, when we were back in Turkey discussing the location of the new Trojan tablet museum with a jubilant Dr. Özlem and an extremely self-congratulatory Mr. Telemakhos. Even so, I knew Nick took the subject of the Amazons as seriously as did I, and that this shared prehistory of ours would serve to bolster our love in the times to come.

For our path—yes, even ours—would not lack enemies or fateful turns, but the jackal from its regal abode assured us that as long as we stuck together, the three of us, we would never stray too far from the happiness that had, as it turned out, been Granny's greatest gift to me.

AUTHOR'S NOTE

DID THE AMAZONS REALLY EXIST? OF COURSE THEY DID. WERE THEY EXactly as we find them portrayed in ancient literature and art? Probably not. As with many other mythical figures and events, the Amazons are a dream, a fear, a seductive constellation of ideas and emotions centered on the place of women in early Mediterranean society. Would women have taken up arms to defend their home and loved ones? It seems impossible that they would not. Would they have assembled entire armies to battle prehistoric Greek military powers? It seems unlikely. But since the dawn of man (and woman), storytellers have sought to spellbind their audiences with abnormal villains and chopped-off limbs. And to the ancient Greeks, the Amazons were bestseller material. Are these remarkable women still around today? They certainly are, in every single one of us. Sometimes we don't realize our inner Amazon until life deals us a numbing blow . . . but she is there, waiting to lend us her strength, I am sure of it.

I have dedicated this book to my wonderful mother-in-law, Shirley Fortier, who was ambushed by cancer the same month I finished the final draft. Despite being unhorsed and outnumbered from the start, she fought to the death with an astonishing courage we never knew she possessed. We miss her dearly and will never forget her.

As for the original Amazons of Greek myth, the legends describing their deeds are so abundant and nebulous—and often contradictory— that no one could ever hope to gather all the strands in a single, comprehensive narrative. I have certainly not attempted to do so, and I hope readers are aware that I deal with the tradition in a playful way, and that this book can by no means replace authoritative nonfiction works on the subject. Therefore, I urge you to continue the Amazon hunt on your own: Gallop apace into your local library, boldly prowl your local bookstores, and allow yourself to indulge in the ancient myths that are available to us even now, millennia later, in so many different intriguing interpretations.

While the events and characters I describe in the book are probably to a large extent fictitious, I have gone to great lengths to ensure that the historical framework is as solid as can be. Several distinguished experts have kindly read the manuscript in progress and given me valuable feedback; above all I am happily indebted to my dear friend, Dr. Thomas R. Martin, Jeremiah O'Connor Professor in Classics at College of the Holy Cross, and I highly recommend his well-known works *Ancient Greece* and *Ancient Rome* to anyone interested in a compelling armchair journey into our amazing past.

I am also immensely grateful to my longtime friend Dr. Timothy J. Moore, the John and Penelope Biggs Distinguished Professor of Classics at Washington University in St. Louis, whose brilliant, generous energy early on made me come to see top-notch philologists in a heroic light, and whose gloves-off, blazing-guns approach to mentoring has done more to toughen me up than any amount of sweetly smiling support could ever do.

My close friends, Mette Korsgaard, senior editor at Gyldendal Business, and Dr. Peter Pentz, curator at the National Museum of Denmark, were kind enough to look at the book from the perspective of the archaeologist. With their counsel in mind, I should emphasize that opinions are often divided when it comes to interpreting ancient finds. Some scholars will certainly disagree with my choices in describing the past—skepticism is, after all, a prerequisite of proper scholarship—but that doesn't necessarily mean things could not have happened the way I depict them. It is my hope, of course, that inquisitive readers will use my book as a springboard for a dive into the many unsolved mysteries of the past and flock to the fields of history, philology, and archaeology, eager to help expand our knowledge of the ancient world.

I should also point out that it was Dr. Pentz who first made me aware of the great efforts undertaken by the National Museum of Denmark to choose a sustainable position in the great and growing battle of artifact restitution. For those interested in reading more about this fascinating subject, I highly recommend Sharon Waxman's excellent book *Loot* as well as *The Medici Conspiracy* by Peter Watson and Cecilia Todescini. Both studies are rich in detail and informed by careful research yet read like well-crafted suspense stories.

I am also grateful for the assistance of my good friend Mrs. Heather Epps, of Storrington, West Sussex, who very kindly read the entire manuscript with a special focus on British-English usage, and who graciously suffered all my Americanisms and naughty little jabs at the eccentricities of British peers and scholars. I was fortunate enough to be a Visiting Graduate Member of Corpus Christi College, Oxford, while finishing my Ph.D. on Latin historians a decade ago, and I trust that the reader—despite Diana Morgan's tribulations—senses the immense admiration and gratitude I feel toward that splendid place and its uniquely gifted people.

My gratitude also goes out to Raatteen Portti Museum Director Marko Seppänen and author Tyyne Martikainen in Finland. It is thanks to their lifelong efforts and expertise that I have come to fully understand the tragedy of the Winter War that ruined the lives of so many thousands of Finns and Russians. Since coproducing the documentary film *Fire and Ice: The Winter War of Finland and Russia* I have been determined to help spread the awareness of the great work done by Tyyne Martikainen and her Finnish and Russian colleagues in an effort to trace the destinies of all the Finnish civilians who were taken hostage and sent away to camps so long ago.

I always tell my students that it takes more than one brain to turn a good story into a great book. That is certainly true in my case. I dread to imagine what Diana's and Myrina's quests would look like without the sound advice of the wonderful editors who helped me beat two wild stories into a manageable shape. What would I have done without the playful wisdom of Dr. Cordelia Borchardt at Fischer/Krüger, the soothing common sense of Iris Tupholme and Lorissa Sengara at HarperCollins Canada, or the relentless expertise of Dana Isaacson at Ballantine/Random House? The mind shudders. And I certainly would have been stranded on many an uninhabitable idea without my marvelously patient editor at Ballantine, Susanna Porter, whose eagle eye and expert touch, once again, have steered me safely home.

Needless to say, many more people have played a role in the birth of this book than I can properly thank here. The wonderful team at Ballantine has made everything a joy and is always there for me. In addition to Susanna Porter and Dana Isaacson, I would like to thank Libby McGuire, Jennifer Hershey, Kim Hovey, Vincent La Scala, Priyanka Krishnan, Susan Turner, Kristin Fassler, Ashley Woodfolk, Toby Ernst, Susan Corcoran, and Lisa Barnes for their enduring support and optimism. And here's an extra shot of gratitude for Paolo Pepe, who created such a stunning cover.

I also owe a special thanks to my friends at Gyldendal in Copenhagen. Merete Borre and Vivi Vestergaard have lent ears to many unwieldy ideas, and their encouragement and can-do attitude have never wavered. Thanks also to the marvelous Danish translator Ulla Oxvig, as well as Anne Hjermitslev and Line Miller at Gyldendal, for working tirelessly until the happy end. Last but not least, a huge thanks to Harvey Macaulay at Imperiet, who—as usual—nailed the Danish cover in the first try.

Since the birth of *Juliet* in 2008, I have come to think of Maja Nikolic, Maria Aughavin, Victoria Doherty-Munro, Chelsey Heller, Angharad Kowal, and Stephen Barr at Writers House as family, and I cannot imagine a writing life without my fabulous agent, Dan Lazar, whose integrity and savoir faire is without compare. What I owe this magnificent team can never be contained in a simple "thank you."

I have not yet mentioned my mother's hand in this book; I simply don't have the space. But rest assured she was there with me, riding camels in the Sahara and striding through the mud in Kalkriese, anticipating my every step and encouraging me all the way. Without her lifelong support and mind-boggling sacrifices I would never have realized my dream of becoming an author; even worse, I would never even have dared to nourish the dream in the first place.

But even with this army of amazing people behind me, I would not be who I am, nor have the drive to do what I do, without the precious love and support of my little girl and my darling husband, Jonathan. It may upset my secret sisters that I say this, but between you and me, if you're so fortunate as to have captured the perfect male, peeling off that chain-mail bikini and becoming a part-time Amazon is not so bad after all.

ABOUT THE AUTHOR

ANNE FORTIER grew up in Denmark and divides her time between Europe and North America. She is the *New York Times* bestselling author of *Juliet*. Fortier also co-produced the Emmy Award–winning documentary *Fire and Ice: The Winter War of Finland and Russia*. She holds a Ph.D. in the history of ideas from Aarhus University, Denmark. *The Lost Sisterhood* is her second novel in English.

www.annefortier.com

facebook.com/AnneFortierBooks

@AnneFortier

ABOUT THE TYPE

This book was set in Perpetua, a typeface designed by the English artist Eric Gill, and cut by the Monotype Corporation between 1928 and 1930. Perpetua is a contemporary face of original design, without any direct historical antecedents. The shapes of the roman letters are derived from the techniques of stonecutting. The larger display sizes are extremely elegant and form a most distinguished series of inscriptional letters.

2/15-12